SAVING SAM

SAVING SAM

Louisa Woods

*For my mother, Maureen Warner,
who taught me to love reading and writing.*

*For my husband, Richard Woods,
who patiently accompanied me
through historical Great Yarmouth*

For SY, who gave me inspiration.

CHAPTER ONE

Great Yarmouth, February 1844

"What *is* that young girl doing in that doorway?" the Reverend of Saint Nicholas' Church wondered aloud. He and his good friend Mrs Elgin were hastening back from the Sunday service. A cold east wind was picking up, driving sleet into the doorway I lay in. Mrs Elgin had been hurrying back from the Sunday service with the idea of treating the Reverend to Sunday dinner.

"I've no idea!" Mrs Elgin moved carefully closer, fearful it was a trap. Some villains were known to pretend to be unwell in order to obtain hand-outs or would suddenly spring onto an unsuspecting victim to rob them. As the pair neared, they saw I was anything but capable of springing on anybody. The Reverend knelt.

"Miss?" He shook me gently. "Wake up; you cannot sleep here." But there was no response. The Reverend looked at Mrs Elgin.

"This child is ill," he said, having put a hand to my forehead. "She doesn't look very old." The pair regarded one another, both undecided what to do, but knowing something must be done.

"I'll take her home with me," Mrs Elgin had already decided. "Poor little thing. Reverend, will you be able to carry her?"

The Reverend looked at Mrs Elgin.

"Are you sure, my dear?" he asked her.

"Yes. I can't possibly leave her."

The Reverend bent and lifted me carefully. My eyes flickered.

"Mamma?" I rasped, and Mrs Elgin's maternal heart felt a surge of warmth.

"I'll do my best to help her, but it may already be too late," she told the Reverend. Mrs Elgin was searching her memory for any herbs that could be used to treat a fever. She had little in the way of medicines, being extremely healthy and vigorous for her age.

We reached Golden Keys Row, which was, fortunately, a stone's throw from Saint Nicholas', and Mrs Elgin and the Reverend hurried up to her lodgings at number 29. Mrs Elgin let herself in, then held the door open for the Reverend. She hastened to the tiny living room and began to feed the fire.

"I'll fetch Helen, shall I?" the Reverend asked. "She may assist you to bathe her. I'll tell her to bring what medicaments we have. She'll know what to do. I'll put her on that settle for now."

Helen Anderson, the Reverend's 23-year-old Scottish maid, returned ahead of her employer having been told about Mrs Elgin's 'poor waif' and entered the room in a brisk and business-like manner in time to see Mrs Elgin filling a bowl of warm water.

"I'll need help with a sponge bath, Helen."

She turned to the Reverend. "Would you mind making up the bed in my spare room?" she asked him. "There is plenty of linen in the ottoman."

"Run, Alice, run."

Helen cocked her head in confusion at the fevered muttering.

Two months had passed since my parents had been foully murdered in Caister-next-Yarmouth in a pick-pocketing gone very wrong.

Having reported their murder to the authorities, and with little hope of finding their killer, the only thing I could do was pay for them to be buried in the same grave. It had taken every penny I had. Already weak, sickened, terrified and grieving, I had taken the stony road from Caister-next-Yarmouth hoping to find work to be able to return to my native Devonshire. I promised myself as soon as I was fit enough, before returning home, I would see that all was right with their resting place. My grandfather would have to know too. Such were my thoughts as I took up the road to Yarmouth.

In time, I would tell Mrs Elgin and Helen the entire tale. Meanwhile, I was too feeble to resist the two women. I knew in the fog of my fevered mind, that somehow, I was being bathed, and my mind took me to my mother who had done this for me as a child. At that moment, I believed myself back in my childhood home.

"Och, look! Ye can count all her ribs!" Helen said, "How old is she? She's no child, I think."

"Well, she's a young woman certainly; perhaps twenty? Come, let's be done. She needs rest."

The women were as gentle as possible. Each was a competent nurse in her own way. Mrs Elgin had reared nine out of fourteen children successfully, and Helen, as one of the eldest in her family, had nursed younger siblings many times.

When I had been washed and decently clad in an old nightgown, I was put to bed. Mrs Elgin had some meat broth and Helen sat at my side, propping me up, whilst the elderly lady managed to spoon some of the meat broth into my mouth. I was fed sips of willow bark. Helen had also brought honey and ginger with which she made a tea. When I had taken a few mouthfuls, she allowed me to rest.

Over the next few days, Helen and Mrs Elgin had dosed me with willow bark, beef tea and soup. Most of the time I had been incoherent, my Devonshire accent broad with the fever, speaking of music halls, my parents' demise, the stabbing and the pickpocket.

Several days later, I woke in the small room at the front of her lodgings, which afforded a view all the way down the row. The room was clean, smelling of soap, with a small cupboard, and a table next to the bed. A washstand stood in one corner, with a jug and basin and a towel. The window was open slightly. I could hear seagulls, horses clopping over cobbles, people shouting. I struggled to sit, feeling terribly light-headed.

"Hello, my dear!" Mrs Elgin laid aside her knitting and got up from where she had been watching me in a rocking chair near the window. I looked at her, utterly confused and feeling extremely weak.

"Where am I?" I asked. It hurt to speak.

"With me. Now, don't be afraid. It's alright; nobody will hurt you. We found you, Reverend and I, four days past."

I tried to recall the time before now, but I couldn't get the fog from my mind. "It's alright." Mrs Elgin came across to put a cool palm on my forehead. "Ah, much better, my dear. Your fever has broken, thanks be to God."

Mrs Elgin went to the door. "Helen! Our patient is awake, and the fever's broken."

Helen clumped up the narrow staircase and entered the room. I blinked. There stood a very tall and well-built girl of around my age. Her hair was long and shiny black, a mob cap perched on her head and eyes of a startling shade of blue. She grinned at me.

"Welcome back to the land of the living, lass!" She advanced to the bed and she too felt my forehead. "Aye! She'll be fine now!" Helen smiled broadly at Mrs Elgin.

So, I met Helen. The broad Scots girl sat heavily on my bed to smile and introduce herself. I liked her at once, but at first, I found her hard to understand. Slowly, as my mind began to clear, I started to tell the pair who I was and what had happened.

The two of them, with the Reverend's help, cared for me until I was able to leave my bed. I felt incredibly weak at first, tiring easily and sleeping much. But with sustenance and medicinal herbs, I was recovering.

Ten days later, clad in one of Mrs Elgin's small nightgowns and wrapped in a shawl, I descended the stairs rather shakily to the small living room to sit at the fireside. Two small soft-looking chairs stood on either side of it. A clock on the mantle ticked, then chimed the hour most delicately. Not everybody had a clock in the house, particularly such a beautiful one.

"It was from a dear friend of mine," said Mrs Elgin, noting my glance in its direction. "We'd been friends since I first came to Yarmouth, many years ago now. She willed it to me."

"It's lovely," I told her.

What a sweet room, I thought. But so small; again, with a nicely swept boarded floor and rag rugs, the fire warmed the room quickly. There was a dresser at the side of the wall with crockery, and along the shelf that was attached to it were some figurines. The window had clean net curtains that hung from halfway. I could see people passing along down or up the row. I swallowed and coughed a little. Helen was at my side in moments.

"Here, drink this," she told me kindly. I obeyed, finding it was more of the willow bark. I pulled a slight expression of distaste.

"Aye, 'tis a wee bit bitter, but that's what's helped ye through," Helen told me, and swapped it for ginger and honeyed tea.

"I don't want to be any trouble," I told her.

"No trouble!" Mrs Elgin reappeared. "I enjoy helping people. It gives me a sense of purpose. You're nowhere near fit enough to leave. All in good time, my dear. I insist you stay here until you are well."

Mrs Elgin rooted around to find something suitable for me to wear since the dress I had arrived in had been unsalvageable. However, one of the other dresses I had carried in the soaking pack had been wrapped in wax paper and, other than being creased, was fine. Mrs Elgin had kept some of her children's clothes, being reluctant to part with them for sentimental reasons, even though they were grown with families of their own. Instead, she gave them to me.

Since then, I had stayed. There was no way for me to travel hundreds of miles yet and besides, I had no money. I was bound to repay this kind lady who had given me so much. As soon as I could, I asked her for a piece of paper, an envelope and a stamp. I had to write and explain to grandfather.

"Take your time, Alice. Explain what you know – you could, perhaps, spare him the knowledge of murder until he has overcome the shock of knowing they are dead, though you may find he already knows. The story was in the newspaper, after all." She smiled at me and stroked my cheek. "You're more than welcome to stay here, my dear," she told me. "You need a base if you are to work. Plus, you'll be company. It's too early for long distance travel yet; besides, you need time to grieve."

"Thank you."

But I couldn't bear to think of their deaths, not just yet. I had to carry on, see that their grave was what they deserved, and try, at least, to seek justice for them.

"It will be good to have someone to look after," Mrs Elgin went on. "I had fourteen children you know; nine survived. I've missed their presence."

"I was the only child," I told her.

"Goodness! How lonely it must have been for you," she stated.

"I didn't know any different," I replied. "Before I travelled with my parents around the music halls, I spent a lot of time with the gypsy children when I was very young, when they came to make a winter camp nearby. I learned palmistry there!"

"Palmistry! You read the future?"

I nodded.

Mrs Elgin smiled. "Did anyone read your palm?"

"Yes, I was told I'd travel far, that I'd have a great loss, but then a great love."

Mrs Elgin hoped that was true, for my sake at least.

I helped Mrs Elgin with some light housework. I also amazed her with my sewing, which I had always enjoyed and had done to help support my family since childhood.

I had found a tablecloth of linen and lace in a drawer whilst searching for some cotton. On seeing it, Mrs Elgin looked sad. "Ah, I can't bear to throw it away. My great grandmother had it gifted to her on her wedding day. When I came here as a girl of sixteen, it was one of the few things I brought with me." She had wrapped it in tissue paper and returned it to the drawer.

When she wasn't looking, I took it to my room where I worked on it in secret for a few days. Once I was satisfied, I took it downstairs.

"What is it, dear?" Mrs Elgin looked up at me from her seat by the fire. I smiled and held out the tablecloth for her inspection. Mrs Elgin removed her tiny spectacles and looked at it in wonder.

"My tablecloth! I can hardly see the join unless I look very closely! Goodness me, Alice! Such fine work! Did *you* repair that?"

"Yes," I told her. "After you said how precious it was, I decided to have a look, see if it was doable, and it was!"

Mrs Elgin wiped a tear from the corner of her eyes.

"I was heartbroken when it tore. I was going to ask the lacemaker; she is good, but she charges so much. I must pay you."

"Mrs Elgin, you owe me nothing. But for you, I'd be dead. I'll do what I can for you, till it's time for me to go home." I closed both her hands around her purse and smiled.

So, I settled with the sweet elderly lady in Golden Keys Row. I had been surprised at the narrowness of the rows, the fact that they could not even get an ordinary-sized cart down between, and instead, used specially designed ones called troll carts. For all many of the rows were cramped, some were filthy, but tiny though our house was, Mrs Elgin was most fastidious. Golden Keys Row was one of the better rows - people kept window boxes or grew flowers around the door. Doorsteps were scrubbed and the cobbles kept free of rubbish. I swept the rooms daily, cleaned the tiny kitchen, kept the stone step clean, and as soon as I was strong enough, I would bathe three times per week in the tin bath.

Helen was two years my senior. She told me about the small croft she had grown up on in the highlands of Scotland, her numerous siblings and her parents. She had come to Yarmouth along with a lot of other Scots girls to work in the herring business, but this was a hard, cold and smelly business. Helen had left after only a couple of seasons. It was dangerous too, particularly in the smoke house. I heard of the endless gutting of herrings, which the town relied upon, salt making fingers sore and cracked, always wet hands and always smelling of fish. Helen had seen the advertisement for a housekeeper for the Reverend at Saint Nicholas' and she had made sure to get the job.

Helen and I clicked straightaway. She adored the Reverend who was one of the kindest men I had ever met. Together, we would go to the market or the rows to shop. Helen's young man was called William, and he worked for the local mews as a driver. He was tall, with silken black hair and a beard. He had a roving eye and was incorrigibly vain. However, the pair suited one another in looks. Helen was a beautiful girl, very strong and well-muscled from years of crofting work. In my mind, she resembled Queen Boudica; Helen laughed when I told her that. "Aye! 'Tis better 'n bein' referred to as a Scots barbarian."

"Who'd be so rude?" I asked. We were walking up Horn Row.

"Woman called Dwyer," Helen answered with distaste. "She's no' a nice woman. Will's best pal is married to her, poor chap!"

"Oh?"

"Aye, Sam. He's forever mekkin bad choices then havin' to suffer the consequences. He's a lovely fella, truly. Quiet, respectable, kind, no like her! I've nae been able to understand why he married her." Helen sighed. "He tries his hardest to do his best and falls flat on his face. He went to London to stay with a relative and got into some unpleasant company. Got talked into marrying her," Helen said, shaking her large head. "His father-in-law's a quack and a criminal. That I do know for certain!"

I looked at her in amazement.

"And he's a *Socialist!* He sells seditious books!"

I looked at Helen for clarification.

"Books that encourage people to rebel against authority and that are against religion!" Helen stated firmly. "Sam's parents are religious, and they tried to knock that out of him! 'Tis disgraceful! Trouble is, he went to London when he was eighteen, and ye know what young men are like. No more sense than my wee finger. The more exciting and dangerous things are, the more they like it."

That very day, we spotted Sam. He was walking toward us along the street. He stopped to reach down and pet a cat. His reddish brown hair, parted in the centre and long at the sides, obscured his face. "That's him, there, wi' the beastie."

I looked at him. Sam was smiling and talking to the cat, which evidently enjoyed the attention and rubbed around his legs. Sam scratched the creature's ears. The cat leaned into his legs, head up, obviously blissful. Helen noticed my eyes follow him as he stood. He glanced at us, and his face showed surprise. I locked eyes with him. Even from where we were, I saw he blushed. He knew Helen, of course, who waved and gave him a cheeky wink. Sam raised his hat, and muttered, "Good morning, Miss Anderson," then walked onward.

"He's nice," I said. "And kind to animals too. People who are kind to animals are good, I think."

We continued through the marketplace, when Helen gasped and elbowed me. "Ugh! Look, Alice, speak of the Devil. That's her!"

I looked. Susan Dwyer was stalking along to her market stall.

"She's a clothes stall here on Wednesdays. The market runs Saturday as well; she sometimes works it then too."

Susan was tall, and older than Sam by five years. Her face was hard but handsome, her hair black and tangled-looking. She glanced across at us, then gave Helen a glower, which Helen returned in full. She made to continue, noticed me and turned. "She's coming over!" Helen told me. "Let me deal with her!"

Susan stopped in front of us. "And what was that look for?"

"Ha! T'was you looked at me!" Helen folded her arms.

"Who's *she?*" Susan asked rudely.

"*She* has a name; it's Alice. She is staying with Mrs Elgin awhile. Not that it's your concern, ye nosy cow!"

"Oh! Wait! I heard something about Mrs Elgin taking in some tramper woman. Now I remember. Well, don't outstay your welcome."

Why was she so bitter and rude when she didn't even know me? I wondered.

"You of all people are the one who shouldnae outstay yer welcome!" Helen pointed out. "Though ye never had one in the first place."

Susan glared. "Bitch!" She hissed, turning to leave.

"Gosh! She isn't very nice, is she?" I said. Helen shook her head.

"No, ye mun avoid her at all costs. Come on, I'll give ye a hand to carry yer spuds."

Easter 1844

Mrs Elgin and I ate fish and potatoes on the Good Friday. "I'm not a fishy person really," I told her making her chuckle. "I don't mind it fried in batter though."

"You don't care for shrimps? Dabs, herrings or that sort of thing?" she asked. I shook my head, pulling a face. "What about eels?" she asked with a mischievous look.

"Eels?" I recoiled. "Ugh! No, Mrs Elgin. I don't! I'd sooner go hungry than eat eels."

"It's as well there are choices of meats then, and that I can afford them. Kippers here are a staple diet. Most people eat fish for almost every meal. Yarmouth is famous for its herring. Have you seen the smokehouse?"

"No, but Helen said she used to work there."

"Yes, she did. But it was rather a small place to work in and Helen doesn't like confined spaces. It makes her uneasy, so when the Reverend advertised for a housekeeper, she applied."

"I like Helen," I told her.

"Ask her to show you the smokehouse," Mrs Elgin suggested as I cleared away. "It won't put her out. She goes regularly to see her old friends there."

I realised I was starting to settle in Yarmouth, and Mrs Elgin told me to address her by her given name, Mary. Mrs Elgin had a Norfolk twang to her speech, but some people were so broad I would sometimes need them to repeat themselves.

We lived close to where Sam had his workshop and I saw him frequently, either in the row or on the denes. On Saturday, I had taken a Penny Dreadful to read on the denes when I heard raised voices.

"Shut yer trap! I do what I want, when I want. Don't play the heavy-handed husband with me!"

There was a sound of flesh striking flesh, and I ducked down behind some scrub as Susan marched past me, dangerously close. As she retreated, I craned my neck to glance across the denes. Sam stood, hand over his cheek. After a few moments, he too left, but in the opposite direction. I was shocked; never had I seen a woman clout a man before.

The unpleasant scene had put me off my reading and so I returned to tell Mrs Elgin what had occurred. The elderly lady shook her head.

"Disgraceful!" she remarked, frowning severely. "Poor fellow. He's too much the gentleman to give her the hiding she deserves. His parents rue the day they sent him to London." She huffed, turning to look at me with a sorry expression.

Mrs Elgin took me along to the Easter fair. "It's been here for centuries!" she told me as we made our way through the entertainments and the booths serving food and drinks. "I've always enjoyed it; I'd bring my children when they were small."

There were tumblers, sideshows and a wagon with bars which held an unfortunate individual who had been labelled 'Wolf Man." His keeper, for want of a better description, bawled to the onlookers that the man had been raised by wolves as a boy and rescued by a priest.

"But even the good holy man couldn't teach him to act human!" the barker stated. "Savage, he is! He must be kept in the cage at all times and I daresn't let him out! He'd run wild through the streets, snatching babes from their mothers' arms to eat raw!" He prodded the man with a long stick and the poor fellow roared in anger. "See what I mean, good people?" the keeper asked.

"What nonsense!" Mrs Elgin sniffed in disapproval. "Poor man. I very much doubt he has done or is even capable of doing anything of the kind. Alice! Where are you going?"

"To see if I can soothe him," I responded. "He looks terrified, not wild!"

Mrs Elgin shook her head and steered me away.

"Come. You can do nothing; I doubt he would even understand you! I despise that sort of freak show."

So did I, though I had seen so-called freaks exhibited. My parents had never agreed with the practice and had taught me not to either.

Suddenly, I spotted Sam, and drew in a small gasp. Sam came over to bid us a good day. Susan stood at his side smirking.

"Hey! Look at 'im!" she hollered, loud enough to turn heads. "Come on, Samuel. Let's see if we can provoke him!"

"No!" Sam stated firmly. "That is not kind."

Susan rolled her eyes in frustration. "So what? I never saw a wild wolf man before; you coming or not?"

Sam shook his head. My eyes met his. Susan frowned, then marched across to the sideshow.

Whilst Susan tormented the caged man, Sam spoke to Mrs Elgin, asking after her health, acknowledging and smiling at me.

Helen arrived on William's arm, and he raised his hat. I wondered where the sweet scent was coming from. I could smell the occasional waft of sweetness from time to time, and soon realised, the man perfumed his beard!

Helen sported a fairing from William which she wore in her hair – a length of green ribbon. I looked to where Susan was standing. The caged man had been roused to fury and Susan stood back, hands on hips, laughing. Sam looked embarrassed. He cleared his throat and nodded to us both, then went to speak to his wife. We watched as she shrugged him off, slapped his arm and stalked away.

Easter Sunday in church; Sam was there. He sat across the aisle from us. I glanced in his direction. He was smartly dressed in a long blue coat, dark trousers, his white shirt high at the collar and a pale blue cravat tie. His neck-length hair was neatly combed. I could hardly drag my gaze away. He nodded to me and gave a half smile. I smiled back, blushing. At his side, Susan looked pale and unwell. I nudged Mrs Elgin who glanced over. Halfway through the service, there was a minor scuffle. Sam was roughly pushed aside, and Susan hastened out of the church. After a moment's hesitation, Sam resignedly followed, evidently much embarrassed.

"Unbelievable!" Mrs Elgin stated as we made our way home. "Running out of church to be sick during the service. It's a disgrace!"

Easter that year had been unexpectedly warm. I walked on the beach and the denes whenever possible, even daring to paddle a little. Small heads bobbed a hundred yards out to sea, startling me at first, with their bulbous black eyes and dog-like faces. Mrs Elgin had explained they were seals and many of them came onto the beaches to have their pups. I smiled, hoping one would lumber onto the sand, but instead, they vanished beneath the waves.

Thursday morning, and Mrs Elgin had sent me to buy some fruit in the row where Sam worked as a cabinet maker. He was outside, taking a draught of ale with William and eating a fresh pasty Helen had made, when I ambled up the row.

"Hello, lass!" Helen was clearly pleased to see me. She delved into her basket and handed me a fresh, still-warm cheese pasty. "Get that down ye, hen; ye've meat to put back on yer bones!"

I accepted the fresh pasty, for all I had had breakfast with gratitude. It was beautifully tasty.

Sam spoke.

"Good morning, miss; are you well?"

I nodded, smiling. "Thank you, I am. And yourself?"

"Thank you, yes. How are you liking Great Yarmouth?"

"I think it's beautiful."

"I heard of your parents' deaths; it was shocking. My deepest condolences, Miss Lawrence. Mrs Elgin, I know well, she's a lovely lady."

"Who's a lovely lady?"

We turned; Susan had appeared and now scowled down at me.

"Mrs Elgin," Sam responded.

"That old witch? And as for *you*, are you still here? *I* heard you're the brat of that music hall duo who got murdered."

Was that a sneer I saw on her lips? I looked at her, hatred brewing.

"I'm not a brat, but I'm their daughter, yes. And don't call my benefactor an old witch!"

Susan looked at me, stunned at my retaliation. She was not used to people who stood up to her bullying nature. Her screeching could be heard up and down Buck Row where they lodged above a shop run by Mrs Elgin's friend, the widow Mrs Townsend. What had Samuel seen in her? I could smell her from where I stood.

"Don't sauce me in that way! I'll call her whatever I want. Anyhow, why should you care? You're takin' advantage of the old widow. You should be gone by now!"

"I do not!" I exclaimed. "I take in sewing; I keep house for her! And *why* should I be gone?"

Susan snorted in disdain. She looked at Sam, then me.

"It's not for you or anyone else to tell Mrs Elgin who she may or may not take as lodger," Sam reminded her.

Furious at being upbraided in front of me, Susan sniffed, then wiped her nose with the sleeve on her arm. I looked away, revolted. She gave Sam such a poisonous look, I knew it meant there would be trouble later. Sam seemed to know it too, since he paled.

Susan scowled and left in the direction of The Three Feathers ale house.

"I apologise," Sam told me softly.

"That's alright," I replied. It's hardly your fault."

I left the three of them, feeling overwhelmed at Sam's impression on me. His collar-length hair, unfashionably long, darkish brown, but mainly with red in it, it seemed to change colour with the light. He wore fashionable mutton chop whiskers, not too long or too thick as some men wore them, but it had been his eyes that had taken my breath away. A deep, clear aquamarine. Something happened inside me that day. Sam felt it too. We had looked at one another intensely for a few moments. There was something about him that drew me.

His mother had urged him, "Wait, Samuel; just wait, and one day, love will walk through your door."

Yet, eighteen-year-old Sam, unwilling to wait any longer, to experience what life had to offer, had headed to London, as had many young men before him, anxious to prove himself a man. He had returned with Susan, and his mother and sisters had wept.

Back at my lodgings, I spoke to Mrs Elgin, who had a broom and was sweeping the passage.

"Let me do that!" I took the broom from her and started to sweep. "I saw him, Mr Dwyer, when I went for the fruit. Helen and William were there."

Mrs Elgin nodded.

"I like him," I said, suddenly blushing. "He's very gentle. Pity one can't say the same of his missus."

"Ah, Susan Dwyer; I don't like her. She frequents ale houses more than some men do and certainly more so than Samuel."

Mrs Elgin continued. "Such a shame he married her. It was her father he knew first – an awful family – rabble-rousing bunch that they are. I was surprised he got involved with them. Sam's always been impulsive, though he ought to know better, and that Susan! She's terrible to him."

"Do they have children?" I asked.

"No, why do you ask?"

I blushed hotly.

"Ah, my poor Alice. You like him, don't you?"

I nodded. "Well, I'd help you if I could, but I don't know..." She trailed off to think.

"How old is he?"

"Sam's 28, she's 33, I think. I was there at his birth. He was always a gentle boy."

I smiled.

Mrs Elgin regarded me. "Ah, put him from your thoughts; there's nothing you can do!"

A couple of hours later and I still looked downcast.

"Go and see Helen," she suggested. "Take these." Mrs Elgin went to the kitchen to take buns from the crock.

"Alright. I shall."

I walked to Saint Nicholas' and went into the back of the rectory to find Helen mangling sheets.

"Alice!" she said, beaming. "Hello again. Will ye stop for a wee drink?"

"Thanks, Helen. Warm today, isn't it? Oh, Mrs Elgin sent these."

Helen unwrapped the buns.

"Och, my favourites. Wonderful. I'll fetch us some ale." She hastened into the kitchen. A man spoke inside, and Helen's Scots lilt could be plainly heard.

"Ah! Miss Lawrence! I shall greet her!" The Reverend came out. I knew him well now and loved him.

"Good afternoon, Reverend," I said with a quick bob. "How are you?"

"Very well thank you, my child. And yourself?"

I nodded. "Well, thank you. Mrs Elgin sent buns."

"Did she now? How lovely. I hope Helen will allow me one later." He winked. I nodded. He knew she would. "I'll leave you girls to chatter then; I must visit Mrs Cronin."

"Lass, ye look troubled." Helen stated.

"That's because I am," I replied.

"Come on, lass. Tell yer Auntie Helen!"

We sat outside to enjoy the early spring sunshine. The trees seemed to have blossomed overnight and there were beautiful bunches of pink and white flowers. Birds sang; a gorgeous day that did not sit well with my heavy heart.

"It's Sam," I told her. "I've seen him about, but this morning, when I met you and William outside his shop, something happened. Something changed. Helen, I, I think I just fell in love!"

My friend looked at me. "Och no, lass!" she groaned. "Ye cannae fall for a married man!"

"Too late," I said. "I can't help what I feel. He is just so... I don't know!" Suddenly, I burst into tears.

Helen put down her ale to put an arm round me.

"Alice, ye poor wee thing. He's a nice man, I grant ye, but someone else's. Ye mun forget him."

"I can't!"

"Lass, ye can do nothing." Helen regarded me sadly. "Listen, why don't I get William to look oot a handsome young man for ye?"

I shook my head. "No, thank you, Helen. I couldn't even look at another man."

Helen sighed.

"Thing is, Helen, I swear I saw something in his face too. In his eyes, oh, such an unusual colour! So clear. He really *looked* at me, Helen. Does that make any sense?"

Helen nodded. "Aye, lass, it does."

I glanced at my hands then back at Helen.

"I *know* he felt something too; I could see it! I've never felt this before. It was so very sudden."

Helen watched as I got up. "I must get back now," I told her.

Helen nodded. "Alright; look, you know you can always come and talk to me, don't you? I'll tek ye round the herring house soon. There's many a good man working there. Handsome, too!"

I nodded and thanked her, and she watched after me, shaking her head sadly.

I walked back along the beach, the long way round. The sea was washing in on a high tide and I heard seagulls overhead. I looked out to sea – a clear blue sky. Love at first sight? Nonsense!

But it wasn't nonsense, because it had just happened, and it had happened to me. When I had looked into those eyes, the feeling had come suddenly from nowhere. Confused, I headed for the denes to sit for a while. He had smelled fresh and clean, of woodruff. Most men smelled sweaty and dirty, especially those who frequented the ale house.

"Stop it!" I told myself firmly. "There's nothing to be done about it."

I spent ten minutes gazing out to sea, wondering if I would see any seals, then, turning with a heavy sigh, went back to my lodgings. I sought out Mrs Elgin to have a heart to heart.

"I'm afraid Helen's right, my dear," she told me sadly. "I do know the feeling. It was the same for my husband and me."

"But he's unhappy."

Mrs Elgin scented trouble. Sam was not the sort of man to be unfaithful and I had no idea what I could be getting myself into.

"Alice, listen to me," Mrs Elgin said. "There is *nothing* you can do and how can you even be sure he feels the same? I know you spoke of the look in his eyes but that could be because you're a beautiful young girl; he was simply admiring you!"

"No, I could sense something," I told her.

"You are young, you're entitled to dream, my dear, but you'll only break your heart if you dream of him."

The following morning, I was tired after a poor night's sleep. Mrs Elgin and I ate breakfast in the back yard for the weather was fine. "Are you alright? You don't look well!"

"Yes; I had a bad night, that's all."

I gave her a sad look.

"'Tis an impossible situation, Alice." She squeezed my hand.

"But you said your families were against you. You still got together. His family had another lined up for him."

"Alice, there's a world of difference between a promise made by parents and a man who's married; for all, it's not a happy one."

"But everyone deserves happiness in their marriage!" I whimpered. "You said Susan's no good. She treats him badly!"

"She does, but your only option would be to become his mistress and then how would people speak of you? Not to mention if *she* found out!"

"I don't *care* what people would say," I said miserably. "Nor do I care what she'd think. She doesn't love him; she doesn't respect him. I've seen her stumbling from the ale house! She's been seen with other men too! What sort of wife does that?"

Mrs Elgin nodded. "I know, but it's impossible, Alice."

A day later, Mrs Elgin glanced into the taper jar and tutted in exasperation. I looked up from the ironing. "Alice, my dear, would you do something for me?"

"Of course." I put the iron down.

"I need some fresh tapers. We are clean out. Would you mind going and asking for a couple from Reverend, please? I only need two. They last a while."

"Yes, course." I put a light shawl around my shoulders and went to the door.

I liked the walk to the church. It was only a matter of yards. The church was huge and truly beautiful. Built in the 12th century, it was known as the Church of Saint Nicholas. I walked to the entrance, wondering if I would see Helen. I did not, but I did see Sam. He was at the door. My heart began to beat faster.

"Mr Dwyer?" I looked up at him and smiled.

"Miss Lawrence. Good morning to you." He reddened a little as did I.

"How do you do?" he asked me, awkwardly.

"Fine, thank you; yourself?"

"Yes, thank you."

I fidgeted slightly then we both spoke at the same time. Sam gestured for me to continue.

"Mrs Elgin needs tapers," I told him.

When I was shy or embarrassed, I tended to ramble. Words came out and there was nothing I could do to stop them. Sam was the opposite - he tended to be tongue-tied.

"He's a generous man. He saved my life, so did Mrs Elgin, and Helen is wonderful. I've become very friendly with her."

Sam nodded. I bit my lip.

'Shut up, Alice! Shut up!' I told myself inside my head. Then, "Isn't it a nice morning, Mr Dwyer? Warm for April."

Sam nodded. He looked into my face, my pink cheeks. 'She's so sweet,' he thought. "Oh, why did I have to fall in love with a girl I can never have?"

'He must think I'm daft,' I thought. Then I spoke more of taking a walk with Helen.

Sam smiled politely. "I'm sure Reverend will allow her to take some time off."

'He's wishing I would go and stop chattering,' I thought.

The Reverend came at that moment.

"Samuel! Alice! My dear children. How may I help you?"

"You were here first, Mr Dwyer," I said but Sam shook his head.

"Ladies first." Blushing, I stammered out my request.

"Of course. One moment, I'll fetch her some. Samuel? What can I do for you?"

"I just needed a word."

"Of course. I shan't be long." The Reverend vanished.

I took the tapers and bid both men a good day. I walked back solemnly. Why did he want to see the Reverend? I wondered. Feeling more embarrassed than I ever had in my whole life, I wandered back.

I went to Mrs Elgin and handed her the tapers.

"Alice? You look troubled."

"Well, I met Mr Dwyer and waffled like a half-wit!"

Mrs Elgin chuckled. "Oh, my dear!" she said, patting my shoulder. "He said he was there to speak to Reverend, but he didn't say why, and I wondered."

"I expect he was there on his mother's behalf."

"Oh?" I asked.

"Well, Ada, that's Sam's mother, does a lot for the church," Mrs Elgin told me. "She usually starts arranging the altar flowers when spring comes. Probably Samuel was there to inquire when Reverend wanted her to start."

"Oh?" I looked at her.

Mrs Elgin shook her head. "Alice, you need to stop thinking so deeply of Samuel."

"That's the trouble, I can't," I answered miserably.

The following afternoon, I went to buy cotton. Ahead walked a familiar figure, his hair blowing in the breeze. It was Sam. As if led by an invisible thread, I followed him, wondering where he was going.

Sam walked swiftly, as he always did, carrying a package under his arm. Sam, for some reason, felt himself being followed and grew uncomfortable. It was not unusual for a pickpocket to choose a victim and follow them discreetly until they turned down one of the rows; and then one lost one's wallet. Samuel stopped dead in his tracks. I collided with him.

"Oh!"

My exclamation surprised him. Sam looked down at me and smiled, relieved it was the small girl he had met that morning. "I am sorry, sir," I stammered.

"That's alright," Sam replied. "My, you are in a hurry."

My face resembled a pink lobster. "Yes, I ah... I am off to get some cotton. For sewing," I added, somewhat unnecessarily.

I looked very flustered, he thought, but then, he had seen something in my face that mirrored his. Since the day I had chatted with him, Helen and William, he had been thinking about me. Sam had looked into my dark eyes and felt something go straight to his heart. His life with Susan was unhappy. His family disliked her intensely. His sister Annette refused to speak to her or allow her into her home. The youngest sister, Maria, feared her. Sam felt I would not be like her. I would have been the sort of wife his parents had wanted for him. But what could he do about it now?

I looked up at him. "I have to go, Sir." I turned and hurried as fast as I could back to the lodgings, forgetting the cotton and my dignity entirely. I scurried off like a tiny mouse.

"Did you get the cotton?" Mrs Elgin saw my red face as I hastened into the lodgings and made to go up to my room.

"Cotton?" I asked stupidly.

"Yes! Cotton! You remember, you can't do your job without it!" But she was smiling.

"I ran into Sam," I told her.

"Oh yes?" Pale grey eyes twinkled.

I told Mrs Elgin about our encounter. "I'd best get to my room," I told her. "I'll go for the cotton later."

Sam, like most people, worked on a Saturday. It got him out of Susan's way and was more convenient for his customers too. Mrs Elgin gave me some cakes to take along to him for his mother.

"Go on, Alice, take these if you've a mind to see him again, though why you're torturing yourself this way, I can't imagine! I would've dropped them round there myself, but I can see you're desperate for an excuse!"

I entered the workshop. It smelled of fresh sawdust. Tools lay neatly in rows on benches or hung from lines of hooks along the walls. Sam looked up and blushed profusely when he saw who his visitor was.

"Miss Lawrence. What can I do for you?"

"Mrs Elgin sent these for your mother; she said to take them to you."

Sam quietly blessed Mrs Elgin and took the tin, which he opened, then sniffed.

"Goodness, Mamma *will* be pleased. She loves these lemon cakes – so fresh. Thank you. Would you take a cup of ale? It's so warm today."

Gratefully, I accepted and settled myself down. Sam chatted as he worked, taking his time.

"Did you get your cotton?" he enquired.

I nodded. "Yes. I am sorry I rushed off rather. I was embarrassed to have collided with you."

"Don't give it any more thought," Sam told me. "It's quite alright. These things happen." He paused then. "Do you make clothes as well as mend them?"

"I can make shirts," I answered. "Nothing complicated. Only plain ones. I use linen and always boil-wash it first, so it's nice and soft."

Sam's mind began to race. If I could mend something for him, it would give him an excuse to see me again. He thought hard, then had an idea. "I, ah, have some shirts that are missing buttons," he said suddenly. "Susan doesn't sew. I wonder, might I ask you to look at them for me?"

"Yes, my pleasure," I said, reddening once more.

"Good. I'll bring them later today; they're at my lodgings now."

"Any time," I replied. "I'll be in all afternoon."

"Sam is bringing some shirts for mending later," I said on reaching our lodgings.

"Oho! Sam now, is it?" Mrs Elgin teased.

"Well, that's his name!" I told her pertly. Mrs Elgin flapped her duster at me.

"Go on, Saucepot! Scrub the kitchen table for me, will you, dear? I'll bake a pie shortly."

Sam arrived at three o'clock, three shirts in a brown bag.

"Good afternoon." He greeted us both. "Here are the shirts, Miss Lawrence. Take as long as you need!"

I took the bag which had three screwed-up shirts inside.

"Yes, Mr Dwyer. I'll do them for you. I don't suppose you have the buttons too, do you?"

"Yes, I put them in a bag," he answered.

"Piece of pie, Samuel?" Mrs Elgin asked.

"Thank you, Mrs Elgin. That would be lovely!"

Sam sat and I brewed him and us some tea whilst a large slice of ham pie was put before him.

"Hmm. Wonderful," Sam said.

Sam told us of the new book he had just begun. "Can you read and write, Miss Lawrence?" he asked.

"Yes, I like reading. Only the Penny Dreadfuls though."

"I've told you about them!" Mrs Elgin said. "Give you nightmares, they will!"

I loved the wild tales of Spring-heeled Jack, Dick Turpin and various vampire tales that I read deep into the night until my candle flickered and died.

Sam left a short time later and I took the bag to my room. I sat on the narrow bed and took out the shirts. I pushed my face into them and breathed deeply. I smelled woodruff. There was a sudden knock at my door and, without waiting to be bidden entrance, Helen walked in. She gaped at me with the shirt in my face.

"Och, lassie! What *are* ye doin'?"

"It's Sam's shirt," I told her, and Helen laughed.

"I hope it smells good!"

"Yes, of woodruff."

"I brought ye this." She held out a skirt. "I ripped it climbing over a fence, on a nail. Is it repairable?"

"Oh, that's a fine, easy job. I'll do it for you."

"*When* ye've finished Sam's shirts, eh? I'll be waitin' a while, I expect."

I looked at the shirt. Then I looked more closely. I pulled the others from the bag, somewhat confused, frowning.

"What?" Helen asked surprised.

"Helen, look!"

Helen examined the shirt thrust under her nose for inspection.

"Nae buttons. Aye. What am I supposed to say?"

"No... I mean, yes! No buttons... but look. They've been cut off! Every single one!"

Helen looked at me still blank of face.

"Well, normally when a button falls off, you get a hanging thread, don't you?"

Helen nodded. "Aye, but I still dinnae follow."

"*He* cut them off!" I said joyfully. "*Sam* cut these buttons off three shirts! He must've! Why would they all suddenly fall off at once? You can see, look, the thread has been neatly cut. And most of all, what man did you ever know saved the fallen buttons, hmm? Or even knew where to find them? Don't you see? Sam did this on purpose, so he could have an excuse to see me!"

Suddenly, Helen realised.

"Aww, hen! Aye, I suppose there is no other explanation for it!"

I smiled so hopefully she could not bear to warn me off. It would do no good in any case. "Just be careful, lass, that's all. The last thing I want for ye is a broken heart."

"I know but I expect it'll happen in any case," I said ruefully.

"What on earth are you lighting up the copper for?" Mrs Elgin stood in the scullery as I was filling the pot.

"I'm going to wash Sam's shirts," I told her, blushing.

"You were only going to sew his buttons on for him," she reminded me.

"Well, yes, but I like to do a good job," I prevaricated. "It's a good day for washing, after all."

"Alice, I know you're out to impress him, but be careful. I believe he returns your interest, but Susan Dwyer is not a woman to be tangled with."

"I'm not afraid of *her*!" I said bravely, and as the water began to boil, I added some scented washing soap flakes.

"Well, you should be!" Mrs Elgin told me, giving me some linen to add to the wash.

Sunday. Sam had to come to collect Mrs Elgin and myself. She did not need to be accompanied really but Sam liked to help people. On arrival, he greeted us politely and held out his arms. Mrs Elgin took one, and I the other, almost swooning. Sam asked after our health. "Fine, thank you, young man!" Mrs Elgin told him. She paused. "Susan not accompanying us?"

"Ah, no she is... er, not too well," Sam said tactfully.

"You mean she had a late night, hmm?" Mrs Elgin asked, and Sam blushed.

He looked at me and compared me, fresh-faced and bright-eyed and smelling sweetly of Devon violets, with the drunken woman who had twice woken him that night, once by coming in and knocking things over, and the second time by vomiting profusely into the chamber pot.

I sat at Sam's side during the service. I thought I felt him press my fingers and when I looked down, his fingers were on mine. I looked up at him with such a sweet expression, Sam felt his heart fill. He felt some guilt, but also resentment. Doubtless, I would not have come in drunk and stinking as she had. My small fingers curled around his. He felt a squeeze. Sam squeezed back, then, in case anybody noticed, put his hands back in his lap and noticed the fleeting look of disappointment. But the message had been sent and received. What was more, it had been reciprocated.

After church, we walked toward Golden Keys Row. Sam frequently took the air after the service, and in any case, Susan would be still in a drunken stupor.

"Will you accompany us for Sunday dinner, Sam?" Mrs Elgin asked. Sam looked surprised but nodded.

"Thank you, Mrs Elgin, that is most kind." He noted the delight on my face, for all I was looking down at my shoes.

"Alice made enough to feed an army!" she went on. "I never saw such a joint of beef other than at Christmas."

Mrs Elgin unlocked the door, and we went inside. "Your shirts need only be ironed now," I said to Sam as Mrs Elgin checked the dinner and put the carrots on to boil. She cleared away the pea pods I had popped that morning.

"Ironed?" he asked.

"Yes, I boil-washed and dried them, then tomorrow I'll iron them."

"Goodness! I didn't expect such service," Sam told me feeling a little guilty. "I was only going to pay you to re-sew the buttons."

"No extra payment, Mr Dwyer. I was washing other things anyway."

Sam did not know what to say, but he thanked me gratefully.

"Dinner smells good!" he said, sniffing the air. I smiled.

"Come on!" Mrs Elgin called. "Table's set!"

We started to eat.

"You've a wonderful piece of beef."

"Ah yes, that is Alice's payment. She mended a lot of things for the butcher's daughter. Alice had about five dresses, didn't you?"

I nodded.

"Well, she suggested paying her with a fine piece of beef so Alice said yes, and goodness me, I could scarce believe it. There'll be enough left cold for tomorrow too, I shouldn't wonder."

Sam nodded and tucked in. There were potatoes, beautifully roasted, and Sam detected a little honey on the parsnips.

"Is there honey on these?" he asked, and I nodded.

"Alice gets these new-fangled crazes," Mrs Elgin told him. "Honey belongs on bread! But I do admit, it's delicious."

Sam reluctantly left around three o'clock. He entered his lodgings and walked up the small, narrow staircase. Susan had roused herself at last.

"Where the bleedin' 'ell 'ave you been?" she enquired crossly.

"Out walking as I usually do," he stated. Then he added sharply, "Get up. Wash and dress yourself!"

Susan was open-mouthed at his cheek. "Got to do the dinner," she said, "but I don't feel like none."

Sam did not want to taste her poor cooking now.

"I'm not hungry," he replied sharply and took up a thick book. "I am going to read in my keeping room," he stated firmly. Susan looked surprised at her husband's non-compliance and distracted air.

Monday found me ironing Sam's shirts with as much precision as I could. Mrs Elgin stood to watch and approved.

"You make a wonderful job of ironing, my dear," she admitted. "Sam will appreciate them."

I smiled and thanked her.

"You do love him, don't you?" she asked sympathetically. I nodded. "Ah, what will be, will be. I've been thinking. Sam is a kind, decent fellow. Oh, he has made some silly choices in the past. For one thing, knowing Harris and Blisset does him no favours."

These men were a local troublemaking duo, always up to no good. One of them, Raymond Blisset, was, in fact, in prison at that time, doing eight weeks. I had seen his partner in crime. They were a dishevelled pair who frequented the ale house as much as they could. Harris, in particular, spent lots of time in Globe Row, a row that was mentioned with hushed tones and a frown, and I had been warned never to speak to these men. Susan was often seen in their company, whilst Sam endured sniggers from others, and he had even been called 'cuckold' to his face.

Mrs Elgin sat to do some embroidery. She watched me at the ironing table, then made a decision.

"I know that fate cannot be denied," she stated. "I see in *his* face what I see in yours. It's very unconventional, but I've decided to do all I can for you both. Sam is as another son to me. I want to see him happy. And he isn't. You snatch your happiness where and when you can, my lass, since we're such a short time on this earth."

I held my breath.

"All I ask is that you both keep it discrete." Mrs Elgin continued, "But be aware, Sam may not even ask you. He was strictly brought up. But, I think, deep down, that he will."

I hugged her hard.

Something Helen, and for that matter, nobody else had thought to tell me, was that George Warne, the organist for the church of Saint Nicholas, was blind. A gentle character, he was fifty-two, and had been organist for a year. Once or twice, I had been in the grounds of the church and had spotted him, usually seated, his face upturned to the sun, eyes shut, relaxing. It had never occurred to me that he couldn't see; his organ playing was wonderful.

That he used a walking stick was irrelevant. Many people did, or men would have walking canes as an accessory. I hadn't noticed, during my love-sick daydreaming, that the stick was white. So, when I noted him looking in my direction one morning, as he had done recently on several occasions, I felt uneasy. I frowned at him to tell him I didn't approve but he continued to stare. Whilst waiting for Helen to finish her chores, I could hear birds singing and the clopping of hooves along the road nearby. I noticed the man once more, so I frowned and hastened up to speak to him.

"Please, sir, must you stare at me? It's very ill-mannered!"

Nobody could have been more horrified than I was when the man smiled.

"Ah! It *is* a young lady! I knew it; I could tell by your step. You are young, from your voice too. Do forgive me; I wasn't staring, I am blind."

Mr Warne could positively feel the shockwave of embarrassment that I radiated.

"Oh no! I am *so* sorry!" I twittered, suddenly realising that the poor soul was indeed sightless; I was mortified.

"I had no idea; do forgive me, sir, I beg you. My late mother would be ashamed of me."

"You are forgiven! People don't always notice. Allow me to introduce myself, I am George Warne, the resident organist here."

I was astounded. "Then how do you play?" I asked, in disbelief.

"Rather well, so I am told," came the reply.

"No! I meant, how? How can you know what you're doing?"

George began to explain and I felt my face go hot. Helen could have thought to warn me! I mentioned this to the man, who laughed. "Ah! Helen! Nice young woman. Hard to understand at times, however. And you, I feel, are also a newcomer here. Am I right?"

"Yes, Mr Warne, how do you know?"

The organist smiled, and gestured me to sit at his side, which I did.

"You've a west country lilt, so you are not from here. I am from London, though I have only a soft lilt."

I nodded, forgetting he couldn't see.

"I believe that to be Devonshire?" he asked and I grinned.

"Yes! How can you tell? Most people can't."

"My ears tell me much, my dear. I see life through my fingers and by using my ears. My remaining senses are incredibly well-attuned to any dialect or tone of voice. I can spot a liar merely by their tone. It's very useful."

I supposed it was. George continued to tell me of how he had come from London to play at Yarmouth. I warmed to the gentleman at once. He was charming.

At that moment, Helen appeared from round the corner. George smiled and turned in her direction. "Helen! Good day to you!" he called. Helen showed no surprise that he had known her rather heavy tread.

"Mr Warne, good to see ye! Ah! Ye've met Alice then, my new friend?"

Helen and I had made plans that day to go to the denes, and Helen spoke of them. George smiled. "How delightful. Alas, I cannot go on the denes or I should fall flat on my face!" He chuckled. "Well, I won't keep you! My wife is making my very favourite of steak and kidney pudding."

Helen got up. "Lovely to chat with ye again," she told him.

I stayed her arm. "Wait, Helen. We'll assist Mr Warne back to his accom-modation."

"No need, my dear! No need! I am quite able to find my way back! I live close by, on Church Plain. There's no difficulty."

We watched as he ambled away. I turned to my new friend. "Helen! I made a right old addlepate of myself. I told him off for staring at me! How was I to know he couldn't see? I felt dreadful!"

Helen had the grace to look ashamed.

"Aye, hen, I'm sorry, I should've said. We're all just so used to him. He enjoys sitting here, ye see."

I wondered how he would cope with villains who might take advantage. Helen smiled when I mentioned that.

"Lass, he mayn't see anything, but there's nothin' amiss wi' his ears. I think he'd crack any unsuspecting felon round the head wi' no bother."

I hoped so. He was a real gentleman, and I would soon get used to seeing him about. I would love to listen to his rehearsing.

Later, and I made my way to Sam's workshop. As the bell jingled and I entered the room, Sam looked up and smiled.

"Your shirts, Mr Dwyer." I handed them to him. Sam observed the neatly pressed linen, sewn-on buttons, perfectly starched collars. Sharp creases in the arms at the sides, as if they had come from a professional launderess. They smelled fresh, of the sea air, and were softly scented too.

I looked around the workshop, intrigued with the tools and odd-looking items he had around the place. Sam explained what each item was for, and even demonstrated.

"Gosh, I would never be able to do all this," I said in admiration. "All those measurements too – I can't add up anything!"

'She has blackberry eyes,' he thought to himself. 'How unusual. So deep. If I got up close, I would see the inner part of her eyes. Such a sweet, pert little nose too.' Sam had to restrain himself from placing a kiss on my turned-up nose. Sam regarded the blonde curls, which looked soft, and he guessed they would smell clean, not like the greasy, ragged locks of his wife. Sam felt warmth go all through him, a wish to hold me close and protect me forever.

I felt myself blush and looked round for something to focus on.

It was then Sam had an idea.

"Miss Lawrence, you have no male protector when you go out, do you?"

I shook my head.

"In that case, should you need an escort, I'd be happy to oblige. I hope that isn't too forward of me. I mean no offence," Sam told me, feeling daring and wondering if he had misread the signs and braced himself for a slapped cheek. But...

"Thank you, sir! I take no offence at all. I'd be happy to accept!" I replied, my face looked radiant.

"Good. Well, with the evenings now so fine, I'd be happy to escort you should you wish to walk. Most people in the town are decent, but there are ruffians abroad."

On Saturday night one went out as a rule. The ale houses would be packed and rowdy with singing, which would become more and more raucous, and fights were inevitable. Mrs Elgin, of course, would not permit me to set foot in there. Sam too hated the noise, the drunken behaviour. He had occasionally indulged but preferred to read than frequent the ale house. Susan always went out.

"It's the centre of life!" she had told him when he had at first objected. "I 'ope you don't expect me to sit at 'ome doin' bugger all, cos I ain't. Me dad and me went along together, so if you don't like it, I don't care."

It was all very well when people gathered to sing, earlier in the evening perhaps, but later, when it got brutish, he would leave. Sam sighed deeply. There was many a truth in the old sayings, and 'marry in haste, repent at leisure' was certainly one of them.

Susan was the eldest of five sisters and three brothers. She and her father were particularly close, and he had raised her like a son, even teaching her to fight in their squalid London rookery. There was nothing Susan enjoyed more than a good Saturday night brawl. Sam had seen her punch a man so hard, he had sailed over the bar, crashing into the glasses behind. Susan's father had considered Sam to be malleable, which indeed, he had been, and Susan's father had used Sam to 'do his dirty work' in his various dodgy dealings, always having a finger in some unlawful pie. He did the moneymaking, whilst Sam took all the risks. Sam, who hated conflict, would acquiesce to his father-in-law's demands, knowing it was wrong but unable to do much else.

The waves lapped the beach and hissed over the stones as they washed back out. Several ships were out, and I looked at them making slow progress it appeared, the wind being from the east. I watched a seagull picking his way along the shoreline. This was truly a beautiful place to live. From what I had seen of the town so far, it was exceptionally clean.

I sat on the shore and set my chin on my knees. If I was to stay here for a time, and I planned to do that, I would need work. Mrs Elgin was happy for me to stay with her – I helped her in the house and provided companionship as well. I had to see about my parents' grave too. Grandfather, since he knew I was safe and well, would not mind my remaining here. I had regular letters from him. Then, there was Sam... I could think of nothing or nobody else but him.

Mrs Elgin and I strolled along the sea front two evenings later.

"A beautiful evening," I said. "I don't want to go home yet."

Mrs Elgin sighed. "My dear, I would continue, but I need to return; my knees are aching. Ah! Look! Here is your good friend Sam coming towards us!"

"Good evening, ladies!" Sam said to us, raising his hat.

"Hello, Sam. What are you doing?"

"I fancied a stroll. Are you on your way back? Might I escort you both home?"

Mrs Elgin smiled. "Thank you, Sam." She took one arm and I the other.

Mrs Elgin had been thinking hard, all the time walking back to our row. She looked at us, easy with one another and so natural, it seemed, to see us together. It was going to happen; she could feel it. She thought then of her late husband. What if he had been married to a scold? It wouldn't have stopped her; she would have done anything to be with him. She made her final decision. She wanted us both to grab what happiness life offered whilst it was possible.

"Well, thank you, Samuel. I shall go in now. Alice, did you not wish to continue to walk?"

I nodded and looked up at Sam.

"Then I will escort her," he told Mrs Elgin. "Is that alright, Miss Lawrence?"

Was it? I nodded with enthusiasm.

Sam and I walked arm in arm along the promenade. It was quiet since many would be in the ale houses at this time. Only a few early tourists ambled about; a child ran by bowling a hoop. Sam and I felt very comfortable with one another. The sun began to sink slowly, and twilight came, bathing everything in a gentle warm light.

"Miss Lawrence," Sam spoke. "I've something to say, and I don't know how you'll take it. It may frighten or offend you and I don't wish that. You have every right to slap my face for my presumption. But I must say what's on my mind."

Was this it? Having nodded, I held my breath.

"I've fallen in love with you," he said softly. "I can't help myself and I had to say something. I'm not happy with Susan; I married unwisely - I wish I'd waited. I hoped things would improve but they didn't. The last thing I expected was for you to enter the shop and steal my heart."

Such a sweet speech had tears come to my eyes.

"Oh, Sam." I reached up to touch his face. "I love you too. I only had to look into your face and I was smitten."

Sam gazed at me. "Truly? You love me too?"

"Yes," I whispered. "I do."

Sam held me close and buried his face in my curls. They smelled of violets.

"Oh, my dear," he sighed. We wandered to a shelf of pebbles, washed up by the sea, to sit side by side. Sam put a finger under my chin. "May I kiss you?" he asked.

"Yes." I could hardly breathe as his lips touched mine. It took only moments for my arms to go around his neck and for his to go around me. For the first ever time, I had a kiss from a man. His tongue touched mine and I was intrigued and thrilled. I had heard of this kind of kiss from friends and had never thought I would ever allow any man to put his tongue in my mouth, but it seemed natural now.

We looked at one another. "That was my very first kiss," I told him.

"And?" He seemed worried.

"It was divine."

Sam touched my cheek. "Your mouth, it tastes sweet, fresh."

"So's yours," I replied.

"I taste mint," Sam said. "You drink mint tea?"

I nodded.

"May I kiss you again?" I nodded once more, feeling warmth spread all through me.

After a time, we wandered back up to the promenade. "I'll make plans so we can meet," he told me. "As long, of course, as you wish it."

"Yes, Sam. What are we going to do?"

"I'm not sure yet. Look, leave things with me. You know I'll let you know, and don't even *think* I want you as a mistress." He added, "This is different; much, much more. Do you understand?"

"Of course. You're so kind, so sweet. I wish things were different."

"Me too," he told me; "but love will find a way." Sam was leaning against a wall. He held me in front of him, arms round my waist as we looked out to sea though it was now almost dark. "She was nice at first, believe it or not. Once she got me wed, then her true nature was revealed, and I was trapped."

Lots of people were trapped in bad marriages. I wondered briefly what my parents would have said and had the idea they, oddly, would not have disapproved.

My mother had married my father, a music hall artiste, very much against her parents' wishes, and they had washed their hands of her.

Sam felt a rush of hope as I mentioned this.

I squeezed his hand. "You know, I was so happy when you first showed an interest in me," I told him. "Those shirts... they gave me the clue."

"What? Because I gave you mending?" he asked amused.

"Yes. I saw the buttons were cut off, snipped neatly!" I looked at him with the wicked look he'd come to love.

"You could tell?" he asked.

"Of course! I sew for a living; I've seen hundreds of buttons that have come away. It's easy enough to tell, and you saved the buttons too. Most men wouldn't have thought of that in a month of Sundays!"

Sam laughed.

We walked back now. I couldn't be out too late. Sam knew that Susan could be in the ale house until closing time. Suddenly, Sam tensed.

"There's Blisset, there, do you see? Staggering along on the other side? I don't doubt he's been thrown out of the inn!" Sam's face showed his disapproval.

The tall man with black hair, who considered himself 'very fine', rather lost his dignity having celebrated his release from prison rather too well. Two other men, staggering but not quite as bad, followed him, bellowing his name for him to wait. We stood watching him with distaste. Suddenly, Blisset went to the side of the road to be sick. I turned my head into Sam's coat in disgust.

"Come on, sweetheart, don't look. He is a vile pig." Sam steered me away from the three, two of whom were bellowing with laugher at their friend's predicament.

"Ha! Best not go to the whorehouse after that!" one called. "She won't want you puking over her!"

"Wouldn't be the first time!" Another of his mates laughed. "D'ye remember? The last doxy had the madam sling him out on his arse cos he threw up down her back!"

There was general hilarity at this recollection, and Blisset spat then moved off. The others followed him, laughing hysterically.

Sam regarded me. "Alice, darling, you *must* avoid him at all costs. The man is a fiend. I've known him many years; we were at school together, but he was a bad 'un, even then."

"Don't worry, Sam, I promise."

He left me at my lodgings, standing in the open door. "I'll see you in the morning," he said softly. I nodded. A last, long and lingering kiss and he left for his own lodgings. I went up to my room and lay on my bed. A soft knocking at the door and I sat up.

"Yes?"

"May I come in?" It was Mrs Elgin.

"Yes, of course."

The elderly lady sat on my bed. "Well?"

I told her what had occurred. Mrs Elgin listened.

"One shouldn't break the sanctity of marriage, ever, but many have done so before and doubtless will do so in the future. Goodness knows, poor Sam has good reason. Listen now, I'll help you all I can. When I knew what he'd wed, I was horrified and distressed. Poor Ada was round here, bawling her eyes out – they hadn't even been invited to the wedding! Sam ought to have invited them, but her old man wouldn't hear of it. Don't worry, Alice. Trust me – all will be well."

"Thank you so much." I hugged the old lady. I knew that Mrs Elgin was going against strict protocol in encouraging any relationship between Sam and myself, but I would ever be grateful.

Indeed, Sam came for Sunday dinner and Mrs Elgin sat us both down beforehand to speak seriously to us.

"You know, most, if not all landladies would never permit this on their premises," she told us. "You're lucky I understand your predicament. I know what it is to feel such a love that you cannot control who the recipient may be; I know how hard it is. People in this town helped Rob and me. I shall help you. You are welcome to pay court to Alice here, Samuel, whenever you wish."

We were both so grateful that Mrs Elgin was touched.

"I'll never forget this, Mrs Elgin," Sam told her. "I thank you from the bottom of my heart."

"So do I," I said and kissed her.

I had been asked to assist Helen. Reverend had come knocking at the door and smiled as he saw Mrs Elgin.

"My dear Mrs Elgin. Helen has injured her wrist," the Reverend told her. "She is able to do some things one-handed but I wondered if Alice could help with washday? I can cook for myself so I would not require her long term."

"Of course. Alice would be happy to help." Mrs Elgin bawled for me where I was in the yard hanging linen to dry.

Having explained Helen's predicament, I at once agreed to help her. "Shall I come now?" I asked.

"If it is no trouble, my dear," he told me.

I joined Helen in the yard. "I'm grateful," she stated. "I'm hopin' the wrist will be better soon. Only I mun rest it and keep it in this splint for a week."

"Of course, that's no problem."

"Will'um has been helping with the heavy stuff. Normally, I can manage as ye know, but och, 'tis painful."

"How'd you injure yourself?" I asked, scrubbing on a washboard.

"I was putting out scraps for the wee birdies when I tripped over one of the chickens that had got oot! That's what ye get for kindness to dumb animals."

"Well, you'll have your reward one day," I told her. "Right, that's all done. Let's get it pegged out and hope it doesn't blow away!"

Helen paused.

"Are you alright?" I asked.

"Aye, lass. Will ye do a reading for me?"

I was surprised at the sudden turn in conversation.

"Yes, of course. What, d'ye want it done now?"

Helen nodded. "Please, if 'tis no trouble." I wiped soapy hands on an apron.

"Come, sit down; I'll do it."

Helen sat on an upturned bucket. She presented her plump paw. I took her hand and regarded it.

"Helen, you must know, I say what I see, whether it's good or no. Do you still want me to continue?" Helen nodded. "Stop me at any time if you're getting uncomfortable," I told her. Then I began.

"Helen. Your hand's one of the most interesting I have ever seen. Gosh, you have changes afoot too. Huge changes. You're going to lead a very interesting life." I looked at her. Helen's face was impassive. She was giving nothing away for all she had plans in her head. Plans that only she and William had shared in the dead of night.

"You're a passionate person. I see problems, though. I don't know what, but it will be complicated. I must be honest. I think that you *will* find your true love." I looked at her rather embarrassed. "But there is a sort of, well, a break off then it continues on smoother." I blushed hotly at this.

"'Tis fine, lass, ye mun say what ye see. I know my man is a wee divil."

"But, at least, oh, Helen, you are going to be wealthy. Very wealthy."

"Are ye sure?" Helen asked. Most palmists said something of that kind. But Helen knew I was truthful. I had told her I had been trained by a gypsy woman as a child when they had camped in an orchard near my home in Tavistock and I had wandered, interested and innocent, to play with the gypsy children. She had picked me out to train, telling me I had gypsy eyes, and it was obviously in my bloodline somewhere.

"Yes, Helen. I see it here."

Helen could see nothing but lines, but she believed me and in fact, it strengthened a decision she had already made in her own mind.

"Children?" she asked hopefully.

I nodded. "You'll have three for certain, or maybe four."

Helen nodded.

"Travel," I said firmly. "You'll travel far." Another pause. "I think you'll come full circle, Helen," I told her.

Helen frowned.

"What does that mean?" she asked me, but I shrugged.

"Thank ye lass, ye've helped me mek a choice."

"I can't go round telling people how to live their lives and what choices to make," I told her rather worriedly.

"Nay, lass, 'tis nothing ye told me that I didnae already know aboot."

"So why ask for a reading?"

"I wanted to be sure I was mekkin' the right decision," she answered. "And I am."

"Will you share it with me?" I asked a little worriedly.

Helen nodded. "I'll fetch us some ale."

She made her way to the kitchen. I followed should she need help and Helen asked me to cut some bread and cheese, or ham if I preferred. As it was almost noon, I did so.

"I hope Sam is having something nice," I mused. "But if *she* cooked it, that's very doubtful."

Helen's lips turned up at the corners.

"I loathe that woman," I told Helen, leaning against the kitchen wall.

"Yer no the only one, hen!" Helen told me. "She's common as muck!"

I nodded. I always felt fury creep in whenever I thought of her with Samuel. She had married him and was with him. I had not. But I would be; Sam deserved better.

Helen and I took our meal back to the garden and sat on beer barrels, a table in front of us. About to speak, I almost knocked over her ale when I suddenly spotted Sam. I waved.

"Lass!" Helen was shocked at the open familiarity, but I simply smiled and went hurrying to the gate where Sam, having seen me, came at once. He took both my hands in his. Helen's knowing mind observed. There was something between us, that was obvious.

"Hello, my sweet," he said quietly. "What are you doing here?"

"Helen's busted her wrist," I explained. "So, the Reverend asked if I could come and help her."

Sam smiled. "That'll make a change for you." He longed to touch my face but did not dare.

"Sam, what do you have for dinner?" I asked.

"Nothing."

"Stay there." I turned to hurry and speak to Helen who nodded and within a few minutes, Sam felt something wrapped in a red and white chequered cloth put into his hands.

"For you," I whispered.

"Thank you, sweetheart." He unwrapped the cloth. Some tempting-looking fresh cheese, bread and a rather large slice of currant cake lay within.

"Goodness! That looks wonderful. I'll see you this evening. Meet me on the denes at 6.30."

Helen watched as I rejoined her on the wall.

"Ye know, Will'um is keen on mekkin lady and gent out of us? He told me we will, one day, have a big hoose, wi' servants, and money to spend."

"Oh? How? Is he going to rob a bank?" I asked jokingly.

Helen then amazed me by explaining their plans to emigrate and make their fortune.

My mouth opened. "America?" My eyes popped. That seemed an incredible distance to me. I had thought Devonshire to Norfolk a vast distance.

"How'd you get there?" I asked stupidly.

"Boat, ye daft lass! Did ye think we'd swim?"

"But that's so far!" I was upset. I had made a good friend of Helen and we were of an age and got on well. Now I had found a good friend, she was going to leave. I tried to swallow down the selfishness. "Helen, are you sure that's what you want? Is that why you asked for the reading?"

"Aye!" she responded. So, she had sought my advice and I had just given her the go ahead to do something wild!

"Ye look sad, Alice; don't be. Will'um will be there to protect me."

"Well, I'll be sad to see you go," I said. "It's a huge decision; you'll never see your folks again."

"I can still travel home every so often," she told me. "We've been mekkin' plans to go to Scotland before, so I can bid my family farewell. We sail from there."

There was nothing I could say.

Cheer up, lassie, 'tis months yet!" She grinned at me. "Now I have told ye my secret, are ye no gonna tell me aboot you and Samuel?"

I blushed crimson. "What do you mean?"

"Lass, 'tis plain as the nose on yer face. I'm nae daft!"

I swallowed with difficulty. "Helen, swear to keep this a secret," I pleaded. "The more people know, the more likely it is to get out!"

"On my word as a good Scots woman." She crossed her heart. "I willnae say a word."

"Not even to William?"

"No, but I think he'll already know. He and Sam are good pals. Does Mrs E know?"

"Yes. She's promised to help us and be discrete. She thinks we are the same as she and her late husband were. She knows we love each other desperately."

"A forbidden love! 'Tis *so* romantic!" Helen clasped her hands together, delighted.

"I'm no' surprised. Susan deserves it! What kind of wife gets doon the ale hoose wi' other men? She doesnae wash, she cannae cook, and she's a gobby wench. William's seen her twist Sam's arm right round his back. Well, if ye dinnae treat yer man well, he'll look elsewhere – my mam told me that! I cannae say I blame ye, lass. So, how did it come aboot?"

I told Helen of the evening on the prom.

The clock struck and Helen sighed, filled with romanticism.

I was ready for Sam at the appointed time, and we nestled in the denes. Skylarks twittered overhead. In between kisses, which neither of us could stop giving the other, I told him of Helen's plans and that she had soon seen how it was between us.

"That's alright, my love. Will does know. It's good to ask his advice. He's wiser than me. We've known each other since boyhood. When I came back married, he couldn't believe it. A man should take a wife, but if he takes the wrong one, he's doomed."

"But sometimes, he is saved."

Sam kissed me.

Sam's mother hastened to his lodgings. His landlady, Florence, greeted her nicely.

"Good morning, Ada, how are you?"

"Very well, thank you, Florence, dear," came her reply. "We're going to the station opening tomorrow! I hope Sam will join us!"

"I'm sure he will. Did you want to speak to him? He hasn't left yet."

"Yes, I need to remind him to swing past Annie's first. Are you coming too?"

Florence nodded. "Of course! Everyone will be there!"

Sam's mother enjoyed being in the shop. It smelled of fruit, rich tobacco and beeswax. Florence was always polite, and they frequently took tea together if there was not much to do.

Susan slouched downstairs, unaware that her mother-in-law had arrived. She had just rolled out of bed, had a terrible hangover and when Ada glanced in her direction, Susan was concentrating on picking her nose. Ada shuddered with disgust and gave Susan an unfriendly look.

"*He's* still washing!" she told her as if it was something inappropriate. "Always washing these days... he's got a fancy woman, that's what I thinks."

It was on the tip of Ada's tongue to say she wouldn't blame him if he had, when Sam appeared, freshly shaved and neat as always.

"Mamma?" he said questioningly, sounding a little worried.

"Nothing's wrong. I just came by to remind you to call at Annie's on the way to the opening tomorrow. Ben's busy, and his master won't let him go, so Annie said can you still come? Tony wants to see you too."

"Of course, Mamma. I'd be happy to." Sam adored his nephew, and his nephew adored him. He was a feisty little four-year-old.

"Nobody's making sure *I* come along!" Susan grumbled.

Ada ignored the remark. Sam merely glanced.

"If you do, I hope you at least wash your face and hands. Your hair could do with a brushing too," he told her sharply.

Mrs Elgin was interested. "Let's go! It's history in the making. Something quite new. It will be rather a nice ceremony; after all, the weather is set fair."

"Yes, of course. I might see Sam!"

Mrs Elgin groaned. "Well, just be careful. Susan's bound to be there, remember!"

1st May 1844

The day was already warm. It seemed the whole of Yarmouth attended the grand opening. The new station, named Vauxhall, was bedecked with flowers, in tubs and made into garlands, there was bunting up, ribbons adorned the waiting area, and a band played cheerful music. The waiting room was full of flowers too and the tea shop served cake, teas and milk or orange juice for the children.

Children pulled their parents' arms, excited to see the new station and everyone dressed in their best. Small girls in pristine white pinafores, shiny black button boots, and straw hats with ribbons or flowers; little boys in sailor suits.

"Look! How delightful!" Mrs Elgin smiled broodily. I had on my Sunday dress; the red one Mrs Elgin had given me with the pretty little white lace hem, straw bonnet and boots. I looked for him eagerly, my arm through Mrs Elgin's.

A fine-looking engine puffed on the track; its brasses shone, and we could smell steam. It was going to give some lucky people a trip to Norwich and back. There had been a raffle to win the journey, and though neither Mrs Elgin nor I had entered, Annette had entered her son's name. She wasn't fearful of the trains but if Tony won, she would let Sam go in her place. Sam was happy to travel on them; it was a novelty. Tony's eyes were like saucers as he spied the train.

"Mamma! Mamma!" he called excitedly. "Look!"

"I am looking – isn't it grand?"

The boy, in his sailor suit, looked delightful. Sam's father hurried to talk to the driver.

The Lord Mayor called for quiet, and the band stopped. He stood on a box.

"This station will be beneficial to you good people of Yarmouth!" he called. "Trains will be running up the city each day, and bring the tourists to us easier, and you know tourists spend money! This will be known as Vauxhall Station." He smiled round at the eager faces. "So, a big round of applause to the gentlemen who made it all happen... Messrs Grissell and Peto!"

"Up the city?" I queried Mrs Elgin, who nodded and smiled.

"It means to go to Norwich," she told me.

There was a round of applause and some cheering, and the high-hatted men stood next to the mayor, smiling.

"Now, I know you're all longing to enjoy the morning, so less of my blabber, eh? I now declare this new station well and truly open!"

Sam stood, his sister at his side, with a very excited little boy. He was jumping up and down and held Sam's hand. Sam's face wore a soft expression whenever he looked at the child. It made my heart ache to look. Mrs Elgin nudged me.

"Alice, be careful. That's his sister and nephew. Don't forget, sour Susan is here somewhere as well."

"I won't," I replied. "She doesn't seem friendly with his sister though."

"Ha! There's no love lost between those two! Annette won't let her in her house!"

I smiled. Perhaps if I could win over Annette, things might be easier. I hated to see Susan next to Sam. Little Tony was a darling in his little sailor suit and I longed to pick him up and cuddle him.

"I wonder where Maria is," Mrs Elgin mused. "I hope she's not unwell." She looked at me. "Maria's a lovely, sweet girl, but rather shy. She dislikes crowds."

The mayor announced the winners of the raffle, and as luck would have it, Tony's name was pulled from the hat.

"Uncle Sam!" Tony squealed. He jumped up and down in excitement. "Do you come with me?!"

Annette grinned. "That's alright, Sam, spend some time with him. I don't mind!"

Sam smiled. "Are you sure?" he asked, and his sister nodded.

"Righto!" The Mayor called over the noise. "Quiet, you rabble! Quiet! Now the lucky winners have fifteen minutes to board the train and off you'll go to Norwich. Once you're there, you get an hour for tea and cake then back you come! Tickets, please!"

Sam just had time to speak to me as the winners formed a line to show their tickets. Susan had found a friend and was sitting with her, running her hand over her eyes to try to dull the headache.

"Alice," he said quietly. "I'm so pleased to see you here." Then louder to Mrs Elgin, "Good morning. Exciting day, is it not?"

"For young people, yes!" Mrs Elgin told him. "I was saying to Alice earlier, I am not enamoured of such rapid transport!"

Sam smiled. "How are you, Miss Lawrence?" He was aware of his wife, who, spotting him talking to us, came closer.

"Fine, thank you," I told him politely.

"This is my nephew, Anthony, a lucky winner!"

"Gosh! Lucky you!" I smiled and squatted to talk to the young boy who grinned, showing tiny white teeth. "Is this your first train ride?"

"Yes, miss!"

"You look so smart in your sailor suit!" I told him. "You'll be the finest-looking boy on the train!"

Tony giggled. He put the end of his finger in his mouth. I smiled at him, and he giggled again.

"He's taken to you, Miss Lawrence!" Sam said, formally, aware that his wife was hovering. And he could not help but add, "Tony seldom takes to strangers!"

Susan butted in. "Are you going on that thing or not, Samuel? They won't wait just for you!"

"Alright, alright." Sam nodded to Mrs Elgin and me.

"Well, enjoy the ride." Mrs Elgin snubbed Susan quite effectively. "And you, young man. Behave yourself!"

"Yes, madam!" Tony glanced uneasily at Susan who frowned at him. Then, to our amusement, he suddenly put out his tongue at Susan who stepped back in surprise. Sam pretended not to notice and turned. As they went to the train, I heard Tony's high little voice.

"Who's that pretty lady?"

"That bloody brat wants a good hiding!" Sarah growled to Mrs Elgin, who shot Susan a look of intense dislike.

We watched as the train whistled loudly making Susan cringe, then pulled off, Sam's father grinning and waving. He had somehow wangled his way onto the footplate and was up with the driver and fireman.

"Would you like me to introduce you to his mother and sister?" Mrs Elgin smiled benignly.

"Just briefly. Don't forget, they don't know about you both."

We walked across to the pair. Florence was heading to the tearoom and nodded to us. "Join me later and I'll stand you tea and cake," she offered generously. I felt nervous as we ventured to the two women.

"Hello, Mary," Mrs Dwyer smiled. "Long time, no see! You're looking very well!"

"Good morning to you both," Mrs Elgin said. "Thank you! And I can say the same for you. I see Simon managed to get up front with the driver!"

The pair chuckled. "Yes, there was no stopping him! This must be the young lady you took in?"

Mrs Elgin nodded. "Yes; Alice, this is Ada Dwyer, and her daughter, Annette Langford." I gave a polite bob to the pair.

"Good morning, ladies."

"Good morning to you. Miss Lawrence. It's nice to meet you. No need to bob to us though, dear."

I felt unaccountably shy and was blushing a little. I kept my eyes down unless I was addressed. But I made eye contact when spoken to. Both women liked me at once, had I but known it.

"No Maria today?" Mrs Elgin asked.

"No, she's filling in for a friend of hers at her job who was desperate to come," Ada said.

Mrs Elgin chatted a little more about the weather and various things before she smiled at me. "Well, Alice, let us take a look around and admire the flowers, then we can have some refreshment."

"Yes, Mary," I said politely. Then I turned to the two women. "It was lovely to meet you."

"Well, they liked you. I could tell!" Mrs Elgin stated. "You were polite and respectful. I'm sure they'd have preferred you to wed Sam. Ada dotes on him; he is the only son and the eldest. She was heartbroken when he brought that creature home!"

We joined Florence at her table and indulged ourselves. Mrs Dwyer and Annette suddenly entered too. "Mary! Florence! Might we join you? It's rather warm to be waiting around outside."

"Of course!" Mrs Elgin smiled as the two seated themselves.

"No urge to travel on the train then, Miss Lawrence?" Mrs Dwyer asked me.

"Oh no, madam. There'll be other times."

"Call me Mrs Dwyer, my dear."

I smiled. "Please call me Alice."

The women ordered tea and cake. As delicately as I could, I was eating a large scone which was laden with jam and cream and wishing I had ordered something less messy. We chatted in a general manner. I really liked his family; they were so friendly.

"Do you know; that line cost £10,000 per mile. Overall, it cost £220,000!" Florence told us. Her head for figures was remarkable.

We were all amazed. I could not even imagine such a sum.

"Extravagant!" Ada stated. "Alice, shall you remain here, or do you wish to return home?"

"I don't know," I told her honestly. "It's strange; my first thought was to earn money to get back to Devon, but I love it here. I must repay Mrs Elgin for saving my life. I need to visit my parents' grave. I'll stay a while longer yet."

"Yes, enjoy summer here at least," Mrs Elgin suggested, suddenly realising herself that she was loathe to let her new companion go.

Then she talked of how I helped her endlessly, including how I'd mended her tablecloth.

"Really? I have some linen that requires close work," Mrs Dwyer told me, looking at me. "I daren't try it myself; my sewing is alright, but this is special. I would love it to be mended. Would you perhaps look at it for me, please?"

"Of course, I'd be glad to." I smiled, trying to hide my delight.

"Then I'll get someone to pop it round to you," Mrs Dwyer replied.

"We'll have to look for a nice young man for you!" Annette joked, and I blushed bright red. The ladies laughed gently.

"Ah, now you've embarrassed her." Mrs Dwyer chuckled, looking at me fondly. "But Annie's right, a young woman needs a husband to protect her."

"Ha! I do not subscribe to that theory!" Florence remarked.

"But you're a widow. You did have a husband," Mrs Elgin pointed out.

"I did, and what a tyrant he was! God rest his soul! Dare to be your own woman, Alice. There are plenty who do!"

Indeed, Florence could take herself off to The Black Swan if she felt like it. Nobody turned a hair, being a widow and older. However, young girls who went unaccompanied to ale houses were deemed to be looking for only one thing and were treated accordingly.

We chatted of other things. I wanted to ferret out more information about Sam, hoping to learn more. Mrs Elgin glanced and decided to speak.

"Sam is so fond of his nephew."

Ada nodded. "He's the best uncle in the world. He'd make the perfect father."

"Don't they want children?" I asked boldly but cringing slightly.

"Susan hates children," Ada said in disgust. "It's dreadful. Still, I don't think any child would grow up well with her for an example. Sam would be perfect, but her?" She shook her head. "He's too soft-hearted. Her father's a *socialist!* He raised Susan like a son, not a daughter. We've met him; rude fellow."

Once started on her errant daughter-in-law, Mrs Dwyer was difficult to stop. She rambled on about Susan's behaviour, her manners and how she wished Sam had never brought her home.

"Well, you never know," said Mrs Elgin, testing the waters. "One day, she might run off with someone."

"Ah! Mary, I could never be that lucky!" Mrs Dwyer grumbled.

The sound of the train puffing back in made us rise. "Well! I must prepare myself for the whirlwind that is Tony!" Annette told us smiling. We bid our farewells and made our way from the station; I looked over my shoulder to try and spot Sam.

We met Helen walking away from the station.

"Helen! You missed all the fun!" I said, upset for her.

"Och, lass, I am sorry, I overslept!" She groaned. "'Tisnae like me!"

"Sam was there," I said. "I got to speak to him and his dear little nephew. I even met his mother and sister."

"Och, 'tis lucky ye didnae reveal yer secret, lass!"

Whenever anyone said something like that, it made me miserable. I realised how fragile our relationship was.

"I have to go," I told them suddenly. "Please excuse me." I hurried off back to our row. Helen looked at Mrs Elgin.

"Did I say something wrong?" she asked.

Mrs Elgin sighed. "No, my dear, but let's leave her to herself. She'll come round. What about you, Helen? You look unwell."

Helen sighed. "I've been sick in the mornings," s]

he told Mrs Elgin. "I think mebbe I've caught!"

"Oh, Helen! Ah well, at least you are betrothed! When do you marry?"

"July," Helen answered and sat on a low wall. "So t'will nae be showing and time it's born we will be in America."

On return to our lodgings, Mrs Elgin noted the tear-stained face and held out her arms. I hurried into them. "Ah, Alice, my dear." She hugged me.

"I love him!" I wailed. "I love him so much. Oh, it's so unfair."

"I know, my dear, but things generally work themselves out. You wait and see. It'll come right in the end. Just have patience."

Patience – a virtue I lacked.

Helen and I walked out to the very end of the jetty. "Lovely fresh air. Breathe deeply, hen, ye'll no get better than this! Except for in the Highlands, of course!"

I did. The slow and deep breathing had a wonderfully calming effect.

"C'mon!" Helen took my arm.

Taking my arm in hers, she strode along to the herring house. I could smell it before even seeing it!

"Hellooo, lassies!" Her loud voice cut through the chattering and working women.

"Helen!" Another Scots girl, dressed in an oilskin overall, dark clothes, a piece of cloth wrapped around her head, sleeves rolled up and man-sized boots came over to Helen and enveloped her in a fishy embrace. I cringed inwardly, hoping she wouldn't do the same to me!

"It's good to see ye! How's the easy life, eh? Rev alright?"

I waited as the pair exchanged pleasantries and Helen then introduced me. I shook hands with the woman, a little reluctantly it had to be said, but she was friendly, and I liked her instantly. She was so small and delicate, I wondered how she could heft the large baskets about.

"I'm showing yon wee lassie here around," Helen stated as we made our way to the herring sheds. "Is that alright with ye?"

"Of course, come and introduce her."

The herring shed both fascinated and appalled me. I had come at the time a fresh catch was being hung and was able to witness pole upon pole of herrings being set into place.

But I enjoyed the visit. It was noisy and friendly, if hot and smelly. Helen jabbered to a young man who'd just leapt from the rafters and was looking at me with some interest.

"Put yer eyes back in, Donald – lass is spoken for!"

That made me smile.

I was given an extensive tour; it was interesting. I had never seen such work in progress. The girls were all gutting fish at a long table, side by side. I wondered they didn't slice their fingers off, the speed they were going. And these girls were strong. They hefted baskets of herrings about as if they were hardly any weight at all. I admired them but was thankful I didn't do such an unpleasant job.

Saturday, and Mrs Elgin was telling me about the legendary late Sarah Martin, who was a local heroine, and had been an unselfish and self-deprecating individual who had done nothing but good in her life.

"She visited prisoners and would sit and read the Bible to them. Give them hope, teach them to read, bring decent food. She did wonders at the workhouse too, teaching the children there; oh, she did so much for people. I don't know where she found the patience – I couldn't do what she did."

I had heard of her here and there but had never got to meet her since she had died the previous year. But her name was still on everyone's lips.

Shortly after, I went with Helen to sit in the garden. We spoke of Sarah Martin. "The Reverend prays daily for her. She ought to have been buried here, a place she loved, but she was from Caistor."

"I *hate* that place," I told her.

Helen, about to abruptly tell me not to be so ridiculous, softened.

"Aye, I know, lass. I'm sorry. I was going to suggest we go there to pay our respects, but that would be too much for you."

I swallowed my grief which felt like a hard lump in my throat.

"Give it time, lass," she advised. "'Tis early yet, but I'll tek ye if ye wish."

Two days later, there was a knock at the door. I went to open it to save Mrs Elgin's legs and saw Annette standing there grinning.

I smiled. "Hello, Annette, do come in."

"I brought Mam's sewing," she told me, handing me a brown paper parcel. "I hope it's not too cheeky. I'm afraid it's rather damaged."

I smiled. "That's alright. Let me see... won't you sit down?"

Mrs Elgin, seeing who the visitor was, told me to sit and she would make tea. As she did so, I unwrapped the parcel and looked. The linen tablecloth set, with napkins, was truly beautiful. There were some doilies too. It had evidently been used a little more frequently than was wise. One side of lace had come away from the tablecloth and hung limply.

"Gosh, what happened to this?" I asked.

Annette reddened slightly. "Captain, our dog, chewed it," she told me. "There was a plate of ham on the table, unattended. Well, you can guess what happened. Mamma was furious!"

I could well understand why. It was a beautiful set of linen.

"Well, don't worry too much. I'll do my best!"

Saturday afternoon, and Sam and I walked to Priory Plain. As we did, we heard the strident voice of Miss Spoonamore. I had had her pointed out to me before by Mrs Elgin who had told me she lived in a beach-front house along with a downtrodden maid who was seldom seen. A formidable ex-Nanny, she was known by the local children as 'Old Iron Drawers.'

"Oh no! It's Miss Spoonamore!" Sam grumbled. "We can't let *her* see us together. She's a dreadful gossip and loves to cause problems. Have you met her yet?"

I shook my head. "No, but I've heard about her! What's she doing?"

Miss Spoonamore was talking at top speed to a bevy of women surrounding her. Sam and I inched closer and hid behind a tree to eavesdrop.

"But my dear, The Cosies are at Gorleston-on-Sea, not here!" a voice spoke up.

"That is by the by!" came the response. "I was born in Gorleston. My brother and sister still reside there, and they tell me the most shocking, disgusting things you could ever hear! Couples kissing! In broad daylight! As for night, well, I cannot bring myself to even mention it."

Peering round the tree trunk, it occurred to Sam that he was a grown man, spying on the miserable harridan of Yarmouth like any schoolboy, but it was fun. Expected to behave as a man by fourteen, working and now married into the bargain, yet he was having a little fun and he was loving it and from the disgust in her voice, it was something too good to miss.

I whispered to Sam, "The Cosies? What are they?"

"They're like little niches where people sit, just as she says," he answered. "They're meant to help with the breakwater at high tide, but they're like seats. They're known for courting couples at night." He winked. I stifled a giggle. So that was what was upsetting Miss Spoonamore.

"So, my sister asked me to start a petition here, to get them removed. I am handing out leaflets in the town."

"But it's nothing to do with us!" A younger woman had joined the listeners.

"It has *everything* to do with us!" Miss Spoonamore had swung round to face her, almost losing her balance. "It is a matter of principle, young woman! Men making free with trollops! It's a disgrace! The decent people of Gorleston-on-Sea are all signing, and it would add a good deal of weight were people here to add their voices too! Modesty and privacy are vitally important. Surely your mother taught you that?"

So severe was she that the young woman blushed, and everyone looked at her as though she was a scarlet woman.

"So, as my sister suggests, I'll collect signatures to demand that it be altered making it impossible for people to sit there. My sister was shocked when she passed and saw a man making free with some tart!"

It was too much, and I guffawed. Miss Spoonamore craned her head to look.

"Run for it!" Sam grabbed my hand, and we raced across the grass.

We ran to the willow tree in the churchyard, a beautiful spot, which gave those under it complete privacy from anyone walking past. "Oh, Alice!" Sam collapsed against its trunk, panting for breath. "That was funny! I haven't done anything like that since I was a boy!" I laughed and fell into his open arms.

The rows fascinated me. Accustomed to the wider lanes of Tavistock, the moor and open meadows of childhood, I asked Mrs Elgin about them.

"They've been here for hundreds of years. They change their names sometimes. Some are named for the people in them, or their trades; they are numbered from north to south and if you're a local, then it's easy. Problems start when the holiday people come. They like the rows numbered so they can find out what's what."

Some rows were gaslit, but most were not. Sea breezes blew up or down the rows, making them fresher than any close-packed city, despite gutters running down their sides, and best of all, the people there were friendly.

Most wives kept their front areas spick and span and fussily scrubbed their doorsteps and swept in front of their houses.

"I like the bricks in some of the houses," I told her. "All different patterns. They look so nice."

Mrs Elgin nodded.

"Yes, they do. Have you seen the houses on South Quay?"

"Yes, so big! Who lives in houses like that?"

"The gentry, merchants, shipping people... the Paget family live in one of them. One of their sons is a doctor; he'll be a surgeon one day. Most are rather stuck up, but James isn't. James is a lovely fellow and will speak to anybody local. If you see him, he may raise his hat to you. Wish you a good day!"

I would meet James Paget sooner than I had anticipated.

I had repaired Mrs Dwyer's tablecloth as well as I could manage. It was no chore to work on something so pretty. It was mending clothes that was boring. But things like this, to me, were a delight. Mrs Elgin admired it.

"You are truly gifted with the needle," she told me. "Ada will be thrilled with this."

I hoped so. I so wanted them to like me.

I returned the linen set that day, curious about the house where Sam had grown up. He knew about the mending I had done and admired it, remembering his mother had been very upset over the table set.

I walked up the row with butterflies in my stomach. The house was much like all the others. There was a set of two raised steps up to the door, with a piece of wood on either side, over the gutter.

Taking a deep breath, I knocked. There was a loud barking inside and I quavered. A loud male voice told the animal to be quiet and Mr Dwyer opened it and stood there. My first thought was how like Sam he looked. He was in his forties and certainly handsome.

"Yes, miss?"

"Good morning, sir! I've brought Mrs Dwyer's linen back."

Mr Dwyer had evidently forgotten about this, since he frowned. "Linen? What linen's that then, mawther?"

I explained and Sam's father nodded. "Oh. Yes, I recall something about table linen. Well, thank you very much, miss."

"Is Mrs Dwyer home, sir?" I asked, hoping for an invite, but her husband shook his head.

"She's at the market. It's alright, you can leave it with me. I'll let her know you returned it. Thank you. How much do we owe you?"

I handed the parcel over miserable now. "Nothing, it's fine, it was a favour."

Mr Dwyer frowned. "But if you've done work for her?!"

I shook my head.

"Please, Mr Dwyer, it's a joy to do such fine work. It's a hobby, so it's greedy to charge. I mean no offence." I paused. "Good morning, sir."

Mr Dwyer looked after me as I walked down the row, confused as to who I was, and whether he had seen me before.

I walked down to Foreman's the Bakers row and bought some bread rolls. As it was a warm and pleasant day, I meandered onto South Quay to watch the hustle and bustle and see if any interesting ships were in port. I looked at the fine houses fronting the quay. I would never be likely to go inside them, however, unless I went into domestic service and that I had no intention of doing, not after the horror stories I had heard.

Suddenly, an excited urchin raced past causing me to sidestep into the road. My arm flew up to prevent my falling and all the rolls went everywhere. I gasped in despair. The urchin looked at me with some trepidation, doubtless expecting a clipped ear, then shot off out of sight. I stood, miserably looking at the rolls. I could hardly pick them up and put them back in the basket. I squatted to examine them. As I was looking tearful, I was suddenly aware of a youngish man standing beside me. I looked up.

"I am sorry you lost your merchandise, miss." The voice was that of a gentleman and his dress proclaimed him one of the affluent. I stood and gave a bob at once.

"Yes, sir, the child made me lose my footing."

"So I saw."

The gentleman observed me. This was James Paget, who Mrs Elgin had mentioned to me. An eminent doctor and assistant surgeon in London, he was home for a family visit and to gather relatives together, shortly before becoming married. Everyone in the town knew him; most were inclined to speak, even if it were just a 'good day.' Everyone except me, that was. His face was friendly, with black, short-cut hair. His eyes were deep set, and he had a large nose. His cheek whiskers ran in a faint, thin line to the earlobe, whereupon they were bushier.

"You are not from here, miss!" he stated. I blushed crimson, at being addressed more than once by someone like him.

"No, sir," another bob, "I'm from Devonshire, sir. I live here temporarily, sir."

James smiled. "Stop sirring me so much. The name's Paget, Doctor James Paget. Now, what about your poor buns?"

"I don't know, Dr Paget," I replied, "I must tell my landlady what happened."

James fished in his pocket. "Here!" He presented me with a whole crown. "Well, take it, young lady!" he said smiling. "You cannot expect the baker to give you more buns for free!"

I was amazed.

"Oh, thank you, Dr Paget, thank you so much!" I bobbed again. The money would have paid for a lot more buns than the four I had purchased. "I'll give you the change," I promised, meaning it.

James waved a hand. "Keep it! Well, as I am going that way myself, I shall walk beside you."

I had never in the whole of my life expected to be accompanied anywhere by a gentleman.

I felt extremely conspicuous. Curious glances came my way, and whispers too. I was overwhelmed as he chattered about his imminent wedding. I did not see Susan standing against a bollard, arms folded, a smirk on her lips.

We reached the bakery.

"Well, it has been lovely to chat with you, my dear," he told me.

The man tipped his hat to me, then waved at the baker.

"Ah, before I go, I did not catch your name!"

"Alice Lawrence."

"Well, good day to you, Miss Lawrence."

"Good day to you too, sir, I hope you have a wonderful wedding, and thank you again." I smiled, still blushing. James thanked me and strolled on, acknowledging people as he went.

In the shop, the baker told me the man was a regular figure, particularly up this side of the town. "You seemed to be having a rare old chinwag with him. For a toff, he's a good 'un and you can't say that about many of 'em."

"He said he's getting married soon."

The Baker grinned. "Well, that's news to me!" he replied. "Hobnobbing with the gentry, eh? You'll be getting an invite next!"

I gave an embarrassed laugh.

I scooted back as swiftly as possible to tell Mrs Elgin what had occurred. She listened; eyes wide.

"Goodness me! Passing the time of day with gentlemen, eh?"

"He was just being kind," I replied. "But honestly, he frightened me to death! I had no idea what to say to him."

"Ah, James is a different kettle of fish," Mrs Elgin told me, spreading the cloth on the table. "He's been known to everyone since he was a boy! He's about two years older than your Samuel!"

Sam heard the news pretty much at the same time I was telling Mrs Elgin.

"What?" He looked at Susan who had come into the shop and was as smug as could be.

"I saw it with my own eyes," she remarked, examining dirty fingernails. "There she was, right outside Paget's place. Taking her payment from Mr James, in broad daylight too! Mind you, it's an *honour* for her. High-class courtesan!"

Sam was seized with fury, jealousy and a feeling of sickness. Surely that wasn't true?!

"Do NOT spread rumours of that sort!" Sam attempted to assert himself and stood. "Mr Paget is friendly to everybody. He has even chatted to you, hasn't he?"

Susan smirked. "Chatting politely is one thing; paying for services rendered, quite another! Besides..." she paused a moment, "they went off together, smiling and chatty!" She regarded Sam. "Ain't that nice and cosy!"

It bothered Sam so much that he could not concentrate. He sat behind his worktable, chin in his hands, seething with resentment. Had my head been turned by a rich, gentleman doctor? Many gentry men had mistresses. Since there were no more customers, he shut up shop and marched off to our row.

Mrs Elgin glanced from the window.

"Alice! Sam's on his way, and he doesn't look happy!" She bit her lip.

"Oh? I expect Susan's upset him again." I put down my sewing.

"Ah, my guess is that he has heard of your tete-a-tete with Mr Paget!" she replied, looking at me.

"What? Already?"

"News travels fast here, you know that by now!"

Sam presented himself outside and raised a hand. Moments later, there was a fierce knocking. "Here goes!" Mrs Elgin winked and opened the door.

"Good afternoon, Samuel!" she beamed. Sam stalked over the threshold, for once forgetting his manners. "Come in, do!" Mrs Elgin told him drily.

"I apologise," Sam said, feeling guilty, "but I must speak to Alice."

Sam entered the tiny room. I stood and smiled. "Sam! I wasn't expecting you! What's the matter, darling?"

Sam's face was a study of misery, jealousy, anger, embarrassment. He knew he had no right to question me, but he couldn't help himself.

"Alice. I would know the meaning of your behaviour with Paget earlier today. I am informed you took money from him. Why?"

Mrs Elgin was torn between annoyance at the man's uncharacteristically arrogant behaviour and amusement. She waited as I explained about our meeting.

Sam listened and his breathing slowed. It was like Mr Paget to help a young lady in distress and make her feel at ease, whatever her station in life. He did that with anyone and everyone.

"Sam?" I asked.

"I'm so sorry, Alice. I heard things differently. Of course, the answer would be something innocent."

"Hmm, and I can guess who from!" Mrs Elgin spoke. Sam blushed once more.

"Sam," I squatted at his side. "I'd never betray you. I *love* you."

Sam believed me and felt a rush of relief.

Helen could hardly believe it when she heard. It was early evening and I had gone to see if she needed any help with the dinner. Reverend was expecting guests and there was much to do, but Helen seemed to be coping well.

"Och, will we address ye as my lady now then?" she teased.

"No!" I gave her a shove. "Don't be daft! Gosh, everyone's on about this... I thought he spoke to all and sundry!"

"Well, aye, 'tis true, he does, but yer a pretty wee lassie."

"He's marrying soon."

"Well, they've been engaged eight years to my knowledge." Helen was putting some potatoes in for baking. "So, my guess is, he's got to mek an honest woman of her sometime, so 'tis probably for decency's sake! Before she has a belly oot to here!"

"You're awful!" I said laughing. "What d'ye think I'll do, hurry up to the altar, shove her out of the way and marry him myself?"

"Aye! Why not? I would!" Helen said with a wink.

Mrs Dwyer had been thrilled with the mending but wanted to pay me. She spoke to Annette about it.

"I don't want to cause offence, offering her money."

Annette laughed. "Well, she worked for it, Mamma, but if she says it was something she enjoyed and wouldn't feel comfortable taking payment, let it go. It's not like mending clothes."

"Why didn't you invite her in, Simon?" Mrs Dwyer asked her husband. "She could have enjoyed a cup of tea until I came back."

"I can't have a pretty young woman in the house when I'm on my own!" Sam's father stated. "Think of the talk!"

Mrs Dwyer elbowed him. "You big ninny. There'd be no talk. Oh well, I'll send her a small gift by way of thanks."

Sam's mother later sent me a pretty basket of sugared fruits.

Later that morning, I went with Helen to take some old clothes to donate to the workhouse. The people of Yarmouth knew about the donations, and most were incredibly generous, despite being poor themselves. Helen and I carried the bag between us, though usually she would have slung it over her broad shoulder. We stopped a moment to adjust the load between us.

"Look at this dear little outfit!" I showed her a baby's smock.

"Oh!" Helen's face softened. Ye can just imagine a wee bairn in that!"

I smiled. "Yes, but I hate to see children in the workhouse," I told her. "It's so sad."

"Aye, I agree," Helen told me. "But they work soon as they are able. Younger ones shouldnae, but I've seen 'em, crawling under them looms. The masters just dinnae care. My weans will want for nothing, I guarantee it!" We hefted the bag once more and continued.

On the way, we met Susan; she was wobbling a little.

"Good God! She looks drunk!" I gasped; "it's not yet noon!"

"I'm nae surprised, hen. Ignore her; we'll walk straight past."

But Susan had no intention of just passing.

"Well, if it isn't the courtesan and the Scots barbarian! Where are you two heading then?"

"Workhoose!" Helen replied. "Want me to enquire after a place for ye?"

Susan spat. "Shut yer gob, you tatty wench! And you, stop trying to curry favour with my in-laws! You slut!"

"*I'm* not the slut!" I retorted; voice full of meaning.

Susan stalked up and slapped my cheek hard. I staggered back but managed to stop myself from falling.

"Well? Gonna slap me back, slut? I know you're hot for my man!"

Helen's large fist bunched.

Susan sneered. "C'mon, Lawrence. Try it!"

Despite the unprovoked attack and the overwhelming desire to slap her back, I raised my chin, then looked at Helen. "Come, Helen, we need to get these to the deserving poor." I walked off with my friend. Inside, I was quietly seething but felt I had done the right thing.

"Lass, ye've a rare self-control. Ye shoulda let me deck her!"

We walked to the workhouse, which was surrounded by huge walls, set with thousands of pebbles. I was fascinated and trailed my fingers along them. We entered the courtyard and mounted the steps into the workhouse. I sniffed.

"Someone's been cleaning!" Helen said. "That makes a change! Generally, it stinks of old cabbage!"

Small wonder this was the place everybody dreaded. Families split up and forbidden to meet. This appalled Helen and I, whose hearts went out to the young children.

An elderly lady hove into view.

"Och, look, one of the blameless. Poor biddy; she can barely walk."

The blameless were those too old or infirm, or labelled as 'imbeciles' and who had nowhere else to go. I loved elderly folk and hastened to her side.

"You need some assistance?" I asked. The old lady turned rheumy eyes to me.

"Thank you, dearie." She hung on to my arm.

"Where are we going then?" I asked her. We were shuffling at a snail's pace. I felt I was holding a fragile bird; her bones were so thin. The old lady stopped and looked at me.

"Pretty," she said, and her tired old hand came up to finger the curls. I smiled.

"Thank you," I replied.

She began to shuffle once more. "Here."

She indicated an open door to a large dormitory where several other old souls were dotted here and there. The beds, in precise lines, were neatly made, but all had as little bedding on them as possible and the mattresses were hard woven straw, most unsuitable for elderly bones. The bedframes were iron and almost coffin shaped. There looked scarcely enough room to move. A chamber pot sat under each one. I took her to sit on her bed.

"Thank you, dearie," she said again and squeezed my hand. Her bones were so prominent. I could have cried.

"What's your name?" I asked her politely. "Mine's Alice."

The lady smiled. "I'm Alice too!"

I wondered if it would be possible to visit her.

"Get some rest, Alice," I told her kindly, kissed the wrinkled cheek and then made my way back to Helen.

Matron appeared. "Ah! Miss Anderson. You have donations?"

Helen nodded. "Aye, Matron. This is my wee pal, Alice."

Matron nodded briskly. "Alright," she said coldly. "You may thank the Reverend on my behalf." She nodded, effectively dismissing us. "I have things to do, so unless you wish to join the inmates here, I suggest you leave! I have had three ins and outs this morning, and they can try the patience of Job."

"Ungrateful sow!" I said as we made our way back.

"Best hope ye dinnae end up there!" Helen nudged me.

"What did she mean by ins and outs?"

"They're a pain in the backside, in truth," Helen told me, "but ye can understand why they want to leave. 'Ins and outs' are folks who leave without notice. You don't need to give a week's notice like ye would to leave a job or something, but they just vanish wi' their uniform on which is no' their property! Then a week or so later, they're back, cos they cannae cope, then a few months later, off they go again. 'Tis a pain for the staff there who need to sort 'em oot when they come back lousy!"

"Helen, don't you think we could help them?" I asked. "The inmates, I mean."

"What do ye think we just did?" She laughed.

"Well, yes, I know, but something better. That poor old duck for one. All the old ones, they need extra blankets. You didn't see their room – those mattresses! Older people need some comfort."

Helen sighed. "Aye, 'tis right y'are, lassie, but what can we do? You'd have the guardians saying it'd encourage 'em to lie abed being idle."

I thought bitterly of Matron.

"Ah! Come on, wench! We'll go to the rows; we haven't done yet!"

Sam heard about my slap. The incident had been witnessed by none other than Florence. She was disgusted but unsurprised, and tutting, she went to her shop but stopped by way of Sam's workshop.

"She what?" Sam asked in horror.

"Disgraceful behaviour!" Florence stated. "I want you to speak to her, Samuel! And severely too! I can't have my lodgers doing that in the road. You're far too soft with her."

"Did Al.. ah, Miss Lawrence hit her back?" he enquired.

Florence shook her head. "No, she merely looked at her and walked away."

Later, when he got back, he spoke to his wife.

"And how did *you* find out so soon?" Susan growled. "Been round here whining, has she?"

"No! Mrs Townsend told me," Sam replied. "She could hardly believe her eyes. She doesn't want her lodgers behaving like that in public."

"Ah, shut up!" Susan snapped, out of patience. "You're just upset 'cos you're sweet on her. You don't control *me*, Samuel! So, don't even try. She's a slut! You just remember, you are *my* man!" She glared, then hissed in a menacing tone, "And I've no intention of letting you go!"

I had decided to square up to the Matron. I had the elderly lady, also named Alice, on my mind a good deal. Mrs Elgin had thought deeply about the situation.

"Workhouse inmates *are* sometimes granted permission for leave, but that's to visit a sick or dying relative in most cases," she told me. "You won't be permitted to visit her, though I think it's sad. She can't come out either; you're not a relative."

I chafed at that and went to Matron in any case, deciding to be as polite as I possibly could. The oppressive building seemed to show me disapproval from its very windows. Bleak misery emanated from the very stonework. I entered the main lobby and glanced about. There was a distant sound of work being done; doubtless, the men were hard at it. I could smell dinner cooking; it would be boiled vegetables today! Very well-boiled, I imagined.

As luck would have it, I encountered the workhouse master, about to take a pipe.

"Hello, young woman!" he said importantly. "How may I help you? After a place, are you?"

"No, Sir!" I replied, a little shocked. "I only wondered, you see, my good friend and I, along with the Reverend of Saint Nicholas' donate things every so often. Well, I met a lady here the other day, called Alice. She was so old and sad looking. I felt I wanted to do something for her, you know, to make her life a bit better."

"She and the other elderly inmates *are* cared for; I'll have you know!" The Master told me a little pompously. "And we have rather a lot of Alices on our books too. Was she complaining?" He suddenly looked angry.

"What? No! She certainly was not! She was shuffling to her room, and I helped her, that's all, but I thought, could I visit her sometimes? Chat to her, and the other elderly ones here? I thought I could read to them or something. I feel sorry for them, with no families."

The man glared at me. "Who do you think you are? Sarah Martin?" he barked. "My wife, the Board of Guardians and I provide for all needs of our inmates, and we're already in receipt of donations from you and your do-gooding friends. Everyone is treated equally here. You cannot single out one for special attention!"

I was disappointed. Helen had said this man was better than the Matron, but he seemed as bad.

"But sir, the old people feel the cold and they don't have enough blankets on the beds to keep warm!" I was feeling desperate.

"Summer's almost here!" he told me, unconcerned. "Now, run along and play, my pretty! I have things to attend to."

Fuming, I walked back along the road and made my way to the beach. The tide had exposed soft sand that I enjoyed the feeling of on my bare feet. Being dry on the surface and damp underneath, it made nice little sounds as I walked.

Three upper-class teenaged girls strolled along towards me at the water's edge. They were chattering and giggling, trying to stop skirt or dress hems from getting wet as the tide washed in. They all wore expensive-looking white or cream dresses, with frills, bows and buttons with sashes of blue, pink, green.

A sudden gust of breeze caught one girl's straw hat and sent it sailing into the water. There was a flurry of dismay among them. I felt my lips turn up. That was the last she'd see of that, unless she fancied taking a dip. They stood, wondering what to do, when one spotted me.

"I say! You there!" The tallest girl with long, sleek black hair called out imperiously. "Go in and fetch Belinda's hat!"

I regarded them. The group approached. "Didn't you hear or understand us?" she asked. "I want you to go in and fetch the hat!"

I shook my head.

The girls looked at me. "You can wade in! It will be alright!" The one named Belinda glanced at the dress I wore – washed-out blue and patched, above my ankles. She looked down her nose at me.

"Not I, miss!" I told her.

The girls grumbled amongst themselves.

They were all so fashionably dressed, but totally unsuited to where they were. One girl had a pinched-in waist, so tiny I couldn't imagine how she could even breathe. I was grateful for my petiteness. I had never bothered with a corset, or even drawers for that matter! I liked to feel free and unencumbered.

"Wretched bumpkin!" one said. "Come, Belinda. You can buy a better hat!" They stalked off giving me backwards scowls. I stood, smiling at the amusing interlude for a few minutes, when suddenly, the hat re-appeared, bobbing at my feet, so I retrieved it. It was of extremely good quality, very pretty, with a white ribbon. I wondered, should I run after them? But the group had disappeared. Taking the hat, I decided to dry it and perhaps I could even wear it myself!

Helen had come visiting, keen to show her new dress for when she attended at the wedding, so she went up to my room to change before coming down to the tiny room and smiling.

"Oh! Mary!" I gasped, "What'll we do? Such a very fine lady in our humble home! You speak to her! I dare not!"

Helen laughed. "Daft wench! Well, what do ye think? 'Tis Reverend's gift, and I'm more than grateful."

We duly admired the dress; it was fashionable, full-skirted, with several dozen petticoats beneath. Lemon in colour, it had a sheen to it like satin. The front had many bows, buttons and the sleeves were mutton leg.

"It's beautiful, Helen," Mrs Elgin told her. "You look dignified and glamorous. It suits your black hair too."

Helen admired her reflection. "I wish Mam could see me like this – she'd no believe her eyes!"

The dress was terribly showy and to me looked too fussy. You couldn't work in it. The skirt would have tripped me up and it had so many frills underneath, I wondered her legs didn't get tangled.

"It makes you look like a handbell!" I told her, giggling, sure that Helen, with her sense of humour, would laugh too, but unexpectedly, she took offence. She gave a "hmph!" sort of noise and stalked out. I looked at Mrs Elgin.

"Oh no!" I groaned. "I thought she'd find that funny, but she does resemble a bell!"

"Never mind, Alice dear, she'll forgive you!"

When it had dried, I put on the straw hat I had found. It suited me well. Mrs Elgin had helped me to dry it out and we had managed to preserve the ribbon too. "I hope you don't run into its former owner, Alice!" she teased. "She may well pluck it from your head!"

"Yes, well, I'd best apologise to Helen! Wish me luck!"

Feeling nervous and guilty, I went to see Helen. I had told Sam how I had offended Helen. He had spluttered.

"Oh, I'm sure she'll forgive you, darling. Take her something to eat and she'll be your friend again!"

So, I had gone looking to see what I could find. Helen, I knew, loved food of all sorts but one of her favourite things was cold sausage. I looked and saw a Cumberland sausage... just the kind she favoured most of all.

I spotted Blisset walking arm-in-arm with Susan and hid up a row as they walked past laughing. Blisset gave a pinch to Susan's bottom, and she yelped and laughed. I scowled as they walked on past. She was out flaunting her behaviour in broad daylight, quite unashamed, whilst Sam and I had to sneak around and hide. I felt bitter indeed as I crossed the marketplace, pushing through the people and heading to Saint Nicholas'.

Helen was in the kitchen. I knocked and entered nervously. Helen gave me a look, a sniff, then turned her head away.

"Helen?" I said tentatively. There was no response. "Helen?" I said again. Still no response. I walked up to her and put down the sausage in the bag in front of her. "I'm sorry I called you a bell!" I told her, humbly. "I didn't mean it; it was a joke. You looked lovely, truly."

Still silence, though Helen's eyes spotted the sausage, and a jar of pickle. She loved this combination. She stopped her work and picked it up, sniffed, then bit into it. She glanced at my worried face. Feeling foolish, she looked at me.

"Och, hen, 'tis alright!" She gave me a one-armed hug. "I should've known ye were joking."

I was most relieved. Helen nibbled the peace offering. "'Tis wonderful!" she told me. "I was feeling a wee bit peckish too. I know fancy clothes aren't your style, Alice. I just love the feeling I get in a beautiful dress. I feel posh and I like that."

I sat on the stool she indicated. "I'll put the kettle on," she told me and proceeded to do so. "I meant to ask ye if ye'd do my hair up on the day," she stated. "Now, I suppose I don't deserve it!"

"Course I will!" I replied, smiling.

Helen admired the new hat, and I told her of the girls on the beach. "They were gone by the time it washed up," I told her, "so, it wasn't stealing. I expected it to float away forevermore, but the tide was coming in."

Helen smiled. "'Tis a comely hat and suits ye, lass!" she told me.

The Reverend had organised a meeting about the workhouse poor.

"I'll come to keep an eye on you!" Mrs Elgin stated. "I know how you get when you're on about the workhouse. You won't get anything if you get angry and cheek Miss Spoonamore!"

"I know. But she doesn't know me, does she?"

"Ha! You'd be surprised, young lady! Nothing gets past her! She'll know all about you, I can guarantee that!"

Two o'clock. Helen had prepared refreshments; all was laid out in the Reverend's parlour. The table, made of solid oak, was spread with different things to eat. Yellow table napkins sat at each plate, done in the fancy manner of a corrugated hand fan. I guessed that was Helen's work. They made the room look cheerful, and presumably were for use at Easter. I admired them very much. If only I could make such shapes. Then, suddenly, I remembered an old trick one of the friends of my parents had shown me as a child. I grinned and took a few of them. I quickly fashioned some of the napkins, rolling them on each side until they met in the middle. I then folded them over and, with a few quick twists and tugs, had produced what resembled a plucked chicken. These I put back on the table and walked innocently away.

I glanced from the window which looked onto the garden – the private green space, filled with flowers. There was a chair and a small table there. I pictured the Reverend sitting there, writing, or observing the birds.

There were two armchairs next to the fire, and a long settle underneath the window. His walls had many pictures – portraits of animals, religious pictures, beach and country scenes – I looked at them all. There were bookcases stuffed full of religious texts, books on flora and fauna, and tales of Aesop's fables.

People began to arrive, and the Reverend welcomed everybody. The Master of the Workhouse, and his wife, Matron, who apologised for the absence of the guardians, Florence, Miss Spoonamore, and a few others. I paid close attention to Miss Spoonamore. Tall, ramrod-straight and extremely thin, with a sharp nose, small, colourless eyes, her nondescript-coloured hair in a very tight bun, her central parting straight as could be, and a cotton blouse, buttoned to the neck. Her skirt was full and grey. She looked formidable!

Having heard about the meeting and keen to impart his opinion, George entered the room. He seated himself on a chair in the corner and beamed round at everyone.

"C'mon then! Let's get this party underway!"

"It's not a party, Mr Warne!" Miss Spoonamore reproved him. "It's a serious meeting!"

"Oh! Beggin' yer pardon, miss!" George grinned and bowed his head.

"Do help yourselves," Reverend said, smiling. "This is not *such* a serious discussion, Miss Spoonamore, so please stand or sit as the mood takes you."

I ushered Mrs Elgin to a comfortable chair, then went in search of some food for us both. She smiled and thanked me as I hurried to George with a full plate, then returned to perch on the arm of Mrs Elgin's chair.

"I hope all are comfortable!" The man smiled benignly on us all. "Now then, we are here to discuss..." A shocked exclamation stopped him. "Miss Spoonamore?" he asked mildly.

She shook a napkin in his face. "Look at that! Ludicrous!" The Reverend saw several 'plucked chickens' and blinked, confused.

"What on earth?" He frowned, then, on seeing what they were meant to be, he laughed. "Dear me! It seems that Helen has decided to inject some humour into our little meeting!"

"It's not funny!" Miss Spoonamore snapped. "It is infantile!"

"It is harmless. After all, God granted us laughter. Now, to return to our theme."

Miss Spoonamore seethed quietly at the rebuke.

"Miss Lawrence," the Reverend spoke, "will you kindly tell us your idea?"

I spoke of visiting the old folk, the thinness of the blankets and how I intended to ask for more.

"What?" Miss Spoonamore barked. "Asking for more is greedy. Families can only give so much, you know!"

I frowned at the woman.

"I wanted only to ask that some thicker blankets be donated. The old feel the cold more readily than younger people." I paused. "Is that not so, Miss Spoonamore?"

"Why, you cheeky...!" Miss Spoonamore stood up, as if ready for battle.

"Please!" the Reverend interrupted, raising his hand. "Do let Miss Lawrence continue." He gave me a slight wink.

"They have adequate bedding," Matron objected, "and we don't want them becoming slugabeds."

Mrs Elgin rose to side with me. "I know what it is to shiver through a winter's night. I've a fire in my room at night, yet still I suffer from cold. The rooms they have are huge, bare, it must be freezing in the wintertime. I second Alice's suggestion."

The Reverend nodded, adding his agreement.

"I third it!" Helen, from the back, added her voice too.

"Absolutely!" George called, raising his glass and almost spilling his drink on Florence's sleeve.

Florence nodded. "Yes! Why should *we* lie warm and snug in our beds when older people shiver? It's hardly an act of Christian charity. I've several blankets you may take. I will let you have them if you come with me after this meeting."

I smiled at Florence gratefully.

"Well, in that case," the Reverend turned to the Workhouse Master and Matron, "might Alice and Helen gather what blankets they can?"

The Workhouse Master nodded reluctantly. He had very little choice really, with the enthusiastic Reverend, and he was one of the workhouse guardians.

Helen would later tell me, jokingly, that I had no scruples when it came to pushing my luck. But I went on. "Please, Reverend, I would like you to ask permission, on my behalf, if I can come and read to the sick and the elderly now and again?"

Silence. Mrs Elgin smiled broadly, as did Helen.

Matron spoke. "Ah! I suppose this is an excuse to visit that dotty old biddy you've taken such a shine to!" She shook her head, arms folded. "My husband told me you asked to visit her. We don't allow visits. Perhaps you'd like to adopt her?"

"I wish I could," I replied.

The Reverend gave a shrug. "I think it a nice idea! Why should anybody object to Alice doing this? It will give them a little pleasure. I second it." He looked round, beaming. Mrs Elgin added her voice too. Even Miss Spoonamore considered, then nodded.

"Well, let us enjoy this little put-together, shall we?" The Reverend smiled, standing up. "I approve wholeheartedly of these plans. We must all do good deeds whenever we can, must we not?"

Nobody could really argue with this, and the group began chattering amongst themselves. I admired the Reverend – he could get round the meanest of people.

A day later, and Helen and I had loaded some blankets onto a small hand cart, and we wended our way to the workhouse.

"I never expected to get all these!" I told her, "It was *so* generous. I just hope that ugly troll Matron doesn't pinch them for her own bed!"

We entered through the large, iron gates and across the wide yard, and manoeuvred the cart up the steps to the entrance lobby.

Matron, standing guard like a dragon, scowled. "Didn't take you long, did it? I had to explain to the Board of Guardians that you and your friend went over my head. Mr Baker was furious! I only shut the wretched man up when I explained about the Reverend liking your ridiculous idea!" She glared like a ferocious bulldog about to bite, then continued. "I hope they have all been laundered?"

I had no idea, but I nodded. The ones we had provided, and the ones from the Reverend and Florence were clean, of course. I gave them to her.

"Good! The last thing we want is an outbreak of lice! I will put these in the cupboards on the elderly dormitory," she explained. "I will have them doled out later. Alright, you may leave now."

"Matron, please might I have a moment?" I spoke so urgently, the large-bodied woman turned.

"What is it *now*, Lawrence?"

"The grey eiderdown, with all the spiral patterns on." I paused.

"What of it?"

"Please will you promise to give that to Alice?" I asked her.

"Is this woman related to you? You seem to care a lot about her."

"No, but she reminds me of my late grandmother," I told her, quite honestly.

"Oh, very well!" Matron, a no-nonsense woman and seldom, if ever afflicted with any caring emotion, nodded.

"Very well. Now, be off with you!" She nodded at us, and we were thus dismissed.

We took our leave of the woman and went out into the sunshine. "Why that one in particular?" Helen asked me, interested.

"Because it's soft and warm, like I said," I answered, sounding embarrassed, trying to avoid eye contact.

Helen stopped me. "Ye took it off yer own bed, didn't ye?" she stated.

"Well, Mrs Elgin didn't mind." I looked out to sea, blushing.

"Yer a great daft ninny!" she told me, exasperated. "But a kind one!"

On Tuesday evening, quite early, I went to the workhouse alone. Matron nodded and directed me to the women's dormitory where I sat beside Alice and read to her. The elderly lady's smile gave me all the reward I needed. Once the others saw what I was doing, they gathered round. Recalling some jokes and songs my parents used in the music halls, I was soon making them laugh and even join in the singing.

Later, Matron, seeing the other dormitories empty, ventured to look. She was annoyed to see such 'time-wasting' and turned to vent her spleen to her husband.

The following day, Sam and I went to Saint Nicholas' to listen to George practising. We sat in the pews and Sam's hand curled around mine. I smiled up at him. George was aware he had a small audience, and after rehearsals, we chatted to him. As he would reveal later, he could tell at once we were in love.

Sam had been horrified to hear that his father-in-law had decided to pay them a visit. Susan had given him no notice whatsoever and 'the old man', as she ever referred to him, was turning up that Friday. Sam told me this as we sat in the denes.

"But don't worry; it just means I can spend more time with you!" He grinned widely.

Sam met his father-in-law off the train with a bad grace. Susan squealed in excitement and went to hug him. He was the only person, it appeared, worthy of her affections.

"Hello, my fine gal!" he said, practically throwing his luggage at Sam to carry. "How are you? That useless excuse for a man looking after you?"

Not really," Susan told him. Her father looked at Sam.

"Afternoon, Samuel," he said.

Sam nodded. "Arternune; how do you do?"

"Alright," he replied somewhat shortly. "Well, come on then, Susie, my queen, what you got in store for the old man then? Something nice, I'll warrant!"

The pair walked off, arm-in-arm as if Sam did not exist.

Back at the lodgings, Susan showed her father where they would be sleeping. "Sam can take the put-up bed downstairs," she told him. "You 'ave his bed, Dad, and I'll be in my own room."

"Ah, you're a good gal!" Her father smiled. "He's actin' a bit odd."

"Yeah, he's sniffin' round some fancy bitch!"

"Oh, is he now?" Mr Bond growled, sounding like a dog himself. "Well, I'll sort the bugger out."

"No, Pa! Let it go." Susan didn't want him interfering. It would make things worse still between them. "It'll wear off in time. Anyway, I wanna sort him out myself!"

"How long you been in separate rooms then, my queen?"

"Since *she* come on the scene!" she replied as they entered Sam's room.

"Bloody Hellfire! Stinks like a tart's boudoir in 'ere!" Susan's father sniffed in disgust, spotting lavender bags dotted here and there along with the dried sweet woodruff that Sam placed in his clothes. The herb smelled of fresh hay and vanilla. Mr Bond was unused to such a sweet assault on his nostrils and shuddered.

Susan opened the window. "I know, he's trying to impress that bitch!" she answered. "So, he keeps on 'avin' baths. I oughta drown him in one!"

"Well, come on, gal, forget him, eh? Have some father and daughter time. What do you say I treat us to a slap-up meal at the ale house?"

Susan shrieked loudly; "Samuel. We're going to the ale house!" Without waiting for a response, the pair went off. Sam turned to head to Golden Keys Row.

"Samuel!" Mrs Elgin beamed as he knocked and entered. "Had enough of the old fellow already?"

Sam nodded. "They're off to the Black Swan," he said sitting down. "So, I decided to use the opportunity to see my little angel."

"She won't be long," Mrs Elgin told him. "We're having cold meats later, with some potatoes. Alice has made some sweet tomato chutney. It's very moreish! Interested?"

Sam nodded. He was famished.

"Well, it will be a treat for Alice to find you here," Mrs Elgin told him. "She wasn't expecting to see you until tomorrow."

Susan and her father were walking to the ale house when she spotted me, walking along in the cheerful and jaunty manner that annoyed her intensely.

"Pa! That's her!" Susan grabbed her father's arm.

"What? Which one?" He squinted.

"The one with the curly blonde hair, pale blue frock. Over there... she been to get summat, I spect, 'cos she's heading back to her row."

Susan's father raised his brows. "Bloody Hell! I didn't realise he was into kids!"

"She's no kid! She's twenty-one, 'cordin' to the old cat!" Susan remarked.

"She don't bleedin' look it!" he replied. "Looks all of thirteen!" His eyes followed me. "Nice tits though!"

"Pa!" Susan screeched.

"Alright, sweetheart. Ah, she ain't a patch on you, my beauty! Don't worry, it's the seven-year itch; he'll get bored."

I entered the kitchen and squeaked with excitement. "Sam!" I put the meat down and hastened to hug him. Sam pulled me onto his knees. "I wasn't expecting you till tomorrow!" I beamed.

"Well, I know, but the old fellow's here and decided to take her to the ale house."

"That's good; with them out of the way, you can stay here a while."

In the ale house, Susan and her father had eaten and were onto the drinking by now. He grumbled loudly about the food, locals, the town in general, and the lack of a good, London chophouse.

"Do you get back to bloody London then!" one man bellowed from his corner.

Mr Bond glared. "Got a right to my opinion, ain't I?"

"Pa, let it lie." Susan knew when the locals were taking offence. "They're all like Sam up 'ere!"

"Useless!" her father bawled. "Bloody useless! You're all soft in this town!" Susan groaned as one large man rolled up his sleeves and advanced.

Late that night, Sam was disturbed from his sleep by the pair returning.

"Oi!" Susan gave a sharp kick to his shins.

Sam leapt. "Don't do that!" he roared, surprising both of them.

"Ooh, he got *some* balls then!" Susan's father sneered. He teetered unsteadily, then overbalanced, and fell sideways into a display and both he and Susan roared with laughter at the splintering of wood. Sam decided a little action was needed and he stood.

"Look at the state of you!" he told her. "It's disgraceful!"

"Don't you call my gal disgraceful!" Susan's father struggled to his feet. "You! I wish I'd never met you! Why I gave my precious angel to you, I can't imagine! You were wet behind the ears then and you still are now! Her first husband... now, there was a *real* man! He was a son to me! Pity he died."

Sam didn't care about the diatribe, or the mocking. He had heard it all before. He merely stood, looking at him, stony-faced. His father-in-law had a black eye and a split lip. Obviously, the man had been brawling. Sam wasn't the least bit surprised.

"Come on, Pa, let's go up." Susan seized her father's hand. "I'll see to your face. Right old shiner you're gonna have." The two began to make their way up the stairs roaring with laugher.

Sam cringed as a nightgown-clad Florence appeared, candle in hand.

"BE QUIET!" she bellowed. "Show some respect! Coming in waking good honest folks from their sleep! And what was that crash I just heard?"

Susan's father, about to make an extremely rude remark, was hushed by his daughter.

"Leave it, Pa. I don't wanna end up on the street!"

They vanished up the stairs.

"Oh no! Just look at my displays! Samuel, I realise that you are a quiet and respectful man, willing to do anything for anybody, but I *insist* you speak to your wife about such behaviour. A woman of her age should *not* be rolling in drunk at this hour and her father should know better! He's a guest in my house!"

"I already have spoken to her, Mrs Townsend," he said, rubbing tired eyes, "and I apologise sincerely to you now. I'll speak to her again, but I fear my words fall on deaf ears!"

"Then a good slap will make her listen!" Florence told him. "It's because of you that I permit you to stay. Anyone else would have been thrown out long ago."

Sam nodded. "I know, Mrs Townsend, and I'm deeply grateful. I'll re-right the displays first thing."

Florence nodded and, after a further look around, tutted and went back to her room.

In the morning, both were sore-headed and unrepentant. Florence was waiting, stony-faced, downstairs for them. "Before you go," she indicated the displays, "your son-in-law put them back upright, those that remain intact, that is, but look at the remnants of my produce! I have lost money over them;

I cannot sell these products now. Now, kindly remember you are a *guest*. In *my* house. Any further horseplay and you leave!"

"Well, sorry I'm sure, Missus!" Susan's father saw that he had overstepped the bounds of a guest. "I'll pay for 'em right and proper."

"See that you do!"

Later, in the privacy of the bedroom, Susan and her father shared their ill-gotten gains. She spoke then, confessing how her pickpocketing episode had gone horribly wrong and had ended in the death of my parents. Her father sat bolt upright, rocked to his core. He took his pipe from his mouth. "Bloody Hell, gal! When was this?"

Susan told him.

"And it didn't occur to you to tell me before?"

Susan Dwyer shook her head. "Don't think badly of me, Pa!"

Her father hugged her. "Of course, I don't, my bird. 'Specially if it was them that bred that little bitch your husband seems to prefer! I'm just a bit shocked! Well, long as nobody saw you, it can be our secret, eh? I'm glad you mentioned it. If anyone should find out, which they won't, but just in *case* they do, we'll think of an alibi, eh?"

Susan nodded, relieved to hear what her father said.

"Thanks, Pa. I had to stick the knife in 'em. Her old man was about to grab me, so I did for his old woman first, then him when he was seeing to her. I would've done that snotty little bitch 'an all, but she ran." She sounded so relieved; her father put his arm round her.

"Think I'd let my best gal take the long drop?" he asked her. "We all make mistakes; now, don't worry. Don't I always think of a way out of things?"

Susan nodded.

Mr Bond chewed the stem of his pipe. "What about her? Did she see you?"

Susan shook her head. "Not really, no. It was dark, raining and she was terrified. Her old man told her to run, and bloody hell, so did I!"

At that moment, Sam and I were in the denes.

"I've made up my mind, Alice. I can't live here and keep seeing you secretly; it's dangerous. We both have a trade, we'll go away, start a new life together. Would you dare to do that with me? It would mean risking your reputation, but I love you, you love me. It can work, Alice. It *will* work."

I nodded vigorously. "That's what I want too," I whispered to him.

Sam felt relief wash over him.

"How about Devon?" I asked. "Grandfather would take us in."

Sam felt that unlikely, but he nodded. "If he'll have us."

I knew we wouldn't be the only ones to run away together. People did. They simply upped and went and when they settled in another place, either merely said they were married, or married each other, regardless of whether one was married before or not.

I asked Sam if he wished me to give him a reading, and having hesitated at first, he nodded.

"Sam, from what I can see, your main troubles are behind you. There is still danger ahead... I don't know what... see here, the lifeline is broken in places, that means accident, great danger. But the future looks smoother." I glanced at his face. Sam nodded.

"It has been difficult," he admitted. "Some years ago, I fell into the Thames, almost drowned, but a stranger dived in and pulled me out."

I sighed with relief as I examined Sam's palm. To me, it seemed as though Sam's future, our future, would be smoother. It surprised me to see signs of wealth later in life, but as long as Sam and I were together, that was all that mattered.

Susan told her father about Blisset. He stroked his chin thoughtfully. "And you prefer this 'un, my princess?" he asked. Susan nodded. She spoke of the man's ill deeds, his lively drinking and camaraderie. In her eyes, Blisset was a daredevil, unafraid to take risks, speak his mind. Just the kind that appealed to her father. Intrigued, they went to meet him.

Blisset at once shook Mr Bond's hand, having first swept off his stove pipe hat and given a short bow.

"It's an honour to meet you, sir," Blisset grovelled. "I've heard so much about you."

"The pleasure's all mine, sir!" her father assured him. "May I buy you a drink?"

The threesome sat in The Three Feathers and, unsurprisingly, got along very well.

"You're the fellow I shoulda picked for my Sue," her father stated, then looked at his daughter. "Now, there's a *real* man for you! What a bloody shame he ain't a Londoner! Eh, gal? He ain't afraid to be on the wrong side of the law to earn a few extra bob. What's your opinion on this bloody soft Nancy boy our Sue wed?"

"He's a nobody. Damn and blast 'im." Blisset growled, "Known him since we was lads. He prefers to be indoors reading than in the ale house. Did you ever hear such a thing?" Blisset rubbed his stubbled chin. "I reckon he's knocking off that Lawrence chit. I'm only amazed he knows what to do with it!"

"Ha! Take it from me, he don't!" Susan blustered. It didn't occur to her that speaking of such things with her father present was somewhat crass.

Blisset nodded soberly. They spent some more time slating Sam and defiling my name before they were finished. At long last, the trio rose, somewhat worse for wear. Blisset clasped Mr Bond's hand.

"I bid you good night, sir, and a safe journey home. I only wish I'd met you sooner! Your daughter's a queen, perfect in every way, and if there was a chance to make her mine, I would."

"You've given me a lot to think on, son," Susan's father told him. "People *can* vanish suddenly or take ill and die!" He glanced at Susan with a smirk. "And London 'ud suit you! I could use a crafty brain like yours. Let's wait and see!"

It was with great relief that Sam was able to bid goodbye to his father-in-law on the Wednesday.

"I wish I could come with you, Pa," Susan said longingly. They stood awaiting the Norwich train.

"We'll think of something! Get you back home, eh? Get that fella Raymond to come with us. I could use a bloke like 'im in the smoke. Sure you want to trade him for Dwyer? Ain't much point hanging onto that lily-liver."

Susan nodded. Blisset was wild, exciting, and supremely dangerous, but that was the attraction. She wondered what Blisset would think of London. You had to be born and bred there to survive it in her opinion.

"Well, there'd be business aplenty there, I don't doubt," he answered after Susan mooted the subject to Blisset. "Your old man's one in a million. Do you let me have a think about it, eh?"

Susan nodded, but Blisset wasn't about to leave Yarmouth with all his current contacts. Susan was his bit on the side and so she would remain. He wasn't the kind of man to commit. He had no interest in anything long-term with her. If she left to return to London, so be it. There were plenty more women.

Thursday the 23rd arrived and there was a palpable air of excitement in the town. Helen was so nervous with the wedding that the Reverend gave her camomile tea.

I turned up early to help Helen, wearing my Sunday dress. Helen suddenly felt extremely overdressed. After all, she was, technically, a servant and it would look somewhat precocious, but she could hardly refuse to wear the pretty dress the Reverend had given her.

"Och! They've arrived!" my friend squeaked in alarm. "Is everything ready? Do I look alright?"

I smiled. "Everything's fine, and you look wonderful. The groom'll wish it was *you* he was marrying when he sees you! Don't panic, or you'll end up dropping something. Ugh! What's this horrible-looking wobbly thing?"

"'Tis a brawn, and you'll no insult it, unless ye fancy it down your front!"

Brawn! I shuddered in revulsion. Jellied pork... more jelly than pork. I prodded it and watched it quiver.

Helen slapped my hand. "Get yer mitts off it! 'Tis no for ye to poke and prod!"

We watched from the doorway as the groom's carriage wound its way into the grounds. They stopped, and the door was opened for them by a man in golden livery.

The groom was assisted to the ground. There was a cheer from the onlookers. James Paget turned and winked at us. I gasped at the familiarity and grinned hugely at him.

George Warne struck up a rousing bridal march and Helen and I squeezed in to watch from the side door. I looked over at the organist. His hands and feet seeming to fly in all directions. I prodded Helen who looked. "The finest organist who ever graced St Nick's!" she told me.

The wedding ceremony droned on and was boring. Helen worried about her brawn collapsing, the idea of which gave me the giggles. At last, the ceremony over, the wedding breakfast took place in a giant marquee. Helen was nervous, but there was little for her to do. The bridal couple had their own servants who managed most efficiently. All that was required of Helen was to be there should anybody need her assistance.

Later, the procession once more wound its way through the street and up onto South Quay.

Helen wiped her sweating brow.

"I'm glad that's over with, hen. I've a headache the size of France! I'll leave the clearing up till the morning."

"Aren't their own people going to clean up?" I asked.

"Aye, they'll do some of it overnight, but ye can bet they'll no' be as thorough as they should be. Well, I'll bid ye a good night, lass."

CHAPTER TWO

July – 1844

I decided to make some shirts for Sam as a surprise.

"You'll need one of his old ones for a pattern," Mrs Elgin stated. "I'm not sure how you'll accomplish that! Pity you didn't think of that when he gave you them to sew the buttons back on."

The back yard behind Florence's shop was incredibly small. Florence used a small line in the back yard or set her things over a clothes horse. Perhaps I could take one from there. Susan did the wash on Fridays, that I did know. She had to wash Florence's things as part of the terms of lodging there, though she would skimp what she could, mainly her own clothing.

It was Friday and I was helping Florence stack some shelves. Florence chattered about the shop, her uncle in Norwich and her late husband. She was never short of something to say. I glanced through the open door. Susan seemed to have finished her chores since she was no longer there.

"Typical," Florence stated when I remarked on her absence. "Slunk off again. Everything done?"

I nodded.

"Alright then," Florence said. "Well, thank you, Alice, you've been most helpful. Shall we take tea and some cake?"

We sat in the small back yard; a rare treat since Florence seldom had the time or the inclination to sit about. The tea was refreshing and the cake moist. I watched the shirts flapping. The other items hung on a clothes horse, or over other items to dry in the sun.

Florence nattered on; privately, she had her suspicions about Sam and me. For all she disapproved, she found she couldn't blame either of us. She was a witness to their arguments all the time. Susan, it had to be said, could outdo a fishwife with her screaming.

"Well, I must return to work. Be an angel, will you, and wash up the crockery? Take some of the cake home for Mary too."

"Yes, Mrs Townsend," I said as she rose to enter the shop. Quickly glancing around, I snatched a shirt from the line and stuffed it inside my bodice. I finished the washing up, cut some cake and bid Florence farewell.

Mrs Elgin laughed when I produced it.

"Alice. What a place to put it!" she exclaimed. "Ah, never mind, I am sure Samuel wouldn't object!"

I grinned. "Nice and cooling," I told her.

Mrs Elgin smiled and took the cake to nibble.

Sam's shirt took little time to dry; I ironed it and soon had it against the linen I had purchased and was marking out the pattern.

Susan knew she had lost Sam and knew too that it was her own fault. If only she had the courage to put arsenic in his food! Then, she would be free to marry Blisset! She had already killed once and got away with it. This time, it would be subtle and slow; foolproof! She would avenge herself for all the imagined wrongs and punish her husband and myself into the bargain.

Arsenic was ridiculously easy to obtain. One had only to sign the poisons book in the apothecary shop. After all, it was used in medicines, tonics, fly-papers and women used it in cosmetics. Having bodged the pickpocketing attempt on my parents, needing to subsequently stab them in cold blood, small amounts of arsenic in food would be simple.

That Wednesday, Mrs Elgin, Helen and I went to the market. I'd decided to make myself a dress and Helen had a thousand ideas for styles.

"I don't want anything fancy," I told her. "Can you imagine the remarks if I went about in the one you have just described? Besides, it'd take me an age!"

Helen had flamboyant ideas about clothing despite her rustic upbringing. She loved full-skirted dresses, and as many petticoats as she could. In truth, the dress the Reverend had bought her for Mr Paget's wedding had been far above her station, but Helen donned it each Sunday with pride.

I hated the stuffiness of too much round my lower half and would have as thin a material as possible. I would wear wool stockings in winter if it was very cold, and to make a semblance of a petticoat, I would stitch linen or lace round the bottom of the dress.

We wandered up and down the stalls. "That's the one where I got the linen for Sam's shirts. It's good quality. Perhaps I could make a linen dress rather than cotton. What do you think, Mary?"

"Either is good," she remarked, "particularly in warmer weather. Linen will last longer though cotton is cool, but the way you keep washing things, Alice, the linen will survive longer. It's up to you, what you feel most comfortable in."

"Linen then."

We went to the stall to look at the cloth. I wondered how much I should need for a dress.

"You're very small, miss. I don't think you'd need more than four yards. Depends on how full you like your skirt."

"She doesnae," Helen said unhelpfully. "She's nae sense of style."

I flipped Helen's arm. "Ignore her, miss," I told her. "I want enough to make this kind of style, please."

I took the linen home wondering how long it would take me. I had only a small amount left to do on the second shirt I had made for Sam.

Whilst making the dress, my mind drifted to the problem of sweating. Sweat was unavoidable. Everyone knew that, but there was a difference between a clean sweat and someone who had not washed in weeks. Sam would be hot and sweaty after a day working, but he would wash himself, not caring for the rancid smell some people had. The smell of unwashed bodies in ale houses could be eye-watering. Even Helen was a little pungent on occasion. I wrinkled my nose fastidiously. Many of the gentry didn't wash much but would merely use strong perfume that didn't mask strong sweat smells.

I had cut away the underarms on my other dresses to avoid sweat stains, and unpleasant smells, which I was always repelled by. However, supposing I could put something in the underarms that could be removed and washed? It would mean I could avoid having to cut around the underarms. Dresses were not easy to wash, unlike shirts or blouses, which could be boil-washed weekly. I would give it some thought.

I presented Sam with his shirts the next morning.

"Darling! These are magnificent! You made these? How? It's like they were made to my exact size."

"They were!" I said, kissing his nose. "You remember the shirt you lost?" I handed it to him.

Sam laughed. "You took it?"

I nodded, smiling cheekily.

"I did, and I stuffed it inside my bodice to get it home!" I responded.

"Oh!" Sam felt himself harden as he thought of that. "You're wonderful, Alice!"

I was pleased he liked them and promised him more.

Mrs Elgin listened to my plan about the dress shields.

"What a good idea!" she exclaimed. "I'm lucky, I don't sweat much these days. Find it hard enough to keep warm, never mind overheat, but look!"

To my surprise, Mrs Elgin took two buttons, sewed them into place, then having made buttonholes in the dress, fitted the shields in.

"Brilliant!" I squealed.

"You thought of it!" The old lady beamed.

"Well, yes, but the buttons were your idea," I told her. "I was wondering how to fasten them so they don't drop out."

"I think it will be very fine," Mrs Elgin stated.

Helen and Mrs Elgin stood back as I came out shyly to show them my new dress.

"Well?" I was red as a berry.

"Alice. You look beautiful!" Mrs Elgin told me sincerely. "That dress lends a semblance of purity; don't you agree, Helen?"

"Aye, I do. Alice, ye've made a very fine job of that!"

I was relieved. "Thank you," I told them. "I wondered how it would look all finished. I didn't think it would suit me really."

"Lass, would ye make me a blouse?" Helen asked. "I'll buy the linen, cottons and stuff and pay ye for yer time."

"Of course! You'd best sketch the kind you want; I know how you like your frills and fancies."

Helen smiled broadly. "Aye, I'll do my best. Thanks, lass, I'll get some material soon as I can."

"And don't forget to let me have one of yours as a pattern," I reminded her.

Helen was intrigued by my linen pads. She suffered greatly from sweating and hated it. I took some of her blouses and dresses and made linen pads for her to attach.

"It saves a lot of washing all the time," I told her, having handed them to her. "All you need do is put them in to soak; they dry quickly and then can be used and re-used."

"Alice, yer a genius," Helen told me. "Ye should mebbe sell them!"

That had not occurred to me before, but it was such a good idea. I could get some more money for our little 'escape fund.' I had been putting money away in a jar I kept in my room. Sam also had a secret fund, hidden beneath a floorboard in his workshop on which stood one of his cabinets.

I put the idea to Mrs Elgin who seized on it at once.

"Helen's right!" She exclaimed. "Why didn't we think of that? Now, how do we do it? Let me think. Perhaps the lady who you bought the linen from can be persuaded to sell them on your behalf. Shall we go and ask her next market day?"

I nodded.

Market day came around quickly, and Mrs Elgin and I ventured to the cloth stall. The lady who ran it observed the pads. She was impressed with the idea and after some negotiation with us, we agreed on my giving her a batch for herself; the rest she would sell, and I would keep the profit.

Later that day, Helen presented me with a blouse and some material. She had also made a sketch of the style she wanted. I almost regretted saying I would do it; she had gone overboard with her design! But it would look beautiful. I regarded the peach-coloured cloth.

"Nice choice, Helen. It'll look well on you."

Helen smiled. "I like peach. I usually go about in blues and greens, so it'll be good and summery."

That Sunday, Florence spoke to us after the morning service, worried about her uncle.

"I have to go to see him," she told us. "He's most unwell. One day he is fit and says he feels fine, the next he lies abed for days. He's lost weight as well."

"What does the doctor say?" Mrs Elgin asked.

"He won't have the doctor!" Florence said in exasperation. "Says he won't let the 'old sawbones' anywhere near him. So, I'm glad I met you both. I was going to ask if you could spare Alice." She looked down at me.

"Alice, dear, will you be good enough to serve in the shop for me? Just mornings. My friend will take over at noon. I shall pay you well."

I could hardly object without inviting suspicion. Mrs Elgin saw my dilemma and spoke for me.

"Well, Alice would be happy to help, of course, but her reckoning is bad. She'd never deliberately short-change a body, but she is more than likely to get it wrong."

"Well, that's not a problem. I'll explain that to the regulars," Florence said smiling. "They'll be patient with you. I'll work out a little table that you can refer to."

What could I say? Now, I would be in the same place as Susan, and she would make things awkward for me.

Later that day, I told Helen.

"Ye cannae be left wi' that spiteful body!" she told me. "I'll call in and sit with ye if ye like. Reverend willnae object."

"Mrs Townsend can't pay both of us though," I reminded her.

"Och, that doesnae matter. I'll do it for you since yer ma wee pal!"

"Thanks, Helen!" I gave her a hug. "You're such a good friend!"

Monday morning came and as I entered the shop, I could hear arguing from upstairs. Goodness! Sam did sound angry. He was shouting; Florence groaned.

"At it again," she grumbled. "Yesterday, all day! And on a Sunday! I rapped on the ceiling with a broom, but it only quieted for a while!"

Florence showed me where things were, how to work the till, and told me I might drink as much tea as I wished, or have fruit or cake, but I was to leave her a list of what I had taken for myself.

I followed her to the door.

"Goodbye, Mrs Townsend. I hope you find your uncle not as bad as you fear."

Shortly after, Sam hurried downstairs, and looked at me.

"Alice," he said quickly and quietly. "You'll be fine, don't worry." A swift kiss and he left. Susan appeared.

"Alright, Lawrence." She folded her arms and leaned against the wall of the shop. "It ain't my choice you're here. Slut! Don't get light-fingered either."

I glared at her. "I don't steal money!" I said annoyed.

"You'd bleedin' well steal my man though, wouldn't you?" came the sharp retort. "Well, you won't get the chance, gal! I'll see to that!"

He wasn't hers either; not anymore, but I kept my mouth shut. The door jangled and Helen came in.

"What are *you* doing here, you great, fat lump?" Susan asked rudely.

"I'm stoppin' wi' my pal." Helen dared her to object. "Helpin' oot!"

Susan looked her up and down, then spat. She turned and left the shop muttering obscenities.

Helen and I stood behind the counter. "I'll work the till if ye prefer," Helen reassured me.

The morning dragged. A few customers asked for their usual and Helen was able to reckon it up in her head well enough.

Near lunchtime, Susan came back in, and having shot a glance at us, ignored us and marched upstairs. Mrs Mackenzie arrived moments later, and I was relieved but as we were leaving, she called us back.

"Miss Lawrence! One moment please." I glanced at Helen. We turned back.

"What have you done to these candles?" To our surprise, she showed us five candles, all bent into almost a C shape. Irritated at my blank look, Mrs Mackenzie gave a huff of exasperation. "You put them in the window. Stupid girl! The sun's been on them. That's why they're half-melted!"

"Oh, I'm sorry, but, well, I'm sure I didn't put them there. I know the sun comes into that window on a morning!"

"You want to use the eyes God gave you, girl! I spotted them at once. Look, in the box at the front! I'll have to inform Mrs Townsend!" the lady told me briskly. "She'll stop your wages for it! Where was your common sense, hmm?"

Helen and I glanced behind her. Susan stood, smug and smirking, against the shop wall.

"But I..." I stopped. What was the use?

"Don't make excuses," Mrs Mackenzie said. "Look, it's not the end of the world; just some thoughtlessness on your part."

Later that day, Mrs Elgin and I went along with Helen to Annie's stall. All 20 sweat pads had been sold and I was handed my shilling wages and told to return with more.

I went to tell Sam and handed him the money.

"This goes into our pot," He assured me. "How was today?"

"I got into trouble for leaving candles in the sun, but I didn't put them there. I've more sense than to leave candles in the sun, for goodness' sake!"

Sam made a murmur of sympathy. "Poor baby," he soothed. "I shall meet you on the beach in our spot at six, alright?"

When Friday came, nobody was more relieved than I. Susan, needing to get rid of Helen, had been making plans. About 11.30, a boy came into the shop in a hurry.

"Miss Anderson!" he told her. "Reverend says do you go straight back 'ome now. He fell off a ladder!"

Helen gasped. "And what was he doin' up a ladder at his age?" She shook her head. "I'll have to leave ye, lass. Ye'll be fine, don't worry."

"I know. Goodness, Helen, I hope he isn't badly injured!"

Helen hastened out, and Susan turned to me.

"Well, you can go; I'll close early. The old cat won't know."

I took off the apron to hang up when a huge crash had me jump out of my skin.

"Ah! Butterfingers!" Susan looked mournfully at the smashed china rose bowl. "Well, I hated that thing anyway. Well! Go! Don't stand there staring!"

When Helen returned, the Reverend was in his room, calmly smoking a pipe and watching the birds. He looked up, startled at Helen's sudden entrance. Panting for breath, Helen spoke.

"Reverend! Yer fine!"

The elderly man looked at her. He smiled. "Of course, my dear child, why wouldn't I be?"

"Laddie told me ye fell off a ladder!" Helen gasped.

Reverend laughed. "No, as you see, I'm fine! Doubtless, an urchin's idea of a joke!" he assured her. "They'll never learn, just like the boy who cried wolf! Did Alice manage the shop?"

Helen sat, deciding it had, indeed, been a joke. It didn't occur to her to ask why and how the urchin had known she would be at Mrs Townsend's shop!

On Saturday morning, I was in my room, leaning on the narrow window ledge, looking at the view of blue sky and warm sun, wishing with all my heart I could be walking on the beach with Sam when I noticed Florence striding up the row. She didn't look terribly pleased.

"Oh no, bad news of her uncle," I whispered to myself. Mrs Elgin answered the fierce knocking and there were voices – Florence's angry, Mrs Elgin's shocked. I got up and moved toward the door to listen.

"ALICE!" Mrs Elgin bawled. "Come down here! At once!" She sounded furious too.

I descended the stairs with a feeling of dread. "Yes?"

"Alice!" Florence stated sharply. "I'm very lenient with anyone in my employ. But, when you break something, I expect you to tell me about it; that is, you leave me a note or that you come to me as soon as you are able! Not leave it to Susan!"

"What?" I was confused.

"My rose bowl. It's been in my family for years!" she responded. "Why were you handling it in the first place?"

"I did *not* touch it never mind break it!" I exclaimed, the penny suddenly dropping.

Florence rolled her eyes dramatically.

"Then why is it in a million pieces?" she asked. Susan says she witnessed you dropping it through an open door and begged her to say nothing about it."

"It was *her* dropped it! She said it didn't matter and that I was to go on home!"

"Then I am informed there is the matter of a box of beeswax candles put in the sun! Mrs Mackenzie spoke for you, citing you'd obviously not thought, for all they are expensive. I will let that go, but the bowl?"

"Wait!" Mrs Elgin said in a sharp voice. "Susan said all this?"

"Yes, she saw her. Alice pleaded with her to say nothing, to put it into the bin as though hoping I wouldn't notice its absence." Florence turned to me. "You really ought to have owned to that, Alice. It's deceitful. I'll take it out of your wages... in fact, that's more than a week's wages, so, you will spend next week, mornings, fetching and carrying for me, and running errands to work off your debt!"

I burst into sobs.

Florence looked at me, feeling angrier than she had in a long time.

"It was *her!*" I sobbed. "That terrible lodger of yours!"

"Florence!" Mrs Elgin stated sharply. "Alice has never been anything but perfectly honest with me. If she broke the dish, she would've told me."

Florence thought. It did seem strange.

"Well, I don't know, I'm sure!"

Mrs Elgin tried to reason with Florence, and I stormed out down the row, where I marched along the sea front and went to the denes to fling myself down and proceeded to call Florence all the worst kind of names I knew.

When I returned an hour later, Florence had gone, and Mrs Elgin sat and handed me a cup of tea. She took my hand across the table.

"I believe *you!*" she said gently. "But there is nothing I can do! These things happen, Alice; you must take it on the chin. She'll think much better of you for it, and so will Sam!" she added.

"Alright, but I don't want to."

"I know, my dear, me neither, but 'tis our cross to bear."

The following week, I obediently worked off my debts to Florence. As things turned out, I quite enjoyed it, taking the handcart with various peoples' orders up and down the rows. The weather was good, and I was able to chatter to the customers as I assisted them with their goods.

Sam had kept yet another black eye Susan had given him from his parents. Susan's abuse was commonplace, but he would never tell them. He knew other men would be scornful of him, and whilst wife beating was not unusual, nobody would believe a wife could beat her husband.

It had been Maria who had seen him as he went on an errand. As soon as she spotted her brother, Maria waved jovially.

"Sam! SAM!"

Sam turned and groaned inwardly. His youngest sister hastened up to him. The smile vanished as she saw his face.

"You've been in a fight!" she gasped. "Are you alright? Who walloped you? That's a real shiner you got there!"

Sam shook his head. "It's fine; don't worry about it, Maria."

"Don't worry? Look, if you were set upon..."

"I wasn't."

Maria shook her head in wonder.

"I have to go, Maria, I'm on an errand."

Sam hastened away, leaving Maria wondering.

Later, Maria informed her parents about Sam's 'shiner.'

"I don't approve of fighting," Simon grumbled. "He should know better."

"My dear, Samuel isn't the fighting sort," his wife replied.

"It'll be one of those good-for-nothings," Maria told them stoutly.

"I don't like Samuel mixing with those sorts," Mr Dwyer said, crossly. He turned to his wife. "Wretched vagabonds! Plus, I've heard some most unsavoury facts about our daughter-in-law too, keeping company with that Blissett. She's been a terrible influence on our son. I rue the day I ever sent him to London!"

"If Sam's been fighting, then you can be sure it was self-defence!" Ada spoke with confidence as she bit off a thread she had been sewing with.

There was an awkward silence as Maria tried to make sense of her father's words about unsavoury facts. She knew she would not be told, even if she were to ask, so she decided it was best left unsaid.

It was the following day that Maria found out the truth, and once she did, she was disgusted, though unsurprised. Her young man, Albert, who worked in the herring business, had been helping to unload the catch. Maria was waiting for him to finish so they could take a walk, when Helen had arrived at the jetty. She had begun to chatter to an old friend. Neither Helen nor Maria knew one another, and Maria would not normally have eavesdropped, but on hearing Sam's name, she froze. Helen told her old friend of how William's friend's wife had punched him and blackened his eye.

"Course, poor Samuel's too much of a gentleman to gi' her the thrashing she deserves," Helen said. "Can ye believe it, Phyllis? Wretched woman! I cannae bear the sight of her. Common as muck!"

Maria could hardly go and ask Helen outright about what she had just said, but she stowed it away in her mind for later. As she and Albert walked along the shoreline, Maria spoke of what she had just heard.

"Do you think Susan beat him?" she enquired.

Albert frowned. "Women don't beat men!" he responded, but he knew what Susan was like. Everybody did. He had heard Sam called 'cuckold', 'weak' and many other unpleasant things which were offensive. Maria adored her big brother, and, in her eyes, he could do no wrong.

"*She* can!" Maria said, with venom in her voice.

Sam's parents heard of the reason for Sam's black eye from Maria and were appalled. His mother wept, his father furious. That Sam had not hit back at her was typical of his good nature and gentlemanly behaviour.

"I shan't say anything to Samuel," Simon told his wife. "But I *will* speak to that wench. I don't want him embarrassed that we know. Assaulting him like that? I'll need to get her alone."

"You're not going to do her any damage?" Sam's mother was suddenly fearful.

"Don't be daft, mawther! When did I ever wallop a female? No! For all that she deserves it, and I'd dearly love to give her the punch she deserves, I'll give her a piece of my mind which'll be just as painful!" With that, he marched out of the house.

Tuesday morning early, I woke to the sounds of the knocker-upper.

"Noisy devil." I rose and opened the window. The sky was dark blue, dawn not far off. The lamplighter was extinguishing the gas lamps. Some early people were abroad, horses' hooves clopping and the occasional shout. A seagull circled and cried. I watched as the sky lightened and the sun rose over the sea. The morning was welcoming, fresh and cool. I watched the man as he lumbered down the row.

"Who knocks up the knocker-upper?" I said to myself with a smile. That had been a tongue-twister my mother had liked to tease me with. Suddenly, a wicked idea came to me and, as the man neared, I bawled from the window, in the deepest voice I could manage, as he rapped the stick on the upper window of the house opposite.

"Bring out your dead! Bring out your dead!"

The man jumped, looking round in annoyance as I spluttered, and the occupant of the house opposite looked out of the window in some concern.

"What're you about, Max?" she asked the confused knocker-upper, who glared up at me. I grinned and withdrew my head.

Mrs Elgin and I took ourselves that morning up Conge Row. I sniffed in appreciation as a pieman walked past. I turned my head, my mouth watering.

"Later!" Mrs Elgin poked me. "You've only just eaten breakfast!"

A small bookseller nearby sold periodicals and she and I were going to find something for our amusement. Mrs Elgin was widely read and enjoyed most things. I preferred Penny Dreadfuls, but she was determined to encourage me to read something different.

"Something not tragic or horrific!" she said as we walked, arm-in-arm. "You ought to try some of Dickens' work –Sam enjoys them."

"They're too long and difficult; such tiny writing."

"At least you *can* write, my dear. Many people still cannot."

"Sam is so clever," I told her. "He reckons all manner of stuff in his head, he reads well, and his writing is beautiful."

"I recall Ada telling me he was head writing monitor at school. She came round especially to tell me. So proud, she was! He was about twelve at the time! I think all children should go to school, don't you, Alice? Reading is a pleasant pastime."

We entered the shop and Mrs Elgin breathed in. She enjoyed the smell of old books where I considered them musty. She went to the proprietor to chat, and I perused the lengthy shelves. Books lined the entire wall, from top to bottom, and lay on various chairs. Suddenly, a title caught my eye. "The Hunchback of Notre Dame," I mused and picked it out. "Victor Hugo. Never heard of him; wonder if Sam has!" I read a little about the plot and decided to buy it. I took it to the counter.

"You have excellent literary taste, young lady!" the proprietor stated with salesman's patter. "Victor Hugo, eh? Make sure you have the English version m'dear, unless you are fluent in French!"

Mrs Elgin nodded approval and later we left the shop with our purchases.

"I expect Sam will ask to read that after you," she told me.

It'll take months to read this."

"Well, you may get so involved in it that you won't take as long as you fear," she replied.

Susan sat seething with rage. Her father-in-law had come to her market stall, telling her that he desired a word. She had been expecting anything but what he actually said. His words left no doubt that the opinion of her in-laws was the lowest of the low. She squirmed with embarrassment at the things he had said, about how she had been a terrible influence on their only son; that her behaviour shamed not only the family, but herself as well. Worst of all, she had cowardly hit Sam, knowing he would never hit her back. He had also mentioned that he had heard about the black eye from his youngest daughter, not Sam himself, who was too much the gentleman to complain. Susan had watched as he had walked away, feeling rage sweep through her.

So, that was his opinion, was it? Very well! She would poison Sam, start with a small amount of arsenic in his food, then, when he was dead and buried, she would be off to London with Blissett, but not before she had exacted some revenge on the Dwyer's family home and those within!

Helen and I were lunching in the rectory garden, Susan making her way along the road, basket on her arm. A sudden volley of laughter came from the church, and she looked to see Helen and I sitting on the inner wall, our picnic laid out on a linen cloth.

"I tell ye, lass, t'was so funny," Helen was saying. "A wee mouse! And Reverend calling me to help! He willnae have it killed. It's built a fine nest in the skirting board now. He doesnae know what to do!"

"Poison the little vermin!" Susan spoke and we both jumped at her sudden, and unexpected approach.

Helen glared. "Who asked your opinion?" she asked sharply.

"I don't need to be asked to give helpful tips, surely?" she asked, swaying lightly. I looked at her with hatred I could not quite mask. "Oh, dear me, Alice! *Such* a look! What *have* I done to deserve that?"

"Ye dinnae need to do anything; merely breathe," Helen replied rudely.

"Ah, she's only jealous," Susan said. "She's upset because Sam and I are so happy!"

I glared. I could hardly say I knew they were not. Helen, though, scoffed. "In fact, we're planning a family," she went on, examining her dirty fingernails. "Won't that be wonderful? We'll have to leave our current lodgings, but I'm sure we can find somewhere nice."

The look on my face became more murderous still. I was biting my tongue.

"Anyway, as I was saying. Get some arsenic, Helen. It will do the job quick as quick. They don't suffer."

"Are ye sure, Susan?" Helen asked mildly. "Can I try it out on you first? I would hate to see a dumb animal suffer."

The insult was plain.

"I'm just trying to help," Susan said. "I'm sure Alice wouldn't mind popping along to the chemist to buy some, would you, eh?"

"I'm not handling that stuff!" I told her sharply.

"Well, I must be going!" With a sidelong glance, she walked off whistling. I turned enraged to Helen.

"Lass! I know what ye are gonna say. Ignore it; do ye really think 'tis true? She's clutching at straws, hen; nothing more!"

"Perhaps. But I didn't like the reference to arsenic, Helen. Not one bit." Helen caught my drift.

"Ye dinnae think...? Och lass, no, surely even she wouldnae do that?"

I said nothing, merely looked seriously at her. Helen puffed out her cheeks.

"Well, it's either him or me! She can't poison me though; she knows I'd never take anything she cooked me or offered me. So, it must be Sam!" Panic surged through me, and I got up and hurried off.

Sam found a small whirlwind entering his workshop.

"Darling! What's the matter?" he asked. "Has something happened?" The look on my face was sheer terror. "Do you come, sit and tell me." He patted his knees. I told him of the encounter in the church yard.

"And I didn't like the reference to the poison, Sam," I told him, seriously. "What if she does put something in your food?"

"I don't eat her food anymore," Sam told me. "And as for starting a family? Ha! There's no chance of that. For one, I'd have to sleep with her, and I cannot bring myself to do that." I looked into his eyes. "Sweet Alice, don't think about it," Sam told me. "Truly, there is no chance of us starting any family. I do not sleep at her side. I do not be intimate with her. I am never going to eat anything she cooks now in any case."

"What about drink?" I asked.

"I'll merely get it as I usually do. After all, she won't put anything in the ale barrel, not unless she wants to poison Mrs Townsend and herself too. As for tea, coffee, I shall buy my own or use Mrs T's. Alice, don't worry she is scarcely likely to say all that and mean it in front of Helen."

Another beautiful morning and the carts rumbled past with people beginning to shout their wares. Later that morning, the sun grew hotter. My small room was hot. I was glad I had decided to 'alter' a couple of the shifts I wore in bed. I chuckled as I recalled Mrs Elgin's amazement when I washed them.

Mrs Elgin had had to look twice. "What *have* you done to those, Alice?" she asked. "Have they shrunk?"

"No, I chopped the bottom pieces off."

"Why, might one ask?"

"They're too hot. I sweat; it's horrible. Don't worry, it's only like what I would wear in the sea!"

Mrs Elgin gaped at me in awe.

Sam had never liked my hospital volunteering. He was terrified I would catch some disease, but this hospital was one of the better ones. Sam had mentioned that some of the smaller London ones were simply charnel houses, with the stench of putrefying limbs and patients lying in their own filth.

"But what about the one Mr Paget works in?"

"The big ones are better," Sam conceded; "They're clean and the one here is decent too; Mamma's friend is a nurse and works on the female medical ward. She's given good reports of the place, or Papa wouldn't let her work there. But I still dislike the idea really."

I stroked Sam's face.

"I'll be careful," I told him.

Yarmouth Hospital was a large, red-bricked building and stood on Queen Street. It had started life as a small dispensary 20 years before but was now a small hospital. A sign outside said 'Hospital: Quiet Please'. It smelled of polish and carbolic soap. A wide staircase led to the wards and painted signs directed people.

"I've to help out with bedpans today!" Helen told me with a wry smile. "Can ye imagine the smell?"

"Ugh! No, I can't! You've a strong stomach!"

Helen shrugged. "I'm used to it, lass. When ye've so many younger siblings, and cows and sheep about the place, 'tis no big problem!"

"I'll be making teas," I told her.

"Ye soft southerner!" She grinned at me.

We entered the inner corridors and went our separate ways. The nurse I usually worked with was on duty and she smiled at me, though she looked to be rushed off her feet.

"Alice. I'm glad you're here. There's a stack of washing up; would you mind?"

"Of course not," I smiled at her. "Want some tea though, Nurse? You look as though you could do with it."

Nurse Bryant glanced round warily. I knew she was looking for the Matron. This formidable woman oversaw the nurses and the domestic staff and was extremely stern. Even doctors had a huge respect and privately, some fear of the woman.

Intrigued, that day I asked if the operations were done on the wards.

"What? Goodness no! Not in front of other patients, Alice. They do it in the operating theatre. That's a large room; it has the table in the centre and a sawdust-covered floor, and all around are seats and standing room for viewing."

"You mean people actually come and watch?"

"Ah, pardon me, Alice, I didn't mean the general public. I meant medical students, other doctors, surgeons. That's why it's called a theatre."

"Can I see it please, Nurse Bryant?" I asked.

"No! Matron would have a fit if she knew! Besides, I think it would alarm you too much. Truly, you are better off not seeing it. Don't forget, what has been seen cannot be unseen."

But my curiosity had always got the better of me. I *had* to see this room. When Nurse Bryant resumed her duties, I glanced at the clock. Helen wouldn't be finished for at least 20 minutes. I saw the sign pointing to 'operating theatre,' and started walking down the long, parquet-floored corridor. The ceilings were high and arched and the windows looked out onto Queen Street. People walked around outside in the lovely weather, carts rumbled by, and I was heading towards the most dreadful place in the building!

I stopped. A set of heavy, double doors, with rounded glass windows. I pushed them tentatively, hoping I wouldn't walk in on an operation, and peered round the door. Inside, light flooded the room from two large windows set high behind the seating, which rose up in tiers, not unlike the theatres my parents had performed in. There was some standing room too, like at the races. There were four tiers with railings for the students to rest notebooks on. These were rounded in shape, forming a circle around the room. At the end of each tier was a bucket. I guessed even medical students might sometimes need to be sick!

Some tables stood at the far end of the theatre, upon which sat bowls, jugs, a pile of rags and a stack of towels. Along one wall hung several capes and aprons, some bloodstained. I grimaced with disgust. On the floor were several buckets filled with sawdust and sand. I wondered if I dared peek into the drawers, since that was where the surgical implements lay! In the centre of the room was the operating table. It was made of wood and had a headrest at one end, which could be put up or down. Two gas lamps hung down on a long pole over the table. Shocked, I saw that the table had three big leather straps on either side and I guessed that this was to hold the unfortunate patient down.

Underneath was a box; I cringed to find it deeply bloodstained. Sawdust lay thickly on the floor; I could smell it, along with the more unpleasant stink of old blood. It was eerily quiet in there, but it wouldn't be like this when a patient lay on the table. How the screams must echo, I thought. I hoped neither I nor Sam would ever have need of one.

Nearby, knives and all kinds of instruments, which would not have looked out of place in a torture chamber, were tidily laid out. I felt queasy at the sight of a massive saw, which, to my horror, still had traces of old blood on it. And what was that thing used for? I wondered at a long copper tube, at the end of which was a fearsome-looking piece of twisted metal. There were numerous syringes, all with large, sharp needles, and even some hammers.

Wishing I had minded my own business, I left, banging the door as I went.

I met Helen outside later and told her what I had done.

"Lass! Whatever possessed ye? Supposing you'd walked in on someone being sawn to bits?"

I shuddered. "I know, but I had to see what it was like. Ugh! Those saws! I'll be dreaming about them now. I don't know how people can stand and watch!"

"I know, but how else can they learn? As long as ye've guts of iron, then it should be alright. I would've been interested to see it, but mebbe, I'm best off remaining ignorant in that department!" Helen shivered.

"Nurse Bryant warned me, so I've only myself to blame," I told her. We made our way to a café along the sea front to take some strong, sweet tea.

It was the morning of Helen and William's wedding, and I was helping Helen to dress. Florence had come to assist with the wedding breakfast. She nodded to Helen. "My dear, you look beautiful!" she told her.

"She does!" I said, squeezing my friend's hand. "The most beautiful bride in all Norfolk!"

Helen's dress was third-hand. It was creamy white. She had got it in Norwich and had bargained hard for it.

Helen looked incredible, her shining black hair piled in large curls on top of her head. She had a long veil, and her dress was stunning. The bodice had frills down the front and the sleeves were tight. The skirt was very full, in the style Helen liked. It graced the floor and swished when she moved.

"Just don't trip!" I teased, imagining my friend falling flat on her face halfway up the aisle. I handed her the posy of lilies.

Sam was assisting William to dress. He was so nervous, he shook.

"Here!" Sam gave him some brandy from William's own hip flask, which was always somewhere about his person.

"Take a nip of this. A nip, I said, not the whole thing!"

William did and fussed with his tie, then his coat.

"Ready?" Sam grinned.

Someone had managed to get hold of a piper from somewhere, and the sound of bagpipes echoed around the church's interior. I had never heard them before.

"What's that appalling screeching?" I asked, shocked, and Helen gasped and smacked my hand lightly.

"'Tis the pipes, ye daft Sassenach! The most wonderful sound in all the world."

Some of the townsfolk who loved weddings attended too. All were seated in the church, awaiting the arrival of the pair.

William arrived with Sam as his best man, looking extremely smart in light grey suits and top hats. Sam sorely wished he could keep his suit, but it had been hired. The pair hastened to the front of the church and then it was our turn. It felt so strange to walk down the aisle, Helen preceding me, with a friend of the Reverend's to give her away since Helen's parents could not attend. Helen was piped down the aisle – something she had argued over and over with her conscience about. To have a true Scots piper... or to have George Warne play?

Helen had struggled for days, desperate to have a Scottish piper at the wedding, but afraid to cause George offence. In the end, she had settled for both.

The ceremony did not take long, and Helen was soon proudly sporting the engraved wedding ring. She felt a huge sense of relief. Now, she was married and respectable. Her child would be born in wedlock. The Reverend smiled, as proud as if Helen were his own daughter. I saw him discreetly wipe a tear from his eye.

Helen and William did not have a honeymoon as such, but they had a few days to themselves. I had volunteered to assist the Reverend in Helen's place. Monday found me at the church to perform Helen's tasks, the Reverend, jolly and humming hymn tunes. I did his laundry. Reverend told me, blushing crimson, that he had already done his 'unmentionables' himself as it was not appropriate for a young lady to handle them. I had had trouble in keeping a straight face at this. I had never seen anyone so embarrassed.

Lately, I had begun to write various recipes and cures in a large, plain-sheeted book; medicinal things at the front and recipes at the back. Mrs Elgin smiled.

"An excellent idea," she said. "You never know when you're going to need them." Mrs Elgin had a wealth of knowledge about all things culinary and healing. Having reared nine children, she knew a thing or two and enjoyed teaching me.

I had also found the Apothecarist tremendously helpful and went once per fortnight to ask his advice. Mr Peterson smiled as Mrs Elgin and I entered his shop. The apothecary was like a wonderland with all manner of items I had never even heard of, never mind used. He stood behind his glass-fronted counter which displayed his wares, including 'ladies' occasional pills' which I knew to be to help with one's monthly issues and cramps.

More alarming was a bottle of snake oil, a dark brown concoction said to be a 'miracle elixir', however, I had no desire to try, miraculous or not! Another bottle by its side contained snake oil liniment of an equally vile hue. There was chill and fever tonic, which Mrs Elgin swore by, and indeed, I had taken some. There was Laudanum, which I would never dare touch, due to its addictive properties. Formalin throat and voice tablets I had seen in our scullery. The chalky Bismuth powder or pills I was familiar with, and the heart stimulant that Mrs Elgin took on occasion. The shop smelled of herbs and cough mixture, lavender and other flowers. I knew he made a lot of his own medicaments and was extremely diligent.

"Ah, dear ladies. What can I get for you?"

"I wanted to know about the whooping cough," I told him.

"Goodness! Nobody has it in your house, I hope?"

"No. It's just for my little book, that's all."

Mr Peterson started to describe the symptoms and how to treat the patient.

"Fresh garlic juice is excellent," he told me. "It's getting it *into* the patient that's the problem! What *is* better for the patient's comfort and taste is to use syrup with a teaspoon of fresh ginger. You can also give ginger root juice with fresh onion juice and if you have access to turmeric, add that too. Twice a day will suffice. It is vital that they eat small meals too; even if they are sick, they should still eat."

I nodded, writing down his words.

Susan had not forgotten her idea of carrying out the poisoning. She had managed to obtain a little bit of arsenic. However, she didn't want to add too much and kill him straightaway. That was too suspicious; she just wanted to make him unwell for now. After some consideration, she prepared a sausage roll in pastry, something Sam had ever enjoyed.

"Samuel!" she spoke to him as he was about to leave. "Look, I am sorry the way I been lately. I just hate that Lawrence girl. Let's try again, eh? We are married after all. I won't see other fellas anymore and I'll stop home of a nighttime too. I'll wash more. Why can't we start sharing a room again, eh? I made you this; it's a peace offering. I know how you always loved them."

Sam found himself the recipient of the sausage roll, and he felt nervous. I had continued to voice my fears about poison. Many people had been able to write off enemies using such a method. It was a favourite method. But...

"Thank you, Susan," he told her. "I think, however, it is rather too late to start again, as you say, though..." He paused and added, "...even if I wished to."

Susan glowered. "Well, you can eat the roll and think about it," she told him. "Can't you, eh? After all, I am your wife, in law."

She moved off. Sam looked at the roll and sniffed it. It smelled alright, but he felt so uneasy that he discarded it on somebody's rubbish dump on his way to work.

Shortly after, a young boy, a street urchin, rooting through old potato peelings and various other items, happened upon the snack, and delighted, he began to eat.

Florence heard on the grapevine and was saddened. She shook her head in disbelief as she was told.

"Poor little bugger. Only about nine. And someone poisoned him? It's despicable!"

Sam entered the shop just in time to hear the news.

"What's that about poison?"

"Oh!" His landlady turned to him. "Little urchin; he was found writhing in agony yesterday. Someone took him to the workhouse infirmary, but they could do nothing. He was curled tight as a hodmedod. They suspected poison due to how he was - said he'd only eaten one sausage roll all that day and he'd always been alright before. I suppose it might've been meat gone bad though."

The shopper shook her head. "Not from what I had described to me. Millie Jenkins works in the infirmary, and she saw it all. Said they were going to open him up and see. How they can tell, I don't know, but obviously they can somehow. Poor little sod. I 'spect it was left there in the hope the rats would eat it."

Sam felt as though he had been doused in freezing water and had to sit down in shock. Never in his life had he felt so faint and unwell, and *he* had discarded it!

"Good Heavens, Samuel, you've lost all colour! Sit down before you fall down!"

Sam took a seat at once.

"It's too hot today," Florence went on. "Get yourself a little fresh ale or something. I have a new barrel just in, half an hour ago. Have some fruit too."

Sam took the ale but didn't fancy the fruit. 'Goodness,' he thought to himself. 'My Alice was right. But that poor little lad!'

He felt terrible now, about throwing the food away, but he had tossed it onto a rubbish dump in someone's yard. How was he to know someone would later go picking through? He would ever feel guilty about that.

Later still that night, he spoke seriously to Susan. "What? Oh, that's bleedin' nice, ain't it?! As if I would poison you! I take offence at that, Samuel. Truly I do. I want to try again like I told you. As for the sausage roll, well, I 'spect it just sat in the sun all day or something."

Sam looked at her. "Let us hope so," he told her coldly, "for if it should ever be discovered that in fact it was something like that, the person responsible would hang! Do you think now, Susan... a little child is dead because of it."

"Ha! Bloody street urchins; what's one less of them, eh? They're no use to anyone – bloody nuisance they are. 'Sides, it *was you* what chucked it away!"

With that, she stalked out, slamming the door.

Monday afternoon the following week, and Mrs Elgin huffed.

"This is not going to go down well," she stated grimly. "Not well at all!" She was talking to her neighbour who lived opposite.

"Alas, I think you're right!" The old lady twinkled her eyes at Mrs Elgin. "Poor girl! Do you think she'll agree?"

"She will when she hears the reason why, but she won't like it. Well, who would?" The two women regarded one another. "I wonder who will explode first!"

Miss Spoonamore had twisted her ankle badly, and that very morning, her maid had had an urgent message to return home with all speed since her mother was very unwell. Miss Spoonamore had therefore made Jane seek a temporary replacement before allowing her to return to her mother and the girl was desperate.

"*Please*, Mrs Elgin," Jane had said, arriving at our house. "She give me leave to go like, but only for a week and I'm hoping me mam will be alright. There ain't anyone else I could ask. Miss Spoonamore said Alice or a couple of other girls, and I did ask 'em first, but they can't do it!"

'More likely wouldn't,' Mrs Elgin thought.

"She doesn't expect her to stay there surely?" Mrs Elgin said. "Not over-night. I won't permit that. What if I need assistance? I'm 20 years older than Miss Spoonamore!"

"She never said nothing about it being overnight." Jane was twisting her apron into a mangled mess; she was close to tears. "If she don't do it, I won't be able to go, and me mam might die."

"Alright!" Mrs Elgin stated. "Tell Miss Spoonamore she'll do it. When will she expect her?"

"Six o'clock," came the response.

Mrs Elgin's eyebrows shot up.

"Well, you tell Miss Spoonamore she can expect Alice at eight. If she complains, remind her that *I* need assistance too. How long will this be for?"

"Well, till the weekend," she answered. "I'll try and get back for Saturday."

Mrs Elgin nodded. "And wages?"

"Oh, yes, she said six shillings at the end of the week."

"Very well," Mrs Elgin said.

I came back from Helen's and entered our lodgings. It was lunchtime and Sam was already there.

"Sam!" I hastened to hug him. Sam hugged me closely.

"Hello, little angel!" He kissed my cheek.

I grinned. "You wouldn't believe the hoity-toity maid we met in the baker's shop!" I stated.

"Alice," Mrs Elgin began. "I want you to listen to me carefully, my dear. I have something I wish to put to you that you are *not* going to like!"

Sam winced as I screeched.

"What? Old Iron Drawers? Oh! how *could* you?"

"Now, calm down, Alice. It's just four days and you'll be paid six shillings. I would've refused, but that poor maid of hers came to me in tears earlier; her mother is extremely ill and if she cannot get a replacement, she won't be allowed to go."

I looked at Sam. Six shillings for four days work was very good and would go a long way in our escape fund. If I refused, the poor maid would not be allowed to see her mother, and if she died, I'd regret my petty meanness forever.

"Alright," I told them both, grumpily.

At eight o'clock the following morning, we arrived at Miss Spoonamore's house.

"Good morning, Miss Spoonamore!" Mrs Elgin stood with me at the woman's door. Miss Spoonamore was leaning heavily on two crutches.

"Alice! Thank you. You're an angel and most forgiving of an old sourpuss like me! I shall do all I can to make as little work for you as possible. You are helping me out tremendously. I'm very grateful!"

She'd better be, I thought, grimly.

"Now, come in. I'll tell you where I need you to begin."

"Wait!" Mrs Elgin said. "Alice *is* here on a temporary basis only, Miss Spoonamore. I need her overnight; I'm 76 and I could be taken ill at any moment, and she will want an hour for lunch each day."

Miss Spoonamore simmered but agreed. Mrs Elgin was fitter than many people who were thirty years younger.

"Very well; now, you'll be starting at eight, is that correct?"

I nodded.

"Can you not begin a *little* earlier? Maybe seven?"

Mrs Elgin shook her head. "No, that's our breakfast time and Alice needs fuel in her if she is to work here."

Miss Spoonamore acquiesced.

"Alright. Well, let us begin!"

I pulled a wry face at Mrs Elgin who winked and smiled. I sighed and followed Miss Spoonamore into the house.

It reminded me of my first day at school, when I had said goodbye to my mother, and I was surprised at the lonely feeling that washed over me.

Inside, everything was neat and clean already. Obviously, Jane worked like a drudge! We stood in the drawing room. A huge bay window overlooked the sea front, and the curtains were a pale lemon colour and tied back with huge bows. There was a chaise longue under the window, made up as a bed. It was rumpled and wanted re-making. Ornaments adorned the mantlepiece and pictures hung everywhere. The carpet was luxurious. Miss Spoonamore noted my look downward.

"Persian," she said with an overly bright tone. "It cost hundreds of pounds!"

I glanced toward the fireplace. Two overstuffed armchairs sat either side of the fireplace and there were a lot of gleaming brass fire irons, a coal scuttle and shovels. The fender glistened brightly too.

I glanced at Miss Spoonamore.

"You can start with the brasses on the fender," she told me. "You'll find the cleaning things in the scullery." She stood over me, pondering.

."You're a good cook, I hear."

"So Mrs Elgin tells me," I answered politely.

"Good. I enjoy my food. I like luncheon at noon; you can have an hour to yourself then."

"Tea?"

"At six o'clock precisely," she told me. "Then you may leave, though you'll have to wash the dishes first thing. There's a menu in the scullery... can you read?"

I nodded.

"Good. I suggest you familiarise yourself with it after you've done this. There's a list of chores there too, with an allotted amount of time for each task. Jane manages well enough; her memory is quite astonishing, for all she doesn't read."

"Yes, Miss Spoonamore," I answered dutifully.

"Now, don't forget to empty *all* the bins. I have wastebaskets in each room; there isn't much in them, but I still want them cleaned."

Finally, she left me to myself, and I was able to get started. I looked at the list of chores and groaned. Surely Jane didn't manage all this? If she did, it was no wonder there was nothing of her. The brasses were already shiny and the hearthstone spotless.

The rest of the morning continued, clean this, clean that. I was tempted to put the wet mop around her ears as I washed the scullery floor. By the time I was ready to do her lunch, I was tired, and I suddenly realised I had nothing for Sam. I always took Sam lunch. I hovered in the doorway.

"What is it, Alice?"

"I just thought. I haven't brought my lunch."

"But I presumed you'd be going back home."

"Well, no, I thought it would mean Mrs Elgin wouldn't need to feed me. I think she presumed you'd allow me to eat here."

Miss Spoonamore drew in a long breath and exhaled sharply; a sign she was getting annoyed.

"Very well. I suppose you may eat something of mine; take what you wish from the pantry."

I left with a sigh of relief. Hot and already tired, I hastened to the workshop.

"Darling!" Sam beamed. "I wasn't sure I'd see you. Oh, you look exhausted already."

"I am." I put the closed sign up and came to him. Sam poured me cool ale.

"I've needed this," I told him. "I'm sorry, I had to take from her pantry to get your lunch. I won't forget it tomorrow."

"Don't worry, it's fine," Sam told me. He cut the beef roll in half and gave it to me.

"No, it's your dinner!"

"Yours too," Sam told me. "We share everything. How's it going there?"

"She hasn't left me alone all morning."

Sam hugged me to his chest.

"You forgot to scrub the front steps," her greeting on my return.

"You didn't tell me about the steps!" I reminded her.

"Yes, I did! Besides, it is on your to-do list. I thought you said you were literate!"

"I am; I must have missed it in all the other chores."

"Alright, don't bite at me like that. Just give them a cursory scrub for now; you can scrub them properly tomorrow first thing. Get a bucket and brush!"

I would dread doing the steps if today was anything to go by. Kneeling and scrubbing with my rear end sticking up, I was the recipient of many a ribald remark. I turned at one comment from a particularly cheeky errand boy.

"Mind your language, you scruffy urchin!"

The lad laughed. He was around sixteen or seventeen, tall and spotty with bright ginger hair sticking up.

I flung the scrubbing brush at him, and it caught him on the ear.

"Ow!" he roared, furious now. Miss Spoonamore, on hearing the noise, stepped out.

"What's going on out here? Leave my maid alone, you disgusting beast! I heard every word!"

The lad glared, rubbing his ear. "She threw a brush at me!" he raged.

"Good!" Miss Spoonamore stated fiercely. "Now! Be off with you or I shall throw another, and I too am a good shot!"

That week was my own purgatory. Miss Spoonamore was a hard taskmaster and I felt I was more than earning six shillings doing four days simply by the amount she gave me to do. If I wanted to leave even five minutes early, having finished my chores, she would snap, "You have five minutes yet, girl! Go and find something to clean!"

Miss Spoonamore didn't like me humming; she didn't like me singing either.

"Alice! You can be heard four rows away," she told me untruthfully. "Why sing when you've a voice like a rook? You could not carry a tune in a bucket!"

Miss Spoonamore liked silence. She read in silence and ate in silence. In the afternoons, sitting on her chaise, she watched people outside. Stiff as a ramrod. Hands in her lap. She could sit for hours like that without even twitching. I would occasionally look over, shaking my head in disbelief. I had never known anybody quite like her.

Miss Spoonamore did nothing but moan. She was sarcastic too and tried my patience to its limit.

"Don't scratch your head. You'll get splinters in your fingers!"

This cheeky remark she made as I removed my cap to run my hands through my curls. I hated the hot, sweaty feeling and I glanced over at her.

Miss Spoonamore's bedroom was not being used at present. Nevertheless, she still wanted it 'doing.'

An iron bed stood in the centre of the room, with immaculate white sheets and pillows, linen folded neatly. It made me think of what a sergeant major's room must look like. There was no carpet, but the floorboards were polished. there were a couple of sumptuous rugs, one at the side of the bed and the other near the dressing table, which had little in the way of vanity upon it – just a brush and a comb, a pot of hair pins, hat pins and some face cream. A hard-backed chair stood in front of the window, presumably so she could spy on people upstairs as well as down!

"Do the windows whilst you're up there!" she bellowed from the bottom of the stairs making me jump. "And the spare rooms too, especially the small room. There are always dead flies in there. I don't know why!"

"Probably from the corpses of people who offend you that you keep under the bed!" I muttered.

I ventured to the other rooms. I was naturally nosy, so I didn't object to looking in them. The 'fly room' was small. It stood bare and empty apart from a trunk in the corner. I wondered what was inside! As Miss Spoonamore had told me, there were some dead flies on the window ledge. I disposed of them and looked out of the window, which had not been opened for years since it was stuck fast.

My interested gaze once again went to the trunk. On top sat a beautifully painted baby doll, which I picked up. I smiled at it, for it was expertly made, dressed in a lovely little gown. It seemed a pity to keep a lovely doll out of the way and not show it off.

"That's a beautiful doll you have in that little room," I told her when I returned downstairs, attempting to make polite conversation. "Was it yours as a girl? I'd've loved a doll like that!"

For some reason, the harridan blushed pink.

"I hope you aren't touching that which does not belong to you!" she said crossly.

"No, I only meant to compliment the doll. Why don't you have it on display? It's lovely. I wouldn't have gone in there, but you told me to!"

"Yes, well, it is my girlhood doll. It is sentimental value only."

Miss Spoonamore had begun the week being reasonable, but, by the end of it, she was back to the tyranny of her usual self. It was because, I thought, she knew I had not too long to go.

However, on the fourth day, Jane sent word she was not coming back for at least another week, and Miss Spoonamore was furious.

"Well, of all the ingrates!" She flapped the message at me. "Letting me down at a moment's notice! I'm sure her mother is now fine; she is merely taking advantage of my good nature! Well! You'll have to stay, Alice. You've done admirably so far. It will only be until Jane returns. It would help me out enormously."

"Well, Mrs Elgin needs me and ..."

"I know that and am perfectly happy to let you continue the hours you have been working. But it would be a great help to me if you were to stay until that dreadful girl returns. Do say you'll stay."

Crocodile tears appeared.

"Alright," I told her.

"Oh, you *are* kind!" She brightened at once. "However, I cannot continue to employ you at six shillings per week. Jane only gets four. I gave you higher wages because of the inconvenience to you but now you are settled and know what you're doing."

That evening, Mrs Elgin listened in horror when I told her Jane wouldn't be returning for at least another week.

"That's ridiculous!" Mrs Elgin shook her head. "Alice Lawrence! You are too soft!"

Miss Spoonamore was the type of person who, 'pushed her luck'. She always got away with it, since she was so formidable and would shout when thwarted and make things so difficult for people, that it was easier to just do what she wanted.

The morning for the cake and tea or cake and coffee arrived.

"I have a nice uniform for you, Alice," she told me graciously. I looked at her questioningly.

"For today. I have taken in the waist some. I worked. For *you*! What do you say to that?"

"Thank you, Miss Spoonamore." This was the only polite thing I could say.

The dress, styled from around 40 years before, had a huge bell-like skirt, tight bodice, buttons up to the neck and long sleeves that would have been tight, had I been a large girl.

"And I want you to wear a proper housemaid's cap." She thrust a horrible-looking thing at me.

"It's awful!" I complained.

"Nonsense! It's just for one morning. That floppy thing you favour is more like a handkerchief. This is a proper, housemaid's cap."

I dragged myself up to Jane's tiny room to dress. As expected, I looked appalling. The cap squashed my curls, came down over my ears and had two strings to tie in a bow. I swore if I needed to go out, I'd change first, no matter what Miss Spoonamore said!

It was then I saw the painting of the sea, waves crashing to the shore and admired it. Then I looked closer. In the corner, written badly, but written none the less, 'Jane.' *She* had done this painting? Then, I spotted another of a sunset; it was fabulous. Jane was a talented artist. She should sell these paintings!

"Alice!" Miss Spoonamore's voice made me jump and I went downstairs to excuse myself by telling her I had been captivated by the paintings.

"Those hideous daubs? Don't be silly."

"Miss Spoonamore, they're wonderful!"

"What do *you* know about art? Well, come on! I don't have all day!" She turned me to face her. "Yes! Excellent presentation. You really do look the part now!"

That was a compliment?

"Last week!" Sam smiled. It was Monday morning and he had come for breakfast. I had been telling them about Jane's artwork.

"As soon as I see her, I am going to say she should sell them. They're incredible. I thought it was professional art!"

"Jane can only write her name," Mrs Elgin told me. "She wouldn't have a clue how to go about it."

"She should get herself a pad in the market or sell them on the sea front! All local views too; the visitors could buy them."

With this in mind, I went reluctantly to my job.

Miss Spoonamore had left a stack of dishes with dried-on food. Also, one of my first more unpleasant tasks was to clean out the chamber pot. She had put one under the chaise to use, but I had not done this the previous week.

"Girls have no stamina these days," she told me in annoyance when I commented on the chamber pot. "I had to clean chamber pots, all day, every day when I was a Nanny. I did it myself last week, but I don't see why I should do your work for you!"

I wanted to empty the lot over her head!

Miss Spoonamore liked to nap after her midday meal. So, that afternoon, when I had returned from my lunchbreak, she was dozing on her chaise longue. I peered at her, mouth open, snores issuing forth. Smiling, I turned and went quietly up the stairs.

The trunk opened easily enough, with a creak that made me cringe and listen, but no sound came from downstairs. I lifted the lid all the way and peered inside.

Good God! I could hardly believe my eyes. In a flat box sat the most curious item of clothing I had ever seen – a bodice of scarlet silk with black lace which was low cut and fastened with hooks and eyes. It looked just the kind of thing a woman of ill repute would wear... not that I was familiar with their type of underwear, but it seemed so. I didn't imagine Miss Spoonamore would even know what one of these were, let alone have cause to wear it. I put it back where it had come from. There were other items in the trunk too. Boots, stockings, items for babies, bottles, napkins. Well, that was not entirely unexpected, given her previous occupation as a nanny, but the bodice? The boots? I cringed. Evidently, there was more to Miss Spoonamore than met the eye!

Miss Spoonamore seemed in affable mood that day.

"Tomorrow, a treat for you. You may take me along the prom in my bath chair. We'll take a picnic. Yes! My mind is made up!"

Wednesday morning dawned bright. Miss Spoonamore was still in genial mood. She positioned herself in her wicker bath chair.

"Comfy?" I asked sarcastically.

"Yes!" came the reply. "Now, let's go. Be careful, unless you wish to tip me out!"

That prospect was terribly inviting, but somehow, we made it to the prom.

People we knew saw us; most merely nodded to the hag in the chair, while others spoke, greeting her nicely, ignoring me, and some chuckled at my cross expression.

Miss Spoonamore now changed tack. The sun was in her eyes, the breeze too fresh, she wanted her shawl around her shoulders for all it was warm.

"Where are the sandwiches?" she asked.

"Ah, I think you're leaning on them!" I said, suddenly remembering, I had put the cloth bag in the bath chair whilst she had taken her time to sit.

"Oh! you stupid girl! Of all the things to do! *In* the chair? Where's your common sense? You *knew* I'd be sitting in here and you put them in on purpose so I would lean against them. Selfish! You think only of yourself!"

"That does it!" I turned to face her. "I'm sick of you! You do nothing but moan! I've done my best for you, but you're never appreciative. Emptying your rancid chamber pots too! I'll bet poor Jane doesn't need to do that, but you make her! Well, you can get yourself back. I've done my last duty for you!"

I turned and stalked off leaving Miss Spoonamore shrilling at me to come back and how dared I leave her stranded, the people on the prom amused, and those who knew Miss Spoonamore laughing hysterically. For many, it was the funniest thing they had seen in a long while. She waved her umbrella at passers-by and called me all the names she could think of. To add to Miss Spoonamore's fury, some local children began to dance round her chair, singing a rude little ditty.

Mrs Elgin looked at me questioningly as I unexpectedly marched into our lodgings and sat down.

"Alice? Have you been handed your sack?"

Mrs Elgin's eyes widened as I explained what I had done, then her mouth became a smile, and she sat, laughing so much that tears came.

"Alice! You didn't, did you? I wish I'd seen that; she deserved it. This will be all round Yarmouth by lunchtime! Go and tell Sam! He'll be amused."

Smiling, I went to Sam's workshop. Sam was surprised to see me and at first worried I had appeared mid-morning. However, as the story unfolded, he too laughed.

"Alice, you are irreplaceable. She will be after you now!"

"I don't care if she is. Stupid old besom. I couldn't take it anymore!" Sam came to hug me close.

"Well, I don't blame you, mawther, still, the money will be useful, and you've more than earned it."

CHAPTER THREE

Sam chose not to tell me about the poisoned sausage roll, but he did discuss it with his friends. Helen and William at once decided Susan's aim had been to poison her husband.

"The sooner you leave with Alice, the better, bor'," William told him. "I hope you bolt your door when you sleep!"

Sam affirmed that he did.

"I feel so terrible about the lad," he went on. "But I deliberately threw it onto a private rubbish tip in someone's yard. I never imagined anyone would go rifling through it."

"Whisht; 'tisnae your fault." Helen handed him a drink of ale. "And as for the poor wean, he's somewhere better now."

Jane returned and was met with an unaccustomed hug from her employer.

"Thank you for returning, dear. That Alice was *dreadful!*"

Jane listened for a good half hour to a recital of my wickedness.

Miss Spoonamore ran out of breath at last. Not a word to ask how her mother was? How *she* was?

"It's tidy now as I had to do it all myself," lied the spinster, "injured though I am!"

Jane was unsurprised at the tirade from her employer, and later, was sent for tea and sugar. Miss Spoonamore generously gave her leave to take an hour for herself.

"Have a walk in the sea air," she ordered Jane, "before setting to with the chores, and buy me my newspaper, will you?"

Jane left the house, her mind in a whirl. She couldn't imagine I had been that bad. She bought the paper and ventured up Golden Keys Row.

"Jane! Lovely to see you again. How's your dear mother now?"

"A lot better, thank you, ma'am; beathing well now. Miss Spoonamore had a lot to say of Alice and none of it good."

"I can well believe it," Mrs Elgin told her. "But it's all nonsense, Jane. Honestly! She worked her fit to drop. I don't know how you do it! Have you time to come in?"

I hurried downstairs.

"Jane! Glad you're back; how's your mother?"

"Very much better, thanks." Jane smiled. "I was saying to Mrs Elgin, but Miss Spoonamore's been going on about you," Jane said. "Did you really walk off and leave her stranded like that?"

"I certainly did," I answered. Jane looked at me with large eyes and spluttered laughing.

"Really? Oh, I wish I had the courage to do that! I bet she was frothing at the mouth."

"She was," I said with a wide smile.

Jane looked at me with eyes wide at my audacity.

"Oh, I meant to say, that doll's nice, isn't it? Fancy keeping it hidden away!"

Jane went red.

"Something I said?" I asked.

Jane shook her head. "No, no, she's a bit funny about the doll, that's all."

"She's a bit funny about a lot of things I think!" I stated. "*And* I looked in that old trunk too. You'd never guess what I found, unless you've seen it?"

Jane blushed to the roots of her hair. "I have, Alice. I was shocked."

Jane hastened on. "I wanted to thank you for stepping in for me and staying on; she can be difficult."

"Try impossible!"

"Yes, that's true, but I think it's because she has remained unmarried."

"Hmm, but the women I know are happier that way."

Jane shook her head.

"No, there was a man she longed for once," she told us, "but he didn't want her. He was in love with someone else, you see. Well…"

"Wait!" Mrs Elgin held up her hand. "If this is going to be a juicy story, we need tea and cake; Alice, get them out, I'll start a brew!"

We seated ourselves round the table.

Jane then proceeded to stupefy us with a tale of how Miss Spoonamore had once confessed lovelorn feelings to the gardener of the house in which they had worked together, however, at her confession, the rather heartless young man had doubled up laughing and told her she had 'no chance,' after which she'd been humiliated and angry.

"It explains the bitterness," Mrs Elgin stated, and Jane nodded.

"When she left, I went with her. I felt so sorry for her. She told me we'd both be better off on our own without men."

"Even so, she shouldn't deprive *you* of a young man," Mrs Elgin told Jane.

Jane sighed. "Yes, but I can't get to meet anybody. Look, I'd best go; she'll be wondering where I am."

"Just a moment, Jane," I stayed her. "When I was doing your job, I went to your room to change. It's alright, I never poked about in there, but I saw some paintings you'd done. They're incredible!"

"Oh, those?" Jane blushed. "They aren't much, I can't sew terribly well, and embroidery gives me a headache, but I enjoy painting."

"You *must* sell some!" I said with enthusiasm.

"What? Who'd buy my rubbish?" she asked.

"It's not rubbish! It's brilliant. Please, think about it. I sell my dress sweat pads, don't I?"

"Miss Spoonamore wouldn't approve."

"It's not her business!" I told Jane. "It's *your* art; the tourists would love them. People buy paintings all the time. Look, just think about it. Please?"

Jane said that she would.

I had received a letter from Grandpa telling me he was thrilled I would be returning and agreed to accept Sam into his home. I sighed with relief; we would have somewhere to go when we left.

Jane was miserable. Miss Spoonamore had told her firmly no to selling her artwork on the sea front.

"It's a ridiculous idea! Nobody will buy them. People will laugh at you! Besides, you cannot spare the time. I need you and you cannot possibly do it on a Sunday. You ought to get rid of them." She sighed deeply. "I cannot believe you even had the presumption to ask me!"

So, Jane, wishing she had not mentioned it, nodded and put her artwork away, ready to throw the paintings out, though it hurt her deeply.

A week later, I ran into her along one of the rows.

"Jane! How are you? Given any more thought to selling your master-pieces?" I asked.

"Miss Spoonamore said no, I was *not* to sell them. She said people would laugh at me. I've no time to do it during the day and I couldn't do it on Sunday! She said they were starting to clutter the place up and I must get rid of them."

This was the final straw.

"Well, she might stop *you* selling them, Jane, but she can't stop *me*!" I said.

Jane looked at me. "What d'ye mean?"

"Simple! We'll fetch them over. I'll get Helen to help and give you the proceeds."

Jane gasped. "You'd do that for me?"

"Of course. We're friends, aren't we?"

"Friends," Jane repeated and smiled. "Would you? Do you even know what to charge? I wouldn't know where to begin."

"Leave it to me!" I grinned.

Four days later, Jane popped in with a message.

"Can you fetch them this evening? She's having a cards night."

"We'll be there!" I grinned at her conspiratorially.

Jane nodded and then hurried away.

Promptly at eight o'clock that evening, Sam, Helen and I waited round the back of Miss Spoonamore's property with a handcart. There was a scraping of a bolt and Jane poked her face out.

"Ready?" She had glimmering eyes as she passed us picture by picture. I imagined this was probably the naughtiest thing she had ever done in her life.

"That the lot?" Sam asked and Jane nodded.

"Alright then, we'll sell 'em Saturday, on the front. I want to be sure you get the money sooner rather than later, so I'll meet you here Saturday evening, same time."

The girl nodded.

We trundled the cart back along to Golden Keys Row and Sam hefted them in and spread them out on the kitchen table.

Mrs Elgin looked over the pictures.

"These are superb!" she told me. "That girl is an artist. Look at this one! Look at the detail! Seagulls, terns, all beautifully done."

Sam and I had debated how much to charge.

"It's the tourists will be most interested," he predicted. "Nice little memento. I think you could get away with bigger prices for the bigger ones, or if they're already framed, and if they want to haggle, they can."

On Saturday, we set up tables on the sea front, with a chair for Mrs Elgin. An interested bunch of people had gathered as we began to lay out the paintings. I had hastily written a sign –

"Portraits of Yarmouth,
by local artist Miss Jane Harrington."

I stood behind the tables, smiling politely. Mrs Elgin, in her best hat, sat looking entirely respectable. Helen called attention to the paintings and soon potential customers were poring over them.

"Look at that one!" A man said to his wife. "Isn't that wonderful? A local artist?" This remark addressed to Sam.

"Yes, sir," Sam replied.

"Well, it is a wonderful painting. She is not here?"

"No, sir, she had to attend a coffee morning and was unable to get out of it," Sam said quite truthfully. He was so clever, I thought; that made it sound as if she was an invited guest and therefore, of the middle class, which would mean perhaps people would be more inclined to buy.

It was going very well indeed. The framed ones fetched more money, particularly the larger ones. We had expected to be there all day, but within two hours, every painting had been sold. Jane painted similar scenes, but each still seemed so very different from the rest and, therefore, unique. Her sunsets were wonderful.

Back at the coffee morning, Miss Spoonamore heard the final guest arrive. Jane opened the door and bobbed.

"Miss Morris. Good morning to you. Miss Spoonamore is in the second drawing room." Miss Morris pushed past the girl rudely as if she did not exist and entered the room.

"Ah, Caroline!" Miss Spoonamore stated. "I thought you weren't coming! It's late!"

"I do apologise, my dear," Miss Morris told her. "I was waylaid. Crowd on the front, you see." She removed her hat and gave it to Jane who waited silently.

"Oh, something going on?" Matron from the workhouse asked.

"No, just some people selling things," she answered, sitting down. "Some artworks or something. I had a quick look but the one I had my eye on was sold. I came away, realising I was late."

"Artwork?"

"Yes, paintings; done locally, I believe." She sat herself down on one of the chairs.

Miss Spoonamore glanced at Jane who had gone bright red. Jane had said she had 'cleared out the paintings' and on checking that she had, Miss Spoonamore found the cupboards empty. She had nodded approvingly and gone about her business. But now, someone selling paintings? The ones in Jane's room gone? It could have been anyone in Yarmouth, but Miss Spoonamore had a suspicious mind. Why did Jane look so guilty? Had she dared defy her?

"Oh?" she asked.

"Yes, they were extremely good. Pity I couldn't get one; never mind, I'm sure they will be back." She smiled and took a large cake. Miss Spoonamore shot Jane a vindictive look.

"Tell me, Caroline dear, who was selling this *incredible* artwork?"

On hearing the woman's description, Miss Spoonamore went white.

"I *know* those people! It's as well you didn't purchase anything from them. The man you saw is Dwyer, a cabinet maker who *is* married, but the girl at his side is not in fact his wife, but his mistress!"

Miss Morris' mouth dropped open with shock, and there was a collective gasp.

"It would seem certain persons who should know better have been frequenting with them." Miss Spoonamore's gaze settled on Jane who paled considerably.

"Wait! Isn't that the one who left you high and dry on the seafront?" Matron asked.

Miss Spoonamore nodded. "Yes, the girl worked for me temporarily for a short time. No better than she should be! Am I not right, Matron?"

"Absolutely!" Matron said vindictively. "She and that Scottish fiend came to the workhouse recently, telling me how to run the place, interfering! Flirting with the masters!"

Miss Morris looked close to fainting.

"And *I* have to concede since the Reverend has got himself involved. This wouldn't have happened a year ago, I can tell you! The Board of Guardians are furious. I don't understand how he's has allowed himself to become twisted around her little finger like he is! He's not fit for his post these days!"

"It's not true!"

Everyone turned. Jane stood; the interruption had been most unexpected.

"They are kind, good friends of mine, and they're selling my paintings for me. I don't know how close Mr Dwyer and Alice are, but they're my friends."

Silence. Nobody could find a word to say at this unexpected outburst.

Miss Spoonamore recovered first and shot to her feet.

"Jane! How DARE you? You have defied me and lied to me. You told me you had got rid of all the pictures!"

"I did *not* lie; I did get rid of them," Jane told her mildly. "I gave them to Mrs Elgin and Alice since they promised to sell them for me and let me have the money."

"You had no right!" Miss Spoonamore bawled.

"Yes, I do! They're *my* pictures! I painted them! You wanted them gone!"

Miss Spoonamore's burning cheeks indicated the level of her temper. The other ladies gasped audibly at Jane's cheek.

"Well! I will not continue to employ such a common, deceitful person as you. I *forbade* you to sell those pictures! When I *think* of all I have done for you, and this is your thanks? You were a decent girl before you started to associate with the likes of *her*!"

Jane had had enough. Reckless now, twenty years of bitterness and withheld emotion flooded forth.

"All you've done for *me*? Like kept me in rags, working me 16 hours per day? Just Sunday afternoons off? I'm not allowed to find a young man and get married! You weren't even going to let me visit my sick mother unless you had a replacement. Well, I went with you years ago because I felt sorry for you after you made a fool of yourself over that gardener! No wonder he fell about laughing!"

Complete and utter silence. All heads turned to look at Miss Spoonamore, whose face was beet red. Jane felt sick. Her entire body shook; now she would be let go, that was certain.

Miss Spoonamore rose, shaking. "OUT!" she screeched. "Collect your belongings and leave! I never wish to set eyes on you again. How DARE you humiliate me like this? You ungrateful brat!"

Jane bravely held her mistress' gaze, then turned and simply walked, still shaking, up to her own room.

We had counted out the money for Jane. "Eight pounds and two shillings," I said in awe.

Mrs Elgin nodded. "A skilled worker's year's good working wage," she stated. "Jane will be able to bank that then get a better job."

There was a knock at the door, and I went to open it.

"Jane!" My shocked voice alerted everyone.

"Alice," Jane said and broke down in tears. I took in the tearful young woman and the bags at her side.

Over tea, Jane told us exactly what had happened.

"So, I'm sacked," she sniffed. "I'll go back home, but oh, I don't know. I'm done for a job in this town. She won't give me a good reference now!"

"*She* won't," Mrs Elgin told her, "But *I* shall. You need a character witness, don't you? I'll say you've worked for me. But return to your mother and take it easy for a bit. You can start looking for work next spring. I'll give you my address in Norwich and am happy to write references for you."

Jane looked at her, relieved. "Oh, thank you so much, Mrs Elgin." She paused. "But I need money. I can't get any from the workhouse now; Matron was there and is upset with me. I don't suppose my paintings made much, did they?"

I shrugged and looked puzzled.

"Well, only eight pounds and two shillings," I told her in a casual manner, as if I was telling her they had made threepence.

"So, I think you can afford to relax just a bit." Then I grinned widely.

Jane's face was a picture. "How much?" she asked.

I deposited the takings onto Jane's lap.

"Eight pounds and two bob!" I told her. "It's all there. We sold every single last one. In fact, it's a pity we didn't have more."

Jane burst into sobs. She hugged me to her.

Sam spoke. "It's a *huge* amount. I think, Jane, that we should accompany you to your mother's house. You can't carry this lot on your own!"

"That's wise," Mrs Elgin said. "Sam, do you speak to William; it's only an hour or so."

Jane spent the weekend with us and enjoyed herself. She bunked down in my room that night and we giggled like a couple of schoolgirls, me talking about Sam, her talking of Miss Spoonamore and how she cast lustful eyes over every man she saw.

Jane returned home with enough money to support them both for a year, and an advert was placed for a new 'live-in housekeeper.'

I was on an errand at the market when I noticed some young girls. There was some pushing and shoving going on and I heard cat calls and the chanting of female bitchiness.

"Hey, freak, did you escape from the circus?" There was then spiteful laughter as they danced round an unfortunate girl. Unable, as always, to mind my own business, I went over to them.

"What's going on?" I asked. There was a girl in the middle of the group. Her head hung low.

"Nothing!" one said, innocently.

"It doesn't look like nothing!" I answered sharply. "What are you all doing to her?"

The girls looked sheepish. One stubbed the ground with the toe of her boot. "Nothing," she said, emulating her companion.

"Are you alright?" I queried. The girl nodded but did not speak or look up at me. Her ringlets hung low, covering her face. I glanced round at the girls, again, about to say more, but they seized their chance and ran.

I turned to their victim.

"Are they your friends? Did they turn against you?"

The girl fidgeted.

"Look at me, won't you? Don't you know it's rude to not look at someone when they're addressing you?"

Slowly, she raised her head. I saw then why she had not wanted to face me, and more to the point, why the others had been tormenting her. A large red stain covered her cheek and half her chin. I was shocked at her appearance, but I schooled my features. My mother had always told me it was terribly wrong and rude to stare.

"What's your name?" I asked her gently.

"Tabitha," she answered.

"I'm Alice, and I'm here to get some vegetables. Why don't you come with me?"

"I don't need your pity!" she retorted, glaring at me.

"Alright! No need for that!" I replied. "I'm not being pitying; I just wondered if you'd like to walk round with me so they don't bother you anymore."

"Don't care if they do!" Tabitha said, sullenly.

"Well, I do! Look, come with me. I need to get some veg; we can get to know one another."

Tabitha grudgingly walked at my side. She was seventeen, she told me, and worked in the family herring business.

"What did you come here for?" I asked. "We can get what you want as well."

"Mother wants some wool; I have to get some socks too." She looked at me.

With the girl at my side, I got the vegetables and then we headed to buy Tabitha's wool. To my horror, she made next for Susan's stall.

"Tab! I..." But it was too late. She stalked belligerently to the stall and presented herself at the front of it.

Susan took one look at her and guffawed.

"Ugh! What in God's name are you? You scared me half to death! Freak!"

I stood at Tabitha's side. "Don't be so rude, Susan! Tabitha's a friend of mine."

"Ha! That doesn't surprise me! A freak for a friend. Freak and the witch! You ought to do a sideshow together. You'd make a lot of money."

Tabitha was used to remarks like this, but she glared at Susan, who spluttered. "*Her* parents were common music hall entertainers," she told Tabitha. "She's a high-class whore too. Her clients are up on South Quay!"

I was furious, and, at that final remark, I swept as many of her goods as I could onto the dirty ground. Susan shrieked.

"Come on," I told Tabitha. "You don't want to buy *her* rubbish."

I took the girl's arm and lead her away.

Tabitha shrugged me off. "I don't need your help!" she snapped.

"Well, excuse me, Miss hoity-toity! I just don't want you wasting money on *her* stall! She's a cow!"

Tabitha looked at me. "Why'd she say all that to you?"

"Because we hate each other. That answer enough for you?"

Tabitha thought, then she nodded.

Able to get along with most people at least, I had decided to match Tabitha's mood. Obviously, sympathy did not work for this young woman.

"Come on; let's see what Eileen has to offer. She's up the other end but at least her stuff hasn't fallen off the back of a wagon."

Tabitha found herself dragged through the crowd to the other end of the market. I heard the snide comments at the girl's face and could see the sidelong glances.

Unsurprisingly, Tabitha seemed to hate people. Having purchased the socks, I asked if she would come back to meet Helen, but she shook her head.

"I'd rather not, thanks."

"Alright, but Helen's nice. You might even know her; she used to be a herring girl. You'd like her, I'm sure."

"I don't like anybody," she told me sullenly.

"Not even me?" I asked.

Tabitha shrugged.

"Thanks, I'm sure!" I replied. "Well, if you change your mind, Tab, I'm at Golden Keys Row. Or Saint Nicholas'. I often go there."

Tabitha turned then to leave.

"Wait! Which row are you?"

"Red Lion," she told me after hesitating. "Number five." She vanished into the crowd.

Tuesday, and a shipment of oranges had arrived. I was surprised at the crowd down at the jetty. Mrs Elgin and I, walking from the marketplace, were going to take some lunch on the prom as a treat.

"Look! Something's up! I wonder what... must be special," she remarked. "Go and see, Alice dear. I can't stand all that pushing and shoving."

At once, I hurried to the jetty.

"What is it?" I asked a townswoman.

"Noranges," she told me breathlessly.

"What?"

"Noranges. You know, fruit! From thousands of miles away!"

It dawned on me she meant oranges. "*Noranges?*" I said with a smile.

"Yeah, ain't you never heard of a norange?"

"You mean *oranges*."

"I know what I means!" She stood on her dignity looking at me. "They're offloading 'em now," she went on. "I'm gonna get one. If I don't, my old man will have the skin from my back. Oi! Get outta me way!" She pushed her way through and was lost in the crowd.

I shrugged and walked back to Mrs Elgin.

"Oranges," I said in an offhand way. My landlady unexpectedly shot to her feet.

"Oranges? Good Heavens! I can't remember the last time I saw one, never mind ate one. The flesh inside is delectable and you can make jam from the peel so the entire fruit can be used. Did you ever eat them?"

"Only once. I prefer pears or plums."

"Alice, they ought to be on the market stalls, but they won't make it that far! They'll be selling them off the jetty and at ludicrously inflated prices too. I *must* have one!"

Mrs Elgin looked so very crestfallen that I patted her arm.

"Don't worry; you wait here."

Forcing my way through a crowd was hard for me since I was so small. I did not have enough money on me to buy two, but a plan was forming.

As if thinking of Sam had conjured up Susan, I heard her raucous voice.

"Come on, my beauty!" she bawled at one of the sailors. "Give us an orange and I'll be yours for a half hour! Do anything you like!"

I pulled a face of distaste. I had no doubt that she would enjoy that. The bluff sailor grinned.

"Well, you'm a saucy wench, ain't you? Alright, come 'ere. You pays for your goods first!"

Susan, willingly, in front of a crowd of women, disappeared behind a mess of lobster pots.

"Please, sir," I approached a large, bearded man covered in tattoos. "Can I get *two* oranges? 'Tisn't for me, 'tis for my ailing grandmother; she needs fresh fruit badly. I only got money enough for one."

The sailor looked down at the poor little moppet who looked at him from black eyes, lips starting to quiver, curls rumpled from the press of the crowd. I held out a hand with what change I possessed. The sailor looked at me. I let two fat tears fall.

Mrs Elgin, watching anxiously, was surprised to see me appear, unharmed, and heading her way.

"Oh, you're alright! Thank goodness." She stood up. "Ah, did you not get any then?"

"Got two!" I opened my deep dress pockets.

"Two?"

"I paid for one, the other the sailor gave."

"Good God! What did you have to do for that?" Mrs Elgin looked as shocked as I had ever seen her.

"Not as much as Sour Susan," I told her angrily. "She went behind a pile of netting and pots and was already hoisting her skirt to...!"

"I don't want to know!" Mrs Elgin squeaked. "Poor Sam."

Later, we made the thick orange jam, so delicious on toasted bread. The following morning, when Sam arrived for breakfast, he was happy to forego his usual eggs and bacon for a sweet start to the morning.

It was a sultry morning, and Sam made his way toward the beach. The sun was rising over the horizon, with sounds of the town beginning to waken. There was already a smell of baking bread and, if he was not mistaken, bacon too. Sam breathed deeply. He loved it at this time of the morning in summer. Now all he needed to do was find the perfect pebble.

Sam wandered along the shoreline. Here, he could put his marital difficulties behind him for a while and think of me... I would be just waking up now.

The waves washed pebbles onto the beach and Sam concentrated. Tiny birds called sandpipers amused him, scurrying up to the wave, then skittering back as the wave came for them. They ran so very fast, tiny legs racing; each bird in the flock of around forty or fifty moved in unison.

He wandered along the beach, head down, eyes scanning. After almost an hour, one caught his gaze. It was a most attractive colour – blue, grey and white. Sam was always constantly impressed with the variety of colours and shapes. This pebble was oval and quite thin and flat. He bent to retrieve it.

"Hmm, now that looks suitable," he muttered. "I wonder!" Pocketing the stone, Sam waked quickly to the jewellers and watchmakers, not far from his lodgings, and he kept an eye out for Susan. Mr Smith had only just opened the shop.

"Mr Dwyer! What can I do for you? You're abroad early!"

"Yes, I wanted to get to you before I went to work," he explained. "I have a job for you. Would you look at this, please? I'd like it set as a pendant."

Mr Smith sat to examine the pebble. "Well, it's flat enough. I think I could do that easy. Be four shillings."

"Thank you, Mr Smith. How long?"

"Well, how long does Susan want it to hang?"

"No, I mean, ah, what I actually meant was how long will it take?" Sam blushed.

"Ah, see what you mean. About a week?"

Sam nodded.

"And the chain length?"

Sam indicated part way between neck and chest.

"Alright, do you leave it with me, and I'll do my best."

Sam nursed his little secret surprise for me with a smile. He wanted to give it to me when he was with me and then he could see my reaction. The week passed, and Sam returned to the jeweller.

"Here ye go, Mr Dwyer." Mr Smith beamed. "Fine job even if I do say so myself!" Sam observed the pretty necklace with its now shiny pebble set in the clutches of the pendant.

"Absolutely first class. Thank you, Mr Smith, you are an artist!"

The man preened and took it to gift-wrap it.

"I am sure your lady love will be thrilled with it," Mr Smith stated. Sam smiled broadly.

"I'm sure she will!" he said, thinking of the little face, alight with pleasure.

He took me to the beach that evening at sunset. We wandered along the shoreline. Sam held my hand then changed his mind and put his arm about me. The sky was dark red; a breeze blew my curls. With the waves washing onto the shore, and the hissing sound of the pebbles, Sam put a hand into his pocket. He stopped.

"Shut your eyes and hold out your hand," he told me. I smiled, did as I was asked and felt a small box pressed into the palm of my hand.

"Can I open my eyes now?"

"Yes," Sam replied.

I did so and looked at the prettily wrapped box. "Oh! A present!"

Sam smiled. "Come on, darling. Open it. I can't wait to see your expression."

I opened the box carefully and gasped. Inside sat the pendant.

"Oh, Sam!" I took it out to look at it. "It's beautiful. For me?"

Sam nodded and kissed my cheek.

"Yes, I had it made especially. In fact, just over a week ago, that very pebble lay on this beach!"

"I thought it looked like the pebbles here! But it's been polished up!"

Sam nodded. He took it and put it over my head where it nestled in the centre of my chest.

"Thank you, Sam, Thank you. It's so beautiful!" I wrapped my arms about him.

I had not heard anything from Tabitha after our initial meeting, but later that morning, I met her along the tide line, heading toward the jetty.

"Hello, stranger!"

Tabitha scowled back. "What do *you* want?"

"To say good morning," I replied simply.

The sea washed around my ankles, and I glanced down at the water as it pulled back, swirling round my feet. I looked up at her and smiled, curls falling over my forehead.

"Helen said she knew you," I told her.

"*I* don't know *her*." Ungracious.

"But you worked with her a time. I know it was years back, but can't you remember her? Big Scots girl."

"They're *all* big Scots girls, stupid!" Tabitha snarled.

"Fine! No need to bite my head off!" I responded. "Where are you off to anyway?"

"None of your business."

I wondered whether it was worth pursuing. She was very hard work.

"Ah, come on, tell me," I pleaded.

Tabitha huffed. "Alright, Miss Nosy, I'm off to see a woman about a post as live-in maid. She doesn't have any family, so I'm not likely to be stared at, or tormented by her rude kids," she told me, frowning, and attempted to continue up the beach, but I stopped her.

"Wait! Live-in maid? Whereabouts?"

Tabitha looked surprised. "Market Place, why? What's it to you?"

"It wouldn't be Miss Spoonamore, by any chance?"

"Yes, Miss Spoonamore. No followers says the advert, ha! Not much chance of that, is there?"

"Are you mad?" I asked, shocked. "You *must* know her reputation! You're a local girl!"

"*I* mind my own business," Tabitha stated. "Unlike you!"

"But you must know how she is!" I told her. "Besides, she's got some pretty strange habits!"

Tabitha pondered. She had heard Miss Spoonamore was tyrannical. She had heard too, of her being stranded on the front. Everyone in Yarmouth had heard that story by now. Even her own parents had chuckled at that one.

"Well, I expect you got on her nerves!" she answered. "Like you get on mine trying to be nice to me all the time!" She stood facing me.

"Tab, don't go, please," I pleaded with her. "I can't imagine she'd have a long list of applicants."

"Good! I should get the job then, shouldn't I?" she sneered. "Then I'll be indoors all the time, and nobody need look at my ugly face!"

"Tabitha! You're *not* ugly!" I burst out.

Tabitha stamped. "Shut up! Stop patronising me!" she shouted. "D'ye think I would *ever* be friends with you?"

Tabitha stalked past me and up the beach. After letting her get ahead of me, I followed.

Tabitha walked quickly to where Miss Spoonamore's three-storeyed house stood. She never looked at other people, nor did she ever look behind her, so accustomed was she to hiding. She marched up the steps and rang the bell. I squatted down by the railing. A few passers-by gave me some odd looks. The door opened and Tabitha was invited inside. 'Now what?' I wondered, chewing my lip. I decided I would stay and see her afterwards; ask her how things had gone.

To my amazement, I heard the stentorian tones of Miss Spoonamore through the open window. I had not expected that, and I glanced up. The front parlour window was wide open for a change, and I wondered whether to leave, but instead, I stood and strained to hear further. Miss Spoonamore had a naturally loud and commanding voice, and now, she was obviously sitting on the chaise longue that was under the window.

"And you are competent with domestic chores?" Miss Spoonamore asked her.

Tabitha began a list of the things she was used to doing at her home.

"Hmm, seems fair," Miss Spoonamore stated. "But. I think this time, I should like a literate maid."

Tabitha affirmed that she could read and write.

"I require all my meals cooked; breakfast too - early. I work out all my menus on a weekly basis and leave them in the kitchen. You pick this up on Monday morning and purchase the ingredients at the same time. Can you cook?"

Tabitha said that she could.

"Now, I do *not*, under *any* circumstances, permit my maids to have followers. By that, I mean young men! Not that it will apply in *your* case, of course!"

Even I was surprised by that remark as I listened outside. What a dreadful thing to say to her!

Tabitha's nostrils flared. She was beginning to think I had been right about this woman.

"Now, I have coffee and cake, fortnightly, with friends," she told her. "You serve these friends with said coffee and cake." She paused to think. "Alas, I don't know about your face. It might put people off! Is there any way you could cover it up, do you think?"

I gasped at this. Even by Miss Spoonamore's standards, it was shockingly rude.

"What *is* wrong with you, by the way?" Miss Spoonamore probed further. "Is it some sort of birth defect? At least here, you'd be hidden away, and...."

"SHUT UP YOU OLD CRONE!" Tabitha stood up, furious. "You *dare* speak to me like that? Who do you think you are? *Why* should I cover my face? It's not my fault I got this mark! I hate it! People are always rude to me! Always staring, pointing, like I was born on purpose with it! Well, you can stick your rotten job up your bony, scraggy arse!"

"And *you* can just leave!" Miss Spoonamore stood and stalked to the door.

"Pleasure, I'm sure!" Tabitha responded curtly. She marched down the steps and bumped into me, squealing in fright.

"Alice! What're you doing skulking about here?"

"I wondered how the interview was," I answered mildly. "So, I decided to listen!"

"Well, you were right about her, I admit," Tabitha fumed. "The old bitch! You should've heard what she said!"

"I did hear; I was listening," I replied.

Tabitha looked at me, amazed, then suddenly she burst out laughing.

"Come to Saint Nicholas'," I told her. "You'll probably remember Helen when you see her."

Tabitha gave in. It appeared somebody, at least, was determined to be her friend. We linked arms and walked along the main promenade chattering and watching the horses clopping along the front, pulling the cabs, while people looked at the beautiful view and children leaned dangerously out of the cabs and were pulled back by anxious mothers or nannies. A particularly grand coach came along the road.

"Cor! Look at them!" Tabitha said in wonder. "Did you ever see a posher coach, Alice?"

I shook my head.

The family inside were extremely well-to-do. That was obvious. The coach was huge, with a padded, red velvet interior. It looked incredibly comfortable.

The woman wore a high-necked cream dress, with tight, long sleeves, which were frilled at the ends. There were dozens of tiny buttons up the front of the dress, and all the way up to the neck. She also had a parasol which she twirled around lightly. She looked very high and mighty and, from the coach, gave us a supercilious look down her pointy nose, then looked away. There were also four well-dressed children. Suddenly, Tabitha saw the woman's face change to one of utmost shock and disgust as the children suddenly started laughing.

"I say! Look at her!" The boy piped up in a cut-glass voice. He burst into laughter.

Tabitha thought they were sniggering at her face, and the woman showing her disgust, but then she turned and almost exploded with laughter. I was clowning at them, making monkey gestures, noises, and leaping up and down.

"Alice!" she chided, embarrassed at my tomfoolery, but laughing.

She laughed still more when a gust suddenly caught the lady's parasol and took it, sailing out of the coach and onto the road, where it was promptly flattened by the horse and coach behind. We watched as the family's coach halted, and the driver started to shout at the driver behind, who leapt from his seat and bellowed back that it hadn't been his fault his horses had trampled the parasol. Before attention could be turned to us, we darted off, whilst both vehicles stopped, and the argument continued between the two cab drivers and the occupants.

"You're naughty!" Tabitha said when we reached the church, and she could catch her breath. "Aren't you a bit old for behaviour like that?"

"Maybe, but I didn't like her snooty look!" I replied. "Besides, I like a bit of fun. I wonder if the two drivers will have fisticuffs! Come on, let's go and see if Helen has any snacks."

We presented ourselves in the kitchen. Helen was just taking a walnut cake from the oven.

"Alice! Ye could sniff out walnut cake from Gorleston, I think, and I see ye brought reinforcements too!" Helen said. "I'm making some fodder for a wake. Will ye help me?"

"Yes, if you give us a slice of that cake!" I told her.

Tabitha did recall Helen. She had been one of the few who hadn't been unkind to her. Helen ignored Tabitha's birthmark, neither staring, nor commenting. I set to slicing cucumber.

"I hate this stuff," I told her.

"'Tis lovely, I think," Helen said. "Always gives me wind though!"

"Most things give *you* wind!" I said cheekily.

We worked in the kitchen. The door stood wide.

"How's yer family, Tabitha?"

Tabitha spoke of her siblings and parents and the interview.

"Well, 'tis incredible Jane stayed for as long as she did," Helen told her. "She was too nice for her own good."

Tabitha, for the first time in her life, spent an enjoyable afternoon helping make sandwiches, then, once they were done, with some odd jobs. When we had finished, she took her leave of us and went home smiling.

It was a warm Sunday afternoon. Mrs Elgin looked at me as if my idea was the worst she had ever heard. "Alice! Are you serious?" she asked me.

"Yes, it was what Reverend said to us this morning, you know, about toleration and understanding, and how we should all help each other."

Mrs Elgin thought of that morning's Sunday sermon.

"Well, it's up to you," she told me. "It's all very well to practice what the Reverend preaches, but Miss Spoonamore is a different kettle of fish, as well you know. Sad though it may be some folks are beyond saving."

"Yes, but I thought, if she could only talk to someone... you know, like I talked to you. How I told you about Sam and me. You helped us."

"But that's different," Mrs Elgin told me. "Still, if you want to give it a try. You never know, she may surprise us all and be thoroughly grateful, but if I were you, I would prepare myself for a showdown! And," she added, "a hasty exit!"

Flushed with my success with Tabitha, feeling in a helpful and benevolent mood, and after the sermon on being tolerant to those whom we disliked, how we should all be good Samaritans, turn the other cheek and help those who hindered us, I decided to risk it. My plan was to talk to her and see if I could help her unburden herself.

"What do *you* want?" Miss Spoonamore appeared at my knock.

"I wanted to speak to you, Miss Spoonamore," I told her nervously.

"Oh, did you now? Not with Mr Dwyer, I see!" She peered along the road as if she expected him to be hiding.

"Miss Spoonamore, I haven't come here to discuss Samuel. May I come in?"

Miss Spoonamore thought, then grudgingly admitted me.

"Well, what do you want to see me about? Have you come to beg my pardon for your disgraceful behaviour when you were here and turning my former maid into a defiant brat?"

I swallowed, suddenly wishing I had not taken the Reverend's sermon to heart after all. We entered her front drawing room. The windows were shut, and it was stiflingly hot in there with the sun pouring in.

"Well, come on. Out with it, girl! I don't have all day!"

I took a deep breath. "I was thinking, you seem very miserable. Lonely. I thought perhaps you'd like to chat, maybe get a few things off your chest? Things that make you sad? I know I can tell Mrs Elgin anything and she always helps."

"What *are* you talking about, girl? Are you drunk? Or is this a joke at my expense?"

"Neither Miss Spoonamore, I thought perhaps, what with the terrible time you had with that gardener, it's no wonder you were hurt and bitter. I mean, it must have been so embarrassing, but there are decent fellows out there. Look at Mrs Elgin... she was married fifty years! There's still time for you to find a soulmate. Perhaps, since you attend functions, you may be able to get someone to introduce you to a likely chap and then you could be happy."

I completed my little speech. To my surprise, her face became redder and redder, her eyes sparking fury. It hadn't occurred to me that I would be giving grave offence by coming to her as I had. I began to wonder if I had been wise to mention the episode with the gardener.

"How dare you? How DARE you?" Miss Spoonamore screamed at me, and got up, stamping her foot. "You insolent little cat! You have the audacity to come in here and make mock of what's private! I suppose Jane told you, hateful little beast that she is! She has probably spread this abroad. I'll be the laughing stock of Yarmouth."

"No, no, Miss Spoonamore, you have it all wrong. Jane only told Mrs Elgin and I; she was very upset and angry at being dismissed after twenty years. I want to help you; you are so unhappy, and it shows."

"Oh? How'd you know I'm unhappy? And how, might I ask, does it show?"

Anyone wiser than I would have quit whilst they were ahead, but I stumbled on.

"Because of the way you are, Miss Spoonamore. You scowl all the time, instead of greeting people with a nod, a smile. It could all be so very different if you were to do that. Nobody likes a sour face or snappy words."

Miss Spoonamore felt more enraged than she ever had in her entire life; more even than with the rejection of her youth. She could barely contain her anger as she roared at me;

"You *really* think I would take advice from a disgusting little strumpet like you? A slut who is blatantly having an affair with a married man? You come here to seek to humiliate me! You damage people, Miss Lawrence! You do!"

"No, no! I don't. I want to help. You have it all wrong about Sam. It's not an affair! You know what Susan's like! Everybody does!"

Miss Spoonamore railed on at me.

"You interfere in matters which don't concern you. And you have the sheer cheek to come round here and mock me, tell me how to behave, and what I must do to win a man! Well, I tell you, Alice Lawrence, you know nothing about me, and you have no right at all to come and preach to me!"

With this, Miss Spoonamore slapped my cheek hard, then she grabbed me by my neckline, dragged me to her front door, wrenched it open and quite literally, threw me down the front steps and slammed the door.

I lay outside the house in shock for a few moments. Then, I sat up, somewhat dazed. Gingerly, I looked at my wrists to ensure there was no damage.

Apart from a bloody scrape from elbow to wrist, and grazed, sore palms, I was unharmed. My face, however, stung terribly. I heard two pairs of feet running towards me.

"Are you alright, miss?"

I looked up at a very young and pretty dark-haired girl of about seventeen or eighteen, who had been walking with a young man. I looked up at them, somewhat dazed.

"Yes, miss, I think so."

"Abe, help her up, please!" the girl asked her young man who obliged at once.

"Goodness me, what *did* you say to the old witch to make her throw you down the steps like that? I never saw such a thing! You might've broken a bone!"

This from the girl.

"I was trying to help her," I told somewhat distractedly. "She didn't appreciate it."

"That's obvious!" The man said as the girl checked me over for any injuries.

"My name's Maria," she told me pleasantly. "Maria Dwyer. This is my young man Albert. We just call him Abe."

Sam's youngest sister! He had spoken of her and described her to me. My face registered shock, which, luckily for me, Maria attributed to being thrown into the road in such a manner. At once, I knew I had better say nothing about Sam!

"Horrid old woman! She should be reported," she huffed in exasperation. "What's your name, by the way?"

"Alice Lawrence. Please excuse me; I should have introduced myself sooner."

"That's alright. Who'd think of that having been flung down the steps like that?" Maria said. "Come, Abe, we'll take this lady home. She's had a horrible shock!"

Maria linked her arm through mine. An irate shout from Albert made us both turn.

"The bitch just threw a full bloody chamber pot over me!" he roared. Poor Abe certainly had been her well-aimed target. Miss Spoonamore stood at the top of her steps.

"Don't come back here again!" she yelled at the top of her voice. "I only wish it had hit all three of you! If I see you near my home again, I shall contact the authorities! You should all be horse-whipped!"

"I am *so* sorry; this was all my fault!" I had kept it together so far, but now I burst into sobs.

"No, don't think that!" Maria put her arm round me. "Come on, I'll get you home. Abe, after you go home and wash and change, do you go to my parents and let them know? I'll walk Miss Alice back."

We began to walk slowly.

"So, you live in Golden Keys Row? That's a nice row."

"It is," I told her. "I lodge with Mrs Elgin. She's been wonderful; she saved my life."

Maria smiled at me. "Where are you from?"

"Devonshire."

"Yes! Of course! I remember now... Mamma and Annette met you at the station opening, and you did all that fancy lace work. Mamma was thrilled with it."

We made it to number 29.

"Do come in, Maria," I said to her.

"Alright, thank you, Alice, I shall. What will Mrs Elgin say about all this, I wonder?"

Mrs Elgin said a lot. She was so angry; I was afraid for her health.

"That dreadful woman!" She sat me down at the table and began to bathe my injuries. "She actually *threw* you down the steps?"

Maria nodded. "She did, Mrs Elgin. I saw it all; me and Abe were out walking. Poor Alice, she just tossed her down to the pavement. I'm only surprised Alice has just a scraped arm. If she'd done that to me, I wager Papa would have had to be restrained!"

Maria watched as Mrs Elgin muttered threats. "I should report this to the Police," she said, once she had finished.

"It's alright," I told her. "It'll only make things worse. But that's the last time I try to help her!"

Mrs Elgin nodded. "I'll be paying Miss Spoonamore a visit shortly! Would you like a cup of tea, Miss Dwyer? We need one to get over the shock."

"No, thank you, Mrs Elgin; it's kind of you to offer but I must get back or my parents will worry. Alice, I hope you will heal quickly."

I smiled and took her hand. "Thank you, Maria. Thank you for walking me home too."

"You're welcome," Maria said as I saw her to the door. "I will see you around town, I hope."

"I give it twenty minutes and Sam will be around," Mrs Elgin told me, glancing at the clock. "Oh, that woman! Just wait until I see her!"

"Don't fret, Mary, she's not worth it," I told her. "Come on, sit down, let's wait and see what Sam will say!"

Sam was at our row within twenty-five minutes.

"He's here!" Mrs Elgin stated glancing from the window. "My, he does look wild!"

Sam was. "Alice!" He hurried to gather me in his arms. He held me so close to his chest that I couldn't breathe for a moment or two. Sam tilted my chin to look at me.

"Good God!" he gasped. To our surprise, tears came to his eyes, and he squashed me once more.

"Sam, be calm," Mrs Elgin told him. "I too am fuming, but you cannot go storming round to her house. Leave that to me. She'll get a piece of my mind she'll positively choke on!"

Sam hugged me closer until I was almost stifled.

"Sit down, Samuel. I've treated Alice's hurts. Have some tea; I understand how you feel, now, let's think calmly."

Sam sat with me on his knees.

Over strong, sweet tea, Sam calmed down, but he was still very angry.

"My parents couldn't believe it!" he stated. "They were so angry for you, Alice. As for myself, I want to go round there and shake her."

"Sam," I stroked his whiskers. "Darling, please, don't go round there, please; you'd be setting us up for a fall. She'd do all she could to stop us leaving, don't forget that."

Sam reluctantly nodded. "Alright, though it sticks in my craw, I shan't go there, but it's for our sake that I won't."

"Now, *I shall* go there," Mrs Elgin told us, having managed to simmer down somewhat.

Sam nodded and we were left to wonder what would happen next.

Mrs Elgin returned within the hour. She smiled.

"Well! That sorted her out!"

"What did you do to her?" I asked worriedly.

"D'ye want us to help you bury her body?" Sam asked.

"I told her you were considering pressing charges for assault, and she went quite white! She doesn't fancy a spell in the Tolhouse, I can assure you, so, she gave me this, and said she hoped that it would 'settle matters.' Mrs Elgin handed us two guineas. I was surprised. Sam too. It was a lot of money.

"Forty-two shillings!" I gasped. Sam too was stunned.

"Well?" Mrs Elgin smiled. "I hope that will suffice. Personally, I'd prefer to have wrung her neck, but you'll do better with the money."

"Thank you so much, Mary!" I said to her smiling.

Helen found out when I told her on Monday morning.

"Evil old bitch!" Helen stated angrily. "Looks as if ye've been in the boxing ring, lass!"

"Well, two guineas will help me forget," I told her.

"We mun get revenge!"

"I think we should forget the matter," I told her. "After all, she gave me money."

"Paying ye off!" Helen said, disgusted. "'Tis time she was taught a proper lesson! Well, at least ye got to meet Maria!"

"So, what revenge have you in mind then, Helen?" I asked.

"I'll think and let ye know," Helen replied. "It should be something she'll no' forget in a hurry."

August 1844

Susan had gone to the post office to collect the letters. One was addressed to her in her mother's hand. As she read it, she frowned. Her father had broken his leg and Susan was required to visit, since she was the only one who could 'deal with him.'

"Damnation!" she muttered to herself. "Now I'll miss the races and all." She folded the letter and put it in her pocket.

She left the post office and went to see Sam. As soon as the door opened, and she came in, his expression grew surly. Susan was angry, but not surprised that her appearance provoked such an expression.

"What is it?" Sam asked grumpily.

Susan thrust the letter under his nose. Sam read it and groaned.

"I can't leave here!"

"I know; you don't have to make excuses," she told him. "Well, fine, I don't care. You have your hobbies here, don't ya, eh? Screwin' the witch for one. I've a mind to take Ray with me!"

"Do you ask him then!" Sam replied with a voice full of meaning. But his mind was awhirl with sudden plans.

The news that Susan was off to London could not have pleased me more. I whooped my delight when we met up for some lunch later that morning.

"For how long?" I queried.

"A few weeks," he answered. "The old man's broken his leg and her mamma is at the end of her tether with him!"

Later, Sam spoke privately to Mrs Elgin.

"I've a mind to take Alice away for a week," he stated. "Do you mind?"

"Gracious!" She chuckled. "Of course not. Where will you go?"

"I thought perhaps Gorleston-on-Sea for five days or so," he answered.

Mrs Elgin nodded.

"Well, how are you going to pay for this? Don't you need your money to travel?" she asked, reading his thoughts.

Sam nodded. "Of course, but I'll work extra. Alice will too when I tell her. But we need some time together without worrying about Susan, or people we know seeing us. Just for us to be a couple like any other."

Mrs Elgin nodded. "I'll give you some money as a gift," she told him.

"What? No! I wasn't hinting at that!" Sam said, horrified.

"I know you weren't, and that is why I'll give it as a gift. It won't be much, but it will help toward board and lodging."

Sam hugged the old lady.

Susan left on the earliest train the following morning. Sam wanted to jump up and down. He hastened to ensure the workshop was shut up securely. A note on the door told customers he would return on Monday week. Sam returned to his lodgings and packed a small bag. He whistled cheerfully as he did so, wondering what my reaction would be.

When Sam told me, I couldn't have been happier. A whole week alone together was a wonderful prospect.

That night, Mrs Elgin spoke to me seriously about what was likely to happen when we shared a bed. I knew what to expect, of course; my mother had seen to that, but Mrs Elgin slipped me some wild carrot seeds she had bought earlier after Sam had mooted the idea. My face was red as she explained why.

The next morning, we were up early and ready to go to the mews. Before we left, Mrs Elgin beckoned me.

"Alice, one thing is most important. Not everyone's as easy going as I am, and they won't let you have a room unless you're married."

My face fell, heart sinking.

"That's no problem; we'll simply say we are," Sam told her. "I regard Alice as my heart wife anyway."

Mrs Elgin shook her head. "The first thing they'll do is look at Alice's fingers. They'll see no ring!"

"Oh no!"

"So, take this."

To our surprise Mrs Elgin removed her own, thin, gold wedding band.

"Sam, put it on Alice's finger!" she stated. Sam, with a wonderfully, warm feeling, did that.

"Are you sure, Mrs Elgin?" I asked. "It's a beautiful ring."

"Perfectly," Mrs Elgin replied, "I won't miss it for a few days, but for goodness' sake, don't lose it!"

"I won't, I promise," I told her. I enveloped her in as tight a hug as I could manage. "It's a precious thing. Thank you! I was so lucky the day you and Reverend found me!"

Mrs Elgin smiled.

"Now, do you go and enjoy yourselves," she ordered. "Bring me back something sweet and I'll be happy."

The journey to Gorleston-on-Sea wasn't far and the weather was warm. I clasped Sam's hand in excitement. We passed the fields, ripe with crops, a reminder that harvest would soon be upon us, and we must be away by the end of September. A curious sense of unease made me nervous.

We entered Gorleston-on-Sea just after 11.15 and Johnny stopped the cab outside the tavern. We got down and Sam gave the lad a tip.

"Let's find lodgings first," Sam said. "Then we can go and explore; enjoy ourselves."

We wandered along the main road that went steadily uphill. There were some guest houses, mainly private homes and a small hotel, all full to our disappointment and Sam was worried. He had not thought of the difficulty of finding somewhere in August. The place was much smaller than Yarmouth and though Yarmouth was growing in popularity as a resort, Gorleston-on-Sea was not, yet. Just as he was giving up hope, at the end of the line of houses, a sign in a window stated VACANCIES.

"Let's hope she hasn't forgotten to turn the sign round," Sam said. We made our way up the steps and Sam knocked.

A smartly dressed maid opened it. "Good morning, Sir, Madam!" She gave a bob. It was funny; neither Sam nor I were of the class to be given such deference. Evidently, we looked smart.

"We wish to rent a room, miss." Sam spoke. "For five days. To return home Saturday."

The maid nodded. "There's just one room left; come in."

The landlady was tall and spare of around fifty or so. With hair scraped back both sides of her head to a tight bun at the back, it looked, as did most of these styles, as if it were painted on. She had on a deep violet-coloured dress, buttoned to the neck.

"Good morning. Brookes tells me you are seeking a room for the week."

"Yes, madam." Sam was firm but polite. "My wife and I have only just got time to take this impromptu..." He paused. "Honeymoon."

"Oh! How nice!"

As Mrs Elgin had warned us, she glanced at my left hand, spotting Mrs Elgin's ring.

"There's just one left, so you are lucky. However, it's a small attic room, at the very top of the house so a long climb upstairs, that is what puts most people off. I have already had one couple turn it down."

"We don't mind stairs," Sam told her.

I smiled at the tone of his voice. He had suddenly acquired an air of authority. The woman nodded curtly.

"Come with me, please. Have you journeyed far?"

"Not too far, Madam, no," Sam told her.

We entered the main hallway. Next to the door was an umbrella stand and coat pegs. A long passage led to the kitchen where breakfast smells still lingered. The walls were covered in pictures, with barely a space between them. To our right, there was a small hatch opening in the wall, and behind this, a desk, some ledgers, an ink pot and a stack of paper. A small handbell sat in front of the window. Eight small cubby holes lined the wall behind. Some had keys in them. The woman entered the room, took a key and returned to the hallway. The stairs looked steep and were carpeted in a dark red-coloured, slightly threadbare carpet.

"The dining room is through here. It doubles as the breakfast room too."

She led us into a pleasant room overlooking the sea front. Windows stood open to let in the breeze. A maid was cleaning and setting the tables, with pretty tablecloths and cutlery, presumably for the next meal. On each table stood a small jar with a posy of flowers in. There were candles on each table, but the main lighting was gaslight.

"Lovely view," Sam said, regarding the vast expanse of sand further down the vista. The landlady nodded.

"Indeed, I have *the* finest spot!" she told us proudly. "Just off the dining room we've a solarium," she added. The large room was mostly glass and it also looked out onto the same view. Windows stood wide. There were wicker chairs, a sofa, cabinets with books, and tables with newspapers. A couple of well-dressed ladies sat in the chairs, clad in white, admiring the vista whilst sipping tea.

"Do you wish to see the room?" she asked and Sam at once affirmed that we did.

We trailed after her up the staircase, which seemed to grow ever steeper and narrower, and arrived at the top. She unlocked the door, holding it open and we walked in.

It was spacious with a sloping ceiling and afforded a good view over the sea. The bed was large and looked comfortable. There was beautiful flock wallpaper, creamy in colour, there were pale blue curtains tied back, and a pale blue rug at the side of the bed. The floor, boards only, were, however, well-polished.

"It's perfect!" The words came from my lips.

"Just us, all week!" I jumped up into Sam's arms the second the door was closed on us. Sam grinned.

"I want it to go as slowly as possible," he told me. I had wrapped my legs about his waist and Sam smiled into my face.

"I'm so lucky," he said softly, "to have you all to myself for an entire week!"

"Me too!" I lay my face against his cheek.

The small seaside place was beautiful; quieter by far than Yarmouth. In our town, there was a theatre, hotels and other such things. Here, there was very little indeed – small eatery and village shops. It rose to a hill and on a good day, one could see Lowestoft. Across the Yare, we could still see Yarmouth and the ships in the harbour.

The breeze blew in and we made our way to The Cosies overlooking the sea.

"These are brilliant!" I told him, settling back. "I can see why The Hag would want them removed, and I can see how they got their name too!"

The sand here was soft with fewer pebbles. It was smooth and perfect for children to run helter-skelter on. I had removed my footwear, as had Sam, and we walked hand-in-hand in the water as we headed to the cove.

Dinner. There were mouth-watering smells coming from the kitchen. We sat at our table, which had the room number set on it, and waited. A maid brought us a menu, then went away again. Sam perused it.

"Roast of the day," he read. "Or there is a steak and kidney pie. I think I shall take the roast; I don't eat offal."

Wine was beyond our pockets unless it was the rough stuff served in the taverns, so Sam ordered ale instead.

Sam put both his hands around mine and looked at me. The candles had been lit but they weren't needed as the sun was still up, for all it was sinking behind the hotel.

By the time the meal arrived, the little dining room was full. The maid bustled here and there, taking orders or bringing food. I could hear Mrs Tanner in the kitchen issuing orders.

In the privacy of our room, Sam put his fingers under my chin to raise my head. My eyes looked into his. "I want to make love to you, Alice, but it's a huge thing to give up one's virginity. I want to assure you that I will love you forever and ever. But if you don't want to, I'll simply hold you all night."

"No, Sam, I *do* want to," I told him softly. "I know what a big thing it is to lie with a man the first time and if I can't have you, I shall remain virgin all my life. It's alright, Mamma told me years ago and Mrs Elgin has given me something to stop a baby. At least for now."

Sam kissed me. For all I had never been with a man before, I felt no fear at all. It all seemed entirely natural to me. Gently, he removed my clothing, whispering endearments all the while. He breathed in the scent of warm, clean skin.

I dared to help him too, encouraged by Sam who found it thrilling. I removed his cravat, his shirt, then stopped, shy now. I had never seen a man naked before, but it thrilled me with a yearning I had never felt before, and I wanted to touch him everywhere... learn about his entire body. I pressed my face to his chest to hear his heartbeat and smell warm, clean skin. Sam asked me to kiss his throat which I did, and he lay with his head back, enjoying the small, shy kisses.

Never had any man touched me where Sam did. The unfamiliar feeling of arousal washed over me, and I found myself wet and yearning. It was a truly wonderfully moving experience. For the both of us. It was so sweet and gentle; Sam was moved beyond all feelings. He slid gently inside and I felt a little pain, but not much, then the feeling of love and desire overwhelmed me. We slept late into the morning, then woke to the sun streaming in. Sam smiled. I touched his face.

In the morning, we asked for a bath to be drawn. We spent a good hour relaxing in it together, each washing the other. Sam had never experienced anything so intense. The warmth of the water was wonderfully relaxing. I washed his hair, his body. Sam sat with closed eyes as I massaged his shoulders.

There was little to do really, in Gorleston – a few holidaymakers who wanted somewhere to walk and bathe, or fishermen unloading their catch. We made as much use of The Cosies as we could, staying so long one night we had to run back to the lodging house.

Friday arrived all too soon. Enjoying our last day, kissing, snuggling in The Cosies, I gave a gasp of horror. I felt my stomach plummet to my boots.

"Sam! Look!"

Approaching us was a woman who was the spit and image of Miss Spoonamore, who stopped to observe us. A frown appeared on her face. I glanced at Sam, who smiled, then, cheekily, he took my chin in his fingers and kissed me. I melted as I always did and returned the kiss, fully, putting my arms around his neck. A disgusted exclamation came from the woman, and she stalked over to us.

On closer inspection, we could see it was not the Miss Spoonamore we knew but was, in fact, her twin sister. I recalled the speech Miss Spoonamore had given that time, over the very places where we were sitting. She wore no pince-nez glasses and was dressed in black. That was the only difference. Smiles appeared on our faces; we simply couldn't help it. We looked at her, then one another, and suddenly spluttered with laughter. The look on her face was murderous!

"What are you doing here behaving like that?" she shot out. "It's a disgrace! It's bad enough when people do this at night! But, in broad daylight? For shame!"

"And who might *you* be?" Sam enquired, rather boldly. "Is that the usual way to address guests in your town?"

I wanted to scream with laughter. The look on her face was priceless.

"It is precisely the way I address people like you!" she snapped. Sam rose, looking terribly indignant.

"I take offence at your words," he told her. "My wife and I are on our honeymoon!"

The other 'Miss Spoonamore' sniffed.

"You should keep behaviour like that private!" the woman spat at us. "I shall bring Arnold here. He'll sort you out!"

"And who might he be?" Sam queried.

"My brother!" she replied. "As a family, we are entirely chaste! You wait and see. He'll be along tomorrow, and if you are still here, he will give you a sermon!"

"Then he'd be wasting his breath!" Sam told her mildly. "We're due home tomorrow!"

Miss Spoonamore flapped at us to drive us both off. We merely sat there. Eventually, unused to defiance, she merely gave us a warning look and stalked away.

I had to buy some nice things for Mrs Elgin and Helen. A pretty cup and saucer for Mrs Elgin with painted flowers on it and a miniature painting of the beach for Helen.

Our holiday was coming to an end, and I was sad.

"But it's been marvellous," I told him. "A taste of what can be for us! Oh, Sam, I want so to be with you."

Sam nibbled my ear. "You will be," he whispered and held me close.

Back in Yarmouth, it had all gone far too fast for my liking. Sam too felt deflated, but he had to continue to make money and, as he kept telling me, it would not be long now.

Several days later, Sam came for dinner, furious and upset.

"My father's watch!" he stated. "He gave it to me before I went to London. It's been stolen. From my very person! I didn't even feel it taken. That's how competent the pickpockets are. It was a lovely watch, for all it didn't keep time terribly well, nor was it expensive, but I'm so angry."

He set himself down heavily at the table and, at once, I put my arm around him.

"Oh, Sam! I'm sorry, really. Are you sure it was stolen? Couldn't it have fallen off in your lodgings?"

"No." Sam shook his head. "I've already looked. Florence too. She helped me, even got down on her knees to look under things. We've scoured everywhere."

I pitied him. To lose something one's parent had gifted you was dreadful. Sam drummed his fingers on the table. "It must've been when I was jostled in the crowd," he told us. "I went to get something for Mamma's headache. It probably happened then."

I was truly sorry, and wished I could replace it. A man's watch and chain were part of his identity, part of becoming a man when he attained his majority.

"I'll need to explain to Papa," Sam grumbled. "He won't be happy. I hope the wretch who stole it gets his comeuppance. Meantime, I'd best see if I can obtain a replacement, though it won't be anywhere near as grand."

Sam's father was upset by the theft, but he didn't blame Sam. He himself had been the victim of pickpockets. They were deplorable, he told Sam. "Don't worry; do you go to Mr Smith, he's a decent range that aren't too expensive."

I took in more sewing to earn money to put away for our escape fund. I would sit with Helen to work, and we'd listen to George's playing. Sam had told me he had spoken to George of our leaving and the organist had been helpful and given some sound advice. He had asked Sam to do a little gardening work, since though his wife enjoyed it, she was not strong enough to do the heavier tasks, and Sam had obligingly done so and received some payment for it. The more we amassed, the happier we would be.

However, it was only a matter of time before Sam's parents discovered the truth.

CHAPTER FOUR

We had both known Sam's parents would have to be told about our plans. Sam would leave with me, with or without their blessing, so he sat and calmly explained our situation, and now they wished to speak to me.

"Don't worry." My earnest lover kissed my brow. "It won't be as bad as you fear."

Sam's parents faced us on the settle, as we sat, hand-in-hand. I answered their many questions truthfully and with respect.

Mr Dwyer spoke. "In the usual way, we *should* condemn you since it's an affair outside of marriage, and marriage is sacred, but, neither of us wish to see him unhappy. I've thought long and hard about this, and had I been married to Susan, then later set eyes on Ada, I must confess, I'd have done the same thing!" Mr Dwyer paused. "Susan and her family had the worst possible influence on Sam. Her behaviour has been inexcusable. So, if this is what you both wish, to begin afresh, together we shall do what we can to help."

The glance I gave to Sam was so full of love and hope. Sam exhaled in relief and bent his head for a moment or two. I had no idea that Sam, having told his parents about Susan's attempt to poison him, had actually been the deciding factor.

"But this *must* be kept quiet," Mr Dwyer said. "We don't want this to be town gossip. We'll help you. Don't tell *anyone* you plan to leave except those you trust. We've some money put away, not much, but you may have it."

"Father!" Sam was unbelievably grateful.

"I suspect we'll have her pounding the door demanding an explanation, but we'll deal with her!" The parents glanced at the dog, Captain, who sat on the rug before the fire, dozing. "*He* won't let her in, that's for certain!" Simon stated.

With acceptance from the Dwyers, I came out of my shell a little more and smiled, warming to them greatly.

Helen had the memory of an elephant, and she was not one to renege on her promises. In her opinion, Miss Spoonamore still had not received adequate punishment for throwing me down the steps.

"Lass, I've a fine joke! Here's what we'll do – we'll send Baker from the workhouse a letter purporting to be from a gorgeous young girl, saying she wants to meet him in secret. Then Spoonamore'll get one purportedly from that jeweller chappie she likes! It'll say that they must each wear a white rose. What do ye think of that then, eh?"

I laughed. "Helen, that's wicked!"

"Aye, I know!" she told me, grinning. "Face it, Alice, they both deserve it!"

I went to find Tabitha to bring her along too.

"Come on!" I took her arm and we walked. The sky was darkening out to sea, with a storm brewing. The wind had strengthened considerably.

As the first drops of rain began to fall, Tabitha and I dashed pell-mell into the grounds of Saint Nicholas.

We sat at the kitchen table listening to the downpour. A huge flash of lightning illuminated the kitchen, followed by a thunderous clap that rolled around the building. Helen took out a piece of paper. She pondered, took some ink and filled the fountain pen.

"Now, let's start." Helen took up a pen.

"*My dear Miss Spoonamore, I sincerely hope you will forgive the familiarity of this letter, but I must speak true.*"

It didn't take long for Helen to draft the letter; on reading it, Tabitha looked at us, astonished.

"So, *Dear Mr Baker....*

Helen scribbled industriously, whilst I watched.

"I'd be grateful if you could meet me at 2 o'clock, this Saturday, at the front of the Hotel Royal. I have admired you from a distance but am too shy to make myself known. I hope you will forgive this forwardness, but I would prefer a real man to a snivelling boy!"

"Please wear a white rose in your buttonhole. I hope you will come and not deny me, for all I am just nineteen. With all the hope in my heart. Yours truly, Cornelia Harrison-Blythe."

Helen handed me the letter. "Now, we deliver these and wait for the fun!"

Susan had been trying to convince Blissett to accompany her to London.

"Come on, Ray, it'll be great! There's all Pa's contacts... plenty of readies to be made."

Blissett looked at her. Whilst he enjoyed her body, he had never been tied to a woman in his life and didn't intent to start now. Besides, he had contacts of his own, and was managing a nice little 'fish racket' with some smuggling on the side.

"We could rob a shop, or a house or two." Susan elbowed him. "Then off to the smoke. It's easy to disappear there; nobody knows your name, and nobody cares either."

"I'll make any decisions as to our future, woman!" Blissett was not about to be ordered about by her. She might rule Sam, but she could never rule him.

"Yeah, course, Ray, just trying to help, that's all."

Blissett thought... there were any number of shops in Yarmouth, but he was not a man to be hurried. Perhaps one of the grand houses up on South Quay? He looked at the eager woman at his side. Really, she was a slattern; small wonder Sam was seeking his comfort elsewhere. Supposing he used Susan to help in a break-in on the quay? A smile spread across his face. An idea was brewing, an idea which would cause little, if any, risk to himself, but rather more to Susan!

Saturday. Helen and I waited with bated breath. We had secreted ourselves behind a large pillar, outside of the hotel.

"Hope she doesn't spot us; it'd spoil everything!"

"She won't," Helen told me with confidence. "She'll be too busy anticipating her date!"

Miss Spoonamore had been amazed at the letter. "So! I had no idea! I thought he did not like me. Now, after so long? I suppose he had no alternative but to send me this missive."

She felt like a young girl again as she titivated herself that morning. Her best blouse, held at the throat with a ruby brooch. Her fanciest hat... she preened in expectation, all with an uncharacteristic, thin-lipped smile on her face. She regarded herself in the mirror and nodded. The long black skirt brushed the floor, and she put a matching jacket over the frilly blouse and pinned the flower onto the lapel.

"Nothing too ostentatious," she muttered. Finally satisfied, she adjusted her hat and made her way out of the house.

Mr Baker had been amused at his letter. The fact that a nineteen-year-old young woman of breeding had written to him was nothing less than miraculous. Too conceited to wonder at it, and suspect, he donned his best cream trousers, frowning a little as he had difficulty in doing up the button over his stomach. His shirt clean, starched collar under the fat chin, he fitted his buttonhole with the desired rose into his short hunting jacket and attempted to comb his scanty hair over his balding head. He regarded himself in the mirror, frowned at his sideways view, licked his fat lips in anticipation of the lively, bold and vulgarly forward nineteen-year-old naughty heiress. He put on the stove pipe hat, nodded, then left the workhouse.

A warm wind blew. The afternoon was quite perfect. Helen elbowed me. We had been loitering since half past one.

"It's Spoonamore!" she hissed. "Look at her! She's early! She cannae wait!"

I peeked. Miss Spoonamore strode along the pavement, a smile on her face. She appeared to be determined to get to her destination as fast as was decently possible.

"Goodness me! She *has* made an effort," I whispered. We watched as she stood, glancing nonchalantly about, beside the low wall. "Do you feel bad now?"

Helen grinned. "Not I!"

Miss Spoonamore positioned herself on the steps and glanced around. She was early, she knew, but she had not been able to help herself. Fifteen minutes passed and Mr Baker marched towards the hotel. He too had evidently dressed for the occasion. His tight-fitting britches and riding boots sent me into a silent paroxysm of mirth at the sight of him. The material was so strained across his bottom, I wondered if he would need to remain standing the whole time, since sitting down was risky!

"Does he think he's going riding then?" I whispered and Helen managed to stop the blurt of laughter.

"Aye! Riding Miss Spoonamore!" she told me. "The skinniest nag at the races!"

The white rose in the buttonholes of each person seemed to shimmer. Miss Spoonamore caught sight of it at once. Mr Baker walked up the steps and stood, a glance at his pocket watch and he turned to look about him. Miss Spoonamore looked at him, and he looked at her. A frown came to her face. This was not Mr Smith! She wondered whether to approach him. Mr Baker, after giving her an unfavourable glance, looked around once more. What were the chances of two entirely unconnected ladies wearing a white rose on the same day to the same meeting place? He felt a shudder. Women, he loved, in all shapes, sizes and ages, but even he had his limits.

"Excuse me," Miss Spoonamore said to him, unable to wait any longer. "Are you waiting for someone? I am expecting a gentleman friend here; he told me he was to wear a white rose, but you are not he!"

Mr Baker looked at the ageing spinster. "Madam, I'm awaiting a young lady if you don't mind." He scowled at her, looking down his nose.

Helen and I held our breath.

"Well, *you* are not Mr Smith!" She glanced at the rose. "Yet you are wearing a rose. I was given to understand Mr Smith would be wearing a white rose! In my experience, men do not go around wearing white roses."

Utterly confused, the two looked at each other.

"I received a letter, not that it is any of your concern, instructing me to do so!" Mr Baker was disdainful. "I'm awaiting the arrival of a young lady, and..." He pulled the letter out of his pocket. Miss Spoonamore took out hers too. They compared the writing.

"Here it comes!" I hissed to Helen.

"These are in the same hand! What on earth?" She looked at Mr Baker, thoroughly confused by now.

"We have been duped!" Mr Baker snapped, catching on faster than Miss Spoonamore. "This is a trick! Damn and blast it!" He looked fit to burst, so great was his rage.

"Indeed we have!" Miss Spoonamore snapped. "Well, I do not find this the least bit amusing!" She stamped her foot in rage.

Mr Baker scowled. "Neither do I! Well, someone evidently wishes to embarrass us and has done so! I wonder who's responsible for this. I can think of nobody, can you?"

Miss Spoonamore shook her head. She had offended so many townsfolk it could have been just about anybody.

"Well, I shall do my damnedest to find out!" Mr Baker snarled, "and once I do, they won't sit down for a month!"

"The culprit may even *be* here!" Miss Spoonamore was not daft. "Watching us!"

Helen tugged my arm. "That's our cue, Alice. Quick! Into the hotel!" She hissed in my ear and the pair of us bolted.

"There! People *were* watching us; they just ran into the lobby!"

Miss Spoonamore picked up the long skirt and followed him up the few steps into the beautiful lobby.

Sedate, upper-class guests seemed to be gliding about on the marbled floor, and there were expensive-looking Ming vases dotted here and there. There was a long, wide, marble staircase, carpeted up the centre in a rich red colour. The reception was beautiful with red velvet sofas to match the carpet. Bell boys carried luggage about.

Helen and I stopped and looked around us. "Up the stairs!" she said and clasped my arm.

"Hurry!"

We hastened toward the staircase, Helen knocking into one bell boy who dropped everything he was carrying. Ignoring his outraged yells, Helen and I bounded in an unladylike manner up the first two flights of stairs we could see, surprising guests, and narrowly missing a maid making her way down with a laden silver tray. Together, we glanced from our vantage point. Numerous shocked faces looked at us, incredulous at what they had just witnessed.

Did you see anybody rush this way?"

The maid nodded. "Yes, sir, I did; they went up the stairs. Almost knocked me flying too!"

Mr Baker scowled. "What did they look like, girl?"

The maid paused. "Not sure, sir, they was that quick!"

"Think! Tell me or I'll shake every tooth from your head! They went right past you!"

"Sir, I don't know. Honestly!" She was now on the verge of tears. Mr Baker made a growling noise and hurried up the steps as fast as his rotundity would allow.

Helen and I reached the second landing.

"Now where shall we go?" I asked. "We need to hide; he's not going to let this go! Try that door!"

"'Tis someone's room! I cannae do that!"

"You can! Helen, try it!"

Helen tried. The door remained shut. "Locked!" she looked at me. I tried the door myself, wrenching the knob, but it wouldn't open.

We heard shouting.

"Where are you? God damn your hides! I know you're here! I will summon a constable! I will birch you myself!"

"Hellfire!" I squeaked. "He means it too! Come on! Back to the landing and up the other stairs. Take care though, Helen!"

My friend nodded and we hurried up another flight, and then another.

"This is as far as they go!" Helen told me, panting for breath. "Now what?"

I looked along the passageway. It too, was beautifully carpeted and the flock wallpaper must have cost hundreds, but this was no time to admire the décor.

At the end was a glass door. "Fire escape!" I said gleefully. "Come on!" Mr Baker could be heard on the floor below. Evidently, someone had called the Hotel Manager, and he was shouting. Mr Baker was positively bellowing at the man that the miscreants were somewhere inside. Miss Spoonamore had evidently caught up with him since her voice could be heard too, getting higher and higher with fury.

I pulled at the door. "It's locked too!" I said in surprise.

"'Tis a fire escape door; push it, ye ninny!"

I pushed hard and the door flew wide, banging on the wall; glass shattered.

"Oh no!" I exclaimed. Helen and I made our way quickly and safely down the iron, twisting staircase, relieved now that the little drama was over.

"Come on, let's get as far as we can from here. Up St Peter's Road, we can mingle in the marketplace. Are you alright, Helen? Oh my God! We just charged up the stairs with you expectant!"

"Aye, he's sound," Helen assured me. "He'll be enjoying the chase!"

We hurried up St Peter's Road, trying to catch our breath, darting nervous looks behind us, then stopped.

"I need a drink," Helen told me. A café in the marketplace was ideal. We chose a table and sat, laughing so much we were almost ejected.

Susan and Blisset sat in The Three Feathers.

"I made a plan, girl, and when we're all set up, we'll leave together," Blisset told her. "Easy money; all it takes is a little bit of guts. You up for it?"

Susan nodded, excitement in the pit of her stomach.

"There's an old dear, lives just two houses down from the Paget's. She's 90 if she's a day. What I want *you* to do is scout round the place over the next few days. You know, servants coming and going, visitors, that sort of thing. You could even go up there, ask for a bit of work, look sad, plead if necessary, even if it's sweeping. Or you can just get one of the servants into conversation. Play on their sympathies, 'specially the old 'un. I heard she don't keep money in a bank; don't trust 'em. She'll have jewellery too, lots of it, accordin' to my associates!"

"Which one?"

"Harris!"

Blisset regarded Susan who seemed agog. It wouldn't take much. She could affect some sort of disguise, perhaps spectacles, a shawl over her hair.

"What about family?"

"There aren't none; not no more. Harris knows the boot boy. I'll sound him out a bit more. Let you know, eh?"

Blissett chucked Susan under her chin and grinned. "Now, off you go, my pretty. Don't make things obvious!"

I sent word to Tabitha to come to see me. Tabitha, having heard the gossip around town, guessed I had something to tell her. She also had an idea of what it would be; she made her way to our row and knocked on the door.

"Tab," I said and hugged her. "I need to tell you something and you won't like it."

Tabitha sat.

"You're going away," she said hoarsely.

I nodded. "We must; we love each other. Susan's already tried to poison Sam, so God knows what she might do next. She hangs around with Blissett and Harris, and you know what they're like – I'm terrified for his safety."

"Well, you have to do what's right and safe for you," Tabitha told me. "I'll always be your friend."

She paused, then spoke; "I know it's not the right time to ask, but will you give me a reading, please?"

"Alright; hold out your hand."

I looked at the small hand she presented.

"Good health. You won't have trouble with illness as far as I can see. I don't see riches or any sort of wealth," I told her with a frown. "But I can see you will have a real love."

Tabitha stopped herself from snorting.

"No, I mean it!" I looked up at her. "Truly, Tab. You *will* marry, but not for some time yet so don't start looking straight away."

Tabitha smiled. "Well, I'll be old and grey, I expect, and meet a greybeard who won't be fussy at his age."

"No, that isn't very likely, Tab, as I see you will have four children."

"Children? Me?"

"Yes," I answered, so definitely that she felt suddenly hopeful.

"When?"

"I don't know, but it's some way off, so don't hold your breath, but don't lose hope either."

Tabitha smiled.

Sam and I bade an emotional farewell to his family, making promises we'd visit, and that they would ever be welcome in Devon. Later, at home, the Reverend paid us a visit. He, too, wished to bid us farewell. I was amazed; had Mrs Elgin told him? Helen? I expected a stern rebuke, but to our surprise, he simply clasped our hands in his and told us he had known about us for a long time.

CHAPTER FIVE

Flight

The last day had arrived. I had barely slept. I was terrified something would go wrong at the last moment, and Mrs Elgin had trouble keeping me calm. I glanced from the window a dozen times; a sea mist had rolled in. I saw Sam then, appearing from the mist, a large canvas bag slung over his shoulder. I grinned.

Sam arrived and held out his arms into which I flew.

"She's been a cat on hot bricks since before dawn!" Mrs Elgin told him as we sat. "I take it that you got away alright?"

"Yes, Mrs Townsend was in the shop. I couldn't say a proper goodbye without arousing suspicion, but never mind. Susan's gone early to buy fish. She wanted to be there when the first catch came in. If I know her, she won't go straight back home either, but to the ale house, then to visit Blisset!"

"Did you leave her a note?" I asked.

"I did, my sweet. I think she'll turn the air blue when she returns."

I wondered when that would be. It was now eight o'clock. The three of us would go to Saint Nicholas' for nine o'clock and meet up with Helen and William, then take a cab to Vauxhall where we would take the train to Norwich, and that was when we would say our goodbyes.

Before we left the house, Mrs Elgin turned to me.

"I have one last parting gift, Alice," she told me seriously. "You *will* take it and you *will* wear it and I want no argument about it, is that clear?"

I nodded, confused. "It is this." To my stunned amazement, Mrs Elgin pulled off her wedding ring. "Samuel, do the honours, if you please."

Sam and I gasped.

"Mary! Are you certain? This is a precious ring!"

"Yes, and what is more, I planned to give it to Alice from the very start," she replied. "I don't want my daughters fighting over it when I'm gone. They'll have my savings and everything else! So, Alice, you shall have it. Do this for me and I'll be happy."

Overwhelmed, I hugged her tightly. "I don't know how to thank you! I really don't."

"Thank me by wearing it for me. It will do my heart good to know it is now on your finger," she replied. She glanced up at Sam. "Well, Samuel? What do you have to say?" Incredibly touched and full of emotion, Sam put the ring on my wedding finger.

"I take you as my heart wife," he told me seriously. "I shall be there for you always, and love you, protect you, forever." I looked at the ring. Sam wore no ring now; he had pawned it.

"Sam, I take you for my heart husband and will ever be yours, obey you in all things, love you and take care of you, forever."

At last, the three of us stood for a few moments looking at the house; I felt a rush of emotion. So much had changed for me in that house.

We walked to the church at the appointed time, Sam and I trundling everyone's luggage on a troll cart. Helen and William were there too. The Reverend, with both hands folded, observed us.

"This is a very sad, bittersweet leave-taking," he told us. "Mrs Elgin, I have known you so very many years. I am glad you are going to your daughter's where you will be waited on and cared for until well into old age."

"I'm already well into old age, Reverend, but thank you anyway!" the lady said with a twinkle in her eyes. "In any case, I'm not going far. We 'll meet on occasion!"

Reverend nodded, tears welling.

"Helen, William, I hope you will be wise when you find what you seek abroad."

William nodded.

"Samuel..." He took Sam's outstretched hand. "Under normal circumstances, I should not bless this union, but I will break the tradition and habit of a lifetime and do so now. You deserve a full and happy life. Both of you, go now and think of me."

"Reverend," Sam spoke, "I'm so very grateful for your understanding and patience." Reverend handed Sam a brown envelope.

"For your new life," he said. "Don't open it until you're on the train! Now, come here and let me hug you all."

The elderly priest had tears in his eyes as he hugged us all, even Sam and William. "Go with God," he told us.

At Vauxhall, I hoped that nothing would stop us now. Sam was nervous too, looking constantly out of the station entrance. I remembered the day of the grand opening. It seemed so long ago. The platform was not too busy, only a few homeward-bound holidaymakers, and children, dragging their feet, not wanting to leave the beach.

We reached Norwich and disembarked. The platform was teeming with people.

William went to check the times of the trains we would need to take. Mrs Elgin's daughter was already there, having sat in the waiting room. She waved and hastened her mother.

I hugged Mrs Elgin.

"I'll miss you so much," I told her, tears streaming. "You've been another grandmother to me, and that is how I'll forever think of you. You saved my life. I owe you so much."

Mrs Elgin felt tears coming. "My little Alice, you have more than repaid me, with your help and kindness and cheery presence. I'll miss you too, but we'll write and who knows? We may meet in the future, since travel is easier by rail."

When Mrs Elgin and her daughter had gone, I cried a good while. I had much to owe to Mrs Elgin. Had it not been for her, I would have died in that shop doorway.

Next, I had to say goodbye to Helen, and it proved harder than I had ever imagined. We had known each other just eight months, but I felt I was losing a sister. We clung to one another.

"I have this for you," I told Helen. "Treat it carefully." Helen took the package.

"May I open it now?" she asked, and I nodded. Helen did and gasped at the beautiful tablecloth. I had purchased it from the market, then I had sewn on some of the Yarmouth lace, all the way around, and put some doily shapes in the middle, but in the corners, I had embroidered the same message "AD & HB, heart sisters."

Helen bawled like a baby.

Tearfully, she handed me some potted heather in a bag. I peered inside.

"Ooh! Heather! Sam! Look!"

"How delightful. Thank you both."

Our train puffed in. This was it, the final parting of the ways.

"I do not say goodbye," Sam told Helen and William, "for I'm sure we'll see you both again. Take care. You have our address safely?"

Helen nodded. "Aye, 'tis here!" She tapped her forehead.

"Write to us. Don't forget! When you are rich and famous especially!" He winked.

Sam and I sat on the train as it left the station and left Norwich behind.

Back in Yarmouth, Florence was having a trying time with Susan. She had indeed, 'turned the air blue' as Sam had predicted. She had had a strange, gut feeling something was wrong when she had marched up Howard Street. Having stalked upstairs to their lodgings, she had entered her room and seen the note on the pillow. She could hardly believe her eyes and had to read it twice.

Now she was throwing things around the room, screeching. In a blinding fury, she tore all the bedclothes off and up-turned the mattress.

"The bastard! The bastard! He ran off with her! Look, Mrs T! Look!"

Florence, who had hastened upstairs in alarm at the screaming, and the sound of furniture bumping, took the crumpled note and read it.

"Susan, I am leaving for a new life with Alice. I hope you understand. Don't associate with undesirables, it will lead you into great misery. Samuel."

"Well, I don't like to say this, but you brought it on yourself!" Florence told her. "You frequented the ale house with other men, flaunted that in his face. How was he supposed to react? I'm only surprised he didn't do this sooner!"

Susan sat on the bed, suddenly run out of steam.

"I'll find out where they went and have him brought back here. I'll learn him, and as for her, I'll find her and have her killed!"

"Susan Dwyer! Don't say such things. You can do nothing but accept what's happened. Think about your behaviour. Pray and ask the Reverend for guidance. Mend your ways, young woman, or it'll be the workhouse for you!"

Susan was infuriated. She stalked out of the door and ran helter-skelter to where we had so recently dwelt where she hammered on the door.

"Open up! Open this door! Now! Or I'll break it down! I swear! I'll wring your scrawny old neck for you too. Where are you? That witch has run off with my man!"

Susan bashed her fist on the door. "OPEN UP!"

A neighbour poked her head from her window. "They've gone!" she stated. "Left early this morning. The three of 'em!"

In a blinding fury, Susan swore. She applied her boot to the door, viciously, then, marched to the Dwyer family home where she hammered on the door.

"Yes, they left." Simon stood at the doorway, forbidding, his arms crossed. His son-in-law stood behind in the hallway. He had been expecting this. A threatening snarl came from Captain at his master's side. "I don't like to see marriage vows broken but, in your case, I don't care. You even tried to poison our boy! Hanged, that's what you should be, hanged! You aren't welcome 'ere, girl; you reap what you sow. Now be off to the workhouse, or I'll set the dog on ye!"

Ada appeared from the doorway and gave her a triumphant look. Susan glowered. Her face was red, eyes wild. The snarl from Captain became more threatening still, his hackles raised. Maria came to stand beside her mother and tittered.

She fixed Maria with a look of hatred, then stalked to Blisset's lodgings.

"Susan!" Blisset had just finished lunch. "This is a nice surprise!" He pushed away his dish, wiping his mouth on his sleeve. His grin faded then at the look on her face. "What's happened?" he asked.

Susan launched into a furious diatribe.

Blisset frowned. "Well, you can do without 'im, can't you? After all, aren't *we* goin' off together?"

"Yeah, course we are but that isn't the bloody point, man. I'm pissed that the louse ran off with her. He got one over on me and I don't like that!"

"Well, all we must do is to find a way of getting back at the pair of 'em! Find out where they went. Shouldn't be difficult," Blisset told her.

Susan sighed; she eyed Blisset keenly.

Blisset smirked. "Ah, forget 'im, Susan, my love. He weren't a proper 'usband to you in any case. You told me yourself how bad he was in bed. I set you screamin', don't I, eh? Well, you won't have no cause for complaints when we're together. Fine house you'll get. Servants. I told you before; nice little horse and carriage to take you to wherever you likes. Now, how's you getting on at the old biddy's?"

Susan had been watching the house, as instructed by Blissett.

"Alright; no family, like you said, carriage comes twice a week to take her and her maid off somewhere or other. Gone for two hours."

"Interesting! So that means house is more or less empty?"

Susan nodded. "Well, I s'pose so, apart from whatever other staff there is, cook, I 'spect, butler, and he's about a hundred."

"And the boot boy, Charlie, he's always on about how little he gets paid, for all she's drowning in money; those were his very words, mawther! Harris got him to look about a bit. There's a housekeeper, but she and the cook take the time to have a good old natter when the missus is gone. The old lady's room is at the front, dead centre; we'll pay the boy handsomely for his silence. After all, he's only a lad. Stays in the background mostly. How's he to know what's going on upstairs, eh?"

"And if he squeals?"

"He won't! He 'udn't dare! Besides, he'll get a sovereign out of it. It's easy. What fourteen-year-old turns up their nose at a sovereign?" Blissett told her with an evil gleam in his eye. "Butler's some old retainer; cook'll be out the way too... it's a really small staff. Now, all we have to do is plan when to get in! I want you to go and search, my queen."

"ME?" Susan screeched, and Blissett looked around in horror. "Why me?"

"Shut it! Want the whole town to know? Yes! You! You can search better. You knows your way round a lady's bedroom, where she'd keep stuff; how do I know, eh? Plus, you can move quicker, light on your feet. See me clomping about in hobnailed boots?"

Susan wasn't at all happy about the plan, but what else could she do? Blissett gave her a loving look. "It's for our nest egg," he reminded her.

"I s'pose. At least the jewels won't attract attention in London."

Sam and I eventually arrived at Bristol, very tired. I now had a pounding headache.

"Poor darling." Sam kissed my forehead. "Don't worry. We'll find somewhere soon, and you can lie down and rest."

We left the station, hauling our luggage. A row of horses and cabs stood outside waiting for weary travellers.

"Ah! Look, we're due the next cab. Come on, sweetheart." Sam assisted me into the coach along with all our baggage.

"We wish to lodge at an hotel close by," Sam said to the driver. "My wife is extremely fatigued."

The driver nodded. "I knows a good 'un," he said, and we set off with a jerk.

The hotel was accustomed to short-stay railway travellers and had some free rooms. It wasn't much of a place, on first impressions, with a drab-looking interior, and threadbare carpet in places, which continued down the hallway. However, with the headache, I didn't care.

Sam looked around, then he looked at me.

"This place doesn't look great. Shall we search for another? I don't want my new wife uncomfortable here."

I squeezed Sam's hand. "Let's stay, darling. I want to get rid of this headache. It's only for one night after all."

Sam paused, then nodded and we spoke to the proprietor, a thin little man who had come out wiping his hands on an apron. He set about booking us in and handed us a key. A shout to a boy to 'take the bags to room six', produced the appearance of a young lad of around thirteen. I doubted his ability to lug the bags that even Sam was having trouble with, but he must have been stronger than he looked, for he took several and sprinted up the stairs with ease.

Our room was nicely decorated, to our surprise, and overlooked Queen's Square. The window was open, and the room smelled fresh. Clean towels had been provided. A jug and washbowl were in good condition.

"Hmm, not bad," Sam told me. "Only for the night anyway." He got up then and glanced into the next room. He gasped.

"Alice! Look! Look at this!"

I poked my head in the door. There was a large bath.

"Gosh. I didn't expect that kind of luxury, from the look of the downstairs! That looks good!" I grinned. "Fancy a bath, Sam?"

Sam winked. "I think we deserve it after all that travelling!"

We bathed together. Sam had asked for some willow bark tea, and this I had drunk. We lay in the water having scrubbed one another with the beautifully scented soap the hotel had provided. Sam had massaged my temples, neck and shoulders, with lavender oil to ease away the headache. I wondered what Susan was doing now. She would be apoplectic; that I did know.

"Mmm, that *is* good," I said.

"Nice hot meal and your headache will go," he whispered in my ear.

We dined early on roast chicken, potatoes, carrots and peas, which was beautifully done, then retired to bed.

"We need to be up for the eight-thirty train," Sam told me. "So, I arranged for us to be called at seven. We'll get to the station for at least a quarter past eight. It will be a shorter journey tomorrow at least. Only a couple of changes, I believe."

I nodded. I turned to nestle into him and slept at once. Sam lay awake for a time, listening to the traffic outside, and somewhere, a barrel organ played, the owner getting the last tunes of the night. His eyes started to close, and he breathed a sigh of relief.

I was refreshed in the morning, as was Sam. My headache had vanished. After a good wash, we ate a large breakfast of eggs, bacon and bread with strong coffee, then, having hefted all our luggage downstairs, Sam paid.

"Was everything to your satisfaction, sir?" The hotelier asked. Sam nodded.

"Unexpectedly good," he answered. "We were impressed with the bath and the standard of cooking here is excellent. The bedroom was beautifully clean, and the dining room most tastefully decorated. Might I be so bold as to suggest that your foyer and front of the hotel get some decoration? We almost didn't stay here due to the carpet and walls. It was only because my wife had such a terrible headache that we did. It's a pity to lose business on first impressions, sir."

The hotelier nodded, smiled and thanked him. "We've plans to do so, sir; it's just taking rather longer than we anticipated. However, thank you for your compliments. I'm pleased you enjoyed your stay."

We boarded the Exeter-bound train. There were a lot of people heading that way. I hoped my headache would not return.

The weather was still good. We had no food for snacks, but there would be a chance to get a quick bite at Exeter. I was pleased we had eaten a good breakfast; it would keep our bellies from rumbling for a while yet.

"It certainly is some beautiful scenery down this way," Sam admitted.

"It is; oh Sam, I hope you won't be too homesick, darling. I know you'll miss the beach but honestly, Dartmoor and Dartmeet are just as beautiful. Truly."

"I'll be fine as long as I have you," Sam told me.

We eventually pulled into Exeter station. Yet another change here for the Plymouth line. Sam glanced at his recently acquired pocket watch.

"Not too long now, angel," Sam told me.

At long last, we reached Plymouth and found a coach that was heading to Tavistock.

"To Pepper Cottage, Blackdown," I said, and the coach set off. Sam smiled. Pepper Cottage – I had not mentioned the name before, and he found it charming and quite unusual. Tired though I was from the journey, the fresh air revived me somewhat and the fact that we were home too, safe. Familiar landscapes passed as we trotted along the dirt and stone tracks to home.

Sam looked at the beautiful countryside. "So gorgeous... so many hills," he said in appreciation.

It was after four o'clock when we reached the home I had grown up in.

Up the slope of a rough, chalky track, that became stonier and dustier as we ascended, then around a corner, a pretty cottage came into view. Thatched roof, with small windows, and a whitewashed wall. There were still some roses around the doorway, though most had died back. There was a small, narrow piece of garden around the front of it, and a tiny fence and gate. Beside the cottage, another gate led to the garden beyond. Sam could hear a blackbird singing.

An elderly man stood at the entrance. The smile on his face rivalled the sun.

"Alice!" he bawled and I leapt from the carriage before it had even stopped and ran to him.

"Grandpapa!" I squealed. "Oh, you are looking fine! You must meet Sam."

Sam had taken our belongings and paid the driver who trotted away. He ventured to my grandfather and proffered his hand.

"Grandpa, this is Samuel Dwyer, my heart husband. Sam, Edward Lawrence, my grandfather." To my amusement, both men bowed politely.

"Mr Lawrence," Sam said. "I cannot tell you how wonderful it is to finally meet you and to thank you from the bottom of my heart for your kindness in accepting our union."

Grandfather nodded, smiling and bade us enter.

We ascended the wooden staircase to the upper floor of the cottage and Sam and I entered the room that had once been my parents'. For all it felt a little strange to be in my parents' room, it somehow felt right too.

The open window faced west, and the sun could be seen, slowly dipping. Sam could smell apples and warm hay, along with the scent of linden trees. In the distance, a sheep bleated, and a blackbird sang. A wooden ottoman stood opposite the bed where the linen was kept. He turned his attention to the neatly made bed.

"Shall we sit, try it out?" I suggested and Sam nodded. We both sat and sank down.

"I think it will be a terrible job getting up of a morning!" Sam warned me. "So comfortable. I have never felt such a comfortable mattress."

Downstairs, Sam could again smell herbs. He glanced up. From the low rafters of the ceiling hung various herbs, obviously drying for use. He saw some lavender, smaller than the Norfolk variety and less bushy; there was thyme, rosemary, marjoram and mint. The warmth from the sun drew the beautiful scent. There was a settle at the fireside in a cosy inglenook with a red cushion to sit on and other cushions on it for leaning against. Another rocking chair sat near the fire, and round the corner was a low bed that Grandfather now used.

The kitchen had a stone-flagged floor, as did the rest of the cottage downstairs, and a small black cooking range, already lit. Another fire was in the kitchen hearth. The kitchen table was snowy white, set with four chairs around it.

"Grandpa, where's Tiger?" I asked observing the old rag rug on the stone floor in front of the fire.

"Ah, my dear, he passed on about a month back. In his sleep. Very peaceful. He was in his favourite place in front the fire. I found him in the mornin'."

"Oh no!" Tears came.

"I couldn't tell 'ee then but I know you had to know. Bless his heart, he went peaceful so we gotta be grateful for that. The old chap was nineteen too. I buried him out back and he got a little wooden marker there. You can see him later or now if you likes."

Sam and I went to stand by the cat's grave.

"Ah, I wish he had lived at least until we came home," I said sadly. Sam put his arm round me and hugged me into his side.

"Me too. But as your grandfather says, he lived to a great age and died in his sleep. That's all anyone can wish for."

Grandfather observed us from inside the cottage. It had given him a huge shock when I had written, first about my parents' deaths, then about Sam and how we had met. That his granddaughter should even consider being a married man's lover had horrified him, and he had been furious at first, and inclined to order me to break off the union, but I had explained everything. Grandfather was a good judge of character, and he trusted my judgement too. I was like my late mother, he mused. She too had defied convention for love, losing her family to marry his son.

After dinner, I struggled to keep my eyes from closing. That evening, with Grandfather in the rocker, Sam and Grandfather conversed quietly. I lay on the settle, my head in Sam's lap as Sam explained the circumstances that had forced us to leave.

Grandfather looked shocked, particularly at the attempt at poisoning.

"I feel terribly guilty about the child that found and ate it," Sam told him. "I never in a thousand years would've imagined that to happen. After all, I threw it onto someone's private rubbish dump. How was I to know he'd scale the walls and go in that particular yard on that particular day?"

"You couldn't have!" Grandfather replied gently. "'T'was a terrible coincidence, my boy; just think, could easily have been you!"

Sam's fingers descended to rub my curls. He looked at me so tenderly that Grandfather grunted in appreciation.

"Ah, I can see you loves her dearly," he stated. Sam nodded.

"With all my heart and soul," he replied. The clock struck ten. Sam got up.

"I shan't wake her." He scooped me up.

"Ah, best not, lad. Well, I bid you a good night. Now, don't forget, this is your home too now, Sam. You'll treat it as such. I'll see you tomorrow, and you'll meet Mrs Fox and Tommy."

I woke with Sam and saw the early autumn sunlight. Sam turned over.

"Hello, sleepy head!" he said, smiling. "You really slept well, didn't you? I did!"

I nodded. Sam pulled me close for a kiss. Once we were up and washing, Sam told me about the conversation he and grandfather had had the night before.

"Oh yes, poor Tommy. I like him; he's a nice boy, but a natural."

"How old is he then?"

"Tommy? Gosh, ah, thirty, I think, or thereabouts."

Sam nodded. He wasn't keen on a young man around me but if he was what people called a 'natural' then he should not be a threat.

"D'ye think Helen and William are in Scotland yet, Sam?" I wondered after breakfast. Sam, polishing his boots at the fireside, thought.

"I doubt it just yet, darling, but I expect it'll be today, or tomorrow. The journey is around ten hours or so and I know they had to make stops and change trains more times than we did."

"Ain't she the one due to go off to America?" Grandfather queried.

"Yes, she and her husband William. He's Sam's childhood friend. They sail at the end of the month."

"I don't hold with all this going off to other lands," Grandfather said. "No good will come of it, I tell 'ee."

Shortly after, there was a shout at the door.

"Edward?" There came a female voice I had not heard in ages.

Grandfather turned. "In 'ere, Mrs Fox! I got folks for you to meet! Alice and her husband are home at last!"

It occurred to me that Grandfather would have had to give a somewhat different account of Sam and I to Mrs Fox who I knew certainly wouldn't have approved but, in my mind, we were married in any case.

The two neighbours came in. Mrs Fox stopped dead in her tracks causing the large man behind her to bump into her.

"Sorry, Ma!" he drawled.

"My God! Just look at you! It's little Helena come alive again!"

She came over to look me up and down. "You be just like your mamma!" she said. "It's uncanny like!"

I smiled. "Hello, Mrs Fox, it's lovely to see you again. This is Sam, my husband."

"Pleased to meet you, Mrs Fox," Sam said politely.

Tommy beamed, holding his cap in his hands and rolling it up and down in his nervousness but pleased to see me none the less.

"Tommy!" I said smiling at him and pecking his cheek, making him blush. "I bet you don't remember me!"

"I do that, miss," he replied.

Sam looked at the young man with the guileless face. For all he was rather slow, he would eventually understand what was required of him and would work willingly. His only fear was the man would become frustrated and hurt me. Sam moved protectively closer.

"Sam, you need to remember that Tommy's harmless," I told him later, when he pronounced his fears over the man. "He's a child in an adult's body. He won't hurt me. Honestly."

September 29th 1844 – Scottish Highlands

Helen and William were spending the last fortnight with her parents and the time had flown.

"Are you sure about this?" Helen's mother asked her privately. "It's no' too late to change yer mind, hen."

But Helen shook her head. "No, Mam, it's the right decision. We'll see you're all alright too and one day we'll come back to visit. I promise."

Mrs Anderson sighed.

"Alright, lass, but I still have a funny feeling. Are ye sure ye ken what you're doing?"

Helen nodded but was struck by a stark foreboding and disquiet deep in her belly.

Helen thought about the small village which she suddenly dreaded to leave... the quiet of the mountains, the lochs and the mist hanging over them. Back in Yarmouth, it had all seemed so simple. She would go to America with her husband, have children, make a lot of money and ensure her family wanted for nothing, but now...?

Helen went for a lone walk that afternoon. She sat on the boulders amongst the heather. Highland cattle grazed, dotted here and there. She could smell the heather, the bracken. The only sound was the occasional lowing of cows, punctuated by bird calls.

The sky was a clear blue, and she could see for miles. To her right, about half a mile away stood a bothy. Helen recalled when she and her brothers and sisters, as children, had spent nights in it in summer, pretending it was their own house. Helen felt tears run down her cheeks. She wished with all her heart she was back in Yarmouth, that she was still maid to the kindly Reverend, that she could still see her friends daily and have fun. But fun times belonged to youth. She was expecting a baby and now had to make a new life. A married woman, bound to obey her husband. She would have the memories at least and my address was fast in her brain. She set her chin on her knee and looked out at the landscape she loved; it would not be like that in America.

She wondered if Sam and I had reached Devonshire safely. She had already written a letter to me, and hoped the mail coach would reach Tavistock. Helen sighed deeply. She didn't want to go; she didn't. All this was for William, the man she loved.

Morning came too soon, for all she had lain awake for most of the night. Her parents had spent all night awake, her mother sobbing quietly, her father equally distraught but attempting to comfort her mother. William had snored throughout.

"Ye'll want a good breakfast!" her mother told her with forced cheerfulness. "Ye cannae be going all that way on empty bellies."

"Not too much for me, please," William said. "My belly is likely to be empty pretty soon after setting sail."

"Ye've two months at sea," her father joked. "You'll be a bean pole time you get there."

Helen looked at the porridge, the staple diet of her family, and knew she would miss it. She cooked excellent porridge, but of course, it wasn't the same as her mother's.

Before leaving, Helen stood in the old room she had shared with brothers and sisters over the years. Next, she stood in her parents' room, the living room, as if she was trying to absorb her surroundings into her very soul.

"Helen."

Her mother's voice made her start. She turned, and Helen's mother came to take her in her arms and whispered in her ear.

"If all fails, lass, ye ken where we are. This'll ever be yer hame."

William and Helen said their final farewells and Helen walked up the gangplank and onto the ship, her legs wobbly. She shook, from head to toe, but she held onto the rail and waved frantically from on deck and her parents waved back, smiling faces masking the terrible pain. Only William was jovial. Helen wanted to get off the ship. She had already changed her mind and was convinced she was making a mistake.

All too soon, the ship set sail. Helen had been desperately trying to stop herself from pushing past those on board and racing back down the steps. She watched as they were taken away and they got under sail. This was it now. Suddenly, the trappings of wealth and wonderful houses, servants and society seemed ridiculous, stifling her until she could scarcely breathe. She turned to look at William hoping for a little comfort. He was looking decidedly unwell already. Helen sighed. Tending to William would, at least, take her mind from things. The ship headed out, and soon she could see no more of her beloved Scotland. Helen knew she had just made a huge mistake.

Devon

Back in Devon, and I glanced at the kitchen clock. It had just gone ten.

"They'll be sailing now," I told Grandfather. "Helen said they were setting off at ten. I hope the weather's alright."

I poked at the fire. "Warm enough, Grandpa?" I asked.

"Ah, I am that." He beamed at me. "Good porridge you did today, girl," he said smiling. "Sam loved it."

A letter had come for me. I went daily to the post office to pick up any mail brought by the large, bright red and black mail coach that came five times per week. It was Monday morning. Sam had gone to the village to do some jobs for the local carpenter, having been recommended by Grandfather, and he was hoping the man could give him a permanent job.

I walked back up the stony path, turned muddy by the recent rain. There were letters for Mrs Fox, for Sam and me. I recognised Helen's writing at once and felt the thick and creamy envelope. She wasn't in America yet, so obviously, this had come from Scotland. I was desperate to open it. I walked to Mrs Fox's cottage to hand her the letter, then continued back to our own place. Sam's letter from Yarmouth, evidently from his parents, I set on the mantlepiece.

Having swept the rooms, and made ready for lunch, I was restless.

"Ahh, go and get him if ye've a mind," Grandfather told me. "You make me nervous, all that flitting up and down!"

I met Sam halfway up the lane.

"Hello, darling!" He held out his arms and I flew into them.

"I'm glad you're finished for the day. Helen has written!"

"Oh? What does she say?" Sam asked.

"I don't know. I haven't opened it yet!" I told him.

"Why ever not?"

"Because I want you there too and today is the day! They'll have started their voyage now."

Over bread and cheese, we read the letter.

"Dear Sam and Alice,

We are safe and well at home. Mam is going on at me to not go but I assured her I'd be fine. We sail on 30ᵗʰ at 10. I'm feeling marvellous and blooming. I hope your granfer is well, and Sam finds work. There won't be any more letters till we dock so don't worry because you don't hear for a bit. We'll be at sea for 6 weeks so hopefully we'll be there come 15ᵗʰ November if God wills.

I miss you so much. You are my sister and always will be. I'm looking forward to a new life but am scared as well.

Weather looks set fair, at least for now. Will's hoping he won't be seasick!
I promise to write soon as we dock. Then I can let you have a return address
when we settle somewhere. Take good care of Sam, I know you will anyway.
Much Love from your heart sister, Helen."

Grandfather and Sam nodded at the letter.

"Only six weeks, she says!" I said. "*Only!* Gosh, I couldn't stand six hours!"
Sam chuckled and kissed my throat.

"Anyway, that's better than the ten we heard at first," Sam told me.

"Well, we must all pray for a fair brisk wind to blow them to the
Americas," Grandfather stated. He glanced outside. "Tell her the heather is
doin' fine once you can write."

I put Helen's letter in a wooden letter rack. I would keep them all.

Great Yarmouth October 1844

Susan's keen gaze lit on the carriage as the butler, who was, as Blissett had
predicted, somewhat doddery and well advanced in years, assisted the lady
and her maid into the carriage. At a signal from him, the driver cracked his
whip and the highly polished landau set off with a jerk. Susan made her way
across to the house. The butler stood, watching until the carriage was out of
sight, then turned and was somewhat startled to see the drab, bespectacled
woman enveloped in a large, red shawl.

"Yes?" He glared down at her.

"Good morning, sir." Susan bobbed. "I've a message for Belinda; might
I take it through to her, please?"

The butler looked stunned. "Who? What? I fear you have the wrong house.
I know of no Belinda, and what do you mean by coming to the front door?"

"I must've been told wrong then." Susan appeared confused. "My sister-in-law told me definitely, number 25, she's Cook's niece, so I s'pect she meant to give it to Cook; it's urgent."

There was something about Susan that the butler did not like, but he nodded.

"I see, well do you take it to the rear entrance. You shall find cook there, doubtless, but do not dawdle, and on *no* account come to the front again. Surely you know better than that?"

He slammed the door in Susan's face, so she spat at the door and made her way around to the rear of the property, where she slipped through the gate. The kitchen door stood open and there was the sound of pots and pans inside. Susan ventured further into the garden, and stood, hidden by foliage, as she examined the house for possible entry points, and kept an eye on the cook's movements. The woman was late middle-age, and rotund, as many cooks were. She was singing as she worked, waddling from here to there.

Later, and the pair sat in The Three Feathers.

"So, what I suggest is this." Blissett took a long draught of ale. "Soon as that carriage calls, and that old boy's helping her and this maid of hers, you sneak in. I'll go to the rear entrance with some good, fat fish and try to tempt her into buying!"

"She can't buy fish just like that, without her mistress' say so!"

"I *know* that! That's why I'm going to generously offer some as a trial, see? She'll be that grateful; I'll turn on the old charm a bit too. Keep her there a while. She might even fry me up a bit! When you're finished, you slip out from a side window or something, and wait for me at Nag's Head Row."

Susan did not like this idea at all. "You suggesting a daylight robbery? Sneaking in the *front* way? Bit bloody risky, ain't it? 'Specially for me, whilst you're sat there charming cook and stuffin' your face with fish!"

"My angel, it's nowhere near as risky as at night. Doors and windows locked! Noise carries more. There's watchmen about, dogs being disturbed, plus it's dark, you'd need lights... No, this way, nobody will be expecting it! Cook'll have her mind on fish, and if, as you say, she ain't that young either, and fat, she ain't likely to move fast, is she? The old boy will probably use the time when his ladyship's out for a snooze. He'll be in the basement anyway; butlers always are. Who the hell's going to notice *you* nipping smartly in, eh? The maid won't be there. All *you* do is get what you can, then slip out a ground floor window. With luck, the old dear won't even notice she's been robbed if she's a bit doddery! What could be simpler?"

Susan nodded. The front door was set back in a large porch; it could be done!

"I want revenge though," she told him. "Revenge on Sam and that bitch. Damn it all! Why didn't I do her when I had the chance, like I did her parents?"

Blisset paled. For a moment, he was silent. Had he heard correctly?

"What d'ye mean? Like you did her parents?"

Susan shrugged and told him about the true events of that terrible night.

"That was *you?*" He removed his pipe from his mouth, stunned. He also felt distinctly uncomfortable for the first time in his life. *Susan* had murdered my parents?

"Yes. I went to pick their pockets and wasn't quick enough. What was I supposed to do, eh? They saw me! I never set out to stab 'em, just rob."

Blisset exhaled mightily.

"Bloody Hell, you're a dark horse. It didn't occur to you to tell me before?"

Shrug from Susan.

Later, and Blissett sat in his house, fingers drumming on the table. Since Susan's sudden revelation, he was anxious. Robbing people and getting clean away was one thing, murder quite another. He felt suddenly cold as he recalled her having put arsenic in the sausage roll she had made for Sam. Blissett shook his head. No! He would go ahead with the robbery as planned using Susan to steal the loot, he would hide it, tell her to pack and be ready to leave the following day, but then he would take the ill-gotten-gains and vanish, probably to Ipswich, he could still work from there.

Devon November 1844

"Alice! Come quick!" Tommy sounded urgent. Fearing something had happened to Grandfather, I raced out.

"Tommy?" I asked worriedly, "What's wrong?!" I noticed a lump under his jacket.

"'Tis this!" He pulled out a small black kitten. I took one look and my heart melted.

"A dear, sweet little kitten! Oh, may I hold it? What's the matter?"

"Farmer Ainsworth was gonna drown 'er!" Tommy told me fiercely and I understood at once what had upset him so much.

"Well, that is just like him, isn't it? Oh! She only has three legs!"

I looked. There was a front leg entirely missing, only a small stump where the front leg should have been.

"Aye, that's why," Tommy said, sniffing. "The others got homes to go to. T'was the barn mouser what had the kittens see. He said she was a runt and deformed and he don't like that so once she was weaned, he was gonna do it."

"Oh no he won't!" I was furious.

"You keep her, Alice; we can't."

"Of course, we'll keep her Tommy."

I kissed the kitten's cold, wet black nose. She started to purr and looked at me with clear blue eyes.

"Will Mr Sam let you keep her?" Tommy asked worried.

"Of course, he will. He loves cats and they're useful too. I'll show him later. Alright?"

I wondered at the kitten's age. She seemed very young, and I guessed her age at around seven or eight weeks. Poor little mite! I thought, rubbing my cheek against hers.

Just as Tommy was leaving, Farmer Ainsworth puffed up the lane, red in the face.

"Oi! You bloody half-wit! Come 'ere! You give me that kitten what you took! Damned village idiot! What d'ye think you're doing?"

I stepped up to the man, the kitten tightly in my arms. Tommy hid behind in fear.

"Farmer Ainsworth. The kitten's now *mine*! I shan't give her up!"

"But it's defected," Farmer Ainsworth argued, then added somewhat cruelly, "just like him!"

Tommy whimpered from behind me.

"Oh, are you suggesting Tommy should've been drowned?" I asked in shock. "Well! Just you say that to Mrs Fox, and then you'll have to run for your life!"

"Alright, I s'pose you can keep him, but it's a useless mouth and how's he gonna catch mice with three legs?!"

"*She* will be fine," I responded. "She was born with just three and I daresay she'll cope. You wait and see!"

Sam and Grandfather arrived back at the same time, having met on the way. They both came in and stopped short at the sight of me with a tiny black kitten who lay in my lap, fast asleep.

"Good grief!" Grandfather advanced. "How'd you come by that then?"

I gave them the account of that morning and Sam sat at my side. He smiled and his gaze softened on the creature.

"Of course, sweetheart. Only three legs! I wonder why."

"Born that way, I suppose," I said. "Look!"

The kitten woke, and after some initial nervousness, she was too curious about Sam and my grandfather to remain shy. Sam adored her from that moment and by evening, there was no way the kitten was going anywhere!

Grandpa had been a little quiet the past few days and it worried me.

"I keep asking him if things are alright and he tells me that they are," I said to Sam in bed that night. "But something's not right."

Sam wondered. To him, the old man was as spry as he had been when he had first met him and was forever at Mrs Fox's doing some small task.

"Would you like me to speak to him?" Sam asked.

I nodded.

Morning came and the last of the leaves were falling. Grandfather was anxious to get round to see Mrs Fox.

"Again?" I asked. "I thought you were going to sit with me while I black-leaded the range, finish that folktale."

"Oh!" Grandfather ran a hand over a balding head. "I was, wasn't I?" He fidgeted.

I frowned. "You're *always* round at Mrs Fox's!"

"How 'bout I send Tommy round?" Grandfather suggested. "He tells funny stories; I'll finish the folk tale this evening!" He adjusted his necker-chief.

I looked exasperated. Now I'd have Tommy clumping about the place in his big boots.

Sam came to kiss me.

"I must be to work, my darling. Don't worry!"

The two men left. I opened the door so that Bundles could chase and play with the leaves that were left.

"Alice is worried about you, Edward," Sam told the old man once they were outside. "She spoke to me last night, asking me to have a word."

"Arr, so she noticed, eh? She don't miss much. Look, Samuel, it sounds daft, but just cos you'm old don't mean you don't feel, and me and Mrs Fox, we got an understanding. Now Alice is home and has you to look after her, we was planning to wed. It'd mean I go to live there, see; you'd have the cottage all yer own. You 'ont need me under yer feet when you got little 'uns, but Alice mightn't approve."

"Whatever makes you think she won't approve?" Sam asked.

"Well, we feels daft at our age."

"Well, don't. There's no age limit on love."

"Then you think she'll be alright with it?" Grandfather queried.

"Of course!"

Tommy watched me blackleading the range, whilst dangling a feather on a string for Bundles.

"You alright, Alice?" he asked.

"Yes; Grandpa's worrying me a bit, that's all."

"Him and ma. They'm good friends."

"I know!"

"Does you and Mister Sam kiss too?" Tommy asked. He blushed at such a question. I jerked upright.

"What?"

"I wondered if you kissed Mr Sam!"

"Of course I do, Tommy, he's my husband, but why ask me that?"

Tommy looked confused. "Kissing's for soppy girls," he stated, his expression disgusted.

I laughed. "Course it's not!"

"Oh!" he said eventually, having processed the thought.

I shook my head. Grandfather would kiss Mrs Fox on the cheek I presumed. But it made me wonder.

"Tommy..." I got up and went to wash my hands. "Tell me why you asked that question!"

My eyes widened as he began to haltingly explain.

So! I sat at the kitchen table. Grandfather and Mrs Fox had been observed, by Tommy, on the settle in their room kissing! It should have been obvious really. Grandfather and Mrs Fox had been alone a long time.

When Sam and Grandfather returned, I stood at the table.

"Well, Grandpapa. When were you going to tell me about you and Mrs Fox? Why did I have to hear it from Tommy?"

Grandfather looked at Sam and gave a groan.

We sat for cider, bread, cheese and cold beef with tomato chutney.

"Grandpa, I'm happy for you, truly," I told him, patting his hand. "I just wish you'd told me before."

"Well, I didn't know how you was going to take it," he replied honestly. "I only told Sam as he was going off to work. We want to wed next year. I'll move into the cottage there, so this 'un'll be yours."

I smiled.

"You have our blessing, Grandpa, really, and we look forward to the wedding!" I told him.

Back in Yarmouth, the day had arrived, and Susan, feeling sick with nerves, glanced at her accomplice.

"Alright, girl, you knows what to do. They'll be out any moment. You go behind that column, slip in once he's tryin' to get the old bat down them steps. Then get to her room. I'll get round the back."

Blissett hastened over the road, his basket of fish under a cover, and Susan, dry-mouthed, made her way to the grand entrance.

"Good morning, mawther! Fine, fresh fish! Caught s'mornin' by my own hand! Would you care to look?"

Cook, used to tradesmen and their banter, frowned. Blissett had a broad grin on his face, he had shaved, he had even washed! His whole demeanour was friendly, and the plump fish, on close inspection, did look very good.

"Do you try one, free of charge, just to show I'm tellin' you true. I can see you're a woman who knows her business and her way round any kitchen!"

Susan found it easier than she had expected to slip unnoticed into the grand entrance hall. It was busy and noisy on the quay that morning, and the butler was having some difficulty with madam's walking, as he and the maid escorted her. Susan hurried up the winding marble staircase and hastened along the landing. Various doors stood open, some shut, but she soon found the elderly woman's room and entered, stopping slightly out of breath. Susan made her way to the dressing table and looked over it. There were numerous jewellery boxes and a silver hairbrush, which she picked up. It was solid and heavy, worth a great deal of money, particularly back in London. Susan began to rummage, stuffing things randomly into her bag – a ruby necklace, a sapphire brooch, a dozen or so rings, and a most ornate casket which Susan found contained notes, tied in bundles. She wondered if there was anything else she could steal. So far, it seemed as if she'd barely made a dent in such a collection. Suddenly, a horrified scream made her leap.

"Who are you? What are you doing here? Thief! Thief! Help!"

Susan froze in shock, then started toward the door, only to find it slammed in her face. To her horror, she heard the turn of a key from the other side.

"You won't be getting away!" the triumphant voice from the other side told her. "Solid oak, this door is! You can't get out the window neither! I'm going for a policeman!"

Susan rattled the door handle, trying to force it open. Who was that woman? Where had she sprung from? Had Blissett set her up? She sank down onto the bed, trembling. Of course, the woman must be the housekeeper. Who else carried a set of keys to every room in the place? She went to the window and looked out. There was no chance of jumping, unless she wanted to break her neck.

Down in the kitchen, Cook was startled to see the appearance of the excited housekeeper who told her proudly that she had disturbed a thief who was now locked in madam's bedroom, and she was going for the police. Blissett went white. He excused himself, told the cook he'd return another time and, once out of sight, he bolted.

Susan heard the door unlock, and gruff, deep voices on the other side. She was in the corner, sitting now, and hugging her knees. To fight was useless; two large men entered the room and surveyed her with distaste.

"Well! What do we have here, eh? A thieving little magpie trapped indoors! C'mon, to the town lock-up with you!" He looked at Susan. "You going to come quietly? Or do we need to cuff you?"

I had saved some money for a new watch for Sam's birthday. I had gone to Grandfather for advice on the best and together we had journeyed into Princetown, where grandfather knew of a good jeweller, on the pretext of fitting him out with a wedding suit.

Sam undid the gift and sat, speechless at first, staring at the watch and chain. He glanced at my smiling face, then lifted it carefully from its presentation box.

"It's a hunter!" he said, breathlessly. "A half-hunter!" He examined the item carefully, then noticed that engraved on the back were the words, 'to my darling Sam, all my love, Alice' then turned to look at me again, incredulous.

"I know! That was why I had to vanish for the day with Grandpapa. I needed his advice on the very best!"

Sam felt tears come. "Alice. This is stupendous! It's... it's... I can't find anything to say, except thank you. Thank you, my darling!"

Sam and I heard by letter about Susan's arrest. She had been placed in the detention cells next to the Town Hall, and in her rage, she had implicated Blissett. Sam's parents spoke of the daring daylight attempted theft, the discovery made by the housekeeper and how Blissett was now being sought. I wondered what her punishment would be. I turned to look at Sam, who whistled through his teeth.

"Caught red-handed stealing off the gentry? Gosh, Alice, she won't walk away from that one! She'll be looking at years and years hard labour, or transportation!"

I hoped for transportation; the further away she was, the better.

There was yet more shocking news. Florence had been found unconscious at the foot of her stairs. When her shop had not opened for the regulars as usual, concern had grown since it was highly unusual, and one of her good friends had asked her husband to break in. It had been lucky that he had. Florence had been there for some considerable time and had suffered not only an almighty bang to the head, but a broken hip as well. She was now in the Great Hospital at Norwich. Ada had been to visit her and had been shocked at her injuries.

In Yarmouth, Florence lay in hospital. She had had doses of Laudanum and now, it was up to her whether she had the strength of will to survive not only the broken hip, and possible infection, but head injuries and shock as well.

The Reverend had not left her side. He prayed intensely for her, hour after hour, whilst the middle-aged woman battled for her life. Reverend glanced up as a doctor came to the bed.

"Will she live, Doctor?"

"It's hard to say," came the reply. "The injury is a serious one, so even if she does, I cannot vouch for her state of mind. Blows to the head often cause irreversible damage. Her mobility will be greatly affected. We have done all we can, but…"

The Reverend nodded.

"Thank you, Doctor." Reverend regarded Florence lying insensible. "I shall pray for one."

April 1845 – TRIP TO YARMOUTH

Incredibly, Florence had stunned everyone by making a very good recovery and was now discussing lodging with the Reverend. We had all been astonished at her resilience. It had been six months since her fall. Back in familiar territory, the priest's help had gone a long way to aiding her recovery. She had begun to sit out in the gardens, enjoying fresh sea air. Florence was determined to overcome her setbacks. The hip had healed, but it had taken a good while, and she would always need a stick. She now had to become accustomed to one leg being several inches shorter than the other, as well as chronic pain.

Susan still awaited her trial at Norwich, and meanwhile, Bissett seemed to have vanished from the face of the earth and he was being sought throughout the county.

The whole family had come to see us. Sam's siblings, of course, had not seen him since he left the previous year, and the talk and laughter went on well into the night.

"We never expected to see you so soon!" Annette said giving us a large hug. "It's wonderful. Look. Greet your new nephew. Isn't he a bruiser?"

Mrs Townsend's shop looked very drab now and had nothing other than a few meagre items in the windows. The door had some panels missing and the gaps had been boarded up. Shutters were closed over one side of the shop. Seagull droppings were all over the entrance. It did not even have an open or closed sign and we wondered if it still, in fact, could serve as a shop.

We meandered to Saint Nicholas'.

"Strange without Helen here," I told Sam. "It feels like we have come back after a hundred odd years or so. Do you know what I mean?"

Sam nodded. "Yes, I feel it too. The only thing that feels normal is being back with the family." We went to the door and Sam knocked. A few moments later and a young girl answered the door.

"Sir? Madam?" She gave a quick bob.

"We are Mr and Mrs Dwyer," Sam told her. "We've come to see Reverend and Mrs Townsend."

"Oh, do you come in; theys expecting you!" the girl said and stepped aside. "Can I take yer coats?"

We handed them to the girl who lead us to the living quarters.

"Reverend, sir, Mrs Townsend, 'tis yer guests arrived."

The Reverend turned and his face lit up as he saw us both.

"Samuel! Alice! My dear children. Welcome back! How wonderful to see you both and looking so well too. Devonshire obviously agrees with you! You'll take tea and cake with us I hope?"

"Yes, please, Reverend, that would be lovely," Sam said. Reverend nodded to the girl who vanished.

"Florence, my dear?" he said softly. "Look who's here. You know these people, don't you?" Florence looked at us and, for a moment was confused, then her mind cleared.

"Samuel! Alice!" she said and struggled up to greet us. "I never thought to see either of you again. How are you both?"

"We are both well, thank you, but how are *you*?"

"Oh, much better these days," Florence told us. "Except for this wretched stick! I was lucky to survive though; many don't. I'm so pleased to see you both. Mrs Elgin is a frequent visitor and tells me all your news, as does Reverend here. Also, news of William and Helen; I hear they settled in America."

"Yes, they've been there since last year," I said. "Helen writes once a month and so do I."

I was very relieved that Florence had found her senses once again, though there was no doubt she had aged a good deal. She looked at least ten years older though that was not to be wondered at. Florence and the Reverend had a comfortable life indeed. I was pleased to see she was almost like her old self. At first, I was terrified when she mobilised around the room, but she waved my protestations to one side, explaining she could manage well.

Florence told us that she still owned the shop but that it had been closed for the duration.

"I'm still undecided as to what to do with it," she remarked. "I could put a few ladies in there to serve and clean it up but it's rather a lot for my mind."

"I'll speak to father about it," Sam told her. "He might have some ideas. Papa is used to running a business after all."

"Hmm, that's worth thinking about," Mrs Townsend admitted. "Yes, do speak to him, Samuel. It's a shame to see it go to waste."

We wandered along the sea front. It was warm, mid-April and not too busy.

"Come on, let's go to our spot," I said, and Sam willingly went with me to the dip in the sand which we had made our own.

Later, we discussed ideas about the shop. Simon was certain something could be done.

"But I don't want to be bothered with paperwork!" he told Sam.

"Don't worry, there'll be someone to do that for you. Mrs Townsend will be the boss, then you, then all the others she can employ under you as well!"

Simon smiled, liking the sound of that.

"And she'll pay the wages too, get someone to sort all that out." Sam's mind was racing ahead. "It could be a nice little place that. Upstairs lodgings too, but they will need a good clean out!"

We left it so that Sam's father would go to talk to Mrs Townsend and the Reverend about what they planned. It would do Florence good, we thought, for her to have something to occupy her mind.

Sam and I took a final walk up Golden Keys Row the following day before heading to the station. It looked just the same. I stopped at number 29.

"Wonder who's in there now?!" I mused and Sam's hand squeezed mine. "Someone is, look." I observed and, through the gap in the lace curtain, I could see a middle-aged woman sitting at the fireside.

Sam smiled. "Come on! You can't peer into other people's houses. Supposing she saw you?"

We paid our respects to my parents' graves at Caistor, then a short, surprise visit to Mrs Elgin in Norwich, much to her delight. Her daughter's town house was magnificent and, for several days, we enjoyed the unaccustomed feeling of being waited on.

On Friday, the two of us travelled home to news of Helen's newly arrived daughter, named for me, which delighted us.

It was Sunday morning when I felt certain. I was pregnant. I knew the signs well enough. I wondered what Sam would think. Our child would be born out of wedlock, but was that really such a bad thing? I wondered. After all, we considered ourselves to be as truly married as if we had been in church. Nobody other than Grandfather and Sam's close family knew the truth.

I looked at myself in the mirror. There was no discernible difference that I could see. I had never been late with my courses in my life, but there had been a good deal of upheaval recently. I decided I ought to tell Sam. I didn't feel nervous exactly, just strange.

Late that afternoon, I was kneeling at one of the flower beds, my mind on my pregnancy. I looked over to where Sam sat, lolled in a chair, a hat over his eyes, legs stretched out and hands folded neatly on his stomach. I got up and went to him.

"Sam?"

"Mmm?" he mumbled, half asleep. I touched his hand. Sam woke properly. He pushed his hat back onto his head and looked at me. My face showed concern.

"Alice, darling? Whatever's the matter? You look scared to death!"

I sighed. "Not scared, Sam, apprehensive. You see, I'm going to have a baby. *We* are going to have a baby!"

Such news had been the last thing Sam had expected. He blinked at me, unsure for a moment.

"Are... are you sure?" His face was unreadable.

I nodded. "Yes. I waited to tell you since I had to be sure. I think it'll be born in November."

Sam seemed lost for words as his eyes gazed into mine.

My nervousness fell away as Sam gasped. The smile on his face became a wide grin. He leapt from his chair, punched the air and bellowed with joy.

2nd May 1845

It was one of the worst days for Yarmouth, and particularly for Sam's family. It had all begun so well, a lovely morning with a light breeze and sunshine. Annette had planned to take Tony along to the Bure River to see Nelson, the famous clown, performing a circus stunt later that afternoon. Posters were everywhere, informing the townspeople of the stunt, from the Bure River, Yarmouth Bridge to the Vauxhall Gardens with a banquet to follow.

Ada was due to go too, but on calling at the house, Annette's father shook his head.

"Sorry sweetheart, yer mam's got one of her headaches. Been up all night with it, but do you go and speak to her. She'll want to see you and she may be better later."

Annette gave her youngest son to his grandfather and hastened up.

"Hello, Mam," she said softly. "Aww, sorry you're feeling poorly."

"It's alright, dear, don't worry," Ada told her. "It's one of my usual ones. I'll be fine once I've slept it off."

Annette murmured soothing noises.

"It's typical, it's not every day you get to see four geese pulling a fellow along a river in a washtub! Call back around three. I'll be better by then; it's not until five after all."

Annette ventured to the jetty. Tabitha was there.

"Tab, are you coming to see Nelson the clown later?" she asked. Tabitha shook her head.

"Shan't have time, Annie, I'm in the smokehouse later. Are you going?"

Annette nodded. "I better had, or Tony would never forgive me!" she told her, smiling.

But when Annette returned, though her mother was sitting out of bed, she was still groggy.

"Sorry, darling, it's only a little better."

Annette nodded. "Of course, Mamma, don't worry. I'll tell you all about it."

Those would be the last words her daughter would speak to her.

Crowds had gathered and there was excitement in the air. A band played along the banks and hot food was being sold. People laughed and jostled one another for the food and the view. The best view would be along the bridge itself and already people were there waiting.

Annette met some friends of hers along the bridge which spanned the River Bure from two piers and was quite elegant to look at.

"Crowded, isn't it?" she said as people joined them, all squashed in tightly.

"Yes! Let's hope the bridge holds, else we'll all be going swimming!" her friend said. She would ever regret those words.

"Look! There's people underneath!" Her friend craned her neck somewhat dangerously over to see men and women clinging to the chains and suspensions. Annette glanced up and down the walkways either side of the railway track that ran across the bridge and felt uneasy.

Suddenly, a cry went up; "Here come the geese!"

The clown's approach was heralded by trumpets and the group on the bridge leaned to watch.

"There he is! I see him!" one woman shouted, pointing. Young children were dangled precariously over the side of the bridge to watch the clown. The small figure came along the river with the geese drawing him along in a washtub. Nelson the clown waved to his audience, grinning. As he approached the bridge, there were shrieks and warning cries from the bank as chains suddenly snapped, one after the other, and people were pitched into the water. Unable to bear the sudden weight on the one side, there was a terrible cracking sound and without warning, the bridge collapsed taking the people with it. What survivors would later say was strange indeed. As the bridge fell, it was in an instant. There was no noise from people who fell; no screams or shouts. The screams began when people hit the water and started fighting for their lives, whilst the bridge itself hung in a peculiar, perpendicular manner. Screaming and struggling people in the water were panicking, some pulling others to the depths in their terror.

Annette floundered gasping. She could swim, but the sheer panic of suddenly and unexpectedly being in the deep river, fully clothed, was horrifying. She went under once, then came up gasping and spitting water. She looked wildly round for her son and screamed his name. Seeing Tony, screaming, panicking and threshing, she grasped him by the collar of his coat, and held him aloft whilst treading water frantically. She looked around for the neighbour's boy, but he was nowhere to be seen.

"Help!" She felt water in her mouth and choked but held her struggling son by his collar as high as she could with one arm, the other flailing, and legs thrashing to try to keep her afloat.

"Help!" Annette roared once more.

A firm hand grabbed the boy.

"Take him!" she cried to the young man who had come to her assistance. "Take him! Please. I can't hold on much longer!"

The young man, seeing the distress the woman was in, seized her boy.

"Swim, mawther," he replied. "I'll go on with the boy. Strike out with your arms! It isn't far. Don't panic, you can do it."

Boats were hastily lowered, and people attempted to rescue who they could. One child was pulled into the boat by her hair, another dragged in by one leg. Annette looked to see a nearby boat and screamed once more, trying to wave, but her strength had gone. She tried but made no progress; the weight of her clothing was like wearing a suit of lead.

"Take him to my parents," she gasped, choking. "The Dwyers." She inhaled water, gagged, and spat. "Mew's Row."

"I know who you mean; hold on! I'll come back for you!"

The man held the screaming and struggling child to him as he struck out with one arm for the riverbank. Annette watched, wanting to see, above all, that her son was saved. She was utterly spent now. She watched, struggling against the water and the weight of her clothes, and the last thing she saw was the man reaching the bank, where he pulled Tony up and held him. Annette sighed and slipped into unconsciousness and when he looked out over the river, intending to swim back to help her, Annette had gone.

Despite rowing boats hastily launched and people pulled from the water, the children first, then women, the efforts were just not enough. There had been upwards of 300 people on the bridge alone, and for all it was wide enough for carts to travel across it, the bridge had held that many people before, but never all in one spot.

Onlookers swung into action with hot drinks and blankets, straight from the local alehouse, some even diving into the Bure to fetch people out. Several barrels full of hot water from the Lacon Brewery arrived on a cart. It was altogether a truly nightmarish sight.

Nelson himself sat, shocked and terrified. It had been his stunt, he thought, caused this. He thought of his own wife and children and wept. He would never recover from the sight.

The injured and dead were taken to nearby houses and inns. Blankets were issued and hot baths drawn for those who had almost drowned to warm themselves and get over the shock. The rescue had been launched incredibly swiftly, but most of the dead were children. All bodies but one would eventually be found.

Devon – Late May 1845

Sam's parents arrived in Devon at the end of May. Sam had been very much anticipating it since he knew how upset his parents were, as we were, about Annette. Her unexpected and tragic death had hit us like a thunderbolt and so soon after we had left too. News of my pregnancy had gone some way to soothing the family, however. I had sent a letter telling them at the end of April, and Annette had died before it had reached them. The two had sent us a message, saying they would visit us as they needed the break.

We met Sam's parents as they came off the train. Sam had wondered at my joining him, but I would not be dissuaded. We had taken a coach from Tavistock to welcome them. I guessed the journey would have been tiring for them and it had been.

They were coping well after the death of Annette, although one could tell how distraught they still were, and now, I watched as Sam's mother wept as she hugged her son hard.

"Sam, it's *so* good to see you both. Oh, poor Annette. We *had* to come down here. I had to get away from consoling people. They mean well, I know, but it just made us feel so much worse."

"Come on, mawther, let me greet the boy!" Sam's father said and his mother smiled and allowed Simon to hug him and slap his back. "And congratulations, son! Such news brings hope to our hearts."

I was more than relieved to hear this. To be unmarried and expectant was an unpardonable sin in most peoples' eyes.

"Alice!" Ada came to me. "I'm so glad to see you, but you look tired."

"I am a little," I told her.

"Well, don't do too much on our account! I can tell you from experience, you need rest."

They regarded our home; "It's wholly marvellous here!" Ada gasped at the living room. "Do you look at that fireplace! Lovely copper warming pans, settle, and that's Yarmouth lace, I know!" She pointed out the cushions and I nodded.

"I hope the lavender grows well," I said. "Grandpa planted it last year. Oh! Take care! It's Bundles; she'll get under your feet."

Sam smiled and picked up the young cat.

Sam's parents fussed her and smiled at her. They told us that Captain was still going strong but had problems walking due to stiff legs.

After dinner, Ada spoke.

"You sit with your feet up, Alice," she stated firmly. "And don't worry about going off certain foods or suddenly acquiring a liking for something strange; it's all quite normal."

I smiled; it was nice to have her advice and experience to hand.

"Whilst we're here, we'll have a nice long chat about babies, birthing and all that kind of thing," she promised me. "I can give you all the advice you need. Don't worry, Alice, you are young, fit and healthy."

We discussed the coming baby.

"Son first, then whatever comes after," Sam said at once.

His mother laughed. "Ah, 'tis well to plan, Samuel dear, but it doesn't always follow."

It was a bright piece of news after the tragic death of their eldest daughter. As it was, we went to visit Grandfather and his wife with the news. She insisted everybody address her as 'granny' and she at once set her mind to work about finding a suitable midwife, citing Mrs Tucker as the best choice.

"I want you there," I told Sam.

"I'll come too if that's what you wish," Sam told me.

"No. I mean, yes, I want you there when I see Mrs Tucker, but I want you there at the birth."

There was a sudden silence in the room, mouths open and faces stunned. They could not have been more surprised had I suggested a trip to the moon!

Sam's father had not been present for the births of any of his children. It was uncharted territory and was just not done.

"What utter nonsense!" Granny said when she could find her voice. "Men in a birthing room! Good Heavens above, Alice. Wherever *did* that idea come from? Since when has a man been in a lying-in room? He'd be worrying, fretting and under our feet."

"But I want Sam there," I said, calmly but firmly. "And it's *our* baby."

"We'll think it over," Granny said, deciding that to humour me for now was the best thing to do. "I'm sure poor Samuel would be far better off keeping your grandpapa company! He won't want all the noise and fuss of a birthing room."

I didn't argue more, since I didn't want to upset Sam's parents, but I was determined. Sam would be there.

Later in the night, as the moon shone down across our bed, Sam spoke to me quietly. "If that is what you wish, Alice, I shall be there with you." I looked at him.

"Truly?" I asked smiling.

"Truly," Sam told me. "They'll have to pick me up to throw me out!"

"Thank you, Sam. I knew I could rely on you."

Ada and I went to the local market and enjoyed ourselves immensely, buying this and that, and the couple treated us to a beautiful little rocking crib found in the village. Sam and I loved it at once. Ada told me in detail exactly what to expect.

Sam's parents left on the 3rd of June, with renewed hope in their hearts. Another grandchild was most welcome.

We heard that Susan had been sentenced to seven years transportation and was even now en route to Botany Bay. I breathed a sigh of relief. Perhaps she would never return, at least, I hoped not. Blissett, found hiding in Lowestoft, for his part in the crime, received five years hard labour. With the future free of them both, Sam divorced her, despite the huge taboos and expense that surrounded divorce. Sam knew he would find only empathy from anybody who had actually known her!

For all that divorced people were never usually permitted to re-marry, Sam and I were able to journey to Yarmouth in August, where we were married quietly by our own dear Reverend.

Devon 21ˢᵗ November 1845

I groaned and sat on the settle at the fireside, my hand on my belly. Sam appeared, having just shrugged on his coat to leave for work, a look of concern on his face. The November morning was dark and heavy with iron-grey clouds. Rain spattered the windows of the cottage. I had even had to light the oil lamps.

"Alice, how do you feel?" Sam's face was etched with concern.

"Fine, darling. Don't worry!"

"But you look in pain!" My husband was all worry, and things for my lying-in had been prepared for several weeks.

"He isn't due yet!" I said with a smile. "Not for another week!"

"Not if your timings are wrong," Sam said sitting at my side.

"Why should they be?" I asked confused.

"I know your reckoning!" Sam replied.

"Well, don't worry, sweetheart, I know the date exactly."

Sam paused, then took off his coat again.

"Alright, but I'm staying home," he told me. He paused, unsure of what to do next.

"Sam?"

He looked at me, startled. "What is it? What's happening?"

I laughed. "Nothing! Look, if you want to do something, you can brew me some tea, then feed Bundles."

Sam rose to make the tea. Since I had neared my time, Sam tried to be as helpful as he possibly could, but he was more under my feet than anything. I smiled after him as he went to make the tea. A twinge had me frown. Then it went away.

"I have your birthday meal to sort later," I told Sam. "Do you prefer boiled potatoes? Ones in their skins? Or...?"

Sam clicked his tongue. "Forget my birthday!" he stated. "I'm more concerned about you."

"My back's aching, but so would yours be, carrying this great lump in front. If you go to the side, in the dresser, that's where your present is!"

The morning went on. Once the rain stopped, a boy from the village raked some leaves from our garden, thinking there little point in truth, since more were surely to fall and they were damp in any case. He had been doing some odd jobs for us to enable Sam to spend more time with me.

I had insisted on having the baby in the room that would be allocated to him or her. When questioned, I had shrugged. So, a bed of sorts had been made for me, and everything laid to hand. The fire was laid ready. All that was needed was warm water. But a pile of towels, soap, rags and who knew what else had been piled on a ledge by Sam under Grandmother's instructions.

"Samuel. I did this five times!" she told him. "My husband was worried, of course, the first time, but after, he simply went to the ale house till it was over!"

"I'll not be going to any ale house," Sam promised her.

"And don't worry when she hollers!" Granny added, having glanced at me. "It's not the easiest of processes. It's painful! You can't predict how long it'll take either, so don't expect it to be over in five minutes!"

Sam chewed his lip worriedly.

"Look, everything is as ready as it possibly can be. All we need now is your offspring! Mrs Tucker is excellent and has attended women up and down the village for over thirty years. She knows what she's doing! She'll be ready at any time. Just send the lad to fetch her once she starts."

Near lunchtime, Sam, about to ask if I wanted anything to eat, glanced at me. I had my hand to my belly and a sudden look of pain crossed my face. I dropped my sewing onto the settle.

"Sam," I looked at him with concern. He shot to my side. "Oh no! Sam! I think something's happening!"

I looked up at him with such fear that Sam, instead of flying into a panic himself, suddenly found himself in control.

A sudden gush of water and I glanced down in horror.

"My flagstones!" I wailed, horrified and disgusted at the mess. Flagstones were the furthest things from Sam's mind.

"Jason! Fetch the midwife! NOW!" he bawled from the window.

I lay on the bed in my old room and started at once to push. I didn't even know what I was supposed to do! Should I be pushing? I couldn't remember what Ada had told me about labour, how to breathe, or anything, and this baby was coming now, whether everyone was ready or not.

Sam deliberated about fetching my grandmother.

"Sam! Stay with me!" I called and Sam nodded.

It would take at least half an hour for Mrs Tucker to reach us. I continued to push, feeling like I had no control over what my muscles were doing. They were doing this for me whether I would or no. I panted for breath, trying to recall my mother-in-law's instructions when she had shown me the correct breathing. Ada had told me she had not given birth until well after her waters had broken.

"Light the fire, Sam!" I said, thinking of heating water. Sam did so at once, with trembling fingers, then returned to my side. I clutched Sam's hand fiercely and made him wince. What a grip I had.

"Alright, mawther. Everything will be over soon, it's all alright."

Sam had no idea whether things were alright or not. I gave an ear-shattering scream that made his blood run cold. He recalled his mother's trials, him and Annette downstairs, hearing the screams, and being scared, or being parked with a neighbour to get them out of the way.

Time passed. It felt like forever, but I would later discover it was only around half an hour. I howled like a wolf, uncaring if the whole of Tavistock could hear me. Then, down below, I felt a searing pain, and I felt as though I was forcing out a huge stone. My body was no longer under my own control. The strange, unaccustomed feeling of a baby's head as it emerged. I felt I was going to split in two. I gripped Sam's hand so hard; he would later bear red nail marks.

"Sam! What's happening?" I asked. Sam glanced and to his terror, saw a head appearing.

"It's coming now!" he exclaimed. He could not look away as the head began to emerge.

"Aaggh!" I yelled. "Damn it all! Bloody Hell! This hurts worse than anything! Sam! Help me!"

Sam was watching, spellbound. Never had he ever seen anything so incredible. He had wanted to be present, but he had imagined sitting at my side, holding my hand as we talked about the impending birth, then being handed a warm, clean, dry boy who looked just like him. He was unprepared for the mess, the blood and the screeching, not to mention the language, but he was the only one here and he loved me.

"Sam! Do something! Heat water!" I managed to say through gritted teeth. Sam forced himself to tear his eyes from the spectacle no man ever usually got to see, did so, shaking, and returned at once to me. Moments later, I yelled again.

"Sam. Grab his head. Don't just stand there gawping! I can feel, he's fully out! Quick!" Sam did so, feeling strange; he was the first person to touch his son as with another push, the rest of him slid easily from my young and healthy body. Sam looked, mesmerised, then he held him up, shocked at what he had just done. Then the sound of a wailing was heard. Sam looked at me, and never would I forget the look of incredible wonder on his face.

"Look!" he gasped, holding our son to show me. "Look what we made!"

"God Almighty! It's here!" Mrs Tucker appeared, sweating in the doorway and gasping for breath. She stood in utter disbelief at Sam who stood, trembling, with a newborn baby in his arms, with me leaning up as far as I could on both elbows.

Evening. I lay in our bed now, bathed and cleaned. Mrs Tucker had gone into action as though at the press of a button. Midwifing for over thirty years, she had seen it all before and had assured Sam that all was well.

"Everything's as it should be," she told him as Little Sam took his first feed. "He's a hefty lad too. I've had a few swift ones in my time but never one produced before I even got there! Most women take hours and hours. But Alice is fine; there is no tearing. She has been cleansed too. Now all you need to do is enjoy your son."

Sam smiled soppily. "The best birthday gift ever!" he said.

Sam sat at my side in disbelief at what the day had brought. Grandmother was there smiling, both anxious to hold him. All was neat and tidy now and Little Sam had just had his first feed. He slept. Grandfather had urged Sam to come and wet the baby's head in the alehouse, but he wouldn't leave my side.

I knew that as a wife, it was one of my duties to provide Sam with children; sons in particular. Now that the ordeal was over, all I could see was Little Sam's sweet face as he looked up at me, wondering who I was no doubt, and how he looked at Sam too.

Sam's parents were thrilled. Neither could believe it when they heard of the actual birth itself. Sam's father told him he himself would have fainted.

"And on his birthday too!" Simon smiled broadly as he showed his wife the telegraph. "Get your bag packed, mawther! We're off to Devon in the morning!"

It snowed hard just before Christmas and there would be no going out or travel just yet. I didn't mind. My in-laws were a massive help with Little Sam. Both were doting grandparents.

"He takes after you!" Sam's mother said. "You went through the night without a murmur. The only one who didn't wake us at all hours!"

Sam chuckled. We had just set up a Christmas tree and Sam and the rest of us stood back to admire it.

"It's lovely," Simon beamed. "Fancy though, a tree in the house; I still ain't got used to it! Makes you feel like royalty!"

"Well, I like the custom," I said. "It's been done in Germany for years and it's catching on here too. It's something very special."

"Oh, this *does* take me back. It's like you all over again, Sam!" Ada gushed with a maternal feeling washing over her as she held Little Sam and rocked him, spoke and cooed to him. She had, of course, years of experience. I enjoyed watching her with him. Little Sam was passed between his two grandparents time and again, since both wanted to hold him.

CHAPTER SIX

Devon September 1852

"Want to be like Papa!" Our Little Sam stood in front of me and Sam.

Time had passed swiftly, and our only child was six years old.

"You will be, Sammy," I told him. "But you do need to do your lessons too! You want to be able to read nice stories, don't you?"

Little Sam reluctantly nodded. "But I don't want learning letters or reckoning!" His little face screwed up in a frown.

"Now then, young man!" Sam got to his knees and looked his son squarely in the face. "You say you want to be just like me, isn't that right?"

Little Sam nodded.

"Good! Well, I learned my letters and reckoning when I was your age. Now, what if you come with me this morning to help me in my workshop, but after noon, you learn your lessons with Mamma?"

Little Sam nodded. "Yes, Papa."

"Good lad! Right then, we shall away to the workshop. Kiss Mamma."

Sam now worked with the local carpenter, and along with cabinet-making, he could turn his hand to anything. I was very proud of him, and our son loved nothing more than 'helping Papa play with wood', a speech that had had us falling over laughing.

Our Little Samuel was such a bright boy. Very kind, just like his father. He had Sam's hair colouring, his eye colouring and his nose, along with my glossy curls and lips. Sam would take him on his shoulders to walk up and down the lane, or run, when I wasn't watching. Now he was already a 'little man.' He idolised Sam, and was his constant shadow, and proclaimed to anyone who would listen that he would be a cabinet maker too. We had both taught him good manners and to be obedient. I sometimes wondered if Sam was a bit too strict, but Sam assured me he had been brought up the same and children were taught to obey and be quiet.

We had lost Ada in 1851 and it had torn everyone apart. Her death had been swift and painless, for which we were thankful, but Simon was still coming to terms with it, and he was grateful to have his family. Shortly after, we had suffered the loss of a newborn girl, whom we had named Dawn, and I had not become pregnant since. Sam and I planned to move back to Yarmouth permanently.

I was thinking of Helen as I ironed; the cottage door stood wide, and a sweet scent blew in from the linden trees. Her letters had worried me, that she and William had grown so far apart.

Sam was hard at work. He was explaining to our son what he was doing. Little Sam's face was screwed up with total concentration as he watched his sire planing a piece of wood.

Suddenly, the door to the workshop opened, and a tall man stood there. He had a large, silky black beard and was dressed in very expensive clothing, striped trousers, jacket and tall, shiny top hat despite the heat of the morning. He wore a very high starched collar and tie. The watch on the chain was obviously gold. Sam glanced at the stranger. Not many upper-class, well-dressed people frequented village carpentry workshops.

"Well, howdy partner! What's a fella gotta do to get some service round here, huh?" The American voice confused Sam completely. Our son stood at his father's side, eyes on the man, nervous but interested in the newcomer. Silence for a few moments as the two regarded each other, the newcomer grinning. Then... the penny dropped.

"WILLIAM!" Sam roared and dropping his tools, he hastened to the man in the workshop doorway and enveloped him in a bone-crushing hug, knocking the top hat to the floor.

Little Sam watched, amused, then he smiled showing little teeth. It was funny to see his father greet someone like that and funnier still that the man's hat had fallen off; Little Sam chuckled.

"Good God! I hardly recognised you!" Sam was stunned at the entirely unexpected appearance of his old friend.

William slapped Sam on the back.

"Sam! You're looking incredible, bor!" The American accent had vanished now and in its place was a voice like his father's own.

"You too, William! When did you arrive? Nobody expected you!"

William grinned. "We docked yesterday at Plymouth and found lodgings in the village! Helen's hardly slept! She's so excited to see you both. Helen wanted to tell you, but I told her it'd be better as a surprise!"

"Where is Helen?" Sam said. William opened the door and in stepped an extremely broad-hipped, glamourous and incredibly richly dressed woman. She wore an expensive hat, decorated with flowers and lace. Her skirt was huge, full and long, the blouse striped. She wore a light coat that looked to be made from cream-coloured velvet. Her fingers were adorned with rings.

"Sam!" She beamed. "'Tis so good to see ye!"

Sam looked at Helen; she too was almost unrecognisable. Helen grabbed Sam to hug him and kiss each cheek. Sam beamed and turned to regard his son.

"Samuel," he said. "You know what to do! These are my oldest friends."

Sam watched proudly as our son walked sedately up to the pair, completely without fear, and proffered his small hand to Helen.

"Good morning, madam. How do you do?" he asked politely.

"I'm very well, thank you!" Helen said, clearly delighted with him. Little Sam proceeded to greet William in the same way.

"Och, such a wee bean!" Helen gushed. She was brimming with excitement. "Wonderful to meet ye! I've heard a lot about ye too, young Samuel."

Sam explained the pair, squatting in front of him.

Helen squeaked, "I *must* see Alice; I cannae wait any longer!"

Sam smiled. "Son, do you escort this lady home."

Little Sam nodded. He went up to Helen without the slightest fear and held out his small arm. Helen chuckled, since she towered above him.

"I'm too tall to take your arm, young man; will ye hold my hand instead?"

Little Sam nodded.

"I'll shut up shop and be along directly," Sam told him.

"This way, madam." Little Sam led the way up the lane towards our cottage.

"Och, ye wee bairn, ye call me Auntie Helen and him Uncle William!" she instructed him, "since we're your parents' oldest friends."

"Yes, Auntie Helen," Little Sam said obediently.

Back in the workshop, and Sam turned to look at William. His smile had slipped somewhat.

"I suppose you know how things are?" William asked Sam. "Helen will have written to Alice."

Sam nodded. "She has, and I can only say how sorry I am, bor'," Sam told him. "But is it so very bad? You have riches beyond what we can ever dream of!"

William sat down. "Ah, it's a long story, Sam. It isn't turning out as either of us had hoped. She doesn't fit in. I blame her; I shouldn't, but I do because she doesn't behave like the other wives."

"Helen's unique. She'll never be anything except herself."

William nodded. "Well, we're visiting Scotland soon; we keep up a front. Perhaps being back in the old country will improve things. We need time to talk seriously about our future."

Sam was much saddened by our friends' troubles. He rose from the stool and the two men left the shop.

Little Sam and Helen walked to the cottage. She was a maternal person who loved all children, but this little chap knew how to seize a heart instantly.

"That's home!" Little Sam stopped to point out our thatched cottage.

Helen observed. Since being in America, she had become used to everything being bigger. Our cottage seemed very rustic and small, but it was typical of its type. The thatched roof hung low; the windows small.

"It looks so sweet and cosy," she said at once. "We'll give your mamma a big surprise just like we gave your papa!"

Little Sam made me jump by bursting into the kitchen.

"Mamma! Mamma!" he called, bright and eager. I was surprised. Obviously, he was excited about something.

"Sam? Where's your papa?"

"At the workshop," Little Sam told me, "and there's a surprise for you!" He seized my hand, pulling me outside. A large well-dressed lady stood grinning at me.

"Hello there, hen!" she called. "Guess who's come to visit!"

I stood, rooted to the spot, eyes wide. I couldn't move for several moments, nor could I speak. Surely it wasn't Helen? Here in Tavistock? And I had been thinking of her only that morning. Then, I hurried forward as Sam had done to William and hugged her, bursting into tears.

"Ye look so good!" Helen said, through her own tears. "Och, ye *do* look well, Alice, and happy, and Sam too. A visit from us was the last thing he was expecting. He leapt on Will'um the moment he saw him!"

Little Sam piped up. "Yes, and Papa knocked his hat off!"

I smiled down at Little Sam. "Did he now? I'm sure you found that funny!"

Little Sam nodded, grinning like an urchin.

"And your wee boy. Och, he is gorgeous! Such a gentleman! Ye can tell he is Sam's without a doubt!"

"When did you arrive?" I asked as we made our way into the cottage.

"Yesterday," Helen said. "We crossed in six weeks; we're spending time in Devon to visit you. Then on to Scotland to see the family before going back."

"Such a journey!" I said, sitting Helen down on the settle. "Why didn't you say you were coming?"

"Surprise!" Helen answered.

I grinned. It was all the better for being so unexpected.

"We're lodging not far away from here, in the village," Helen told me as Little Sam climbed onto her knee.

"Well, you can tell William from us to have your belongings sent here!" I told her at once. "We want you to stay with us!"

"Och, we dinnae want to be any trouble," Helen said.

"It's no trouble! Sam and William can go and get your things later today. He'll insist on having you here too!"

Helen beamed. "Thank ye, hen. As long as you're sure!"

At that moment, Sam and William entered the cottage. Sam smiled to see Helen and I sitting together with our son on her lap.

"William!" I rose to greet him. "Good to see you; Sam, darling, I said they must stay with us."

Sam nodded. "Absolutely! I wouldn't hear of such close friends lodging with strangers. We'll eat now, then go to the lodgings, bring your belongings here. Where are you staying?"

"With a Mrs Andover," William said. "She's nice enough, but we'd much rather stay here."

"Can you stay a long time?" Little Sam asked. "I want you to tell me about America and the ship and the sea!"

"Aye, we'll stay long enough for that, dinnae worry," Helen told him.

Helen regretted not bringing her children, but they had been too young to make the voyage. I was disappointed but understood.

The guests sat along with Sam, Little Sam and I to enjoy the soup I had made my own from potatoes and it was Little Sam's favourite.

"Lovely!" Helen said sitting back. "It's ages since I tasted real home-cooked food. Ship's meals are nae so good, isn't that so, William?"

William shook his head.

"No, not that I eat them really. I must've lost a stone on the way out! Still, at least I had a better crossing this time!"

Bundles walked over the lawn. She spied the newcomers, and after some hesitation, came to investigate. Helen, she sniffed, then rubbed.

"Och, ye pretty wee thing!" Helen said, smiling at the cat. William craned his neck to look. To him, Bundles looked useless; an ornament and no more. He didn't mind cats however; cats were useful. But this one, with just three legs, William would not have allowed to live had she been in the litter in his home. Bundles gave him a severe look, as if she had guessed what he was thinking, and wandered off again to the edge of the garden where it bordered onto a field. She stood, stock still, then wriggled and pounced; this was followed by a sharp squealing noise, hastily cut off.

"She catches mice?" William asked in surprise.

I nodded. "She's a fine mouser."

"She caught seven, when mice got into the workshop!" Sam stated proudly.

Later, we went to the edge of the village to fetch the Blake's luggage. I made up the spare room with Helen assisting me.

Helen wore jewellery of all descriptions whilst I had only my thin, gold, wedding band along with the pebble pendant. Yet I wore both like they were the crown jewels. Together, we fitted the sheet on the bed.

Now that we could have a girly talk together, I asked, "So, how's it been, Helen? Your letters sounded sad."

"Och, 'tis a problem with Will'um's wandering eye. We had some trouble when I found out he'd been seeing a wench from the shanty town. They sling up these cheap houses, bars, shops and things like that to live in whilst the go prospecting, ye see. The wives stay in the town houses. I was mad as Hell, Alice." She sighed. "He's let money turn his head, trying to climb the *society* ladder! I'd sooner be at home."

"I hope it won't be too boring for you here," I told her.

"Ye must be joking, hen! I cannae wait for the peace and quiet, I'm sick of the endless parties, calling on folks and that, but, oh lass, I was so sorry when I heard about Dawn."

"Thank you," I told her. "When I told Little Sam he was going to be a big brother, I asked him if he wanted a brother or a sister. He thought, then told me he preferred an elephant!"

Helen roared at this.

"I explained how large they were in real life, and that only its head would fit in the cottage."

Helen laughed again. "Ah, the things they say!"

I decided on a chicken stew that night. Little Sam shared his father's predilection for dumplings and so Helen and I made them that afternoon.

"'Tis only right I help," she told me, "since ye've two extra mouths to feed, and big ones at that!"

I laughed. I enjoyed working with Helen in my kitchen. It was just like old times. The men returned with Little Sam and the luggage to find us in the kitchen, up to our elbows in preparing the stew.

Helen and William sat back, replete. William had said to Helen privately that he would take Sam to the local ale house that evening, but Helen had been annoyed at such a suggestion.

"Ye cannae do that on the first night, Will'um! Where are your manners, mun?" William sniffed with disdain.

"You're a fine one to talk about manners, aren't you? We can't even hold our heads up in some places because of your behaviour!"

Helen had glared. "Alice says he doesnae go to the ale house, ever."

William shrugged. "Well, he never was keen, so I suppose we can stay here. It's bound to be a dreadful place anyway, full of mumbling yokels," William told her. Then he thought. "I wonder if he has Bourbon here!"

"Don't be daft! Sam won't have even *heard* of the stuff, never mind have any!"

William rolled his eyes and nodded. He was fed up with his wife's bossiness.

For all their wealth, neither Sam nor I were envious. Helen and William had maids and a cook. The house was gigantic. Their clothes were the very best; yet the relationship between them was not as it was between us. I was sorry about that.

"I hope ye can come to see our house one day," Helen told me. "'Tis a long way across the sea, I know, but ye'd like it." She thought then.

"Something wrong, Helen?" I asked.

"Not really, lass; 'tis just strange. I didnae know how homesick I had been until I came back and saw ye. Doubtless I'll be worse still when we reach Scotland."

I felt sorry for my old friend. Her trouble with the local women, not being accepted, William's overly high expectations of her... I personally felt she would be better off back in Scotland, but we could hardly interfere. I enjoyed Helen's companionship at least and we made several journeys to the surrounding area.

As the visit progressed, I became more aware of William's snobbery. He had spoken to Helen unaware I was nearby and able to hear, complaining about the flagstone floors, no gaslight and how dark the place was. He mocked the clothes I wore, liking them to domestic servant garb, and the food was far too plain. It took all my strength not to go in there and batter him!

I was relieved when they finally left – sorry to say goodbye to Helen, but not William. I didn't dare mention what I had heard to Sam.

Great Yarmouth June 1853

"I can't believe my eyes!" I stood on the promenade with Sam and our son. We were in Yarmouth to visit Sam's father and greet Maria's new baby and to attend the christening at Saint Nicholas'.

"What?" Sam queried.

"Look!" I indicated the tall, spare female stomping along the path a trail of about seven girls meandering after her. The two in the front were imitating her every step.

"Miss Spoonamore!" we said in unison and laughed.

The little group approached.

"Well, as I live and breathe!" Miss Spoonamore stopped, arms folded. She regarded us. "What are *you* doing here?" She glared at us icily.

"Visiting family," Sam responded cooly.

"I see." Miss Spoonamore looked at Little Sam. "And who might this young man be?"

"Our son, Samuel," I replied, daring her to make an unkind remark.

"Born in wedlock, was he?" she asked.

"Yes!" I replied in an offended tone.

"Hmm, that's more than these were!" She indicated the girls behind her. "I'm taking them for their daily airing."

Florence's former shop had been turned into an 'academy for wayward girls.'

"Ungrateful beasts! None of them can keep a civil tongue in their heads. Their long-suffering parents have asked me to take them and help them to become decent members of society; I get so many letters from desperate mothers now," Miss Spoonamore boasted to us. "My little academy is becoming quite the thing."

This, we already knew. Sam's father spent as little time as possible discussing any form of business with her and could not stand Miss Spoonamore in the same room as himself for more than five minutes.

"Yes, Father said," Sam replied nonchalantly.

"The horrible creature has developed a thing for me," Simon told us later, when we mentioned meeting her. "Ugh! She pretends to be all proper and correct, but under it all, she's man-mad!"

Sam chuckled at the idea of his father being chased by Miss Spoonamore.

"Florence was on about the shop; we were having a meeting about it in the churchyard, the Reverend, me, and Florence and along comes Miss Spoonamore and says, 'I've an idea, to those who will listen!'"

I laughed. "And even for those who won't!"

"Hmm, that's true," Simon agreed. "Well, she puts forward her idea of a school for wayward girls, where she can teach them the three Rs, if they don't already know, and how to behave. Well, she sits down uninvited, then trots out this idea! Well, we laughed, I admit. She's got the hide of an elephant and didn't realise we were laughing!"

"I want an elephant!" Little Sam informed his grandfather. "But Mamma says we can't!"

Sam's father laughed.

"Well, she's right, bor! They are enormous! You wouldn't get one in your house!"

Little Sam sighed with regret.

"Anyway, next thing we know, she comes along with drawn-up plans for the place! She'd been up overnight, designing everything herself. I couldn't believe it!"

This, we had to see!

Simon ensured we got a tour of the school. With an impish sense of humour, he approached her for 'permission' to take us round. Miss Spoonamore, flattered to have been asked and wanting a chance to ingratiate herself with the handsome, widower, agreed at once.

Miss Spoonamore had been awaiting our arrival. She stood outside, stiff as a ramrod. As we passed the window, we saw seven girls grinning at our approach and one pulled a face.

"Come in! Ah, Mr Dwyer senior. I'm *so* glad you came; there are a few matters I would discuss with you after your tour."

"Good morning, Miss Spoonamore," Sam said pleasantly. "It's good of you to show us around."

We entered what had been the main room of the shop. The last time I had been here, it had had displays in the window, a counter, shelves with goods and had resembled any grocers. Now it had desks with an assortment of wooden chairs. Miss Spoonamore had her main desk at the front of the class, near the window. The girls all stood behind their desks and Miss Spoonamore gave them a withering look. At once, all chorused:

"Good morning, sirs, madam," with some giggles from the back. I grinned at them.

"This is where I do my instruction!" Miss Spoonamore stated. "You shall find it different from when you lived here, Samuel," she stated. "We have prayers in here first thing, then to breakfast, where we all cook our own."

"What's breakfast, Miss Spoonamore?" I asked.

"Slop and mouldy crusts!" came one voice.

"Silence, Millicent!" Miss Spoonamore snapped, then turned to us.

"Oh, mainly porridge. Toasted bread. I don't encourage gargantuan appetites, but it is good to have something inside one."

"Oh, it certainly is, Miss Spoonamore." This came from Millicent. "I love a good hot sausage in me!"

There were screams of laughter. Sam and his father turned red but had to stop laughter of their own. I guffawed, not caring if she took offence.

"Millicent! Any more filthy remarks like that, and I shall beat you!" Miss Spoonamore shot out.

"What?" Millicent effected an innocent air. "I only meant that I love sausage, bacon..." she paused, "and that kind of thing!"

"That you love 'that kind of thing', young lady, is precisely why you are here!" Miss Spoonamore yapped. She scowled at the girl, then continued.

"Then, lessons; as each girl is at a different stage, I cater for them individually. They learn domestic chores so they can go into service."

"We're her drudges!" piped up Millicent.

"That will DO!" Miss Spoonamore stamped her foot. Millicent struggled to hold back laughter. "You are treated very well indeed, considering your disgraceful conduct!"

"What's the age range here, Miss Spoonamore?" I asked.

"They range from eleven to fifteen," Miss Spoonamore told me. "Of course, the fifteen-year-olds will be going out to work as soon as they have learned to behave. After all, nobody wants a domestic servant who is disobedient, do they? I've told them all about going into service. It's not a bad life. One is fed, clad and has a roof over one's head."

Miss Spoonamore turned an unkind look on the girls.

"If they do not improve, then it'll be the workhouse for them!" she stated in a threatening manner, then glared at the girls, feeling spiteful.

"Millicent here had a baby two months ago." Miss Spoonamore, it seemed, was determined to shock us no matter what. "It was given to the workhouse."

"That's awful!" I said loudly, embarrassed for Millicent, and angry that a newborn would be merely handed over to the workhouse.

"I agree!" Miss Spoonamore told me, unexpectedly. "A child. At fifteen, and out of wedlock! It's scandalous!"

"No! I *meant* it's awful that someone took her baby away from her and put it in the workhouse like it wasn't even important!" I stated. "*And* the fact you have just mentioned it in front of strangers!"

"Nonsense!" Miss Spoonamore replied in a dismissive manner. "Everybody knows anyway. Besides, she can't possibly want a little bastard, can she?" Miss Spoonamore, entirely devoid of any feeling, spat at me.

"I think that should've been kept private, Miss Spoonamore," Sam stated.

"Ha! she doesn't care one way or the other," she admitted.

But Millicent did care. She cared very much. It hadn't been her choice that the child had been taken from her, and she had objected vociferously at the time. Her face had lost its cheeky expression and had been replaced by a morose one. I racked my brain for a suitable remark.

"Well, once she has a trade, she can get the child back!" I stated. Miss Spoonamore looked at me as though I was stupid.

"Who'd employ her with a bastard brat in tow?! Talk sense, Alice!"

Despite the presence of Miss Spoonamore, I spoke to the girl. "Millicent, would you like your baby back some day?"

Millicent nodded; her eyes were downcast now.

"There you are!" I said triumphantly.

"Nonsense! Out of the question!" Miss Spoonamore told me. "Kindly do not interfere, Alice. You're incapable of minding your own business! Besides, I doubt she can remember whether it was boy or girl never mind its name, assuming it had one in the first place. It would have been absorbed into the workhouse populace by now!"

She glanced around, attempting to calm down.

"I shall take you to see the dormitory now!" She glowered at the girls. "Get on with your work. There is to be no talking, or I'll be applying my ruler to palms!" She turned with a swish and led us up the stairs.

"Interesting!" Sam told her. "I never imagined you could turn the three old rooms into a dormitory."

"Miss Spoonamore, do you live here now?" I asked. "I mean, overnight? I thought you had a house."

"I still have a house," she told me briskly, "and a maid. I employ a couple of women for the night duty here."

I looked at Sam, wondering if we knew these women.

"Well, on we go!" Miss Spoonamore clumped back down the stairs again. There was an instant hush and the scratching of pens.

"Very interesting," Sam said. "Thank you for the tour."

We made to leave but Miss Spoonamore spoke; "Ah, Mr Dwyer, before you go, there are one or two matters I should like you to attend to!" Sam's father looked at us, a look which plainly said, 'don't dare leave me here with her!'

"Of course; we'll wait here, shall we? Unless you don't want us to?"

The look Sam's father gave me made me chuckle.

Whilst Miss Spoonamore and Simon spoke, I had been thinking. "Wait here, Sam!" I entered the classroom.

"Hey, Milly," I said, going to her desk. "Listen, tell me, if you really do want your baby back, I can try to help you."

Millicent looked at me suspiciously. "Why'd you help me for?" she asked sullenly.

"Because I was pregnant out of wedlock too, and it must've been incredibly hard to give up your child. What was it?"

"Daughter," she told me, looking down at her hands in her lap, twisting her fingers around her pinny.

"What's her name?" I asked.

"Bea."

"Aww, that's a lovely name!" I replied.

"Ha! Won't do her much good in the bloody workhouse!"

"What about the father's family. Would they look after her for a bit?"

"*He* didn't want to know; said she weren't his, though she bleedin' well is! Anyway, I don't want him getting his hands on her. His mother would sell her!"

"I see. Well, I'll try to help you if you like," I told her. "Tell me when she was taken in. Was it the one here?"

Millicent thought. "14th of June," she answered. "And yes, it was, but it won't be any good fetching her back. I can't support her here, can I?"

"No, but, supposing I could arrange for a foster mother? Someone I know and trust who'd let you see her and not make things difficult? Then you could visit her whenever you liked."

Millicent glanced at the door Miss Spoonamore had vanished through with Simon. Sam stood in the doorway; head cocked. I beckoned him to tell him my idea.

Sam had not expected to be asked such a question and he had no idea.

"Well, I can speak to Maria," he stated. "She'd help a small baby, but Abe might not allow it. I'll ask, but I can't promise anything. It's Albert's decision."

"We can only ask; then here's Tabitha, or her mother. I reckon she'd do it. Mrs Bostock can't get enough of mothering!"

Sam hoped I wasn't rushing headlong into trouble. He could have forbidden it, but when he saw how hopeful Millicent looked, he relented.

"Can't *you* take her?" Millicent asked. "You're nice, I like you."

"We'd love to, Milly, but we're here on a visit from Devon and that's so far! Let me talk to my friend, my sister-in-law, and see what we can come up with, eh?"

Millicent nodded.

"Now, before that old bat comes back, do you sew?"

"Yes, I'm pretty good at it, though not much else. I made this apron."

"That's really good work, Milly. Now, if you want, I can show you other methods before I go, draw some patterns and you can do some practice pieces. Do you read and write?"

Millicent nodded.

"Great, I'll do that, and you can follow them and practice. Once you're out of here, you can find lodgings, support yourself and Bea. What do you say?"

Millicent burst into tears and hugged me.

Finding a foster mother was important; buying and selling of babies happened. Couples desperate for a family would advertise in local newspapers. It was a common practice which I was in two minds about. On the one hand, a deserving couple could obtain an unwanted child, taking it from poverty and possible cruelty, but the practice was abused by unscrupulous baby farmers.

Later, I spoke to Maria.

"Well, that's all very good in theory, Alice," Maria told me, "but don't forget, she's very young. She won't know what she's doing, and what landlady will allow a fifteen-year-old unmarried mother onto her premises?"

I grinned. "One who thinks she's eighteen and a young widow!" I answered promptly.

Maria laughed. "Fibber!"

"All in a good cause," I remarked.

"Well, I'd be delighted to take her, but Albert must agree. Come on, let's ask."

On 1st September, Maria and I stalked to the workhouse with Albert in tow, though he was reluctant to lie.

"You *have* to bend the truth a little," I explained. "It's for the baby's sake. You can't let her suffer life in the workhouse through no fault of her own. Besides, it'll be me doing the talking."

The place had changed little. Still with the big, echoing foyer, and as soon as one entered, it brought an almost suffocating feel of misery. I could smell old, stale vegetables, and from somewhere on my right, I could hear looms clattering.

Matron took us into her office; she looked formidable behind her oaken desk. She looked at each of us in turn. I had no qualms about looking her in the eye.

"What can I do for you?" she asked us. "Something about a child, was it not?"

Maria looked at me as though indicating for me to start. I smiled.

"Madam," I said politely, "we're here to discuss fostering a young baby from you. She's been here two and a half months and is called Beatrix Barker. She was brought in, *without* her mother's consent, on 14th June. This lady and gentleman were asked to be godparents, but they've been in Ipswich tending a sick relative. They've only just heard about Bea and are shocked. They wish to foster her, until her birth mother recovers."

Albert glanced at me. Were it not for the baby, he would have got up and walked out for shame at the lies I was telling.

The office was oppressive. The warmth of the September sun streamed in through the shuttered window. From without came the dulled sound of people, of pots and pans clattering. I watched dust motes dancing in the sun's rays. Matron was silent, tapping fingers on the desk. She examined her ink blotter as if it were the most interesting thing she had ever seen. Damn the woman. Was she never going to answer? The large clock on the wall ticked louder and louder.

"I see," Matron said, eventually. "Well, this is somewhat irregular, however, the child is blameless after all. She should be given a decent chance. I should put it before the Board of Guardians, but..."

"Reverend is happy with the idea," I interjected. The woman's eyes bore into mine, but I held her gaze politely.

Matron rose and moved slowly to her bookcase, where she took a ledger from the side and ran her finger slowly down a list of entrants.

"Beatrix Barker... ah, yes, here she is. Illegitimate." She frowned and glared harshly at me.

"Madam, your information is incorrect," I said at once in a shocked manner. "The girl, though young, *was* married and alas, her husband drowned at sea. He was a friend of this gentleman here." I indicated Albert.

"I see. I was given to understand the mother was a worthless little fifteen-year-old trollop. If she's a widow, why did she not wish to keep the child?"

"She did, Matron, but she was distraught, being so soon a widow. Her neighbour took the baby to help, but she couldn't manage, and her mother was too unwell and grief-stricken. The neighbour had no right to do this, dumping the child here, though I suppose she thought she was helping, and now we are in this mess."

Matron huffed. She put down the ledger and thought. There were already too many children in the workhouse, and it would be years before Bea could earn her bread. Matron glanced round at us once more. Obviously, Maria and Albert were a respectable married couple. Maria was as tense as I had ever seen her. Albert too seemed rigid.

"You work, I take it?" she asked Albert who nodded.

"Yes, Matron, my family's in the herring business. I don't go to sea now, however. My job's smoking herring."

She nodded. "Where's the child's mother now?"

"With a good friend of ours," I lied. "She has, to add to her troubles, broken her leg. If you wish, I'll ask Reverend Thomas from Saint Nicholas' to vouch for us; he's happy for the fostering to go ahead."

"Ah, very well, I'll have her brought to you. Please remain here." She left the office.

Maria leaned to whisper to me.

"Good Heavens, Alice! You'd best go straight to Reverend after this! Have him absolve you for all those fibs!"

She was smiling though.

Matron re-appeared with Beatrix and handed her to Maria. "The child is healthy, though forever hungry. She's had a recent bath, so she doesn't stink too badly!"

That was the Matron's opinion. I had never let Little Sam get so fragrant! Maria's face softened and her eyes teared.

"She's beautiful! Look, Abe! Just *look* at her!" Albert smiled and tickled her belly.

"We'll take her!" Albert, instantly besotted, spoke firmly.

"Very well." Matron made some notes in another column by the child's name. "All I need is your address, if you would, please."

Albert gave the Matron the information she required, then we were permitted to leave.

"I'll give her a nice bath," Maria told me as we headed up to their row. "I expect you'll want to get hold of Millicent, won't you?"

I grinned, nodding.

Having spoken to the Reverend, I went to the school. Miss Spoonamore grumbled at me.

"What is it, Alice?" she asked me abruptly. "We're busy with some sums."

"I wish to borrow Millicent, please." I told her cooly. "I'm scrubbing my father-in-law's floor and I'm tired!" Miss Spoonamore frowned.

"Well, she's in class at the moment!"

"I know, but I wanted to do it before we return to Devon," I explained. "I'm halfway through and I can't manage any more. My arm hurts."

Miss Spoonamore tutted. "You young women aren't what we used to be! You all want pampering these days. Very well, if you must, it will be good for her soul! Millicent! Leave your work and go with Alice."

Millicent got up with a very bad grace and stomped outside.

"I thought you were my friend!" she rounded on me. "I thought you were different!"

"I am!" I told her. "Keep your drawers on! I've a surprise for you. Come on; scrubbing floors was just a ruse. How else was I meant to get you out?"

"Where are we going?" she enquired as we hurried up to Quay Mill Row.

"Wait and see!" I grinned.

On reaching Maria and Albert's house, I knocked and entered.

"Alice!" Maria smiled as she appeared with Beatrix in her arms. Now bathed, and warmly wrapped in a shawl, she smelled sweet. Her eyes were open, hair all soft, belly full of milk; she was most content.

"Here," Maria handed her to Millicent. "Say hello to your daughter!"

Millicent gasped on taking her, unable to say a thing, and gently rocked her. Silent tears streamed down her face.

"She's *so* beautiful," Millicent said when she could find her voice. "Oh my! She's heavier since I held her last. How sweet she smells. You took her out of that terrible place!"

Maria smiled; "We'll foster her until you are able to work. I'll give you a good reference. We'll say you're a young widow, but you *must* add three years to your age! In the meantime, you can visit her whenever you wish. Is it very difficult for you to get away?"

Millicent nodded, sitting in a fireside chair and rocking Bea, beaming at her. I noted she had not once, yet, taken her eyes from her baby's face.

I suggested the idea that Maria needed Millicent to help her with heavy household chores along with sewing instruction. Miss Spoonamore couldn't object, since she had already stated she was training them for service.

"And Reverend will back us up too!" I added.

Before we left for Devon, we had settled an arrangement with Miss Spoonamore.

"It will do her nothing but good!" she told Maria. "As you are Mr Dwyer's daughter, I'm happy for her to assist you. He is a fine man, your father. Very fine indeed!"

Devon November 1853

Little Sam at school for the afternoon, I was finishing off washing the dishes and had put some fish down for Bundles, when I heard the clopping of hooves. They stopped and I glanced over to the door. Strange! We were not expecting visitors. Suddenly, there was a knocking on the door. Puzzled, I went to open it.

To my utmost amazement, there stood Helen. At her side were three youngsters.

"Hello, hen; might we come in? We won't be staying long. We've rooms at the boarding house down in the village."

I stood, unable to say a thing, so great was my surprise. My mouth opened.

"Alice?" Helen commented. "Does the cat have yer tongue? Do say something!"

"Helen! What are *you* doing here?" I asked her stupidly. "Where's William? Oh, please come in. Sam will be home shortly. What's happened?"

There was no sign of the jolly old Helen, and the woeful-looking youngsters that surrounded her seemed troubled. Helen, in fact, looked rough.

She had lost weight and there were lines on her face that had not been there before. I was horrified to see some streaks of grey too, where her hair had been a vivid blue-black only eighteen months before.

I was grateful that Sam came home as soon as the small family had seated themselves near the fire. I made them tea and gave the youngest some fresh milk. Only then were we able to sit and listen to Helen's tale of woe, of how they had divorced, which was, apparently, easier in America, and Helen, with a generous settlement, was heading to her beloved Scotland.

"Helen, we're truly, truly sorry to hear of such a dreadful thing." Sam spoke for us, since I was lost for words. "I can hardly believe it!"

Helen sighed. "I know, but ye warned me, didn't ye, Alice? All those years ago?"

I bit my lip, unsure. "Helen, I said there'd be problems, but that it continued on smoothly after."

Helen shrugged. "Well, 'tis open to interpretation, I s'pose. Anyway! Enough of my woes!" She broke the difficult silence. "I'm a rich, free woman now. Where's that lovely wee laddie of yours?"

"He's at school," I replied. The three children sat on the couch at Helen's side, all mindful of their manners, particularly the eldest girl, Alice.

"Well, welcome to our home," I said to them, unable to think of anything else.

Helen had told them on the way over, not to make any unkind remarks about the size or the look of our home since it was bad manners. I had imagined they would be traumatised over the split, but as Sam reminded me, they had been at sea for almost two months. They told us about the voyage and how, once they had got over the shock of Helen's taking them away, they had enjoyed it. It appeared that Alice and Elspeth had been relieved to go.

But they had arrived the day before Sam's birthday, and indeed, Little Sam's birthday as well. I tentatively broached the subject.

"Och, 'tis fine. Look, we want a wee rest before going home again, so, we'll leave ye to celebrate in peace. I want to take mine to show them Plymouth before we sail to Aberdeen."

My mind was working. "Helen, I've an idea!" I told her brightly.

"Oh no! Same old Alice. What mischief have ye afoot this time?"

"No mischief," I said. "We'll all go to Yarmouth, and you could introduce your brood to Reverend and Florence. They'd love to see them. We could see our family at the same time!"

We had only just returned, having been in August, but it seemed a good idea to Sam. I looked at him for his permission and Sam smiled.

"Yes!" he stated. "That'd be fine."

"Wonderful! We'll tek ship from Plymouth," Helen announced.

Sam looked at my face. Seldom had he seen such a horrified expression. He smiled, a little amused.

"Ship?" I gasped.

I boarded the ship with great trepidation. Little Sam and his companions hastened aboard, full of excitement. I held tight to Sam's hand. For all Sam was afraid himself, he wouldn't show it. But he bravely nodded as Helen showed us to our family cabin.

"Now, dinnae panic, lass. Ye'll feel a bit of swell; there's creaks and bangs too. 'Tis normal; the weather's good, really calm."

Helen saw my face and laughed.

"Lass! Ye'll find 'tis so much fun! Just wait and see!"

For me, it was anything but. A few miles out and the wind picked up. Almost at once, I began to feel sick.

A couple of hours and at least two more days to endure. Brisk and efficient, Helen hauled me from my bed and had me up on the deck in moments to sit at the front where I could see the horizon.

By night, I sweated in the hot, airless cabin. Sam and Little Sam slept pretty much at once, Little Sam worn out from playing at pirates, and Sam himself, tired with looking after me and making sure our son did not go overboard.

I cheered up the next morning. Yarmouth was in sight.

"Look at that!" Sam beamed. He had found his sea legs after the first day. We watched as the familiar sight of masts, sails, harbour, beach, a lighthouse and the windmill on the denes came closer. Little Sam leapt up and down.

"Look, Mamma! Look!" He pointed eagerly. "Yarmouth! We're going to see Grandpapa!"

As it was November, it took little time to find rooms for Helen and the children.

"Hotel Royal," she told me, with an impish grin. "This time, as a well-behaved guest!"

We had all gathered to go to Saint Nicholas'. Helen looked around. "'Tis hard to believe it's ten years since I left." She shook her head in wonder. "And for all that's happened, it doesnae seem long. I still feel like I did at 24."

We made our way to Saint Nicholas', Helen very much looking forward to it.

"Let me go in first!" Helen said, stopping at the gates. "I want to see what his reaction will be."

"Don't frighten him too much," I told her. "Don't forget, he's over eighty!"

Helen smiled. "I shan't."

Helen had found the kitchen door ajar. She stepped inside. Whoever was maid now was not doing as good a job as she had! She could hear the Reverend's voice and Florence's too.

"Hellooo there!" Helen stepped into the room. "Forgive me for not waiting to be invited in!"

Reverend glanced and his mouth dropped open. For half a minute, neither person spoke. The Reverend removed his spectacles and peered closer, the only sound, the ticking of the grandfather clock.

"It cannot be! Helen? Is it you?"

Helen grinned. "Aye, Reverend, in the flesh!"

Then the Reverend, his smile bright, got up and walked over to her, where he flung both arms round his former maid and stunned everyone by bursting into tears.

"My dear child! I thought never to see you again. What are you doing back here?"

"I'm fine, Reverend, truly," Helen told him. "I'll tell ye everything. Dinnae cry. I'm so happy to see you again; you too, Mrs Townsend. You look so well."

Florence smiled. "Thank you, Helen dear. I feel it."

"Might I bring my children to meet you?" Helen asked, and Reverend nodded.

"Of course you may; I'm longing to meet them."

"Good, they're waiting outside with Sam and Alice and their wee laddie."

It was a wonderful reunion. The Reverend had met Little Sam on several occasions, as had Florence, but the three others, who they had not, behaved exceptionally well. The Reverend introduced us to his new curate, a thin little man with curly brown hair and glasses. He nodded to us but hardly said a word.

We spent a pleasant time with the Reverend, his assistant Rupert and Florence. I advised Helen to speak to Reverend of her marital troubles.

"I cannae heap my troubles on such elderly shoulders, lass!" she told me. I shook my head.

"Nonsense, Helen. He's been hearing stuff like that for years. He'd want to help you. He need only listen, advise. Besides, Rev's climbing the walls for something to do!"

Sam and I wandered along the sea front. Helen had joined us. The children were at Saint Nicholas' since they had all taken to the Reverend very much and Florence adored them.

"It's busier now, by far, than it was ten years ago," Sam stated. "Even if it is November. There are a lot of ships docked. I reckon people are thinking about wintering over or something."

People did – from foreign climes, they would stay in Yarmouth to avoid rough sea conditions. We passed a chop house that seemed busy.

"At least businesses are picking up," Helen stated. "I remember when I first came here, fifteen years ago, there was nothing for visitors; it was much quieter, even in summer."

We stopped to look in the chop house window. I felt my belly rumble, but the place was packed.

"Look!" I said with a groan. "Look at that pie!" Sam and I gazed hungrily. "And look!" I poked Sam's middle. "That family there, they've finished all their food and they're just sitting there! Why don't they get up and let others sit there?"

I felt a kiss on my forehead.

"Probably wanting dessert!" he said. "Come on! There'll be somewhere else."

We sauntered on. Helen spoke of American food and how it differed from here, when suddenly, there was the sound of running feet behind us.

"Dwyer!"

The voice made us all leap.

"Hey! Stop!"

I spun round, as did Sam, no doubt thinking someone had decided to accost us, even after almost ten years had passed. But in front of us stood a stranger. He was huge, well over six feet tall, tight, curly black hair, slightly greying and a greying stubbly beard. The man had the darkest brown skin I had ever seen – the colour of dark oakwood. My mouth opened in surprise, but the wide smile on this man's face showed us he had no ill intentions. He made a move toward Sam, who stepped back, uncertain, despite the man's grin.

"Don't you remember me, Samuel? I saved your life! Remember? The day you fell into the Thames!"

I had heard of Sam's falling into the river, and the subsequent rescue, but that had been all. I had been more concerned for his health at the time.

"Manoa?"

Sam's grin suddenly equalled that of the man. The confused look on his face turned to one of happiness. "It *is* you!"

To our amazement, Sam grabbed the large man in a hug, the pair slapping one another on the backs.

"Long time, not see!" Manny grinned. "I knew it was you! I never forget a face! I was just having lunch. I had to slap the money on the table and leave before I lost you! You haven't changed a bit! It's been years, man! Years!"

Sam nodded. He still had the smile on his face.

"Sam?" I prodded him.

"Oh! Darling! I'm sorry! Alice, meet Manoa Wadaa. We knew each other in London. He's the man who pulled me from the Thames. I told you how I almost drowned!"

He took my hand and proudly introduced me.

"Wife?" Manoa asked, amazed. "What a pretty girl she is! What happened to Susan, if you don't mind my asking?"

"She got transported," Sam answered with no trace of emotion. "I'll tell you all about it, but right now, this is Alice, my wife; we met here ten years ago. The other lady is Helen Blake, a very close friend, who has spent ten years in America but returned home."

Helen's eyes met Manoa's; they clicked at once, and I would later tell Sam, I could almost hear two souls colliding. Having lived in America, Helen had met more people of colour than I had. Most were treated in a despicable manner, but Helen had been one of the few who had opposed that violently. She looked up at him in admiration.

"Come and chat to us. We've plenty of time," Sam told him. So, the four of us made our way to purchase pies and took them to eat in a shelter in the sea front garden to keep out of the chill.

Manoa came from North Africa originally. He had taken to the sea at just ten years old, as a cabin boy, narrowly escaping slave traders. Since then, he had sailed around the world and had seen wonders and terrors alike. As we ate, Sam brought him up to date on his story over the past decade.

"You've a son? I'd love to meet him!"

"You will," Sam promised. "Papa's taking him round the ships now, and Helen's three are at Saint Nicholas'. You'll meet everyone in time. Where are you staying and for how long?"

"I'm at Mrs Quinn's, Tooke, the Baker's Row," Manoa replied. "I stayed with her twice before. She appreciates the help. I always come back here now."

Helen could not take her eyes from the man's face. She had seldom seen someone with an almost permanent smile.

"I'm getting too old to keep going round the globe," Manoa told Helen.

"And does yer wife nae object?" Helen wondered, fishing, I could see, for information.

"I'm a widower," Manoa said sadly.

"Och, I'm so sorry."

Manoa nodded. "Thank you. I never felt I could want someone else after her, but, well, now, I...." He stopped talking and I smiled. I caught Helen's eye. She blushed to the roots of her hair. Most unusual for Helen!

"We really must be getting back," Sam told him. "Samuel will have worn out Papa by now, I should think."

"I must get back too," Helen informed us.

Manoa looked at her. "I hope to make your acquaintance again soon, Mrs Blake." He took her hand and raised it to his lips. I could practically hear Helen's heart racing.

"Call me Helen," she told him, "as you're so friendly with Sam. He and I go back many years."

Manoa nodded. "Helen," he stated. "Like Helen of Troy!"

Helen went an even brighter red at the compliment and smiled.

Back at the Dwyer house, Little Sam excitedly raced out to meet us, stopping in his tracks at the sight of Manoa. I could see his little brain whirring in confusion, fear and the knowledge we would expect him to be polite.

"Papa! Mamma!" He hastened up, longing to tell us of his morning but wanting to know who we were with.

Sam addressed our son. "Samuel. This is Manoa; he's an old friend of mine from a long time ago."

Little Sam, seeing the man's smile, held out his hand.

"Good afternoon, Sir, how do you do?"

"Very well, thank you, young man!" Manoa answered shaking his small hand.

Manoa's hands were like shovels. He topped Sam by a head and a half. Sam was of average height at around five foot eight, but this man made him look small. He turned to us.

"What a charming young gentleman!" he stated with a beam.

"Come in!" Sam said, holding the door open for the man.

Simon had not met Manoa, though he had, of course, heard the tale. He hid his surprise at the sudden and unfamiliar appearance of the large man. He rose to greet him at once.

"So, you're the fellow that pulled my boy from the river! A belated thank you, sir!"

Manoa beamed. "Call me Manoa."

It was surprising how the pair got along at the first meeting. But then, most people did, with Manoa. He was cheerful, extremely friendly with a smile showing good, white teeth. I would later find out that it was impossible not to get along with him. His accent, I found, was the strangest I had ever heard, yet it was wonderful. I felt I could listen to him talk for hours, though sometimes I couldn't understand what he said.

We sat around the fire and Manoa told us about some of his childhood friends who had not been as lucky as he had been, having been taken for slaves.

Sam wondered.

"Manoa, do you read and write?"

The man shook his head. "No. I was on board ship all my life."

"Ah, that's a pity," I told him.

"Maybe Helen could teach you. After all, she's a good letter-writer." Sam smiled. "If you can untangle that scrawl she calls handwriting. Why don't you ask her, Manoa?"

The man wondered, then nodded. Not that he expected to be able to learn at his age, but the thought of spending time with Helen was too tempting to turn down.

Manoa's face went soft.

"What is it?" Sam asked.

Manoa bit his lip. "She is beautiful woman," he said. "Very beautiful woman."

I smiled and Sam nudged his friend.

"We don't have very much longer here!" I told Sam that night in bed.

"I know, but darling, we'll stay until the end of the first week in December." He hugged me closely. "Besides, I wish to pay our respects to Mamma, Annette and the others."

Whenever we came back to Yarmouth, we would always put flowers for Sam's mother and sister, plus his siblings who had not made it through their first year. We also took a trip to Caistor. My parents now had a fine headstone, and this year, we took Little Sam and I explained who they were.

I went to see Helen who seemed somewhat out of sorts.

"You alright?" I asked as we sat in the fine drawing room of the hotel, looking out to sea. I felt distinctly ill at ease, and it wasn't just the room, with its golden curtains, luxurious wallpaper, huge, gold brocaded chairs and the fireplace that seemed as big as the wall of any row house.

"Aye," she responded.

"You don't seem to be."

"Sorry, hen, I'm thinking."

"That makes a nice change; what about?"

"Nothing."

"Well, that explains the vacant look," I told her. "Come on, Helen, how long have we been friends?"

She turned to look at me, then back out to sea.

"No, 'tis a daft thought. How long are ye stopping here?"

"Til the 7th," I replied. "Sam wants to spend an extra week, then we can take father-in-law down to Devon."

Helen smiled. "Aye, well, we mun enjoy the time we have left."

Helen seemed disinclined to leave, and I wondered why. It was now the 2nd of December and we had spent time with our family, visiting the resting places of loved ones, and walking to 'our spot' though it was too cold to stay for long.

I met Helen for a beach walk. We would also go round the market to see what Christmas gifts we could buy.

"Helen, you seem weighted down with problems," I told her. "Come on, tell me! You know I'll understand."

"Would ye?"

"Of course I would. Look, let's finish our shopping and get a nice hot drink."

We ventured to one of the street stalls that sold hot food and drink. From the way Helen looked around her at the familiar sights and sounds of Yarmouth, I took it to mean that she was keen to remain and wondering what to do. I understood that. I felt it myself. There was a biting wind, and I was grateful to get my fingers round the cup, my mittens only venturing as far as my knuckles. We stood on the sea front. "Come on, out with it! This is like pulling teeth!"

Helen glanced at me, took a breath and decided.

"Lass, dinnae scream at me." She looked at me.

"Fine, I shan't scream at you. What on earth have you done?"

Helen bit her lip.

"Manny asked me to marry him, and I accepted."

It took several moments for the startling news to sink in.

"WHAT?"

I looked at her, incredulous.

"Are you mad?" I asked, shocked. "You don't even *know* him! You only met him a week ago! Now you're engaged? What are you playing at? You've three children to consider! Is he wanting to be a kept man? Helen! Think!"

"Ye said you wouldnae yell at me."

"That was before I heard you'd done something so stupid!"

"'Tisnae stupid. We love each other. We're neither of us getting any younger. Why wait when we both know?"

I recalled the looks that had passed and the vibes I had felt between the pair, but marriage?

"I offered to teach him to read and write; it meant I could stay a wee while longer. He said yes, he'd like that, but then he told me he had to say what was on his mind, so he did. And it was the same thing I'd had on mine."

I could scarcely believe Helen's recklessness. She had just come thousands of miles to escape one man, only to jump straight into a relationship with another. And this was one that she barely knew.

"He's after your money!" I said angrily.

"I didnae tell him about the fortune!"

"Helen!" I wailed. "Look at the way your children are dressed... you're staying in this hotel. He'd need to be plain daft to not realise you've money!"

"He's not like that! He has his own money!"

"Ha! That's what they all say!" I snapped indignantly.

"Look, we discussed it, all night. He said he knew from the first he wanted me. He's enough money to buy a house, here, or Scotland. He wants me to be happy and the wee ones to have a good life, and I want to stay here. I love Yarmouth. Perhaps I can get my old job back."

I liked Manoa - he'd rescued Sam - but I could only look at her. Helen, so headstrong, wilful.

The wind blew harder, and the sea crashed onto the beach.

"Helen! If he ever hit you, you'd be knocked out cold!" I warned. "I've seen smaller shovels!"

"Is it because he has coloured skin?" she asked me. "Ye dinnae approve of a mixed marriage? I know it's going to shock a lot of people."

I swung round, enraged. "How DARE you say that to me? It's because you *don't know him*! How d'ye know he doesn't have a temper?"

"Alice, I am *totally* safe with Manoa. I can tell."

"I don't believe *this*!" I roared. "I don't believe *you*! What if you needed help? We'd be hundreds of miles away!"

"Ye always return," she told me. "Several times a year! Besides, I've friends here... there's Reverend, Florence, Maria, Tabitha!"

"I see! So you'd steal all *my* friends, would you?" I told her unreasonably. "When I come back next, none of them will want to know me!"

"Alice, yer being childish and unreasonable."

"It's YOU that's childish and unreasonable. Selfish too! You've had it your own way for too long!"

Helen bit her lip. "I'm sorry, Alice."

I turned and stomped up to the Dwyer home.

Everyone was surprised when I hurried into the room, I set down the packages, burst into tears, and poured out the story. Sam was surprised, but not upset, and tried to soothe my fears. Manoa was a good person. Who leapt into a filthy river to save someone they didn't know? Nobody bad would do that.

We left Yarmouth in a shower of sleet to travel back to Devon. I was in a sulky mood. Sam spoke to Helen and Manoa, who would spend Christmas with her parents. They would then return in April to Yarmouth. Helen would resume her duties at Saint Nicholas'. The Reverend had told her he would be 'thrilled' to have her back. Once married, they would take up residence there.

I was still angry over the argument, but I was terrified for Helen and her hastiness.

We returned to the appalling news that Grandfather had died suddenly.

CHAPTER SEVEN

January 1854

We had come home to Yarmouth; I couldn't remain in Devon after Grand-father's passing. Our new house was in Half Moon Row. I looked at it, and instantly fell in love with it. It had three bedrooms, and a decent-sized back yard. The roof sloped down, with small, tiled overhangs between the dormer windows. There was a kitchen and living room and a workshop area for Sam. The front of the house had been freshly whitewashed. The door was a deep brown, patterned with spirals and shell designs. Two wooden steps, scrubbed clean, led down to the flat cobbles. Pretty pebbles sat all around the door. It looked so welcoming.

The front door opened directly into the front room. Everything looked fresh, and it smelled beautifully clean. A fireplace, with brass fire irons each side, was lit already to welcome us into the small room, and the coal scuttle shone like a mirror. There was a warming pan too.

Over the fireplace sat a mirror, with seagulls etched around its perimeter. There was a cupboard against the wall, a small writing desk, a settle at the fireside like the one in the cottage, and a chair facing it. Against the wall was a glass-fronted cabinet

In the kitchen was a small stove, a wooden dining table, and a stone sink. A dresser stood against the wall for our china and cutlery. A small stable-type door opened onto a small yard which had a gate.

There was even a water pump in the yard, as well as the rainwater tank, which would make us the envy of all the neighbours.

A large tin bath hung on a hook. There was a copper for laundry with every implement needed for washing day. The pantry was dark and slated. I nodded in approval. Things would keep cool enough in there.

The master bedroom was large for a row house. The windows, like the ones downstairs, had half-net curtains and looked out onto the row. To my surprise, the drawing curtains had been made by Millicent as a gift for our homecoming.

Little Sam's room was similar but smaller. The tiniest room was only meant for storage, but it could be a bedroom. There was a chest in each room for linen and clothing and a rack to hang dresses.

"Bundles!" I said gently to the cat. "Come and see your new home, but we'll let you get used to one room at a time. It's all a bit overwhelming for you, isn't it?"

"You'll need to butter her paws," Simon told me.

"I will. Oh, this is wonderful. Thank you so much, Papa. Thank you!"

That evening: "It feels like home already," I said as we sat round to eat a stew Maria had brought us. "This meal is remarkable, Maria, truly delicious." Maria smiled and blushed.

"So, what are your plans then?" she asked Sam and I.

"Get Little Sam into my old school. Some work I can do from here, in the kitchen corner." Sam nodded to where the workspace had been created; an old keeping room, now altered to make the kitchen a bit bigger.

"This is one of the best rows of the lot," Sam's father said. "This, and ours."

We would forever love the house he had found for us.

We settled in. With the fire in the grate, we sat as a family close to one another. Bundles fell asleep on the rag rug. It smelled familiar and the warmth of the fire, along with our presence, was calming... that and a belly full of fish. She slept as if she had been here for years. The musical box chimed gently in the corner and Sam smiled, his eyes slowly closing. Home.

On the third morning, we woke to the knocker-upper though it was a different man now. Sam kissed my forehead. "Nice, this, comfy bed, warm wife... I don't want to get up!"

"Me neither!" I replied and I smiled at him. "Sam?" He felt my hand descend to his thighs. He leaned in to kiss me.

"Mamma! Papa!" Little Sam burst into the room like a whirling dervish and bounced on the bed. We groaned.

"You're up early, little man!" Sam said.

"Yes. I want to see my new school!"

I hoped that he would be just as enthusiastic when he had been attending for a few weeks!

"We'll go to the school shortly," Sam told me at breakfast, starting on his cup of tea. "Father's already enrolled him, so there's no paperwork. I just want to take him and show him round. If he wants to, he can stay, though really, he starts next week. Father wanted to make sure we were settled first."

I nodded. I put the bacon, eggs and fried bread onto the plates and poured more tea.

At a little after nine o'clock, we went to the school.

The Charity School, built in 1713, stood in the marketplace and was not far to walk. A large, red brick building, it was imposing. The windows were high, arched. There was a small playground area, and the iron gates were huge. It looked extremely foreboding and made me think of the workhouse.

"Don't worry, it looks better inside," Sam assured me.

Inside, it smelled typically of schools. I wrinkled my nose a little, and Sam chuckled. "It smelled the same when I was here. Some things never change!"

There were two floor levels to the school, the upper forms on the higher, the lower on the ground floor.

We were in a corridor, with a flight of stairs to the left, and there was a large window at the top of the stairs, a classroom to our right and another further down the corridor. Through open doors, I could see a hall.

"That's the dinner hall." Sam squeezed my shoulder.

Little Sam observed the school. It was hard to tell what he was thinking. His face showed no expression. He pulled at Sam's coat sleeve.

"Papa, can I be in your old classroom?" he enquired.

Sam smiled. "Well, bor,' I don't know which one they'll put you in and I can't tell them, but you never know, you may be."

We were greeted by the school matron, who looked efficient and brisk in her white apron and starched cap. Little Sam appeared confused; there had been no such nurse at his previous school.

"Ah, Master Samuel," she stated. "I was told you'd be attending today. I'm Matron."

"I wish to meet the form master," Sam stated. "My wife will wait here, but she'd like a tour. I was a pupil here, so I know the place, but my wife doesn't."

Matron nodded. "Of course. Take young Samuel to the form room. It is Class 2, with the green door. Once he has met the master, come back, and I'll show you around. I think you'll find we have not changed much since you were a pupil."

Sam went off to the form room with Little Sam trotting at his side. He recalled the way as if it had been yesterday. Matron indicated I sit on a hard bench.

Sam took our son to the door of the form room. "I *was* in here," he said to Little Sam. "When I was seven, actually."

Little Sam gave a tentative smile. Sam knocked and the master, having been told to expect the interruption, turned to look.

"Ah, Dwyer!" Mr Brook said. "Excuse me, Mr Dwyer. Old habits die hard."

"Yes." Sam was not terribly pleased to see his old form master again. He had hoped the man would have gone by now. He was a tall, spare man, with greying thin hair and a grey goatee-style beard. He was known for his fiery temper and fondness for the cane. For a moment, Sam felt unhappy at letting our son stay.

"Master Samuel Dwyer!" Mr Brook held out a large, dry and, from Sam's occasional experience, very hard hand. Little Sam shook it.

"Good morning, sir; how do you do?"

"Very well, thank you! Glad to see you've manners. No worries about beginning a new school?"

Little Sam shook his curly head.

"No, sir!"

"Excellent! Speak up! I knew your father well. He was head writing monitor! Shall you be the same?"

Little Sam, to his credit, held his head high. "I hope so, sir!" he answered.

"Good!" Mr Brook smiled slightly. "Will you remain with us for the morning? Get a taste of school life? Or do you prefer to return home with your parents?"

Little Sam wanted more than anything to come back with us, but he knew first impressions were everything. Sam had also told him to never show fear, even if he felt it. The option of 'returning with Mamma and Papa' would make all the difference in his reputation with the other boys right from the start.

"I'll stay if I may, sir!"

"Good! That is exactly what I hoped you would say. Brave lad! Sit next to Rix there."

"Alright, Samuel," Sam spoke stiffly, and frowning to his son, not in the usual way he would, knowing his son would be better for it among his peers.

"I'll require your help this afternoon. We need to re-cover the kitchen chairs, and it's a difficult job, so..." he added a little sternly, "...do *not* be late."

Sam left the classroom feeling hot under the collar. He had not expected to feel so bad at leaving his boy with the others, but he did.

Back with Matron, I was waiting anxiously.

"Where's Sam?" was the first question on my lips. I rose at once.

"Now, darling, calm down," Sam told me. "He's fine. I left him to attend morning school. Don't worry! He was happy to do so. He'll be the better for it."

We saw over the whole school. I had insisted on seeing the upper floor, even though Little Sam would not be there yet.

Classrooms were situated around a large hall and was where the boys had assembly. This doubled as a drill hall too, when wet, and there were also pieces of gym equipment. To my astonishment, having turned around, I observed a small stage, equipped with footlights. A huge lectern also stood nearby, in the shape of a monstrous brass eagle.

"Headmaster takes assembly from there!" Matron explained, "We have shows at Christmas. It gives the children a sense of maturity and achievement to perform in front of their parents."

"That's new," Sam observed. "We never had that in my day!"

I hoped very much that Little Sam would get himself involved. It would be fun for him and delightful for us.

Little Sam sat beside Roland. The school dining hall was big and noisy. Each child had a table monitor who would collect the food and bring it to the table. There were mounds of boiled potatoes, soggy-looking, pale-coloured cabbage, which Little Sam eyed with great suspicion, and meat stew. Roland saw his look and laughed.

"It tastes better than it looks," he told him. "Does your mamma cook well?"

Little Sam nodded.

"Yes, she does." He sampled the potatoes, suspiciously.

"You must eat *all* your food," Roland warned him. "There's always a teacher on dinner duty. He stands behind anyone with leftovers and makes them eat it all."

Little Sam seldom had trouble clearing his plate.

The boys chattered over the meal.

"What's the form master like?" he asked Roland.

Roland pulled a face.

"Horrible! He leans over you when he's checking your work, he stinks, and his teeth are black. He's bad-tempered too. He's got his favourites though. They never get told off."

Little Sam began to feel miserable.

"Don't worry, I'll be your friend," Roland told Sam. "Look, you can have this if you like, till next week."

He slipped his hand into his pocket and brought out a large matchbox.

"What you got matches for?" Little Sam asked.

"'Tisn't matches; look, it's my pet, he's called Alfred."

Little Sam smiled as a huge, black and shiny beetle was revealed.

"What do you give him to eat? Does he ever come out?" he asked, fascinated at the shiny-shelled insect.

"Yes, I built a little pen for him at home. It's only cardboard, but he has grass in there. I give him some leaves, a piece of fruit if I can get it, some wood."

Little Sam beamed, "He's lovely!" he told Roland.

Roland brought Little Sam to the bottom end of the row.

"See you next week then."

"Yes. Do you come in and meet Mamma."

Roland thought. "I should for politeness, but I'd best get back. I don't fancy the cane across my arse."

Little Sam nodded. "Alright. See you Monday. I'll look after Alfred!" The pair shook hands and Little Sam watched as his new friend charged back the way they had come.

"How was it?" I could not help racing to him and asking.

"It's alright," Little Sam told me. "But the food's horrible. Your dinners are loads better!"

I hugged him and Little Sam squirmed slightly. I sighed. He was getting too old for cuddles now and would, no doubt, soon believe big boys like him did not need cuddles from Mamma!

Little Sam looked after the beetle very well. He obtained a small box and, as instructed by his new friend, he put in grass and some leaves and watched, his chin on his fists, as the creature ambled about. I didn't mind; I just hoped Bundles wouldn't eat it!

"I had a wormery when I was small; would you like one of those? We can build one together if you like. I'm sure Mamma has a jar she can spare." Sam smiled at the eager boy.

Little Sam obtained a second beetle, for himself. I produced an old jar and once more, the two went out to dig for worms.

"What with beetles and worms all over the place, I feel I'm living in a zoo!" I told Maria later.

Maria laughed. "Luckily, I won't have that trouble, with a girl!" she smiled fondly at Annie.

On Little Sam's first morning, I worried and fretted.

"Now, you remember the way?" I asked him, dusting at his jacket and fussing with his hair.

"Yes! Mamma! I don't want my curls brushed down!" Little Sam ruffled at the hair I had combed back with water to look tidy. He glared at me with a fierce look on his face. I groaned.

"Sam! I just did your hair!" I tutted.

Sam came and stood, arms folded, grinning.

"He looks fine, mawther. Don't fuss so. He's a big boy now!"

Little Sam nodded fiercely.

"Alright, now come straight home at four o'clock. No dawdling!" I stated to him. "Don't speak to anyone you don't know. Mind what Mr Brook says too." I looked at our son who gave an expression of exasperation, just as his father would.

Sam patted his shoulder. "You'll be fine. Enjoy it! Work comes around all too soon. Don't forget to give Roland back his beetle!"

For all his bravado at home, once he got to the school, Little Sam looked up at the iron gates. They were large and imposing; he felt a frisson of fear and a longing to be back at home, or even his former school where he had known everybody. Children wandered into the grounds and met up with friends. Some chased each other round; others had a ball. Little Sam glanced. A gaggle of girls were heading to the other gates separated off from the boys' school. He wrinkled his nose in disgust. He was glad there were no girls in *his* school.

The huge, red-bricked building loomed up in front of him and he craned his neck back to see. Five high set windows at the top storey, another five at the bottom.

He walked up to the main entrance and went inside. The parquet flooring had been polished over the weekend and he looked down at his boots. 'Papa bought those,' he thought. 'For me!' Suddenly, Little Sam was overcome by a terrible feeling of homesickness. He wanted more than anything to turn and race back the way he had come. The feeling became stronger when Mr Brook strode by at alarming speed. He felt tears threatening and was about to cry, when suddenly, he heard a voice behind him.

"Sam! There you are! I've been looking for you!"

He turned to see Roland's smiling face. "D'ye have my beetle?" he asked, and Sam produced the matchbox. Roland looked inside. "He looks fine. I think he's a bit bigger! You been feeding him?"

Little Sam nodded.

"Come on, I'll show you where to put your coat."

The first day passed quite well. Roland took Little Sam under his wing so that he did not have a chance to feel lost. Roland was pleased to have a friend. He had recently lost his other best pal from the previous term when the boy's parents had moved away.

The morning lesson had been reckoning, at which, thankfully, Little Sam did not take after me, but after his father. Mr Brook saw no reason why he should go easy on the newcomer, but Little Sam was more than capable of standing up for himself and winning the respect of his classmates if not the form master.

He was naturally curious, friendly and bright. He and Roland became the very best of friends. I welcomed him into our home, and it seemed I had two sons rather than one.

I had eventually written to Helen. There was a lot of news to impart – some bad, some good, but I would keep her up to date. After all, she had had her problems too. I suddenly felt selfish for not being happy for her with Manoa, and even managing to get her old job back. I knew I had acted stupidly. I hoped she would forgive me.

I went along to Saint Nicholas'. The Reverend told me he looked forward to Helen's return and subsequent wedding.

"Helen returns in March with an Easter wedding on April the 7th. I can hardly let her start and spend her honeymoon here."

"Sam won't mind if I do it till then," I told him. "The money will come in handy, and it will keep me out of trouble!"

"I'd be delighted, Alice, but do get Samuel's permission first."

I promised that I would. Reverend smiled and took my hand in his.

"I am so glad I was able to marry you and Samuel," he told me. I leaned in smiling and pecked his cheek.

Rupert, the shy curate, entered the kitchen and on seeing me, he stood where he was, wondering what to do. I gave him a cheeky wink, at which he stumbled over his own feet, blushed hotly, and hastily excused himself.

Sam agreed at once to my helping the Reverend and I took some sheets for repair and mended them nicely. Millicent watched me.

"Last time I repaired a sheet, I just stuck my foot through it again," she told me jovially. "Spoony was furious! The sheet was thin as a church wafer! I told her, you can't mend that', but she wouldn't listen."

"Miss Spoonamore? Not listening? You do surprise me!"

Millicent grinned. "Are you going to be there when I leave?"

"Of course. When does she kick you out?"

"Friday afternoon. She makes a big thing about girls leaving. We all have to stand and wish them well."

"I'll be there!" I promised.

I enjoyed helping Reverend. He was full of funny anecdotes and interesting tales. I asked Little Sam to help with some of the winter gardening that needed doing. He and Roland could both be seen pushing wheelbarrows about and assisting here and there.

Friday afternoon and I went with Maria and the two babies to Miss Spoonamore's school for Millicent's sending-off. Millicent had her bags with her and stood in front of the other girls.

"Well, Millicent! We say farewell to you!" Miss Spoonamore stated with a grim look on her face. "I sincerely hope you'll do well, though I very much doubt it. You were the most difficult girl I have ever had in this academy!"

Millicent smiled. "I'll do extremely well, thank you!" she answered pertly. "I've lodgings and work!" She paused. "*And* my daughter!"

Miss Spoonamore's eyes widened. "What did you say?"

"I *said* I have lodgings, work and my daughter!" Millicent repeated loudly. "See?" She indicated us waiting by the door. "I'm staying with Maria. And that's little Bea that Alice is holding!"

I gave her a cheeky grin.

"But... she was in the workhouse!" Miss Spoonamore said, floundering for something to say.

"Yes, I know; taken without my permission. Maria and Albert have been fostering her for me. Matron agreed to it, and now I'm going to live with them and work there whilst raising my daughter."

Miss Spoonamore's mouth was agape. "That is not at all appropriate! And what do you mean by 'without *your* permission'? Who needed your permission?" She stamped her foot, then pushed past Millicent to go to the door and stepped out in front of us.

"What are you playing at?" she ranted. "Why would you interfere and take in this little slut and her bastard? Are you mad?"

Maria took offence at the words, and she stiffened.

"No, Miss Spoonamore, I'm not! Milly's no slut either; she's a hardworking and respectable young woman. Besides, it's none of your business who my husband and I have in our home, is it?"

"Well, on your head be it!" Miss Spoonamore pushed Millicent out of the door. "You'll be sorry! You mark my words!"

March arrived and the weather slowly became that bit warmer. Both Sam and I were amazed at how easily we slipped back into Yarmouth life. Little Sam became very firm friends with Roland who was one of the most mischievous children I had ever met.

"He's such a little monkey!" I said to Sam later that day.

"What's he done this time?" Sam asked me. He was busy, but I loved to have him working from the kitchen, and if mess was kept to a minimum, I didn't need to worry.

"He put a toad in my sewing box! A great big, ugly toad! How'd he get hold of a toad? There aren't any places for toads in Yarmouth!"

Sam smiled. "What happened to it?" he asked, smiling when he recalled the horrified scream that had come from the living room. He had come dashing in, heart pounding.

"It hopped away," I said.

Roland had also been responsible for a chicken in our bedroom. I had screamed in alarm when I went in to change the bedding and saw a large biddy hen, peering at me from my side of the bed.

I found that I was expecting again; Sam was thrilled and at the same time petrified. So was I.

"You *will* take things slowly!" he told me sternly. "I'll come with you and speak to Reverend; I'll do any heavy work he needs."

I smiled and squeezed his hand. "I'll speak to Maria about a midwife too. The one she and Ann had."

I caressed his mutton chops.

"Alright. I suppose we must tell Little Sam now. I do hope he won't be jealous!"

Little Sam was older now and he listened carefully as I explained I was due to have another baby. His eyes were very round.

"When?" he queried.

"Around November time again!" I told him.

Little Sam nodded, but I could see by his face that he was not thrilled at the news. He pouted a little. I knew he was thinking of Dawn.

"Sam. Listen to me!" his father stated. "You're a big boy now. This time, all shall be as it should be. Don't worry, we'll take extra good care of Mamma," he assured him.

Roland was most matter of fact about the new arrival. "Do you make sure you tell your brother to do what you say when he's born! Mamma's *always* having babies; I've three older sisters." He gave a world-weary sigh. "They're *so* bossy!"

We had gone to visit Mrs Elgin in Norwich. She had been thrilled to know we were back to stay in Yarmouth. Little Sam had behaved impeccably, and Mrs Elgin had commented on what a beautifully mannered young gentleman we were raising.

We spoke of my third pregnancy and Mrs Elgin wished us every joy and luck. I had written about Dawn, and Mrs Elgin would speak to me, privately. She too had lost children at a very young age. She couldn't think of any woman who had not, in fact.

Her two eldest grandsons were doing well at work. The youngest girl, Rosie, was at boarding school. Elsie, now sixteen and lovely with it, was to head off to a finishing school in Switzerland. She was incorrigibly vain, and dreadfully spoiled too. Even Mrs Elgin was disappointed with her granddaughter.

We heard her stomping down the staircase. "I won't have a governess now!" she shouted. "I am too old for one! I am going to Switzerland in September!"

Elsie's governess hastened down after her charge. The door opened and Elsie stalked in. She stopped short having been unaware of any visitors. Her face showed confusion, then she frowned, taking in our plain clothes. Elsie herself was dressed in a beautiful white dress, with pink and blue bows, and lace. Her hair was long, a mass of waves and curls, which positively shone. Her sharp little face looked disgusted.

"Grandmama, who *are* these people?" she asked peremptorily, as if we were urchins off the street.

Mrs Elgin blushed. "Elsie! How dare you speak in such a tone? They are my dearest, oldest friends, Mr and Mrs Dwyer and their dear son, Master Samuel."

Elsie peered at us. True, we were plainly dressed, but we were clean. Elsie wrinkled her pert nose.

"Oh, is *she* the one you picked up off the streets then?" she asked. "I remember you telling me about that!"

Mrs Elgin was scandalised. "Off the streets? You keep a civil tongue in your head when addressing my guests! How *dare* you?"

Elsie shrieked and stamped her foot. "You can't tell me what to do!"

Mrs Elgin fixed the girl with a hard stare. "I can, young lady! How dare you speak to your grandmother with such blatant disrespect? Go to your room and think about your rudeness. Miss Perkins, do you take her, please."

The Governess nodded. "Well, you heard your grandmother. Up you go!"

Elsie stamped a booted foot once more.

"I'm sorry about that." Mrs Elgin was terribly embarrassed. "None of my girls were ever so difficult, nor my sons. She can't bear to hear about my living in the rows, or how Robert and I ran away together. She seems ashamed of mine and her mother's past."

Despite this, during our visit, Elsie developed an intense crush on Sam! She had never seen such a handsome man. His clear, blue-green eyes, red hair, the straight nose and sensuous mouth. When she got as close as she dared, she could smell the woodruff on his clothes, soap and fresh linen. She liked his Yarmouth accent, his sweet and gentle demeanour and smile. What would she give, she thought, to have a man like him? Elsie would sit as close as propriety would allow, and Sam didn't like it one bit.

Just before we left, I accidentally went into the wrong bedroom. I had hurried to fetch a handkerchief before dinner and, with my mind elsewhere, I suddenly found myself in Elsie's room. I gazed around in wonder. The bedroom was huge. There was a double four poster bed, piled with white cushions of linen and lace, the bedside rug luxurious. The carpet was thick and brightly coloured.

"What are *you* doing in here?"

I spun round. Elsie stood behind me, hands on hips.

"Oh, forgive me, Miss Elsie, I was aiming for our room! I needed a handkerchief."

Elsie regarded me. She hated me for being with Sam. She, as I had been, was utterly smitten. I sensed the undercurrent that she was sweet on my Sam.

"Well, of course, one does make mistakes in strange houses," she told me, swiftly recovering her composure. "Well, now you're here, what do you think of it?"

I duly admired the room. Privately, I thought it a shocking waste, but;

"It's beautiful," I told her, smiling. "You're a lucky young lady, Miss Elsie."

"I am," she affirmed, "and I *always* get what I want!" she added slyly, then paused, and gave me a sidelong glance. "Do you?"

"I have what I want, and I don't want anything more," I stated.

Elsie smiled. "Of course; how I wish I could see your home. I would love to see Grandmamma's old house too. I've never been to Yarmouth. Do you think I could stay with you over the summer? For a week? You could show me around!"

It was incredibly rude to invite oneself, as Elsie doubtless knew, but then this young girl was accustomed to having her every whim granted. I struggled for a reply.

"Well, our house is very small. Our master bedroom is half this size, probably less... I'm sure you'd hate it."

If Sam was there, Elsie decided she wouldn't mind.

"I realise that." Elsie examined her faultless, and highly polished fingernails. "I'll ensure Papa pays you well!"

I didn't want this spoiled little madam in our home. However, Elsie spoke about it over dinner, as though I had already invited her. I was angry at being put in such a difficult position. Julia felt embarrassed.

"Really!" Her mother dabbed at her lips with a napkin. "You cannot expect people to 'put you up', as it were, for goodness knows how long!"

"But Mrs Dwyer said!" she objected, petulantly, daring me to contradict her. Sam shot me a look, but I frowned at him. "I want to see Grandmamma's old house." She looked at her mother then, petulant. "When I wasn't interested in Grandmamma's origins, you chastised me; when I show an interest, that's wrong!" She sat back, sulking.

"We'll see," was all her mother could say.

I was furious and I told Sam later as we took a bath together that she had blatantly invited herself. He believed me. We took our leave the next morning and I hugged Mrs Elgin and whispered to her.

"I *didn't* invite her!" I looked so desperate; Mrs Elgin smiled.

"I'll do my best to prevent your unwanted guest!" she told me. "And I really don't blame you!" She winked.

Sam and I wandered along the sea front, looking at the various changes that had occurred during our absence. We could see quite a difference.

"But the rows are the same at least," I said, squeezing Sam's arm.

"I hope they never alter," Sam told me.

Suddenly, we saw, walking towards us, Miss Spoonamore and her sister, identically dressed, with a squat little man at their side. The two women were taller than him. Without a doubt, it was The Spoonamore sisters and their brother.

"Two of them together!" I exclaimed.

"I know – one's bad enough," Sam answered.

"Good afternoon!" Sam said politely. "How *delightful* we should meet!"

Miss Spoonamore huffed. She could tell sarcasm when she heard it.

"This is Eleanor, my sister; Arnold, my brother. They have recently moved from Gorleston and now reside with me."

Anyone else, I would have pitied, but they seemed well-suited!

Eleanor will help me out with the school, as will Arnold," Miss Spoonamore continued. "So, you'll see them around the town."

Unable to resist, I spoke. "Miss Spoonamore, ah, the other Miss Spoonamore, I mean," I said when the regular Miss Spoonamore looked at me. "Did you ever manage to get rid of The Cosies?"

Sam bit his lip. It took a short time for the comment to register. Then there was recognition on the sister's face.

"Not as yet!" she answered sharply. "However, we live in hope!"

"That particular project has had to be abandoned, alas," Arnold put in. He eyed me keenly. "But we plan to re-visit it." His eyes met mine and I could see at once that this man was a lecher. He licked his lips, and I repressed a shudder.

Sam and I nodded to them, then took our leave of them.

Helen returned on the 14th of March. I answered a knock at the door and found her and Manoa there, grinning widely.

"Lass!" she squealed, and before I had time to react, she enveloped me in a bone-crushing, stiflingly perfumed hug. She had gained more weight and was what my father would have called 'strapping.'

I gasped for breath as she set me down.

"I've missed ye so! I'm so sorry about yer granfer. Ye poor wee thing. Such a shock too; 'tis no wonder ye never wrote. Well, I'm back and it'll be like old times again!"

She rabbited on without drawing breath.

I smiled, feeling a little awkward, remembering our parting. Helen, however, seemed either to have forgotten about it, or had chosen to disregard it.

"I hope so, Helen!" I said when I could get a word in. "It was wholly unexpected to find he'd died. I'm so grateful for Sam and my wonderful family."

Helen nodded. "Aye, hen, you are much loved!"

"I've looked after Reverend as best I can, with Florence's help, but Sam's had to do the heavy work!" I gave her a meaningful look. Helen glanced at me as I took them both to sit near the fire.

"Och, lass; ye mean?"

I grinned and nodded. But deep inside, I was afraid. Never would I forget our sweet little Dawn.

"I'll be at the birth if ye want me, and this time, all will be well," she told me.

Sam came in. "Ah, I thought I heard your dulcet tones!" he told her. "Welcome back! Manoa, did you like Scotland?"

Manoa shivered. "Freezing! I've been cold on board ship but at least I could go to my hammock! I never felt such cold as I did in Scotland; it's very beautiful though."

"How did the family like you?" Sam asked.

"They were wary at first. When we walked into their house, their mouths dropped open. Then they were interested in me, my background. I told them all about my homeland. The little ones were afraid at first, but they soon got over that, and then, I couldn't get rid of them!"

Helen laughed. "Aye, I marvelled at his patience. Mam cried when we left, but I told her, I'm no setting foot south of Yarmouth ever again, so dinnae worry." She smiled and kissed Manoa's cheek.

Suddenly, she spluttered with laughter.

"Ah, I must tell ye this; 'tis a rare honour! Da got Manny a proper kilt made for our wedding! He looks incredible!"

"I never saw a fellow wear a kilt before," I told them.

"Well, ye'll see! Which reminds me, Alice, ye'll be chief bridesmaid? Ye cannae refuse. I'll have nobody else! Alice and Elspeth are bridesmaids too.

We want your wee laddie to be a page. And, Manny has something to ask ye, Sam."

The large man smiled. "Be best man for me?" he asked, and Sam beamed.

"Yes! I will! Thank you, Manoa! It'd be an honour!"

Helen continued. "Will's giving me away!" she continued. "When I told him that, he was pleased, then says, 'Can ye no' bring the wedding forward then I can give you away sooner'?!"

We all laughed at that.

Maria was delighted when I informed her of my pregnancy.

"How wonderful! I'm thrilled for you both. It's time you had another. I'll not be long behind you! If I can help in any way, just tell me."

I started to say about the midwife and Maria listened seriously.

"Mrs Thatcher was mine. She was good, clean, so nice. She's four daughters and two of them are learning her trade. "

I felt relieved.

Miss Spoonamore was shocked when she saw Helen with Manoa, Sam and me, strolling along the sea front. It was Sunday afternoon. Since her pupils were so disruptive, Miss Spoonamore had reluctantly been forced to eschew the Sunday service and now her brother gave the religious instruction.

"Oh no!" I said. "Helen, this is a bad time to tell you, but Miss Spoonamore's brother and twin sister have come here to live."

I smiled at my friend's horrified expression.

"What? And ye didnae think to tell me this ghastly news before?" she asked. "I thought I was seeing double!"

"Sorry, I meant to," I told her. "The misses Spankmore!" I said, and Helen laughed aloud.

"Great God!" Miss Spoonamore exclaimed and squinted. "Now, girls! There are two examples of womanhood you should definitely *not* follow!"

The seven girls observed us. "One, you know; she has already proven that with her conduct toward Millicent! That showed exactly how devious she is."

Miss Spoonamore drew herself up to her full height and looked down her nose in fury.

"And as for that Scottish creature. Walking down the prom with a black man? He isn't in livery, so I presume he's not a servant."

"That's her boyfriend, miss!" stated an impish voice from behind her.

"What? How do you know that, girl?"

The girl giggled. "I saw 'em snogging in one of the rows!"

Miss Spoonamore turned, scarlet-faced and scandalised at the remark, and the others laughed. Miss Spoonamore's sister looked equally cold and disapproving.

Appearing to forget her charges, Miss Spoonamore marched up to us.

"Here comes trouble!" I said with a grin. "Double trouble! Manny! I apologise in advance for what she's likely to say. Just ignore it! She doesn't know any better."

Manoa, confused, watched as Miss Spoonamore stalked up.

"How *dare* you conduct yourselves in such a disgraceful manner?" she stated.

Helen and I looked at her innocently.

"How should we conduct ourselves?" Helen asked. "We're having an afternoon stroll, my friend with her husband and me with my fiancé!"

Miss Spoonamore's mouth opened and closed like a fish for several moments. "Do you mean to tell me you are going to actually *marry* that man?"

"Aye!"

"But that is outrageous!" she spat vindictively. "Completely outrageous; it cannot be allowed! What are young people coming to?"

One of the girls had the audacity to call out,

"Hey, miss? Is it true what they say?"

Helen looked at her quizzically.

"You know, about what's worn under the kilt?" The look on the girl's face was pure mischief. She made a lewd gesture with her hand.

Helen roared. "Aye!" she affirmed. "'Tis indeed the truth!"

The girls screamed with laughter.

"You foul-mouthed slut!" Miss Spoonamore yelled at the girl in her charge. "I will see Arnold fetch you a birching later!"

The girl merely sneered. "Ha! How d'ye even know what I mean if *you're* so innocent?!"

Miss Spoonamore's neck and face flushed an alarming shade of red in her fury.

"Well, we shall see about this, young woman!" Miss Spoonamore snapped.

"About what? Whether 'tis true? Well, if ye've any doubt, come to the wedding. Being April, it'll be a breezy day, and Manny's promised to wear a kilt like all good Scotsmen at their weddings and ye'll be able to judge for yerself!"

This was too much for Miss Spoonamore's little entourage and the girls bent double with laughter. Miss Spoonamore stamped her foot.

"Stop it! Stop it at once!" she raged. "What I mean is that we will see about your marriage!"

Helen and Manoa's wedding day dawned a bright, sunny morning, with just a few puffy white clouds and a mild breeze. Helen fidgeted as I put the finishing touches to her hair. I smacked her hand as she reached up to feel what I had done.

"Helen! Stop fiddling! You'll make the blossoms fall out!"

"I'm so nervous!" she told me.

"Why?"

"The Hag was complaining to Reverend about the marriage!"

"Yes, and he gave her short shrift for it," I replied. "Forget her, Helen. This is yours and Manoa's wedding day."

Helen nodded. "Aye, 'tis true. Well. Will I do?" She looked at her reflection.

"What do you think, Helen? Course you'll *do!*"

Helen gave a huff. "At least Mam and Dad are here this time."

I nodded. "And your father didn't mind Will doing the honours and giving you away?"

Helen shook her head.

Helen stood tall and proud in her cream-coloured dress; it was quite different to the style she had had before in that this one had the fullest of skirts I had ever seen. The underskirts made it billow out widely. It was a sumptuous dress of satin, and all over the skirt were swirling patterns in a diamanté effect, full at the bottom of the skirt, then they tapered upwards to very little design, just plain satin. That was, until it reached the waist, where the entire bodice and tight sleeves were all fashioned with the same patterning.

As head bridesmaid, I wore a lacy, net dress, with long sleeves that were loose until they reached the wrist, where they became small, neat cuffs, which Sam had exclaimed at. Little Sam, honest to the point of bluntness as children are, had done himself no favours when he had asked me, quite seriously,

"Mamma, why are you wearing a dress made from window curtains?"

I had liked the dress when I had first seen it, so had Sam, who had never seen me clad in anything quite so dramatic, but I had changed my opinion after our son's comment.

Sam was having trouble with a nervous Manoa who groaned he was 'not worthy' of Helen and what if she changed her mind? But, at length, he was ready. Manoa looked quite superb in his highland dress. Little Sam had once again almost blotted his copybook on exploding into giggles at Manoa's 'skirt'. It took some time to explain a Scotsman's kilt and Sam hoped the lad wouldn't giggle through the ceremony.

Mrs Elgin had come all the way from Norwich – no mean feat now that she was eighty-six.

"I wouldn't have missed it for the world!" she told Helen who was delighted to see her. She was a little older-looking and slightly slower now, but she walked well enough, with Florence and Elsie at her side 'just in case', and they were given the front pews.

I was annoyed that Elsie had accompanied her; as soon as she had heard about the wedding, she had demanded to attend, and her mother, needing some space, had agreed.

Elsie regarded my dress with a sneer. 'What', she thought, 'was I wearing?' She sniggered at the bridesmaids dressed the same way. Helen might be a rich woman, but her clothes? She had no idea at all!

Elsie hurried to me in an unladylike manner. "Hello, Mrs Dwyer! How are you?"

I gave a tight smile. "Very well, thank you, and yourself?"

"Yes, er, where is Mr Dwyer? I'd like to greet him if I may."

"He's with the groom," I replied.

"Of course!" She nodded. "Well, I'll see him later, I hope. Perhaps he would favour me with a dance?"

I gave her a scowl.

The Reverend welcomed the congregation. Most people liked to attend a wedding even if they didn't know to the couple.

Nobody had met Helen's parents before, except for Manoa and Helen's children. Helen's father had a huge ginger beard and a voice like a foghorn. Helen's mother was an older version of her daughter. Both seemed extremely jolly, and they greeted Manoa so warmly, I knew things would be alright with them. Helen introduced Sam and I, along with the rest of our family and Mrs Elgin, and they made much of us.

The wedding began, with Helen 'piped' to the altar. Little Sam, I was amused to see, had both hands over his ears and a comical look of disgust on his little face.

Miss Spoonamore had crept in, unnoticed. Now, she stood in the nave. The Reverend welcomed everyone, and the service began. At the very point where Reverend posed the question, did anybody know why they should not be joined in matrimony, there came a shout.

"I DO!" she thundered. Every head swivelled round. Sam groaned, I jumped, and gasped in shock, as did Maria. Miss Spoonamore marched half-way down the aisle, with every single pair of eyes fixed upon her. The silence was almost deafening.

"Miss Spoonamore! Please!" The Reverend said curtly.

Rupert, the shy little curate, ducked swiftly out of sight.

"But you have asked the question, Reverend, and I am answering. My objection is that it will not be a true marriage. This man is no Christian. He is from foreign climes!" She stalked the rest of the way up the aisle, and stood, arms folded.

A shocked gasp went round. Foreign people were readily accepted in Yarmouth, it being a port with sailors from just about everywhere. Helen was on the verge of tears. Helen's father opened and shut his mouth like a landed fish, wondering what to do. There was silence before the Reverend spoke. This sort of thing had not occurred in any wedding ceremony he had conducted in his entire career!

"Rubbish!" he exclaimed at last. "There is no sacrilege! Manoa was baptised!"

Miss Spoonamore was silent for a moment. Then she continued.

"Nonsense! When was this?"

"When he was a boy!" Reverend replied. "In his own country."

"Well, then, that doesn't count!" Miss Spoonamore objected.

"Ah, but it does, Miss Spoonamore. Do not forget, the word of God is worldwide, not just in this country. Manoa's parents were much involved with the church there and had been for many years. They were the ones taken against their will. By people like us... like you! The *slavers* were savages, Miss Spoonamore!"

Miss Spoonamore stamped her foot, outraged. "How dare you, Reverend? I won't stand for such insult!"

By now, Helen was in tears. Manoa tried to comfort his bride. Elspeth had begun to cry. I was infuriated that the old besom could even have contemplated this, upsetting the bridal couple, making the children cry.

"Hold this!" I thrust my posy into the surprised Maria's hands, turned and stalked down the aisle. Had I been able to, I would have rolled up my sleeves!

The congregation watched spellbound, Sam amused, and faintly embarrassed. Little Sam's eyes were rounded, and he gaped. Elsie glared; trust me to draw attention to myself, she thought, grim of face.

"Come on, you! We've heard enough nonsense from your clack-box. Out!"

To everyone's amazement and Miss Spoonamore's shock, I turned the woman round by her shoulders and marched her out of the church. Miss Spoonamore was so taken aback, she could only protest, volubly.

"How *dare* you lay hands on me! I shall have you charged with assault!" There were various other threats, of which I took no heed. For all she attempted to resist, I simply propelled her along, shoved her outside and closed the door, putting the bar across it, ignoring the hammering and yelling that began outside. I walked back up the aisle, dusting my hands. Then, suddenly, there was a round of applause.

The Reverend smiled around, and then held up a hand for quiet. "Might I continue? I hope nobody else objects?" He said it with a smile, and nobody else made any objection. Little Sam glanced up at his father, who grinned and winked.

"It was as well she came alone," I said to Sam after the ceremony had been performed. "Can you imagine if all three of them had come along?"

"Well, at least Helen's alright now," Sam stated. "Manoa was speechless!"

Little Sam giggled. "I thought it was funny!"

"Me too!" Roland piped up.

Mrs Rix chuckled. "I would've had no idea what to do!"

"Ah, Mrs Rix, I have never forgotten, nor forgiven the time she threw me down her steps!"

Mrs Rix's eyes bulged, and I had to give her an account of the event.

The wedding breakfast was outside due to the lovely weather. Helen's parents chatted to the bagpiper, who stood dressed in a lovely red tartan. Mrs Anderson told us he was the best.

Elsie ventured to Sam. She had hung around watching him. When was the dancing going to start? Surely, even ordinary people danced at weddings? Her crush had not lessened, and the wedding was the ideal chance. She had her parasol and held it at a certain angle, which, as with a lady's fan, according to gentry etiquette, meant that she was urging him to talk to her, alone. Sam did not even notice the silent, secret message. Frustrated on realising this, Elsie wondered how to attract his attention.

Elsie had been furious to learn that I was expecting, but she was not one to give up her quarry. Not for me... not for anybody. She chewed her lip, then suddenly appeared to stumble.

"Oh! My ankle!" Elsie gasped and pulled a grimace of what passed for pain. Sam turned.

"Miss Elsie?"

"My poor foot!" She looked up at him from the ground. "Oh, it does hurt so!"

Sam was embarrassed. "Ah, might I assist you?"

He reached out his hand and Elsie grasped it. Sam pulled her up.

"Oh!" She fluttered her eyelashes at him and gave a little sob. "I cannot put any weight on it."

She put one arm round his waist. Sam was shocked at such familiarity and looked round for help. Still with Mrs Rix, I had been joined by Helen and Manoa. Sam looked around hoping to see Mrs Elgin. On spotting her, he indicated, with a wave, but Mrs Elgin, being not as keen-sighted, didn't see him.

"Please Miss Elsie, let me go; it's not appropriate."

"I'm injured!" she said in a plaintive voice.

"Do you sit on a bench and rest. Raise your foot; it'll soon be alright," Sam told her, attempting to disengage himself from her clutches. There were benches dotted here and there, and Sam looked for the nearest one.

"I don't believe I can walk to one," Elsie cooed. "Might you be so good as to carry me, Mr Dwyer?"

Sam blushed red. "I cannot!" he answered, shocked. "One moment."

Sam hailed us across to him. "Elsie's fallen," Sam told us. "Would you escort her to a seat so that she can rest a moment?"

My eyes met the girl's, which were sly.

Helen and Maria joined hands to make a seat. This was not what Elsie had planned, when she found herself transported in an undignified manner to the bench and Helen spoke; "Manoa, shift yer great arse, mun! I'll fetch Mrs Elgin."

I was furious when I heard, and angry at Sam who had found it amusing.

"Manoa should've slung her over his shoulder like a sack of spuds!"

"Alice, really!"

"Ha! I was a sixteen-year-old girl once, Samuel!" I snapped back. "And I *know* how sixteen-year-old girls think! Especially when a handsome man's around!"

Sam merely chuckled.

I seethed. "She sits as close to you as she can, and why come to the wedding of someone she doesn't even know?"

Sam smiled. "To be with her grandmother, of course. You're being fanciful!"

"It's *you* she fancies!" I stated, frowning.

Sam laughed at me.

"It's true!" I told him. "Why else is she hankering after an invitation to stay in Yarmouth? You know I never said any such thing about inviting her!" Sam stroked my cheek.

"You're beautiful when you are angry!" He chuckled. I stalked off in a huff.

Later, Sam and I lay in bed, drowsy. As soon as Little Sam had been in bed, to my husband's astonishment, I had grabbed his tie and pulled him up to bed, which Sam had enjoyed very much.

"Sam," I whispered. "About Elsie."

Sam held me close and regarded me in the moonlight. "She's a fanciful child, nothing more," he whispered. "You are my wife, and I love you. I feel nothing for her."

The Easter fair had come to Yarmouth as it always did and there were many to attend it. There were stalls that sold all kinds of things – sweets, hot food – and there were the usual fortune-tellers and sideshows.

There were displays by acrobats which delighted the children and not a few adults. I hoped Little Sam would not attempt to imitate them! We watched in delight as they bounded over the flattened grass, somersaulting and backflipping all around the square which had been specially laid out for them. He and Roland, who had joined our little group, stood open-mouthed and wide-eyed.

Later, we came across the most absurd sight we had ever seen. There was a fenced off area, decorated with flowers and ribbons, and inside sat a small table with little chairs around. A woman ventured out of a tent and was setting the table with plates, cups and humming as she did so.

"Ah! Sweet!" Maria beamed. "I suppose it's a little party for young children!"

It was, but it was also something else too. A gypsy-looking man came out whistling. He grinned at us, gold earring flashing in the sun.

"Fancy joining the party?" He had noticed Little Sam, whose expression at being asked was offended outrage.

"No, thank you, sir!" he stated with firm politeness. "I am *far* too old for that!" The man guffawed.

"Ah! Sorry, young master! I see that now! But this *is* a party with a difference. You won't see it's like elsewhere!" We soon saw what kind of difference as the man started to call.

"Chimps tea party starts at three! Bring your young ones!"

"Whatever's that?" Mr Dwyer asked.

The man bowed theatrically. "Me and my missus got some chimpanzees – baby ones – they enjoy a party, and 'tis fun to watch! All dressed up they are, just like kiddies. They eats and drinks with them!"

"I want! I want!" Elspeth screeched, leaping up and down, something like a monkey herself.

"Alright, simmer down!" Helen told her. "Goodness me! Try to act the wee lassie, will ye?" She turned to the gypsy man and handed over some money. Elspeth made to march into the small circle. "No! We must wait in line, and if ye start one of your paddies, ye'll no go at all," Helen added, seeing her youngest daughter prepare for a tantrum. This seemed worth waiting for and so we stood in our little group to await the other children.

The unusual sight soon attracted several youngsters.

"Five is all we can take!" the man's wife stated. "Now, there's room for four more of you; one penny each."

We stood to watch, Sam behind me, his arms around me, Little Sam in front of me. Manoa had seen such animals before, but these had been in his childhood, living naturally in trees, and he was horrified to see them all troop out, holding their owners' hands, wearing outfits. The male chimps wore sailor suits, the females pink chequered dresses. To Sam and I, who really knew no better, it looked amusing as it did to the others, like a circus act, but there was no smile on Manoa's face. In fact, he looked thunderous.

The youngsters settled themselves at the table, a chimp at each side of each child. Suddenly, one bared its teeth and I felt fear almost overwhelm me.

"Look at their teeth!" I gasped and looked up at Sam. "Gosh! What if it bites?"

"They won't. They're used to this, and they're getting a treat. I don't expect they'll be aggressive."

Manoa frowned. "Bad to do this to animals," he said crossly. "Making them like people!"

He sounded so annoyed that I looked in surprise at him.

"It's not normal for them!" he explained. "I didn't realise what the party was, at first, but these animals live wild in my old home." He continued to look on with a frown of disapproval, and almost fetched Elspeth out, but he knew that would bring on a tantrum of epic proportions.

The party was organised chaos, with the chimps reaching for things and gulping the drink.

"You got no manners!" Elspeth squeaked at the chimp next to her. "Like this, look!" She demonstrated with her small china cup. The chimp, a female, watched, interested and clapped her hands. This, of course, delighted Elspeth. She laughed. "You smell!" she told the chimp, who did not appear offended at this remark and merely reached for a bun.

The spectacle had drawn a crowd who watched indulgently. It was an altogether fun afternoon, except that Manoa was becoming more and more uncomfortable. He was, I noticed, starting to sweat.

"Are you alright, Manny?" I asked, and Sam turned to look at his friend too. Manoa glanced at us.

"It's so wrong!" he stated again. "What are they eating? They don't eat that kind of food in the wild. It'll make them ill. It's dangerous too; adult males can be extremely aggressive."

"But these are babies," I pointed out.

Mr Dwyer laughed. "Reminds me of when you lot were small!" he told his son with a grin; Sam laughed.

The party came to an end and the messy chimps and children left the table. Elspeth shot up to her parents.

"That was fun!" she squealed.

"Och, look at ye!" Helen produced a handkerchief to wipe the mess from her daughter's face. "Ye look as messy as one of the monkeys!"

"Apes," corrected Manoa, thankful she had come to no harm. "Chimps are *apes*." He lifted her up. She grinned at him.

"Funny!" She chortled, wrapping both small arms around his neck.

Little Sam and Roland had hurried off to do a little exploring of their own. Just up ahead, Manoa was speaking to Helen in a quiet but serious manner. Her children were with Maria, who was listening to the conversation. Sam's father joined us.

"He's giving her a talking to!" Simon told us. "He's upset about the monkeys."

Even though Manoa was very upset, he wasn't angry with Helen, merely explaining about male chimps' tendencies to aggression, and the folly of treating wild animals that way. Helen bit her lip; it hadn't occurred to her at all. Elspeth would not be having any further treats of that sort. She glanced at the five-year-old girl with some anxiety and Manoa touched Helen's cheek.

"It's alright, not your fault." He pulled her into his huge embrace.

It was time for a spring clean. We went to Simon's house first, but owing to my condition, I would only wash the delicate ornaments in warm, soapy water, a task I could do sitting down. Little Sam was to assist and one of his jobs was to sort out the drawers and bring anything threadbare, or odd socks to us so that we could sort things out.

"Don't forget – let us know if there are moths," I said to our son. "Then we can deal with them."

Simon's bedroom was spartan and small. He had moved into the other room after Ada had died, unwilling to sleep in their old room. Little Sam opened the drawers and wardrobe to inspect the clothing. There wasn't much – old shirts, waistcoats, trousers, plenty of boots, old, but perfectly serviceable, clean; then he started in surprise. Right at the back of the wardrobe there appeared to be an animal curled up. Little Sam prodded it gingerly, expecting a growl, but none came. What was a dead animal doing in the wardrobe? He prodded it again; still, nothing. Little Sam reached out to grab it.

He found to his amusement that it was, in fact, a wig, a long wig, all grey curls. He looked at it, then set it on his head, looked into the mirror, and exploded with giggles. These had once been fashionable; even poorer folk had had them, but nobody wore them now. Little Sam peered at himself in the mirror, turning this way and that. He took the walking cane, struck a pose, and strutted around the room, pretending to be an upper-class young gentleman. He wondered what his father would look like in it. Had his grandfather worn this? Forgetting his tasks, he marched down the stairs.

Little Sam caused outright laughter when he strutted into the room with the wig and walking cane.

"Look at me!" he squeaked, "I'm a swell!" He then gave a flourishing bow. I burst into laughter, as did Maria. Mr Dwyer roared.

"Well! Of all the things! Where'd you find that, bor'?"

"At the back of the wardrobe," Little Sam informed him walking to stand in front of his grandfather. "I thought it was an animal!"

Sam and Albert came in and stood, surprised at the boy's outfit. "That wig was my father's," Simon told him. "I recall him wearing it; very proud of it he was. He gave it to me, but nobody wears them now. I kept it though, for him. Let's try it on!"

Mr Dwyer donned the wig and looked about him with a regal air.

"Suits you!" I told him.

Maria laughed. "Papa, how is it you never showed us before?"

Simon handed the wig to Sam who put it on.

"I clean forgot about it," he answered. "It was always stashed in the spare room wardrobe. I never got rid of it though, since it was my father's. Well!"

We sat down to lunch after the morning's work, chuckling at past fashions.

Helen was delighted when I told her Sam had allowed me to volunteer again. She listened to Sam's long lecture on what I should and should not do.

"I know she's with child so don't think I'll forget!" Helen forestalled him, when Sam would have continued.

At the hospital, we met the Lady Almoner.

"You've worked here before, you say?"

Helen nodded. "Aye, Madam, about ten years since. I was on female medical. Lass here is especially good wi' wee ones and the elderly."

The Almoner, whose late husband had been one of the best surgeons there, was a kind, very large lady known as 'Lady Betts', for all she had no real, bestowed title. On hearing this, she nodded. "Excellent! I can make good use of your help. Now then!" She turned to me. "And you are?"

"Alice Dwyer."

"Can you recall who you worked with last time?" she queried.

"Nurse Bryant."

"Hmm, well, she is still here. Good Nurse, she is. Matron material. Very dependable. Alright, I'll take you up. Mrs Wadaa, wait here a short while. I need to get hold of the Matron for female medical."

I followed the woman up the massive staircase. It all looked and smelled the same. After walking down the long, echoing corridor, which I remembered, Lady Betts stopped. She knocked on the door of the sluice room.

"Come in!" came a voice from the other side.

"Nurse Bryant, I've brought an old friend of yours!"

Nurse Bryant rose to greet Lady Betts and looked at me. She had barely altered at all. Then, she smiled brightly.

"Alice! My dear! How wonderful to see you again!"

I was delighted at her response.

"Nurse Bryant! Good to see you again too." We exchanged cheek kisses.

"I'll leave you two to chat," Lady Betts told her. "But not for too long! Matron's about!"

"Alice, I can't believe it," Nurse Bryant told me. "Sit down. I can hear Matron's shoes so we'll be alright for a while. I was disappointed when you sent word that you couldn't come back, though I understood. How have things been for you? I heard you left with Mr Dwyer. So, you're married now?"

I nodded. "Yes, all respectable now. We've a son, called Samuel. Oh, that reminds me, I am three months expectant and Sam's strict about what I can and can't do."

Nurse Bryant soon set me some light tasks; it felt good to be doing something useful.

Two days later, Sam's father was round at ours, having promised to take Little Sam and his faithful friend Roland to the beach after school.

Running footsteps up the row heralded Little Sam and his pal Roland.

"Here come the whirlwinds! Papa, don't let them drag you too far!"

"Not in me dotage, you know!" He smiled at me. The door opened and
the boys came in, but instead of the smiling anticipation I had expected,
Little Sam looked miserable. I could see he was desperately trying not to cry.
His rounded cheeks were red, as were Roland's, who was standing with his
arm around his friend.

"Go on! Tell your mamma. It's not fair."

Little Sam shook his curly head.

"Tell me what?" I squatted to look at my son. "Darling! What's wrong?"

We all looked at him. Sam knelt too. "Son?" he asked, brushing a curl
from his forehead. Little Sam's eyes were wide, his lips pressed tightly together.
I could tell he was forcing back tears. Simon glanced; Little Sam was holding
his hand inside his jacket. The expression on his face showed pain, the way
he held his hand a dead giveaway.

"Sam, sweetheart, what's wrong? Are you hurt? Let Mamma see."

But Little Sam shook his head and then it all became too much – his face
crumpled, and he burst into sobs. "Darling!" I exclaimed and hugged him
closely, looking to Roland for help.

"Brook caned him!" he stated, angrily.

"What? Why?" I asked horrified. Both Sam and his father prepared themselves to hear of his offence, but we were shocked when Roland started to tell
us the scene as it had unfolded.

"So!" Mr Brook told his class that afternoon, "We'll be celebrating the
birthday of our dearest Queen Victoria with a fine tea in the dining hall. The
school will provide *some* of it, but you'll need to ask your mothers to help.
After, there's games and races in the playground."

Mr Brook paused. "We'll have a collection for a small gift for her." He
added, "She would remember something from a school where the boys had
generously given even a farthing, if they can, in order to buy her a handkerchief, a pair of gloves, or something small. Imagine, she might even write a
letter of thanks! We'll start by signing a card."

Mr Brook brought out a beautifully hand-painted card, with delicate lace in an oval shape.

Mr Brook had ever had delusions of grandeur. A fanatical royalist, he recalled the coronation, and the fact that the Queen, on looking at the crowds, had smiled benignly and waved. She had happened to be looking in his direction at the time, and Mr Brook had taken the gesture to have been especially for him and had since told others of his 'encounter with The Queen', and this had grown in the telling, until he had been 'having speech with her.' He then had glanced at Little Sam and Roland. "What are you whispering about, Dwyer?" he asked, sharply.

Little Sam had turned large, dark, nervous eyes upon the schoolmaster.

"Well? Speak up, boy!" Mr Brook stood over Little Sam. Roland was frantically trying to think of an excuse.

"He said that's exciting, sir!" Roland said breathlessly.

"I did not ask you, Rix! I asked Dwyer!" the schoolmaster roared into Roland's face. There was instant silence. Nothing immediately brought complete stillness to twenty children like Mr Brook being angry and towering over another pupil. Little Sam spoke. As he did so, his words were inaudible to the class. But Mr Brook's eyes popped, and his eyebrows raised. "WHAT? What did you say, Dwyer? Come to the front of the class and repeat it so that your schoolfellows may hear!"

Little Sam got up, shaking, but he moved with courage and stood at the front.

"I said, Mamma won't want to help as she doesn't like the Queen."

A gasp went round.

"There is more, is there not?" Mr Brook was merciless.

Little Sam faithfully parroted my words.

"Mamma hates the Queen, as she let a boy of ten be hanged just for stealing bread, and she waxes fat from her empire whilst poor children starve."

Mr Brook inflated with fury.

"Nonsense! How *dare* you believe such tripe? How *dare* your mother spout such treason! *All* women are hysterical, especially your mamma!" Mr Brook's voice was deafening.

Little Sam turned fiercely to the annoyed man, and, with an enraged look on his face, he had responded, "She is *not*! She's wonderful!"

Mr Brook's face had flamed. "You defiant boy! How *dare* you answer me back? Hold out your hand!"

Little Sam had done so, and three strokes of the cane were delivered. All the boys had been caned at one time or other with varying degrees of severity, and to many, it had little effect. Canings were given on the seat of one's trousers or, for more offending cases, on the hand. Roland winced as Little Sam bore the punishment, his teeth gritted. He wanted badly to cry but he did not. He looked at the man with intense loathing. Hard though his canings were, he had never applied it quite so savagely before. Being caned on the hand, as Sam would later tell me, was excruciating, particularly if one got it on the end of the fingers.

Little Sam, however, despite the agonising caning, refused to allow the tears to fall, so Mr Brook was even more incensed.

"Well, since you feel so strongly, you won't attend the party! Instead, you'll sit with me and do sums. Now, return to your place! As for you, Rix, up here!"

Roland went up miserably. He received one stroke of the cane on his backside for lying to the form master. The rest of the boys looked in awe at the pair. Mr Brook had not spared himself in caning our son and he had taken it without bawling. Afterwards, lessons continued, no boy daring to move or speak without being spoken to. Little Sam had put his damaged hand inside his jacket. The stripes burned and his whole hand ached.

Now back at home, the three of us listened to young Roland's tale in silence. I was horrified. It had been my beliefs that had caused this, this beating of my angelic little boy. He had defended me and had been beaten for it. I held him close. "Darling, darling!" I then wept myself. "How *dare* he do that? I'll be speaking to him!"

Sam's father fumed. "That man!" he exclaimed. "For such a reason! Every Englishman has the right to speak his mind and defend those he loves!"

I felt a surge of anger so strong that I wondered I could control it. "Sam, speak to me; show Mamma your hand."

Little Sam showed me, and I bristled in anger at the red, sore marks. "Come, darling, let me treat it."

Little Sam nodded miserably. Now he was home and with those who loved him, he felt better. I fetched some water and began the gentle treatment to cleanse and wrap the wound.

Sam breathed through his nose as he looked at our boy's hand, his expression irate, teeth gritted. It certainly would hurt for some time, and it looked raw, with the skin broken. Sam had seldom felt such intense rage as he did now.

"Mr Dwyer," Roland's little voice made Sam look down.

"Yes?"

"Sam never cried," he told him. "I've seen boys bawl like girls when they have been caned. Mr Brook was angry he wouldn't cry, so did it harder."

Sam regarded Roland, then he turned and went to get his coat.

"Now, be careful, son!" Simon spoke warningly. "I know you're angry and so am I! But don't go and punch him or you'll be having an assault charge and that won't do Little Sam, or any of you, any good!"

"I'll try to restrain myself," Sam stated, pulling on his coat.

"But, Mr Dwyer, school's finished for today!" Roland pointed out.

"Well, he may still be there. The teachers sometimes stay for a while. Alice, do you see to his hurts." He nodded to his father and left the house.

Sam strode along the row, fists clenched. He was burning with fury. Had it been for a deliberate offence, then it would have been understandable, but the severity of the blows had been dreadful! He knew from experience just how much a caning hurt. He reached the school in record time.

"Brooky's long gone," a woman with a mop told him. "Went off soon as the kiddies did."

Sam nodded curtly. "Thank you!" he said. "I'll be back in the morning."

"You want to leave a message, sir?" she asked.

"No!" He paused, then added, "I wish it to be a surprise!"

Sam turned and left the school grounds. He glanced from left to right in case he could spot the tall figure of the schoolmaster, but Mr Brook, fortunately for him, was nowhere in sight. He stalked back to Half Moon Row, wondering at the wisdom of sending him to the same school he had attended after all.

Back at the house, I soothed my son's little hand. Roland watched. "You alright now, Sammy?" he asked, concerned for his friend. Little Sam nodded.

"Yes, better now. I *hate* Mr Brook!"

"Well, don't worry, Papa will sort him out! He won't hit you again!"

But when Sam came back, he told us the man had already gone home. "Luckily for him!" he said. "But I'll return tomorrow!"

"Me too!" I snapped.

"No, I am sorry, darling, but I cannot permit you to do that!" Sam stated.

I stood. "Samuel Dwyer! I am his mother! I *shall* be with you!"

Sam glanced at his father, who nodded at his son. "Your mamma would've done the same, son," he told him.

"Alright darling, but do try not to kill him!"

"I'll try."

"Now then!" Simon smiled. "Do you young men still feel like going to the beach? It's a lovely day. We can bring everyone back some fish and chips if you like, and I've heard tell there's a fresh batch of cakes at Tooke's!"

The boys nodded. I knew that many things were made 'alright' for a boy once his belly was filled. Fish and chips were cheap and plentiful here and already a few new shops had opened, the popularity of this dish having gone sky-high.

Little Sam's caning had taken place on a Thursday, therefore, we could and did, accompany him with Roland on the Friday. The boys ran off to play before the first bell. I had inspected and treated Little Sam's hand several times and was satisfied there was no infection, for now at least, but I had warned him to let me or the school matron know if the pain worsened, or the dressing came off.

Mr Brook was in the staff room at this hour, standing at the window, smoking a pipe and drinking tea. There was half an hour before assembly. He was looking forward to finding out whether Little Sam was absent that day, and if he were, it would be a chance to demean him on Monday morning, or whether if he did attend, he could further inflict misery on him.

"Friday at last," he mentioned. "Thankfully, a weekend clear of those little monsters! Devilish! Every one of them! I had cause to cane Dwyer yesterday! The boy's just like his father! He was nothing but trouble when I had him."

"Oh really? I recall young Samuel," another teacher spoke. "He always conducted himself well. I thought you'd made him a monitor."

Mr Brook scowled. "I did, to attempt to teach him some responsibility," he snapped. "Anyway, we are discussing Dwyer's son, here five minutes, and now, he comes out with treason about our beloved Queen! That's his mother's influence; damned females! It's a pity she can't wear a scold's bridle! She certainly needs one. She wants whipping through the town! If she were my wife, I'd give her the hiding she deserves and..."

Mr Brook trailed off. The other men and one or two females, who had been tutting and about to speak up themselves, went totally quiet as Sam and I marched into the staff room, slamming the door behind us.

"I say, what are you doing here? You have no right to..." His complaint was cut short as I stalked to the man, more swiftly than Sam had ever seen me move before, and before he could stop me, I slapped his face hard.

"How *dare* you?" I screamed at him. "You callous, evil man! He's just an eight-year-old boy! Those marks on his hand are disgraceful!"

"Alice, leave this to me," Sam said firmly and loudly. He was already behind me, a restraining hand on my shoulder. "Now! You listen to me, Brook. I'll be taking this to Headmaster!"

Mr Brook gave a sharp bark. "Ha! For what reason? Punishing a boy who makes insulting, treasonous remarks?" The teacher was holding his hand to his face. I had slapped him as hard as I could manage, and he was sure I had dislodged a tooth.

Sam held onto his temper. "All Englishmen and women are free to hold an opinion!" he stated harshly. "I *share* my wife's opinion. Now, the issue is not over the fact you have caned our son for a punishment which had been deserved, but that you have caned him with excessive severity! Not only that, but you have also maligned my wife in public, to which I take very serious offence!"

Mr Brook snorted. "Damn it all man! Surely you don't believe all that claptrap?"

Never had I seen Sam so furious.

"Have you seen his little hand?" I screamed at him. "Those are deep, deep cuts! He was awake all night with the pain. You're despicable! A disgrace to your profession!"

Now there were rumblings. Most of the staff there fully supported the corporal punishment which was part and parcel of school life. How else to control misbehaviour? But few liked Mr Brook's methods. Just how badly had this lad been beaten?

"Perhaps I was *slightly* harsh." Mr Brook could only back down at the look on his former pupil's face.

"*Slightly* harsh? His poor little hand!" I raged. "If it goes bad, I will hold you *fully* responsible and you will be paying for his care from the finest doctor I can find!"

"Darling, calm down; remember your condition," Sam warned me.

Fortunately, at that moment, the Headmaster walked in. One of the older boys had come and told him what was occurring in the staff room. The last thing Headmaster needed was a showdown in the staff room with doors and windows wide open.

"Excuse me, ladies, gentlemen. Might I suggest we continue this in my office?" he asked in a loud voice and looked behind him. We then noticed a large group of wide-eyed boys, thoroughly enjoying Mr Brook's encounter with us. Now it would be all over the school.

"Hey! Dwyer! Your mamma's a tigress!" one delighted boy who had witnessed the incident said to Little Sam. He was panting hard, having run to find him. "She went up and slapped old Brooky, right across the chops!"

The lad's face showed his glee that his hated form master had been walloped.

Little Sam's eyes widened in amazement and Roland grinned.

"Your parents. They went storming into the staff room! And your papa is set to tear off his head. Gosh, I wish my old man would come down here and do for him like that! Brooky's caned me a million times!" The bearer of this news hopped up and down in excitement.

Mr Brook was having a bad time in the office. "You insulted Mrs Dwyer!" the Headmaster said, once he had heard the tale again. "You expect her son to sit down under that, do you? Would *you* have borne such insult to your mother? I think not! Also, as Mr Dwyer so rightly says, we are a nation that prides itself on freedom of speech. Of course, there are certain things that *are* better left unsaid in public, perhaps, but the boy is only eight."

"Alright, but the insult to the Queen!"

"What of it? She can't hear it in London!" came the rather surprising response.

Mr Brook's mouth opened, and he looked stunned. The Headmaster could not have shocked him more had he come in wearing a frock.

"Listen, Brook, your treatment of the boy was overharsh. I am all for discipline. I have caned more boys than I can count, but *only* when the offence is deserving. From what Mrs Dwyer tells me, the marks on her son's hand are appalling." He paused, then rang a bell.

A maid entered. "Yes, Headmaster?"

"Bring me the Dwyer boy, if you please, miss. Tell him not to worry, he's not in any trouble, I merely wish to see the damage."

Shortly, the maid entered with Little Sam. He had been told to not worry, but he still did. His rounded eyes looked full of fear. He came to stand in between us.

"Samuel." The Headmaster addressed the boy by his given name. "Let me see your hand."

"I'll do it," I told the Headmaster. I bent to undo the bandage as carefully as I possibly could. "There!" I said softly. "Now, show Headmaster what *he* did to you."

Meekly, Little Sam held out his hand. The Headmaster sucked in his breath. He had seen, and in fact, doled out beatings on numerous occasions, but his method was to make the offender bend over, and any application of the cane was onto the seat of the clothing, certainly not on soft, young flesh. Mr Brook began to wish he had merely made Little Sam bend over.

Headmaster, for all his sternness, was horrified. Good God! If this got round the town, he would be seeing pupils taken away in droves. He fervently hoped the wounds would not fester.

"I can see your mother has dealt admirably with these wounds," the Headmaster told him kindly. "But just to be on the safe side, you must see Matron. Mrs Dwyer, kindly take him to her. Mr Dwyer, I'd ask you to remain.

Ah, once he has been treated, take him back to his form room. Morning school's already begun. Miss?"

The maid was hovering.

"Do you go to Mr Falstaff and ask him to look in on Mr Brook's form, set them some reading or something."

The door closed and we walked to Matron's room. "Is he getting told off now, Mamma?" asked Little Sam.

"Oh yes! He certainly is! Come on, darling, take me to Matron. I can't remember the way."

Mr Brook returned to his class. I hoped that he would be giving Little Sam kid glove treatment from now on. As we all left the school, I spoke once more to Mr Brook.

"Don't *dare* touch our boy again," I told him. "I hope you bloody well drown!"

"Witch!" he hissed.

Sam and I walked to Saint Nicholas' to calm ourselves down. Helen was there along with Manoa. To our surprise, Sam's father was also present.

"I've been telling them about poor Little Sammy!" he said. "I knew you'd be coming here as soon as you could. What happened?"

I let Sam tell the story. I was exhausted. I had put a lot of venom into my voice at the end of the visit and I had been tired out with the experience. Florence had put the kettle on and was making us tea. Helen, as expected, appeared to go flying straight up to the ceiling and stayed there citing what she wanted to do to Mr Brook.

We considered the matter closed. Nothing further happened that Friday and Little Sam bravely returned to the classroom on the Monday. His scars would heal quickly and without problem, but he would forever bear slight red marks. Little Sam found himself quite a hero. The injuries had been nasty and none of the others had experienced such a 'whopping'. Little Sam went up in the other boys' estimation.

However, Mr Brook had other ideas. Angry at our interference, furious at the derogatory remarks about the Queen, who he adored, with a seething hatred of myself, and annoyance that his colleagues cold-shouldered him for disciplining a child, which they all did, Mr Brook appeared to 'let the matter rest.' However, he planned extra humiliation for poor Little Sam. He was furious and it made him reckless.

"Darling, are you sure you want to attend the party?" I asked Little Sam that morning on 24th May.

"Yes, Mamma, everyone's going. Otherwise, I'll have to do lessons with Brook."

"Ha! He wouldn't dare keep you for a lesson now!" I replied. "Now, off you go, enjoy it and tell me all about it later."

Little did we know, it would soon involve another trip to the school.

The dining hall was decorated with long tables set out in a huge square. The tables had crisp white tablecloths, flags descended from the rafters, and a large portrait of the queen on the wall in the dinner hall frowned stonily down at everyone.

Little Sam and Roland sat in class that morning, wondering at the side-long glances the teacher gave them. At the end of the morning school, all the boys rose, and Mr Brook stood by the door.

"Alright. To the dining hall with you! Though you don't deserve it in my opinion." The boys spilled from the form room, but Mr Brook shouted, making everybody jump.

"Wait! Dwyer! Where are *you* off too?"

Little Sam looked up at the large man. "Party, Sir. I thought I could go after all."

"And go you shall!" Mr Brook suddenly looked down with a hateful smirk. "But just a moment, young man, there is something I must attend to first. What are you staring at Rix? Get along before I cane your arse for you!"

Roland looked at the man fearfully, then looked at Little Sam, unwilling to leave his friend. "I said GO!" roared Mr Brook and brandished his cane. Roland fled.

Little Sam looked up at the man, his lips quivering slightly.

"Don't worry, Dwyer. I'm not about to cane you again, if that's what you're afraid of!"

"I'm not afraid!" Little Sam told him stoutly.

"Hmm, well you should be! I'm not finished with you. You spouted treason against our Queen, for which you should be imprisoned in the Tower!" Mr Brook's face was inches from Little Sam's.

The form master reached into his desk drawer and pulled out a piece of cardboard. On it was a string which he hung around Little Sam's neck. "Now others will see what your wickedness has led to and do not *dare* tell your parents, or the punishment will be worse next week!"

Little Sam felt terrible as he looked down at the card around his neck which bore the word – 'TRAITOR'

The children went deathly quiet when Mr Brook and Little Sam came into the hall; Mr Brook had a firm grip on his upper arm. He walked to a box that he had had put in the centre and lifted Little Sam onto it.

"Now, stand there, silent, and watch your friends enjoy," Mr Brook told him maliciously. Little Sam regarded the man full in the face. He wanted badly to cry, but he would not give the man the satisfaction. Instead, he held up his head, much to the man's annoyance.

"Well? What are you waiting for?" roared Mr Brook, annoyed at the sudden hush among the boys. None of them had ever seen any such thing before.

Little Sam, standing on a box, labelled a traitor, with the big schoolmaster at his side, a fierce and spiteful look on his features.

"Get on with your food!" he bellowed. The boys resumed eating, but it was suddenly a very different atmosphere from before. There were glances, whispers and muttering. None of them dared defy him and go to speak to Little Sam, but there were many uneasy glances in his direction. Roland was horrified.

"Swine!" Roland hissed to his neighbour. "Look what he's done!"

The boy looked, feeling sick. "Go and tell the Old Boy!"

"Not I!" Roland said. "But I'm going to get his parents. Shuffle your seat up so he won't see I'm missing."

Before the boy could respond, Roland had checked to see Mr Brook had his back to them, then he slipped from his seat.

"Mr Dwyer! Mrs Dwyer, come quick!"

Recognising Roland's voice, we hastened down the stairs.

"What's happened?" I asked in fear.

"You have to come!" Roland was in tears now. "Brook's stuck Sam on a box right in the middle of the hall and made a sign saying traitor for him to wear."

Sam was thunderstruck. "He's done WHAT?" he roared.

We hurried to the school. Sam and I hastened behind Roland. We entered the silent playground and Roland led us to the dinner hall. The double doors once more slammed behind us and everybody looked.

Mr Brook, who had been walking round the boys asking if they were enjoying themselves, went pale. The sneer fell away. "Dear God! How did they find out?" he asked himself.

Sam and I stalked to our son. Sam glanced at the card with disgust, turned a look of anger in the man's direction, and tore it off, flinging it to the floor. I screamed at Mr Brook. Little Sam clung to me, terrified.

"Good God, Dwyer! Can't you take a joke?"

Sam strode to Mr Brook, drew back his fist and punched him. Mr Brook fell into the tables and the boys sitting at them scattered. I winced. I clutched at my belly. Pain.

It was late afternoon. Five o'clock chimed in the Headmaster's office. Mr Brook had been sacked without further ado. This would be all over town and the Headmaster could well do without that. Parents would not be paying to send their children to that school if masters like him were still teaching. The Headmaster had never seen a lad humiliated to such a degree before. Now, he had to deal with the fall out, which was considerable. He sat at his desk and sighed. A breeze blew in through the open windows. A few papers blew across the desk, and he slapped his hand down on them to stop them escaping. It was the end of the school day. It had been fraught.

"Tea, Headmaster?" the maid asked tentatively.

Headmaster nodded. "Please! I need it after today. I cannot believe it! All these years, coming up to retirement, and he does that! How many others have suffered in silence, I wonder?"

"Probably lots," the maid told him. "That was awful. Poor little lamb, stood there like that. I heard he was so brave too. I heard his little lip was trembling, but he never cried! I do hope as Mrs Dwyer's alright, Headmaster. I heard she's expecting. She don't need shocks like that!"

The Headmaster had been forced to make his sincere apologies and assure Sam that Mr Brook had been dismissed. Discipline was one thing: humiliation quite another.

Thankfully, after an hour or two of spotting blood, it had stopped, and the pain had rescinded.

Helen bustled, moving pillows behind my back. Nurse Bryant checked my temperature and nodded. "Normal, good. Alice! What a thing to happen! I couldn't believe it! I was fuming."

"So were we!" Sam stated.

"It was horrible," Little Sam told us, eyes wide.

"It was, and you bore it well," Sam answered. "I'm proud of you, son. You've an excellent friend in young Roland! Well, don't worry, Brook's gone now. He'll not teach again!"

There was a temporary master for the boys for the next two weeks, highly recommended from a colleague at a school in Gorleston. An ex-Army man, hero of a rebellion put down by the British in 1849, he had lost an arm on the battlefield, and the boys plagued him for tales of bravery and gruesome details. Young and handsome with black wavy hair, black eyes, pale skin, tall; add to that his heroism and he was quite a catch. The boys had liked him at once when Headmaster had introduced Corporal George McIntyre, feeling the impressionable lads could have no better role model.

For the next fortnight, all we heard was Corporal McIntyre's name. Mrs Rix had met him, telling me, "A brave soldier! Just you wait till you see him! His smile will knock you sideways! His teeth are so good too!" She blushed and I giggled.

"Ah, I only have eyes for Sam!" I told her.

Early June

Tabitha and I took a walk along the beach. Despite my predictions, she had given up hope of meeting and marrying anybody now. "*You're* the one stopping it, not your face!" I had said exasperated. "You hide yourself away; you never attend anything."

"Drop it, Alice!" Tabitha said firmly. "I know I'm destined to be a spinster forever and end up like Miss Spoonamore."

"Good God! I hope not!" I told her. "One of her was bad enough, now we have two to contend with; if you end up as a third, there'll be nothing left to smile about!"

We sat at the water's edge and dabbled our toes. Tabitha seemed very downcast, and I was more worried than usual.

"Trouble is, if I don't find someone soon, I'll never have children," she muttered.

"Ah, you've time yet; look at me! I'm thirty now and expectant. I don't doubt for a moment that Helen will have another too, don't worry."

In Norwich, Elsie had not forgotten Sam. Her obsession had grown since the wedding, and she was determined to get him, somehow. Elsie lay on her bed, squeezing the frills of her pillow savagely. She decided, such a man would be a fool to pass up the opportunity of comfortable living with her! The thought of my being with child was something she could not even entertain in her mind, so angry did it make her. Revenge, she decided, was the best option. She would get Sam and she wouldn't no for an answer.

The holidays for the children had come and nobody was happier than Little Sam and Roland who had been looking forward to six weeks. Roland still had to help his father at home, and Little Sam would be at Sam's side, learning his father's trade, but the afternoons were theirs.

Mr Brook still suffered the backlash. The people of Yarmouth did not take kindly to those who hurt and humiliated children. Clips round the ear for cheek was one thing, a whipping from a father was par for the course, but his actions had been outrageous.

Comments were made in his hearing, and Mr Brook was the recipient of many an angry mother, telling him they were glad he had lost his job. The local children made it a thrilling dare to cheek him or run up and touch his person. The bolder ones would leap out in front of him, yelling, to startle him. His only allies were the Spoonamores.

That afternoon, Little Sam and Roland sniggered at the sight of their former form master striding along the seafront.

"Look! It's old Brooky! The smelliest teacher in the school. Hey! Mr Whiffy! Washed your socks lately?"

Mr Brook showed them a fist.

"He stinks! We should give him a wash!" Roland suddenly shouted, and the boys began to swipe handfuls of the water from the horse trough at Mr Brook, who backed off at once.

Miss Spoonamore chose that moment to walk along in the opposite direction. "Hey! Look! It's Miss Spankmore! That's what he's doing, he's meeting his fancy woman!"

Shrieks of laughter were heard, and Miss Spoonamore began to set about them with her umbrella, which they neatly dodged.

Little Sam jumped up and down. "Smelly Brook!" he called, "Ha! My papa knocked you down!"

Mr Brook longed to wipe the grin from Little Sam's freckled cheeks. He showed his fist once more. "You wait till you're older, Dwyer! You and your friend will end your days on the end of a rope!"

The boys laughed and, after more catcalling, chased one another onto the beach.

Miss Spoonamore snorted in disgust. "What a family!" she said bitterly. "You were entirely within your rights, Mr Brook, to chastise that cheeky brat! There's no discipline anymore and those of us who do employ it are vilified."

Mr Brook nodded.

"Miss Spoonamore, you should apply for my post!"

"What?" Miss Spoonamore looked at him in astonishment.

"Well, you've been a Nanny all your life, haven't you? Your school achieves good results."

Miss Spoonamore thought. "I don't know, the school is for boys!"

"Matron is female... just think on it, Miss Spoonamore. Think on it!" He paused momentarily. "After all, you're known to be particularly savage, and I mean that as a compliment!"

He raised his hat and strolled off whistling, leaving Miss Spoonamore standing there, her mind awhirl with plans.

The domestics were on their knees, scrubbing floors and walls, when Miss Spoonamore walked in and stood, hands folded before her, observing them as though she were their employer.

"Get right into the corners, young woman!" she stated to a domestic who jumped in fright at the sudden order, then gaped at her cheek. "Well! Go on! Dirt and the filth of an entire term is in them!"

The young girl was about to make a reply when Miss Spoonamore heard her name called. She turned round.

It was Matron. She wondered what the woman was doing there.

"Hello, Miss Spoonamore. Might I ask what you are doing here? It's not your usual port of call."

"I know, but I met Mr Brook, and he recommended I apply for his post!"

Matron looked stunned and could not speak for a moment. How like Miss Spoonamore to have the effrontery to march in like that, ignoring all the usual protocols.

"What? I thought you were busy with your school!"

"I am, but my dear siblings are wonderful assistants."

Matron nodded, then spoke; "Very well, I'll see if he's free, though really you should apply in writing once an advertisement has been submitted. However, since you have taken the trouble to come..."

Surprisingly, the Headmaster agreed to see Miss Spoonamore. He hated tedious interviews and all that went with the employment process.

"So!" Headmaster said as Miss Spoonamore sat opposite him. "What leads you to apply for this post in such an unconventional manner?"

Miss Spoonamore gave him one of her so-called smiles and began to speak.

"I could work mornings," she explained. "As I was telling Matron, my sister and brother help at my school. I could manage that easily."

"Allow me to think on it, Miss Spoonamore," the Headmaster said. "The post *is* full time, but maybe Corporal McIntyre may wish to share. Let me think."

Much to Miss Spoonamore's delight, two days later, she was asked to return. Corporal McIntyre was there, his tufted, wavy dark hair sticking up. Miss Spoonamore eyed him appreciatively. He was thirty years old, and incredibly attractive, his dark eyes giving him a very romantic look. The Headmaster spoke to both individuals, and a deal was struck. Miss Spoonamore would do the mornings and hand over to Corporal McIntyre at lunchtime.

Mr Brook stalked along South Quay in a fearsome temper. He had not truly expected Miss Spoonamore to get the job! He hated women who did not 'know their place.' He had married young, and his wife had been little more than a downtrodden servant to him. Terrified of his evil temper, after only six months of marriage, she had run off with another man over forty years before. So deep in thought was he, that he failed notice a long, thick rope lying on the quayside. Mr Brook caught his foot in it, staggered and gave a roar as he toppled over the quayside and into the deep River Yare. Shocked to find himself in the water, he panicked, and kicked his legs to try to right himself and came to the surface.

"HELP! he bawled. "Help! I can't swim!" He sank once more then thrashed wildly, the salty water gushing into his eyes, ears, nose and mouth. He could hear a muffled voice, the actual sound of the water in his ears. This time, he surfaced, spat and choked on the river water, and yelled once more. Several sailors, on hearing his yells, came to the quayside.

"Man overboard!" one bellowed.

A rope was thrown, and Mr Brook attempted to grasp at it, but his panic was so great that he couldn't grip. His clothes weighed him down. His chest pained him intensely, his lungs filling with water. The river tasted foul, salty, dirty. Again, the rope was tossed out, but his shaking hands couldn't grasp. He gasped and choked as he swallowed yet more of the river. The deep, dark and swirling water went over his face, his head, to pull him to its depths.

A sailor leapt into the Yare, swimming to him, but Mr Brook had gone under for the final time. The man took a breath of air and dived down. The sailors watched anxiously from the quayside. Someone had gone to get a blanket. The sailor surfaced with Mr Brook in a headlock, and swum to the side, and hefted him up to his friends. Arms reached to grab the sodden man, and he was dragged onto the quay. The man grasped hold of a rope and pulled himself up with the assistance of one of his shipmates.

"He's a goner!"

The limp and lifeless body of Mr Brook lay on the quay. It was too late to save him. Someone dropped a blanket over him, and a ship's boy was sent to alert the police.

The news of the drowning flew around the town.

Manoa was chopping wood when a delivery boy hurried up to the outbuilding. Dropping a sack of rags, he advised Manoa of what had just occurred. Manoa's eyes bulged.

"Drowned?"

"Yes, sir. I heard it from my pa. He works up on South Quay. He seen him trip on a rope and go right over into the Yare!"

I sat in our kitchen, watching Sam work in the corner. Windows were open wide to allow fresh sea air into the house. I was making a stuffed bear for the baby. "It doesn't look very much like a bear!" I said dolefully. Sam glanced over and grinned.

"No, it doesn't, darling!" he agreed.

"What? You're meant to say, 'yes it does, darling, it's a brilliant bear'!"

"Well, I don't suppose he or she will mind."

I decided I would make some coloured balls too, maybe sell them as a side-line. I gave a hefty sigh. I was a seamstress by trade; surely that meant I should be able to make something as simple as a toy bear? I made mine and my family's own clothes.

"Alice! Sam!"

Helen barged into the house.

"What is it?" I asked seeing her urgency.

"Lass, ye'll no guess what's happened." Helen entered the kitchen, breath-less.

"Sit and tell us then!" I got up to make a drink. Helen sat at the table. Her eye fell on the toy I was sewing.

"What the very devil is this thing?" She picked up the bear.

"It's a bear, for the baby," I told her filling the kettle.

"What? It doesnae look much like a bear to me! More like some kind of fiend! Do ye wish to frighten the child out of its wits, hen?"

"Stop insulting my bear, unless you want a bucket of cold water down your back!" I said. "What's the news anyway?"

"That horrid teacher who hurt wee Sammy has just drowned!" she exclaimed.

We stopped what we were doing in amazement.

"What? When?" Sam and I took our seats at the table.

We were silent as Helen told us. It was wrong to speak ill of the dead, but I would never forget Little Sam's hand or the sight of my little boy standing on a box in the middle of the dining room with that appalling sign around his neck.

"Well, I don't know what to say," I told her. Then suddenly, I felt cold wash through my body. 'I hope you drown' I had told him. Why had I chosen that particular thing to say? I felt the blood drain from my face.

"Alice?" Helen looked at me. "You look shocked, lass. Come on! He was a horrible man; nobody liked him. He got his just desserts in my opinion."

Sam agreed. "I know, it's wrong to speak ill of the dead, but come on, darling, his behaviour to Sammy was unforgiveable."

"Yes, yes, it was, it's just that I'm a bit stunned, that's all." I pulled myself together.

August, and the races attracted people from far and wide – those who came purely to enjoy themselves and have the odd 'flutter', and those, of course, who were dead set on making money too, but not by any honest means, and these men were known as 'Welshers'. They took bets from as many people as possible, then disappeared up the rows. There was very little chance of finding them after that. Manoa and Albert would be acting as lookouts.

In Norwich, Elsie had been keeping to her room until she could make a run for it. She was determined. Somehow, she just had to see Sam and talk to him. Race week would be ideal; she could go unnoticed in the crowd! She planned to ask permission to take a short turn around the square since she needed exercise and fresh air. Perhaps her mother would allow it, then, Elsie would be off.

The first day of the races had been much anticipated. Helen was to join Manoa, much to our surprise.

"I start tomorrow," Helen told us proudly. "Wi' my man!"

"I wish you luck," Sam told them. "Please be careful; you never know who may have a knife!"

The races would begin at two o'clock in the afternoon, and Helen and Manoa, along with Albert, were looking forward to their jobs.

The two men and Helen made their way to the denes. The racecourse, a long, flat piece of land, was perfect. There was a lot of business already taking place and money changed hands rapidly. Horses were being led by the owners or trotted up and down the course by their jockeys. There was a good deal of noise going on; men's voices raised.

It was difficult to determine who were tricksters and who was genuine. But if one knew the type to look for, the sly and crafty manner, watchful eyes, the pushy kind of way they had, and the haste in going from one to another to collect bets, one could winkle them out from honest folks. Helen spotted one man and she decided to follow him discreetly. She looked out for Manoa, who was easy to spot, and gave a slight tilt of her head. Manoa wended his way through the crowd to join her.

"Someone?" he asked her quietly and Helen nodded.

"Aye, yon fellow, high hat, black cravat, grey trousers, unshaven, scruffy devil."

Manoa caught side of the man and nodded. "I'll trail him."

Manoa was not exactly inconspicuous, but he used that to his own advantage, hiding in plain sight.

The conman had amassed quite a bit of money and instead of making his way to one of the Nelson's pillar to wait, he glanced around, then scurried off to the rear of the crowd. Manoa followed him.

"Hey! You!" Manoa roared at the man who was making his way as fast as possible across the denes. "Wait! Where are you going? That's peoples' hard-earned cash you're making off with!"

The man glanced round and was horrified to see Manoa, who was well over six feet tall with huge muscles, chasing him. At once, he broke into a run and slithered down a small rise in the denes onto the sand. He fell for a few seconds, then, getting up, he took to his heels, ignoring the hat which fell from his head. Manoa was a good runner. His huge thigh muscles were strong, and he pounded along the sand after the man who, on glancing round, was terrified to see the giant man bearing down on him. The man, who was almost fifty, did not usually run anywhere, but now, he was spurred on by his pursuer.

Manoa had only intended, as he told us later, to grab the man and make him turn out his pockets. He had never expected the man, thinking Manoa was out to kill him for the money, to charge into the sea.

"Hey!" Manoa roared as the man sloshed through the waves, looking back fearfully over his shoulder. He would, he knew, be shortly out of his depth but he continued out.

"Come back! I'm not going to harm you! I just want back what you stole from those people!" Manoa roared. But the man was not about to trust Manoa. He had been chased before and endured a spell inside the Tolhouse.

Helen arrived, breathless, on the sand next to her husband. "Och, the idiot! He's gone into the water!" she exclaimed. "Hey! You!" she screamed, "come on out! 'Tis a turning tide, ye barmpot! It's going out and it'll take ye with it!"

But the man was too scared to return to the shore, particularly with Manoa there. He shook his head, trying to steady himself against the pull of the tide and almost losing his footing. "Manny! Ye mun do something!" Helen stated. "He'll drown."

Manoa removed his boots, went to the water's edge and plunged into the sea. The thief in the water had not expected this and, with an exclamation of horror, tried to swim.

Helen watched, wringing her hands in anguish; the chap was sure to drown out there. She saw Albert pelting across the beach to her.

Manoa swam, pacing himself against the waves, hoping he would reach him. The current was with him as he swam out, but that would change on his return. It seemed to take forever to reach the man who was now tired out and had already gone under twice. He grabbed him and spoke to him.

"Don't panic and don't struggle. You're safe."

The trickster coughed up some water.

"Leave me, bor'. I ain't going to no Tolhouse – better to drown!"

Manoa was now swimming strongly back to the shore, striking out with his right arm.

"Not gonna let you drown, man!" he told him. It was fortunate that the man was too weak to struggle. Unbelievably, Manoa, though up to his chin in water, suddenly felt the sand under his feet, and stood. Helen and Albert at once waded out to assist in dragging the man to the shore, where he lay, limply, against the wet sand, still coughing up sea water. Manoa staggered out, weak after his efforts.

Helen crouched at his side and she and Manoa checked him over.

The man groaned. "Soon as you lot are gone, I'll go back out there," he told them morosely. "You 'ont stop me!"

"That's self-murder," Helen informed him, "a mortal sin and something ye cannae do. Ah, Manoa, what are we to do with him?"

Manoa thought.

"Take him back," he suggested. "Rev'll know."

Albert scooted off to let the Reverend know of his unlikely guest-to-be.

The Reverend met Albert squelching his way up to Saint Nicholas'. He had been putting some notices on the notice board and gasped at him.

"Albert! My son! What *have* you been doing? Are you alright?"

Albert nodded, then proceeded to explain to the bemused cleric what had transpired. "He'll need a hot bath, Reverend; change of clothes. Can you help him, please?"

'Gus' was his name. He spent four days in bed having been very ill after his near drowning and was insensible and feverish for much of the time. Helen sent Manoa to tell us they had a patient at the church and could she 'borrow my medical book' for a short time. I nodded at once and handed it to him.

Saturday: Gus woke and looked around the room. He had no idea where he was. He smelled freshly laundered bedding. The window afforded a view of trees and was open, the curtains were blowing gently, and the scent of many different flowers came floating in on the wind. Cabs rattled past a hundred yards away; children's voices. A clock struck two and he jumped.

"You're back with us then!"

Gus turned, alarmed at the close, female voice. There stood Helen, arms folded across her chest. He frowned, and blinked, trying to recall where he had seen her and when. Manoa entered the room and the whole adventure came flooding back. He groaned. So much for the pretty view and comfortable bed then!

"Alright, put the irons on me," he groaned. "But I ain't running!"

Manoa came over and sat on the bed. "Nobody's going to put chains on you, man!" he told him. "You're safe at Saint Nicholas'. D'ye remember what happened?"

Gus screwed his eyes up. He remembered. He nodded, ashamed. Helen handed him some strong tea.

"Here. 'Tis very sweet and strong. We brought you here after your disgraceful conduct at the races rather than have ye arrested, or worse, drowned!"

"Why?" Gus asked.

Helen shrugged. "We just did. So, don't make me regret it. Now, do you have a name?"

Gus hesitated and nodded.

"Is it a secret?" she continued when the man remained silent. Gus shook his head and sipped the tea. He looked down at the sheet and the coverlet, observing the way the patterns curled and curled round.

"Gus," he told her reluctantly.

Florence had been horrified that the Reverend had taken in a ne'er-do-well at first, until she had met him. Then, she recalled him.

"Well, I never!" she stated, on seeing the man in his sick bed, and tapping her foot. "Gus Fishwick! Turned up like a bad penny I see!"

Gus blushed, and a pained expression came over his face.

"Mrs Townsend; good to see you again! Nice to see you're still alive!"

"Hmm!" She turned to Helen. "This chap was a neighbour of uncle in Norwich. Always up to something, isn't that right, bor'?"

"Well, not anymore, my dear good woman!" he told her.

"Oh! So, what possessed you to go for a swim fully clothed, then?"

Gus merely groaned. "Not as from now on, is what I means." He sent her an appealing look. "Please, Mrs Townsend, I'm changing my ways for the better. Honest I am!"

"Ye know this fellow then, Florence?"

"I do. Ah, he's not all bad, just a bit of a rogue. He knew uncle back in the day. Uncle liked him, strange though it seems. Isn't that right, bor?"

Gus nodded.

Florence later told them what had happened. His wife, three sons and two daughters had died in a house fire in Norwich fifteen years before. Gus had been at work, and the loss had all but destroyed him. He had gone to the workhouse having lost his job shortly after the fire. In the workhouse, he had been at his lowest ebb. He had eventually left and attempted to start a business with a man he had known for several years, but his business partner had robbed him of everything he had left and fled. Now, he was here, in Yarmouth, trying to survive.

Helen shook her head. "Poor fella. Well, let's try and make things more bearable for him; what d'ye say, Rev? Everyone deserves a chance, don't they?"

The Reverend smiled.

Gus soon proved to be what people called a 'lovable rogue,' and would do anything for anybody.

"If you want to stay here, you must abide by the law!" the Reverend told him sternly. "I can't have the police knocking on my door at all hours! There must be no thieving, Gus."

Gus grinned and promised he would behave. The Reverend set Gus to tending the graves, something he did very well, since he had no family ones to care for and it gave him comfort to tend the graves of others.

Sam and I met him unexpectedly. Little Sam and Roland had been helping in the church grounds, as they often did, doing odd jobs for Reverend during their summer break, and had met Gus then. The two boys reminded Gus of his own sons, and they soon endeared themselves to him, a fact that nobody thought to mention to myself or Sam. But 'Uncle Gus' was full of funny stories, and not averse to a ball game once the chores were done.

I decided a visit to Florence and Helen was in order, so Sam took me along. We admired the bright morning.

As we neared Saint Nicholas', I saw the two boys in the grounds. They were with Gus. He wore his battered old hat, his chin and cheeks covered with stubble, mutton chop whiskers as scraggy as could be. He was talking to them, a smile on his face and nodding at them. He handed something to each boy. Then, after patting Little Sam's head, they walked away in the direction of the shrubbery. I squeaked in fear. Who was this person? We had always warned Little Sam against talking to older men he did not know and had stressed to never accept things from them.

"Sam!" I exclaimed. "Who's he? What's he up to? HEY! YOU!" I bellowed for the whole of Yarmouth to hear. "What are you doing with my son and his friend?"

Sam's face had gone red. He knew what happened to young boys who went off with strange men and he stalked up to Gus.

"Leave them alone!" Sam roared in a fury.

"Papa! Papa!" Little Sam jumped up and down. "He's our friend, he's Uncle Gus!"

"Is he now?" Sam's eyes were murderous as he regarded the man. I puffed up to the foursome. "Alice. Mind your condition!" warned Sam. I glared at Gus and grabbed Little Sam toward me, hugging him protectively.

"Mamma!" he objected, much embarrassed, and almost suffocating with his face in my belly.

"Leave our boys alone!" I fumed. "Don't you *dare* touch them! I'll have you arrested! Taking little boys off into the bushes!"

Gus was trying to explain, Little Sam squeaking up at me, Roland pulling at my sleeve. "No! Mrs Dwyer! Mrs Dwyer!" he exclaimed. Sam's fist had bunched.

"I'll knock your block off!" he roared.

"No! Wait!" We turned to see Helen hurtling toward us. "You're mistaken! Truly! Reverend'll tell youse! Gus is a friend. He lives here now! The boys help him around the grounds!"

In silence, we all looked at Helen. Little Sam looked up at me.

"I tried to tell you, Mamma!" he said crossly.

"I think an explanation is called for!" Sam said angrily.

And so, we met Gus. Half an hour later, and I would be eternally grateful he hadn't taken offence. We had both apologised profusely. Of course, Gus realised how it had seemed, but he was not that type of man, luckily.

"We been planting stuff." He indicated the seed packets the boys had. Those, I saw, were the packets he had handed over to them. "We do weeding; clear rubbish." He looked somewhat hurt. "I ain't *that* kind of fella," he said in disgust, realising what we had been thinking.

"You really should have told us about Gus," Sam told the boys, annoyed, and still embarrassed at his reaction. "Particularly if it's a grown-up. Not all grown-ups are nice; besides, it prevents embarrassing mistakes like this!"

Gus smiled. "It's fine, Mr Dwyer, really, they remind me of my boys. Twins they were. Lovely little chappies. I'd never hurt little 'uns, honest I wouldn't."

Gus later became a firm friend of ours.

Elsie smirked as she made her way to Norwich station. She had left that morning, having obtained permission for her walk. Unobserved, she had vanished through the gate into the square, which she walked through quickly and out the other side. She hurried a few streets away and waved a horse and cab to a halt. She had never been out alone before, and excitement almost overwhelmed her. She was off to see and claim the love of her life!

Now to find the train to Yarmouth; she had never been in a railway station alone in her life. People everywhere, so much noise. There was the smell of steam as a train pulled in. People spilled from it onto the platform, hollering for porters. Elsie went up to one of the destination boards and traced a cream-gloved finger down it, frowning in concentration. A woman appeared at her side.

"What's the matter, dearie?"

The female voice startled her, and she spun round to see a middle-aged woman, who was quite plain and ordinary-looking. Certainly not of Elsie's class.

"I want the Yarmouth train, Mrs..."

"Tomlinson." The woman spoke; "Are you here alone? You shouldn't be, you know; you meet all manner of undesirables!"

The woman smiled; she was poorly dressed, in a patched, stained skirt. She had the smell of unwashed about her and her bonnet was broken in several places. Elsie managed not to shrink back.

"Next Yarmouth train's at five and twenty past six! That's a long time. Listen, by chance, I'm going in the same direction. Stick with me, young woman; much safer. Shall we have some tea?"

They sat to watch the trains pulling in and out.

"Off on your holidays then? Bit young to be alone, aren't you?"

Elsie shook her head. "No, I'm sixteen now, and am meeting my man friend there."

"Oh?" Mrs Tomlinson smiled. "I gets the feeling your folks don't know. You're running away, ain't you?"

Elsie blushed. "Well, that is so, madam. I admit, I'm going to my swain without my parents' knowledge. He is going to leave his wife and marry me!"

Mrs Tomlinson's eyes were sparkly and bright. "Is he now?" she asked. "Well, I never! Hmm, there's an intriguing little tale and no mistake."

Elsie wondered what she meant by that but didn't have time to wonder, for the woman leaned forward in a companionable manner. "Tell you what, how's about we gets there a bit sooner, eh? Take a cab?"

Elsie frowned. A cab would be better than waiting four hours, plus her absence, when noticed, meant they would be out searching and might come here. She had no doubt in her mind that this woman wanted to get to Yarmouth quickly and would expect her to pay the cab fare, a more considerable sum than a train would cost. Well, if that was what it took!

She was, however, hesitant about doing this. Her mother and governess, not to mention her grandmother, had forever told her about not speaking to strangers and going anywhere with people she did not know. But what harm could a middle-aged woman do? She smiled and nodded.

"Yes, why not? I'll pay."

Mrs Tomlinson smiled. "Good! Let's go if you've finished. Come along, my chick."

They made their way out, and round to where a line of horses and cabs waited. One normally approached the front cab, and Elsie made to do so, but Mrs Tomlinson had other ideas. A particularly drab one was at the end of the line. Elsie would never have given it a second look, but the woman headed straight for it, and with her arm firmly through Elsie's, the girl had little choice but to follow.

"Where to, Missus?" the driver asked. Elsie looked up at him. He was shabby-looking, young, with a small moustache and a large mole on his nose. He wore a stovepipe hat.

"Yarmouth," she told him peremptorily.

The cabbie nodded. "Right y'are, ladies."

Elsie hesitated, then gathered her skirt and ascended to the cab, putting her small bag at her feet. Mrs Tomlinson joined her and settled back at her side. She turned to smile at the girl, but there was something strange in the smile that made Elsie uneasy.

The journey would take around two hours or so. Once in the cab, Mrs Tomlinson spoke little. Elsie, to fill the awkward silence, spoke of 'the love that awaited her in Yarmouth.'

"So, leaving his wife for you, eh!" Mrs Tomlinson gave her a sideways glance. She had already marked out this little minx for being no better than she should be, and that, after all, was all part of the fun! These kinds of girls deserved it. Spoiled gentry girls... who did they think they were? What gave them the right to behave with such disregard to those of the lower orders?

"And child!" she mocked.

Mrs Tomlinson's expression was almost feral.

Elsie had never taken a cab to Yarmouth in her life and wondered just how twisted the road was. But as time went on, the road became a lane, and the lane, a track, and a bumpy one at that. She looked at Mrs Tomlinson fearfully and banged on the ceiling of the cab.

"Stop!" she called out. "I want to get out!"

Mrs Tomlinson regarded her. "Don't worry! We're stopping shortly!"

"We aren't on the main road; this is a farm track!" Elsie stated, sudden fear making her heart thump at twice its normal speed. "Where are we?" Mrs Tomlinson did not speak at first, and merely stared into Elsie's face.

"Pretty little duck you are," she said, putting a dirty finger against the smooth cheek. "Hmm, we might keep you a while."

"Keep me? Whatever do you mean? Keep me?"

The cab stopped so suddenly, Elsie fell forward. "You'll see!" Mrs Tomlinson answered.

Suddenly realising she was in danger, Elsie shouted up to the driver, "Help!" She opened the door and stepped outside, grasping her bag to her chest. "Let me go!" she ordered. "You can't do this to me! Hey! You!" Elsie addressed the driver who had clambered down from his seat. "Why don't you help me?"

Elsie was pushed, roughly, up the dusty, stony path to a ramshackle cottage that was well hidden amongst the trees. She resisted and then, suddenly, breaking free, she pushed past the woman, heading back down the path toward the cab, her intention being to run; however, she got no further. The driver blocked her way. Suddenly, Elsie knew, she was trapped here. The driver picked her up easily, and flung her over his shoulder, laughing loudly.

"Where'd you want her, Ma?" he asked, grinning.

The woman cackled a laugh. "Inside, of course. Usual place!"

Elsie struggled, she kicked and screamed and battered the young man's back with small fists, but it was no good. He was young, strong, well-built and used to carrying struggling females. Elsie was whisked into the old house and set down. The door slammed and the key turned. The woman put the key in a pocket somewhere in her skirt.

"We're home!" she grinned at Elsie, who felt sheer panic. Her hands went to her mouth in horror. "Don't look so shocked; enjoy this, you will, at least till Fred here tires of you!"

September Term

The new term had begun, and I had fussed round Little Sam making sure he had the cleanest and nicest clothes we could afford. "Mamma!" he stated crossly as I fiddled with his hair on the first morning.

Roland called and grinned up at me. "Now, behave yourselves!" I told them, giving Little Sam his dinner money. "You're in class three now. Have a lovely day and we'll see you at teatime."

The boys in the form room sat on the desks and chattered about who would be teaching them that term. Mr Brook would not be missed. One boy, on watch, scooted to the front of the class. "It's the Old Boy," he exclaimed, "and you'll never guess who's with him!"

The boys rose as the Headmaster entered the classroom. "Good morning, boys! Welcome back for another year. You shall have plenty of hard work in you, I hope. I would like to introduce you to Miss Spoonamore. You know her, I am sure!"

Roland nudged Little Sam and made a 'sick' face. Little Sam smiled.

"Now, she will be teaching you five mornings per week. After that, she'll hand over to Corporal McIntyre, who'll take you five afternoons per week."

That piece of news was wonderful for the boys. There was a buzz of excited whispers and smiley faces. "Well, I'll leave you to it!" He turned and left.

Miss Spoonamore stood importantly behind the desk. Her eyes ranged over the young faces in front of her.

"Well! Good morning, boys. Do not get any ideas of playing me up simply because I'm female. I am hard as nails! Let me assure you!" She glared round the class, hoping she looked intimidating.

Neither Sam nor I could believe our ears when Little Sam and Roland beat a hasty path to our door after school.

"Miss Spoonamore? You joking, bor'?" Sam asked, but the boys shook their heads.

"No, Mr Dwyer!" Roland said, gleefully. "It *was* her. She's taking old Brook's place. Only the mornings though, and she won't dare wallop us, 'cos a woman teacher can't. Arternune's are with Mackie!" The pair stood, grinning widely.

Helen and I worked in the churchyard, or rather, she worked and I watched. It was my task to keep the lemonade, cakes and biscuits coming. Helen stood and wiped her brow. "I'm sweating cobs, lass! Ye'd never think so many weeds could come up at once."

"Let's have some lemonade," I suggested, and Helen nodded.

I nibbled a cake. "What do you think happened to Elsie then?"

Helen sucked in her breath. "Och, God knows, Alice. What was the last piece of news?"

"Mrs Elgin wrote that she'd gone walking in the square, and that was it!" I told her. "Perhaps she's run off."

"Young ladies like her dinnae tend to run off," Helen mused. "They've no clue how to look after themselves; ye know how they are, expecting to be spoon-fed."

Elsie's terrified mother had reported her absence to the police and a search was underway. A photograph had been printed and copied and distributed all over Norwich, as well as in the newspaper. It had been almost three weeks since her vanishing and, as every day passed, finding her seemed more and more unlikely. A sighting had been reported at the train station in Norwich, but nothing more. If she had gone to the station, it was likely she was no longer in the city.

Four days later, tragedy had struck. Sam and I had been horrified to hear Elspeth had died. The Reverend had sent us a message to 'come with all speed'.

Whilst playing on Priory Plain, Elspeth had chased a ball right into the path of an oncoming coach and had died instantly under its wheels.

"It was quick, Helen," I told her, unable to think what else to say. "She died at once. She can't have known anything about it."

Helen nodded. "Aye, I know that. Ye ought not to have come; 'tis too sad for an expectant lass."

"What? You're my sister!" I told her. "I know what you're feeling."

Dawn might've been stillborn, but Elspeth had been active and healthy and had been sure to grow up. My mind went back to Helen's reading ten years before. Three children, possibly four. Well, she had only two now.

During her mourning, Gus proved invaluable. He and I understood exactly what Helen was going through, having suffered just the same, and all three of us became closer.

Late September

We had only just recovered from Elspeth's untimely death when I got another shock. Little Sam brought home a note from the Headmaster which he handed to me. I glanced and bit my lip. "Sam! Come and see this!"

Sam came to me and, like me, his face paled. The note, to all the parents, told them of an outbreak of scarlet fever at the school.

"Does that mean I can't go to school? Roland said it does!"

"Yes, for the time being, Mamma will teach you, like she used to, alright? I'll teach you reckoning. Meanwhile, I'd best go and speak to Corporal McIntyre, so we know what we're doing."

The last thing Sam wanted was for me to contract this disease being seven months pregnant. I felt sick and edgy as Sam made his way to the school to speak to his form master.

Miss Spoonamore, of course, was most practical about it... even blasé. "It won't spread that badly," she stated in the staff room. Corporal McIntyre was by the window getting fresh air since he did not wish a dose of the scarlet fever which he had had as a youngster.

"You cannot be sure of that, Miss Spoonamore." The young man felt vulnerable being alone with this woman. He hoped someone else would enter the staff room shortly. "I think Headmaster should close the school; he was thinking about it."

"Nonsense! It'll never happen!" Miss Spoonamore stated, assuredly sidling up to the young man. "Still, if *you* became ill, I would help you, should you need it."

Corporal McIntyre decided he would rather take his chances alone. Being nursed by Miss Spoonamore was something he wished to avoid, at all costs.

"Mrs Rix came round whilst you were out," I told Sam. "She's doing the same. She's just found out she's got another bun in the oven too!"

Sam rolled his eyes. "Again! Alright, well, I suppose it's up to her husband to collect any work. Now, young Sam. You do as you are told. Work steadily through this book and if you need help, ask me or Mamma."

Three days later, in the evening, Sam was tired and said his head ached.

I was alarmed; Sam was never ill. "Don't worry!" he told me, reading my mind. "I've been doing a lot of close work today. Maybe the time's come to wear spectacles."

Next morning, I felt I had not slept at all. I looked at Sam and felt fear. His face was red and rashy. He was burning hot, and the skin felt strangely rough. "Alice, I don't feel at all well," he rasped.

I observed, with a sinking feeling, a whitish coating over his tongue. "Sam, you must have scarlet fever," I said softly.

He shook his head.

"Sam! Listen to me. You *do* have it. I know the symptoms; it's at Little Sam's school. Now, lie still. I'll fetch you willow bark extract."

Sam lay back on the pillow, his head pounding.

Now I had a dilemma. I didn't want Little Sam sickening, and being seven months pregnant, I was extremely vulnerable. I forced myself to think clearly as I made up the willow bark. Calamine lotion for his sore and itchy skin. Cool water to drink. What else? I bit my lip.

Little Sam entered the kitchen. "Mamma! I'm hungry!" he told me. He seemed to be alright, for now at least.

"Sam, listen to me. I want you to wash and dress yourself. After that, go to Grandpapa's house. Your father isn't well this morning, darling, so I need to look after him."

Little Sam's face was confused. "Why?"

"Because sometimes people get ill," I answered.

"I want to see Papa," the little voice squeaked.

"He's sleeping. He's a bad cold and needs rest. Now, be a good boy and do as I ask."

I hastened up to Sam. "Here." I helped him to sit up against the pillow. Sam sipped the concoction. "Sorry, I know it's not very nice."

Sam merely grunted.

"I'll send Little Sam to your father," I told him quietly. "Tell him to occupy him for a while. I can't have you both in the same house, but I don't want to risk your father getting sick either." I looked at him. Sam shut his eyes.

"Papa?" Little Sam stuck his head round the door.

"Sam! What did I tell you? Do you go to Grandpapa's and tell him your father is unwell and to look after you a bit."

"What about my breakfast?"

"Grandpapa will give it to you," I told him. I scribbled a quick note and put it in an envelope. "Now, give Grandpapa this the moment you get in the house," I told him. Little Sam looked up at me. There was an urgency in my voice that he had seldom heard before.

"Alright." He frowned. "Will Papa be alright later?"

"I expect so; now go on. The sooner you leave, the sooner I can help Papa."

Sam's father was much alarmed, but he covered it well. As he made them breakfast, Little Sam told his grandfather of the fact he couldn't see Sam.

"Mamma said I couldn't. That isn't fair, is it?"

"Well, she needs to look after him, and help him get better, so it is really."

Little Sam considered, then reluctantly, he nodded.

"So, do you stay and keep your old grandpapa company, eh? We'll go to the beach later if you like."

Little Sam nodded, unaware of the whirling of his grandsire's mind at that moment.

"Now, don't worry; eat your breakfast. Just let me write a few notes!"

"Everybody's writing notes today!"

Mr Dwyer despatched two notes, one to Maria and one to Helen. He wanted to see how Sam was but would need to rely on my sending messages.

Gus, hearing of our situation, at once marched round to our home. "You send me a note if you want anything, mawther, and I'll do it at once!" he told me firmly. "Sam'll be fine. I had that too. He'll be pretty sick a day or so, but he's strong, and he'll get better."

I smiled at Gus. "Thank you, I'll send if I need you. I.." I paused, and a tear came. Gus looked at me, his head on one side. "I don't know," I told him despondently. Gus hugged me.

"Don't forget the little 'un there!" He indicated my belly. "We're here for you."

I felt grateful as I closed the front door.

I sat at Sam's side. He was burning with fever. His throat was raw. "It's alright, darling," I said soothingly. "I'll take care of you."

Sam shut his eyes. His head thundered; the willow bark had begun to wear off.

"Drink," he said and I supported his head so that he could take some sips. He lay back, exhausted. I looked at the man I loved. The rash on his face seemed to have spread to become one red rash rather than small spots. His tongue looked like a strawberry. I stroked his head, his hair.

With Sam sleeping, I took my little book to look over to see if I had missed anything. I fed Bundles, set some water to warm, then rummaged in the scullery. Taking out carbolic soap solution, I poured it into a bucket and then immersed a sheet. When it was ready, I sent it through the mangle and hastened back upstairs. I hung it up haphazardly, planning to ask the next person who called if they could hang it properly. Once I had done that, I felt better. Checking Sam again, I went to prepare some soup, wondering if he would, or could, take any, when I heard a knock at the door.

Albert smiled at me. "Keep away, Abe!" I said worriedly, peering from behind the door.

"It's alright, I know. Maria sent me. Simon said something about speaking to Helen, so I think between them they are sorting something out."

"That's one thing off my mind," I said.

Albert nodded. "Well, don't worry, Alice. Maria says give me a list. She and Milly will sort it all."

"Thanks; some more carbolic soap, if you please, and some bread – I don't feel like eating."

"Well, you must!" Albert regarded my belly.

"I know, and I will, but I don't feel like it. I'll settle up later." I hastily scribbled a small list. "Thanks, Abe; thank Maria and Milly for me. I must get back to Sam now."

Albert nodded, tipped his hat and left and I returned to the bedroom.

Sam tossed and turned when his fever rose. I watched, wondering what I could do to relieve the symptoms, other than what I was doing. It broke my heart to see him so. He and our son were my life.

Night fell and I lit the candles and oil lamps as I sat beside Sam, cooling him with water, over his face, his forehead, neck and chest. I washed his hands lightly too. "I love you, Sam," I told him. "I'll get you better. I'm here to look after you and I shall."

Sam groaned. "Alice." His voice didn't even sound like his own. Pretty soon, his mind started to wander. I stroked his forehead and hair. His hair was sweat-soaked, tangled. I would wash it for him when the fever left him. I looked out of the window. The moon shone into our bedroom. Were there ever such long hours? I wondered. The clock showed just after two in the morning. The candles I replenished, but the smell of the carbolic from the sheet was nauseating. I said my own prayers and sat doggedly on. I put some cooling cream on his face, neck and chest. It would sooth the itching and cool at the same time.

He poured sweat and it was all I could do to keep cooling him off. He seemed to smell of illness. His usually sweet breath was rank.

"Alice?" he spoke again. His eyes suddenly opened. "Where are you?"

"I'm right beside you," I told him gently.

"Don't go!" he told me, swallowing painfully.

"I won't go!"

Throughout the night, I tended Sam. I would need to change the bedding; it was sweat-soaked. Deciding it would be sensible to leave it until morning, I continued talking to him, bathing his face, giving small drinks whenever I could. I glanced at my stomach. "Hang in there, Bump!" I whispered. "I'm making your papa better so he can be proud of you when you come out."

Morning came at last, with a warm sun, and I was beyond tired. Sam seemed to sleep easier, but he was still hot. His throat, when I looked, was red raw. I would never get any food into him. I still had to make him drink liquids, somehow. This could, I knew, last for up to a week. I had done just two days and already was exhausted. A knock came at the door and I hastened to open it.

Corporal McIntyre stood outside. "Hello!" I said, surprised. "I am afraid, if you want Little Sam, he's at Saint Nicholas' due to the outbreak."

"I know, I heard. Might I come in?"

"What? No! Sam's infectious!"

"I've had it, and I'd like to help you," he told me. At a loss what to say, I admitted him.

"Just because you've had this once doesn't mean you can't catch it again."

"I know, but I'm a tough old soldier. Takes a lot to knock me off my feet! What help do you need, Mrs Dwyer? I can relay the fire, heat up water, do anything."

"Well, I need help with Sam, actually," I answered leading him up the stairs and wondering if I was doing the right thing. "I want to change him, his bed. Could you help me support him, do you think?"

We entered the room. Sam was still feverish, but he appeared to be slightly less so. He was certainly fighting the disease.

Corporal McIntyre assisted me, taking Sam's full weight, rolling him to one side, right to the edge of the bed, supporting Sam against his own body, his arm around him, so I could change his bedding and nightgown.

"Ah, that's better," I said, as he assisted me to lay him down again.

Corporal McIntyre helped me to hang the carbolic sheet more securely. I was surprised at his dexterity with only one arm. He grinned at me. "I'm not totally useless!" he told me.

"Goodness, Corporal! I think you're a massive help!" I replied.

"Call me Mackie – everyone else does!"

After Mackie had left, I opened the door to Tabitha. She held a bag of oranges. "I'll squeeze these for you. It'll do Sam good," she stated as I let her in, a little reluctantly. "Don't worry, I shan't get too close; I'm pretty hard to kill! But these will be good for him. I realise he won't be eating, but he must drink."

"Thanks, Tab."

"You look terrible!"

"Hmm, and it's only just the start of it," I said dismally.

"I dropped by Maria's," Tabitha added. "Here's your bag of tricks."

I was profoundly grateful as I accepted the bag. Inside were candles, more carbolic, all that I needed.

"And fish! Only the best silver darlings for puss!"

Already, Bundles, having smelt the fish, was nosing the bag.

Gus chose that moment to show up. He tipped his hat to Tabitha. "Arternune!" he told her and looked at me. "Sack of coal for you 'ere, mawther."

"A whole sack?"

"Yes, where'd you like it?"

"In the yard, please, for now." I watched as he walked through the house. I wondered where he'd got all that from, deciding it was better not to know!

Gus glanced at Tabitha. "Shall I escort you 'ome, mawther?" he asked cheekily.

"No, thank you!" Tabitha returned frostily. "And it's Miss Bostock to you!"

I thanked Gus and watched as he stalked away, then looked at Tabitha.

"I'd best be off," she said quietly.

Everyone was worried for Sam; his father, unable to stay away, came to the house.

"I had to," he told me when I scolded him mildly. "I'll be alright. It's not as if I wasn't around when they were children and were ill. I can't help worrying about my boy, for all he's the finest nurse in Yarmouth."

"Alright then; but not too close," I said. "Put your handkerchief over your nose."

Simon came up to the bedroom. He pulled a face at the sheet. "Ugh, I remember these stinking things," he told me.

I let him take over for a short time on the promise he would wake me if anything changed, and I fell asleep the instant I shut my eyes.

I slept for several hours. On waking, I rose to go to him. "Still not with it," Simon told me as I heard the feverish mutterings. "But he's fighting alright."

Sam grew very hot during the late afternoon and evening, and I was terrified. I had no way of measuring his temperature, but I could guess it was well over 100. I knew now, he was having the chill phase. Why was it called a chill when he was burning up? I wondered. I chewed my lip. "Sam!" I spoke to him. "You can fight this. Get better, darling. I need you; we all need you."

Sam seemed agitated and he rolled and kicked at the bedclothes. Just as I was thinking I might have to send a message to the doctor, Sam relaxed. He gave a lengthy exhalation, then, with an effort, opened his eyes. The sweat had cooled. He glanced round at me weakly.

"Alice?" he whispered.

"Papa!" I bellowed down the stairs, and Simon came up as fast as he could. "His fever's broken! He's come through the crisis," I said and burst out sobbing.

"Come on, mawther, no time for that now!" Mr Dwyer told me. "Sam! My boy!" Sam held out a hand to me, which I took at once.

Now that Sam was no longer infectious, I sent word to Helen. Little Sam, on hearing he could at last come home, thanked Helen nicely, shook hands with everyone, walked sedately to the churchyard gates, then ran at top speed to our row and charged upstairs.

"Papa!" he screeched and leapt on the bed full of excitement.

"Whoa! Steady there, bor'!" Sam smiled as our son flung his arms round Sam's neck.

"Papa. Are you well now? Truly?" He looked at his father, critically. Sam nodded.

"I am, bor', I am. Oof! You're squashing me. You've gained some weight whilst you've been away, and I swear you're taller!"

Little Sam smiled and hugged his father again. I watched. It was such a sweet sight.

Little Sam was happy to sit with his father, amusing him with stories, doing puzzles with him, and running for things I needed. Sam was weak at first and easily tired, but he soon recovered. The fever had taken a lot of flesh from him, and I began feeding him up with suet puddings and creamy rice pudding.

Mackie arrived with a meat pie. "I got this from Bill's," he said. "He heard about Sam and sent it with his blessings."

"I'm getting hungrier by the day," Sam stated. The door opened and a voice called out.

"Hello? Can I come up?" It was Tabitha.

The second Tabitha laid eyes on Mackie, she felt a jolt. She gathered herself quickly. "Alice, Samuel, I made this." She showed me a bowl containing soup.

"Thank you, Tab. Smells good!"

Mackie glanced in her direction.

"Good afternoon, miss." He greeted her formally, with a nod.

"This is my dear friend, Tabitha Bostock," I told him. The man smiled and shook hands politely. Tabitha could only gaze at him.

Late OCTOBER 1854

October, and my favourite month. I loved autumn, with misty mornings; the first frost. Sam was now completely well and back at his work.

Elsie was still missing. I had been uncomfortable at the fact a constable had come to make enquiries.

"How should I know?" I had snapped at him. "My husband has only just recovered from scarlet fever and I'm eight months pregnant and worn out!"

Sam had cringed at the way I had spoken to him, but the constable had merely glanced at my belly and nodded.

"You misunderstand me, goodwife," he stated. "I'm merely enquiring if you've heard anything, since you know the family."

I had shrugged wearily. "We heard from Mrs Elgin that she was missing, and then saw the article in the paper. Other than that, you know as much as I do!"

"Of course, I didn't mean to distress you, my apologies, but if you should hear anything, do you come and tell us."

"Of course, I shall."

Sam spoke. "Does nobody have any idea where she's gone?"

The constable shook his head. "No. There were mutterings of someone resembling her at Norwich station, with some woman, but nothing more."

Since their first meeting, Tabitha had fallen hopelessly in love with Mackie. Mackie clearly did not return the feelings, and poor Gus, he had fallen hard for Tabitha.

"It's a problem!" Sam stated as we watched some children chasing a dog round, scattering sticks and leaves. "Gus adores her, but she just gets annoyed with him."

I sighed. "We'd best wait and see how things turn out. I daren't interfere!"

One damp, misty morning, and there was a hammering on our front door. I opened it to a furious Helen, who marched in, tearful and red-faced, and sat at the kitchen table so heavily I wondered the chair didn't break. She was ranting in a fury about Manoa.

"He's an idiot!" she bawled. "Stupid, stupid man! I wish I'd never set eyes on him!"

"Helen. Whatever's happened?"

I had been prepared for anything, from being caught with another woman, to a slapped face, but I did not expect to hear what she spluttered at me.

"He's joined the lifeboat crew!" she told me, sniffing and wiping her eyes.

"Is *that* what's upset you?"

The lifeboat was invaluable to a town where so many worked on the sea for their livelihoods. Volunteers were expected to be able to row, fast and furious. Manoa's arms were huge; he was ideal.

"What do ye mean? To endanger himself each time some person gets themselves in trouble?"

"Helen, don't get in a state," I told her. "You should be proud of Manoa!"

"Well, I'm not! I could strangle him wi' my bare hands! And after losing our wee Elspeth too. Does he want me to be a widow?"

"Helen, calm down." I presented her with some tea. "Manoa knows what he's doing. He's spent his life on board ship! I expect he meant it as a surprise for you, make you proud."

Helen sniffed and wiped her eyes.

"Not when they carry his lifeless body back home. Plus, we'll no' be permitted rest at night now. Soon as trouble's spotted, we'll have the watch pounding on the door and he'll be off."

I looked helplessly at Sam.

"Where's Manoa now?"

"I don't know, nor care!" she spat. "I thought ye'd understand! I'm going!" She left, slamming the door.

"She's out of her mind with worry," Sam said, putting an arm round me, and drawing me close.

Sam found Manoa on the jetty, assisting the unloading of a ship, and was speaking to him casually. Manoa had been disappointed with Helen's response. He told Sam about the practice run they planned that afternoon and had hoped Helen would watch. Sam promised to try to persuade her.

Later that afternoon, Sam had asked me about watching the lifeboat drill. "That would be fun!" I replied. "Come on, let's get the boys; they won't want to miss that!"

"What about Helen?" Sam asked when we were outside Saint Nicholas'.

I made my way to the kitchen where Helen sat alone, drumming her fingers on the table.

"Hello, grumpy!" I said to her as I lumbered in. "Come with us. We are going to see Manoa having a lifeboat drill!"

Helen looked at me, miserably.

"Come on, girl, this isn't like you! Just watch, eh? Manoa told Sam he was really disappointed with your reaction. He wanted to make you so proud of him!"

Helen got up. "Alright, I'll come."

Gus looked up, hopeful. "Yes, you too!" I told him, grinning. "The sun's coming out; it'll be nice."

The six of us journeyed to the lifeboat station. Manoa was already there, wearing his hat and holding his cork vest.

"Helen?" Manoa asked uncertainly. Helen stepped up to him, then hugged him.

"Go on then. Show me what it's all about."

Manoa smiled.

Tabitha was impressed on hearing of Manoa's volunteering. "It's wonderful that people put their own lives at risk to save others," she told me as we sat by the fire. "My folks are out there most days. When they heard there was a lifeboat starting up, they couldn't have been more relieved. Helen should be so proud."

I saw Gus march past our house; he grinned and waved.

"Gus is dewy-eyed over you!" I said to her, and Tabitha looked stunned.

"That rogue? I may dream of marrying and having children, Alice, but I'm not desperate!"

"Don't you like him then?" I asked, wondering how anybody could not like Gus.

"No!" Tabitha seemed insulted.

"He's not *that* bad!" I told her. "He's had a hard life!"

"Huh! Haven't we all!"

"But you haven't seen the way he looks at you! I reckon if you'd only give him a chance, you'd click at once."

"Thanks!" she said, sarcastically.

I shook my head and gave Tabitha the story of Gus' life. She seemed to thaw a little, but she shook her head. "Well, alright, I feel for him, but he's fiftyish, I should think!"

"Fifty on Thursday, actually," I told her, nibbling some cheese which I had cut wafer thin, the way I liked it. "We're having a birthday party for him. Fancy coming?"

Tabitha glowered as if I had grossly insulted her.

"Excuse me!" she snapped. I watched as she flounced off. Sam glanced across as she stalked out. His raised eyebrows questioned me, so I went over and told him what had happened. Sam shrugged.

"Her loss!" he told me. "Gus is a good fellow. We trust him with our firstborn. Can't think of any better recommendation than that, can you?"

I shook my head.

Tabitha had long since resigned herself to the life of a spinster. She was offended that I had seemed to think she and Gus would be good together. He was a scruffy individual who shaved once per week, if he remembered. He looked a mess in the battered old hat and coat. His clothes were ironed now, thanks to Helen, but otherwise, he wouldn't have bothered.

She wandered along the sea front. It was a cold, blustery day. She spotted Gus stomping along on the other side of the road and glanced, her lip curling in distaste. She thought he was probably drunk, having come from one of the many ale houses. This thought was suddenly swept aside, however, when she saw an elderly man, who had been walking in front of Gus with some degree of infirmity, drop his wallet on the floor, having fished a handkerchief out of his pocket.

Gus glanced, then swooped to retrieve it. Tabitha's lips set hard, and a frown came to her face. She checked for traffic and was half-way across the road to berate him for stealing it when she stopped in her tracks.

Gus had tapped the man on the shoulder, and he had turned and looked at him with some trepidation. Gus had then handed the man his wallet and smiled, the two exchanged words, then there was a handshake. Gus spoke further to the elderly man, who, after a moment or two, nodded and allowed him to escort him up a row. Tabitha was thunderstruck.

"Hey! You! Get outta the road unless you want trampling!"

Tabitha realised she was standing right in the way of the horses and cabs and made her way swiftly to the pavement.

She followed the pair up the row, still not quite convinced that Gus wouldn't rob him, but she watched as the elderly man beamed, and made his tottering way to his house. Gus smiled and turned to go back the way they had come.

Tabitha stepped in front of Gus.

"Miss Bostock!" Gus said awkwardly, raising his hat. "Such a fierce look. What've I done now then?"

Tabitha realised she was still looking cross. She then surprised him by reaching out and taking his hand, which she squeezed, smiling and then walking away, leaving him stunned.

Gus' birthday arrived. Helen told Manoa to take him out of the way for the afternoon so that she could arrange a surprise tea. I had gone along to help, but Sam had made me just sit and observe. "So much for helping!" I said. "I am capable, you know!" But Sam wouldn't hear of it.

"You've done enough already," he told me.

Helen chuckled. "Aye, lass, he's right. Look at the size of ye! I've some yellow cloths here; will ye make up some of yer funny chickens? He'll like that! You can help with the birthday greeting sign too."

"Who's coming?" Sam asked as I sat down to fold the napkins into chicken shapes.

"Tab, and Mackie," Helen answered, wielding a rolling pin perilously close to Sam's head. "I think she's over him now; she was in love with him, but she realises 'tis no good."

"She hasn't spoken to me since I told her she and Gus would make a good couple," I admitted. "I think they'd be good. Don't you, Helen? Gus thinks she's wonderful."

Helen pondered. "Aye, mebbe," she told me. "For all he's a rogue at times, he's a heart of gold."

There were gifts wrapped for him which we had put by his plate where he would sit at the head of the long table in the warm kitchen. Everything was ready.

"How much longer are they going to be?" I looked at the kitchen clock. It was nearing four o'clock. Almost dark.

"Anytime now!" Helen replied. "Ah, I hear footsteps!"

Everyone waited quietly, then, as the kitchen door opened, called out 'surprise!' and into the kitchen stepped Tabitha.

"Thanks, I'm sure!" she said smiling. "But I thought it was Gus' party!"

"Tab! You came!" I was thrilled to see her. I reached out to pull her to sit next to me.

"I did," she told me. "I even have a gift for the old devil too. Now, you'd best be ready. I saw him and Manoa, and they'll be here in two shakes of a lamb's tail." She looked at me. "Sorry, Alice, I didn't mean to snap your head off. I know you only want the best for me."

Helen swooped. "Alright, but I think you'd better sit alongside him! Pardon me, Alice!" Helen pulled Tabitha from her stool, ignoring her squawk of surprise, and deposited her at the side of the birthday guest's chair. I smiled, seeing that she had put the two together intentionally.

Gus entered the kitchen at that moment, and once more, we all chorused "Surprise! Happy birthday!"

Gus stopped and gaped. He couldn't remember the last time he had marked his birthday, even to himself, and to have everyone here with a surprise party for him was beyond belief. He grinned as he looked around. "I wasn't expecting this!" he said, as Manoa urged him to the seat at the head of the table, and he spied the presents next to his plate. Even better, Tabitha sat next to him, and better still, she was smiling.

The party was enjoyable and cosy in the warm kitchen. Gus opened his gifts and was thrilled with the variety of presents. He was grateful, and even a little tearful. He bellowed with laugher at the chickens made from napkins. I had to show him how it was done, and Gus copied me to make one too, the curious party trick amusing him no end.

Gus had been moved to tears by the friendship that he had been shown. He had suddenly looked at Tabitha with such gentleness, that she realised that she was, indeed, quite in love with him. The sudden realisation surprised her. Gus was older, he wasn't the snappiest dresser, nor was he the least bit handsome; but she had been watching him. The elderly man who had lost his wallet... he could have picked up and put it in his own pocket, but he hadn't. Gus was kind and honest. That, she decided, was more important than looks. But, that look, just now. Suddenly, she was sure. To his delight, she returned the look and smiled.

Elsie's whereabouts remained a mystery. I still half expected her to turn up on the doorstep. It would be just like her, I decided, the last thing I wanted whilst heavily pregnant. Mrs Elgin had come for a visit and was staying at Saint Nicholas'. She told us that Elsie had not been seen since the morning of her vanishing, and had been missing for two months, despite searches. Mrs Elgin shook her head in despair. For all the girl was wayward, she was her granddaughter.

"Do you know, I've half a mind to live back here!"

Mrs Elgin had come to our home. She sat at the fireside with Little Sam.

"Yes!" he squeaked. "Come back, then we can visit you every day!"

Mrs Elgin smiled at him.

"Really? What, give up all that comfort?" I wondered aloud.

"Yes! Comfortable it may be, but there's a very strained atmosphere in the house now. Still, I suppose it's to be expected."

Mrs Elgin sighed. "I wonder all the time where Elsie is," she stated. "It's a real mystery. I begin to think that she is, well..." she left the word unsaid. I had thought that from the start.

Mrs Elgin looked at my stomach. "Soon then, Alice!" she said with a smile.

"Yes, end of the month, hopefully. I'll be relieved. My back aches so much."

Mrs Elgin nodded with understanding.

My labour pains began very early on the morning of 21st November. I could scarcely believe it. What were the chances of giving birth on the same day exactly nine years on? Helen, Maria and the midwife attended me. Sam stayed at my side, despite objections from the midwife and her daughters.

"He's my *husband*! He put this baby in me so he can be there when it's born! I don't care what anyone thinks!"

Little Sam looked unsure – it was his ninth birthday and normally he would be being fussed over. We had organised a birthday tea with Roland, but now he wondered what was going to happen about that.

Mr Dwyer patted his grandson's shoulder. "Come on! We'll celebrate when we return. Mamma needs your papa there; we'll go out for the day. What would you like to do, bor'? Do you tell me what treat you want, and you'll have it. Your papa told me you're to choose the new one's name too. Let's hear what you got in mind."

Early evening and our second son had arrived.

"Lass! He could be Sammy's twin!" Helen was ecstatic. The newest member of the Dwyer family had been bathed and fed, and warmly wrapped up.

I smiled, sore and tired now, but with a feeling of relief.

"What will you call him?" Maria smiled as Sam held his second son.

"It's up to Little Sam to name him!" I told her.

Maria beamed. "Come on, brother! I want a go on him now!"

Sam handed his second son to his youngest sister. She rocked him gently. "Aren't you the beautiful one?" she cooed.

Helen took him next and beamed. "Fat cheeks!" she said. "I love fat cheeks on a bairn."

"I love their fat little starfish hands with dimples best," I said. "Especially when they grab your finger!"

Little Sam and his grandfather came home with Roland. I lay in bed, warm and clean. "Come and see him!" I said to our firstborn. "He's asleep at the moment." Little Sam sat on the bed. He looked uneasily at his father, still unsure about the new arrival. "Would you like to hold him?" I asked.

Little Sam thought. "Alright, but I don't want him to wee on me!"

I spluttered with laughter.

"He won't, he's a nappy on. Now, very carefully. He's quite heavy. You need to hold him like this. Don't let his head fall back."

So, Little Sam took charge of his baby brother. At once, the baby opened his eyes. He looked at Little Sam with great interest, it seemed. Little Sam smiled. "He's looking at me!" he said, entranced.

"Of course! He's thinking, gosh, is that my older brother? I've a lot to live up to!"

Sam smiled. "So then, young man, what's his name to be?" Sam and his grandfather had discussed names on their day out.

"Kit. I want him called Kit!" Little Sam said.

"Oh, what a delightful name!" I was thrilled with our son's choice. "Kit? That's lovely! Clever boy!"

Our eldest son grinned broadly. He was very proud to have been asked to choose a name. Names, after all, stuck with you forever. Roland looked at him.

"He's bigger than my brothers were," he told us.

"Yes, do you know how much he weighs, Samuel?"

"About nine pounds from the feel of him," Sam answered.

The party for Little Sam went ahead as planned. There was no way I would deprive him of it.

Kit was baptised on the same day as his father and brother had been. Miss Spoonamore, who had been wandering through the churchyard, looked in disapproval as we brought young Kit to his baptism. "Another Dwyer brat!" she hissed to herself. "Hmm, I wonder, I could put it about that the child is not Samuel's... that would teach her!" She watched as we entered the church and sneered.

We had a small party back at home, just our immediate family and very close friends. Mackie was invited of course, and Miss Spoonamore, seeing him come out of the church, had immediately accosted him, asking if he cared to take tea with her.

"I'm attending Kit's celebration at their home," he replied, a little shortly. Miss Spoonamore fixed him with a furious stare.

"Ah, I see, well, it is only natural that you would wish to be there, after all, he is *your* son!"

Mackie was left open-mouthed with shock as she marched off. His son? Where had she got that idea from?

CHAPTER EIGHT

Maria, Helen, Tabitha and I were in the marketplace when we heard a commotion. A group had gathered and shocked, raised voices could be heard. "Has someone sent for a constable?" I heard one woman shout in horror.

"What's all that about?" Tabitha wondered. We ventured to the edge of the cobbles where the market ended, opposite Saint Nicholas'.

"I'll go and see!" Helen rushed towards the gathering crowd. As she learned of what had been found, her expression turned to shock. We ventured to the gathering of people.

"There's a body been washed up along the tideline! Two wee laddies found her. 'Tis awful!"

We all looked at one another, totally shocked.

"Drowned?" I asked as we made our way hurriedly to the beach.

"No, lass. 'Tis worse than that. 'Tis murder been done! The constables have been summoned. They say 'tis a young lassie." Helen paused. "She was found with her throat cut!"

We continued over the denes and onto the sand. There were several policemen carrying the body, now wrapped in a blanket, up the beach. We stood, watching, shivering in the cold north-easterly wind, the small crowd trailing back up the beach after them chattering excitedly. Helen hastened across to one woman.

"You saw her?" she asked, and the older woman nodded, crossing herself.

"I did! Poor little mawther. No clothes. Dunno how long she been in the water. Quite some time from the look of 'er. All bloated up, skin all purple, no eyes, and..."

"Thank you! We don't need any more information!" Maria told her, feeling sick.

Later that day, I informed Sam about the body. He made a face. "Poor thing," he stated. I picked Kit out of his playpen, and he bellowed in my ear.

"What? You want to go back in?" I asked.

"He needs a change," Sam informed me.

I grinned. "I know, I can smell it. Nothing to stop you from doing it you know!"

Sam pulled an exaggerated face of distaste, making me laugh, as I went to clean and change Kit.

The weather was freezing. We had over a week of hard ice, and I had to be careful walking outside. I slipped and earned myself a big bruise. I dreaded the sound of the knocker-upper tapping on our window with his jovial cry of, "Wakey-wakey! Rise and shine, my booties!"

I would groan, cling to Sam and snuggle into him. He would mumble something about getting up and I would brave reaching out from under the warm blanket and eiderdown to strike a match and light my candle. It took a lot of effort to slide out of bed, wrap myself in my thick shawl, put on the fur-lined slippers and then go to Sam's side of the bed, light his candle and go downstairs to light the fires and oil lamps and start the water heating for our washes. At least my family came down to a warm kitchen and warm room whilst someone, usually Sam, would mind the breakfast as I hastened to wash and dress, then do breakfast for everybody.

Nearing Christmas, the school would hold a concert. "What will you do?" Sam asked our son.

Little Sam stood, thoughtfully. "I don't know. I don't think I'd like to be in front of an audience."

"Well, what's Roland going to do?" I asked. I was feeding Kit and Little Sam watched as his brother took his milk.

"Play the penny whistle. He's good at it."

"Well, what about a step dance?" I asked him. "I can teach you. I used to do that at your age."

Little Sam nodded.

"And I've an even better idea," Sam said. "What if you dance along to Roland's tune?"

Little Sam's face was bright with enthusiasm.

Roland liked to play a traditional English folk song called 'Portsmouth.' I had seen this done in music halls with the dancers all dressed as sailors.

Rehearsals began and Little Sam enjoyed the step dancing very much. I sewed little sailor costumes for them both. I enjoyed helping at rehearsals. Mackie oversaw them, and as soon as Miss Spoonamore found that out, she elbowed her way in.

I persuaded Helen to help, and we were put in charge of refreshments. Mackie looked at me with wistful eyes, and Miss Spoonamore, on seeing this, simmered with anger.

At the market the following day, Maria revealed their Christmas plans.

"We'll have Father for Christmas dinner," she told me.

"I hope he tastes nice then," I stated, "though he might be a bit tough at his age!"

Maria laughed.

"You know what I mean! Will you visit us though?"

"Of course! When do you want us?"

"You're welcome any time, you know that."

"Hellooo!"

We turned to find Helen, arms round several boxes. "Mind if I join ye? I hoped ye'd be here. Hello, Kit! Ye get handsomer every day!" She smiled;

"I'm glad I met ye both. I've news for you!" We waited, anticipating what she had to say.

"I'm expecting again," Helen said, beaming from ear to ear. "Midwife reckons, 'bout three months she said."

"Oh, Helen, that's marvellous!" I exclaimed. "Does Manoa know yet?"

Helen shook her head.

"What wonderful news." I was pleased; this would help her recover somewhat from Elspeth's death.

Mid-week, we received shocking news. The girl who had drowned had eventually been identified as Elsie. It was estimated she had been in the water for some considerable time. She had vanished in August and had been seen by several people in Norwich speaking to a woman and getting into a cab driven by a younger man with a moustache, a large mole on his nose, and a stovepipe hat. A search for the people was underway.

We read the story in the paper over dinner that evening, and at once sent our condolences to the family, particularly Mrs Elgin.

The evening for the dress rehearsal came and we made our way to the school.

The boys hopped alongside. Snow was falling thicker now, and already, a covering lay on the cobbles. The wind was so icy, my cheeks felt hot. I blew on my finger ends too, grateful I had on stout boots and thick, woollen black stockings. The gaslights hissed and glowed eerily against the dusk, and snowflakes whirled around them. Horses wore sacking boots now. If it got much worse, the cabs would be off the street.

The school was warm and welcoming for the many attending the dress rehearsal. The first person I saw was Mackie. He smiled at me, and his cheeks flushed.

Little Sam and Roland hastened toward him. "Mackie!" they bellowed.

"Ah, boys! Welcome! I'm looking forward to seeing your dress rehearsal! Good evening, Alice."

"Good evening, Mackie. It's bitter out."

"I'll take you to get some mulled wine," he told me. "I'm afraid The Spoonamore is in charge of it though."

"I'll risk it," I said, chuckling.

"Boys! Wait a moment!" Mackie called. "Go to your form rooms and change into your costumes. Then come back here, no messing about. It's a serious rehearsal. Tomorrow night, you'll be doing it for real."

We watched them scamper off to change and I went with Mackie to Miss Spoonamore who stood, looking most formidable, behind the table on which stood pots of mulled wine.

"Miss Spoonamore, would you be good enough to give Alice, I mean, Mrs Dwyer, a glass of your finest mulled wine?" he asked.

Miss Spoonamore's eyes narrowed. She had not missed the use of my first name and was tempted to sling the lot over me. She put some into a small tankard.

"Is your *husband* not here?" she asked meaningfully.

"No, he's work to finish," I replied.

"And is Corporal McIntyre your escort?" she asked, with a hint of sarcasm.

"Of course, he is!" I replied cheekily, and Miss Spoonamore shot him a look, full of venom. Mackie paled considerably.

"That is wholly inappropriate!" she bit out at him.

"Nonsense," I told her briskly. "What's inappropriate about it?"

"You of all people should know the answer to that!" Miss Spoonamore answered spitefully.

"Oh, really? Why?" I asked.

"You know why!" Miss Spoonamore snapped. She looked at Mackie. "You'd be well advised to steer clear of *her*," she stated. "She is loose-moralled."

I laughed at her.

"Take no notice, Mackie. I'm most grateful to you, particularly for your assistance home." I shot Miss Spoonamore a quick look and with my arm through Mackie's, made my way to the main hall.

"Alice, you shouldn't provoke her so!" he told me, cheeks scarlet. "Have a care for your reputation."

I laughed loudly at this. "Ah, Mackie, nobody takes any notice of what she says!" I told him.

Mackie bit his lip. "She likes me," he said, flushing a bright red. "It's dreadfully embarrassing!"

"The only person she's embarrassing is herself," I told him. "There are things I could tell you that'd curl your hair!"

Mackie could imagine it.

At the top end of the hall was a proper stage with curtains, installed by a former theatre enthusiast Headmaster. I was worried to learn there were real, gas-powered 'footlights' on the stage.

"But that's dangerous, with children performing!"

The music halls my parents performed in had had gas foot and wing lights. They changed the colours in them by stretching coloured linen over a wire frame. My parents had told me about a theatre that had burned to the ground from an accident with footlights.

"Headmaster knows what he's doing!" Mackie attempted to reassure me.

In theatres, the lights were controlled by the 'Gasman' who sat at a gas table, from where he could change lighting during the performance. I was also aware of limelight, a strong beam of light that could centre on the main performer. This was concocted of oxygen mixed with hydrogen which, in turn, heated a block of limestone, thus producing a brilliant white light. However, they required several operators. There had always been a 'safety curtain' in the theatres, brought down between performances. I spoke of this to Mackie, who patted my hand sympathetically. Miss Spoonamore noticed and seethed with fury.

Little Sam and Roland were next up. I clasped my hands together as Roland played the pipe and Little Sam did the step dance, exactly how I had taught him. Both in their little sailor outfits, it made my heart soft.

Mackie observed the look on my face and felt his own heart melting.

The following evening came, and everyone was excited. The boys ran off to get changed. Mackie, looking out for me, spotted Sam. He put on a straight face.

"Alice! Sam! Good evening. Oh, your father's here too!" He nodded at Samuel senior and shook his hand. "Good evening, sir, I hope you find the concert enjoyable." He smiled at us and showed us to our seats.

Miss Spoonamore, once more at the mulled wine, glanced across. She was feeling sick with hatred. "Little slut!" she muttered to herself. "Making free with George whilst her husband is at her very side."

We had all arranged to sit together. Miss Spoonamore's gaze fell on Kit who was barely visible, so wrapped up was he. "I don't mind betting that brat is not Samuel's," she muttered once more. "I bet it doesn't resemble any of the Dwyers. More likely my George. And mine he is, though he doesn't yet know it, poor man; he doesn't know what's good for him."

That it was physically impossible to be Mackie's did not cross her mind. He had not even come to Yarmouth until late August and Kit certainly resembled his sire. But Miss Spoonamore was determined to make whatever trouble she could and had no intention of letting Mackie get away.

Helen elbowed me. "Yon Miss Spanker's looking at ye like the very Devil!" she hissed. I nodded and turned a smile in her direction which made her slam the ladle into the mulled wine in a temper, splashing herself and making her angrier still.

The concert was thoroughly enjoyable. I was so proud when the boys did their hornpipe dance. I smiled broadly, as did Sam, when our Little Sam, standing at his friend's side and having been introduced by another staff member, spoke to the crowd.

"This is a folk tune," he announced suddenly, his little speech entirely unrehearsed. "Roland's playing it and I'm going to stepdance to it. Mamma taught me how. It's called 'Portsmouth,' but we're calling it 'Yarmouth,' 'cos Yarmouth's better!"

There was applause at that little speech and remarks of 'Hear! Hear!' before Roland put the pipe to his lips.

Sam and I sat riveted, thrilled with the dance. Mrs Rix beamed round, and Mr Dwyer and Maria looked equally proud. Tabitha beamed, and Gus, sitting beside her, roared his approval. Miss Spoonamore willed Little Sam to trip and fall flat on his little face, but he did not. At the end, we all applauded. The two boys stood there grinning.

The end of the show culminated in the entire cast singing some carols along with the audience. Miss Spoonamore fussily arranged the children on the stage, snapping out orders. "Tallest at the back, little ones at the front. Come on! Use your common sense, Bernard, if you have any that is! You can't possibly be seen back there!"

She fidgeted and fussed so much that the audience began to mutter. Miss Spoonamore shot them a look. From somewhere in the audience, a voice called out "Miss Spankmore!" and she turned an infuriated and venomous look at the disembodied voice. There was a ripple of laughter.

The carols were sung, and I smiled at my father-in-law whose face was a rosy glow of happiness as he belted out the carol of Good King Wenceslas, which was my utmost favourite.

"That was wonderful!" I said, as the boys joined us after the concert had finished. "You were easily the best act!"

Miss Spoonamore waved to Mackie. "Oh dear! I'm being summoned," he stated grumpily.

"Ignore the old trout!" I told him.

"I dare not!" Mackie answered. "Well, good evening to you all. I hope you all have a wonderful Christmas. A happy new year to you too, Samuel! Roland! I look forward to seeing you next term. 1st January, nine o'clock sharp!"

Outside, we bid Reverend and our other friends a good night. As we did so, Sam noticed Miss Spoonamore talking to Mackie at top speed.

"Shall I rescue him?" he asked with a grin.

"Yes! Poor fellow. I don't doubt he can fight any enemy and win, but she's someone he will never defeat!"

Sam hastened across to the pair. "Excuse me, Miss Spoonamore," he said firmly. "I need a word with this fine fellow." Before she could object, Sam had whisked Mackie back to our group.

Miss Spoonamore was furious. 'How dared he?' she stated to herself. As Mackie got into our carriage, Miss Spoonamore fumed more.

"Good God above! Like as not he's taking him back so they can all be in bed together! Well, I won't stand for that!" She watched as the carriage rolled off.

At that time, I had no idea that Mackie had fallen for me. I could not see it at all. He was so friendly and likeable that anyone would want him for a friend. Even Sam didn't notice.

Christmas was wonderful. Little Sam was delighted with his new skates and even more impressed with a cart on wheels that Sam had made. His face was a picture and he squealed, "A red cart! A red cart!" He leapt up and down, then promptly sat in it. "Can I take it out today?" he asked.

"Well, it's snowing," Sam told him. "You can't make it work on snow, but I shall clear the yard for you; it won't take long, then you can go round in the yard if you like!"

Little Sam beamed. "Thank you, Papa!" he squeaked. "It's the bestest cart in all Yarmouth!"

February 1855

I was not one to make much of my birthday, and never had been. But this year, Sam told our son that there would be something special. Knowing my love of musical boxes, he had decided to make me one.

Little Sam looked at his father and listened, a serious expression on his small face. "You can do it, Papa!" he said beaming. But despite his son's confidence in him, Sam wasn't sure. Cabinets were large - musical boxes were on a much smaller scale and required much detail.

One could find mechanisms for musical boxes in Norwich. These varied in size, and Sam had seen ones in snuff boxes, when his grandfather had been alive. I had obtained several over the years. I had one that I used for Kit to send him to sleep.

"So, we'll both go up the city together, bor'" Sam told him. "But getting away is likely to be difficult. So, we must think of a good excuse."

Meanwhile, Little Sam was despatched to the beach. "I want some nice pebbles," Sam instructed him. "But they can't be too big. Get nice, patterned ones."

Little Sam nodded. "I'll find the nicest pebbles on the beach!" he promised and went off then and there.

Little Sam enjoyed the beach and seized any excuse to go there. He pottered about on the tide line, noting the shiny, wet pebbles. It was cold, but he scarcely noticed the wind. It took only a half hour to select some pretty stones and he hastened back to his father.

So it was I found myself occupied with a small tea party, which was most enjoyable, particularly as I got to spend some time with Millicent, of whom I had seen little recently.

Sam and our son boarded the train to Norwich and arrived shortly. "Now to find somewhere we can get a hold of a mechanism," he stated. "We need to find a song she'll like too. This might take some time, son!"

They wandered about, and eventually found a shop that sold musical instruments. This kind of place would have been far beyond the reach of Sam's pocket in the usual way, but it wasn't an instrument he wanted.

The bell tinkled gently as they entered the shop. The door, once closed, shut out all street sounds. The sudden silence was strange. The proprietor regarded them uneasily, and was about to make a remark that they leave, when he caught Sam's eye. Plainly dressed he might be, but there was a certain air about him, the way he removed his hat and nodded politely, that told the proprietor he was not there to cause trouble. On explaining what he wanted, the proprietor nodded.

"I've some things that might suit," he told him.

"It needs to be a pretty tune," Sam told him. "For my wife."

"Allow me to show you."

They listened to several mechanisms; the proprietor was becoming mildly impatient. Surely the fellow had heard at least one he liked?

Sam nodded at a sixth rendition of a little tune. "Yes, this one... it's gorgeous," he stated and the proprietor concealed a sigh of relief.

"Thank you. An excellent choice, sir; most appropriate too – it's called 'For My Lady!'"

Sam nodded, a big smile on his face.

"Then it's just right."

Having wandered around, they made their way back to the station. Sam needed the gents. Little Sam preferred to wait outside and watch the trains.

"Alright but stay here."

Little Sam enjoyed the sights, sounds and smells of steam. Railway stations were busy. It was good to watch the comings and goings.

Suddenly, he detected a presence at his side. "Hello, bor'!"

He looked up at the woman. She didn't look very clean, or friendly. Little Sam moved away slightly.

"Lost, are you?" she enquired. "Where's your mamma? Nanny then?"

"Papa's in the room of easement," Little Sam replied in a polite voice. "I don't have a nanny, and Mamma is at home."

"Is he now? Well, come with me and I'll buy you a bun whilst we wait."

Little Sam shook his head.

"Come on. My name's Mrs Tomlinson; what's yours?"

But Little Sam still shook his head.

"No, thank you!"

"Would you like a bull's eye?" She produced a bag brimming with sweets.

Little Sam said nothing.

Suddenly, the woman's demeanour changed; he felt strong fingers around his upper arm. "Come with me!"

Little Sam let out a piercing scream, making heads turn. He struggled. "Let me alone! Let me alone! PAPA!" he bellowed.

"Shut up you! None of that noise now. You come with me!"

Little Sam struggled, and kicked out, screeching. He would have been pulled away, had not Sam heard the screech, and knowing his own son's voice, came hastening out, trousers half-buttoned.

"What are you doing with my boy?" he bellowed, grabbing Little Sam to him. The woman cringed as heads turned in their direction.

"I thought him lost, sir."

"No! She was trying to take me away!" Little Sam howled.

"Is that so?" Sam was enraged.

The woman turned and shoved her way hurriedly through the crowd to the shabby coach waiting outside. Her son sniffed and wiped his nose along his sleeve.

"Didn't you get no one, Ma?"

Mrs Tomlinson shook her head, gasping for breath.

"Damn! I nearly got caught then," she told him. "His father came out. We need to be more careful, bor', change our method. It's already in the papers, after that Elsie brat! Pity though, he was a plump little chicken!"

"Are you alright, bor'?" Sam asked. Little Sam nodded. He was shaking now, almost in tears.

"Yes, Papa. She tried to take me away!"

"Well, you did right to holler and struggle like that. Good boy. But don't tell Mamma; she'd be hysterical."

Sam hugged his son closely; the near abduction had terrified him more than Little Sam.

They made their way home on the train. Sam's heart had gone back to its normal rhythm, having been sent double its speed. He would speak to the police back in Yarmouth. Another child might not be so lucky!

Despite the incident, the police could not do much, but it was as well to know if there were unpleasant persons of that sort about. The constable noted down the 'kidnapping attempt', as Sam strongly insisted he put it.

"Well, Mr Dwyer, we'll get a description out to Norwich station. We can't do a lot, but at least we know there's some bad bugger on the loose."

Sam put the finishing touches to the box. "That's all done!" he told Little Sam. "Now to put those pretty pebbles on and varnish them and the box. Gosh, it's taken me ages. I didn't think it would take so long!"

Little Sam nodded, admiring the box. "It's lovely, Papa," he said, beaming. "Mamma will love it."

Sam hoped so. Later, he carried it gently to his father's house, where it could dry in secret.

"It was much harder than it looks." Sam pondered as he took some coffee with his father. "So much smaller!"

Sam confided to his father about the attempted kidnapping. "Gosh, did he holler!" he said, shaking his head. "To think what might've happened. I daren't tell Alice!"

Simon nodded. "Hmm, best not to, bor', and you did right to tell the police as well. If they know what this biddy looks like, then they can keep their eyes open at the station."

Sam nodded. "I was terrified!" he told his father. "Seconds later, and he'd have been gone." He was silent for a moment. It was then Sam lost all colour and he turned to his father. "That woman! Why didn't I see it? She looked like the description of the person last seen with Elsie." He seemed about to faint. It was a sickening thought.

"Do you go back to the police then, bor', and tell 'em. I'll come too."

For my birthday, we were having a tea at home. Our friends were invited. Everyone brought something so that I need not cook. Helen turned up with a whole shoulder of ham, Millicent brought a syllabub that she made her speciality, and there were other cold meats and roast potatoes; I was thrilled. But what thrilled me most of all was the beautiful musical box Sam had made me. I gasped as I took it in my hands and held it gently.

"It's pretty sturdy, don't worry," Sam told me. "You won't break it."

I marvelled at all the beautiful pebbles on the top.

"I chose them!" Little Sam told me proudly. "I chose them, all by myself!"

"Well, you did marvellously, darling!" I told him. "They're beautiful!"

"Listen to the tune." Sam wanted to know what I thought of the music. I wound up the key and listened in delight as the tune played out.

Late that night, we lay close together. "I'm so glad I found you," I whispered to him.

Sam kissed the tip of my nose. "Me too," he replied.

March 1855

Little Sam still loved his cart. He and Roland took it in turns to push or pull one another. They could just about squeeze into it together and they rattled down the rows.

I was horrified when one morning, having hung laundry out to dry, I chatted to our neighbour for a short time, then returned to the kitchen to sort out the ingredients for a cake. I turned to pick up Kit from his playpen and found him missing.

"SAM!" I screamed loudly, making him jump violently.

"Darling? What's the matter?"

"Kit's gone. Oh no! How could he have got out of that playpen? There's no way! He can't even walk! Sam! Someone's taken him!"

"Calm down, sweetheart!" Sam then shocked me to the core with his next words. "Little Sam took him out for some fresh air!"

"What?" I felt faint.

"Well, he's doing his duty as an older brother!" Sam replied, unable to see the reason for my horror. "I didn't think it a problem. You want them to bond, don't you?"

My husband looked at me, evidently not understanding my concern.

"He's four months old!" I wailed. "I'm going out to look for them."

"Alice! I was entrusted with Maria when I was only a year older than him," Sam pointed out.

I pounced at once.

"Yes, and I heard you parked her somewhere and came home without her!" I reminded him. Sam winced slightly. "Men!" I exclaimed exasperated.

"Alice, they'll be back shortly. I only let him take Kit to Tooke the Baker's Row! That's only six rows up!"

Just as I was about to let fly, I heard boyish laughter from outside and at once flung the door open.

"Hello, Mamma!" Little Sam stood there grinning, Roland at his side. A babyish squeal and giggles alerted me to the passenger in Little Sam's cart. There, cushioned against several pillows, sat Kit, his face bright and little arms jiggling about. Evidently, he had enjoyed the ride. I swooped to retrieve him, and Kit's little face crumpled.

"Here's the bread, Mamma!" Little Sam pulled out the rolls, considerably flattened now since Kit had been sitting on them.

Kit started to bawl, annoyed that his ride had been so abruptly terminated. I rolled my eyes and popped him back in. Kit at once stopped his bellowing. About to start reprimanding our first-born, Sam stepped in.

"Don't scold him, Alice, it's my fault. He asked me if he could take Kit out. You were at the laundry line. I never thought till you mentioned it!"

Of course, I forgave them. Later, I recounted the tale to Helen, who gave one of her belly laughs. Maria too found it hilarious, though she had, of course, no memory of being forgotten by her elder brother.

Gus had decided to propose to Tabitha. He had come to our house in something of a flap, wondering how to do it, where to do it and whether to get a betrothal ring. Sam smiled. "Over to you, Alice!" he said, sitting back, and stretching out his legs. He lay Kit on his chest for a nap. For some reason, lately, Kit would not sleep during the afternoon unless he was laid on his father's chest. Putting him down anywhere else resulted in loud bawling.

I beamed. "I've the very thing!" I sat him down and poured a cup of tea. "Now then, you old romantic!"

Gus held up a hand. "Less of the old, if you please, mawther!"

"Alright, romantic, now, she'll be overwhelmed at this. No girl could refuse. Even practical ones like Tab." I told him of my idea.

Gus began to smile. "D'ye think she'll accept?" he asked me when I had finished. I nodded.

"If she doesn't, then more fool her," I replied. "But I reckon she will. Who could resist?"

Gus trembled. It was so nerve-racking. He didn't recall it being as bad with his first wife. But now, he was about to ask Tabitha to be his wife. What if she refused? What if she laughed? But she was here now; Gus had sent word she was to come to the park, urgently, to meet him just before sundown. He spotted her, walking through the trees. She waved cheerfully.

"How now, Gus? What's this? You know I supervise the smoke house on a Thursday."

"Yes, but I had something important to say and it couldn't wait," Gus replied. Tabitha saw he was worried and took his hand.

"Is something wrong?" she asked, suddenly afraid he was going to tell her he was leaving town. "Come on, Gus." She looked at him when he remained silent. "You can tell me."

Gus sighed. The sun was now setting, and they could see it, shining a brilliant red through the trees, heavy with blossom, all pink and white and scented the evening air. He turned to take both her hands in his.

"Look!" He indicated the red sun, sinking slowly in the west through the blossom covered trees. Tabitha looked and smiled. "Beautiful, isn't it?" Gus said. "Just like you." Tabitha opened her mouth to say he was 'being daft', but suddenly, Gus dropped to one knee. "Marry me, Tab," he said. "I know I'm a gruff old rogue who doesn't shave nearly as much as he should, but I'm honest, loyal and I'll love you forever."

Tabitha gasped. She looked at the pretty betrothal ring that lay on his work-roughened palm. Usually, women only had the wedding band, unless they had money. Gus looked up at her, imploringly.

"Yes!" Tabitha choked out the word, overwhelmed.

Gus rose and roared in delight.

Smokehouse forgotten; they hurried round to tell us. I squealed with joy and hugged them both. Sam shook Gus' hand warmly. I looked at Tabitha.

"See?" I said. "I told you, didn't I?"

Tabitha smiled. "I know, it's been years, but you did warn me I'd have to wait."

I smiled at Gus, who was grinning all over his face.

"Well, it was worth waiting for, wasn't it? We expect a wedding invitation!" I said to them sternly.

Tabitha nodded. "Of course. Oh, Alice, I've never been happier!"

On my way home from market, I met Mackie. As we walked, I mentioned Tabitha. "She's rapt," I told him. "The wedding's in June."

Mackie smiled; "I'm relieved," he answered. "She's a nice girl and I like her, but Gus is the man for her."

"He is. Well, would you care to join us for dinner tomorrow night?"

"Alice, I cannot really accept the invitation."

"Why?"

"Because, for all you're married, and I know how dearly you love your family, I cannot entertain thoughts of any other young woman. I love you, Alice. You must be aware of it."

"Oh, Mackie, truly, were it not for Sam and our sons, it *would* be you! I know it's bold and forward to say it, but I have feelings of great warmth and friendship for you, Mackie. You're a wonderful person, and I want to see you happy with someone who'd look after you."

"I'm grateful for that," he said dismally. "But you have feelings too."

I blushed, shocked to find that I was very attracted to Mackie. I nodded, eyes down.

"But there's nothing I can do about it, Mackie."

"I don't expect you to; just knowing that makes me happy. But will you just allow me to kiss you, Alice? Please? Just once?"

I nodded, and Mackie leaned forward and planted a soft kiss on my lips.

"Thank you," he whispered.

Miss Spoonamore stopped in her tracks. On the other side of the road, she was unable to believe what she had just witnessed, and in broad daylight too! Now she was sure; Mackie and I were having an affair. Kit was Mackie's and that was all there was to it. Miss Spoonamore stormed across the road, almost mown down by a horse and cab. The animal shied and jerked the reins and the driver cursed her, but she took no heed. She entered her house, slammed the door and hurried upstairs, where she vented her fury in her bedroom.

"My dear! Whatever is the matter?" Eleanor, having heard the commotion, hurried to her twin's side. Miss Spoonamore thrashed wildly on the bed, kicking her thin legs, biting and tearing at the bedclothes in a fury. Miss Spoonamore's twin was alarmed; she had indulged in these peculiar fits of temper occasionally in childhood, but not recently.

"The slut! Whore! I saw her kissing that schoolteacher! In broad daylight, like the wicked strumpet she is!"

Eleanor was shocked. Miss Spoonamore's eyes were wild. She rose from her bed and swept the contents of her dressing table to the floor.

"She did what? Kissed him? In full view of everyone?"

"Yes! Along by Angel Row. I couldn't believe my eyes. I *told* you I saw him holding his bastard son too! He should be mine! MINE! I'd earmarked him for my own!" she spluttered, uncaring now of what her sister thought.

"For your *own?* Goodness me! I thought we were going to remain chaste all our lives! Did we not take an oath on that?"

Miss Spoonamore sniffed. She gave her sister a furious look which unnerved the woman. She grasped hold of the bedpost and started to seethe. Breathing hard, nostrils flaring, a peculiar, strangled-type growl issued from her throat. Her eyes were wide.

"I've been infected by her," she hissed. "Her lax ways; she is a known witch in any case, spreading her immorality like she spreads her legs!"

Eleanor did not know what to say. She was truly afraid of her sister's behaviour.

"Now, let us tackle this calmly. We'll go to Arnold, tell him what you saw. He'll pray with us. You *must* rid your thoughts of her, my dear."

Miss Spoonamore managed to calm somewhat and rose to tidy herself. She faced her sister. "Good. Now you are calm. Come, let's find Arnold."

I met up with Tabitha. It was warm and we planned a picnic.

"Alice, I cannot tell you how happy I am now. Gus! When we first met him, he wasn't the man I had in mind!"

I grinned. "I think Gus is what they call a rough diamond."

"He is. I never thought he could be so sweet. He's a terribly wicked sense of humour too!"

I laughed as she continued. "I just suddenly seemed to see it at the birthday party we had for him. It'd been staring me in the face, all that time, obvious to everyone but me. I, of all people, should never judge by appearances."

"Well, at least you came to your senses in time," I told her.

Tabitha was keen to wear her mother's old wedding dress.

"I'll alter it to fit you."

"You'll have rather a job on," Tabitha admitted, shamefaced. "Me and my sisters would dress up in it as kids. There's a rip our Sal put in it when she stuck her foot through the hem."

"Don't worry," I assured her. "I'll sort it out."

I had no idea what I was letting myself in for.

Monday morning, and the boys were driving Miss Spoonamore to distraction. Eventually, she lost her temper.

"Shut up!" she screeched. "We shall spend the first part of the morning with reckoning. After playtime, you will study your catechism. You're a bunch of heathens! I'd like to see all your heads on spikes at the town gateway, like they used to in the olden days." With this heart-warming remark, she turned to the board.

Roland nudged Little Sam and he almost laughed aloud. His friend had drawn an image of Miss Spoonamore's severed head on a spike, dripping copious amounts of blood, whilst her mouth still appeared to shriek. As a caricature, it was incredibly good.

The next morning, she entered the classroom and the boys stood in respectful silence. But there were certain looks on all the little faces. Miss Spoonamore knew that look. They were all trying to stop laughing – every single one.

"What are you all looking so pleased about?" she had ranted, banging a book down on her desk and creating a cloud of chalk dust. Nobody dared move, but 20 pairs of eyes were fixed on the board behind her, and turning around, she spotted Roland's comical drawing of her. In a fury, she whipped it off the board where it had been pinned.

"I suppose there is no hope of my finding the perpetrator of this malicious piece of spite!" she shrieked, shaking the piece of paper at them. "Well? One of you admit to it, or I keep you in this breaktime and lunchtime!"

Nobody spoke. Losing two breaktimes didn't matter; it was worth it to see the look on her face. Miss Spoonamore shrilled at them again, so loudly that Headmaster, passing on his way to assembly, and wondering why she still had her class in session, looked into the classroom.

"Miss Spoonamore! Is anything wrong?" The Headmaster asked mildly. Every boy in the room suddenly glanced at one another, feeling worried now.

"This! THIS!" Miss Spoonamore thrust the paper under Headmaster's large nose. "Look!" She pointed at the paper. "An image! Of my own head! On a spike! Did you ever see such malice? Evil! Every one of them!"

"Calm down, Miss Spoonamore," the Headmaster said, taking the drawing from her. "It is a boyish prank, nothing more!"

Miss Spoonamore stamped her foot. "Prank? It's disrespect of the highest degree!"

The man regarded the drawing. Really, it was extremely well done, and he wondered who the artist was. True, it was disrespectful, but the woman tried his patience to the utmost and beyond. He glanced over the 20 nervous-looking boys.

"Well?" he asked. "And who is the budding comic artist?"

Silence. Roland felt queasy; but decided it best to get it over with. The old boy didn't whop one too hard!

"I did it, Headmaster!" He rose. Little Sam looked at his friend and rose too.

"I helped."

"Hmm, a joint effort I see!" His deep voice rumbled. He glanced at the paper. It was very funny, and the Headmaster disliked Miss Spoonamore intensely. However, one could not condone rudeness of this sort.

"We are late for prayers," he told her sharply. "Leave this with me, Miss Spoonamore! I shall deal with it. Come on, boys, assembly is about to begin!"

The class filed out of the form room behind the Headmaster.

Later that morning, Headmaster told Miss Spoonamore it was not up to her to administer the cane after she had threatened them with it in his hearing.

"You'll refer any floggings to me, Miss Spoonamore!" he stated, standing upright, thumbs hitched in his braces. "It is not appropriate for you to cane any boy; it is demeaning to be beaten by a woman!"

Miss Spoonamore restrained herself with a massive effort.

The boys heard her clopping heels along the corridor and Miss Spoonamore entered the form room to 20 hard-working mice. She eyed them evilly. "Don't think I believe you have all been industrious whilst I've not been here! I know what you're all like... lazy, dishonest, ill-disciplined!" She looked at the 20 little faces and her eyes rested on Little Sam for a moment, malice in her face, then she added, "You are the most dishonest boy in the class!"

We heard about this over our evening meal.

Little Sam pulled a face. "She's horrible to everyone. Nobody likes her. She said we were all dishonest this morning!"

"What?" Sam put down his fork, angry. "Why?"

"Because when she came back from Headmaster, we were all quiet and busy," he told us.

"What's dishonest about that?" I asked. "Isn't that what you're supposed to be doing?"

"Yes, but *she* said she didn't believe we'd been like that whilst she was away!" Little Sam said.

"Hmm and what had you been doing?" I asked.

"Just talking," Little Sam told us. "We heard her shoes and started working when we did."

"That's not dishonesty, that's common sense," grinned Sam.

"She said I was the most dishonest boy in the class!" Little Sam added, crossly.

I gasped. "WHAT? How dare she? I'll be speaking to her!"

"The other day, she told us she wished she could see all our heads on spikes at the town gates!" he added to our horror.

Little Sam then spoke of the drawing Roland had done and the three of us laughed, particularly at the Headmaster's reaction. "We're still waiting for his punishment," Little Sam told us. "I don't think he's going to do anything though. He was trying not to smile at it."

I hoped he wouldn't be too hard. I had no idea, however, that the cartoon had, in fact, been pinned to the Headmaster's notice board and he had no intention at all of taking any action.

The following day, I accompanied Little Sam to school.

"I'd like a word, Miss Spoonamore!" I told her sharply.

"What do *you* want?" she asked rudely.

"Just to say that I don't wish to hear of you saying such dreadful things to the boys again," I told her. "Heads on spikes? Good God, woman! Whatever possessed you to say such a thing? And, I will have you know, my boy *is* honest!"

Miss Spoonamore peered at me down her nose.

"Well, I speak as I find. I found them dishonest. Every time I look around in class, they are whispering, particularly your son!"

I was stunned at the vitriol. "You're disgusting!" I snapped, furious at the remarks.

Miss Spoonamore merely sniffed. "Don't pretend to know more than you really do, Alice. It merely betrays your ignorance! Besides, you've no right to be so smug. You're having an affair with George McIntyre. The whole town knows!"

With that, she strode off.

On a wet, Saturday afternoon, Tabitha brought her mother's wedding dress round. I took it from its brown paper and my face fell. "Tab!" I exclaimed, reproach in my voice. "Whatever made you and your sisters treat such a beautiful dress so roughly?"

Tabitha looked very guilty. "I know, Alice, I 'm sorry, but we were just little girls. We didn't understand. We wanted to play at the dressing-up, being brides, princesses... you know the kind of thing. Mamma would skin me alive if she knew."

I'll do my best, Tab!" I told her brightly, but inside, I felt hopeless. The dress would be better off in the rag bag.

Later, I spoke to Sam. "That dress, Sam! It's going to need so much work! It's falling apart at the seams."

Sam nodded. We both looked then at Little Sam who was sitting on the other side of Kit's playpen. He moved the coloured wooden balls up and down; "red, green, blue, yellow!" Little Sam turned to see we had been watching him, and smiled a little sheepishly, but I beamed at him.

It was not the first time I had caught him 'educating Kit.' I had found him a few days ago, Kit on his knees, as Little Sam counted the pudgy little fingers, one to five, then would set Kit squealing with laughter by tickling his palm. He was such a good older brother, a fact I never failed to tell him.

Work began on the dress. It was almost 40 years old, but I could make it a little more modern. Tabitha's mother would be proud of it, I hoped. I decided to get more Yarmouth lace and netting, yards of it. I would make that dress pretty if it was the last thing I did.

June 1855

It was ten o'clock the next morning when I heard a knocking at the door. I wiped my hands on my apron and hurried to open it.

"Mrs Dwyer!" the urchin spoke "Mrs Wadaa says please hurry, babby's coming!" I nodded.

"Alright, young man, thank you. I'll be there shortly."

Manoa was in panic mode; for all he had faced so many dangers from childhood to adulthood, escaping slavery by a whisker, dangers of the sea, storms, venomous snakes, even pirate ships, none quite compared to his wife giving birth.

"Come on, man!" Sam patted his broad shoulder. "She'll be fine. She's young and strong. Come and show the boys the ships; there must be someone you know there who'll let them on board."

Having successfully got rid of Manoa, the women got down to business. Helen had started and I was pleased none of the children were about. Her language would have made a docker blush.

The midwife was bossy and efficient. Helen roared like a lioness, and four hours later, their new daughter was born. Cleaned and wrapped, she was handed to Helen who at once began to feed her. I looked at the newborn. The child was a deep, dusky colour, part Helen's skin tone and part Manoa's, eyes black. Her hair was black and as tightly curled as Manoa's. She was unbelievably beautiful.

"Oh, Helen!" I gasped. "I never saw a prettier baby. Just look at those fat cheeks! Those eyes! She's gorgeous!"

Helen beamed. "Aye, that she is!"

"What will you name her?" The Midwife asked.

Helen smiled. "Manoa wants to call her Iffey."

"Call her what?"

"Iffey; 'tis a lovely name."

"It is!" I said, smiling. "And it suits her too. I was expecting some Scots monstrosity!" Helen made a rude noise at me.

"Florence," Helen said, "please will you see to the wages? We are happy with her services."

Florence nodded. She and the Midwife went to sort out what she was owed. Helen looked at her daughter.

"Well, suppose 'tis my poor pal who must go and tell Manoa," she told me.

"Alright, well, do you need anything else?"

Helen shook her head.

"No, hen, thank ye for yer help. Manny can get all I want, and I promised to send word the moment she was born."

I could hardly wait to go out and show off Iffey with Helen. One week on, and Helen was readying her daughter for her first outing.

"Lass! Yer keener than I am!" Helen told me laughing. "Dinnae rush me, or I'll forget something!"

Iffey, in the perambulator, gazed up at us, eyes wide.

"Her eyes are like saucers!" I said. "She's going to be a heartbreaker one day!"

"Nay, lass, she'll no leave my side!" Helen stated firmly. "No man, I don't care how rich he is, will *ever* get his lustful hands on my lovely, pure wee lassie!"

"Ah, you can't mean that, Helen. You can't deny her a home and children of her own one day."

Helen frowned. "I said, no man, I don't care how rich he is, will EVER get his hands on my lassie!" she repeated. I didn't take Helen seriously; it was just the newness of motherhood, I decided.

As it was a beautifully warm morning, we trundled her along the front. Kit, now seven months old, was around 18lbs in weight and I couldn't possibly carry him for long. He too was in a perambulator and took in his surroundings with interest. We met a lot of people. Iffey was received in many ways. People we were friendly with cooed and exclaimed over her, but others frowned their disapproval, some downright rude.

"That poor child!" one woman said, having peered into the pram. "You can't expect her to come to much, Mrs Wadaa. Mixed marriage! Half caste children! I've seen a few in the workhouse!"

Helen snorted. "Ye mind yer own business, ye evil busybody! My lass will want for nothing. And *if* she enters the workhouse, it will be to do as I do and give charity to those who need it! So, you can take yer ridiculous opinions and stuff them up yer fat arse, 'cos I don't care whether ye like it or whether ye don't!"

We stalked on leaving the women totally shocked. "Goodness, Helen!" I said, fanning my red face. "That was horrendous!"

"Well, if it makes ye uncomfortable, ye don't have to stay!" Helen told me feistily.

"Now just one moment!" I stopped her. "I didn't mean *your* comments, and well you know it! I meant *her* attitude! Whatever's the matter with you?"

"Aye, I'm sorry, I'm just so protective of her. Well, c'mon lass, to the park. Mebbe wee Kit'll want to get out."

We sat in the shade, while Kit crawled in the cool clover enjoying himself. Helen had fashioned him a toorie and I had him wear it whilst he was still too young to object and clamour that it 'made him look daft' as Little Sam had done, fortunately, not in Helen's hearing.

As we sat talking, the familiar figures of the Misses Spoonamore came into view. "Och no!" Helen said. "Here comes trouble!"

Miss Spoonamore's eyes bore into mine as she approached, and I could see her teeth were clenched. At her side, her sister was speaking earnestly to her.

"Calmness, my dear. Calmness. Don't forget! Do not drag yourself to her level. You want to win, do you not?"

Miss Spoonamore nodded. The pair came closer, and I grabbed Kit from pure fear and a surge of protectiveness. He squawked in objection and surprise.

"We are scarcely going to kidnap your child, young woman!" Eleanor stated haughtily. "There is no need to snatch him from our path!"

"There's every need," I replied. "I don't trust you! You'd kick him and say it was accidental."

"Well! What have we here?" She peeked into the pram to look at Iffey who gazed back at the woman. "What *have* you brought forth, woman?" Eleanor said in such disgust, one would have thought Helen had had a snake in the pram.

Helen bristled. "A wee baby! What do *you* think?"

Miss Spoonamore looked at the baby with a curled lip. Helen prepared herself for battle.

"And just *how* do you think it will cope?" Miss Spoonamore asked. "It is neither one race nor the other!"

Helen boiled over.

"IT?" she bellowed, surprising the duo. "IT? *She,* if ye dinnae mind, and *she* will do wonderfully well! Her name is Iffey, and I'd be obliged if ye'd use it from now on!"

The sisters looked down their noses.

"Children like that are born evil!" Eleanor snarled. Before Helen could react with violence, I reached into the pram and held Iffey up in front of the spinsters' faces.

"Take a good, long, look at her!" I snapped. "Look at that face! Those eyes! She's an innocent child! A baby just born! Does she look evil to you? Not a bad bone in her body! Unlike you pair! Go on! Look at her and you tell me what evil you see!"

Kit roared his disapproval at his mamma with another baby and Helen attempted to soothe him.

"I think we should leave!" Miss Spoonamore told her sister. "Come along, Eleanor."

"Yes! Leave!" I snapped. "And if you want to see evil, look in your own mirror!"

They trailed off together with loud remarks about rudeness and bad manners, and I turned to look at Helen who was jogging Kit. I put Iffey back and took Kit whose howls stopped.

"Alice! Thank ye. But attitudes like that are precisely what I need to protect her from."

"Not everyone's like them." I sat with Kit. "Most people are alright." But I had the unpleasant feeling that it had affected Helen far too deeply and thus would affect her daughter too.

"Stand still or I'll stick a pin in you!" I chided Tabitha as she stood in our bedroom for her final dress fitting. "Now, all I need is to take it up just a tiny bit more."

Tabitha nodded. "You're a magician, Alice!"

I laughed. "No magic, Tab, only 25 years of practice. Now, that should do it!" I rose from a kneeling position.

"I think you've worked wonders," Tabitha told me. "When you consider the state of it. I'm so glad Mamma didn't catch sight of it like that; she'd have wrung my neck. She'll be so happy to see it now though."

I smiled at her. I always felt so pleased when someone complimented my work.

A sudden disturbance next door made me go to the window to look. "Nosy!" Tabitha told me, coming to observe as well.

"Ha! You can talk! Why are you looking too then, eh?" Tabitha laughed.

"New neighbours," I told her. "I hope they're decent. Goodness! Look at her! Did you ever see such a size?"

Tabitha looked out over my shoulder. The lady who was to be our new neighbour stood at the troll cart's tail, looking about her with a haughty expression. Her face was pasty, rounded, with small eyes of an indiscernible colour. She had tight curled hair, almost grey in colour, under a small white cap. She gave a sniff of disparagement.

"She doesn't seem to like the look of her new home." Tabitha told me.

"She doesn't, does she? But the houses in this row are lovely."

The woman shouted. "Robin! Robin! Come here!"

A very tall, thin man appeared next to her. He had snow-white hair and high cheeks that were rounded and rosy.

The pair appeared to be in their late forties. Tabitha looked at me and I looked at her. We spluttered with laughter and the pair looked up. The woman frowned.

"Oops! She's seen us!" I withdrew my head. "What a mismatched pair!" Tabitha took off her dress, folding it neatly and put on her skirt and blouse. As we descended the stairs, Little Sam hastened up.

"Mamma, there's a big, fat lady outside!" he told me excitedly.

"I know, we were looking," I answered.

"Well, thank you Alice," Tabitha told me. "See you Saturday morning, bright and early!"

I grinned. "We'll be there. Wish us luck with the new people!"

Tabitha did, and left, glancing at them and their items on the troll cart. I peeped out under the net curtain.

Sam hissed. "Alice! For goodness' sake, don't let them see you're watching!"

"Whyever not? I'm sure she'd watch us, and besides, we have a right to know what new neighbours are like."

Sam groaned. There was never any point arguing with a curious woman.

The neighbours would soon make their presence felt. Not that they were noisy; they weren't. Anyone living in the rows was used to sounds of living next door, morning ashes being raked, coal deliveries, troll carts, people chattering – all manner of things one just didn't even hear as a rule since it was background noise, and normal. But the very next morning, the woman was on my doorstep, knocking loudly.

"Must you rake your ashes so early?" she asked me crossly, without even a hint of a greeting. "It woke my husband and I this morning."

I folded my arms. "Good morning, madam. Welcome to Half Moon Row," I replied rather sharply. "I am Mrs Dwyer."

The woman blushed.

"Of course, I apologise. I am Mrs Floyd; it's just that we enjoy a lie in of a morning and your raking ashes disturbed us."

I looked at her. She appeared to be the kind of woman who was used to instant obedience and the attitude irked me.

"Mrs Floyd, my husband and I need to rise at between six and seven so I can get their breakfasts going before my husband begins work and my son his school," I told her. "And as you know, raking ashes isn't a quiet job. I expect I'll hear you doing yours!"

Mrs Floyd pursed her lips. "Not before nine o'clock!"

"Well, perhaps you and your husband are able to begin your day later, but we cannot," I told her pertly. "Some of us have to get up for work!"

Just as Mrs Floyd was digesting this somewhat rude remark, Sam came to the door wondering who I was talking to in such a snappy voice. He nodded at the huge woman. "My husband, Samuel," I told her. Mrs Floyd barely acknowledged him.

"Alright, well, I'd be obliged if you *could* try to make *slightly* less noise," she told me, then spun round, almost toppling over, entered her own home and shut the door. Sam and I looked at one another in disbelief.

Mrs Floyd was certainly what Sam's father called 'an odd duck.' It didn't take long to realise that she and her husband had come down in the world rather. It explained the somewhat haughty attitude. Later that day, she frowned over the yard fence where I was hanging up laundry. Noting Little Sam's red cart and several balls, skates, and a skipping rope, she spoke.

"I see you have children!" she barked at me, as though she was noting I had some nasty disease. I jumped for I had had my back to her.

"Two, actually," I answered. "Our eldest, Samuel, is ten this year. Our youngest will be one." Then I smiled impishly. "With room for more."

"There isn't enough room in these tiny places for two people, let alone more!" she snapped. "Poor Towser won't have enough space."

"Who's Towser?" I asked.

"Our poodle!" She replied.

"How much space does a poodle need?" I asked.

Mrs Floyd frowned. "He used to have the run of the lawns where we lived before," she stated, as though it were my fault she and her husband had moved here. I shrugged.

"There's over a mile of beach, you know." I pegged up a small shirt of Little Sam's. "Plus the denes, but they aren't encouraged as they leave mess everywhere." I pulled a face thinking of that. Mrs Floyd made an impatient sounding snort.

"I can't walk all that way! Besides, dogs must go somewhere. People should be more careful where they put their feet," she replied sharply. I said nothing to this. There was no polite response one could make.

I hung up a pair of Sam's drawers and noted the look on her face. I wanted to laugh. I hoped the dog wouldn't be the yapping sort that drove neighbours mad.

"Why don't you come and have some tea, Mrs Floyd?" I decided to attempt to be neighbourly. "Bring your husband as well. We should like to meet you properly."

Mrs Floyd looked at me, appearing to consider it.

"Very well. We ought, I suppose, to meet you formally."

I shook my head. "Nothing is formal in the rows, Mrs Floyd. We are in and out of one another's houses, without all that calling card Society nonsense!"

"I'll bring Towser," she said. "It's as well to get to know a dog."

"*Not* the dog," I told her. "Our cat is eleven and I don't want her upset; she hates dogs."

"Towser is extremely well-behaved."

"I'm sorry, Mrs Floyd, I must ask you to leave the dog behind," I replied. "I don't allow dogs in here in any case."

Mrs Floyd looked at me as though I had taken leave of my senses. "Oh, very well!" She nodded and turned. "We shall call on you at three." With this remark, she marched back into her house.

Sam grumbled when I told him about the new neighbours. "Well, we need to get to know them," I reasoned. "But I am not sure they're going to be easy to get along with!" I looked at Kit, just waking from his nap. "Come on, little man!" I picked him up. "Better get you washed and changed before the visitors come."

The two presented themselves at the agreed time. Sam admitted the couple and they sat around the kitchen table. I could see Mrs Floyd disapproved of sitting in the kitchen. She took charge of the conversation at once, and told us she had been Head Cook at the manor house she and her husband had been employed in. Her husband had been Head Gardener. "We were *not* domestic servants!" She stressed the point once more. "But since we were employed there, the lodge house went with the job, didn't it, Robin?"

Her husband nodded.

Still domestic servants, I thought, smiling politely.

"Do you have children?" Sam asked.

"Oh no!" Mrs Floyd said. "Towser is our child. You should've let us bring him."

"My wife and I don't like dogs in our home," Sam said politely. "They cover everything in hair."

"Towser wouldn't, he's a poodle! Their hair doesn't shed!" Mrs Floyd argued.

Little Sam chose this moment to enter the house. He came in, in his usual jolly fashion, calling for us, then spotting the strangers, stopped dead.

"Ah, Sam, darling! Come and meet our new neighbours."

Our son approached cautiously, not liking Mrs Floyd much. He greeted both politely and the two nodded to him. But it was patently obvious they were most uneasy with him. Mrs Floyd stared at Kit as if he were something nasty. This made me bristle.

Little Sam, having greeted the newcomers, spoke quite innocently; "Gosh, Mrs Floyd, I didn't realise ladies could grow moustaches like men!"

I cringed, Sam covered his face with both hands, Robin actually sniggered, and Mrs Floyd was at a loss for words for several heart-stopping moments.

"I *beg* your pardon?" she exclaimed in horror.

"I said..."

Hastily, I intercepted Little Sam. "Darling, go and change your shirt," I told him. "Quickly now..."

Little Sam nodded and hastened upstairs, leaving me to apologise to the couple.

September 1856

Breakfast, and Kit sat at the table too. I had begun to wean him, and Kit was doing marvellously on a combination of milk and soft fruits or potatoes, mashed up with added butter. He also had a penchant for scrambled eggs, like his older brother, and would wail loudly to get them whenever I cooked

them, flailing little arms wildly until they appeared in his dish, which produced instant silence.

We had just finished when there was a knocking at the door and a white-
faced Helen came in, Iffey strapped round her front. I looked at her. "Helen!
You look terrified. What's happened?"

"I've bad news," she told us, and at once, Sam and I sat either side of her.
"Well?"

"I had a letter this morning. From my folks. I've nae idea how to tell ye
this, but well, William's back in the country."

I gaped.

"He came to the croft; Mam says she didn't recognise him at all. Thought
he was some tramp! Och, what if he comes here? He's bound to!"

"Why would he do that? He won't know where you are."

"He was born here. Where else would he go other than his old home?"
Helen reminded me, and I saw she was right. I felt extremely uncomfortable.
Helen then admitted she had not only failed to mention re-marrying but
hadn't told him about Elspeth's death. If he did return, Helen would have
a deal of explaining to do.

"Don't worry, we'll stick by you," I told her, and Helen breathed a little
easier. After all, what could William do?

Late September, and I found I was pregnant once more.

Helen beamed. "Tab's expecting too!" she stated, and I nodded. Tabitha
was excited, Gus a bundle of nerves. As it was a half-day holiday for the
schools, Little Sam and Roland were out somewhere, chasing one another
up and down the rows.

"Och, look!" Helen indicated two figures charging along the sand. I stood
up, suddenly worried.

"Mamma! Mamma!" Little Sam waved frantically, bellowing as loudly as he could. My concern left me when I saw there were smiles on the boys' faces. They both stood, panting in front of us.

"What's all this about?" I asked.

"Mamma, you must come! You must!" Little Sam grabbed my arm. "There's a big to-do in Conge Row. Come and see!" Evidently, something had excited them. "Come ON!" He almost pulled me off my feet.

"Alright! I'm coming!" I told him as we hastily packed up the remains of the picnic and rug.

A crowd had gathered to watch what was unfolding. People were chuckling, calling out to others to 'come and see!' I could never have even guessed, nor believed it, had I not seen it for myself. Helen and I, with the boys, made our way to the front of the crowd.

"What's happening?" Helen asked a woman. Her face showed disbelief at first at the woman's explanation, then she roared one of her deep belly laughs.

Earlier that day, a burglar had decided to try his luck. He wasn't a terribly competent thief at the best of times. That day, he was less competent still. The young man had climbed into a house through an open window, thinking nobody was home. Indeed, he had been initially correct having seen the woman who lived there walk off down the row with a basket on her arm. Smiling, he had checked about him; no others were around, so he slipped through the window. He had not bargained for the housewife's swift return as she suddenly remembered the open window. Nor had he bargained for the appearance of the woman's eldest son, who had arrived to visit his mother unexpectedly.

So it was that the burglar had begun to poke about, opening drawers, looking at the cutlery... anything he could steal that he could maybe sell on. He was so intent on his business that he was suddenly startled by a shrill scream as the woman spotted the intruder.

The man froze in terror. Alarmed by his mother's shriek, the son had come into the small room. "Hey! You! What the bloody hell you doing in our house?"

The young man cringed, since this fellow looked handy with his fists and was huge. There was no chance to get through the window since the woman had positioned herself in front of it, arms folded, looking furious, and still less chance of getting past her enraged son. So, he did the only thing he could possibly think of, and that was to climb up the chimney, his intention being to be off over the rooftops and away, a trick he had learned in his earlier days. However, he had been much smaller then.

"What the...?" The woman's son looked stunned as the villain, terrified, scrambled to the chimney stack and vanished up it. Both mother and son looked in sheer disbelief at one another.

"He won't escape that way!" the mother told her son. "That 'un needs sweeping. Besides, it narrows halfway up!"

It certainly did and the unfortunate burglar found himself tightly wedged. He started to struggle, but the more he struggled, the worse stuck he became. His mouth and nose were choking with soot. His fingers scrabbled against the sides of the flue, dislodging soot as he did so. He coughed and spat. The chimney had not been used for some time, but it still felt hot, and it was claustrophobic.

"HELP!" he bawled. "HELP! I can't move!"

Outside, we watched. The goodwife had come out of her home and shot off, whilst her son stuck his head from the window and addressed the crowd. It was such an unusual situation, everybody thought it mightily funny.

"He ain't going nowhere fast!" the son said, suddenly now seeing the amusing side of the situation. "Serves him right. I dunno as how we'll get him out!"

"Smoke him out!" called one man.

There were numerous witty suggestions of how to get to the burglar. I looked at Helen and we both laughed.

"Mamma! Mamma! He's stuck up the chimney and can't get out!" Little Sam informed me.

The approach of the constables' pounding boots on the cobbles made every head turn.

"Alright now. What's this side show?" One of the constables looked around.

He frowned and entered the house. Inside, soot lay everywhere, the policeman glanced to see boots protruding from the chimney stack.

"Oi! What you doing up there?" he asked, annoyed.

"Get me out!" a muffled voice came back to him. "I'm stuck!"

The policeman scratched his head. "We'll try!" he told him, wondering what on earth could be done to free him.

At first, the constable hailed his colleagues to assist. The strongest was set to pull on the fellow's legs as hard as he could, but he remained stuck fast.

The constable cleared his throat and spoke rather impishly. "Stay right where you are, bor'!"

There was an oath from the trapped man. The policeman came out of the house and addressed the crowd.

"We're going to have to dismantle that chimney to get at the bugger!" he added cheerfully.

There was a squawk of outrage from the housewife.

"You're going to do what?"

The policeman turned to her. "'Tis either that, goodwife, or you has him up there forevermore!"

"Well then, he'll pay for the damage!" She tapped her foot, angrily.

The constable nodded. "He will. Now you lot, s'pose there ain't no way you're gonna disperse, is there?" He smiled at the crowd; it was a good-natured lot, thoroughly enjoying the spectacle.

The careful dismantling of the chimney took much of the day, but the captive was eventually freed. He came out with the policeman who had not even needed to handcuff him since the poor fellow shook like a leaf and was weak from exhaustion. He was taken off to the Tolhouse looking very sorry for himself.

"Ah, I do hope they won't be too hard on him," I said as we walked home. "It can't have been very pleasant stuck up that chimney after all."

We heard later that the man had spent only a week in the prison, and then had been made to repair the stonework himself without pay.

1st December 1856

Another Christmas on the way. Sam was thrilled to find out another baby would be with us come June.

Sam and I had heard the real reason for the Floyds coming to Yarmouth. I had been in Tooke the bakers the month before, when a local woman, Mrs Laine, had prodded me in the back. "You want to be careful with your new people right next to you!" she had told me, and I had looked at her questioningly. "Bad lot!" she had hissed, loud enough for the other customers to hear.

"Bad?" I asked, confused.

"Well! That tall fellow. Right eye for the ladies that one. Got a young girl in the family way, he did."

"Are you sure? He doesn't look the sort. He's so mild-mannered."

Mrs Laine snorted. "It's the quiet ones you got to watch!"

I pressed her for more information, which she was happy to give.

According to Mrs Laine, Robin had chased the women servants at the house, seducing them, seemingly without trouble, and he had produced one or two illegitimate heirs on various females in the village.

"How do you know all this?" Sam asked me, when I had brought home the news, wide-eyed with disbelief.

"Mrs Laine told me."

Sam blinked. "But how does *she* know?" he pressed.

"Her great-niece has a friend who worked there at the same time," I said, taking Kit from him. "She couldn't stand him, so she left. Shocking, isn't it?"

Sam nodded. Wherever one was, there was always a grapevine.

Kit watched Bundles washing herself with interest, fingers in his mouth. "Hey, fingers out, young man!" I told him. "Or they won't grow!" Kit looked at me with large, dark eyes and smiled.

"Fingers!" he said, and I nodded. I went on to have a question-and-answer session with him – where were the eyes? The nose? And Kit would point at my face.

"Where's Samsam?" he enquired.

"He's at school!"

"School!" Kit parroted.

Now, in the first week of December, I went to the marketplace with Maria.

We chattered about our neighbours, and I told her what Mrs Laine had said to me. Like anybody else, Maria loved a good gossip and was delightfully shocked.

In the corner of the market, a small band played carols and Maria and I stopped to listen. People were singing alongside the band and a small crowd had gathered.

William Blake sat against a wall. He was unrecognisable now – very much thinner. His face was filthy and weather-beaten, with lines and dirty creases the like of which he never could have imagined he would have. His nails were ingrained with so much filth, he doubted they would ever get clean. He was dressed in ragged old clothes and a thick, filthy coat, stained with mud and other, more unpleasant liquids. His hat was battered. He carried a cloth bag with a few possessions in. His boots were worn and had many holes. His beard was now matted and stinking. William sat thinking bitter thoughts of days gone by, when his beard had been silky; his pride and joy, washed and carefully barbered every week. His clothes had been perfectly tailored. He thought how he had had his nails clipped and buffed regularly, and daily baths. Then, he had smelled fresh, his linen had been crisp – a clean shirt every day; now, he itched as lice crawled within his clothes.

Back in America, William had, with the help of another inmate, managed to escape from the prison in San Quentin. After weeks on the run, he had worked his passage over to Plymouth, carrying out the foulest jobs, but he had managed it. Once in Plymouth, he had begun the long trek to Scotland. He hoped Helen would take him back, even if just for the sake of the children.

William had stolen a man's wallet in Plymouth and secured himself a third-class seat in a carriage, the cheapest class on a train to Scotland. It had taken almost six months from the time of his escape to reach Scotland, with Helen and the children always in mind, and so it had been a shock to reach there and find Helen absent, not to mention the heartbreak over Elspeth's passing.

The family had not recognised him at first, taking him for what he was, a vagrant. Helen's father had threatened him with a shotgun. Later, William had blustered and wept, insisting he needed to know where his ex-wife and children were, and that as their father, he had every right to see the children. How could she not have had the decency to inform him of that?

Now, seven months later and back in Yarmouth, he determined to find out where Helen had gone. It would not be easy.

So, he sat, in the marketplace, looking about him. He observed Maria as we walked arm-in-arm. He had been jolted by her appearance, recognising her face, but having problems recalling who she was, but knew she was one of the Dwyers; that he could tell by the features.

It had been some years since he had seen me, and I had barely changed. William had been stunned to see me, unable to believe it at first. Well, if I was here, then so would Sam be. Perhaps we were visiting for Christmas?

He was only guessing that Helen would be here. If she was not, then surely, I would know her whereabouts, since we had kept in regular contact. He decided to follow me, and unintentionally, I led him to Saint Nicholas'.

"Helen!" I reached the kitchen. "Where are you?"

William's dirty face broke into a smile. He could hardly believe his luck. Again, he wondered if there was a chance she would take him back. Would she forgive him? The door stood ajar, even though it was December. Helen was doing laundry, and the copper was boiling. How beautifully warm it would be in there! He could smell soap and longed for a clean body and clothes.

"What you doing 'ere?"

William jumped violently at the unexpected voice. Gus stood, glaring down at him. William thought fast. He needed to get on this man's right side if he was to somehow get to Helen.

"Sir!" He took off his hat and bowed his head. "I wanted a bit of warmth, sir, warmth and a crust of bread. Nothing more. I thought the church gave alms to people like me!"

Gus observed the man. His whole demeanour spoke of desperation, the whining voice of the beggar. Gus was not unsympathetic to anybody who had genuinely fallen on hard times. Had he not been so himself? And the Reverend was happy to feed the poor, allow them warmth, and was known to be the softest touch in all Yarmouth. William held out a filthy mittened hand.

"Please, sir, have pity!" William permitted some tears to fall.

Gus paused. "Wait there!" he ordered.

When Gus came to him in the vestry to speak of the beggar in the church-yard, the Reverend nodded.

"Poor fellow." Reverend sighed. "I so pity the destitute at this time of year. Alright, Gus, you may bring him to the kitchen."

Gus shook his head at once. "I daresn't, Reverend!" he told the elderly man. "Helen'd have my hide! Filthy, he is."

"I see, then tell Helen to give him some food... soup. Tell her to find something in the donations box too, like gloves and a scarf. She'll know what to select."

Gus came into the kitchen and we both smiled at him. He kissed Tabitha and asked her if she felt well, to which she replied that she did. We heard the request and at once, Helen nodded. There was a stew bubbling on the fire, some of which she ladled into a bowl.

"There are cold sausages, bread, cheese." Helen bustled about getting the food, even some cake which she wrapped in a cloth.

I went with Gus to the donation box, glanced inside, and picked out a scarf, mittens and a woollen hat and gave them to Gus, who took it and the food and made his way back outside. William was waiting.

"Sir!" William said. "You are blessed; truly, a Good Samaritan."

Gus nodded. "You know, you ought to try the workhouse," he told William. "I know it ain't nice, been there myself, but better than outside."

"Yes, sir, thank you. I will." William took the food and, giving a polite bow, left the churchyard.

Having bid Helen, Tabitha and Gus farewell, I ventured out of the kitchen to return home. As I got to the road, William suddenly stepped out in front of me on the small, icily grassed plain, hand stretched out in pleading.

"Alms, miss, for pity's sake." I squealed in alarm and jumped. I could smell him from where I stood.

"Please, miss, please."

I rooted inside my glove and dropped some coins near his feet.

"There, that will suffice, I hope?"

William bent and retrieved the money. "Thank you, miss; don't worry, I shan't hurt you!" he smiled. "Bless you, charming lady. I'm grateful."

I was edging away from him. William edged a little closer. I felt extremely ill at ease. "I shan't hurt you, miss! It's just lovely to look upon such a pretty face and hear such pretty speech."

I thought. "Are you the fellow Gus got food for?"

"Yes, miss. A goodly man if ever I saw one. I'm not ungrateful, I know he gave me food, but it only lasts so long and it's bitterly cold."

I was wondering what to do. I very much wanted to help him, but I wanted to get away from him too. I heard familiar whistling and glanced around. Never had I been so glad to see Manoa! The towering man walked swiftly toward me.

"You alright, Alice?"

"Yes. I was just giving this man some coins."

Manoa glowered at William. "You've got what you wanted! Now let this young lady pass."

Manoa turned to me. "Is Helen there?" he asked and I nodded.

"Yes, she's doing laundry."

William stood, open-mouthed. Who *was* this individual to his Helen? Surely not her husband?

Manoa spoke once more. "You got what you came for, now go."

William turned to shuffle away, boiling with rage. *He* had his Helen now? He wanted to scream.

William knew he wouldn't be recognised. He wondered if anyone would know him from his voice, but I had not, however, it would perhaps be pertinent to change it a little and adopt more of a Suffolk twang.

William needed somehow to get Helen alone, but how? She wouldn't come willingly, he mused. He decided to watch Saint Nicholas' for a few days, observe her movements and think things through with the utmost care. He had been shocked to find out what had happened to Elspeth. Nevertheless, he still loved Helen.

William set about the crowded marketplace to attempt to pick a pocket. Women, he found, were more careless and he managed to swipe two purses from the tops of women's baskets whilst they jabbered with friends.

He went round some stalls in the market and purchased some decent-looking clothes, a winter coat, hat, some boots he badly needed and a shirt, all second or third-hand, he thought with disgust. He would never have even dreamt of wearing such rags before, but he had little choice.

William obtained lodgings on Ramp Row. He had changed his filthy clothes to the clean ones but was longing for a bath. He deliberated, should he shave off his beard? Helen had never actually seen him without a beard; surely, she would not recognise her former husband clean-shaven? By the time he had done with his self-barbering, not even his own mother would have recognised him. He was shocked to see the whiteness of the lower half of his face, the rest, still tanned, despite his imprisonment and time in his home country. The last time he had been beardless was when he had been a boy.

Pleased to see the public baths, William bathed for the first time in months. He enjoyed the feeling of the hot water over his body. It took several repetitions before he was completely clean. He dug his fingers into his scalp, rooting through the oily, messy hair. He would find a barber shop to have it cut closely later. After a thorough scrubbing, he shut his eyes and inhaled the scent of soap. He lay in the water and looked about him, then called for more soap and hot water.

Back in Rampart Row, William glanced morosely at the walls of the house where he had his lodgings. He wished he had left it until he had been able to wash properly and dress in clean clothes. The landlady who had permitted him the room was none too particular regarding cleanliness and didn't care who had the room so long as they had the wherewithal to pay. He would need better lodgings, even if it were for just a short time.

Mould was halfway up the wall of the front of the house where the window was. It was cracked and draughty. There was a table with a chair against the wall which looked as though it would fall to pieces if one sat on it. He could smell mice. The bed was little more than a frame with a stained, damp and disgusting mattress on it, onto which the landlady had heaped a sheet and some blankets, leaving him to sort it out himself. The chamber pot was cracked, with dubious-looking stains inside. William's lip curled in disgust. Even the fireplace could not support a fire, having been kicked in a rage by the previous occupant.

William made his way to The Three Feathers Inn. He desperately wanted to see his children again and wondered where they were. He would need to engage someone who knew them in conversation. He looked around to see if he recognised any faces. However, for all the tap room had changed not at all, the people seemed to have; William couldn't recognise anyone. It would not be wise to ask too many questions either. Why would a stranger suddenly want to find Helen or her children?

William went to the church in the hope he would see Helen, but that morning, the house door was firmly shut, and instead, he walked into the nave. The organ produced melodic Christmas carols and he stopped to listen. He had not heard these in years. He felt miserable; this was where he and Helen had married, and he thought of their wedding day, many years before, and couldn't help himself as tears rolled down his cheeks; he wanted Helen badly.

It took almost a week, but William, having formulated a plan, ventured to the mews where he used to work, recognising Johnny. The man was similar to how he had been a decade before and was mucking out the stables. William walked casually into the stable yard. Icy and muddy puddles cracked under his boots. Manure steamed in a corner.

"Good morning, Johnny!" he stated. Johnny, intent on his job, jumped and swung round.

"Sir?"

"Got a light, bor'?" he asked, and Johnny fumbled in his britches for matches, handed them to William and watched as he lit his pipe, puffed several times and handed them back. "What're you doing? Shovelling shit? You were a driver once!"

Johnny hung his head.

"I kept gettin' it wrong," he stated dolefully. "I lost the way that many times, Mews Master got sick of complaints, so he demoted me. I been doing this now for eight years."

William shook his head.

"Damned shame, bor'!"

Johnny squinted at the man. "Sorry, sir, but how d'ye know me? I don't know you!"

"I think you'll discover that you do, bor'! What time d'ye knock off for lunch? Fancy an ale and some pie?"

Johnny nodded.

At half past noon, William bought himself and Johnny a pie and ale. Johnny was stunned to hear of his old friend's return. Johnny could barely write his own name; he was an innocent, that much was obvious –not entirely stupid, but he was gullible. William told him his unfortunate tale and by the time he'd finished speaking, Johnny was willing to do anything he asked.

He agreed that he would 'work for' William as his assistant. He didn't query how William would pay him; he was amazed to be asked to be William's right-hand man, in 'business.' It was easy to get Johnny to allow him to share his lodgings, which, though not of a good standard, far exceeded those he was in now. He told Johnny that nobody was to know he was back in Yarmouth.

William spoke of Helen, of how she had re-married. Johnny recalled Helen and Manoa's wedding; William listened, miserable, as he learned the entire story.

"All I need is time with her, bor', persuade her... time alone; that's where you come in!"

It didn't occur to William that his incredible scheme would have repercussions. In his misery, he simply could not see it.

They left the tavern to return to William's squalid lodgings. Johnny looked around, the distaste on his face evident.

"I know, bor', it ain't glamorous."

Johnny nodded. "Well, come and stay with me! My room isn't bad."

William pretended to think. "Hmm, why not, eh? It'll be a sight warmer there! What a good lad you are, Johnny. Well, the Mews Master's loss is my gain. I need a faithful friend by my side. Do you go and tell that fella to stick his job. You work for me now! Oh, and I want to see my son too; d'ye know where he is?"

Johnny thought deeply. "Well, I dunno for certain, but he's at a posh school," he told him.

William smiled. It wouldn't take long to find out.

They hastened back to Johnny's lodgings. They were untidy and smelled strongly of sweat and the mews, but William wasn't concerned. This room was better than the one he had just left. At least it was dry; there was no mould or cracked windows. Johnny hesitated. "You'd best take the bed, sir, seeing as you're my boss now!"

William accepted this gracefully. He laid a hand on his shoulder. "You're a great friend, bor'. I'll see you right; you see if I don't." He sat on the bed and watched, as Johnny laid some blankets on the floor in the corner for himself. "Now, time we got our heads down!" William said. "Work begins on the morrow. Straight after breakfast, do you go in and tell the Mews Master where to stick his job. You'll enjoy that! But *don't* mention my name, eh, bor'? We don't want people knowing I'm back."

Johnny took little time to fall asleep. William lay, hands behind his head, whilst he looked at the flickering candle flame.

In the morning, they went to a chop house to breakfast. Johnny then made his way to work and sought the Mews Master, striding into his office without even knocking. The Master stared at him, open-mouthed with shock, as the young man gleefully told him, 'Do you stick your job where the sun don't shine, 'cos I got a better one now!"

He walked away, very pleased with himself, leaving his old boss speechless, gasping in indignation and anger, and returned to his lodgings, where William explained to Johnny what he needed him to do. His tasks were to find out the whereabouts of his son, and to see what else he could learn about his ex-wife's marriage. Johnny listened closely. He did not want to mess up this job as he had the previous one.

"I want to visit my Elspeth's grave too. Talk to that gardener fellow. Make an excuse."

Making excuses was beyond Johnny's imagination. William looked at his new assistant. "Can you read?" he asked, as an afterthought, but the young man shook his head.

"No, sir."

On a piece of paper, William wrote Elspeth's name and date of death. "Now, I know you don't read, bor', but you can match these letter shapes against what's on the headstone. Look at the newest kiddies' ones. If what's on the stone matches what's on the paper, then that's it!"

William toyed with the idea of approaching Sam, as his oldest friend, but he rejected the idea. "D'ye know much about the Dwyers?" he asked, as he stirred a pot of tea. "Where'd they live?"

Johnny tried to recall. "In one of the nicer rows," he guessed. William had nodded. Johnny, he knew, would try his patience, but he had to be good to him. He needed his help.

"Have a good think, Johnny bor'."

"Half Moon Row. The last house up from the ale house there," he said, grinning at his ability to recollect. "They got two nice boys; littlest one's sweet. All curly hair. Real smiler he is. So's their eldest. Nice manners too."

"Half Moon Row." William noted it down. "Might take a turn up there later!"

William did, but he made sure he was well muffled over the lower half of his face. His hat pulled down, so that only his eyes were visible, he walked up the snowy cobbles of Half Moon Row. It was quiet and the snow squeaked under his boots. He came to our house and peeked in. I was busy cooking by the seem of it. Sam was in the front room, poking at the fire and Little Sam stood with Kit in his arms. It represented the perfect family home and all content within. Suddenly, much to his shame, William wanted to cry. He turned to lean against our wall and took several deep breaths whilst he regained control.

As it was advent, the atmosphere was cheerful in the town. The weather obliged with snow, making it more festive still. William was hoping to be able to get to Helen at least before Christmas; all they needed was time alone.

Johnny was well known in the town and people gossiped with him. Knowing he was also a little lacking in intelligence, they generally told him more than was wise, considering him 'harmless', which indeed he was. There was no spite in Johnny at all. But he was careless.

Johnny wandered along to Saint Nicholas'. The church doors stood open, ever welcoming anybody who wished to pray. Braziers warmed the huge interior.

Johnny meandered to the newer part of the churchyard. He had gone to at least thirty small headstones and he was cold. Not much snow had fallen along the paths protected by trees, but little drifts of snow had accumulated, and they made him think of mountains in faraway lands. Then, among the bare branches of the willows, he saw a fairly fresh-looking grave with a magnificent headstone. It was small, indicating that a child lay there. Johnny pulled out the piece of paper and laboriously examined each letter on the stone that corresponded with the ones written on the page. He smiled. He had found the grave. William would be thrilled. Pocketing the paper, feeling very clever, he made his way back to his lodging.

"Sir! I got where she is." Johnny sat and took off his mittens, chafing cold fingers together. "She's near the centre, where the big tree is."

"Can you take me to her?" he asked, and Johnny nodded eagerly.

William patted Johnny on the back. "Good work, bor. We'll visit later."

A week later, and Miss Spoonamore was in the market. She was selecting some items as gifts for her twin and her brother. These normally un-exciting gifts would take the form of handkerchiefs, socks and gloves. She huffed in exasperation as she spied Johnny, who was at a stall. He turned.

"Morning, Miss Spoonamore!" he said politely, tipping his hat to her. Miss Spoonamore sighed. She could not stand this man and privately referred to him as a 'drooling idiot.'

"Good morning, young man. Selecting a gift for your sweetheart, are you?" she asked him spitefully, knowing Johnny had no girl.

"Not me, miss." He blushed. "I don't have a sweetheart. I'm looking for something for my new master."

Miss Spoonamore looked surprised. "Oh? What new master is that? I thought you worked at the mews!"

"I did!" Johnny told her proudly. "But now, I got a better job. A proper one." He grinned, showing brown teeth. "I'm assistant to Master William Blake!"

His hand shot to cover his mouth in shock. One week on the job and he had already let his master's name slip, having been expressly told not to. He was so horrified that Miss Spoonamore wondered, what was so odd about having a master named William Blake? She regarded Johnny, who was red as a berry and looking shifty. There was something strange here!

"William Blake, you say?" she asked with a frown.

Johnny nodded. Miss Spoonamore trawled her memory. The name rang a bell. She wondered why the man looked so worried. "Well, I'm pleased you have something decent, but why so horror-stricken?"

Johnny mumbled an excuse and made as if to leave hastily, but Miss Spoonamore's hand shot out and grasped his sleeve.

"Wait! I haven't finished. William Blake. The name *is* familiar to me." She hesitated. Johnny stood, looking down at the ground. Then, it came to her. "Do you mean the same William Blake that left for America?"

"Yes, Miss Spoonamore, but he told me no one must know. Nobody!"

"But why? I don't understand!" Miss Spoonamore replied. "So what? He's from here, is he not?"

Johnny looked so uncomfortable that Miss Spoonamore smelled a rat. She patted the man's arm.

"Is something amiss?"

Johnny could not help the guilty look on his face, and he blushed. Miss Spoonamore wondered deeply. Now, listen, don't worry, you can trust me. Come with me. I'll buy you tea and a cake. Would you like that?"

Johnny nodded.

The pair went to a small eating house along by Market Row, where Miss Spoonamore ordered tea and buns.

Miss Spoonamore, for a change, actually sat and listened as someone else spoke. Suddenly, she saw a way of avenging herself on Helen... everyone who had felt her spite over the years. She questioned him, and Johnny, not understanding where her leading questions would go, simply responded with the truth. Miss Spoonamore nodded sympathetically. "I always felt that man was done wrong by." She sipped her tea.

Johnny was still worried, nibbling at his fingernails with concern that he had said what he should not have. Miss Spoonamore gave him what she thought was a reassuring smile. "Don't worry young man!" she told him. "You haven't made a mistake in telling me. I can keep secrets very well! Take me to your lodgings. I'd like to re-acquaint myself with your master. It's been a long time!"

Johnny led Miss Spoonamore, scampering in front of her like some strange creature. They turned into his row. Miss Spoonamore's lips curled as she picked her way through the ice and snow. Even snow-covered, this row looked dirty.

William was horrified when the tall, spare figure of Miss Spoonamore entered the room ahead of Johnny. He stood and wondered whether to bolt or bluster. In the end, he needed to do neither. Miss Spoonamore regarded William. After ten years, he was scarcely recognisable, particularly without the beard. But, as usual, she took control of the situation. She sat, uninvited, at the table, somewhat grudgingly, since neither seat nor table were too clean. She smiled at both men and informed them, much to William's stunned amazement, that she would be 'willing to assist him in any way she could.'

"Are you sure, Miss Spoonamore?" William asked in surprise and with suspicion.

"Naturally!" she responded. "Though I fail to see what you can achieve by forcing the issue."

"Once we're alone, somewhere quiet, she'll listen, and want to come back to me."

To his amazement, Miss Spoonamore appeared to relish the idea. Far from being concerned she might be 'found out', she seemed positively excited by the admittedly mad scheme William had in mind! She thoroughly disapproved of Helen's current marriage. She would aid the man in getting Helen 'back where she belonged to her lawful husband'.

Later that day, William went into the churchyard to re-visit Elspeth.

"I'm sorry, Elspeth. If I'd had you by my side, you'd be here now, excited for Christmas."

Gus, out doing some last-minute maintenance before Christmas, spotted him and wondered what he was doing. He moved closer, but seeing him with head bowed, murmuring, evidently paying his respects, he left.

Early on the morning of the 21st of December, Helen was out delivering some cards. She enjoyed a little gossip with one or two people, and jumped when Miss Spoonamore, lurking just inside one of the rows, tapped her smartly on the shoulder.

"Och! Miss Spoonamore. You gave me a start!" Helen told her. "What're ye doing lurking inside this row?"

Miss Spoonamore smiled. "I've been looking for you!" she answered, with false jollity. "I thought I might see you about."

"Oh? Why? Decided to enter into the Christmas spirit at last? Has only taken ye over fifty years!"

Miss Spoonamore smirked. "I've a present for you! A special surprise! Follow me!"

Helen, a little stunned and a mite concerned, and wondering why she was obeying, followed her, walking quickly up the row, then turned into an icy half row and entered a small house.

"What *are* ye up to?" Helen asked crossly. "I've cards to deliver! I've nae time for jokes!"

"No joke!" Miss Spoonamore assured her.

The door shut loudly behind them, making Helen jump. Miss Spoonamore led her into the back room of the house. An oil lamp glowed eerily in the gloom. A man was standing, looking out the window at the tiny back yard. His hands were loosely clasped behind his back. He turned slowly.

"Helen," William said to her in a smooth voice. "Long time, no see, eh?" He removed his top hat and gave a bow.

Helen's mouth dropped open in shock. The man standing in front of her was very different from how she had last seen him, but his voice, she would never forget. For a moment, she found she couldn't speak, then;

"William? What are you doing here? Oh no!" Helen suddenly realising she was trapped, made to turn and run, but felt strong arms grab her from behind.

"Easy, my dear, it's for your own good."

Little Sam's school was having a Christmas party later that afternoon. Sam was busy finishing up his work and I glanced at the puddings I had made; the smell inside the house was incredible. A mixture of brandy, rich fruits, lemon, ginger, oranges, all mingled with the pine from the tree in the window. There were other Christmas pieces dotted here and there.

I addressed Little Sam. "Please take a pudding round to Aunt Maria. Don't drop it! Then stop by Grandpapa's and tell him Sam'll fetch him ready for the party at three o'clock."

"Yes, Mamma!" he said, and hugging Sam and I, he hastened off. I grinned at Sam who winked and grinned back.

"I'll go to Saint Nicholas' now." I put on my thickest shawl. "Shan't be long. I'm taking Kit. I expect he'd like to see Iffey."

Sam nodded. "Don't be long!" he told me. "I fancy a nice, long cuddle!" Another grin and a wink.

I was keen to involve Helen, but on arrival, I found Helen gone. "Ah, that's a pity. I was hoping to invite her to the school party!" I told Manoa.

"Well, she said she wouldn't be long, but that was an hour and a half ago. She only went to deliver cards," Manoa replied.

"Well, you know Helen, she's probably gossiping," I replied, shifting Kit to the other arm. He burbled at Iffey who gave a wide grin.

"Can I give her a message?" Manoa asked.

"Tell her if she wants to come to the Christmas party at Sam's school, to be at ours for 3.15pm."

I went to give my greetings and gifts to Florence and the Reverend too. I gave them an open invitation to the school party, though I doubted they would come. They were too elderly to go out in such freezing weather.

Gus and Tabitha agreed to come along to help in the chaos. "Only if you're sure, Tab," I said, looking at the woman's belly.

Tabitha laughed. "Ah, what can possibly go wrong?" she asked with a wink.

The rest of that morning, I was busy with preparations for Christmas and Boxing Day, so when Manoa arrived at one o'clock, I smiled at him. "You're early, Manny!" I told him. "Where's Helen?"

Manoa sat. "I don't know!" he told me in a worried voice. I looked at him in confusion.

"What do you mean, you don't know?" I asked.

"Well, she went out five hours ago! She hasn't come back!"

Sam and I exchanged glances. The first flicker of worry came into my belly. I started to fill the kettle, then joined the men at the table.

"Well, she probably got lost in the excitement of shopping," I said. "Or she met up with someone– you know what she is when she gets chatting."

Manoa nodded miserably. I looked at Sam for help.

Perhaps she had had an accident and was lying unnoticed in a quiet row. My mind showed me Helen, shivering, with a cracked head, or worse still, unconscious, slowly freezing to death.

"We'll find her," Sam said to Manoa, who rose. "I know it's silly to say don't worry, but… well, all her friends are out looking for her."

"Thanks. I'd better get back home; she may be back already."

Late afternoon. I was impatient with waiting. "Ah, it's no good!" I said to Sam and my father-in-law. "Helen isn't coming; what's she playing at? It's getting dark." I looked out of the window for the umpteenth time, hoping to see Helen and Manoa marching up the row. "Well, there's no reason for the children to miss the party. Let's go."

The school was warm and welcoming. There was the sound of happily raised voices, and squeals of excitement. Mackie was attempting to keep some form of order and failing dismally.

I was worried. Helen would not have missed this party; I knew her. Perhaps she *was* lying injured somewhere. That *must* be it. I spoke of my fears to the men. "Something terrible's happened," I told them. "I can feel it!"

Manoa had already organised a search with his crewmates from the lifeboat. The police did not seem bothered, much to his disgust, and had simply told Manoa that she must have needed a break and would come home in time; they couldn't interfere. Even Manoa's pleas that she may have had some sort of accident failed to yield any help.

"If we searched for every wife who forgot the time nattering at market, we'd be forever searching, and villains would be running wild!" he was told in no uncertain terms. "It's not up to us to discipline her!"

By seven o'clock, the party was over, and we collected the boys. Simon would go to Maria and Albert's home that night and stay. He would then make his way to our home in time for Christmas dinner. Then they would all be at our home on Boxing Day.

I slept fitfully that night, as did Sam. Around midnight, I rose, and shrugging my shawl about me, I looked out of the window. The moon, huge and bright, shone down on Yarmouth. Ice glittered on the cobbles; there was no wind at all. A few drunken revellers could be heard making their way home. My breath misted the windowpane and I opened it to crane my neck up and down.

"Alice! Back to bed. At once! Leaning out into the freezing night air!"

I turned, smiled at Sam, shut the window and went back to snuggle into his warm body. His arms held me closely,

The morning dawned bright and crisp. Sun glinted on the snowy patches, and ice, making it look incredibly pretty, but my heart was heavy with worry for my friend. Had she come home? I resolved to go and see as soon as breakfast was finished.

Helen had not returned, and another search party had been organised. Sam and Manoa headed out, leading the volunteers.

From the window of her front parlour, Miss Spoonamore peered out around the lace curtains. "You won't find her," she whispered. "Look all you want, but you won't find her!" She gave a sudden cackle which unnerved her sister very much.

I ventured into the church. Everything was ready for Christmas and the evening's service, but it felt flat and empty knowing my friend was missing. Helen and I always enjoyed 'doing things up' to make it look Christmassy, and I had sorely missed it. I sat to wait until Reverend came to a stop in his prayers and spoke. He turned around and smiled.

"Alice, dear child. We are doing all that we can." He smiled at Kit who grinned at him. "Kit, come to me that I may bless you."

I took him to the gentle Reverend who placed a hand on Kit's curly hair.

The sergeant heard Manoa out. He had just come on duty and was preparing for what he hoped would be his final Christmas working, having decided on retirement in the spring. The searchers had been out for two whole days. It was Christmas Eve, and something more had to be done. Since she had not been found injured or dead anywhere, she must be being held somewhere. She wouldn't have left her children at Christmas. The question was, why? By whom? And most of all, where? He sat near the fire, a mug of tea in his hand, and thought hard.

He decided he would gather the people in the marketplace. Then, he'd get someone to address them on the matter of Helen's sudden disappearance. He got up and hurried to Poppy's Row, where the town crier lived with his wife and six children. What better way to draw a crowd?

At midday, the town crier and the policeman hurried to the bustling marketplace where he stood on a platform and bellowed for silence, ringing his bell to get attention. It took a little time, but seeing him there, calling, the people soon gathered, knowing there was important news.

He spoke of Helen's sudden disappearance, and asked them to check their yards, outhouses, coal sheds, anywhere someone could lie unnoticed. He asked them, that if they had seen anything, seen Helen with anybody, to speak to the police and it mattered not whether it was man, woman or child. Any information was welcome, and any information would be well-rewarded.

Things had already been set in motion, for all we had no idea at that time. A street urchin had seen Helen and Miss Spoonamore together, heading up Row 87 ½. The lad, Bertie, had followed them, thinking to cadge something, since Helen was known for her generosity; when they had vanished into one of the houses, he had waited, but only Miss Spoonamore had come out. He had thought nothing of it at the time, having shrugged and gone elsewhere. Now, having heard the town crier's appeal, he put his sharp wits to work. He might get a reward for the information. Perhaps she was trapped! He trotted off to the police station and, for once in his life, voluntarily walked in.

The Sergeant on duty was not pleased to see a dirty urchin enter and still less pleased when the boy told him he had information, and if he wanted it, he should give him some money. With all the usual cheek that only a street urchin could muster, he leaned his arms on the desk and spoke.

"Oi, mister, I got something to tell yer!"

"Be off with you, you little toad!"

"But I knows something!" he shouted as the man seized him by the scruff to toss him into the road. "'Bout that woman what's missing!"

The policeman halted, the urchin dangling from his grasp by his scruffy jacket collar. "What did you just say, bor'?" he asked.

The sergeant digested this startling news. "Miss Spoonamore? Are you sure?" he asked, and Bertie nodded.

"Course I am. Everyone knows the hag! They was walking together. The hag got her as a prisoner, I bet! She come out and went off, but Mrs Wadaa never."

The sergeant considered. What on earth could Miss Spoonamore hope to gain by taking Helen prisoner? It seemed highly unlikely, but every avenue must be investigated, no matter how absurd it seemed. He looked fiercely at the child.

"I hope you're not pollywigglin' me, bor'. Those that do that spends the night in the lock-up!"

Bertie shook his head. "No sir. I ain't. 'Tis true."

Having given the lad a spare set of clothes, the policeman smiled down at the boy.

"Now then, if you can show me the house where she took Mrs Wadaa first, then there'll be a warm place for you for the Christmas period; good food too. Can you show me?"

The urchin rose.

"Yes, SIR!" he answered, excited now and feeling most important.

The pair made their way up Row 87 ½. The lad pointed to the ramshackle house and the policeman entered with some caution. Bertie followed him. It was an abandoned place, but there were signs of recent occupation. His eye caught a pile of scattered envelopes, addressed to various people in the town. He picked them up and looked at them. So, as Manoa had stated, Helen had gone out delivering cards. She had, for some strange reason, come into this house with Miss Spoonamore and now all that remained were the undelivered cards.

"Anyone there?" Sergeant Collins called, but there was no answer other than a thin moan of wind from the chimney. The policeman glanced at the boy. "Do you stay here." He turned then and went up the stairs hoping to find Helen safe and well, if trussed up, but there was nobody.

Sergeant Collins made his way back to Bertie, boots thumping on the wooden stairs.

He stood, finger against his lips as he thought. To Bertie, it looked like a good place to squat. "Hmm," the sergeant thought, looking down at the dirty little boy.

"Sir?" Bertie spoke again.

"It's alright, bor' I'm just thinking. Well, there certainly have been people here recently."

"I told you!" the boy stated firmly. "Now, can I get me warmth and food like you promised?"

The man smiled down at him. "Shortly, my boy. First, we need to pay Miss Spoonamore a visit, but I need another chap with me. Come! Back to the station. I need to speak to her; you brave enough to come along with me? Just to make sure it *was* her you saw?"

Bertie agreed.

Miss Spoonamore's maid opened the door to the two policemen who stood on the doorstep, accompanied by a ragged street urchin. She looked surprised to say the least.

"Good afternoon, miss!" the sergeant said in a pleasant manner. "Where is your mistress? We wish a word with her!"

The maid bobbed. "She's in the kitchen, sir," she answered. "I'll get her." She eyed the boy who followed the two policemen into the house. Miss Spoonamore was not going to want that boy in her clean home!

Miss Spoonamore came out, confused at the girl's message, and even more surprised at the news that two policemen were in her parlour with a street urchin and wanted to speak to her. She frowned, and worriedly, made her way into her parlour.

"What can I do for you?" she asked stiffly. "And more to the point, what *is* that malodourous child doing in my house? He will bring in fleas!"

The sergeant looked down at the boy.

"Well now, young fellow. You sure she is the woman you saw?"

The boy nodded. "Yes, sir!"

Miss Spoonamore felt a cold trickle of unease make its way down her spine. "What?" she barked. "What do you mean, *her* you saw? Why have you brought me a disgusting child? Am I being expected to feed and clothe urchins now?"

The sergeant looked intently at the spinster, and Miss Spoonamore felt butterflies in her stomach.

"No, Miss Spoonamore, I have come to ask if you could accompany us to the station. We would like a word with you regarding the disappearance of Mrs Helen Wadaa!"

Miss Spoonamore looked at the man in horror. "But... but... what does that have to do with me? I seldom spoke to the woman! How would I know where she is?" she blustered.

Sergeant Collins knew a guilty face when he saw it and noted her shaking, that the colour had drained from her face.

"Chappie here says he saw you with her. Going into a house in Row 87 ½. You come out, but she never!"

Everyone heard the crash as Miss Spoonamore, who had been clutching onto the tablecloth, fainted, pulling cloth and crockery down with her, bringing her sister, brother, and maid in at a run.

It took some time to bring Miss Spoonamore round. Her twin and brother protested, but nothing could prevent him taking Miss Spoonamore, limp as a rag doll, to the station for questioning.

The sergeant looked at her.

"Now then!" he stated firmly. "Is there anything you wish to tell us?"

Miss Spoonamore, head down, spilled the story in its entirety.

"But it wasn't my idea!" she wailed. "Nor my fault. I was *forced* to cooperate!" She burst into sobs of rage. "All he's doing is taking back his legal wife! How else was he to make the horrible woman listen? Mr Blake made me bring her to him! That half-wit from the mews drove them, and I heard Mr Blake say to Somerton."

Christmas Day came, and Sam and I opened each other's gifts, then watched Little Sam open his as Kit explored everything with great interest. The multi-coloured stuffed ball made a large grin appear on his little cheeks and he hugged it to him. My mind, though, was on Helen. Sam hastened to fetch his father to assist him through the snow. He spoke to Maria and Albert who offered him mulled ale before leaving, which Sam accepted.

"Any news?" Maria asked, but Sam shook his head.

"Not that we've heard. Poor Manoa! Alice is thinking of the effect it must be having on little Iffey too."

"Oh, The poor little thing!" Maria's eyes teared. "I expect Manoa can cope with her, but a child that age needs her mother."

At Saint Nicholas', there was sudden hope. The sergeant had walked jauntily down to Helen's home, the urchin trotting at his side, and in the warm kitchen, he informed Manoa, Helen's other children, and Florence of everything that had occurred. Gus came in and stood listening, Tabitha at his side, her face suddenly alight with hope.

"Reverend's doing the morning service, but he won't be much longer," Florence told him.

"When can we fetch her home?" Manoa asked standing bolt upright and looking around for his coat. "Where is she? We must go. Will? Come with me!"

Sergeant Collins gently put both hands on Manoa's shoulders and pushed him back down in his seat. "That's already happening. Right now! She was taken somewhere a couple of hours away. Miss Spoonamore, we questioned yesterday afternoon, and it wasn't long afore she spilled the beans. We know where your wife is, and with whom."

"How did Miss Spoonamore get involved?" Florence queried.

"By accident, apparently. She swears she was made to co-operate. This boy saw everything. I promised to find him a place. It's thanks to him we found out what happened. I wondered if you'd give him houseroom this Christmas and perhaps find a place for him after? If you cannot, I shall."

There was no question about turning the lad out.

As they waited, and Manoa went to assist Gus with settling the new member of the household, Florence wondered if a message should be sent to us, and a mild argument developed. "Sam and Alice deserve to know," Florence stated fiercely. "They're worried sick. At least if they know, they can rest easier."

"But we do not know if she will be found well, or even alive." Reverend spoke calmly. "We can only hope William has not harmed her. Then we can send a message."

With this as the decision made, they sat, nervously waiting for Helen's return.

25th December

Helen never spoke to any of us about her time with William; only later would she speak privately to the authorities.

The lights in the kitchen at Saint Nicholas' burned brightly and late that night into the small hours. Helen was home at last. She had bathed and dressed and now she sat at the kitchen table, Iffey asleep in her arms. Alice and Will were sat on one side of her, with Manoa on the other. She looked at her family. "I'm fine," she said stoically. The Reverend pottered here and there, attempting to be of some assistance. "He didnae hurt me. But I cannae believe I was so stupid as to go with Spoonamore."

"That was scarcely your fault," the Reverend told her. "How were you to know what would happen? Nobody would have even imagined in their wildest dreams what she was capable of."

Alice nodded. "Yes, Momma, I'm so glad you're home." Alice began to sob, and Helen slipped Iffey into the crook of one elbow so that she could hug her elder daughter.

"Youse all need to open yer Christmas gifts," she told them, attempting normality.

"We'll do that tomorrow," Manoa told her. "Right now, you're the only gift we want!"

26th December 1856

Boxing Day morning and it was icy cold. The snow crunched as Little Sam marched round, crunching the icy-topped snow in the yard. Kit saw it and squealed in excitement.

"No!" I told him, "Looking from the window is all you'll do, young man! You are far too young to go out in the snow!"

When Kit realised he was not to enjoy the outside with his brother, he bawled, little fists clenched, legs kicking. Sam smiled and picked up his second son.

"Stop yer blartin'," he told him. "Mamma's right. It's too cold for your little feet. Look! Go and see Grandpapa."

Kit was passed to his grandfather who began to chatter to him. "Now then, Kit, do you stop all this noise," he told him, "or Mamma might not let you have any mashed potato!"

Kit's lower lip stuck out and tears welled once more.

"Gosh, but he is *so* like our Annie was," he said, with a reminiscent smile. "D'ye remember how she used to take off like that?"

Sam shook his head, smiling.

We were content to gather around the kitchen stove or living room fire and enjoy ourselves. Maria and Albert arrived to complete the gathering. Dinner that day would be potatoes with cold meats. Maria had brought some sweet chutneys she had made to go with it, along with some ham and beef offcuts. I was as ravenous as a starving wolf but tried not to eat too much.

"A friend of mine has a sister in service," Maria began. "She was telling me this morning her sister had been refused leave to go home! I know they don't go home as a rule, but this year she'd been promised she could, just for the day, but they changed their minds and told her just as she was putting her coat on! She was in floods of tears, but they said to be quiet and get on with her work. Her folks were waiting for her, looking forward to the visit. It's terrible, don't you think?"

I nodded; the poor maid would be expected to attend to her duties as if nothing was wrong, and any sullenness would be reprimanded.

Meanwhile, Helen was adjusting to being back at home. It seemed like weeks since she had been taken to that cottage, yet it had been just four days.

"I want to send a message to my friends," Helen told Bertie as the kitchen began to fill with the delicious smells. "Will ye run this envelope to Half Moon Row, number 29?"

"Yes, Mrs Wadaa."

"Tell them I'll call soon. Tell Alice *not* to come running; she's expecting a baby, and she'll fall and do herself some damage."

The hammering on the door made me jump.

"You Mr Dwyer?" Bertie asked. Sam nodded. "Message for you and your missus from Mrs Wadaa!"

"Helen?" Sam exclaimed and hearing her name mentioned, I ran to the doorway. Sam shrieked at me to remain calm.

"Who are you? What's that about Helen?" I asked at once, and almost dragged the boy inside.

"Now, calm down, Alice!" Sam stated. "This is no time for hysteria. Who are you? Is Helen at home?"

So, Bertie began his tale.

We sat and listened as Bertie sat at the fireside and told the story. Little Sam looked wide-eyed at him. I wanted to go to Helen, but Sam shook his head. "She says to wait, Alice. She'll need time with her husband and children," he told me gently. "You'll soon get to see her."

"Can I go now, Mrs Dwyer?" Bertie asked. "We got a goose in the oven!"

"They expect her to cook Christmas dinner?" I exclaimed in horror.

"No, mawther, the others are doing it," Bertie informed me. "She said she was starving and wasn't gonna let anyone spoil her dinner!"

"Now, *that* sounds like the Helen we know," Sam told me. "Alright, tell her we'll wait for her to say when we can visit, and we're hugely relieved she's home."

Mackie, on his return from a family visit on 30th December, was oblivious to the drama. He called round with the usual smile on his face to ask if we were bringing the children to the park for the old year feast.

"Of course!" I told him. "But I doubt Helen will. I haven't seen her yet. Sam said it was better to leave her to settle a while and be with her family."

Kit, in his playpen, spied Mackie and roared for his attention.

"Maaaackiee!" he screeched at ear-splitting volume, and struggled to get out of his playpen, climbing part way up with frightening ease.

"Goodness me! What a noise!" Mackie chuckled as I lifted Kit to give him to Mackie. I smiled as Kit settled down.

Helen surprised us all by attending the feast in the park on New Year's Eve. She came first to our home. The moment I saw her, I hastened to hug her. "Helen!" I sobbed.

"Och, ye soppy wee lassie, look for yourself; I'm alright." She smiled at me. "Let's go. I don't want to miss this!"

"Are you sure you're up to it?" I asked, and the glint in Helen's eyes told me that she was! Shrugging, I glanced over at Manoa who merely gave me a helpless look. "Alright, let's go!"

We headed over to collect Sam's father, everyone dressed warmly. I had made a special outfit for Kit, from sheepskin-lined material, a little suit of trousers, with jacket and hood. I had sewn the jacket to the trousers and the front could be opened with buttons. Then I had the task of stuffing Kit into the little suit. It was the same kind of thing as his all-in-one suits, but stiffer and more difficult to get into due to the thick material. Once on, however, it was so warm that Kit would invariably sleep in it. It was hard for him to walk in it, though, as his legs and arms stuck out rather, and with the hood up, Sam had said he resembled a starfish.

It was a fun evening. A huge bonfire had been made, and the crowd counted down from ten as they waited for the lighting. Some snowflakes were starting to fall once more, and the hot roast was much appreciated. Helen came to me. "I love that wee suit Kit has on!" he told me. "How'd ye make that? Ye'll show me?"

I nodded. "Yes, if you like; it's not hard. It's the same as his other little suits, but a lot thicker. It's lovely and warm for him." I paused. "Are you sure you're alright? D'ye want to talk about it?"

"Give over, will ye? No, 'tis best I get back to normal straightaway."

But I could see she was struggling.

"It's so like Helen to hold things inside," I told Sam quietly. "If she doesn't let it all out, she'll make herself ill."

Having seen the old year out and the new one in, we all repaired to our homes. Kit was fast asleep, and Sam carried him. "I don't think Helen's right though, Sam," I told him. "She's acting like nothing even happened!"

January 1857

Kit had looked pale for the last few days, and was off his food, which was enough to worry me. He had started a cough, and I felt his little forehead, which was hot. I gave him some watered-down willow bark, but it was a job to get him to drink it. I added honey and Kit took it, but he was reluctant.

During that night, Little Sam shook me awake.

"Mamma! Wake up! Kit's coughing."

I listened. He certainly was and there was something else too. The sound of his non-stop hacking made me cringe, when he suddenly drew breath noisily in the characteristic long whoop.

"Oh no!" I whispered to myself. "Alright, Sam. Good boy for telling me. You wake your father; I'll see to Kit." I lit a candle with trembling fingers and carried it into the boys' room.

Kit was clutching at his sheets, puce in the face, eyes streaming tears and unable to control the terrible hacking, wrenching coughs which had made him sick too.

"Hey, bor', what's up, eh?" Sam soothed. He looked at me. "I'll take the bedding down. Put it in the copper," he offered. "Sam? Pour Mamma some water into the wash basin and then wring out a flannel so she can cool his face and head and give him a face wash."

Little Sam at once did as he was bid. I sat with Kit as he coughed and cried, working himself into a terrible frenzy of fear and distress. I wiped his hot cheeks and head. His curls were plastered to his head with sweat. I spoke to Kit softly, trying to get him to breathe more slowly. Kit was tiring. To my relief, the coughing subsided and Kit sank onto the pillow, worn out, his cheeks red as fire, his small body soaked in sweat.

Whilst Sam took over with Kit, I hastened to the kitchen to make up a remedy. I mixed some apple cider vinegar and warm water, with syrup for sweetener. I glanced at my herbs. I had some spices too, and I caught sight of the bright yellow turmeric that had been part of a gift from Manoa. I tried to recall his remarks when I had seen the bright yellow grains. Hadn't he said something then about its medicinal qualities? I bit my lip. A sudden burst of coughing again from upstairs, and I took the turmeric to add to the mixture.

I spooned it into Kit's small mouth. Now, I was having little bother getting it in – he was so exhausted, his only option was to lie back and swallow. But even then, it took a while to get the stuff into him.

"I'll stay with him for the rest of the night," I told Sam.

Sam gave me a hug. "Alright, darling. Oh, my poor boy. I hope he can sleep a while. He needs the rest."

I sat on Little Sam's bed, ensured the candle was still burning safely, and lay down, where I dozed on and off for the rest of the night.

In the morning, it was hectic. I had had to use three sets of bedding for Kit. Sam sent Little Sam to Helen to ask her assistance. Since he was needed at home, Sam dashed off a note to Mackie and sent it to the school.

Helen arrived swiftly and took every bit of laundry with her since the rectory laundry room was far bigger and better equipped to deal with a larger volume, thus giving me ample time to nurse Kit.

For all I had been reluctant to add to Helen's troubles, she affirmed it 'kept her from thinking too much,' and fortunately, within a fortnight, Kit began to recover without complications, and everybody was relieved. I thanked Helen for her help, but would be even more grateful when I knew the problem she carried with her.

March 1857

We sat around our kitchen table in silence; Helen was pregnant, and needed her friends around her, with advice for her and Manoa, who was enraged. It was bad enough that she had pleaded for clemency for William, but to want to continue the pregnancy left him enraged.

"There's no question of abortion," Helen said firmly to us all. "I willnae have an innocent babe murdered. It's unlawful and dangerous. That's what I'm trying to explain!"

Manoa was in a most unenviable position. He was happy to have Helen home, unharmed, but expecting William's child to live with them was too much. I glowered at him.

"I'm surprised at you, Manoa!" I told him. "How could you expect Helen to put herself through something so dangerous? So dreadful?"

Manoa put his head in his hands. He had gone much greyer since the ordeal.

"Besides which, Will and Alice are *his*!" I added crossly. You love *them*! So, what's the difference?"

I was furious, trying to make him see sense.

"It's not the child's fault, is it? If it bothers you that much, take ship and sail away. We won't miss you!"

Sam put a hand on my arm. "Alice! Enough! Calm down. Helen, you're certain it's not Manoa's child?"

"Aye, I am," she stated. Then she turned to her husband. "Manny, the babe isnae to blame. I tell ye, I *wasnae* forced. Ye see, it was…"

"I don't want to know!" he roared, and standing up, he strode from the house, slamming the door.

William had received five and a half years in prison for abduction, and he would have a bad time with 12 hours hard labour, every day except Sunday, limited rations, and sleeping in a freezing cell.

As for Johnny, he had entered the workhouse, unable to cope after his part in the affair. Miss Spoonamore had been committed to the asylum, suffering from brain fever and jealousy, along with hysteria. Whether she would recover was anybody's guess.

Over the next few months, Helen coped well with the unplanned pregnancy, yet Manoa could not, and things became more strained between them.

14th June 1857

"Twins!" Sam looked fit to burst with pride.

Ever since Sam had first set the precedent of being at my side when I was in labour, he would not change it now.

Both twins were a very healthy weight. Two identical boys, named Oscar and Ollie, with butter-blond wavy hair, which, I hoped, wouldn't turn darker.

I looked at Sam who held both, one in each arm. He was beaming, silent, with tears streaming down his face.

July, and Kit stood watching the sleeping twins. There was a small frown on his face. Sam crouched at his side.

"What's the matter, bor'?" he asked two-and-a-half-year-old Kit. "Don't you like them?"

Kit shook his head. "They're noisy."

Sam smiled. "Yes, but that's because they haven't yet learned how to ask for things nicely, like you do. They'll be better once they can speak." He ruffled Kit's curls. He understood Kit. He had been extremely jealous of Annette at first and had been just Kit's age when she had arrived into the family.

"They pooh too much!"

Sam stifled a giggle. "Well, babies tend to, bor'."

"Can't Mamma give them to another lady?"

"No! We can't do that, Kit! That'd be unkind; you are their elder brother. They'll love you as they grow up. Don't you love Little Sam?"

Kit nodded.

"Well then, just think, as they grow up, they'll be wanting you to help them, show them things like how to play. You'll enjoy being a big brother once they're a bit older."

Kit wasn't sure. For a while after, I found him demanding and difficult. I couldn't blame him; he had always been the baby of the family. For all he was toilet-trained, he would sometimes 'forget' and I would have to leave his siblings to tend to him.

"You can throw them away!" he told me, frowning fiercely, small arms crossed, after one particularly trying morning.

"No, we can't," I replied. "Come on, Kit. You're a big boy now. Let's go to the marketplace and you can choose a toy for yourself."

Leaving the twins at Saint Nicholas', which was much appreciated by Helen and particularly Iffey, Kit and I went to the market where Kit chose a small steam engine, then we went to the beach. We sat on a blanket under a parasol that Helen had given us. It was huge, frilly and white and extremely pretty. Sam had fashioned a wooden block for it to stand in when we sat out in the yard. Now, I could enjoy the sunny days without worrying about sunburn. The sun was warm, and Kit happily paddled under strict supervision. Suddenly, he paused and glanced downwards.

"What is it, darling? What've you seen?"

"Look!" Kit's small finger pointed to some peculiar looking things on the sand, indicating translucent sea gooseberries that lived in the water. I squatted and prevented Kit from touching them.

"No, sweetheart, they're all slimy. Well, these are called sea gooseberries! Isn't that a funny name? They are jellyfish, I think; your papa will know for certain."

Kit laughed. "Jellyfish!" he squeaked. "Fish made of jelly!"

I hugged him to me. "Well, I don't think these are alive, Kit. They don't live out of water; I expect the sea carried them onto the beach."

Kit pondered. He didn't understand death yet and I didn't want him to; not yet.

"Can we take them home, Mamma?"

I didn't particularly want dead jellyfish around the house, but I had an idea.

"Alright, let's see if Auntie Helen has a clean jar, shall we? We'll put them in water, in the jar, then you can look at them!"

I didn't know how long they would last in a jar, but as Kit was interested, I got up, collected our basket and headed back to Saint Nicholas'.

Helen, who had never seen them before, was interested, so having left Ollie and Oscar with Florence and the Reverend, she returned with us to the beach.

The children were fascinated by the creatures, even if they were dead, and soon we were picking them carefully up with tweezers and putting them into jars of sea water. As we were doing this; we heard the familiar voice of Mackie who hailed us.

"Ah! Sea gooseberries!" The schoolmaster squatted and Kit ran to him and put his arms round the man's neck. He beamed, giving Kit a hug, and watched as he went back to look at the jars. Mackie continued; "They catch prey with long tentacles, but I can't see any. Perhaps they retracted them; they can do that. They live in groups, so that's maybe why there are so many. They eat tiny worms, and they, in turn, are eaten by our very own herrings!"

I smiled at such fascinating information. I had not known they were eaten by herrings; I wondered if Tabitha knew.

September 1857

Mrs Elgin had returned to Yarmouth and was living in the rear parlour; it was good to have everyone back together. I would drop Kit off on a morning so he could spend plenty of time with his 'granny Elgy'. I had spoken to her about him being jealous of the twins, and she had come up with some ideas.

"I'll see what I can do," she told me. "Don't worry, Alice. It'll all come right."

Helen too shared her ideas for coping with jealous siblings.

"I recall I was terribly jealous of my younger brother when he came along," she told me, "so, Mam found something I could do. Wait a bit and I'll show ye!"

So it was that I surprised Sam a good deal when I came home with some old potatoes, which I cut into shapes. I then took paint and some paper and taking Kit, I gave him the potatoes. Kit's smile was huge as he dipped the shapes in the paint and made shapes over the paper.

"Ber-tater painting!" he proudly exclaimed. I got Sam to put up the 'paint-ings' Kit did for us on one of the kitchen walls. I told Kit how good they were, and how proud I was of him. He did some for everybody, and thus kept himself occupied.

Helen's labour had begun. Neither she nor Manoa had come to any agreement of what should be done when the child was born. I told Sam it was ridiculous they had not yet worked out a solution, with the impending birth just days away. I wondered if any childless couples would be interested in adopting the baby. Tabitha and Gus had assured her they would be happy to adopt the child along with their own. Helen agreed, but Manoa objected, and this made me fume.

Bertie had come to bang on the door. It was a warm morning and he had come to pick up Little Sam and Roland to go to school. "Mrs Dwyer!" he called loudly. "Helen says to come quick."

I was ready for the call and nodded to Sam.

I had expected it to be half over by the time I got there. Helen had had all four previous children in no time, big babies at healthy weights that had caused no trouble, but this time, there was a problem.

Florence met me in the kitchen. "It's not going well," she told me, fearfully. "Not well at all. Oh, Alice, I hope that midwife can do something."

I patted her shoulder and hastened up the stairs.

Upstairs, Tabitha was cooling Helen's forehead. I entered the room and found it stuffy, smelling strongly of sweat and slightly fleshy; I shuddered.

"She's straining, but nothing's happening," Tabitha told me, looking worried. "Even the midwife's concerned."

I looked at Helen. I had never seen her look so wan, so tired.

"The waters broke, but that was ages ago," Tabitha told me, taking me to the other side of the room. "She ought to be making more progress than this, surely?"

"It's still early, Tab; how long's it been? Only a couple of hours. As a rule, she just pops them out and gets on with things; well, that's what she tells me anyway."

But Tabitha shook her head. "No, she started last night, Alice. Just never told anyone. Then the waters broke; that was what woke Manoa."

I gasped. "So how long has she been at it then?"

"Well, it's five and twenty to eleven now, so probably around ten or eleven hours or so! You know what Helen's like. She never makes any fuss and would have no reason to think this birth would be any different."

The midwife from Norwich, who had delivered Iffey, was speaking to Helen in a serious voice. Helen answered weakly, nodding, "Yes, do it."

The midwife then greasing her hands, attempted to turn the baby, eliciting a terrible howl from Helen. Tabitha went white. I cringed, and looked away, feeling sick. Tabitha gripped my hand hard. This was a breech birth!

Sweat poured from Helen's body, her face a mask of agony. I wanted to cry, but what use would that be? Helen had roared like an angry lioness during her other births – that was normal for her – but this yell was different, speaking of excruciating pain.

This was so dangerous; I had known two women die in normal childbirth, let alone this kind.

"The child isn't presenting right." The midwife was speaking now to Manoa outside the door. "Plus, it's very large. It should be presenting head down." She glanced at Helen, who had appeared to stop pushing altogether. Her face was pure white, dark circles under her eyes, that were scrunched up tightly. Having screamed so much, she now appeared exhausted.

"I am afraid your wife is in extreme danger, Mr Wadaa, and it's a choice to save her or the child. I've tried to turn it myself but no luck."

He looked at the midwife with incomprehension.

"She *must* go to the hospital," the Midwife told Manoa, seeing he had no idea what to say. "I can do no more; it's for the doctors now. If we don't get her there fast, she'll die. So will the baby. In fact, I have a terrible feeling, it may already be too late... for the baby at least."

Manoa breathed hard. He couldn't make any decision at all.

"Well?" The midwife shook Manoa's arm.

"MANOA!" I screamed at him, slapping his forearm. "Do something!"

He looked down at me, then hastened down to the kitchen.

A cab rattled to a halt and Helen was carried, or rather, dragged between Manoa and Gus. She couldn't walk and her feet dangled, scuffing along the ground in the men's haste to get her to the carriage, blood staining her nightgown. The midwife assisted to get her in. She sat at Helen's side, holding her up, since Helen barely clung to consciousness. Manoa got in the other side. I felt numb... I should go with her to the hospital, but there was nothing I could do. We watched as the driver was told to make all haste to the hospital and disappeared.

The baby had been stillborn. Helen had had to have her stomach opened, in what was called 'Caesar's operation.' It was incredibly risky to undertake. But without the baby removed, Helen would have died. Manoa had given his permission for the operation to go ahead, and Helen had been taken to the operating theatre so the urgent procedure could begin.

I went to south beach and wandered along the water's edge.

The tide was on its way back in again, and where it had been several hours before, the sand was thick and smooth, and I wandered barefoot along it, liking the feel of the sand beneath my feet. I turned to look back at the prints I had made, then walked round in a circle, and made more marks. I stood and breathed deeply, thinking of Helen in the operating theatre. What did it feel like to come around from such an operation? How much pain would there be?

The following day, Florence came to visit and told us Helen had survived another night, but it could still go either way.

"Reverend has been all night at his prayers," she told us, sitting at the kitchen table and accepting tea. "He's sleeping now; I had to nag him to rest. Manoa's seen her and says she's very distant."

I ground my teeth. "What can he expect?"

Two days later, I plucked up my courage and went to see her. I was directed to her bed and walked nervously down the middle of the ward. It was clean in here, pleasant, with windows open and fresh flowers. Helen sat in the bed; at least she was upright and talking. I hugged her. Helen sighed and I took her hand.

"It just wasn't meant to be, lass," she told me. "I'll be alright. We'll have a service for her. Other than that, I cannae bear to speak of it, so please don't ask me."

"Alright, but if you change your mind, you know you can talk to me."

I did not refer to the matter again, and Helen seemed to be coping. Their third daughter was buried near to Elspeth and had been baptised Mandy.

October 1857

Things had settled down. I was relieved. Helen was recovering from the operation. She didn't speak about the event, not to me, nor even Manoa; only to the Reverend.

Halloween was approaching and this year, as most years, we hollowed out a pumpkin and set it in the yard. Kit was almost three now, and I told Little Sam he would understand more this year, and so to be careful not to frighten him.

I could always forgive our boys anything. Kit, despite his little temper tantrums, was a sweet boy, and very cuddly. He idolised Little Sam. His newly discovered hobby of drawing, or painting, absorbed his mind still more. He loved the colourful wooden bricks Sam had made him too.

On Saturday, I was making pastry in the kitchen. Little Sam was asking if he could leave school early, and Sam was explaining why he could not, when I spoke.

"It's suspiciously quiet in there," I told Sam, meaning our living room. Sam looked at me, then he nodded.

"I agree."

Suddenly, afraid Kit had managed to get out of the front door somehow, I shot into the room and gasped, both in shock and relief. Kit sat in the middle of a neatly ironed pile of clothes chuckling to himself. He was also holding something, visibly intrigued.

"Kit, what do you have there?" I asked.

"Hodmedod!" He beamed, having used the local word to describe the hedgehog. He held it up proudly and I squeaked in horror.

"Oh! Sam! Look, he's got hold of a hedgehog!"

Kit had indeed! The creature had, of course, curled itself up, and only its tiny snout was showing. Sam laughed.

"Oh no, he's put it in all my clean laundry!" I was quite cross. I loved to watch the hedgehogs – I knew how beneficial they were too, and I liked their sweet little faces, but I didn't want one in my nice, clean laundry pile, fearing it would bring fleas. "No!" I told Kit firmly and picked up the hedgehog to put it outside. "Hedgehogs go outside. Not in the house."

Kit set up a wailing and I groaned.

"Hodemedod!" he bawled, setting the twins off too. "Hodmedodddd!" Small arms and legs flailed and kicked; his little face puce with rage. "MINE!" he screamed. "MINE!"

"It's out a bit late," Sam said loudly over the bellowing. "I know, I've an idea." He hurried to fetch a box, into which he put some ripped-up newspaper. He then went into the yard to pick up the hedgehog and put it in the box. "Kit!" He looked at the boy who was still crying at the sudden loss of his potential pet.

Little Sam watched with interest.

"Kit. Listen to Papa!" Sam spoke firmly. He squatted and took the boy's flapping hands. "Stop yer blartin'. Hodmedods belong outside."

"NO!" he bellowed. "MINE!"

"He's a wild animal," Sam explained, "and needs his freedom. It's cruel to keep them as pets."

Kit looked up, lower lip drooping. He looked to Little Sam. Feeling very much the big brother, Little Sam looked down at Kit.

"Hodmedods sleep all winter," he explained importantly. "But they can't sleep in a box in the house. We'll take him to the park; there's lots of cosy places there for him to sleep and be safe. Besides, what if he has a wife and children somewhere? They'll be wondering where he is!" He looked up at Sam. "Can we take him, Papa?"

Sam beamed down at our eldest. "Of course! Now then, Kit, we can't make Mamma's nice clean clothes all dirty now, can we? And we can't leave Mrs Hodmedod without her husband or the hedgehog babies without their papa."

It worked like magic! Kit stopped crying and looked at the hedgehog who was snuffling in the box.

"Come on, you two!" I picked up the twins. "That's enough! Let's go and see Auntie Helen, shall we?"

"How'd he manage to get hold of a hedgehog without pricking himself?" Helen asked me. We were taking a slow walk around the churchyard. Helen was benefitting from the gentle exercise after her ordeal.

"I've no idea!" I answered. "He dumped it in all my clean laundry. I shook all the clothes outside, but if we end up with fleas, I'll know who to blame!"

Helen scratched her belly. The scar still itched on occasion. I had not seen it and didn't wish to. Helen had refused to show even Manoa the scar which she considered hideous.

Helen looked at her daughter, proudly stumbling alongside her. She had the plumpest dimpled knees I had ever seen. She was exquisite with huge eyes. Helen paid her more attention than anyone else. Will wasn't the least bothered, but Alice was becoming increasingly difficult. Helen bemoaned that fact now.

"I think she's jealous of Iffey." I pointed out the obvious to Helen.

"What? Whyever should she be? She's the best of everything. She's at the best school, has the nicest of clothes..."

I nodded, but it was not enough really. Alice was thirteen and when she was home, she resented the attention paid to her younger sister. But there was no telling Helen that.

"I suppose I ought to expect the attitude!" she said grumpily. "She began her courses the other month, and just before they start, och, she's impossible! Worse than I ever was! If I'd spoken to my parents that way, I'd have got a hefty clip round the ear!"

I nodded. We would all echo our parents down the years.

Although Helen didn't discuss such things openly with me, in a round-about way, I gleaned the information that she and Manoa were no longer intimate. He had moved into another bedroom, and whilst that was not uncommon, Helen would never have tolerated such an arrangement a year or two before. I didn't wonder now why Manoa seemed permanently in a bad mood. I thought it perhaps for safety's sake, Helen wanting no more children after such an ordeal.

Summer 1858

It was June, and once more, the town was full. The twins were a year old, Kit was nearly four and Little Sam twelve.

Both twins were already able to say Mamma, Papa, Sam and Kit. Oscar, who loved trying out new sounds, made a funny little noise, which sounded like a constant; 'toooktoooktoook' and Sam had at once nicknamed him 'Mr Tucker', which made me giggle.

It was the hottest summer anyone could remember. I was grateful for the sea breezes. All our windows stood open; the back door too. Laundry dried in a moment, and I had done double the amount I usually would, even washing things that didn't need it, telling Sam I may as well take advantage of such weather.

The children spent time on the beach; Little Sam and Roland loved running up and down the sand and splashing in the sea. The twins I parked in the yard, under the large parasol, ensuring plenty of drinks came their way. I had to ensure Kit stayed with me and drank plenty too. I filled the bath with cool water which I then set in the yard in a shady bit so the boys could play in it or sit in it as they liked. Even Sam and I took turns to sit in the water, laughing as we poured jugs of cool water over each other's heads.

I wore my shortened shift in the house. Sam had been shocked at first, but knew I found it far cooler when working. I even ventured out in the yard wearing it. Mrs Floyd was scandalised and was not afraid to tell me so.

"Well, you can sweat if you like! I intend to keep cool. Besides, I'm in my own yard."

Mrs Floyd tutted her annoyance. She wore a full, mid-blue skirt and a long-sleeved blouse buttoned to the neck. She must be sweltering, I decided. But it was like that for a lot of people. Sam and I would dress as cooly as decency permitted whilst in public, but in our own home, we did as we pleased. The gentry wore their usual clothes and I had seen people parading along the promenade, gentlemen sweating in shirts, ties, dark jackets and hats, the ladies wilting under their parasols. More than a few of them swooned and a makeshift tent was set up on the beach so that they could sit and rest there, whilst gathering their dignity.

"I don't understand how you can wear something so *indecent!*" she snapped, folding her meaty arms across her vast chest. "I suppose it's to flirt with my husband!"

I laughed so much at that, Mrs Floyd made a noise of disapproval and stormed back into her house, slamming the door.

"Alice! That shift!" Maria chuckled when she visited with Annie. She fanned herself vigorously as she sat in the kitchen with fresh lemonade I had made that morning.

"I know, shocking, isn't it? Such a hussy for a sister-in-law, but at least it's cool."

"I wouldn't *dare* wear something like that!" she told me as Sam and I joined her. "Do you change if Papa comes round, Alice; the sight of your bare legs would finish him off!"

"Why? They aren't that bad!"

"You know what I mean! Legs are private!" Maria blushed deeply.

I chuckled at that.

Maria finished the lemonade and I poured more, then sat astride Sam's knee as Kit clambered onto the vacant chair to grin at his Aunt Maria.

"I've brought a morning paper for you." She fished it out of her basket. "I picked up two by mistake. I thought I'd bring it round. I'll go back with another penny in a bit, but I must have a rest first."

Sam began reading a piece about the Thames River in London. Due to the heat, the open sewer had become sluggish, and with no rain, the effluent was becoming more and more of a problem to the populace of the city. Sam cringed as he read it out. "I remember it stank when I was there 20 years ago, so I hate to think what it must be like now."

"Ugh!" I said. "Smelly river!"

"Stinky pooh!" Kit chortled, and Maria nodded at him.

"Yes, because there are too many people living there."

"Well, something ought to be done about it," Sam stated. "It'll be hotter there than it is here. We think it's boiling here, but the sea breezes are such a relief."

July, and the heatwave continued, becoming worse, if anything. Helen's two eldest had broken up for the summer. Will was having problems adjusting to his father being in prison in Norwich, Alice was becoming more difficult, and Helen never stopped complaining about them.

Following an actual brawl, Alice had already been sent home from school in disgrace, to think on her 'wicked ways'. It had been that and the castigation from Helen that had finally pushed her into seeing her father, for all the prison shocked her to the core. She determined to help her brother when their father had done his time.

"We should be thankful!"

So, the Sunday service ran, with Rupert.

"This heatwave brings disease and death to Londoners and no sign of it stopping. We shall pray for them and be grateful that whilst it is hot, here we have the breezes from the sea, good fresh air, and are not sickened by the miasmas that afflict our fellow brethren in the capital. Even Her Majesty, The Queen was affected, having taken a boat to experience the dreadful situation herself! It was said she sickened and was stricken by an episode of extreme nausea."

I hastily covered a laugh with a cough.

On the way back home, I carried Ollie and Sam had Oscar. Little Sam was swinging Kit's hand as they walked. I was still laughing.

"The indignity of it!" I chuckled. "Vicky, the vomiting queen!"

"Hush, Alice!" Sam glanced about him, but there was nobody to hear. But to me, the idea of her, in all her finery, with head hanging over the side of a boat, tickled me. That would put a dampener on her dignity!

The news was ongoing, and people read avidly about the situation in London and how carbolic and lime were poured into the Thames in an effort to lessen the stench. Sam was reminded of his few years in the capital when he, as were so many, had been afflicted with 'summer diarrhoea', a noxious disease that occurred annually in any case, which had been made far worse that summer. The newspapers made for grim reading. I was particularly horrified by a drawing in the paper of a skeleton in a cloak, rowing up the Thames, with the caption beneath of 'the silent highwayman.' I told Sam not to let Kit get a hold of it. It would give him nightmares. As it was, I had dreams of skeletal harbingers of death myself.

January 1860

The New Year rolled in, freezing with snow.

It was later when Little Sam came home, and he was full of excitement, eyes bright, as he hauled his bag onto the table where I was preparing to cook.

"Mamma! Mamma! Guess what?!" His face shone.

"Hmm," I told him, "give me a clue." Little Sam paused, screwed up his face and thought, then he beamed.

"It's to do with a ghost!" he told me, gleefully. Kit looked somewhat apprehensive at this, and I smiled.

"Well, it won't hurt us. Alright, you saw one?"

Little Sam shook his head. I thought once more. "I can't guess. You'll have to tell me!"

So, I heard the news. It was all over the school! The residents of nearby Southtown had been terrorised by the nightly appearance of the supernatural entity, 'Spring-heeled Jack.' An avid fan of the Penny Dreadfuls still, I gasped. Whether these creatures existed or not was debateable, but it was thrillingly scary to believe. Mindful of Kit nearby, I giggled.

"Oh! How exciting!" I told Little Sam. "Goodness me!" Little Sam's dark eyes glowed with excitement. "Can we go and watch for him, Mamma?" he asked me. "I want to see him! People say they wait up to watch him skip over the marshes."

"What? I'm not shivering on the marshes at two o'clock in the morning!"

Kit wondered who Spring-heeled Jack was, and Little Sam enlightened him.

"He's a wicked goblin, tall and thin, and has a face like the Devil. His eyes are red fireballs, and claws dripping blood..."

"Oh Sam!" I reprimanded, as Kit began to wail. The door of the house opened, and Sam came in shivering. He popped his gloves on the table, removed his hat, scarf and coat and glanced at our middle son.

"What's up, bor'?" He picked Kit up. Kit whimpered as I explained. Little Sam chewed his lip. He hadn't thought of the effect the description would have on his smaller brother.

"Aww, come now," Sam told Kit. "I heard different, I heard he *is* tall and thin, but with the appearance and manners of a gentleman. He leaps about in the marshes with a lighted lantern, otherwise he'd fall down a hole! He just likes to scare those who are up to no good!"

But the reports were quite serious. On the Saturday, although it was still snowing, I went with Maria to the market. She too had heard the reports and we delighted in scaring each other. Southtown wasn't far, though it was on the other side of the Yare.

"He's a lot closer to you than he is to us!" I teased her. "He'll come bounding up your row one night, knocking on your door!"

Maria shivered.

"You'll hear his icy voice, calling, 'Maria! Maria! Come with me!'"

"Oh no, Alice! I'll be too scared to answer the door now!"

I laughed. "He'll scoop you up in those freezing arms of his, and spirit you away across the Yare back to his freezing, dingy hovel, where he'll kiss you with lips of ice!"

"Stop it!" Maria laughed, slapping my arm. "I've got goose skin now!"

There had been numerous sightings and the local paper proclaimed, 'Fiend at large'. He appeared impossible to capture, since he sprang away from any pursuers with an evil laugh.

But the curious phenomenon was soon brought to an abrupt end, and the so-called fiend was discovered. Sick of the creature frightening old folk and children, a watch had been set up to catch, or at least to send the thing on its way, so one night, five local men sat to watch out.

"There 'e goes!" one man hissed to the others, catching sight of the tall, skinny, leaping figure, his cackling laugh splitting the cold night. "C'mon, fellas, let's catch the bugger!"

The man who had assumed the role of the legendary fiend was startled to see five large men, armed with shovels and a pitchfork, appear from nowhere and chase him. He uttered a shriek of alarm and ran. They chased him to the railway line, surrounded him and 'Spring-heeled Jack' looked about him in fear. One fellow advanced and received a spirited punch to the jaw which knocked him senseless. Whilst one of his colleagues bent to assist him, the three others grabbed the squirming creature, and began to unmask him.

The news declared a local man responsible, clad in a skintight, white dress, wearing a pair of goat's horns on his head. He had been taken roughly by the arms to the local constable and dealt with accordingly. Sam hooted with laughter on reading the story.

"He'll be lucky if he avoids either the Tolhouse or Saint John's," Sam said. "He's from Southtown. Once they finish with him, he'll be having to watch his step. I don't expect his neighbours will be impressed!"

I smiled, hoping that the man would not be badly punished. It had only been a practical joke.

Early May 1861

Life had been smooth and uneventful, and time seemed to speed onwards. My family were healthy and happy and growing. Maria had a daughter and two sons.

Our patriarch was sprightly as ever, refusing to be 'mollycoddled' by Maria or myself. I was glad, since it kept him well, in both body and mind. We only helped him with the housework.

We had lost Bundles that winter, but she, as her predecessor Tiger, had passed peacefully in her sleep. However, everyone had been heartbroken. We had since acquired a lovely Tabby that Sam had brought home one afternoon, having bought it from a man who had been selling them outside an ale house as mousers. He was now huge, with the appetite of a tiger and the nature of a lamb.

The academy Miss Spoonamore had run had been, conversely, turned back into shops; a grocer's and apothecary. The shop floor was open-plan; one entered the shop and went left for groceries, or right for medicines. The new shopkeepers in there were pleasant people.

Kit was very interested in the reconstruction going on, and every time we went out, I had to stand with him watching the building works. Sam had previously made him some building blocks from pieces of wood and painted them different colours, and Kit played with them endlessly, the only issue being when his younger brothers knocked them over, bringing about howls of outrage. I wondered if he'd become a builder!

On entering the hospital one morning, I heard heartrending sobs coming from Nurse Bryant's room. A young woman came out and slammed the door.

"Hello, what's the matter?" I asked. "Is there anything I can do to help?"

"Not unless you can get the law changed!" came the bitter response. "It isn't my fault! All I want is to be a children's nurse, but thanks to my parents, I can't, ever!"

The girl gave one last bitter sob, picked up her skirt and vanished down the long corridor, sobs echoing. I looked to Nurse Bryant.

"Poor girl," she said with a sigh. "She came to me to plead to train her as a nurse, but Matron wouldn't allow it."

I looked at her questioningly.

"Kathryn's illegitimate," she explained. "She's the daughter of a housemaid, and her father was transported when she was three."

I knew that children born out of wedlock were held to be a disgrace and affront to society and its morals; that the children were believed to have inherited their parents' lack of morals and thus, were shunned by so called decent society. All in all, it was absurd.

"Really, Alice! It's ridiculous; that girl would be a wonderful nurse! I can always tell!"

"Tell Matron her parents *were* married... that her father died; Matron won't know! After all, he might be; not everyone survives transportation."

Nurse Bryant looked undecided.

"Come on! Isn't it worth some fibs to get a dedicated young woman onto your staff? Why waste it because of what society thinks? Don't forget, all these stupid ideas are brought about by the gentry and that stuck-up sow who sits in London on her fat arse!"

Nurse Bryant's cheeks flamed. "Alice! Really!" she exclaimed. But then, she thought. Twenty years was a long time. Kathryn's mother wasn't likely to broadcast the news that she had had a child out of wedlock. It might work.

"Alright, I will. But if Matron ever finds out, she'll flay me alive!"

I grinned.

"How's your family anyway, Alice? How's that eldest son doing?"

I willingly told her the latest news, and she smiled, nodding.

"And your unfortunate friend?"

"Ah, Helen," I said, sadly. "We had a massive argument. In front of everyone too. As a result, we're not speaking."

Helen and I had been in the marketplace with Kit and Iffey. Iffey was being difficult since she had recently made two good friends from a most respectable family, who lived on South Quay, who attended a very exclusive and small, private girls' school run by two spinsters in Gorleston. Iffey wanted to attend also, but she had a governess. Iffey was desperate to go to the 'brilliant school' her friends did.

"I've told ye a hundred times, lass. No!" Helen admonished the girl who had begun, once again, to plead. "I want ye home where I can be sure you're safe. I hired the best governess in Yarmouth. You wouldn't like school."

"Helen, that's not true," I told her. "Iffey has friends who go there already, don't you, Iffey?" The girl looked up at me and nodded her head fiercely.

"Well, I say no," Helen told her, pulling the girl along with her, whilst Iffey dragged her feet.

"No! It's not fair! I want to go to school with Sally and Lucy!" Her small foot stamped.

Helen shook her head. "No! 'Tis my final word!"

Iffey started to wail loudly.

"Stop that at once!" she snapped, smacking the back of her legs. "I'll send ye to your room for the rest of the day!"

Iffey glowered, resentfully.

"You're mean! I hate you!" she shrieked.

Helen didn't appear hurt at the remark, where I would have been devastated.

"I'm not mean! You'll soon find out for yerself just how unkind people can be. School isn't all it's cracked up to be!"

Iffey stamped her feet in a fury. Helen shouted at her to keep still.

"What are the families of the other girls like?" I asked, trying to insert a little calmness into the outing.

"Och, nice wee lassies, I suppose. I don't know them well though. Their parents live up on South Quay and ye know what they're like up there!"

"Helen, why not let her just try it at least?" I asked. "Just until Christmas. It'd do her good. Kit's starting early; he can't wait."

Helen merely shrugged.

"But Iffey will make more than just two friends when she goes; it'll be fun. New faces, new things. I went to school, and it never did me any harm!"

I had said this lightly, smiling, not expecting Helen's response, so I was shocked when she stopped and turned to face me.

"Och WILL ye mind your own business, Alice? You always interfere! Ye drive me mad poking your nose here and there! I don't *want* your advice! I'll do as I choose! Iffey is *not* going to go to school, and there's an end to it!"

I was furious at being spoken to like that, not to mention embarrassed, particularly in front of people.

"FINE!" I roared back at Helen, oblivious to Iffey's bawling, and Kit's stunned surprise. "I'm fed up with you too! You're stifling Iffey. How could you deny her a childhood full of friends? I've always been there for you! I resent that remark about interfering!"

Helen was enraged.

"Well, if that's how ye feel, ye can take yerself off. Dinnae come calling on me anymore!"

"You're not the only person living there you know! If you don't like it, stay out of my way! But I *will* see my real friends!"

Kit and I hastened to buy some vegetables. He was quiet; realising he was upset, so I sat on a seat and sat him at my side.

"I'm sorry you saw that, Kit. I shouldn't have shouted in front of you, but sometimes people make us shout when they won't listen to reason."

Kit regarded me seriously. "Aren't you friends with Auntie Helen now?" he asked.

"No, darling," I replied. "Sometimes grown-ups argue, you know!" Kit's lips turned down.

"I don't like Auntie Helen now!" he told me fiercely. "She was horrid to you!"

I hugged him. "I know, Kit, but I think Auntie Helen is not feeling well. Come on, let's go home and later we'll have fish and chips."

Having successfully persuaded Nurse Bryant to fib to the Matron, I walked to Ramp Row to try to find Kathryn. I knocked on the first door and was directed by a girl of about eight to her house.

Kathryn herself answered my knock. I introduced myself and told her I had come from speaking to Nurse Bryant. Kathryn's eyes were still red from crying. "Oh, you're the lady I spoke to," she recalled.

"Let's go somewhere we can talk privately," I told her. We wandered off together.

"I spoke to Nurse Bryant after I overheard you," I told her. "Sorry, Kathryn, I've been told about minding my own business more than once, but it's a good plan, you see! She wants you; we thought it'd help you."

Kathryn's eyes widened. "But if anyone finds out?"

"They won't. I bet your mamma would be proud if you were to become a nurse." Kathryn nodded.

"She would. Thanks, I appreciate this. I long to be a nurse. I love children. They seem to like me too!"

I regarded her. "Look, why not come back to our house? You can meet my children, my husband. We'll have some tea, then see what we're going to do."

Sam was surprised when I walked in with our unexpected guest, but he nodded his approval.

I introduced Sam, along with Little Sam, who smiled at her, then Kit stomped up to say hello and shake her hand. The twins, Oscar and Ollie were shy at first, but soon, I discovered she had a real way with children. The twins did not take long to take quite a shine to my new friend when she began to speak to them. We planned to see Nurse Bryant later that afternoon.

Sam was saddened about the argument with Helen. He urged me to go to speak to her, but I refused.

"Helen's cooked her goose well and truly this time!" I said, tapping my foot in annoyance.

Kit looked at me. "Mamma, if you're not friends with Auntie Helen, she won't let you have any of her goose!"

Both Sams laughed at that.

"No, she won't, and I don't care!" I told Kit.

The rift between Helen and myself was obvious to everyone. Helen had stormed into the kitchen, seething, and clamouring that I was the worst friend she had ever had and nosier than she had ever realised. Florence had shaken her head and told Helen that good friends in this life were 'rarer than hen's teeth.' But Helen merely glared and said I should 'learn to mind my own business!"

Not even the Reverend could move her. "Helen, surely I've taught you better than that! It's Christian to forgive, and she has really done nothing wrong."

Helen shook her head. "No! I'm sorry, Reverend, but she must learn not to interfere in people's lives."

"She isn't interfering, my child," he told her. "You've been friends for so long; don't throw it all away."

But Helen was intractable. She had always been stubborn, but now, she seemed to positively wallow in it.

I went to invite Gus and Tabitha to dinner. As soon as I reached the open kitchen door, Helen stuck her bulk in the doorway.

"NO! Whatever ye've brought me won't make any difference. Ye cannae win me over with tasty grub! You're no coming into *my* kitchen!" she told me, glaring at me menacingly. Her large frame filled the doorway.

"I haven't come to see *you*, and it's not *your* kitchen, it belongs to Reverend," I snapped. "And if you've got the idea I've brought grub for you, you can think again! Not everything revolves around you and your ever-hungry stomach! Now let me in!"

"Well, if Reverend says ye can enter, I'll step aside, but 'tis unlikely, since he isnae here!" She looked so smug, I itched to slap the look from her face.

Helen raised her chin and looked at me from her not inconsiderable height.

"Move me!"

"Don't be so childish!" I told her angrily. "I've come to see Gus, or Tab, if she's here, to invite them to dinner, if you must know. Now, do you mind?"

"I live here, 'tis my home, and you're no welcome."

I shook my head in disbelief and made to push past her, but Helen resisted firmly. In that moment, I hated her. Truly, she could be maddening.

"Gus! Tab!" I bellowed right next to Helen's ear. "Get this stupid Scots lump out of my way, can you? I want to come in!"

From behind, I heard Gus.

"Helen! For God's sake, what are you playing at? Let her in!"

But Helen refused. Once more, I went to push past her, but Helen set both hands on my shoulders and pushed me away. I stumbled backwards, landing, fortunately for me, on soft grass. But I was irate. Helen smirked.

Kit began crying and wrapped both arms around my legs. "Mamma!" he wailed.

"HELEN!"

I looked round at the shocked voice. Tabitha dropped her basket, oblivious of its contents, and hastened up behind me. She assisted me to my feet. "Are you alright, Alice?" She glowered at Helen. "What possessed you to do that? You great idiot!"

Helen looked at me in a lofty manner.

"She's no' welcome here."

"Not by you, obviously, but by everyone else she is," Tabitha snapped. Then she turned to me.

"Alice, come in; I'll make some tea." She looked at Helen reproachfully. "What? Are you going to stop *me* from coming in?" Tabitha's voice was angry. "Or will you push me over too? You don't *own* this place!"

Helen stood, unrepentant, and Kit, on seeing my tearful face, suddenly let go of me and stalked over to Helen, where he kicked her leg as hard as he could manage.

"I HATE YOU!" he screamed. "You're mean!"

No reprimand came his way and Helen was outraged. She raised her hand to clip Kit's ear, but I seized it.

"Don't you *dare*!" I snarled.

I followed Tabitha into the kitchen. Helen made a noise of exasperation and stomped outside.

I was more shaken than I realised. I was trembling now, as Tabitha poured me tea.

Gus came to sit down too. "She's off her rocker."

"I never expected her to turn against me like that," I told them, shakily. "We've had our fallings out... who hasn't? But this? All because I said about Iffey going to school, and how it'd be good for her!"

Gus thought. "Can't Manoa get through to her?" he asked. "He's her husband after all!"

Tabitha shook her head. "No, you know what she's like, she'll stand up to him every time. Manoa once said he didn't want an obedient wife, he wanted a strong one; well, he certainly got that!"

With Gus and Tabitha accepting my dinner invitation with thanks, I went home. "Ignore what she says," Tabitha told me as we parted ways. "You're always welcome here; you know that Reverend would be furious if he thought you were being forced away!"

I told Sam of the incident, and he was angry, and planned to speak to Manoa.

Kit pushed me gently towards the settle, telling me; "do you sit down, Mamma; you've had a shock", which made me want to laugh at his serious little face, but I thanked him and did as I was bidden. Little Sam brought me a cup of strong, sweet tea, and to my surprise and delight, Kit began to tell me a story. The twins came to listen too.

Manoa tried to placate Sam. "Man, I'm sorry! I never imagined she'd be so..." He paused then sighed and continued, "...aggressive. Will's a nuisance too. I know he goes to visit his father, does as he likes, whatever we say. I don't want to make an enemy of him!"

"I see you've your share of problems, Manny, but I do *not* wish to hear of any further assaults upon my wife. I was shocked when I heard. It's made me angry. Really, very angry. Do I make myself clear?"

Manoa nodded sadly.

That evening, Kit presented me with a drawing of a large house, with dozens of windows, a garden with trees, and several chimneys on the roof.

Kit had even drawn oblong and rounded pebbles on the house wall. It was an amazing drawing for a six-year-old.

"What a wonderful drawing, Kit!" I said to him; and took it to show Sam. "Look at this! Will you build this house one day, Kit?"

Kit beamed. "Yes. That's the house I'm going to build for you and Papa and Sam and the twins. We'll all live in it, and it'll be on the denes so you can look at the sea and watch the ships when you're old!"

"Thank you, Kit!" Sam told him solemnly. "We'd be proud to live in such a nice house."

I took the picture and pinned it to the wall, along with the others he had done.

The situation with Helen worsened. If I chanced to meet her in the marketplace, she drew herself up with a sniff and looked haughtily the other way. Such direct snubs made me sad. One morning, Helen had glanced, seen me approach, and had walked around me! Kit, at my side, yelled after her.

"Don't be mean to Mamma! You're horrible, and you smell!"

Helen had marched on without turning her head. Kit was furious on my behalf. He looked up at me. "Did she hear me, Mamma?" he asked.

"I'm certain she did!" I told him.

Kit scowled. "Good!"

Kit knew how upset I was and had seen me cry over it. Kit was a very sensitive boy – creative, like his sire and elder brother. He thought about how Helen had spoken to me, and the resentment in him grew. In fact, his indignation reached hitherto unforeseen proportions in a child so young. Helen was being mean to his mamma, and anyone mean to his mamma deserved to have nasty tricks played on them. Kit thought about the problem between Helen and I a lot.

After breakfast, since Kit wasn't yet attending school, I gave him some lessons to be getting on with, whilst I did the household chores and chatted to the twins. Both were doing well, and their speech was excellent; I was proud of them. Both chatted non-stop. Their little accents were already strong.

"Mamma, can I go out to play s'arternune?" Kit spoke.

"Yes, of course, darling."

Even at six, it was normal to allow children to run free. Indeed, I had vanished from dawn to dusk at his age. Kit had recently become friendly with a boy from Angel Row called Stanley, who was seven. I didn't like him much; he was always up to something, usually nothing good.

Little Sam was still friendly with Roland, who now worked on South Quay alongside Manoa, who had taken the job since he had missed the companionship of his shipmates, and lately, needed some peace from Helen.

Later that afternoon, Stanley led Kit up to South Quay.

"We shouldn't be here," Kit said. "Mamma said not to."

Stanley looked at his friend.

"There's Roland!" Kit pointed out the tall lad. "He's my brother's friend. He's nice." Roland obligingly waved back. Manoa saw them and he, too, waved, but Kit pointedly turned his back. "I don't like *him* anymore either!" he told Stanley. "He's married to Helen, and Helen pushed Mamma over!"

Stanley had heard about this and had been amazed that a woman would do that.

Both boys, having looked at the ships a while, turned back down another row.

"You should come to school with me when I go. Ask your parents."

"I don't want to! All those masters with canes!"

"But you won't be able to read and write if you don't!"

"I'm going to be a soldier. They don't need to read and write."

"My brother's old teacher was in the Army. He got his arm shot off. I'd like to keep mine. I'm going to be a builder! I'll build the best houses in Yarmouth and people will pay hundreds and hundreds of pounds to live in them!"

As they walked, the lads chatted about Helen and her behaviour. "She's so horrible to Mamma," Kit said. "She made her cry. She's fat, old and ugly!" He kicked a stone in frustration. "And she won't share her goose with her now either!"

"Let's pay her out!" Stanley said and applied his agile mind to his mischief. "Got any money?" he asked, and Kit fumbled in his pocket.

Stanley looked at the pennies in Kit's palm. On counting them out, Stanley gave a wicked urchin-like grin. "Come on, I know what we'll do!" He leaned in to whisper in Kit's ear.

In the market, Kit, urged on by his friend, bought a half dozen eggs. "I wish they were rotten eggs," Kit said. "Then she'd stink even more!"

At the next stall, they bought flour. "Now what?" Kit asked.

"We make a flour bomb!" Stanley told him. "I'll show you how."

They ventured to the end of the market, and Kit spotted some bruised pears on the floor. He grinned wickedly, picking them up. Stanley nodded his approval.

Like most children, neither boy considered the long-term effects of showering Helen with eggs and flour, or rotten fruit. They were more concerned with the here and now, and a little revenge!

Near the church garden walls, the pair put the flour into the bags, and screwed the tops round. He had, it seemed, done this before. "Come on!" Stanley led the way.

"The kitchen. That's where she is," Kit told Stanley. He had been worried at first, but now, he felt intense excitement. This was, he knew, extremely naughty, but Helen had been hateful.

"Throw them when I tell you," Stanley whispered. "Do you throw really hard. Use all your strength."

The door was half open, so Stanley sent one flour bomb at the door, which exploded on impact. Kit threw some eggs which smashed and dribbled down the door into the flour.

"Helen! Helen! Helen's the Loch Ness Monster!" Stanley bawled to get her attention. Helen appeared at the door.

"What are ye doing? Ye wee demons!" She glanced at the mess on the ground and the door in shock. "Och, ye wee divils! Oho! Kit Dwyer! I might've known it'd be *you*, laddie! Wait till I tell yer father! He'll tan yer arse for ye, and you too, Stanley McShane!"

Stanley laughed and thumbed his nose. He threw another flour bomb at her, which exploded, dead centre on her chest. Kit tossed the eggs, two of which caught her on the shoulder. He then launched two pears, one after the other. One caught Helen on her thigh, the other next to her foot.

"You're mean!" Kit called out to her. "You pushed my mamma over and made her cry! Meanie! Meanie! Helen's a meanie!" The boys danced round, just out of her reach, pulling the worst expressions they could. Inside the kitchen, Iffey set up a roaring.

"Now look what ye've done, ye nasty wee savages! Upset my wee lassie! You just wait, the pair of yese!"

"*You're* the Loch Ness Monster!" Kit said loudly, pointing at her. He pulled a further extraordinary face at her. "Helen's big and fat, with smelly drawers!" Kit bellowed, unable to prevent the pent-up frustration and indignance, trying to think of the rudest things he could possibly say. Stanley laughed as Helen swiped at them with a fly swat.

"I'll wallop the pair of yese!"

"You got to catch us first!" Kit called, and both boys charged, roaring insults, down the path and into the marketplace, leaving Helen yelling at the top of her voice.

Gus had been on his way back to the kitchen in the hope of some afternoon tea and perhaps cake, if Helen was in a good mood, which, these days, was unlikely. He stopped in amazement at the sight of the mess on the door, the ground and over Helen too. His first thought was that he'd get no cake today. His second was how funny she looked. He couldn't help but laugh; she was in a dreadful mess! Her face was red-cheeked with fury.

"What happened here?"

Helen turned to face him. "Kit Dwyer, the wee demon, and Stanley McShane... och, that a laddie with Scots heritage should be so bad. They came shouting insults, then hurled flour and eggs my way. The door's a right mess and so am I!"

"So I see!" Gus stated. His lips twisted, trying to hold back more laughter. Helen thumped a meaty fist on the table.

"I might've guessed you'd find it amusing!" she snapped, as Gus' reserve broke, and he began to laugh loudly.

Meanwhile, the miscreants charged up Half Moon Row. "Oh, that was funny!" Stanley said. "What'll we do next?"

Kit frowned. "I don't know, but we'd best stay out of fatty's way!"

Both boys came into the house ready for some snacks. I cut them a large slice of cake each, along with some freshly made lemonade.

"Well, what've you two been up to?" I asked. "Is there anyone in Yarmouth still speaking to me?"

The boys mumbled, both red-faced, and I looked at them. I knew guilt when I saw it. I was about to remark on it when Ollie let out a squawk of complaint as his sibling took his piece of cake. He opened his already cakey mouth to put as much inside as he could.

"Oscar! That's very naughty. You've eaten your cake; let Ollie have his." I picked Ollie up and held him on my lap so he could eat in peace. When I looked back, Kit and Stanley were speaking to Little Sam who nodded, and after asking his father, he joined the lads out in the yard. I frowned with suspicion. I had not been the mother of four boys without picking up a *few* things!

"Guess what we did!" Kit idolised his big brother and was eager to boast of their exploits.

"I shudder to think!" Little Sam replied. Kit whispered and Little Sam looked shocked and, at the same time, delighted. He laughed.

"Well, do you keep a low profile and no mistake," he told them. "She'll be thumping her way up here in a bit!"

Kit didn't like the sound of that at all. "Will Papa wallop me?" he asked, worried.

"I don't know, bor'!" He shook his head. "How much mess *did* you make?"

Helen was still spitting fury over the "attack" as she called it. She ranted to Gus about it, who told her she was making a fuss over nothing and escaped to the peaceful grounds. Helen, fuming, sent an urgent message to Manoa via a passing boy, telling him to come back 'with all speed' as she had been 'attacked.'

Manoa, horrified at this message, dropped everything and raced home, charging down the rows in panic, his mind full of fear and irrational thoughts, expecting Helen to be lying cut and bleeding on the floor. He charged into the kitchen to find Helen with a mixing bowl under her arm stirring vigorously. Iffey sat at the table, playing with some pastry bits.

"Helen?" he asked, hastening to her. "Are you alright? Who attacked you?" His fist bunched.

"Kit Dwyer, the nasty little beast!" she snapped.

Manoa's mouth opened as Helen recounted what the boys had done.

"You sent me a message that scared me half to death 'cos a couple of kids of six threw eggs and flour at you?" He was stunned and extremely reproachful.

"And rotten pears!" Helen stated. "I was assaulted! Look at me, mun!" She put the mixing bowl down and stood in front of her husband. "I left the door to show you! Look at the mess! I'm going to send this dress to Alice, and *she* can get the stains out!"

Manoa looked. He hadn't noticed the door at first, in his haste, expecting to find the stuff of nightmares.

"Now, *you* get around to the Dwyer's place and drag that wee demon back, by his ear if necessary, and stand over him whilst he cleans it off. He'll apologise to me too!"

Manoa rubbed a bristly chin. He was confused.

"I'll give him a hiding he'll no' forget!"

Manoa shook his head. "No, you can't do that, Helen. I don't want Sam or Alice round here in a paddy!"

"I don't care about Sam!" she hollered. "And I certainly don't care about Alice! Go and tell him what their brat's done. Go on! Now! I'll no' stand for it!"

Manoa groaned. He nodded and left the kitchen.

Kit and Stanley were sitting at the workbench with Sam and Little Sam when there was a knock at the door. Kit looked at his friend uneasily. I rose from where I was sewing and answered the door.

"Oh, hello, Manoa!" I was surprised to see him. I wondered what he wanted. I had no quarrel with Manoa, just his wife! The two boys were not happy at the visitor and glanced at each other uneasily.

"Alice, I'm sorry to come to you like this, but there's something you should know! Is Sam here?"

Manoa entered the kitchen to tell a stunned Sam and I about what Kit and Stanley had done. The two began to slip quietly out the back way, but Sam stopped them.

"Oh no you don't! Do you stay here! What do you have to say about this?"

Kit looked at Manoa then his father. Kit stood, defiant, hands on hips. He wasn't afraid of his father; none of the boys had any cause to be. But Sam did look most annoyed. Kit glanced at me and spoke to Sam.

"Auntie Helen was mean to Mamma. She wouldn't speak to her in the market. She made her cry and pushed her over, so we don't like her now; she won't let her in to see anybody. She's rude and mean, and I'm *glad* we made her messy!"

The angry little explanation convinced Manoa it had been no more than small boys 'getting their own back'. He felt embarrassed and had no idea what to say.

Sam cleared his throat. "I see, well, you shouldn't have done that. The quarrel is between your mamma and Helen. Howsumdever, I know it upset you very much to see your mamma hurt."

He looked at Manoa. He was acutely embarrassed. He wondered what his own father would have done, had he done similar. All the Dwyer children had been strictly brought up, but none had ever needed severe punishment, and Sam had no intention of beating Kit, as was doubtless expected by Helen.

"I know, Sam, it's not their fault. It's all blown out of proportion." Manoa wiped his face with his kerchief. "Helen sent me a message saying she'd been attacked. Naturally, I feared the worst. I expected to find her lying on the floor, bleeding! I won't punish them, but they should at least wash the door, and apologise to Reverend; it's his door after all!"

Sam nodded. "I agree. Kit, listen to me, I understand your anger, but you *must* leave these matters to us."

Kit stamped his foot. "NO! I don't want to clean the door!"

"Kit," I said, before Sam could get annoyed at such defiance. I took his small, grubby hands in mine. "Listen to me, sweetheart. It's the Reverend's door, not Helen's. You like Reverend, don't you? He's always kind to you. Won't you clean the door for him?" I was stroking his hair as I spoke. Kit thought, then nodded, miserably. He looked about to burst into tears.

Stanley spoke up. "It was my fault really," he said. "It *was* my idea to get her back because Kit was upset."

We all looked at him. I came to sit between the boys and gave them a hug each.

"Thank you both. Look, I wasn't hurt and I'm alright. I was just angry and shocked. Now, let's see what we can do to make this all better, shall we?"

The boys went to Saint Nicholas'. Sam and Manoa joined them in case Helen became difficult. I stayed with Little Sam and the twins, wondering what was happening. I gave them some chalk and some slates and watched as they drew, or scribbled pictures.

Little Sam hugged me. "Don't worry, Mamma. It'll be alright."

"Oh Sam, you look *so* like your father! Your voice is breaking too!" I knew he was a bit embarrassed about the squeaky high voice, which made him sound as if he had a cold one minute and then the deeper voice, like his father.

Little Sam smiled. "Yes, I'll be glad when it stops! Why do boys' voices do that?"

"I don't know, darling; you'll have to ask your father," I replied.

Manoa went into the kitchen to fetch some water and rags. "Don't start on them!" he stated to Helen, so fiercely that she actually backed down. They were going to refuse to clean the door, but your one-time friend persuaded them to do it for the Reverend's sake."

Helen seethed. Sam frowned at her. He took the bucket and passed it to the boys in case she decided to throw the contents over them. Helen saw how angry Sam was, and it was not directed at the boys.

When the job was done, Sam nodded. "Good day to you then, Manoa," he said, and went outside, ignoring Helen completely.

I resented Helen for stopping me from visiting Mrs Elgin, so, one morning, I looked in through an open window to see her, glasses perched on the end of her nose, reading the morning news. I grinned, tapped on the partly opened window, and the old lady looked up. I waved.

"Alice!" She beamed at me.

"Helen won't let me in!" I said. "But it's not up to her!"

I shoved the window up further, then hitched up my skirt and simply climbed into the room over the windowsill and plopped down into the room. I grinned at her.

Mrs Elgin chuckled. "You hoyden!" she told me, smiling. Having given her a hug, I sat opposite her. "Alice, my dear, shall we have some tea?"

The thought of getting Helen to make and serve me tea was almost irresistible, but I shook my head. "None for me, Mrs Elgin, though you go ahead if you want some. She might spit in mine!"

Later that week, I needed a break and a walk along the tideline seemed to be calling me, but I couldn't leave yet. Sam had been concerned about a possible leak in our rainwater tank and he was up there with a plumber.

The twins had been particularly tiresome, I had a headache, and my nerves were frazzled. I had a complicated dress to finish repairing and the whining of their spinning top was grating on my nerves.

"That's enough now, twins. Please put that top away; it's distracting me."

"Shan't!" Oscar said defiantly. I glared at him. Since they had begun to go to a kindergarten club, the twins had seen how some children behaved and 'shan't' was a new and thrillingly defiant word.

"Oscar! You naughty boy! Don't say shan't to me!" I turned to frown at him.

"Shan't! Shan't! Shan't!" Oscar said making Ollie look at him. I stood up. Little Sam, working in the corner, became aware of something happening and came over.

"Do you stop this, the pair of you! Do you either be quiet or go with Kit somewhere else. Mamma and I are working!"

The twins looked tearful at Little Sam's cross voice. Kit glanced from where he was practising writing. He put the writing away happily enough. They had been bothering him too.

"Shall I take them out, Mamma?" he asked and I nodded.

"Yes please, Kit. Anywhere! I can't put up with that top any longer!"

Kit duly took a protesting twin in each hand and hastened down the row to the marketplace. He looked down at Oscar, who now, in a temper, stuck out his tongue and kicked Kit's shin. Kit jumped.

"Ow! You rotten little egg!"

"I hate you!" Oscar yelled at his brother. "You're mean! Mamma's mean! Papa's mean too!"

Kit shook Oscar's arm. "Well, I hate you too, and I don't want you in our house anymore. You're horrible, and Ollie's horrible too!"

It was that which gave him the idea. Everyone was shouting their wares. Kit considered.

Ollie, who had not said a word the whole time, began to sniffle. Oscar once more stuck out his tongue and trod on Kit's toes. Kit exploded with rage. For him, it was the final straw. He took a deep breath.

"Twins for sale!" he bellowed as loud as he possibly could. "Twins for sale! Come and see them! Twins for sale!"

Both boys struggled, but Kit held them fast, and continued to shout, drawing quite a crowd.

"For sale, eh?" A grubby looking man rubbed his bristly chin. "Seems they don't wanna be sold, bor'!"

"Nooo!" Ollie cried, terrified. "Want Mamma!"

"They're my brothers and they're annoying!" Kit snapped; cheeks flushed. "I can sell 'em; Mamma said to take them away! I don't want them in our house anymore!"

A lady nearby chuckled. "I don't expect she meant for you to sell them!" she told Kit, who stood looking angrily at her. "I think, perhaps she meant take them from under her feet!"

"No! She said I was to sell them and bring back a guinea!" Kit's ire was well and truly up, and his jealousy of his younger siblings was getting the better of him. "They're naughty!"

"Well, nobody will buy naughty twins!" the woman told him.

"I want to sell them!" Kit said, and stamped his foot, oblivious to the still-wailing twins. "They're rotten. Will you buy them? Or just one? This is Oscar!" Oscar found himself jerked forward. He howled.

"A guinea is rather expensive!" The lady chuckled. "Besides, I wouldn't want naughty little boys; I'd only want good little boys. I think perhaps you'd best take them back home – there are some folks that really 'ud buy them and then what would your mother say?"

Kit knew I wouldn't be happy, but he had had enough of them.

The lady tried again. "Look, little man, what's your name?"

"Kit Dwyer and I'm six."

"I see, well, Kit Dwyer, do you take those poor little blighters back home," she told him, "or you might lose hold of them, and then they'll be gone!"

"Good!" Kit grumped; lips downturned.

"Now, now. I know small brothers can be a perfect nuisance," she stated. "I had three myself when I was young. Come on, let's go to your home, eh? Come with me!"

Kit unwillingly found himself following the woman up to our row. The twins now, seeing where they were headed, had stopped struggling but were still in tears, with Ollie wailing.

I was stunned, therefore, when there came a knock on the door and outside stood a grumpy-looking Kit, a pair of excited twins who had flung both arms round my legs the moment they saw me, bellowing for 'Mamma', and an amused woman who explained that Kit had had it in mind to sell his younger brothers.

I gasped as I admitted the four of them. "Sell them? Kit! Really! Whatever were you thinking?"

I sat in the chair with the twins snuggled close, whilst Kit stood, sulkily digging the toe of his boot into the floor.

"They were being mean," he said, tears ready to fall. "They were being rude. Oscar kicked me and stamped on my toes! I thought you wouldn't mind, 'cos then you could get on with your work!"

"Oh, Kit!" I said, hiding a smile. "I don't want them gone! I don't want *any* of you gone! I love all of you, equally. All I wanted was a little peace and quiet to get on with my sewing."

Sam, having settled the price of a repair with the plumber, had left him to get on with the work, and came to kneel and take his middle son in his arms. Kit was now crying, terrified he was going to be in trouble.

"Now then, bor'. Let's not get all upset. It's alright now. Everyone's safe at home." He smiled at the woman.

"Thanks for bringing them back, Mrs...?"

"Dilwyn," the woman told him. "That's alright. I thought I'd better before someone really did go and buy them!"

"How much were you asking for them, Kit?" Little Sam asked Kit.

"One guinea!" Kit replied.

"Ah, no wonder you didn't have any offers, bor'!" Little Sam chuckled. "Far too expensive!"

"Sam!" I admonished, and Little Sam grinned.

June 1861

William sat opposite his son. Since coming to prison, William had been a model prisoner – attending the chapel, reading to other prisoners, requesting the chaplain's company and repenting as much as he could, all the while, desperately trying to assure he was a reformed character. He had the cleanest cell in the place since he had asked for a broom, water and bucket. He had even volunteered cleaning duties elsewhere in the prison. Now he had become a Trustee.

"I'm sorry you have to put up with your mother being like she is," William said to his son. "It's not her fault, it's mine."

His son shook his head. "No, Pa, it's hers. If she behaved as a woman should, instead of like some hoyden, you'd be at home now."

William thought for a moment then asked, "You'd welcome me back?"

Will nodded. "I would. I wish I was old enough to move out, Pa. Get somewhere of my own. You might be released early for good behaviour. I'd stand surety for you!"

William clasped his son's hand over the rough, wooden table which was placed outside the cells in the small communal space, where the more well-behaved prisoners took their meals and received visitors.

"Thank you, son," he said quietly. "Listen, bor', you're working. You could probably find lodgings for yourself soon."

Will nodded. "When you're released, we'll get a place together!"

"I'm so proud of you, son. You aren't a boy anymore; you're a man, and a man to be proud of! But I don't want to marry again. Leastwise, not any other woman. I still want your mamma back." He looked very sad.

"How's your dear sister?" he continued. "She didn't come with you today."

"No, she wanted to, but Mamma locked her in her room," he told him, quite truthfully.

William was saddened to hear that, but unsurprised. "When I get out, I've a mind to do as Sarah Martin did. I'll become a prison visitor."

Will agreed.

"We'll see what ideas we can come up with!" he promised his son, patting his hand.

Sam and I heard from Florence that Will had left home. Helen told everyone she had thrown him out, but he had left of his own accord. Manoa had tried to prevent him, telling him it would cause a rift beyond healing, but Will had merely shrugged.

"I don't care. My father suffered thanks to her. Elspeth died due to her negligence. She should have been watching her!"

Manoa was at a loss to try and explain to him.

"And you! You could convince her! Why *shouldn't* a son see his father? I don't care what he's done; it's not like he murdered anybody! Anyway, when all's said and done, you're not my father, and you *can't* control me!"

Manoa watched sadly as the young man turned and stormed out once again.

"Helen is not a well woman!"

Florence was speaking to Sam, Little Sam and I at the entrance to the church grounds. I had come to see the Reverend who was unwell. We all knew we were about to lose him, and it was devastating. "You'd think she would be more considerate of the poor Reverend; have you come to see him?"

Sam and I nodded; lately, Helen's hostility bordered on frightening.

"Come on," Florence said, and we made our way to the church. "I'll let you in at the side door," she told us. "I don't want Helen shouting!"

I had no qualms about taking her on, but with the Reverend lying so poorly, I wouldn't dream of it. Helen, though, caught sight of us and marched up to the four of us.

"Florence! What have I told you about not permitting the Dwyers any-where near here?" she asked, pugnaciously.

I regarded my former friend. She had put on yet more weight, her chin was sticking out, a fierce scowl on the once-cheerful face, and her hair now mostly grey, for all she was not much older than I was.

"Now, just a minute!" Florence told her stiffly. "This nonsense must stop. Sam and Alice are our dearest friends. They're coming to see Reverend, not you! Also, I might remind you to show some manners to your elders. I am sixty-four! Therefore, I expect you to treat me with some respect."

Helen gnashed her teeth.

"Fine! What do I care? He'll be dead soon in any case!" She slammed back inside.

Florence cringed and shut her eyes in disgust. Sam and I could not have been more shocked.

Florence recovered herself. "You see what I mean?" she said quietly as we went up to the Reverend's room. "She is not herself."

We entered the quiet room. It pained us all to see Reverend lying there, so fragile-looking now. He was ninety-three; an incredible age. I felt sadness overwhelm me. It would not be much longer; I could feel it. We sat at his side. After some moments, the Reverend's eyelids fluttered, and he woke. A smile came to his face.

"Ah, Alice, Sam, and Little Sam! Though not so very little now." He gave a smile and a glint appeared in his eyes, making him look very much like his old self.

We spent as much time with him as we could. The Reverend passed peacefully four days later, having seen us and the children.

I sobbed hard at his funeral. Sam held me tightly. He was also struggling not to let the tears flow. The Reverend had been known to Sam since the day he had been born, had married his parents, baptised him, his siblings, and our children too. It was a terrible and painful wrench.

We had planned a small wake, but as had the funeral, it turned into a big one. I was unsurprised to see how many people had loved him. He had been such a kindly man, so generous and selfless, and even those who had not been a member of his parish had wanted to attend, and the Reverend was laid to rest in the chancel itself; a high honour for the man who had done so much.

Mrs Elgin had passed peacefully shortly after the Reverend. We had been utterly devastated. It was like losing my parents all over again. I had grown to love the dear, sweet elderly lady who had taken me in and given so much; and coming so soon after the loss of the Reverend had been unbearable.

Rupert saw to it that she was buried in the quiet, beautiful grounds, which was what she had told him she wished for, in her husband's resting place. Once more, Saint Nicholas' was filled with mourners.

July 1861

Yesterday. What an horrendous day that had been. Helen had been taken to The Great Hospital at Norwich. She had finally had a serious breakdown, having been found by Tabitha wandering in her nightgown.

Helen had been diagnosed as suffering from severe melancholy, relapsing mania, female hysteria and brain fever. I was horrified to hear such words – people with those afflictions almost always ended up in insane asylums. But the doctor was disinclined to merely put Helen under the label of 'lunatic' and for this we had Nurse Bryant to thank.

"Helen worked with me for many years," she had explained, "and never truly recovered from her stillbirth, or the subsequent passing of the Reverend. She isn't mad, Doctor, and I don't think an asylum is the best place for her.

She can be treated at The Great Hospital. There is a separate ward there for people like her. Treatment is peace and quiet, rest and nice things to do.”

Most, if not all men, in particular a doctor, would have been shocked, not to mention furious and insulted, to have a nurse speak her mind so thoroughly, but Doctor Stevens was young. He was also progressive, and diseases of the mind were his speciality.

So, Helen was admitted to the Great Hospital in Norwich. I hoped Helen would recover. Could people recover from her malady?

After a four-week interlude, I wondered about visiting her, and so, with Kit and the twins in tow, I went to see Nurse Bryant.

“It can do no harm,” she stated. “I expect she’d benefit from the familiar. Most do. They need quiet, where they can recover properly, with no noise and no distractions. Doctor Stevens says healing a broken mind is like healing a broken leg... with care, and the right setting, so, yes, do go. Only be warned; you may find it distressing.” I nodded.

“Don’t take the younger children,” she told me as an afterthought. “I think it would upset them. Your eldest may go, but it would be wise to leave the twins. They are too young. As for Kit, er, well, I...”

I smiled. “I know what you’re trying to say, Nurse Bryant. Kit’s been a bit of a monkey where Helen’s concerned. I won’t take him.”

“I’m not a monkey!” Kit exclaimed, indignant. “I’m a little boy!”

Nurse Bryant smiled at Kit then at the twins who beamed back at her.

I had spoken to Manoa about Helen. He had been several times to visit her, and would have stayed near the hospital, but he had not wished to disturb Iffey.

At first, Helen had screamed when Manoa had approached her. She had, however, taken a liking to Iffey after seeing her a couple of times, since she was a young child and she had petted her, and kissed her cheeks, much in her old manner, and Iffey had been extremely brave for one so young. Manoa and Florence had done their best to explain that her mother was 'poorly' and needed special treatment.

"She's better than she was," Manoa explained to Sam and I later that day. "At least she knows me now. But it's going to be a while before she's back to her old self. She's so nervous."

Will was now living full-time in lodgings in Church Row. He had 'disowned' his mother, and Alice hoped to join him. They were making plans for when William was released, and William continued his model inmate behaviour. He had even become a mentor to younger prisoners, or new admissions.

"I won't try to stop Alice if she wants to stay with her brother," Manoa informed us. "I know she's underage; well, so is he, but he can still be responsible for her. There's no sense in talking to them – they won't listen to anything I say."

Sam and I decided to visit Helen. "I shan't take Kit and the twins," I told him after considering. "They're too young. Besides, it might set her back a bit if she sees Kit."

I looked over at Little Sam. "Will you come with us?" I asked, "Or would you prefer to stay here and keep an eye on the little monkeys?"

Little Sam pulled a face. "I think I prefer the monkeys," he told us. "Sorry, Mamma, but I don't like the thought of that place."

Sam nodded. "Of course, bor, we understand, but it won't be as scary as you think; it's not an asylum. Still, it's probably for the best. Helen won't want too many visitors all at once."

We took the train to Norwich. On arrival, I clutched Sam's hand.

"Would you rather have something to eat, then do some shopping instead?" he asked me. "I don't want you upset."

I looked into Sam's kind face.

"Thank you, darling, but, no, I *must* do this. She's my friend; had the boot been on the other foot, she would've come to me."

Sam and I walked to the hospital entrance and glanced at one another. "Come on." Sam held out his arm, which I took.

We could smell polish, carbolic... something else I couldn't quite identify, but it smelled clean to me.

We were directed down a long corridor with a sign that read 'Sanatorium' and a pointed finger drawn on it. I had brought Helen her favourite treats, a book and some flowers. After what seemed a never-ending walk, we reached the doors and peered inside. I could see nothing but a usual hospital ward. Right at the very end was a large sunny-looking room which, in turn, backed on to a lovely garden, and there were chairs and some tables. Sam pushed them open.

"Good afternoon!" A nurse smiled, having appeared from a side room, and held out her hand. "Who have you come to visit?"

I found my mouth so dry that I couldn't speak.

"Helen Wadaa," Sam answered.

"Ah! Good! She's in the day room, down at the end."

Sam hesitated. "How is she?" he asked. "I mean, what's she like?"

"She's doing very well actually. Her husband has visited with her youngest child. She was fretting about her, but I told her children that young are always a bit confused if they visit. We don't normally encourage it, but her husband thought it would help her."

Sam and I spotted our old friend. She sat in a wicker chair at the end of the room near the open window. She was reading. I glanced at Sam. She seemed to have aged a lot in four weeks.

The nurse spoke again. "Don't be worried; she's doing well. Next week, we're taking them out for the day – a picnic – then they can watch a cricket match."

I looked surprised. "What?"

The woman nodded. "Yes, we find it benefits them greatly."

"May we see her now?" I asked, and the nurse nodded.

Sam and I walked carefully into the day room. I felt as though I was treading on eggshells. I half expected someone to leap out at me. Asylums of our time were dreadful places, but this was not an asylum, as I kept reminding myself. Helen had her back to us and was sitting in a comfortable chair, watching the birds in the garden.

"Helen?" I went up to her tentatively. "How do you feel?" She turned to look at me. There was a glimmer of a smile on her lips.

Since I seemed to be unable to say a single word beyond the initial greeting, Sam had to take charge of the conversation. But as the talk went on, Helen responded better. She smiled, thanking us politely for the basket of treats. I looked at the other patients who sat in the sunny room. Some were chatting to visitors, others reading. It wasn't as bad as I had feared. This seemed more a place where one could rest, a convalescent place like ones people sometimes went to after a long illness. It was spotlessly clean; I couldn't fault it.

After an hour, we had to leave. Helen looked at us sadly.

"I wish I could come home with you," she told me.

"You have to stay here and get better, Helen," I told her gently. "Once you're well again, you'll be home."

Helen looked sad. "Give the Reverend and Mrs Elgin my love," she said. "And see if Florence will visit me. I'm being wrapped in a bit, so you won't be allowed to stay then."

I hadn't the heart to say that the Reverend and Mrs Elgin had died and I realised she didn't remember those sad events.

I spoke of her curious comment to Nurse Bryant when I next went to volunteer at the hospital.

"Wrapped? Oh! Yes! I see what she means. It's actually known as 'wet-packed'; it's where wet sheets are wrapped around the patient at varying degrees of temperature. It has a calming effect, for some reason. Yes, it's a new technique," Nurse Bryant informed me as we changed a patient's bed. "They also dry-pack them too. I think it's quite good. I mean, if you feel cold, miserable, and agitated, what do you do?"

"I take a lavender bath," I told her, though I seldom felt miserable or agitated.

"Exactly! The hot water and scent of lavender all combines to calm you. It's the same with the patients, just a bit easier than giving them all baths!"

Summer was hot, broken only by huge downpours and thunder. The town was extremely busy, and many tourists or day-trippers flocked in.

Kit and Stanley were on the beach collecting pebbles when they spotted a young man 'limbering up' as he called it. The two boys giggled at his squats and arms windmilling around. He wore a black and white striped bathing suit that came just below his knees, and the pair asked him what he was doing.

"Swimming to that sandbank out there!" he replied, indicating Scroby Sands. Both Kit and Stanley looked at one another. Living by the sea, all parents instilled into their children the perils of going out too far, too deep, rip tides, and all the other dangers the sea presented.

"It's dangerous out there, mister!" Stanley told him. But the fellow had laughed.

"Ah, don't worry, chappies! I'm a fine swimmer."

"But the tide's on the turn," Kit pointed out.

"What does a tiddler like you know about tide times, eh?"

Kit regarded him. "A lot, sir; I live here."

The man grinned and ruffled Kit's hair. Manoa had told them much about the sea, and just how treacherous the currents around the sandbank were. Scroby Sands was visible at some times but wasn't a solid island. It could shift and change according to the water, sometimes long and thin, at others, more rounded.

"There's strong currents round there, mister!" Stanley said. "You'll get drowned!"

"Well, I'll watch out! Might grab me a mermaid, eh?"

The boys scoffed. "No such things!" Kit told him stoutly.

"Well, don't worry, little 'un! I know what I'm about! Cheer'ho!" The man smiled at the boys, then stalked into the sea. Moments later, a woman hastened along the sands. She was waving at the man.

"Howard!" she had called shrilly. "Howard! Oh, you madman! Get back here. You can't swim all that way!"

But Howard turned. "I'll be back for dinner!" he called out cheerily, waved and plunged forwards into the waves. The boys watched his head bobbing up and down until they could see no more. Stanley turned to the woman who stood, wringing her hands, still shrieking at him to come back.

Kit looked at her. She was certainly not of the gentry – her voice had a London accent, and from some of the words she used, Kit knew he'd better not repeat them.

"He swims in the local lido; nothing more!" she told them in anguish. "He won't make it all the way out there, and if he did, he'll be too tired to get back!" She looked out to sea, miserably.

"He your husband, mawther?" Stanley asked, and the woman nodded.

"Yes, he is, for my sins! Ah! What am I to do?"

Kit thought. "If he don't come back by the time you got dinner on, do you ask Manoa to fetch him!" he said, brightly. The woman concentrated on Kit's broad Yarmouth accent.

"Who's Manoa?" she queried, wondering if she had heard aright, and listened as the boys explained who he was and what he did. The woman nodded. "Well, thanks, lads. I may just do that!"

The next day, we heard the lifeboat had been summoned to Scroby Sands to rescue the man there. He had made it to the small island but had been exhausted. He had flopped on the sand and had fallen asleep for several hours, waking to find the sea washing round him, and painful sunburn. He'd been alarmed to find he could barely see Yarmouth, and stood, wondering what to do.

By this time, it was afternoon, and Howard's wife had felt it necessary to go along to Saint Nicholas' to ask for 'Manoa'. She had been startled at his appearance, but had quickly told him about her husband, and how he had not returned. Manoa had left the woman in Florence's charge and had hastened to the lifeboat station. Howard had been rescued in the nick of time.

It was a perfect summer day. The twins and I were walking where some of the grander houses stood. I was wondering what it must be like to live in one, but smiled; the little row house we had was truly home, and I didn't desire a grand house. As we walked past the beautifully kept square with railings all around it, I stopped. The twins looked at me and made to go toward the open gate.

"Come on then!" I smiled at the twins. "Though we really shouldn't, you know!"

Normally, I wouldn't dare enter 'the square.' These were places reserved for the gentry, and young, finely dressed ladies with parasols would walk there. Anyone eligible for the square had a key for the locked gate. But today, it was open. The boys had always looked longingly at the place, with its duck pond and its beautiful trees. There were only a couple of places like this in Yarmouth. The plains were the usual places for the ordinary children to play and were dotted all over the town. This square was in the middle of some extremely well-to-do houses along the sea front. With another glance at the four-year-old twins' faces, looking expectantly up at me, I beamed and lead them in. Nobody else was about.

As luck would have it, at the side of the boating pond lay a beautifully crafted toy boat. It was on its side and a couple of the sails and the rigging had broken, but otherwise, it was sound. I wondered if the child who owned it had thrown it away on purpose. I decided it was likely – children of rich families would have something new. Why bother to have anything repaired? I picked up the toy and turned it over in my hands to examine it. I could repair those sails! Sam could repair the rigging. It was a good-quality toy.

"Would you like to play with this?" I asked Oscar and Ollie. The boys nodded at once. "Alright, now, remember to take turns; don't let it go out or we won't be able to get it back, so keep hold of the string. I expect somebody threw it away."

I sat on the grass and prepared to enjoy the warmth, the fresh air and watching the twins.

Suddenly, a shout was heard. I recognised the voice and turned to wave and smile as Mackie hurried over.

"Alice! What *are* you doing in here? You'll get shot!"

"Gate was open," I answered. "Anyway, there isn't anyone else here."

"That's not the point, Alice. You know it's just for the people who live here!" Mackie was worried. Technically, I was trespassing, but the sight of the twins with the boat made him smile. "That boat looks a bit worse for wear," he told me.

"Yes, I found it at the water's edge. It'll be fine. I'll sew new sails, and Sam can do the rigging bit."

Mackie groaned again. "Alice, that's stealing!"

"Rubbish, Mackie! It was left broken, by the pond. The ungrateful brat who owned it before obviously threw it away. Probably has a new, bigger and more expensive one by now!"

Mackie had to admit that was true. But he still felt awkward about it. I rose to join him, and he offered me his arm and I took it graciously. Mackie decided that in his schoolmaster-type of clothing, it wouldn't be quite so obvious, so we were able to enjoy the square for some time.

We strolled for a time before Mackie's nerves got the better of him.

"Oscar! Ollie! Come along now. Your mamma and I are going for ice cream. Bring your boat!"

We walked to the sea front, Mackie thinking how pleasant it was that we looked as if we were a couple with children. We found an ice-cream seller and the twins settled down to eat with great enjoyment. Mackie and I joined them.

"That was lovely," Mackie told me as we made our way back to our row. "Thank you for letting me come, Alice."

"Pleasure is all ours!" I grinned.

November 1861

Helen looked around her own kitchen. It felt strange being back. But it was warm, homey and cosy. She was happy to be back within her family once more. Iffey had been more than helpful, doing all kinds of things for her mother. I had come visiting, nervous in case she lost her temper with me, but Helen had smiled and hugged me warmly.

To make her laugh, I told her about Kit trying to sell the twins.

"I can imagine!" she replied, grinning like her old self. "Poor babies. 'Tis lucky he didnae succeed. There's villains aplenty who'd buy them." She thought then and continued; "Lass, are we going to go back to doing things for the workhouse?"

"Yes! If you feel up to it!"

I was pleased. This was just the sort of thing that would improve my old friend.

"I'll speak to the master and matron soon as I can," I promised her, and Helen nodded, smiling pleasantly.

Helen had been in the hospital for exactly thirteen weeks. After the initial phase of getting used to her surroundings, talking to the doctors and nurses,

Helen had begun to adapt, and her mind to heal. It had been a long struggle, but Helen had won the battle. It wasn't the same between us now, however. There was an awkwardness that had never been there before, even when we had fallen out. I realised that I felt a little afraid of her now.

We had explained as succinctly as we could to Kit that Helen had been ill in her mind and asked that he be nice to her. Kit was still upset at how she had been, and no longer called her 'Auntie Helen', which, though it was understandable, did upset her somewhat. He would speak to her politely, but I could see he was very uncomfortable in her presence.

15th December 1861

We had awakened to the news that Prince Albert was dead.

"Forty-two!" Sam gave a low whistle. "That's three years younger than me! He died yesterday. Says it was typhoid, but I think there'd be more to it than that. Especially with the way his eldest son behaves! D'ye recall that article a few weeks back? About how he got into trouble over an affair with that actress?"

I nodded; it had been quite a juicy scandal in the newspapers up and down the country.

But now, just before Christmas, the celebrations countrywide were expected to be muted for a week at least, and that morning, I hurried out with dozens of other housewives to get my hands on provisions before the shops shut for the mourning period.

I was at Saint Nicholas' assisting with the preparations for the carol concert, and as George rehearsed, I was listening to Helen who was talking of Alice's 'young man.' Her eldest daughter had found herself a boyfriend and had been seen about the town arm-in-arm with him. This news had been brought to her by one of the local busybodies and Helen had been annoyed.

"I don't approve of him!" she stated firmly. "He's a grocer's lad; we haven't even met him yet!" She stuck a candle so firmly into its pricket, I winced.

"William's expecting her and Will over Christmas!" she stated. "Honestly, why don't they just let him out and be done with it? I'm told they're spending Boxing Day with him for a few hours."

It was the children's right as well as choice to see their real father, but I knew better than to say so.

"I'll forbid her to see this boy, though," Helen stated. "If he cannae show himself and be introduced, he's something to hide!" She finished the candle display. "There! That looks good, does it not?"

I nodded. "Alright, Helen, you know best, but don't forget, if you forbid her, she's more than likely going to sneak out and see him. She takes after *you*, remember!"

Reverend Rupert had, after much thought over whether it was appropriate after a royal death, organised a nativity play, and I had been thrilled when the twins had been asked to be angels. With their golden curls, pink cheeks and sweet smiles, they were ideal. Kit was to be Joseph.

Rupert had spoken to him. "How about you lead in the donkey all the way up the aisle to the front?"

This idea had appealed to Kit immensely. I was pleased and I spoke of it now, to Helen.

"The girl playing Mary's too scared to ride the donkey in front of everybody, so, she'll just come on stage from the side."

Helen nodded. Kit loved animals too and the donkey was a gentle creature. He had retired from the beach and spent these days in a field. To my knowledge, he was over twenty years old.

The day for the nativity arrived, and we had rehearsed it. The donkey had ambled slowly, and most obediently, up the aisle on a leading rein with Kit, and had stood quietly for the whole rehearsal. A small, low stage had been erected, decked out as a stable, with fresh straw scattered.

Simon was delighted with his two youngest grandsons.

"Look, Grandpapa. We're angels!" Ollie trilled and smiled up at their grandfather. Mr Dwyer beamed and made to pick Ollie up, but rather to his surprise, Ollie took a step backwards remarking, "You'll squash our wings, Grandpapa!" This tickled Sam's father and he roared.

"Of course! I'm sorry! Can't be squashing wings now, eh?"

That afternoon at four o'clock, as snow fell softly, we made our way to Saint Nicholas', carrying lanterns, and with the boys dressed in their costumes. Rupert welcomed everyone at the door.

"Donkey's round the back," he said to Kit. "Now, all you need to do is, when Gus tells you, you lead him in, up the aisle and onto the stage we have built. Just like we did when we practised it."

Our family settled in our usual places and Rupert began. He had grown in confidence lately and was looking far more at home.

"Welcome, welcome, good people of Yarmouth, on this beautiful Christmas Eve. May I wish you all the blessings of a very happy Yuletide. Tonight, we shall begin our service with some well-loved carols, after which, the dear children will re-enact the nativity from long ago. First, I will lead you all in prayer for our dear, departed Albert, Prince Consort."

Prayers said, we began to sing, accompanied by the tuneful organ. Mr Dwyer, next to me, sang lustily along with Maria and her family, Florence and Helen, Manoa and Alice. Will had not turned up and Helen fumed quietly, since he had told her through his sister that he would attend. I squeezed Sam's hand and glanced up at him. He favoured me with a wink. I smiled at him.

Once the carols had been sung, the nativity began. I saw Ollie and Oscar make their way out, being gently ushered onto the stage under the care of

Tabitha, who had been keeping them quiet at the side of the church. An older boy was the narrator, and he started to haltingly tell the story of the nativity, in a thick, Yarmouth accent.

Kit began to lead the donkey up to the stage and people smiled at the charmingly innocent scene. Suddenly, however, the donkey stopped, and no amount of encouragement from Kit would make it move. "Come on, Donks!" I heard him say in an encouraging voice. "You can't stop now, bor'!"

"Hmm, that's typical," Little Sam stated. "I hope he won't start blartin'."

So did I, but then, the donkey decided that it was time to 'relieve himself' and stood as his droppings fell to the floor. I tried desperately not to laugh. Kit, however, had no such compunction, and having seen what the donkey had done, he burst into laughter. So much so, that he doubled up.

"Ugh! He just poohed!" Kit announced to all and sundry with much glee. I cringed. Everyone stared, some people chuckled, others tutted or looked annoyed. I glanced at Maria, and she too was straining to keep back the giggles, while her children laughed aloud. Albert frowned in disapproval.

"Oh! Oh, dear me!" Rupert came hurrying up the aisle. "Goodness! Alright, Kit, come this way; don't take any notice of what's happened. Let us continue – we can attend to this shortly!"

"*I* hope you'll attend to it now, Reverend!" One rather stuffy woman stood up. "That creature has done its duty right next to where we're sitting!"

Gus laughed loudly, uncaring of any offended sensibilities, and moved off to get a shovel. Rupert nodded. "Thank you, Gus. Ah, madam, please, do not blame the donkey; it is a poor dumb creature and knows no better."

There was a short interlude as Gus removed the donkey's droppings, and went outside, chuckling to himself. I nudged Sam who smiled.

That year, Christmas was held in Mr Dwyer's home, with a warm and happy atmosphere.

Kit presented me with another drawing and asked my approval.

"Wonderful, Kit. Truly a beautiful drawing."

Kit smiled. "I'll build houses when I'm a man!" he told me proudly and I nodded. But it seemed as though he might be more an architect than a builder. He had a natural ability. The only problem was, architects were skilled craftsmen and boys from Kit's background seldom got a chance of that kind of employment, unless he managed to get himself a good master.

Easter 1862

Helen, I decided, had been right to be concerned about her eldest. I was taking the twins through the park, enjoying the first day of spring. I sat on a park bench and watched as Ollie and Oscar found a new game of sitting in the fallen blossom and scattering it over each other's heads. Suddenly, I heard a giggle, then spluttering laughter.

"If we get caught, we'll be done for!" The accented voice of the female made my blood run cold. I only knew one girl who spoke that way. The giggles became squeals.

I gritted my teeth. I could just imagine what she was up to! I had been no different, with Sam during the days we had fallen so deeply in love, but she could have chosen a less public place.

Before things went too far, I stood up and looked over the hedge. Alice and the young man were in a passionate clinch. I cleared my throat. Alice screamed and jumped.

"Oh! Thank God! It's you!" She sat down, hand to her thudding chest.

"Thank your lucky stars it was!" I told her. "Good God! Couldn't you go somewhere more private? What if I'd been your mother?"

The guilty pair joined me on the bench. "Please, Aunt Alice, don't tell Momma; she'd go off her head!"

"I know, and of course I shan't tell. But you should've introduced Brian by now."

Both young people looked guiltier still, and I recalled Helen saying she had forbidden their union. I sighed; this could only lead to disaster.

Later, I spoke of this to Sam who whistled. "Trust you to bump into them!" he told me. "Best not let Helen find out you know!"

Kit would ever be full of mischief, but with Stanley's influence, it was worse. One morning, the pair caused chaos. The tide was unusually low, lapping onto the mudbank under The Haven bridge on Hall Quay. The boys had gone onto the mudflats to see if they could find anything valuable. I had told Kit time and again not to go there, but Stanley had insisted.

The previous day, the pair had found a strange, large doll dumped behind one of the shops. The boys looked at it, mystified at first, then Stanley burst into laughter.

"I know what it is, Kit! It's a dummy, like tailors use! It's got legs though; it stands in the shop wearing an outfit so you can see what it looks like! Come on, nobody's looking. Let's take it!"

"That's stealing!"

"It's not, it's broken."

"But *why* do you want it?" Kit asked, truly puzzled.

"I got an idea!" Stanley said, and grinned, then enlightened Kit as to his plans.

Kit gasped. "We'll get into terrible trouble," he told Stanley, but the boy shook his head.

"We won't! Come on, let's get it."

Very early that morning, the pair met up on the corner of our row, Stanley with the mannequin, now in a dress, stolen from one of his sisters.

"Right, tide's low, it's a shame it's so early, but there's enough people about. Come on, and don't slip."

Together, the boys made their way under the bridge, down the steps, which were covered with green, slimy seaweed halfway down, and Stanley squelched out, then deposited the dummy, face down, at the water's edge. Kit squeaked as he slipped, and Stanley glared. "Shut up!" he told him. Kit twisted to look round at the seat of his trousers, now stained a muddy green, but Stanley laughed. "There! Doesn't it look good, bor'?"

Kit agreed. It did look, for all the world, as though a child of around five years old or so had come to grief. So realistic did it look that Kit shuddered.

The boys hastened to the highest step, and Stanley made a trumpet of his hands and called out. "HELP! HELP! Somebody! A girl's in the water! HELP!"

He nudged Kit, who also began yelling. It wasn't long before their cries attracted the attention of several burly men, who, on seeing the 'body' face down, hastened down the steps.

"Look, mister! Look!" Stanley would have made a fine actor from the way he let tears run and howled.

"Alright, boys, do you calm down. Aww, poor little cherub. Why wasn't her mother looking out for her? Just a titty-totty!"

One of them made his way, gingerly, to the river's edge, to rescue what he believed to be a child. He glanced down at his boots, caked in thick, sticky, stinking mud, and frowned. As he reached the mannequin, he paled considerably. The child was alabaster white! Her small legs were sticking out. He reached to touch her, to pull her onto her back, hoping it wasn't a child he knew, but was stunned at the cold, hard feel. Realisation dawned as he turned the mannequin over so that it faced upwards. It was obvious now that the thing wasn't even real. He turned to the two boys who had got to the top of the steps. Stanley was laughing, thumbing his nose at the man.

"You bloody little sods!" he roared at them.

"Ha! Ha! We got you there! Fancy trying to rescue a broken doll!"

The man shook his fist. "I'll find out where you lives, and when I do, you'll get a bloody good hiding! You just wait!"

The boys hared down the nearest row, and puffed onto the denes, flopping down, safe now from the irate sailor.

"Ha! Ha! That was funny!" Stanley told Kit. "Did you see his face? I thought he was going to burst!"

For all Stanley's glee, Kit felt uncomfortable. He sat staring at his boots whilst Stanley chuckled.

Word about the mannequin in the mud had quickly gone round. Manoa heard and was frustrated that anybody could do something so stupid.

"KIT DWYER!" I screeched like a fishwife as he stomped into the house. Kit and everybody else leapt in fright.

"Take those boots off! At once! You've walked mud and sand all over my clean floor! You ought to know better! Don't you think I've enough to do without cleaning up after you?"

Kit mumbled an apology and took off the mucky boots.

"Where have you been?" Sam asked him, a frown on his face. Boots obviously, got muddy and sandy, but that was from merely walking about outside. These boots had mud up the sides.

"Nowhere," Kit answered.

"Well, take more care in future!" Sam told him. "Do you go into the yard and clean them yourself."

As Kit trundled into the yard, I spotted his trousers. "Hey! Wait! What the very devil have you been sitting in?" I frowned, looking extremely cross. Kit swallowed hard.

"Sorry, Mamma, I slipped!"

I frowned at him.

"I'll scrub them, Mamma!" he promised.

Mollified, I nodded. "Make sure you do, Kit. I don't need extra laundry. Be a bit more thoughtful next time."

Kit nodded, and began to clean the boots, whilst I quickly mopped up the mud.

"That stuff stinks!" I complained to Sam afterwards. "I bet he's been up on the quay!"

Sam frowned and spoke.

"We warned you about going up there. Don't forget that not all the sailors there are nice, like Manoa and his friends."

Kit nodded, looking sheepish.

The misbehaviour was forgotten until later that afternoon. Mrs Floyd was outside, scrubbing her step.

"I hear there was quite a to-do up on Hall Quay this morning," she told me.

"Oh?"

"Some jokers put a doll in on the mudbank. Face down. What a thing to do. A trick like that is wicked and irresponsible. If I knew who they were, I'd have them flogged!"

An unpleasant thought suddenly occurred to me. Kit had had muddy boots from the quay. The mud had been on the seat of his trousers too. Surely, it wasn't him? I went to speak to Sam who glanced over at Kit. Sam frowned. He patted my hand. "I'll deal with it," he told me. Then, he went over to Kit.

"Kit, I'm going to ask you a question, and I want an honest answer," Sam stated.

With much reluctance, Kit admitted to the ridiculous trick he and Stanley had played.

We were angry, but instead of punishing Kit, Sam spoke of the stupidity of the prank.

"Do you remember the story of the boy who cried wolf?" he asked. "What if you really saw someone in trouble? Think anyone 'ud believe you now? You won't be seeing that Stanley again, bor!"

I was relieved. Stanley had got Kit into trouble too often for my liking, and when Stanley called a few days later, Sam very firmly told him he was no longer welcome.

May 1862

"As if poor Helen didn't have enough to contend with!" I was sitting peeling potatoes in our back yard. Sam, busily working on some shoes, door open, agreed. "I wonder what she'll do!"

Alice, at sixteen, had become pregnant and her mother was beside herself with fury, not knowing what to do for the best.

"Ye slut!" Helen bellowed into her daughter's face. "What did I do to deserve this, eh? Do ye want to drive me to Saint John's? Fancy letting him go that far!"

Helen regarded her daughter, but Alice merely looked defiant. Helen looked angrier than I had ever seen her.

Sam and I sat, incredibly embarrassed.

"You can't yell and call me names, not when *you* did the same!" Alice stated.

Helen itched to slap the girl's smug face. "I was two months off getting married, young lady!" she pointed out. "Besides, I was a grown woman!"

"Well? I don't see the fuss! Brian's offered to marry me!"

Helen attempted to simmer down slightly.

"He'd bloody well better!"

Sam and I exchanged glances. Helen noted. "Can youse two believe this?"

"Helen, be calm. A grocer's son's decent enough."

Helen sighed. "I don't know why I even asked ye!" she grumbled.

I shrugged "Well, he seemed a nice lad."

Alice glanced my way and I felt suddenly very awkward. My expression told Helen all she needed to know, along with the crimson blush. She bashed her fist on the table.

"Ye mean, ye *knew* about this, Alice Dwyer?! Did it not occur to ye to tell me? Her mother?"

"I'm sorry, Helen, I didn't think."

"No, ye never do!"

An awkward silence ensued.

"I'll go and ask him now to call for Sunday tea," Alice told Helen, who nodded.

"Ye make sure ye do! Meantime, I'll go and attempt to smooth things over with Manoa! He willnae be happy at this news."

On Sunday, we dined with Sam's father, chatting about Helen's dilemma. Simon shook his head. "Sixteen!" he said, disgusted. "It's a disgrace!"

Little Sam wiped his mouth. "Has she got one in the oven then?" He chuckled.

"Samuel! Really!"

"What's she cooking, Mamma?" Kit asked me.

Little Sam smiled at his brother. "A bun!" he replied at once.

"Well, if she's only baking a bun, why is everyone so cross about it?" Kit asked in general.

His remarks made me smile; the day when he knew what all the cryptic comments meant would come far too soon.

Alice sat at the table in the kitchen, her head in her hands, sobbing brokenly. "I'll be ruined now!" she wailed. "Ruined! I can't believe it! He PROMISED!"

The family had expected Brian at five o'clock, and he had told Alice he would be there to speak to her parents formally. That promise had been made the previous morning, and Alice had been satisfied, and looking forward to introducing him. She was proud of her incredibly handsome, though feckless young man.

Manoa had taken it better than expected. He didn't approve of the fact Alice was pregnant at only a couple of weeks past her 16th birthday, but a hasty wedding was preferable to none. Having a baby in his culture was something to celebrate, and girls married and gave birth very young, and he had not been raised with the excessively formal, Victorian customs.

So, the family had waited, wearing Sunday best, the table laid with the very best china. Except, five o'clock came and went and there was no sign of him. Helen glanced at the clock and soon, her fingers began to drum on the tabletop.

"Well!" she stated, testily, "Your fine fellow doesnae seem to know how to tell the time."

"He'll be here," Alice had told her.

Helen's eyes met Manoa's.

"I'll go and see what's kept him." Alice rose hurriedly, feeling uneasy, and made for the door.

Alice hurried as fast as she could to his row and banged on the door. Brian's mother looked out.

"Who are you and what the devil do you mean by creating such a disturbance on a Sunday?"

Alice sobbed out that Brian was expected at the rectory for Sunday tea and that she was his young lady. Then she told of his promise to marry her. The woman could hazard a guess what had occurred. *Again!* She cursed her wayward son inwardly.

"Well, he ain't here!" she told Alice truthfully. "He left, suddenly, yesterday afternoon, saying as he'd heard of a job in London, so off he went."

Alice stood, shocked. She felt as though all the breath had been drawn from her body. "London? But he's due to meet my family for tea. I spoke to him yesterday; he promised!"

"I'm not his keeper! I can't stop him leaving, can I?"

Alice knew, deep down, she was lost. "But I'm, I'm…" She paused, unable to say the word, looked down at her boots, cheeks flushed red.

"You mean you're in pod, eh? Dratted boy! Well, it takes two to make a baby. You should've told him no!"

Alice reappeared in floods of tears, and Helen fixed her a baleful look.

"So, my fine lady! What d'ye suggest we do now?"

May 1863

To Helen and her immediate family, Rosie, her new granddaughter, was just that. To the rest of Yarmouth, she was Helen's. I hoped for Alice's sake the truth would remain secret.

William had been released from prison, and Will secured new lodgings for them both along King Street, near the marketplace. William was soon getting back on his feet. He had even secured a post at draper's shop as a clerk and was a changed man. He brought news of Blissett who, having done his time, now languished once more in prison for receiving stolen goods. It appeared some people would never learn. That brought Susan to mind. Was she still alive? I wondered.

William kept his distance from Helen, only seeing his children. Alice had been nervous, but William had nodded, saying that everyone made mistakes, and she could be assured she could rely on him. She was his daughter and he loved her dearly.

A fine morning found me doing laundry in the yard. I was scrubbing vigorously, when Mrs Floyd's voice was heard over the fence.

"Good morning, Alice! Hard at work I see!"

She turned to her companion, and I observed a thin, bespectacled lady of about 20, hair parted, and trained into coils round her ears, a frowning face and downturned lips. "You see, my dear? How nice and clean she keeps everything. Never saw any of that family with so much as a smudge on their noses! I don't know how she does it."

Grace nodded, but without change to the sullen expression.

"Where's that eldest son of yours?" Mrs Floyd asked, then, without waiting for an answer, turned to Grace. "Now, *he* is the young man I had in mind for you. You can tell by his father just what an industrious fellow he is. Handsome too!"

So that was it! Why had I not guessed?

"Now, wait, just one moment!" I said. "What d'ye mean? We haven't discussed anything like this!"

I didn't want our eldest son to meet this woman. But he and Sam had heard the chattering and had come outside. Mrs Floyd beamed. "And here he is! Good morning to you both. Father and son, aren't they alike, Grace dear?" Sam glanced at our son, who looked horrified. Grace looked at Little Sam, and I was reminded of a fox sensing a juicy chicken.

Grace became a fixture next door, staying with the Floyds. She had gone to Saint Nicholas' and badgered Rupert about starting a Sunday School. Rupert had trembled, fidgeted with his spectacles, blushed and nodded without asking anything further, anxious to be rid of her, then retreated into the calm, and mercifully female-free interior of the church. He took to hiding whenever he saw her coming and Helen became used to finding him in the pantry, and, on one occasion, up a tree!

An old friend of Mackie's, acrobat and violinist, Charles Marsh, had come to Yarmouth for the summer, not only to earn some money with his antics, but during that time he planned to scale the Nelson Monument and play his violin from Britannia's shoulders. This crazy bet had been made some weeks previously, despite Mackie's shocked objections, and Saturday afternoon at three o'clock was the time planned for the ascent.

Sam and I had been introduced to him, and we at once liked him. He was typical of music hall artistes - flamboyant, funny and a little outrageous. My father had been much the same and I lost no time in telling him tales of my youth and the music halls I had seen when I had accompanied my parents.

But this stunt was ridiculous, and I was not afraid to tell him so.

"Are you mad? You'll fall!" I chided him. "Have you seen how high it is?"

But Charles had merely grinned at me. "It'll be fine; I know what I'm doing. I've been climbing and balancing all my life."

"Not that thing! Do you have a safety rope you could use?"

Charles blinked at me. "A rope? Certainly not! I don't need a rope - I'm an acrobat!"

He grinned. "Fear not, dear lady, it will be a tremendous feat!"

Saturday came, and I had been edgy all morning. Mackie had joined him and had asked him not to attempt it, but word had got round, so many had gathered to watch the daring ascent, and he wound up the spectators like a music hall compère. He then bowed, and vanished through the door, which lead to the spiral steps, the audience cheers following him.

The audience watched, chattering amongst themselves. He appeared at the viewing platform and waved frantically. Now full of confidence, Charles began the ascent. He looked up at the six caryatid figures that held the circle of stone on which Britannia stood, then, he began.

He concentrated on his job, making short work of the caryatids, and clung to the statue's feet, observing the sculpture, then slowly but steadily, he made his way up, clutching at what handholds he could find. He could hear the light wind... the rushing of blood in his ears as his heart hammered furiously. Seagulls flew here and there. Charles shut his eyes, took a few deep breaths, composed himself for a moment, then continued. Right up. Right onto the top of the statue's shoulders, he sat astride, one arm holding on, and bellowed his victory.

The crowd cheered and roared.

Charles looked around. He had no fear of heights. In fact, they thrilled him. He felt so free, like a bird must feel when it perched and looked about it. The sky was mainly blue with only a few fluffy white clouds, though something appeared to be building on the distant horizon. He could see that there were darker, heavier clouds out to sea; the heavy, threatening sort that generally came in on a hot summer's day to round it off with the perfect storm. He could see the entire town; all the rows, the tented city that was the market, the plains, Saint Nicholas' with its grand spire, seemingly to be level with his gaze. He might try to climb that next!

In the crowd, necks were becoming stiff from so much looking up. Mackie glanced, fearfully. The crowd were becoming somewhat impatient. They had seen him climb up and wanted him to play the violin.

A low chanting became audible. "Charlie! Charlie!"

Up on his vantage point, the man smiled and took his violin. Hanging on for dear life with feet, his knees pressed hard against the cold stone. A cheer from the crowd below made him feel all-powerful. A swift tune, then he prepared to come down. As he moved from the shoulders of the monument, his footing slipped. A thrill of fear charged through him, and he scrabbled for a handhold, but there was none on the smooth stone and Charles Marsh, acrobat and violinist, fell to his death in moments.

In the moments when he fell, he wasn't frightened; they seemed to go past in slow motion. But he felt annoyed. Then, he hit the ground, and there was nothing at all, not even pain.

Mackie stood, so horrified he could barely move. The crowd buzzed; several women close to the accident site fainted.

Monday, and Kit came home from school, visibly upset that his schoolfellows had told him Charles had been 'in a million pieces' and other horrific descriptions, which small boys felt gory and exciting. But Kit had not found it so and he had nightmares. So terrified was he, we had taken him in with us.

Mackie listened, nodding sagely. "Alright, Alice, I'll sort things out; don't worry." I looked at his face; he seemed suddenly to be ageing, but still, incredibly handsome. He was only my age, yet seemed older. His hair too was starting to get that salt-and-pepper look, and he looked unbelievably distinguished. I pulled myself together and thanked him. I realised he must feel terrible, having seen it happen.

Mackie had some very sharp words for his class that day. He left everybody feeling terribly guilty. When school finished, Kit found Stanley waiting outside. He made to go past him, but Stanley caught at his sleeve.

"Where you goin', bor'?" he asked.

"Home, of course."

Stanley grinned. "Come on with me, down the denes."

"No! I'm not allowed to see you anymore."

"Come on, I've got a knife. Look at it. Isn't it sharp? I'm going to cut some of the nets, then all the fish will fall through!" Stanley laughed, evidently thinking this highly amusing.

Kit was shocked. "You can't do that!" he gasped. "Those nets cost a lot of money!"

"I can so!" Stanley replied. "I don't care if they cost £100! And if you don't help me, then you're a chicken, and I'll beat you up."

Kit fled.

Over the next couple of weeks, when school was finished for the afternoon, Kit would leave the playground, cautiously, looking this way and that, then he would run all the way home without stopping.

For all that Kit could vanish up the rows if pursued, so could Stanley. More than once, Kit found himself in someone else's yard, having nipped smartly over the wall. He would then squat in a tiny ball until it was safe to climb over again. Later, when we found out, I was thankful he hadn't jumped into a yard with a dog in it.

Each day, Stanley would wait, lurking either near the gates, or somewhere along the road to waylay him; always somewhere different, where he could be sure Kit would pass by. Kit would either be thumped or kicked or, as today, tripped up by a foot sticking out from behind a wall. Kit, hurrying as usual, went flat on the floor. He was more shocked than hurt, though he would feel his scraped hands and knees later. He lay where he was for a few moments, then, suddenly, felt himself lifted by his collar and thrust against the wall, coming face to face with Stanley.

"Well, if it isn't Dwyer!" he sneered. "The chicken! Still too scared to do dare, then? Big girl!"

Kit glowered. He was afraid, but didn't show it.

"It's stupid, cutting the nets," he dared to say. "People won't have enough to eat."

"I don't care!" Stanley snarled into Kit's face.

Kit twisted. "Let me go!" he snapped.

Kit entered the house, and I turned to smile at him. But the smile soon vanished.

"Kit!" I hurried over to him. "Goodness me, you do look hot and dishevelled. And what have you done to your knees?"

Kit hopped up onto the kitchen table for me to take a look.

Sam glanced over. "You alright, bor'?" he asked with concern, and Kit nodded.

"I fell over."

I was already filling a bowl with warm water. "So I see. Oh, Kit! Slow you down! Don't worry, I'll clean your knees up." I set about his injured knees; the twins watched with interest.

"Kit fell over!" Ollie said with concern, frowning.

"Yes, he did! So Mamma is making his knees better."

Ollie went to his toybox and handed Kit his favourite coloured ball which made me smile at such sweetness.

Kit seemed none the worse for his scraped knees and, not knowing the real reason for it, I soon forgot the incident.

Next day, Kit asked permission to leave school early and Mackie, none the wiser, granted it.

Children were not forced to attend school. Those who did were often required to take time off in order to help their parents, so the request was not unusual. Sometimes, it was to save on the 'school pence' which was given to each child to hand in once per week, generally Monday.

Kit had been delighted with this and felt much relieved. The plan worked well for a while. Stanley wondered if he was off school, unwell, and lurked by the house to find out, but he knew if he came to the door, he would no longer be welcome. Mornings might be a good time to waylay him, he decided, stalking back along the row. He decided to try it then.

Kit was alarmed to see Stanley lurking by the school gates. He held up his head, and went to march past, but a hand shot out and caught him deftly by the wrist. Kit found himself roughly yanked off his feet and dragged against the wall.

"Leave me alone!" Kit snapped.

Stanley scowled.

"Where've you been? After school? Found a secret back way out, eh? Bloody chicken!"

"No, let me go!" Kit tried to pull away, but Stanley held him fast.

At that moment, one of the masters came out to ensure there were no stragglers and spotted the pair. That Kit was struggling to get away was obvious. He stalked over to then.

"What are you doing to that boy?" he asked Stanley, towering above him, grey eyebrows knitted together in a fierce expression. "Let him go! At once!" The man turned to Kit. "Dwyer, isn't it?" he asked and Kit nodded. "Alright, in you go, young man, and as for you, scoundrel, don't let me see you hanging around here again. I can still take my stick to you, pupil or not!"

Kit hurried in gratefully, and Stanley, rather unnerved by the fierce schoolmaster, skulked off, hands in his pockets.

Later that day, as he washed, Kit saw an enormous black and purple bruise on his arm. Hastily, he pulled down his shirt sleeve. It would never do to let me or his father see that.

Kit began to ask if I would accompany him to school in the morning. I was surprised by this, since it had not been so long ago that he had told me he was 'big enough to go by himself.'

"Oh? Why's that, darling?" I asked, surprised.

Kit shrugged. "I like it when you walk with me," came his response.

I beamed. "Of course I will. Shall we take the twins too?"

Kit had nodded; thus, Stanley was thwarted once again, but not for long.

The long summer holidays passed peacefully by. One morning, I went to the front door to shake out a mat, but when I looked down, on the doorstep was a piece of what looked like bacon, but it was covered in wriggling maggots. I screamed at the top of my voice.

Sam had got rid of the disgusting creatures, and now sat at the kitchen table, his arm around me. I was shaking.

"I expect a seagull dropped it," he told me to comfort me. "You know what those blighters are like, forever picking up bits from people's rubbish."

But I wasn't convinced. The vile mess had been put there, deliberately, I thought.

September

On the first day of term, Kit lay in his bed and complained of a headache. I put my hand to his forehead. "Well, you don't have any fever," I said. "Alright, sweetheart, stay in bed, Would you like a drink?"

Kit nodded.

"Do you want to stay home today?" I asked and Kit looked suddenly very much brighter. By noon, he was eating as he usually did.

On his return to school, Kit spotted Stanley. It was breaktime, and the boy held onto the bars of the main school gate. Kit went up to him, feeling brave with the bars between them. Stanley sneered, showing bad teeth.

"How'd your mam like her little present then?" he asked. "I was round the corner, and I heard the scream!"

He laughed and Kit's small fist bunched. He couldn't attack his enemy through the bars, however, but he wanted to plant his fist into that sneering face.

"I *knew* it was you!" he told him angrily. "You're horrible, you are!"

Stanley merely laughed.

"I'll tell on you!" Kit threatened, but Stanley suddenly shot a hand through the bars and grabbed Kit's shirt front.

"Ha! I'll get you, Dwyer – you see if I don't!"

It was Grace who unwittingly drew our attention to Kit's truancy as Sam and I tended pot plants in the yard.

"I thought your boy went to school," she stated. I turned and looked at her.

"He does," I said. "Why?"

"I saw him. Yesterday afternoon about two o'clock... he was hanging round the market," she responded.

"Was he now?" Sam frowned.

Playing truant was much frowned upon, particularly as it cost us money to send Kit to school. We discussed it in bed that night. Neither of us had spoken to Kit yet.

"There's something up; got to be," I told him. "Kit's always enjoyed school. Now, suddenly, he's truanting, telling me he doesn't feel well. Do you think he's being bullied?"

Sam nodded in the moonlight.

"Probably, Alice. It explains why he was suddenly so keen to have you take him to school, and all these headaches as well. We'll speak to Mackie. Maybe he can shed some light on the matter."

In the morning, Kit got ready for school. He seemed sad, but Sam had told me to say nothing. I took the twins and Kit and left. Sam readied himself for speaking to Mackie. I was to wait outside the school and join him once Kit had gone inside.

Sam appeared and smiled at me. "Ready, darling?" he asked, and I nodded. The playground was silent now, and from one classroom's open window, we could hear rhythmic chanting of times tables.

"We used to do that," I told Sam.

"Hmm, and you still can't remember them!" he replied cheekily.

Having been summoned by a staff member, Mackie joined us in the corridor.

"Sam, Alice, what's the matter?" he asked. "You look terribly serious."

"It's Kit. We're very worried about him," Sam told him. "Is he being bullied? Lately he's had a lot of headaches. Is his work not up to standard?"

Mackie looked surprised.

"Not to my knowledge, no," he responded. "There were some unpleasant comments after poor Charles fell from the column, but I dealt very firmly with that. Kit's work is very good. He's a very well-behaved little boy, but I was meaning to say to you, I appreciate he needs to do his chores, but taking so much time off school isn't doing him any favours."

We looked at Mackie. "What do you mean?" Sam asked, perplexed.

"I'll fetch him out." Mackie looked at the clock. "It's almost time for morning break – look, go into the nurse's room. She isn't here today. I'll bring him along, alright?"

Kit was alarmed to be taken by Mackie along to the Nurse's quarters. Mackie wasn't angry, but Kit could tell he was worried. When he saw us, me sitting on a chair, Sam standing behind me, his heart dropped.

But instead of anger or shouting, Sam went up and squatted. He took Kit's hands. "Now then, little rascal, suppose you tell us what's been going on, eh? Why have you suddenly started missing school?"

There was nothing for it. Kit knew he had to confess, but he burst into sobs and blurted out the entire story.

We sat, listening, not interrupting him until he had finished. I felt a growing fury inside me.

"Calm down, Alice, *I* will deal with this," Sam told me. Kit rolled up his shirt sleeve to show us bruises and even his little legs where Stanley had grabbed him, kicked him, were covered in huge purple bruises. I gasped in horror. Mackie too was most concerned. A boy bullying another in the school grounds he could deal with, but not if it was happening outside the school.

Kit said that it had been Stanley who had left the mouldering bacon on the doorstep, and his idea to cut the fishing nets.

"I'll speak with his father," Sam told Mackie. "We can't have this! I don't suppose his old man will be happy he's been destroying nets! Well, Kit, don't you worry about going to or from school. Little Sam or one of us will see to it, until that brat has been dealt with. He'll leave you be in future, bor', I promise!"

When I asked why he hadn't told us, Kit hung his head and told us he had been too ashamed to admit he couldn't stand up for himself.

"It's alright, Kit, don't be ashamed. He's older and bigger."

I insisted on us taking Kit home for the rest of the day and made a fuss of him, doing all I possibly could to make him feel better. Even the twins came to cuddle up to him. Sam was furious at our son's bruises.

However, Sam had got short shrift when he went to complain. Stanley's father didn't seem at all bothered about his son beating up a former play-fellow.

"You'd best teach your lad how to defend himself then, hadn't you, bor'?"

He stood on the doorstep, arms folded defensively. He was dirty, unshaven and Sam smelled sour sweat on him along with stale beer. "All boys fight; I certainly did, didn't you? You mollycoddle him! You can't come round here tellin' me what my boy can and can't do. Teach him some defensive skills!"

Sam had been most annoyed at the response, but he couldn't truly say he was surprised. The only thing that made Stanley's father angry was hearing about cutting the fishing nets.

"Alright, Dwyer! Fair enough. I'll deal with *that*," he told Sam. "But don't come round 'ere whining your boy's getting beaten up. Teach him some moves, and if our lad comes home with a bloody nose, well, it's just the way things are. Your middle lad's too soft." He had then slammed the door in Sam's face.

The next day, I ventured to the hospital to do my volunteering work. Nurse Bryant smiled at me and gave me a list of various things to do. She was busier than normal.

"I've a ward full!" she told me, wiping her hands on a towel. "It's like bedlam in here the last few days."

"Don't worry, let me sort things," I told her. "I'll even take the bed pans round, but I'm not collecting them, mind!"

Nurse Bryant cackled. "I wouldn't expect you to, Alice. You're saving me a lot of work as it is."

"That's alright. Just make sure you make time for a tea break!"

I duly went onto the ward, bed pans piled on a tray. I was concentrating hard on not dropping them as I made my way round, asking if patients wanted one, and if they did, putting the screens round their beds, ensuring they had a tiny handbell within reach so they could summon assistance once finished.

"Knock! Knock!" I called at one bedside which had screens around it already. "Do you need a pan, madam?"

A strange, rasping noise came from the bed, and concerned the patient had been taken ill, I glanced around the screens. What I saw horrified me so much I dropped the tray with a tremendous clatter and clapped my hands over my mouth to keep from screaming. There in the bed sat a woman of around my age. The poor woman had much of her lower face missing. Where cheeks should be was an open wound, her teeth and gums clearly visible. On seeing I was not a nurse; she threw the sheet over her head.

"Alice?" I heard Nurse Bryant come speeding up the ward to me. "It's alright, look, come away. I'll send someone else round with the pans; come and sit down."

It was as well she took hold of me, since I had felt a whooshing noise in my ears, and I would have pitched forward had it not been for her.

"I am so, so sorry, Alice. I clean forgot to warn you. The lady, Mrs Pullin, has what's known as phossy jaw. You may have heard of it?"

I nodded dumbly, but I had never seen it, until now. Phossy jaw was a terrible affliction, suffered by workers in match factories. It was due to the type of yellow phosphorus used in the 'strike easy and anywhere' matches... matches I had at home. This terrified me, but Nurse Bryant explained that it was the workers who made them, day in, day out, year upon year that suffered the horrid disease that ate away at the bones of the face. It would begin in the teeth and gums, but tooth extraction did little to alleviate the pain. Far advanced cases, like Mrs Pullin's, were the result of a sudden splitting of the skin of the jaw. Foul stinking pus had been discharged continuously, and the only chance was surgery.

"She came in yesterday," Nurse Bryant explained, handing me a strong, sweet tea. "Her only option is to have her lower jaw removed, but how is she to survive that? We're getting our finest surgeon to see her later today. There was a case in America where the sufferer had her jaw removed and survived, though I don't know for how long."

"I never saw anything so terrible. That poor woman. Will she live?"

"It's doubtful; most sufferers don't, not when the disease is that far advanced. The operation is brutal, despite everything having rotted away. She should be kept well sedated until, well, the end."

"I'd like to apologise to her," I told Nurse Bryant. "That was an awful way to react."

The woman frowned a little. "I expect she's used to it, but if you wish to, be my guest."

I walked to Mrs Pullin's bed on wobbly legs and peeked round the screen. Two huge, beautiful blue eyes regarded me. I kept my eyes on hers and went to the bed, where tentatively, I took her hand.

"I'm sorry I jumped," I told her. "I've never seen such a disease before. I was just shocked."

Mrs Pullin managed to nod and attempted to speak. She could manage some words though talking was difficult.

"I understand."

"Thank you." I squeezed her hand as Nurse Bryant joined me.

"How are you feeling, my dear? How is the pain?"

Mrs Pullin shook her head. "'ad." she rasped.

"I'll dose you again," Nurse Bryant told her. "Now, Mr Peek is coming to see you later. I'll be back with the laudanum very shortly."

"I really hope something can be done for you, Mrs Pullin," I told her. "If you work with this horrible stuff, you should have safer conditions, even wearing masks as you work, then you won't breathe it in. I'll see if I can get some people together to do something about it." I leaned in and kissed her forehead.

Safety in the workplace was always a massive worry. Only recently had laws come into place regarding working hours, child labour, and a 56-hour week. However, many places disregarded these laws. Young children still cleaned highly dangerous machinery, often whilst it was still moving. People still worked with dangerous materials. The Employers' Liability Act had yet to be made. There were factory inspectors, but many of them could be bribed, and there was little if nothing in the way of compensation for workers injured or killed. Smaller businesses might compensate, if the master was good, and the workers valued, but big industries, factories and mills were dangerous and unpleasant places to be. Employers, technically, had a duty of care for their workforce, but since 1835, the numbers of employers paying out for their employees could be counted on one hand.

The next day, I heard she had died. I was upset, but Nurse Bryant visited to tell me in person. She said it had meant much to have someone treat her kindly. I told Sam and Little Sam about the woman, but not the younger children.

This project, I decided, would need Helen's input. The plan was simply to sew and provide masks to the girls and women who worked in the match factory in Norwich. Perhaps the wearing of cotton or linen masks would go some way to helping stop the inhalation of the deadly phosphorous.

November 1863

Helen, Maria, Tabitha and I, with a mask that Nurse Bryant had produced for a pattern, had sewn many linen masks that would tie at the back of the girls' heads. These we had made around the kitchen table at Saint Nicholas'.

Everyone who worked in that industry was aware of the danger, but they had no choice. Those who had been there since childhood already showed signs of disease – aching teeth, bleeding gums. It might be too late, but it could, perhaps, slow the process a little.

Monday, and Helen, Maria, Tabitha and I ventured to Norwich on the early train, and hurried to the match factory, ready for when the workers came in at eight o'clock.

The gates were opened by some men who gave us surprised looks, and a trickle of women started to make their way in. As they did so, they stopped, surprised at the unexpected little reception committee. I had delegated Helen to be our spokesperson and she at once went into action.

"Masks!" Helen called. "Help to protect yese from the dreaded phossy jaw! Come get 'em, lassies. They're free!"

We drew quite a crowd. Women came up to us to look at the masks, having never seen the like before. Maria and I stood either side of the boxes of masks we had fashioned and had begun handing them out whilst explaining what they were for and how to tie them. We were surprised and pleased at the women's reactions. Almost everyone took up a mask. I was particularly concerned that the young girls got them.

"They look strange," I said to one girl who was around ten years of age. "But it means you don't have to breathe in all the nasty fumes that'll make you ill later in life."

Mrs Pullin had worked at the same factory, and I spoke with some women about her and her condition before she died. I knew I could rely on them to spread the word. None of them could afford to stop working, but they could protect themselves as far as was possible.

Of course, such action was bound to attract attention, and the factory boss soon learned that there was 'a bunch of women making trouble outside.'

The boss sat behind his desk, chewing a huge cigar. He drummed his fingers impatiently. He had it in mind to open longer hours, regardless of the 10-hour-day law, and was just deciding to speak to his staff, when an excited knocking at the door interrupted his thoughts.

"Come!" His voice showed he didn't want any interruptions and what interruptions there were, had better be good!

"Mr Bask, there's four women outside; they're approaching the workers. I dunno what they're up to, but they looks like trouble."

"What the bloody hell are you talking about, Fipps?"

"Look!"

Down in the courtyard below, the boss saw the gaggle of females at the gate. His workers walked into the factory, tying things around their faces. Mr Bask looked at his foreman askance. He at once made for the stairs.

"Hey! You four! What trouble are you stirring up?"

We turned at the shout. A squat, middle-aged man clutching a cigar strode towards us.

"We're issuing workers with masks!" Helen stated.

"What the bloody hell for?"

"So they don't breathe in so much phosphorus," she responded. "Do ye recall a lady called Mrs Pullin who worked here?"

"Good God! I've a workforce of over five hundred here. No, I bloody well don't!"

"Well, my wee friend here knew her. She worked here for years and now she's dead, and when she died, she had half a face left. It was because of phossy jaw!"

Mr Bask knew of the condition, and why people suffered it too, but he wasn't about to be dictated to by Helen.

"Well, that's not my fault, is it? Everyone knows the risks. She should've chosen a different job! Why are you worried? You don't work here! Damned females, who don't know their places. Do you get back to your cooking pots and children before I gets the police involved!"

"I'll bet you wouldn't work with all that poison!" I shouted at him. "What harm have we done, eh? They can still work in masks!"

Helen nodded. "Alright, ladies! Let's get on. We did what we came here to do!"

"You all want a bloody good thrashing!" Mr Bask snarled. "Don't your men discipline you?"

Just as we were packing up to leave, we were approached by two men. One carried a huge and awkward-looking camera. The other held out a press card in his gloved fingers.

"Mr Bell from the Norfolk News!" he said to Helen. "My friend here is Mr Palmer, a photographer. Would you give us a statement, madam? Come and have some breakfast, courtesy of The Norfolk News. Might as well be comfortable whilst we talk!"

I grinned at my friends. Sam would never believe this!

We were taken to a good café and indulged with breakfast; Helen and I held forth without drawing breath for some minutes. The reporter scribbled eagerly; defiant women outside of a factory was a wonderful story.

December 1863

That year, gales blew in, and nobody dared put to sea. The water rose high on the quay and blasted itself into the house fronts, and domestic servants could be seen with mops, buckets, until it became impossible to do any more.

I needed to go shopping, but Sam was not at all happy at me going out in such weather.

"I'll be alright, darling, besides, we've nothing for tea. I need potatoes, some meat. I said I'd stop off at Saint Nicholas', pick up Helen."

"I come too!" Kit bounced at my side.

"I'm going to Saint Nicholas' first," I warned him. Kit frowned. "Come on! Brave boys come with me to see the storm and help carry the heavy things Mamma can't."

Kit at once put on his little short coat and cap. He stood and grinned cheekily up at me.

"This is horrendous," Helen said as I entered the warm kitchen. "Hello there, young Kit! Would you like a piece of gingerbread?"

Kit nodded, silently.

"Kit?" I prompted, and Kit lisped;

"Yes, please."

Helen smiled at him and plonked some cake on the plate, along with a glass of milk. I was presented with a piece too, and we sat to munch.

"That wind, it's kept me up all night long."

"We didn't have a good night either."

"Aye, 'tis a mite breezy, though I've known worse," Helen said. "Well, best we get along. Manoa says it's set to double in strength later."

Shopping completed, we wandered to the quay. The wind had worsened, and we saw many ships, moored up for the Christmas season, rocking dangerously. I looked at Helen shocked. I had never seen them riding the waves like that before.

Several men were aboard trying to steady the ships, offloading where they could, tying them, seeking desperately to find some way of securing them more safely, preventing them from banging into each other. A couple had begun to drift, dragging their anchors, and this caused great panic amongst the men, particularly to those on board. There was no stopping a massive ship weighing many tons. Whatever must it be like out at sea when our quay was so violent?

I shivered into my shawl, glancing at Kit to make sure he was alright. The wind was blowing right into our faces and I had already lost my hat.

"Come on; it's too cold to stand about here anymore. "We need to get home, or your papa will be worried."

I turned to Helen. "You coming?" I asked. Helen nodded, gathering her wits.

"Aye, there's baking to be done."

During the afternoon, I stoked the fire and settled with Sam and the children, Minnow the cat on my knees as I read to them. Little Sam sat on the other side of the fire, eyes closed, dozing, wondering what we would think of our Christmas gifts.

Helen had been waylaid in the marketplace longer than she had anticipated, having met a woman who normally held a market stall who was lamenting long and loud about the storm causing the market to temporarily shut. Helen was concerned at being out so long since Manoa became worried; she was glad to get indoors at last. She was soaked and Florence clucked in annoyance.

"Helen! Get those wet things off at once! I've had the water ready for a bath for ages!"

Helen nodded and dutifully went up to get some dry clothes, and towels for after her bath. Iffey sat, swinging her legs, on the kitchen table. With Helen well-screened in front of the fire, she listened to Iffey's chatter.

"Uncle Gus is afraid for the trees," she told her mother. "He thinks some might come down. What if one crashed down on our kitchen, Mamma? We'd be killed."

Helen glared round the screen.

"Be still with that kind of talk!" she told her sharply, settling back, since she was enjoying it. But, at her daughter's next comment, she sat up in horror.

"Oh! I nearly forgot. Papa said to tell you he'd be back at six or just after."

The words sent shock through Helen. She sat silent for a moment. Then, "What do you mean? Back by six? Where's he gone?"

She shut her eyes in fear at the reply.

"He's gone to help the sailors on the quay, of course!"

Manoa shielded his eyes from the driving rain and sleet. The wind was storm force. Two ships had headed for the open sea, one beyond reach, and was being battered by winds and waves; he had no idea if it was manned. On board another, which was nearer, men shouted for help, clinging to rigging. The gale had blown 'The Lady's Maid' almost sideways, and the river was a raging beast. Huge waves slapped the quayside, and foam rolled onto the land carrying debris, swilling right over the road, into people's front gardens.

Dreadful sounds of creaking, ripping, and splintering, cracking wood were heard. The sounds of the ships' bells, in varying tones, sounded like some terrible dirge. It made Manoa shiver with fear, but no mariner would ever refuse assistance to a fellow sailor.

"How can I help, mate?" he asked.

The skipper recognised Manoa at once.

"Follow me, shipmate," he answered and took Manoa up to the quayside. He indicated the skipper of the lifeboat, who was attempting to lower a rescue craft.

"You're a member of the lifeboat crew, aren't you? Well, there's no time to get that thing out; do you give him a hand, bor'. They're going to try to get the men off that ship afore 'tis smashed to bloody matchsticks." He looked at Manoa in fear. "My three lads are aboard."

Manoa charged up to where the lifeboat skipper was hauling out the smaller vessel, an ordinary rowing boat. He seemed most relieved to see Manoa.

"I knew you'd come," he told him. "Round up a few more chaps, then we'll put this in the drink. 'T'ain't our trusty lifeboat, but it's better than nothing and 'tis all we have."

Chaos on the quayside. Manoa brought back some strong, young men and the six of them began to lower the smaller boat as safely as they could. Some way off, another one was being lowered too.

At Saint Nicholas', Helen was in turmoil.

"You *cannot* go up there!" Gus had hold of the struggling Helen's arms. "Listen to me!"

Helen sagged, shaking her head.

"You can't do anything to help. Do you stay with the children! Manoa would have me shot if I let you to go up there and something happened to you!"

There was nothing to be done but to sit and wait it out.

At our home, there was the smell of roasting potatoes, along with meat. Sam sniffed the air. His stomach rumbled loudly, and Little Sam chuckled. "Storm's getting worse!"

"I'll go to see if Papa's alright," Sam told me. "Don't worry, I'll be back for dinner." He said when I objected.

"Alright but go there and straight back." I waved a wooden spoon at him.

Much to my relief, Sam returned quickly. "He was just off to Maria's," he told me, hanging up his coat and scarf. "Abe was there; he's been up the quay, and he said it's awful up there."

Manoa and his fellow crew members were attempting to row the water up to where the river met the sea. Rain lashed down, hurting his skin, and waves began to wash over the small boat; the sea merely mocking their attempts to save the stricken vessel and crew. It could toss a ton of ship about like a toy, so it made short work of the small boat.

Even the skipper knew they were getting nowhere, and now they too were victims... playthings of an angry river that crashed, spilling all of them into the waters. They had been foolish even to attempt the rescue.

Manoa swallowed a mouthful of water and spluttered. His legs kicked and he tried his utmost to swim, but the waves continued to crash over him, water up his nose, in his ears, mouth. He was tiring. He was freezing. He made a grab for a piece of mast that had toppled from the ship and been swept into the river and managed to haul himself onto it. He coughed once more, struggling to breathe, then with a final thought of Helen and Iffey, he closed his eyes. "I'll just rest a moment," he told himself.

CHAPTER NINE

Little Sam busied himself with the last of the gifts – new slippers for everyone, made by himself, which he was proud of; small toys for the twins, Kit's drawing things, oranges, nuts and other Christmas pieces. He was startled, therefore, to hear an urgent hammering on the door. Frowning, he went to open it and saw Gus looking deadly serious.

"Gus! Are you alright, bor'?" he asked, as the twins came to cling to a leg each. Gus looked dreadfully upset. He removed his hat. Tears were in his eyes.

"May I come in? I must speak to your parents urgently."

Little Sam nodded but spoke of our absence. "They went to get some last-minute things," he told him. "Why? Whatever's happened?"

Gus sat, and took the proffered tea, with shaking hands. He looked awful, tired, unshaven, exhausted.

"It's Manoa, bor'. He went to the quay yesterday afternoon, to help in the storm. I just come back from there. Some chap told me they lost twenty ships; worse, they think they must've lost over a hundred men! Two ships broke away and I know for certain that one had crew on board."

Gus stopped and sipped his tea. Little Sam listened, appalled.

"I got home in the early hours since Tab would be frantic. Then, I went there again this morning to see if I could find him, since Manny joined the other rescue attempts yesterday afternoon. He's missing. Somehow, I got to tell Helen all this."

Little Sam sat; it felt as though a lead weight had dropped into his belly. Helen didn't know yet? But then, it was still early in the morning.

"Wait till Mamma and Papa get back," he told Gus. "They'll know what to do, I'm sure. I mean, knowing him, he's helping someone and forgot to send word."

Gus nodded. He wanted to delay telling Helen for as long as possible.

We returned in merry mood, one that was dispersed at the look on the faces of Gus and Little Sam.

As Sam and Gus started to speak of Manoa, I felt sick. Gus was almost in tears once again.

Sam decided he and Little Sam would return to the quay with Gus to search again.

"Go careful, Sam," I told him, kissing his face as he put his coat back on. "There'll be all manner of debris about."

Sam promised. "Come on, bor', let's go."

I looked at Sam. "What about Helen?" I asked, as Kit bounded to my side and seized my hand, face beaming.

"Send her a message," Sam told me, wrapping a scarf around his throat. "Say we're all searching. Tell her to stay put; he's probably back there by now, though, or is making his way back." I nodded and took some paper to scribble a note.

"Kit," I said to him, brushing his curls. "Can you deliver this for me, please? It's to Auntie Helen."

Kit nodded. "What's it about? Why is everyone looking so sad? It's Christmas Eve tomorrow."

I looked at him. "Well, we're just a bit worried over Manoa," I told Kit. "We're not sure where he is, so Papa and Sam are going with Uncle Gus to see if they can find him. Now, you give that note to her, alright?"

Kit nodded.

"And once you've done that, if Auntie Tab is there, tell her Gus is fine. If she's not, pop along to their house and tell her. Can you remember all that?"

Kit nodded. "Yes, Mamma."

"Mamma?" Ollie lisped. "Where's Uncle Manny?"

"Well, that's what we're trying to find out, Ollie. Now, don't worry; shall we make some pastry Christmas trees?"

Florence greeted them. "Hello, Kit! Have you come to see Helen?"

Kit nodded. "I got a note to give her," he explained. "Papa and Sam and Uncle Gus are up the quay, looking for Manoa."

Florence nodded, her face worried. "Thank you, Kit. I'm keeping Helen quiet for now. I'll give her the note when she wakes up."

Christmas Eve, I usually went to Saint Nicholas', helping Helen to organise things, visiting my father-in-law and Maria, then home to bake and prepare, but this year was different since Manoa remained missing. After breakfast, Sam took the boys to the quay to resume the hunt for Manoa. I took the twins to the church.

"Florence?" I peeped round the kitchen door having expected to see Helen. Florence, in a floury apron, sighed.

"My dear Alice. It's terrible. Still no news of Manoa! He's been missing two days now; whatever can we do?"

"My lot are up on the quay," I told Florence. "There's always hope."

The parlour was warm when I went to see Helen. The fire burned, lamps were lit, and Helen sat on a sofa, staring at the floor. Tabitha glanced up as I came in. Gus nodded to me and whispered he was going up to the quay. I sat at Helen's side.

"Helen?" I took her hand. "Let's try to stay positive, shall we? I know it's easier said than done, but we can do little else."

Helen nodded. "I'm trying to, for Iffey's sake. But I know something bad's happened, Alice; it must've, else he'd have sent a message." She looked at me and then broke down.

Christmas Day dawned bright and sunny. The snow had turned crisp. We all proceeded to the church for the Christmas Day morning service. Helen was nowhere in sight.

Rupert gave a good sermon. He then spoke of the disaster and led us all in prayers for the missing and the deceased. We heard that 120 men had been lost or were missing. There were so many widows now, with children, that anything anybody could give, no matter how small, would help.

"There is a box near the entrance," he affirmed. "You can donate anything, not just money, but food, clothes... especially for the children. I'll be here throughout Christmas and will take donations and provide what comfort and advice I can."

Afterwards, I spoke to Florence who emerged from the side entrance. "If I hear anything, I'll send word," she told us. "But there's nothing you can do. Don't let it spoil your celebration. Go home and enjoy yourselves."

January 1864

By 10th January, Manoa was listed as 'missing.' Sam and I sat discussing the matter with Simon. "It's been three weeks," Sam said. "I don't honestly think there's any hope, do you? Poor Helen. She'll end up with another breakdown."

I nodded. I had gone to visit her the previous day, but she had taken to her bed and refused visitors.

Light. A very bright light. Manoa half-opened his eyes, but the pain of the light, and the swimminess of the room made him shut them again and he tried hard to concentrate. His head hammered painfully. He felt sick. His leg was painful too. It felt strange, stiff – there was something on it. Manoa carefully reached down and was startled to find wood! He opened his lips to speak, but no sound came, other than a raspy noise. A gentle hand applied a cool compress to his forehead.

"Alright, don't try to speak; you take it easy."

Manoa once more opened his eyes. Whoever that was, he couldn't see properly due to his blurred vision.

"Right. Do you sit up slowly now."

Manoa found himself assisted upright in the bed.

"Giddy, eh? I'll bet. You been flat on your back for ages. Now then, what's your real name, eh? Mine's Peggy, and this old devil here is Bert, my old man. We been calling you Johnny, but that ain't your real name, I bet."

Manoa regarded the couple who he had never in his life seen before. The man was obviously an old sailor. He could tell his kind anywhere. His rough skin from the sun and wind. Deep lines round his eyes and mouth. The seemingly obligatory greying beard. He smelled of rum and fine tobacco.

They both had very friendly faces.

The room he was in was very small, smelling faintly of herrings. It was daytime and the room faced east. Outside, the snow gave off a blue-white light that illuminated the room. His bed was low to the floor and extremely hard.

Manoa managed a smile. "I'm Manoa Wadaa," he rasped, "and I think I'm missing. Where am I?"

"Ness Point," came the reply, and Manoa blinked. Ness Point? That was the most easterly point of the country. The coastline here was incredibly rough. It looked out towards Dogger Bank.

"How'd I get here?" he asked hoarsely.

"You were found, bor'." Bert took up the tale. "By our son, down on the sands, still clinging to a piece of wood. Thought you was a goner, but somehow, I dunno how, you survived. Your leg was a mess, all broken... you're lucky it didn't mortify; and you was that cold! Since then, you've had terrible agues."

So that explained the wood, Manoa thought, reaching down to feel the cast once more. He had been incredibly lucky to survive.

"How long have I been here?" he asked.

"Five weeks," Bert went on. "We thought you'd have someone but didn't know where, so we thought we'd nurse you better and then let your folks know. I guess they're Yarmouth or Gorleston folk?"

Manoa nodded.

"Well, you wait a moment whilst Peggy gets you some soup. You're rake thin, m'lad. You must be pretty fit to survive all that."

He turned his head to see heavy snowflakes falling thickly. Bert tutted and lit his pipe. "Bloody snow!" He grunted. Peggy returned to the room with a bowl of soup on a tray.

Manoa swallowed with difficulty. His throat ached and even the act of sitting up and attempting to hold the spoon made him break out in a sweat. His lungs felt they were on fire. He was breathless at what he had just done. Peggy waited whilst he gained some control, wiped the perspiration from his face, then assisted him to eat.

"We gotta get a message out somehow, but there's no getting through that snow. Can you write, bor'?"

Manoa shook his head. "No."

"Well, few more weeks won't do any harm," Bert stated, thoughtfully. "Soon as it's safe, we'll get a message out. You rest easy, bor'. The worst's over with."

February 1864

William sat next to Helen on the settle in the parlour. He sighed with contentment. The fire was warm and bright, the snow had lessened, and traffic was slowly getting back to normal. It was Valentine's Day and Helen had received chocolates, candied fruit and a beautiful card. Late afternoon and she sat now, with her head on his shoulder. Strange how natural this should feel, considering what had happened.

Eleven-year-old Iffey sat, her gaze fixed on her mother and her ex-husband. She felt angry and couldn't understand why her mother wasn't more upset about Manoa. Iffey was old enough to understand that he had probably drowned, but nobody would talk about it, and Iffey had a hundred questions she wanted answers to. Now, William was coming to their home more and more often. It was Valentine's Day. Why was *he* here?

"I've never felt happier," William stated; "I can't tell you how glad I am you've let me back into your life."

Helen kissed his cheek. "Me neither," she stated, regarding him. He seemed to have aged so much. He was forty-nine now but looked ten years more. His hair was grey, but Helen had to admit he did look distinguished.

"I feel old," she told him suddenly. "We've a grandchild, our eldest bringing his young lady home for the first time..."

William smiled and nodded.

"I got a letter from Mam," Helen said, suddenly. "I forgot to tell ye! I told her about how we were friends again, how kind you are now, how you'd helped me, and they were pleased."

William felt relieved. Not every parent-in-law would have been happy at his return and initially, they had been horrified, but Helen had always done as she pleased and always would. If she was happy, they were willing to forgive their former errant son-in-law.

It would soon be my birthday and Sam had decided a night at the Hotel Royal along the sea front was perfect. Sam was brimming over with plans. He spoke of them to Little Sam. "I daren't tell the others; they're too young and will let it slip. Well, son, d'ye think she'd like a Norwich shawl as a gift?"

Little Sam laughed. "You bet she would!" he told him. Sam nodded and laid a hand on his son's shoulder.

"How'd you fancy learning to cook, bor'?" he asked and chuckled at Little Sam's shocked face.

Over at Ness Point, Manoa sat on the chair. He had walked around his bedroom several times on some home-made crutches and was improving daily. His legs, however, had become so thin, during his severe illness, as had his arms. His shin itched unbearably, but Peggy had informed him that was a good sign, and they would take the cast off at the weekend, but he would need to expect to see unsightly scars from the injury. Manoa knew to do strengthening exercises for his legs and arms, but it hurt a good deal.

He longed to return home. He missed his family more than he had ever thought possible and wondered constantly how they fared without him. Helen must have given up hope by now, but then, he shook his head and smiled. He could rely on Helen; she would know instinctively that he was alright and thinking of her and that he would return as soon as the weather allowed.

The day before my birthday and Helen and I entered a tea shop. We had been out to get shopping, and the snow had stopped three days before. Helen was 'taking me to tea' and asking me to choose a gift for myself. Knowing what I was like about getting older, she had tactfully not mentioned it, but had merely told me we deserved a treat. She had also told me she was organising a memorial for Manoa.

Flabbergasted, I clutched her arm.

"What? So soon?"

Helen sat to study the menu. "Relatives have memorials for people, if they die overseas, or in battle and suchlike."

"Yes, I know, but that's when they've been missing for some time!" I pointed out.

"And you don't consider almost two months a considerable time?" Helen regarded me.

"Well, not really, no. Still, it's up to you! But his body hasn't been found, don't forget," I told her, seeing a defiant expression cross her face. "So, what's happening with you and William then?"

Helen smiled. "That's *my* secret!" she told me, maddeningly.

"We never kept secrets before," I replied, disgruntled.

Helen smiled again. "Aye, lass, 'tis true, OK, but you'll no like it! William wants us to try again, and I think we should. After all, we've two children and a grandchild together. All the fighting, animosity, doesnae do any good. We'd end up with a family feud that went on for years!"

"Oh!"

"Lass, William's changed," Helen told me in a persuading voice. "For goodness' sake, you and Sam were the ones encouraging me to forgive him after he came out of prison."

"Forgive him, yes, not re-marry him!" I stated.

"I didnae say anything about re-marrying, did I? For the time being, we're together, unofficially if you like."

"And if Manoa comes back?"

"He won't; how can he? I loved him dearly, but I've a life to lead! I want to be happy."

Back home, I told Sam about the memorial service. Sam sat bolt upright.

"What? Isn't that rather jumping the gun?" He sounded appalled.

"I told her that, but she won't have it! Wait a year, or six months even, but she's determined."

On the morning of my fortieth birthday. I sat up in bed. "Forty!" I groaned. "I'm an old woman now!" I gave such a heavy sigh that Sam awoke. He looked at me, bleary-eyed from sleep, and grinned.

"Happy birthday, my darling!" he told me. I looked at him. My face was so dismal, lips turned downwards; he pulled me close.

"Don't look so sad, darling. You 're beautiful! Now, let's wash and get to breakfast, for there's a treat for you this morning. No work for you today."

I was amazed to be greeted by the smell of frying bacon and bread. There stood Little Sam, cooking really rather well. Men never cooked for themselves, not if they had a wife or mother to do it for them. It would never have occurred to me to teach any of our boys to cook.

"Sam!" I went up to him. "Whatever are *you* doing cooking?"

He leaned in to kiss my cheek. "Cooking your breakfast, Mamma. Everything's done; there's no work for you this morning. Do you sit and enjoy your breakfast! Happy birthday! Now, go and sit with Papa at the table."

Bemused and pleased, I sat and the boys came to wish me a happy birthday.

Little Sam put plates of hot food down before us all. I had to admit, it looked and tasted as good as I could have done. I wondered where he had learned to cook!

"Aunt Maria," he explained when I questioned him.

"Goodness! She taught you very well. These eggs are *just* the way I like them!"

Sam placed a soft package before me. "Happy birthday to the most beautiful, precious wife in the world."

I felt tears fall as I opened the package to reveal the shawl. I sat in total amazement. The small label proclaimed its veracity, but I would know a Norwich shawl anywhere.

"Oh!" I gasped, when I could find my breath to speak. "A shawl. A Norwich shawl!" I felt tears start. "It's beautiful!" I said, holding it to my cheek to feel the softness. "Oh, thank you, Sam. I can't believe you got me one of these."

As a rule, nobody made much about birthdays, unless it was the children's, and I had never bothered about myself, so I was once more amazed when Sam told me to pack my best clothes.

"What? Why?"

"We're staying overnight at the Hotel Royal!"

Little Sam grinned. "You can trust me to look after everyone here whilst you're away," he promised.

The hotel had a fabulous view of the beach. I smiled as we entered the lobby, recalling the last time I had set foot in here.

The room we had overlooked the sea and it was gigantic.

I gazed at the beautiful furnishings, especially the four-poster bed. It was the biggest I had ever seen. Sam sat on it and bounced a little. "Hmm, splendid-looking bed, but it's nowhere near as soft as ours."

Chippendale furniture stood around the room. On the floor was a brightly coloured Turkish carpet. Floorboards shone, having been highly polished. The fireplace was very ornate and had been laid ready for lighting. A bell-pull next to it, we presumed, was to summon the maid.

We entered the bathroom which was attached to the room and gasped at the bath.

"Sam! You could get all the family in here at once!" I gasped.

"Hmm, two at least!" He winked at me.

We went down to dinner that evening and were seated with a sea view. I glanced around the dining room, which was full, the diners dressed extravagantly. The men were in white ties. Sam glanced down at his blue cravat. "I seem to be a little underdressed!" he told me.

"You are the most handsome, stylish man here!" I replied, squeezing his hand.

But we were obviously somewhat 'out of place'.

Huge, glittering candelabras decorated the ceiling, shimmering like diamonds, and the wallpaper was beautiful. The large, high-backed chairs looked like they belonged in a palace. There was a large fireplace with china artefacts along the mantlepiece. Ming vases stood either side of the fireplace, each containing a dried flower display. I glanced downwards and wrinkled my nose at the smell of bad eggs that seemed to emanate from the vases.

We regarded the menu. This was one thing Sam had not bargained for. He had presumed the meals, like the breakfast, would be included in the stay, but dinner, however, was separate. It was also horrendously expensive.

I gasped. "Oh, Sam!"

Sam looked worried. Starters equalled a week's wages and the main course, not to mention sweet, was still more expensive. Sam sat, wondering how we could gracefully withdraw, and I became aware of looks in our direction. There were people whispering to each other, some discreetly, others more blatantly.

I frowned. Wretched snobs!

"Wait a bit, Sam," I told him. "I know we need to leave, but not yet. Those folks over there have got their eyes on us and *he* even asked the waiter whether we ought to even *be* here or not."

Sam nodded. "Cheek! But why wait?"

"I don't want them to think they've scared us off!" I told him quite truthfully. Sam nodded and the pair of us pretended to study the menu further. The waiter came over to inquire whether we were ready to order. Sam shook his head, and he drifted off elsewhere.

As soon as I saw the other diners had become bored with giving us mean glances, we rose quietly and went out into the foyer. "Now what?" he asked. "My belly's rumbling."

I took his hand. "Come on, Sam! I've an idea!"

Sam couldn't help but laugh as I took him to one of the many fish and chip shops. We bought a large fish and chips to share, and even a cheap bottle of wine from an ale house.

"They won't let us take this up to the room!" Sam said, as I hid the supper inside a bag. I shrugged.

"We won't let them see it!"

"See it? They'll smell it!" Sam told me, but I grinned.

We sat on the bed, between us a pile of fish and chips wrapped in newspaper, and the bottle of wine.

"This is far better than eating downstairs!" Sam told me, blowing on a chip to cool it a little. "What a good idea!" He beamed and raised his glass. "Happy birthday, Alice, my darling."

Breakfast was a luxurious affair. Dishes were set on hotplates, as in the houses of the gentry, and people helped themselves. I stood alongside a woman of about my own age; her waist was so tightly corseted that I wondered how she could even breathe, let alone eat.

The attitude of the guests was appalling, though why I should have expected better, I didn't know. Sam and I watched as waitresses dashed hither and thither, attempting to serve multiple people at the same time.

"Hey! You girl!" A lofty-looking man put up a hand and a timid waitress went to their table.

She bobbed. "Yes, sir?"

"This toast. It's burned! D'ye expect my wife to eat charcoal? Get more. Now! And whilst we're about it, that cook needs sacking! Raw, rubbery kidneys. The tea is cold! I thought an establishment like this provided decent fodder! It's not good enough. I shall be speaking to the manager!"

The waitress was nodding, bobbing and getting more distressed. She had not been in service long and was afraid of losing her job. I guessed she was all of thirteen. In her haste to placate the customer, she tripped over her skirt, sprawled headlong, and burst into tears. A man sitting nearby roared with loud laughter and pointed at her. Other diners enjoyed the unexpected sideshow too, laughing; one woman flicked open her lorgnette to get a better look.

I put my napkin down and hastened to assist her to her feet.

"Are you alright?" I asked her in concern.

"Yes, madam," she whimpered through tears. I was furious, embarrassed for her and outraged at the man whose humour turned to outrage, as, spying a full sauce jug on his table, I seized it and emptied it liberally over the bacon, eggs, kidneys and sausages. Sam cringed, not so much in surprise, but rather because we would now have to beat a hasty retreat. He was only grateful I hadn't emptied over his lap, or worse still, his head!

"Damn your hide! You insolent wench! How dare you!" The man stood, grabbing his napkin from his shirt front. Sam also rose, as the room fell silent.

"Damn yours!" I retorted. "She's only a young girl and she fell! How'd you like to have a roomful of people laughing at you?"

The Manager, made aware of an 'affray in the breakfast room', entered demanding to know what was happening. By now, Sam had joined me.

I explained that the 'fussy old toad over there had complained about the food and terrorised a child servant who had tripped and fallen, then had had to endure the humiliation of being laughed at by an old stuffshirt sitting at this table who should have known better.'

Since all this had been delivered at top speed and volume, the Manager had not been able to get a word in edgewise. He looked furious; his lips had grown thinner and thinner he had compressed them so much, and now, with arms tightly folded, eyes bulging, he looked like a butler about to reprimand the tweenie.

"That is true, young man!"

We all turned to see an elderly lady seated in the window area.

"That poor child did trip." She turned to the fellow who had laughed. "And *you* should know better!"

So fierce was she, the man paled slightly. His cheeks then flooded once more, full of righteous indignation and embarrassment.

"Well, this woman has ruined my breakfast! Look what she did!"

He indicated the food, now swimming in sauce. The Manager bit his lip.

"My apologies, sir." He gave a short bow. "James?"

A snap of the fingers summoned another maid, hovering in the doorway, her eyes drinking in every detail to spread to the other staff later.

"Fetch this gentleman some more breakfast; take the other plate to the kitchens."

"Yes, sir!" The girl bobbed and went to fetch the disgruntled diner more breakfast.

I looked at the Manager.

"I suggest you pack your things and leave!" he told me haughtily.

"We're leaving anyway after breakfast!" I responded. "But before we do, this girl's been good as gold. She's been most helpful, even though we had her running round after us. I hope you'll overlook her accident."

"Very well. Do finish your breakfast and leave!" He swivelled on his heel and left the room. The maid gave me a smile and a bob. I winked at her and took Sam's hand to return to eat.

"I can't take you anywhere!" he told me, laughing. "Alice, why is it that any time you come to this hotel, something outrageous happens?"

I chuckled.

I hurried to show my shawl to Helen. There had been a thaw, but it was hardly noticeable. Heavy grey clouds threatened sleet and rain, and horses splashed on the road, sending muck, slush and all manner of things over passers-by and I endeavoured to keep away from the kerb.

As always, the kitchen door stood open. I heard a giggle from inside.

"Just like old times!" Helen's voice sounded girlish. A second chuckle brought me up short.

"Ah, the good old times, though, not the bad ones. Never again, Helen, my oath."

I frowned. Was this what I thought it was? Before I could overhear more, the twins shot into the kitchen.

"Auntie Helen!" Oscar bawled heading over to her. I followed, finding William sitting in the chair at the head of the table.

"Morning to you both," I said, feeling somewhat awkward.

Helen set the kettle boiling.

"'Tis the wee buttercups! Would youse like some fresh milk?"

As she poured for the twins, I stood, waiting. Helen glanced over. "Well, sit ye down and tell me about your birthday treat, leaving out the naughty bits since the bairns are here!"

I smiled but continued to stand. Helen blinked and came over.

"Ye gone deaf, lass? I..." She paused and squinted, then was over to me in a flash and seized a piece of the shawl in her fingers.

"Och! My days! 'Tis a Norwich shawl ye have there!"

"Yes, it's a birthday present from Sam. Isn't it beautiful?"

Helen nodded. "I'm green-eyed, lass! 'Tis gorgeous. May I try it?"

I nodded.

William cleared his throat. "Helen, it's time we told Alice."

I didn't need to be told. I could guess. What had I told her when I had read her palm years ago? That she would have a turbulent love life? Well, that was certainly true. I had seen something about full circle too, and this certainly appeared to be full circle!

"I don't quite know what to say," I told the pair.

"Say nothing then!" Helen stated in a jolly voice. "Or say what ye feel! That we're just plain crazy! Or that it's too soon. Either way, we'll no take offence. We know ye've our best interests at heart."

I sat on the kitchen chair. There was little point in my saying anything in truth. I only hoped they both knew what they were doing.

"I've organised Manny's memorial service," she told me, sitting down, having poured the tea. "It's to be on the 15th of March. You'll come?"

The Ides of March? That was asking for trouble! But...

"Naturally," I told her, but I felt strange. Manoa had been missing for ten weeks but his body had not been found, not in the local area at least, but I supposed he could have been washed further along the coastline, and perhaps would never be found. Either way, with no news about him, no sightings, and after so long, there really was no alternative than to assume that he had perished in the storm. But it was indecently too soon to think of another man, even if he was her ex-husband.

"Are you planning on marrying again then?" I asked, deciding that I may as well come straight out with it.

Helen glanced at William who nodded.

"In June," Helen said. "It'll be six months by then."

I nodded but was uncomfortable with the idea.

"What does Iffey say?" I asked.

"Well, we need to break it to her gently," William stated. "But she's a young lady now. I'm sure she'll understand."

On leaving, I popped in to see Florence. At 68, she was sprightly and fiercely independent. I told her about the impending marriage, and she sighed heavily.

"Alice, it's a disaster waiting to happen! How *could* she even entertain such an idea, with poor Manoa not even cold?"

I agreed.

I had noted Helen wore lilac, the colour for half-mourning, something one usually donned once a full year was up, and if it was a spouse who had died, then it was full mourning forever.

Sam received the news of the intention to marry without surprise, though he too thoroughly disapproved. She was charging ahead without thought.

We assisted in organising the memorial. Afterwards would be a kind of wake held in the kitchen at Saint Nicholas', where there would be celebration of his 'homegoing', and since Manoa had led a different kind of life than he would have traditionally, had he remained in his own country, it was only fitting that a 'little of each' be incorporated into his memorial service. Helen had convinced herself he had drowned. Now, she had begun to feel that perhaps she was meant to come back to William. Why wait a year? Six months was long enough, and to those who didn't approve, Helen would merely thumb her nose.

On hearing her mother was to re-marry, Iffey had stormed out, slamming the door so hard that the ceiling plaster cracked.

At Ness Point, Manoa would soon be leaving. The path from the couple's home was just passable. A messenger was dispatched to Yarmouth very early that morning, and Manoa wondered what Helen would say when she received it. In his mind's eye, he saw her sitting at the table in the darkened kitchen, weeping into a handkerchief, then, on being passed such a note, leaping for joy, wrenching down the black curtains.

Thomas, the messenger, whistled as he rode briskly along the winding roads to Yarmouth. It was a fine spring morning, and daffodils reached for miles in a beautiful golden carpet. He was being entrusted with the horse as well as the message which sat in his saddlebags, since the creature belonged to the local mews. He rode slightly inland but kept the coastline in sight.

He broke the journey for lunch on the cliff watching the sun glint on the water, then continued. He had been back in the saddle for some time when a rabbit, startled from the bracken, made the animal shy. It staggered and reared, neighing in fright, throwing its rider to the floor. Thomas sat up and roared as pain shot through his wrist up to his elbow. He then watched in horror as the horse, perilously close to the edge of the cliff, lost its footing. The clifftop grass was already sodden from months of snow, and though its feet scrambled for purchase, neighing in terror, with eyes wide with fear, the unfortunate and panic-stricken creature toppled over with a blood-curdling scream that the young man would never forget, and hurtled down to the rocks below.

Thomas staggered to the edge to look over, holding his arm against his chest, but he could only see a little of the horse, being tossed on the waves. Now, he had to walk eight miles back and explain to the Mews Master what had happened. He rose, rubbed his bruises, and set off, the message still in the saddlebag of the doomed horse. He doubted he would get back before dark.

The sad day arrived, and Sam and I got ready for the memorial service. I buttoned my dress and frowned. I had a black, serge dress that I had got from the market, and it was itchy and uncomfortable around the neck. It also had a high, buttoned collar which I hated. I glanced at Sam, who looked equally ill at ease in funereal garb.

It was exactly eighty days since Manoa had been swept away. At Ness Point, Manoa had breakfasted well, and Peggy had put some meat, cheese and bread in a pack.

He hugged Peggy so hard she felt her bones might crack.

"It's not goodbye, '*mamma*'." He told her. "I'll visit with my wife and child as soon as possible."

Manoa felt good. That his message had not got through didn't worry him; so much more a surprise for Helen, though he pitied the horse.

Manoa took a hansom to Yarmouth, but once he reached Gorleston, he stopped the driver, and, despite his leg, decided to walk the remainder of the journey.

The fresh air with its tang of salt spurred him into song, some of the sea shanties he and his shipmates used to sing.

Manoa strode forward towards Yarmouth. He could not stop the smile that came to his face. The leg throbbed slightly, but he ignored it.

We all met up at Saint Nicholas'. Iffey stood stiffly some way off from Helen. She had decided she would leave home, and this service would be the last time she displayed any form of obedience; she owed that, at least, to her father. We found some seats near the front to be next to Helen as she wished us to do. Tabitha was already dabbing at her eyes. The rest of the congregation were seated, and Helen sat upright in the front pew alongside William.

Reverend Rupert put on his spectacles and moved into the pulpit, having thanked the organist for the stirring rendition of 'Life on the Ocean Wave,'

Sam and I had gaped at each other, aghast, but, as Sam whispered, this was for Manoa.

I sniffed and Sam passed me his large handkerchief. Little Sam held my hand and squeezed it.

Yarmouth was in sight, and Manoa stopped to admire the view. There was the spire of Saint Nicholas'... the huge Lacon brewery, smelling of hops as usual. Manoa picked up his stride, feeling as fresh as a spring lamb, and as if he had the heart of one too. He went across the bridge and was on South Quay in minutes. It felt as if he had left only yesterday.

Helen stood, stiff-backed and dutiful, head bowed. Nobody could have faulted her demeanour, at least not outwardly.

Manoa reached the house and smiled. Home! At last! He hastened to the kitchen door, ready to surprise Helen, imagining her screeching with fright, dropping whatever she was doing, berating him for scaring her like that, then running into his arms. But nobody was there.

"Helen!" he called into the empty house. "HELEN! IFFEY! Where are you? Guess who?!" But his calls went unanswered. He looked at the table, stacked with plates, cutlery neatly wrapped in serviettes. There must be some kind of function going on. He noticed the black curtains and presumed they were for him.

Manoa looked everywhere; no sign of Florence or even Rupert. Still, he wasn't expected, so Manoa decided to try the church itself. He shut the kitchen door and moved toward the ancient building.

The door was open and Manoa walked into the nave. The church was unexpectedly full of people. Manoa genuflected, and was about to back up and leave quietly, when a shrill scream from a woman at the back who had looked his way on hearing a latecomer made him almost leap from his own skin. The congregation, startled by the shrill scream, all turned to look. Nobody spoke. I gaped in shock, as did Sam. Manoa, aware and embarrassed that he had caused a scene at a sombre gathering, held up a hand in apology. The look on Rupert's face was utter disbelief, as his words died away.

"Do forgive me. I meant no offence. Please, carry on." Manoa spoke uneasily.

But there would be no carrying on. Not now. William had risen from his seat, sheet-white at the sudden appearance of Helen's second husband. Helen herself stood, rooted to the spot, and her expression, too, was sheer disbelief and shock, but something else too... horror.

Manoa spotted Helen at the front. Iffey too. He frowned, confused. Helen gave a groan and slid into her pew in a dead faint. Sam struggled to hold her. Iffey, having glanced, saw her father, and heedless of watching people, ran toward him screaming, "PAPA!"

Neither Sam nor I could believe what, or rather who, we were seeing. I clutched Sam's hand in fear. All we could do was stare at the figure of the man people believed had drowned.

Iffey had no such compunction and now she was clinging to her father and wailing loudly. Manoa smiled down at her.

"There, there, my bokkie," his voice soft and comforting as she clung to him and sobbed. "It's alright. I'm alive and well, as you see." He looked over at William with a frown.

The congregation was in an uproar. Nobody had expected to see Manoa back, much less at his own memorial service.

Manoa looked at William, who was near Helen, fanning her face. I reached into my pocket and brought out some smelling salts, glad I had had the forethought to do so.

Manoa, aware of the disturbance he had caused, smiled awkwardly, but then, his gaze fell onto William and Helen once more. He felt a little sick. Something was very wrong.

Rupert stood; he had no idea at all what to do. Florence gathered her wits and went up to him and spoke quietly. Rupert nodded. He climbed back to the pulpit, raising his hands for silence, then addressed his buzzing congregation.

"Please, good people, if you would be so kind as to disperse. I am sure there's a rational explanation for this, and we'll find it in good time. Manoa's sudden appearance is most unexpected, but very welcome and we must all thank God he is still with us. Meanwhile, I beg you to give the family some air. If you wouldn't mind?"

The crowd dispersed into the grounds, each chattering to their neighbours in amazement. Some went off to spread the word, and by the evening, the whole of Yarmouth would know that Manoa had 'come back from the dead.'

Manoa wondered what to do. He had expected his sudden appearance to cause a stir, but not like this, not inside a packed church, and certainly not the horrified looks from his own wife. He became aware that Iffey was pulling at him, but away from her mother. Manoa was shocked to see that William was at her side.

Iffey spoke. "Papa! I'm so glad you're back. Now Mamma can't marry that horrid man!"

Marry? His stomach felt as if it had plummeted to his boots.

Sam and Little Sam hastened to him.

"Manny! Thank God! We all thought you drowned!" Sam gave him a hug. "Where the devil have you been, bor'? This is your memorial service!"

"So I see!" Manoa said grimly. "And I hear from my daughter that Helen, my *wife*, is set to marry that reprobate William! Would you care to explain?"

Sam nodded. "Of course; let's go."

Helen had come to herself and was sitting, whimpering, her pale face covered by her hands with shock. "What am I to do? What am I to do?" she murmured over and over.

I would never forget the look on my friend's face. It seemed her entire world had come crashing down.

Will took her arm.

"Come now, Momma, none of us expected this! Let's go and sit and talk things through."

"You were gone!" Helen explained, breathless. "All that time! No sighting, no message! Nothing! The last I heard you'd drowned in the Yare."

We sat at the kitchen table. Reverend Rupert was there too, not knowing how to handle such an awkward situation. Not for the first time, he wished he had never taken over at Saint Nicholas'.

"But to re-marry *him*? Of all people? I was gone just three months, woman! That's no time at all! I was almost dead when I was found, clinging to a piece of driftwood, my head injured, my leg broken. I almost *died.* From injury, drowning, fever! Do you know who my last thoughts were of before I went under? Do you? Have a guess and tell me!"

Helen rubbed at her forehead. She could well imagine who Manoa had thought about in what he had imagined to be his final moments.

"Well?" Manoa wasn't going to let this go.

"Me and Iffey." She seemed about to faint again, and I put my arm round her shoulders.

"Correct!" Manoa told her bitingly. "D'ye have any idea how I felt when *you* were away? I wasn't swanning around with another woman!"

Manoa was furious.

Helen stood angrily to defend herself. How dared he judge her like that?

"And how was I to know that, eh?" Helen ranted, angered by the unfairness of it all. "The last I heard was that ye'd been swept out to sea. Nobody else survived. Besides, I was gone for just three days, mun!"

Manoa shook his head.

"You could've sent word!" Helen yelled at him, her hands planted firmly onto the table.

"I was snowed in!" Manoa raged back. "There wasn't any way *to* send a message! Not at first! Then I *did* send one, three days ago, but it didn't get through! But I still didn't expect to walk into my own memorial service, and worst of all, to hear *you're* planning to re-marry, three months after I'm presumed drowned!"

Silence. We all felt so awkward. I felt we shouldn't even be here.

"I'm no psychic, mun! Why'd I think just *you* had survived? And yes, I did mourn for you. I didn't just jump straight into the idea of another marriage by New Year!"

"But with *him?*" Manoa was incredulous.

"He mended his ways. He's my first love, my first husband."

At this, Manoa let out a bellow of rage, disbelief and scorn.

"Well! What are you going to do? Decide now. *I* am your legal husband."

Helen sat down again, staring at the boards of the freshly scrubbed table. She had never expected this to happen. She had convinced herself of Manoa's death and had processed it in her mind. Now he had returned, and everything was confused, churned up and changed. Over the past three months, Helen had fallen back in love with William. She found she resented Manoa for his sudden appearance.

"I don't know!" she said, miserably. "I just don't know."

Manoa's eyes were in danger of watering now.

"I see. Well, your answers to me are answer enough." He looked down at Iffey. "Will you come with me, or will you stay here?" he enquired. There was no such indecision for Iffey.

"I'm coming with you!" she responded firmly.

"Alright, we'll go to an hotel until your mother makes up her mind which of us she wants!"

Sam felt awful for Manoa. He had come home, after a near tragedy, expecting Helen to be delighted on seeing him. How deeply must he be hurting?

Helen kept her eyes on the table. The silence grew until it was deafening.

Along with Gus and Tabitha, Sam and I left before anything inflamed the situation further, and outside in the fresh air, we heaved a sigh.

"I could hardly believe that," Sam said. "Come to the ale house. We need a drink!"

Manoa and Iffey settled in at their hotel. Iffey was pleased to have her father back, alive and well, and paid scant thought to her mother back at Saint Nicholas'. Her thoughts didn't go much beyond the fact that her father was alive, but Manoa waited for word from his wife. Each day, he woke, hoping for a message, and each night, he went to bed disappointed. He grew angrier and more miserable with each passing day.

Manoa stayed on at the hotel with Iffey, hoping Helen would come to her senses; I marvelled at his patience. He had initially said he would wait one week. That had been three weeks since. Helen, I knew, would choose William. I'd known her so long I could guess. She was terribly upset about Iffey, who refused to speak to her, not even acknowledging her if they met by chance.

I had met Iffey in the marketplace, but when I had spoken to her of showing respect to her mother, she had laughed in my face.

Saturday morning and all I could hear were screams of outrage and bumping coming from next door. I had been about to cook a late breakfast, and the boys sat around the table, waiting.

"How could you? How *could* you? Right under my nose! And as for you! Shameless hussy! You'll be going right back to your parents! That or the streets. When I think of all I've done for you! I never would've imagined it!"

Next, there came the sound of glass smashing, and Robin's voice was raised in anger. Our sons bolted to the kitchen window and door to look out.

"Alice!"

I leapt at Sam who had entered the room. I was there, with my ear pressed against the wall. "What are you doing?"

"They're arguing next door!" I told him.

"So I hear. So can the entire row, I should think," Sam replied. "Hey, you boys, you're as nosy as your mother!"

But this was a piece of drama. Robin and Grace had been quietly having an affair together. Nobody had suspected a thing. The staid, upright, prim and proper Grace had been discovered, writhing in ecstasy beneath Robin's sweating form in the marriage bed that very morning, using obscenities her aunt had never dreamt existed. The screams from her house had been heard at the other end of the row and some people had stopped outside, thinking murder was being done.

"How long's this been going on? I'd never have known if I hadn't forgotten my purse and come back. No wonder you were so eager to stay behind! Slut! Whore! And as for *you!* You're an old man! I'm amazed you can even get it up anymore!" Somebody yelped and I thought perhaps a blow had been struck.

The front door opened, and things crashed onto the cobbles.

The door slammed and we glanced outside. Grace was there, her hair in disarray, red-faced and sobbing, attempting to gather her belongings which had scattered all over the row.

"Can we have breakfast now?" Sam asked, mildly.

Autumn 1866

Manoa still lived in Yarmouth, despite having given Helen just one week to make up her mind. He had managed to get a good house, up on South Quay, much to Helen's fury. He now lived with Iffey, who attended an exclusive day school.

Will and Lucy had married earlier that year and now lived on Laughing Image Corner. Lucy was already expecting. Helen had flouted all custom and she and William had now moved to Angel Row, not far from us. One very frosty morning, I went to visit Helen via Church Plain. I looked down at the carpet of red, orange and yellow leaves and swooped to pick up the nicest coloured and shiniest. There were a few conkers, and I took them too, shiny and huge from their green, spiky cases.

I entered Helen's home, her door as ever, unlocked.

"HELEN!" I roared, and from upstairs there came an answer.

"Up here, hen!"

Helen lay in her bed, grumbling. She had had stomach pain on and off for weeks now. Sometimes she was fine, but at others, she would be confined to her bed for days at a time.

"Not again, Helen?"

"Aye, I've to rest. 'Tis a mighty nuisance. Hello, what have ye brought me?"

She laughed as I deposited the leaves and conkers.

"I thought you'd like a display for the kitchen, Helen, but if you prefer, I'll arrange them here."

"Aye, might as well... I'll be up for a while."

This alarmed me and I turned to her but she smiled. "Ach, 'tis only me bein' lazy! I could get up if I'd a mind to, but I rather like bein' waited on. Well, those are pretty. Thanks!"

I smiled and regarded my friend. She seemed pale and tired. Despite her words, I knew there was something quite wrong. Helen never lay abed.

I glanced from the window. William was walking up the row. It had been remarkable, their getting back together. What was more, it had worked, and they were happy. William had even bought her a wedding ring. They behaved as a married couple and Helen had firmly stated that anyone who didn't like it could lump it. She had just recently begun to see Iffey again. They had not spoken for some time after Helen had chosen William, but Lucy had told Iffey that she should make amends. Otherwise, she would one day bitterly regret not doing so.

Manoa remained steadfast in his refusal to give her a divorce.

What upset me was the fact that the relationship between Helen and Manoa had turned so very bitter. Their whirlwind romance and passionate love was gone.

"He willnae divorce me; not because of the stigma, but he doesnae want me to marry Will'um."

This I could understand, but why make it so difficult? Helen and William were together anyway, wedding or not.

"Maybe he's hoping you'll come back."

"Not a chance!" Helen growled. "I'll no' forget my wee babby either, the one Manoa told me would be evil. Anyway, enough of my miseries. Tell me all the gossip!"

As I did so, Helen winced.

"Helen?" I asked, concerned.

"Ach, 'tis nothin', lass, a wee twinge."

"She keeps refusing the doctor!" William entered the room and sat on the bed taking both Helen's hands in his. "Don't you? We all know you're a tough Scotswoman, but you really do need to see one!"

"I don't want doctors poking me about!" Helen told us both. "Did ye put the victuals away in their correct places, or have ye put tins in the refrigerator and ham in the fruit basket?"

"All is in its correct place!" He smiled and kissed her brow. "Your hands are hot!" He frowned in concern.

Helen huffed. "I've had my fingers round a mug of tea, mun! What do ye expect?"

"What *are* your symptoms, Helen?" I asked.

Helen shrugged. "Nothing much; every so often I get pukey, and I cannae *go* properly. William's tried prunes, syrup of figs, Valentine's meat juice... That's no good, it doesnae stay down more 'n five minutes."

I shuddered. It made a lot of people sick, and I never used it.

"But you said the pain was on the right."

"'Tis nothing. Stop fussin', Alice! And that goes for you too!" she added to William who set a warm compress over her belly.

Later, William and I went to the kitchen, where he set the kettle to boil. William was quiet, worried. "What is it?" I asked him. William sighed and looked at me.

"I can't say, Alice, it's too far-fetched. Besides, I could be wrong."

"Go on," I urged. "I can see she's unwell, and something's bothering you."

William stood, his back to the fireplace. He sighed.

"Iffey's been here," he told me. "I'm happy they're reunited. I always make myself scarce when she comes round so they can be private. But it seems odd; after her visits, Helen gets the tummy pains. Iffey brings round food for her."

I looked at him. His hint was unmistakeable.

"What are you suggesting William?" I asked quietly. "Iffey's trying to poison her own mother?"

William shrugged. "I don't know. That's another reason I want the doctor from Norwich; he'd know."

Poison was a favourite way of ridding oneself of unwanted relatives, or enemies, and was readily available in chemist shops. I could never forget Susan's attempt to poison Sam.

"William, you need proof of something like that," I told him quietly. "Something that would stand up in court. Iffey's a child. No, William, it's just coincidence."

"I hope so," William told me. "I can't help being suspicious." He pinched the bridge of his nose with his finger and thumb; he looked extremely tired. He had refused assistance, wanting to care for her himself.

"William!" Helen's voice came down the stairs. "I'm gonna be sick!"

I cringed. "I'll, ah, leave you to it," I told him. "Sorry!"

William smiled. "Don't worry about it!"

I took William's suspicions home to Sam.

"Food poisoning?" Sam suggested. "William cooks. What if he doesn't wash up right? Men aren't made for washing up... or cooking for that matter; we don't notice dirt."

"Perhaps, but then, he'd be ill too, wouldn't he? Anyway, William only cooks simple things or does sandwiches, and he generally gets food from outside and brings it home."

Sam nodded.

"It's not like Helen to stay abed either." I drummed my fingers on the wooden tabletop. "So, she must be feeling proper poorly."

I sought out my little medical book and perused it, but I could find nothing.

"I know! I'll ask Nurse Bryant!"

I went to her lodgings and poured out my suspicions. Nurse Bryant listened and nodded.

"Alice, the symptoms you described don't match those of poisoning," she told me. "If that was the case, Helen's symptoms would be different. No, I don't think it's that at all. Does she have any numbness in her fingers? Toes?"

I shook my head. "Not that she's told me."

Nurse Bryant pondered. "It sounds more like her caecum."

"Her what?"

"Caecum. It's a piece of intestine."

"Can anything be done about it?"

"Well, yes, but it's very risky. It's been successfully treated in London, during the last century, I believe. A child was operated on. He lived."

"Well, can you speak with a doctor, please?" I asked her. "I'd feel a lot better if you did."

I went to visit Helen the following day, hoping that she was a little better, and ran into Iffey coming up the row with a covered dish.

"Good afternoon! What do you have in there?" I asked her.

"It's a vegetable curry. Papa said not to take her meat as it's harder to digest."

I looked at her, trying to detect signs of nervousness, but there were none. She merely regarded me out of jet-black eyes.

"Iffey, how is your father? I heard he spat at William's feet the other day!"

"Well, what can he expect?" Iffey asked at once, defensive. "*He* broke up our family. We were happy till he came along. Now Papa won't see anybody."

"Well, I'm sorry how things have turned out, but it isn't that simple! When you're grown up, you'll understand."

Iffey nodded. "I suppose so. I'm trying to be nice to Mamma. Lucy said I'd regret it if I didn't, one day. That's why I take her stuff," she answered.

"Well, come on, let's go and visit her."

Iffey shot a look of loathing at William, who nodded at me. "I'll leave you to it," he said, and kissing Helen, he left. Iffey's expression as she glared after him was pure venom.

"Lass!" Helen smiled at her daughter. "I'm happy to see you. How are you?"

"Well enough," she told her. "I cooked this for you. Eat it whilst it's hot."

She fetched some cutlery and deposited the meal on a tray and put it on Helen's knees.

Helen didn't feel the least bit hungry, but she told the girl that it smelled delicious.

"May I try some?" I asked, suddenly. If there *was* poison in the food, Iffey would not let me eat it, would she?

Iffey thought, then she nodded and spooned some onto a plate for me. I wondered if I was doing the right thing, despite Nurse Bryant's remarks.

"Come on, Iffey, join us in the meal. You've done plenty," I said, encouragingly. Iffey paused, then to my sheer relief, she spooned some onto a plate for herself too. We all three began to eat.

"This is delicious, Iffey," I told her – rather too hot for my liking, but I had to admit it was enjoyable. Helen's appetite recovered somewhat, and she was able to eat most of what was on her plate.

Later that afternoon, however, Helen was horribly sick again and William sat stroking her head.

I returned that evening, in another attempt to persuade her to see a doctor.

"Ach! 'Tis a mild distemper, nothing more."

I took her hand. "It's a bit more serious than that. Sam said he had heard of this kind of pain, but he can't remember what it's called. He knows that operations can be done."

I bit my tongue at her immediate retort.

"Operation! I'll no have another of those!" Helen said firmly.

"Helen, it would be different this time. Please, just think about this. Go into the hospital. Let Nurse Bryant have a look. *Please*, Helen!"

My friend shook her head. "Whisht, Alice! I'll be fine. You'll see!"

The following morning, I went round to see Helen to find her curled up on her side, knees up to her chin.

"That does it! I'm getting Nurse Bryant round for you. You know her; you worked with her too." Helen realised she would get no peace until she agreed.

"Och, alright! If it'll stop yer nagging!" my friend exclaimed, out of patience with me. I sighed in relief. William was at once relieved and told her she was making the right decision.

I ran to Nurse Bryant's lodgings, unwilling to waste time or give Helen an opportunity to change her mind. Alarmed at my hasty explanation, she at once accompanied me.

"Show me where the pain is, Helen."

Helen pointed, and Nurse Bryant nodded. "May I feel?"

Helen shrugged. "I s'pose so, but dinnae press hard."

Nurse Bryant lightly touched Helen's lower right quadrant and my friend yelped. Sweat broke out on her forehead. It felt hard to the nurse's touch.

"I'll get Doctor Hill to come round. He's a good man! Don't worry, Helen. I'll send a message at once."

Helen nodded. "Alright, if it'll stop everyone fussin' and nagging me!"

Doctor Hill arrived, nodded to Helen and asked her to lie down flat, which she did. He then observed her stomach. He palpated it softly, noting, as Nurse Bryant had, that the right side looked to be harder. On touching that side, Helen shrieked, and everyone jumped.

"I apologise," Doctor Hill told her. "It is as Nurse Bryant thought."

Next, Doctor Hill opened his black bag and produced a strange-looking object. It was a thin tube, about six inches long, made of glass, and none of us had seen the like before.

"What're ye gonna do wi' that?" Helen asked, with extreme concern. "Don't ye dare put it up my arse, young man, else ye'll have great difficulty in pulling it oota yer ear!"

"It's a thermometer. Don't worry, it sits under your tongue," he told us, smiling. "It measures how hot you are. Five minutes should do the trick."

We all waited, Helen feeling ridiculous with a glass tube in her mouth, unable to speak.

When he was satisfied, he glanced at it, raised his eyebrows and shook it. He looked at Helen.

"Well, madam. You need to come into the hospital. You've a temperature of 103! That's far too high. I insist you be admitted immediately."

Helen looked at William. "Please," He pleaded with her. "I love you, Helen. I can't lose you, not again!" Helen sighed and nodded. For all she was terrified at the thought of another operation, she knew she was very ill.

Sam and I accompanied them to the hospital at Helen's insistence. Nurse Bryant spoke to the Sister on the ward, who was startled at her old colleague's sudden re-appearance, and nodded as they spoke in hushed whispers as Helen was settled into a bed.

The Ward Sister came to Helen's bed. She wore the obligatory starched white apron and a very ornate type of hat, denoting her rank.

"Now, Helen, say your farewells. It's time for the lights out. The surgeon shall operate first thing, and you'll see your family after. Don't look so alarmed! We've the latest equipment, and everything is clean. You won't know a thing about it either, since he'll give you chloroform. You'll drift into a lovely sleep, then wake with the pain gone."

It sounded like magic.

Sam and I said goodnight to Helen.

"Now, behave yourself!" I told her, giving her a hug and a kiss on the cheek. "Do what you're told for once, and I'll see you after the operation, if they'll let me."

"Goodnight, hen," Helen said, smiling. "I'll see ye tomorrow. Give my love to the weans."

December 1866

I sat at the kitchen table. Helen was dead. She had died the previous morning at eight o'clock. Sam sat at my side, his arm about my shoulder. On hearing the news, I had bawled like a baby, alarming my family. Now, silent hot tears flooded my cheeks. This was the last thing we had expected. Helen had been 45 years old, and had died, not from poison in her food, as we had suspected, but from a burst appendix. By the time the surgeon had opened her belly, the appendix had ruptured. There was no way Helen would have survived the poison flooding her bloodstream. At least this way, she had been relatively peaceful.

Little Sam set down some ginger wine. "Here you are, Mamma," he said softly. "Do you drink this."

Sam nodded his thanks to our eldest. His fingers caressed my shoulder. I had been numb for pretty much 24 hours. The gut-wrenching news had hit me hard.

"No-one'll call me 'hen' anymore," I said, stupidly. "I always thought it a queer sort of term of address. Now I miss it."

Sam kissed my cheek. Helen and I had sometimes had quite a rocky relationship. She had, at times, driven me quite mad with her stubbornness, but we had considered ourselves sisters.

William was in pieces. Having got Helen back after so long, to lose her again was terrible and he was full of remorse, regret and misery. He looked older still now, and sat in his lodgings with Will, who was desperately trying to keep himself together.

Two days later and William had come to see us. Dressed in mourning, he informed us that he would be meeting Helen's elderly parents at the station that afternoon, and the following day, we would all travel to Scotland for Helen's funeral.

"All?" I managed to say, and William nodded.

"Well, the two of you, I mean. Helen would never forgive me if you weren't there. Forget the expense; I'll pay. Helen would've insisted."

"What of Manoa?"

"He won't be coming."

The terrible day dawned, grey and freezing, but with no wind. We walked in a solemn procession to Helen's kirk, led by a solemn piper. The kirk was packed with members of the family and Helen's childhood friends. The vicar talked at some length about Helen. Sam supported me, fearing I'd faint. Iffey stood alone by choice, stiff, silent, head bowed, not looking at or talking to anybody. There were a few hymns, including Helen's favourite – 'Lead, Kindly

Light.' I found myself unable to sing at all for the lump in my throat, and below a black net veil, tears streamed silently.

Never had I expected to be doing this. Never had I even thought about Helen dying. She had always been larger than life. Now, she would lie in her beloved Scotland forever, with her family close by, and one by one, they would join her.

In the late afternoon of the following day, I knelt at the graveside, reluctant to leave my closest friend in the cold earth.

"Remember when we tricked Miss Spoonamore?" I said softly, arranging red-berried holly with care. I smiled sadly at the memory. "Trust you to have such a wild idea! But it was so funny. Gosh, she never forgot that did she?"

"Alice?"

I turned at Sam's quiet voice. "Come, we need to leave now." I looked at him and Sam squatted at my side. He took my hand. "It's starting to snow. Helen wouldn't want you to catch a chill." I sighed and got up. I knew we would never come back here again.

Back in Yarmouth once more, I tried to speak to Iffey, but she merely turned and ran, vanishing through the station entrance like a whirlwind.

On New Year's Eve, determined to see how Manoa fared, Kit and I ventured to visit him. It was a cold and frosty afternoon; the sky was blue. The temperature had steadfastly refused to rise, and the ice was treacherous. I rang the doorbell and waited. Nobody came. I frowned slightly and tugged harder on the bell pull. I could hear it jangling inside, so there was no question of any occupants not hearing it.

"We'll go round the back, Kit. Maybe they're in the kitchen."

I peered through the window, through a small hole made in the frost by my gloved fingers, but there was nobody there. "They must've gone out," I muttered to myself.

"Mamma! Mamma!" Kit's voice squeaked; and I glanced. "The door's open. Look!" He indicated the back door, slightly ajar; I pushed it open and peered inside.

"Manny! Iffey!" I called into the kitchen. But there was no answer. I ventured right in. The range was stone cold and obviously had not been lit for some time.

Suddenly, a terrible fear washed over me, so that I almost passed out. What would I find in the house? Had Manoa been so overcome with grief he had harmed himself and his daughter? This did not bear thinking about.

Telling Kit to stay where he was, I ventured cautiously into all the rooms, but none showed no signs of recent occupancy. I leapt with a scream as a clock chimed the hour.

Clutching my thumping chest, I ventured upstairs; this, if anywhere, was where I would find bodies, though I sincerely hoped I wouldn't.

Upstairs was as empty as down. A large clock ticked in Manoa's room. I wandered around, knowing I had no right to be there and feeling guilty. I checked the wardrobes but could not tell if any clothes were missing.

"Kit! Fetch your papa, would you? Something's wrong here!"

It seemed to take forever for Sam to arrive. He hurried into the house, confused by Kit's breathless tale of a deserted house. I was relieved to hear him coming up the stairs.

"Alice! Whatever are you doing in here?" Sam asked. "You do know you're trespassing, don't you?"

"Sam, something's wrong. We've been here ages; they haven't come back!"

Sam shook his head. "Really, darling! They'll have gone for a walk. I expect Manoa forgot to lock the door. Come on! What d'ye think he'd say to catch us snooping around his house, nosing here, there and everywhere?"

"But the range is stone cold!" I objected. "No fires lit; it's all cold! Sam, something *is* wrong, I know it. Even if they had gone out, the range would be still lit, fire still warm!"

Sam looked at me. I was much in earnest. He ran a hand through his hair.

"Alright, you do look worried, and it's strange there are no fires; we'll come back tomorrow. They've probably gone visiting. Look, there's a key in the back door, do you take it and lock up."

At Ness Point, Manoa and Iffey sat near the fire. Manoa had hated descending on Bert and Peggy so suddenly, without any warning at all, but as he told them, they couldn't remain in Yarmouth any longer. The elderly couple nodded, both terribly sympathetic.

"You'll stay here long as you want," Bert told him. "Our home is yours too, you know. I'm that sorry to hear your tale though, bor'. I'm afraid our hospitality ain't what it should be, but you're welcome, even so."

"Thank you." Manoa lifted sad, dark eyes to the pair. "I'm truly grateful. We shan't trouble you for long, only until I sort us out a crossing."

Iffey spoke. "But we never said goodbye," she objected. "Nobody knows we're gone. We never even left a note!"

"We'll send word."

Iffey sighed. "But we left all our things behind."

Manoa simply shrugged. "Things are things, Iffey. Alice will know what to do with them. Doubtless they'll be given to the needy. She's bound to come looking when we've been missing a while, that's why I left the door."

Manoa turned to look at Iffey.

"You'll enjoy Antigua, I promise. It's warm all the time. The people there are extremely friendly, always happy. There are lots of celebrations, bright colours, music. There are flowers, fresh fruit, a warm, clear sea, fish all colours of the rainbow. White, soft sand, big palm trees with juicy coconuts, coloured birds, hundreds of them. I'll find you a nice young, respectful, handsome man. You'll feel like you've come home."

I stood behind the police reception desk, Sam, Tabitha and Gus at my side.

"Missing? Everything left?" The sergeant regarded us.

"Yes, and what with Helen passing like that, it's been ten days now and no sign. It's a wonder the house wasn't ransacked. I found the key and locked it up. But where are they?"

"The Police can do nothing," he told me, honestly but unhelpfully. "If he's decided to take off with his daughter, there's nothing to be done about it. It's his choice. His right."

July 1870

Time raced on all too swiftly. Little Sam, at 24, was still at home and had no intentions of marrying, happy to remain a bachelor. He had become as proficient at his craft as his father. There was plenty of business put their way, so much so, they'd had to move into a bigger workshop in the next row. Yarmouth was growing, both as a town and a resort.

At fifteen, Kit had left school and was working in an architect's office, where he had assumed the post of apprentice draughtsman. The qualified draughtsman had initially been reluctant to take him on, not having had a grammar school education, but Kit had packed up his drawings into a leather artist's portfolio that we had bought him on leaving school and had presented them to the man. The fellow had been looking for an apprentice draughtsman and had been expecting one of rather more mature years, with a grammar school education and the kind of parents who lived up on South Quay.

He had looked at Kit, thunderstruck at his cheek, and was about to order him out of the office, preferably with a smacked head, but Kit had been ready for that.

"Do look, Sir; I assure you, I am in earnest." So saying, Kit had opened the portfolio.

Kit's apprenticeship had begun then and there. The man, a Mr Critchley, had looked, stunned, at the beautifully designed buildings, complete with measurements, and had looked at him, wondering if his leg was being pulled, but Kit had assured him he was the person who had done these plans and now, Kit worked alongside him up near South Quay. Mr Critchley, a great believer in never looking a gift horse in the mouth, was thrilled by his new apprentice's natural skills.

The twins at thirteen were doing well too. Ollie planned to become a teacher, and Oscar a gardener. Gus promised he would help him find something in the line of horticulture when the time came. Mackie had told us that when Ollie turned fourteen, he could try a little teaching of the younger pupils at the Charity School.

Sam's father was now eighty-three and slowing down a little, but his mind was as sharp as ever. We visited him daily. He also liked to spend the day with us.

The previous year, we had, at last, received communication from Manoa and Iffey. I had been amazed to learn they were now living in a place called Saint John's in Antigua. I had never heard of it and when Sam and I had looked for it on the map, we had been surprised at how far away it was. There had been a return address and so I had written to them.

Initially, I had been somewhat annoyed at being left with the house and all its contents to deal with, not to mention upset that they had simply gone without a word. I had tried to understand why. Sam had told me it would have been so hard for them to face us, but Manoa had, quite literally, 'given it to us' and we had been humbled at such generosity.

The letter from the solicitor had been so difficult to understand that Sam and I had taken it to Mackie, who understood more. Manoa had 'gifted' the house and its contents to us, to live in or sell, as we pleased.

However, I had had no inclination at all to move from our dear row house which I loved, and so, after a lengthy family discussion, we had sold it and put money in the bank with accounts for the boys. It had taken months to sort out, but the solicitor, and Mackie, had been incredibly helpful and had taken the work from our shoulders.

1872

It was a quiet year for us all. June saw the town receive a visit from Edward, Prince of Wales. Maria, hearing of the visit, was delighted to tell me about the scandalous rumours that attached themselves to the royal person. It was well known he had had liaisons with actresses, ladies of high rank and dubious morality, and even prostitutes. It was also said that his mother blamed him for her 'Dear Albert's death' and could not bring herself even to look at him.

Sam read us the story in the morning newspaper. "Well, at least his mother's not coming! He's staying at Shadingfield Lodge! Poor old Cudden! I bet they're quaking in their boots. They'll house his hangers-on too, who'll eat him out of house and home. Still, 'tis a big honour for him. There'll be a big celebration in the town as well – illuminations, fireworks, hot food – it'll be quite a day!"

"They want volunteers, Mamma!" Kit teased me. "I bet you'll be trampling old ladies underfoot to get to the head of the queue."

The twins laughed.

It turned out that Tabitha had offered to help and had badgered me to join her. To keep her quiet, I eventually agreed, and was somewhat less than pleased to hear I would be joining her in Shadingfield Lodge.

"Oh, *Tabitha!*" I groaned. "I thought you meant *outside!*"

But she grinned and winked at Sam.

"What's wrong, Alice? You've always wanted to nose round that place from the inside!" Sam said, jokingly. "Well, now's your chance!"

Tabitha's youngest sister was a housemaid there, and the regular domestic staff would never manage such an entourage by themselves. They had exhausted the agency staff, and had advertised for extra help, to be paid a sovereign for their efforts, so Maria was eager to join us. The royal staff would consist of His Majesty's valet, Master of the Household, Deputy Master, his secretary, various footmen, stewards and a food taster to mention but a few.

Shadingfield Lodge was a beautiful, two-storey home, with bay windows and a fabulous sea view, set in glorious gardens. I couldn't understand why the Prince of Wales would even want to stay here, in somebody's private home, but Tabitha told me it was customary for royals on a progress to dump themselves on their 'favourites', and whilst this kind of grandeur held much prestige, it didn't do much for one's pocket.

The three of us marched up to the house and I yanked the bell pull.

"ALICE!" Tabitha roared, horrified, hastening up to me and pulling me away. "What *do* you think you're doing? Front door? Want to get us kicked out before we've even started?"

Belatedly, I remembered. The servants' entrance, of course. I grinned and tugged my forelock at her. But at that moment, the door was opened by a butler, who looked anything but pleased to see the three of us. Tabitha gave a deep curtsy. "Beggin' yer pardon, sir, we made a mistake. We couldn't find the servant's entrance."

The butler looked down his long nose. "It is around the back, woman, where servant's doors generally are."

"Of course!" Tabitha nodded.

"The door is, I believe, open. Present yourselves to Cook, who needs extra hands, and Johnson, the Housekeeper." Without further ado, he shut the door in our faces.

"Come on!" Tabitha gave me a gentle shove. "Really, Alice! Front door indeed!"

We hastened around to the back of the house, and for all I despised roy-alty, I suddenly felt a sense of fun take hold. I dearly wished that Helen was here with us to enjoy the day. I could imagine what she would have been like! Doubtless, we would have been sacked after half the morning!

Cook was a fearsome-looking woman – squat, with a huge bosom, her hair neatly under her cap. She wore a print green dress under the white apron. She was only about four foot ten, and as wide as she was tall. I had hoped the three of us would stay together, but it wasn't to be. Instead, Cook chose Tabitha for the kitchen work since she was the heftiest. I looked at Maria who glanced anxiously at me.

"We were hoping to stay together!" Maria said politely, as Johnson, the Housekeeper, beckoned us over, where a few other girls hung around her.

"Stay together? What? Are you children that you cannot bear to let go of your friend?" she asked sarcastically. I felt my hackles rise and had opened my mouth to respond. Johnson frowned. "Are you going to argue with me? If so, you can turn round and go straight back home!"

Maria squeezed my hand. "It's alright, miss, Alice won't argue. I'm sure you're right. We had merely hoped to be of help together."

"Well, the best person is the one who is right for the job. Now, come along with me. Is that everybody?"

It appeared no more were arriving, so Maria and I left with the House-keeper to venture to the main lobby where she told us to gather round her. Another female joined her and looked over us with some disdain.

"Is that the lot?" she asked her superior, and Johnson nodded.

"Seems to be." She turned to us. "This is our First Housemaid, Gibbons. If I am not around, you will refer any problems to her, is that alright, Myrtle?"

The other woman nodded.

"I had an Aunt Myrtle once," I told Maria. "We used to call her Myrtle the spurtle."

Maria snorted with laughter, and I received a withering look from the Housekeeper.

"Don't be so childish!" she scolded me. "Now, your work!"

She smoothed her immaculate apron and glanced over our little gathering.

"His Majesty and his entourage arrive at two o'clock," she told us. "I cannot emphasise enough that you are to stay out of the way as much as possible. His Royal Highness does not care to look upon a bunch of scruffy domestics. The staff at the palace, the lower servants that is, see very little, if anything, of their employers. However, should you by chance encounter him, you will give a proper curtsy. None of this bobbing nonsense; you will do a full sweep downwards, like so!" She demonstrated. "You will also curtsy to his immediate staff... Valet, Master Secretary and so on. You need not worry about meeting his wife; she is not here. He is accompanied by some very important persons too... the Earl of Leicester for one, and, if, I only say *if*, the chances are one in a million, any *one* of the royal party should speak to you, you will address them correctly and do not look directly at them. Do you all understand me?"

Heads nodded. Maria could almost read my mind; 'Curtsy to domestic staff? Not I!'

"Very well, I shall give you your tasks."

Maria and I were directed to the blue room; we opened the door and stood. The carpet looked thick enough to sink to one's ankles. The bed had blue velvet curtains around it, with delicate, fine, pale blue netting on the inside; I had to try it. Maria, who had come into the room with linen in her arms, squawked in alarm to see me lying fully stretched, head on a pillow.

"Alice! What if somebody should see? For goodness' sake, get off that bed!"

I laughed at her horrified face. "We'd hear anyone coming. You try it, Maria, go on! Just don't fall asleep. Gosh, imagine if we had this bed in our homes. We'd never be up to do any work!"

Maria glanced into the hallway, looked up and down, then lay down too.

"Oh my! I have never felt anything so soft. It's wonderful! And it's a *spare* bed! The ones the master and mistress sleep in must be softer still!"

Reluctantly, we rose and started to tidy the room.

"Look, all the carpet and furnishings muffle any sound. I wish we had thick carpets at home. You can hear our Annie coming a mile off, and the boys, clomping about in hobnailed boots!"

There was a white bearskin rug, with the head still attached, its dark brown, shining eyes gazing sightlessly, which I found rather sad. I knelt to feel its fur. Maria watched as I caressed the creature's head pityingly and fondled its small ears.

"Oscar would hate to see this," I told her. "He hates animal cruelty. He doesn't approve of fox hunting, deer hunting or anything like that. If he could see this, he'd be devastated. Poor, magnificent creature. Imagine how this would be in life, Maria."

"It'd bite off your head, Alice!" Maria said with a grin. "Look at those teeth!"

As I was cleaning one of the windows and Maria was polishing a table, Johnson came in, making us jump.

"Good! I see you are working. I meant to remind you too, *no* pilfering! I'll be searching you thoroughly before you leave!"

Before I could retaliate, she left. My face was a picture of offence. Maria giggled.

"Search us, eh? I'll hide the silver spoons in my drawers; she won't dare look there!"

Maria and I got a sheet between us to throw over the bed. The sheet had to look flat, with no wrinkles in it. I turned to look at Maria to make a jocular remark when suddenly there was a rip. Maria looked horrified.

"Alice? What was that?"

I glanced down. I had managed to put my hand through the flimsy net curtain whilst tucking the sheet underneath. I looked at my sister-in-law with a grimace.

Maria cringed.

"I'll tuck it in," I told her.

Maria hissed through her teeth. She sincerely hoped the netting would not be discovered until the following day when the occupant of the room could shoulder the blame.

Maria regarded the settle by the window. "That's what Romans used to lie on, eating grapes. Look at all the gold leaf! Blue satin cushions. I don't even mind betting nobody uses the thing either. It's a decorative piece."

The clock on the landing chimed midday, and I realised we had been in the room for three hours. Nothing looked hugely different, apart from the bed being made.

"I'm starved," Maria stated. "Shall we see if any grub's going?"

We found the kitchen along the long back corridor, full of noise and bustle. The smells made our mouths water and the two of us ventured inside. There was steam, the smell of baking bread and roasting meats, making us feel even more famished. Somebody was basting an almighty turkey, and I groaned, holding my empty, grumbling stomach. I had never seen such a massive oven either. "Imagine having to blacklead that great monster!" I said to Maria, who nodded. I could hardly believe the noise level. A cacophony of pots being bashed, spoons, metal on metal, high voices, orders being shouted... I spotted Tabitha stirring a large pot and we hastened across to her.

"What are you doing here?" she asked, her face red and sweating. "You ought to be upstairs!"

"We know, and we have been. We just wondered if there was any food going. We are allowed a break, aren't we?"

Tabitha was about to comment that she didn't think so, when Cook spotted us and came bustling over, demanding to know what we were doing in her kitchen. On hearing we wanted something to eat, she hesitated, then she nodded reluctantly.

"Very well, I suppose you can have something. You can tell you're not true domestic servants. We'd never have the cheek to ask!" She looked so cross, short arms folded across her large bust.

Maria spoke. "Please, Cook, we've been working flat out all morning. I know we shouldn't ask, but please, if you would be so kind, we'd be extremely grateful."

"Very well; wait here. I'll find something, but don't stay here to eat it. You'll get in the way, and don't sit in the garden either, you'll be in the way there too. Go to the servants' hall along the passageway."

She pottered off to bring something and Tabitha chuckled. "You two! Really! Most others brought their own sandwiches you know!"

"How're you getting on?" I asked.

Tabitha groaned. "I spent all morning lugging spuds about. See that girl over there? She has the job of peeling them all. It's horribly hot and noisy in here."

We looked to where a young, scrawny girl stood amid mountains of potatoes. I felt as though I peeled hundreds of potatoes for the men in my family, but it was nothing compared to how many she had done, and still had to do.

Cook returned with some food under a cloth. "Here!" she said, shoving it into our hands. "Take it away, please. You'll find a treat in there too. Hot chocolate. It's not every day you get to sample such, I'll be bound."

Maria and I sat on the beautiful settle in the blue room to eat the noonday meal, eschewing the servants' hall, having given it a cursory glance.

We munched on the pie and potatoes. It was delicious.

"Hot chocolate too!" Maria said. "We are living high off the hog!"

I agreed. I had never tasted hot chocolate, and knew it was a reserve of the upper echelons. Maria swigged hers.

"Hmm, not what I expected, Alice; it's actually quite bitter."

I tasted mine and pulled a face. "Ugh. You're right. The upper classes can keep their hot chocolate." I wiped my lips and set the mug down.

The window was open, and we breathed in the fresh sea air and the scents of the many flowers in the garden below. Outside, I could see people hurrying about various tasks – gardeners making miniscule adjustments to flower beds, grass verges.

"Oscar had a great idea the other day, Maria. He said when he's older and working, he'll design a garden for blind people."

"What? How?" Maria asked.

"Same as you would any garden, but he said he would choose flowers that were the most beautifully scented so they could enjoy the smells, sit and hear the birds. He got the idea from George who told him how he enjoyed sitting in his garden smelling roses."

Oscar and George had struck up an unlikely friendship, despite an almost 40-year age gap.

"That's a kind idea," my sister-in-law told me. "How nice!"

I sighed and withdrew my head.

"You know, what this family's spending on all this nonsense would feed and clothe every single house in every single row for a whole year!" I told Maria. "And what's more, oh no!"

Maria squealed in horror as my gesticulating hand had met with the mug of hot chocolate on the arm of a chair sending it to the floor. We watched in despair as the dark liquid seeped into the carpet.

"It's a colourful carpet," I told Maria, clutching at her arm. "D'ye think they'd notice?"

"It's pretty obvious, Alice, don't you think? Clumsy oaf!"

"Well, what are we going to do?" I asked, chewing my lower lip.

"I don't know, but I think you've forfeited your guinea," Maria answered. "You ripped that netting, now you've soaked the floor in hot chocolate." She looked at me, my face so horror-stricken that she chuckled. "Ah, never mind. Come on. Let's try and get it out; it may come up alright."

We spent some time scrubbing at the stain, but it still showed. Maria suddenly knelt up straight.

"I know, we'll put the rug over it, then nobody'll notice!" This we did and left the room, looking back nervously.

Johnson inspected our work, then nodded. "Well, you have some spare time. His Highness will be here at any moment. Go and watch the arrival if you wish, but then return to me. I 've hundreds of napkins I want folding." She bustled off.

We weren't interested in the arrival, but we joined the others who crowded the window. Comments floated in the air along the lines of; "Ooh, isn't he handsome? I wouldn't mind being in service to him!"

"Look at him! Look at that beard. I wouldn't mind feeling that along me bits, would you, Bertha?"

"Play your cards right and you never know!" a housemaid said. "He's had lots of lovers already, got a mistress now!"

Maria and I exchanged glances. I indicated sickness, with a smirk. Truly, I was ready to take my guinea and leave. I'd had more than enough of grand houses, with self-important upper servants and gentry.

Maria and I found ourselves in the dining room, with, as promised, hundreds of napkins.

"I dare you!" Maria told me, grinning.

"A pity they're not yellow or orange," I told her. "Come on, hurry up with yours, Maria, you'll take all day."

When we had finished, I had placed the napkins for the royal party, subtly hidden, but nevertheless in the form of plucked chickens. Maria grinned at me.

"If we end up in the tower for this, I'll know exactly who to blame!" she told me, smiling.

The royal party arrived. I could tell by the racket. Maria glanced at me.

"I s'pect he'll go to his room first," she stated, "to freshen up. I hope he *does* see these chickens. It might amuse him!"

"Well, I hope so, because if he has his mother's sense of humour, its 'orf wiv 'er 'ed!" I replied. Maria spluttered with laughter again. Having put the finishing touches to things, Maria and I left the dining room.

"Now what are we to do?" she wondered.

I stood, wondering. No doubt Johnson would find something. As if thinking of her conjured her, Johnson appeared.

"Don't dawdle!" she snapped. "There's plenty still to do. You're not being paid for standing around looking useless. Now they're here, they need refreshment. I have trays going out of the kitchen to be taken along to the rear parlour. You'll soon see where it is as people will be to-ing and fro-ing. Fetch some trays. They'll be heavy so be careful. The door is open to the room itself, though the one in the passageway is not, so again, be careful. When you get to the parlour, you'll hand the tray quietly to a lady called Mrs Spratt."

"Mrs Spratt?" I spluttered.

"Don't be infantile!" Johnson's withering remark had little effect on my schoolgirl humour. "Now, do as I say. Quickly."

We went to the kitchen and were handed our trays, upon which were silver teapots and an array of cutlery. Maria's had many silver teaspoons on it, all beautifully crafted, with the family crest on them, some serviettes and various other things. We chattered as we walked briskly along the corridor to the back parlour, Maria behind me, telling me she might hide some spoons in her drawers! As we approached the passage doorway, I looked behind to laugh at what she had just said when, without warning, the door opened. I collided with the person coming through and the tray crashed to the floor spilling everything; fortunately, nothing breakable. Furious I glared at the well-built, bearded and finely dressed man.

"You clumsy clod!" I snapped. "We're ferrying things to the rear parlour this way. Why don't you watch where you're going?"

The man looked at me in stunned amazement. The flushed cheeks, the cross expression... I stood, hands on hips, looking at him the way I looked at Sam when he had used his handkerchiefs to wipe up glue, or some other messy, sticky substance.

"Alice!" Maria's voice was barely more than a squeak. "Shut up!"

I began to clear up, muttering and telling people in general that I wasn't going to be scrubbing up coffee stains, since it had not been my fault that I couldn't see through wooden doors. As I rose, I became aware that everyone behind me had sunk to the floor. I turned round. Maria looked terrified. She tugged at my skirt.

There was complete silence; heads appeared round the doorway; some people had come into the corridor to look. Mr Cudden gaped, shocked. There was a small moan from Mrs Cudden who looked about to sink to the floor. Maria again pulled at my skirt.

"Alice!" she moaned; her voice hoarse with fright. "That's His Royal Highness, the Prince of Wales you've just insulted!"

I felt my blood run cold.

Just when I thought it could not possibly get any worse, Johnson appeared, wondering at the loud crash. She took in everyone, their horrified expressions, me, standing looking shocked, and Prince Albert 'Bertie' Edward standing there.

"What have you *done*, Dwyer? You stupid woman!" Her voice was pure terror.

Suddenly, against all expectations, the man started to laugh. Everyone looked at everybody else.

"Get up, everyone!" he called jovially. "Don't look so shocked! It was entirely my fault, bursting through that door without a care! Come, my dear! Accidents happen!"

I had no choice but to take the outstretched hand. There was an audible gasp behind me.

"Thank you, sir," I said in a dutiful manner.

"His Royal Highness, Dwyer!" Johnson squawked from the back.

Prince Albert Edward laughed again. He leaned in closer to me; "*You can call me Bertie, you cheeky minx!*" he said and winked. A blush flooded my cheeks scarlet. "We shall be staying here a while," he stated, "so, we hope to see *you* again, what?" With that, he strode off down the corridor past the fluttering females, who once more sank floorwards.

"We were lucky to get out of that place without shackles!" Tabitha told me as we left to return home. "Good God! I can't believe it, though I'd love to have seen it. It's as well he's known to be a jovial, friendly sort."

Sam laughed like a drain over the unexpected meeting with the Prince of Wales, the invitation to call him 'Bertie', not to mention the veiled remark at another, potentially more private meeting. He was glad I had not barged into the queen herself, however, whose reaction would have been anything but jovial. It would take a good deal of time to live that particular episode down.

Summer 1873

Another hot summer. Florence had died peacefully in spring. Sam sat at my side, his arm around me. I inclined my head against his shoulder.

"We still have each other," he reminded me. "And our fabulous family! Let's enjoy the time we have left together, however long it may be." I nodded and looked into his face. I was so grateful to have had him at my side. We had been together now for almost thirty years.

On South Quay, the house where the Paget family had lived had been renovated to make a small private school. Kit's firm had had the contract and Kit was responsible for re-designing the kitchen and servants' quarters into a classroom – an honour for one so young. There had been logistical concerns, and Kit's explanations had gone entirely over my head, but I boasted of it to anyone who would listen. Kit himself was far too modest.

Mr Paget had come to oversee the renovations, and to install a beautiful memorial window which was to be placed in their local parish church, commemorating his parents, brothers and sisters. Kit had told us about it and had suggested I come along to meet him.

"Are you mad, Kit?" I gasped. "Look at me!" I stood, duster in hand, a coal-dusted apron, even a smudge on my cheek. "It'll take a while to heat water for a bath... I need to wash my hair, and..."

"Not *now*, Mamma! "I mean this afternoon. You know him, after all!"

"Kit, I met him once! *Once!* Years ago! He won't remember me!"

"'Course he will! Besides, you've no reason to be nervous, not when you're so chummy with royalty!"

I smacked Kit's arm playfully.

Kit grinned and I sighed. "Well, I'll have to bathe and change. Tell your father. He's out the back." I hurried up to our bedroom to attempt to find something decent to wear. I had made myself several dresses over the years, so I had a reasonably good choice, but they were all simple, workaday clothes. Sam came in to see me with every single garment I possessed spread on the bed.

"Darling, you could wear sackcloth and look stunning, but do you wear the pink and grey check; it's my favourite."

I donned the dress and glanced at myself in the mirror. It didn't look too bad and was my newest one. I thought of Maria's latest addition to her wardrobe – a bustle. To me, they looked ludicrous, were torture to wear and prevented one from even sitting comfortably. When Maria had first visited wearing hers, I had burst into laughter. But many women, of all stations in life, wore them. Apparently, they made women 'irresistible to men' for all I couldn't fathom why this should be. I had told Sam not to expect me to have 'an arse that stuck out a mile', at which he had roared with laughter.

That afternoon, everyone in Sunday best, fresh from our baths, we all trooped round to the parish church to see the incredible stained-glass window set in place. I held my breath, thoughts of the beautifully crafted work falling to the ground and smashing, but fortune was with the glaziers who managed to set it safely into place, where the sun streamed through to make pretty patterns on the wooden floor of the inside.

Mr Paget himself had congratulated Kit, who had bowed and been genuinely thrilled at the eminent man's praise. Kit had spoken to him quietly about meeting his parents, telling him that the story of his giving me money so long ago to buy more buns had been told and re-told numerous times, and I had been rendered almost speechless when Mr Paget, who was far too mannerly to remark that he barely had any memory of it, had strolled casually over to speak to Sam and myself.

"You must be very proud of your son!" he told us, smiling. Sam nodded and shook the man's hand. Mr Paget smiled. "Ah, I recall you, my dear! The young lady who lost her buns! How are you? You don't look a day older! And Mr Dwyer, sir, your son has told me of your romantic tale!"

December 1873

Kit was bringing his young lady, Charlotte, to meet us for Boxing Day. He had been invited round to her family's house for Christmas Eve for a meal and I was still upset at that. Christmas was a family time; I wanted Kit with us, but Sam had made me see that it was only for the evening and that it was important for Kit to meet her parents too. So, I didn't object, at least, not in Kit's hearing.

Maria and I went out to search the market for Christmas pieces as we always did. Some Christmas trees graced the walkways, all for sale. I looked at them. "This one's nice," I told her.

Maria agreed. "Have it put by then; I'll take this one next to it, and Abe and Sam can fetch them later."

We sat for some refreshment.

"Are you nervous about meeting Kit's lady friend?" Maria asked.

"Yes, very. What if I don't like her? What if she's awful?"

"And what if she isn't?" Maria said smiling. "Don't worry, Alice, I'm sure things will go smoothly; don't forget, she'll be the one who's more afraid. Don't you remember how afraid you were when you met Mamma and Papa the first time?"

"It's not her especially," I told Maria. "More us; we feel so old. It doesn't seem long since Kit was sitting there with his thumb in his mouth or scream-ing in a fit of tantrum."

Maria laughed. "I know exactly what you mean!" she told me. "Annie's engagement shocked me, for all she's been walking out with him for ages." She looked then, reminiscing.

"First time we met Annie's fellow, we went there for dinner. Alice, you should have seen it. There was a calf's head on the table! They'd splashed out, especially for us. Well, our Annie's always had a soft spot for cows, baby ones in particular. She burst into tears when she saw it! Me and Albert had no idea what to do!"

I laughed, having heard the tale several times. Maria had ever been grate-ful the family hadn't taken offence.

We celebrated our Christmas in the usual way and were introduced to Charlotte, who did appear nervous of us. It was over the meal of cold meats and potatoes, along with some sweet chutneys. I couldn't warm to her though; she seemed domineering. So had Helen been, in a way, but at least she had had a warmth about her which Charlotte didn't have.

The new year rolled in; Oscar was working in the grounds of Saint Nich-olas', invaluable to Gus, who had been somewhat rheumatic recently, and Ollie was a student teacher.

Recently, Maria had become friendly with one of the servants who worked for a gentleman, a Mr Stafford. This man was rather eccentric, and keen on animals. Maria spoke of a fine young otter that had been caught a few miles from Yarmouth.

"He took it home. He decided to make a pet of it since it was young," Maria said, grinning, "and it caused havoc! It chewed everything it could get its teeth into. It bit one of the other maidservants, ripped apart some expensive furniture and ran up the curtains! His wife was terrified of it. One night, about three in the morning, Belinda said her Mistress woke the entire household with her screaming. The Master and everybody else went running to her room, and it was the otter! It had got into her room. She had woken to feel something tickling her face, you see. So, she looks and sees this furry face looking at her. I'd've given anything to have seen that."

"Oh, that's priceless, Maria! An otter! I love them; such sweet faces! Then what?"

"It ran and leapt on to the dressing table, doing more damage. She insisted it be killed, but Mr Stafford refused, and in the end, had it taken to a local zoological garden."

A few days later, and everyone had been shocked to hear that Sam's father had been taken to the local hospital, having tripped and fallen down the bottom two stairs. He had lain there for several hours, too shocked and weak to rise, before being found by his horrified daughter, who had immediately sent a messenger to Albert and Sam. There had been no more than bruises and a sprained wrist, and a night in the hospital had seen him recover.

A doctor had checked him and had come to the conclusion it had been nothing more than a case of tripping over the old carpet. Since then, he had gone to live with Albert and Maria. Sam had put his foot firmly down and insisted upon it, citing that next time, he might not be so lucky. Simon soon found out that far from losing his independence, he was still permitted to do as he pleased, was waited on, was warm and comfortable.

"I should sell our house," Sam's father told us as we joined them for Sunday dinner. He paused, then, thinking. "Sam, Alice, d'ye think Kit would like it for when he marries?"

I turned to Kit, who sat at my side, red as a berry at the mention of marriage.

Kit was overwhelmed. "I'd be delighted, and very grateful, Grandpapa," Kit told him. "Thank you!"

Simon grinned. "It's a wedding present then! Keep it in the family, for generations of Dwyers to come! I know you haven't reached your majority yet, bor', but do you make it yours anyway." He looked around the table. "That alright with everybody?"

It seemed that it was.

September came and the term had begun. Seventeen-year-old Ollie had gone off whistling cheerfully to the school. Several new schools had opened in Yarmouth in recent years, but he still taught at the Charity School where all the Dwyer boys had been educated. I smiled, watching him stride off down our row. Next, Oscar was out of the door, heading toward the church grounds. He had been drawing up plans for the garden he had thought of for the blind and had been deciding on the most beautifully scented flowers and whereabouts they would be planted.

I decided to walk to see Tabitha and we could do a little shopping to cheer ourselves.

Tabitha was happy to accompany me, and we headed up to South Quay. As it was a nice, warm morning, we decided to watch as some ships docked.

"Gus is happy with Oscar," she told me. "He's such a help. Poor Gus, he has terrible hip pain now. Some days he can hardly get himself going."

I nodded; it was a common complaint in the older generation and Gus was a good 20 years Tabitha's senior.

"Get a cabbage at the market," I told her. "Tell him to wear the leaf next to his skin, all the time; change it daily – it's good for easing joint pain. Papa's been wearing one for several years."

Tabitha smiled. "I'll try that, Alice, anything to stop his moaning. Oh! What's that?"

We ventured over to the bridge. I hadn't spotted the parcel from where I stood, but Tabitha had, and she pointed at it. The brown parcel, wrapped with string, sat on the ridge of the bridge. We looked at it, full of curiosity. My first thought was ill-gotten gains.

"I'll bet there's valuables in there," I told Tabitha excitedly. "Jewels, money... you know, these thieves stash stuff anywhere unusual. Burying it in the denes seems to have gone out of fashion. I suppose it was done at night, them thinking nobody would spot it."

Tabitha picked up a long stick, then, reaching out, managing to hook the stick under the string. "I can get it, Alice. Best we take it to the police station. Whatever it is, it's heavy, and, ugh! Wet. Soft." She dragged the parcel in, and it fell with a thud onto the quayside. Tabitha looked closer. Then, she squatted beside it. Suddenly, she spotted a vile watery, reddish liquid coming from within the parcel. There was a foul smell coming from it. Horrified, she rose and took a step backwards. She put out an arm to stop me looking.

"Dear God!" she gasped. Where the brown parcel paper was separating slightly, Tabitha could see pale flesh, small fingers.

To our horror, the body of a new-born baby lay within the confines of the packaging. Tabitha turned away. I hastened backwards several steps, shocked. For a moment, neither of us could move.

"Tab, stay here, I'll run for a constable." I turned and bolted for help, shocked to my core.

Back at the station, we were questioned.

"*We* don't know anyone who'd do that to a baby!" Tabitha exclaimed, angry and indignant. "Whoever she is, I'd love to get my hands on her!"

I nodded agreement.

"But why put her on a bridge?" Tabitha continued.

"Possibly so it could be discovered and given a decent burial," the Constable said. "As indeed it should!"

"*She*, not it!" I snapped at him. The constable bowed his head slightly.

"I apologise, Mrs Dwyer, of course, she."

"Can you find out how she died?" I asked.

"I've sent for the Police Doctor."

He rose as if to dismiss us.

"Sir!" I said, standing. "Where will she be buried? I mean, she doesn't even have a name!"

The constable frowned. "Pauper's grave, I'd imagine."

"Please, don't let her be buried like that. I'll speak to my husband. He can talk to the Reverend. Perhaps he can still baptise her and pay for a decent burial."

The constable looked stunned. "Why are *you* so bothered, Mrs Dwyer?" he asked me, a hint of suspicion in his voice.

I looked at him. "Because I'm a mother myself, who had to bury my own baby years ago," I replied.

The man blushed scarlet. He nodded. "Very well, we will see what can be done."

Tabitha and I made our way dolefully out of the police station. "So much for cheering ourselves," I said, dismally. "That poor little thing. Oh, Tab! Wait till I tell Sam."

Nobody ever found out how or why the child had ended up on the bridge. The mother would never be found. Sam and I ensured she had a good resting place, under a tree in the churchyard. We named her Elaine.

That August, the entire town was talking about a 'trickster' who had conned many out of their money. I had wondered what the people of Yarmouth would do were he to show his face in the town again, but of course, he never would. His likeness had been sketched and wanted posters appeared.

Bill posters appeared proclaiming that a brand-new steamer ship, which boasted every comfort on board, with all kinds of meals served, was due to arrive at the end of the jetty on July 30th at 8.30 sharp and would take residents and tourists alike to Cromer for the day, for 2s 6d per person. Booking the tickets in advance was highly recommended due to the demand.

We were observing a neatly printed poster now, with a picture of the steamship. There was a list of the destinations, with the Cromer trip in bold capitals, reading; 'BOOK EARLY AND AVOID DISAPPOINTMENT. Tickets on sale from 25th July at the jetty kiosk. Only 2/6d per person. Children 1/6d'.

"I'm going!" Maria told me. "I love Cromer; the crabs there are huge!"

"Ours are better!" I pointed out. "Yarmouth has better everything than Cromer!"

Maria laughed. "Spoken like a true Yarmouth girl," she told me. "But it'll be a change; it doesn't take long to get there. It's bang up to date too."

"It's the 'bang' that worries me," I told her. "These things aren't reliable, Maria – what if the boiler explodes? That's happened before."

"It won't!" Maria said with confidence. "You worry too much, Alice. Well, I'm sorry you won't join us; sure you won't change your mind?" She gave me her large smile.

Though I had no intention of going, I accompanied Maria to the ticket booth on the jetty. The man sat in a deckchair outside, smoking a pipe. He smiled at us both and rose. "Two fine ladies for the steamer to Cromer?" he enquired.

I shook my head. "No, just one fine lady. I never set foot on a boat if I can help it!"

The man removed the stem of his pipe from his mouth and sighed. "Ah, pity, m'dear, you'd enjoy Cromer." He grinned and took Maria's fee. "Well, I'm here all day if you change your mind, mawther!" he told me. "Tomorrow morning as well!"

On the morning of the trip, I stood on the doorstep of our home. I glanced down the row and breathed in the fresh sea air. It was very warm. I thought of Maria, Tabitha and Gus. They'd be in Cromer by now.

Mr Dwyer was spending the day with us and had Minnow on his knees. I had fed my family, cleaned the house, and was just about to shake out and beat the rugs when suddenly, Maria came striding up the row, the look on her face thunderous. I had seldom seen my sweet-tempered sister-in-law so angry.

"Maria?" I queried. "What's the matter? You look furious."

Maria slung down her fussy, feathery hat and folded her arms, a deep frown on her face. "The whole thing was a hoax, Alice! A hoax! There were 20 of us, all waiting on the jetty, kiddies all excited, in their best, Tab and Gus all looking forward to it, and no boat shows up!"

"Well, it might've had a problem," I told her. "What makes you think it was a hoax? What if it had something wrong and couldn't get here? It's probably just late, Maria."

Maria shook her head. "No, we went to that ticket booth, you know, and it was shut. The posters have all vanished. That little fellow wasn't there. We all waited. One man said there hadn't been any such day trip in the first place. He was saying the bloke we got the tickets from had been taking money right up to four o'clock yesterday afternoon. He said that the ticket office would be open again today, but he wasn't there, and the shutters were up. Everyone's fuming. We looked out to sea for ages. It ought to have come at 8.30 and it's almost 10 o'clock now! That's 2 and 6 I lost! Swindling swine!"

"Ah, Maria, I am sorry," I told her. "It's a beautiful day, and who wants to go to rotten old Cromer anyway? It's much lovelier here!"

To ease Maria's annoyance, I packed up a hamper of food – we went along to fetch Tabitha and Gus too – and went to the beach to have our own picnic. Sam joined us; Little Sam would stay to keep his grandfather company. We sat in the denes on a large blanket with a hamper between us, full of ginger ale, hard boiled eggs, cheese, bread rolls and cake. I lay on my back and shut my eyes, letting the warmth seep into my skin.

The irony was that eventually, a steamer *did* go to Cromer. Maria had said she wasn't about to be swindled again and refused to go. Tabitha had decided to risk it, though Gus decided not to, citing that the weather would turn later in the day, and he had no stomach for heavier seas.

Tabitha had always had good sea legs; plus, she was stubborn. Having failed to persuade anyone to accompany her, she had gone alone, and had then regretted it, since the boat had steamed off well before its passengers could alight for the homeward journey since, as Gus had predicted, the seas had become rough, and every single person who had taken the day trip had been left stranded in Cromer to make their own arrangements as to how they were to return to their homes.

The following morning, Tabitha, along with other disgruntled passengers, had stamped their way down to the office to complain volubly. So much so, the man at the passenger desk had been forced to shut his window and retire into the rear office, whilst the manager had had to calm the excited crowd with apologies and their money back.

Three weeks later. About to start on the family's breakfast, Sam was whistling as he dressed himself, anticipating a full plateful of bacon, sausages, eggs and fried bread when there was a frantic and constant hammering on the door. Frowning, I went to open it to find Tabitha, who almost fell into our house; she was sobbing, shaking, and not making much sense at all.

"Tabitha! Good God! What's the matter?" I asked, practically having to drag her to sit down. Tabitha gulped for air between sobs. Her hands were clenched into fists and her hair was all unbound.

"It's Gus, it's Gus!" she wailed. "I can't wake him up and he's all cold!"

My eyes met Sam's. His expression spoke volumes. Swallowing my own shock, I rose to pour her some strong tea, which I had fortunately just made. "Alright, Tab. Look, drink this. Try to breathe more slowly. Sam will go and see what's happened."

Sam was already calling to our two eldest and shrugging on a jacket. Fortunately, the pair lived just a couple of rows away from us. He looked at me seriously, hoping that the man was just sleeping very deeply, and Tabitha was panicking for no reason. Sam and the others hurried along to their row and entered the house.

Gus lay in bed. He had been dead for some time. Sam pulled the covers over Gus' head and went to the window to breathe some fresh, cool air. Little Sam and Kit stood looking at one another, wondering what to do. Gus had been in his late 70s, so it wasn't entirely unexpected. But it was still hugely upsetting. Sam turned to our sons. "Come, lads," he said, gaining control of himself. "We'll say a quick prayer for him, pay our respects. Kit, do you go and fetch Dr Sanders. He's the best one I know of. Tell him exactly what's happened, bor'. Sam, you go back home. Tell Alice what's going on and try to get Tabitha to come here; the doctor will want to speak to her without a doubt."

In the kitchen, I was attempting to console Tabitha. I had made her drink some strong, sweet tea and she had at least got her breathing under control and was shaking now. The twins sat, feeling awkward, not knowing what to do.

"He's gone, he's gone, I know it," she whimpered. "He was fine last night at bedtime. His usual jokey self. He tickled me, he rubbed his stubble over my cheek, like he often did to annoy me, 'cos I always told him it was rough, and he should shave. There was nothing to say he felt ill. Nothing! Only his rheumatics. We just lay down and went to sleep. Everything was all normal, and when I woke up, he was, he was…" Tabitha bawled into her handkerchief.

"I am *so* sorry, Tab," I said quietly. "I hope you're wrong, I truly do, but if you can't wake him and he's cold…"

Tabitha was struggling, fighting off the belief of what she knew to be the stark truth.

Little Sam came in and we both looked up, Tabitha with forlorn hope. He came to look at our good friend and shook his head.

"I'm sorry, Tabitha," he said.

Tabitha burst into a further flood of tears and wailed in despair.

Oscar was devastated to learn his mentor had died; he had learned much from the elderly man. He took his hat and went to sit in the denes whilst he gave way to his grief in private.

Over the next few days, I sought Maria's assistance in helping Tabitha to organise the burial. Tabitha donned the black dress that she would wear for the rest of her days. She was lost without Gus. Tabitha's children rallied round and took some of the pressure off Maria and myself. They convinced her to come to stay with one of them for a short time. It was a miserable autumn for us all. We had all loved Gus with his wicked sense of humour.

Easter 1876

"Alice! Alice! Get a wriggle on!" So bawled Sam up the stairs. Maria chuckled and went to yell back down at her brother.

"Simmer down, Sam! She's all fingers and thumbs up here!"

"I know, I can imagine, so am I, but we need to get going!"

What was happening? It was Kit's wedding day. I could barely believe it. Our little bubble-headed Kit was marrying, and all I wanted to do was cry.

"Alice!" Sam bellowed. "Come ON! We're going to be late!"

I looked at Maria. "Well? How do I look, Maria?" I asked. My sister-in-law chuckled.

"Terrified!" she replied.

Sam thundered up the stairs. "Look! Look at the time!" He produced his pocket watch and shoved it under my nose. "Alice, we're the parents of the groom. We *have* to be there before anyone else!"

Little Sam was, of course, best man. He was nervous; but would acquit himself well. The twins stood in the front pews. I had no duties as mother of the groom, and I was glad about it. I would have been useless, so great were my nerves. I looked at Charlotte's mother, who seemed quite self-assured, but I knew she too was trembling inside. She had been pleased her daughter was to marry Kit. She had liked our middle son from the first moment she had seen him. A great pity, I thought, that I could not feel the same about her daughter!

Ollie held my hand. I was grateful since I was convinced I'd have fallen flat on my face had he not held me up.

Unable to prevent it, I started to cry as Kit took his vows. Sam, as well as Ollie, held me closely in case I fainted, which, for once, I felt just like doing. Our little boy, getting married! He looked so like Sam in his wonderful wedding suit.

George played the organ beautifully. Kit had insisted it be George and nobody else. The elderly man had been pleased to play for him. He played most Sundays now, and the occasional wedding.

Mackie was there. He had not been well recently, and his hair had gone grey, almost white. He still taught, and was still mentoring Ollie, though he insisted Ollie didn't need it.

He congratulated the newlyweds and then came to Sam and I. "The passage of time!" he said with a sigh. "I remember Kit's first day at school. He was a true delight to teach, as were all your boys! I am sure he'll do well and provide you with a host of grandchildren!"

That was something else I couldn't imagine. Our little Kit, having a woman in his bed!

William had shaken Kit's hand and congratulated the pair too. They would stay tonight at the hotel. So would Ollie and Oscar. I would go to our home with Sam and our eldest son.

Kit's first child was born at the beginning of December that year; a hefty girl named Dawn. Kit had insisted on the name, thus creating his and Charlotte's first argument in what would be an ongoing theme throughout their marriage. Kit had a short fuse, but he wasn't violent. Charlotte had always had a tempestuous nature and it was inevitable the two would clash.

March 1877

During that month, it was alternatively warm one day, cold the next. Recently, Mackie had been unwell, and I was sad and worried for him. He hadn't been good for some time now, but it had mainly been aches in his arm and the left stump at the shoulder which, for all he had not really felt it for years, had suddenly become painful indeed. He hadn't gone out of the house since Kit's wedding now; and wasn't able to be at the school either. I decided I'd visit him.

Having checked this was alright with Sam, I made my way to Mackie's home.

"Mackie!" I called up the stairs. "It's me! I've come a-visiting!"

"Alice! Thank God! I was bored to tears!"

I smiled, poking my head round the doorway. "Hey, what are you doing in bed!"

Mackie grinned. "Waiting for you, of course!" He winked, and I came to sit at his side.

"Cheeky devil!" I told him. "I thought you were ill."

Mackie sighed. "Ah, it's nothing, Alice, just a headache. I feel a bit run down really. I'm glad you're here though."

We chatted for a while, then Mackie winced. "You alright?" I asked him, worriedly. Mackie nodded.

"Yes, just a bit of a twinge." He looked at me. I looked at him.

"Have you seen a doctor?" I asked, but Mackie shook his head.

"No need for one of those."

"Mackie?" I asked, with a frown. Mackie seemed a little awkward. He wanted to ask me something, but wondered if it was appropriate. He decided to ask anyway.

"Alice. I know I shouldn't ask this, but, well, would you just lie at my side for a while?" Mackie asked. "Cuddle me? Let me cuddle you? I won't do anything I shouldn't. I promise, but I feel quite tired, and my head is bad. Just hold me close for a while, I just fancy a nap. Stay a while, would you?"

I nodded. "Of course, Mackie," I told him. "You do look so pale and tired. You'll feel better for the rest. Just a moment."

I removed my boots and lay on the bed. Mackie snuggled into me until I held him close, his head on my chest. I kissed his head and hugged him closely. "Mmmm. Nice," he said softly. "I do feel all warm and safe like this. You smell of lavender. I like that."

"You are warm and safe," I answered. "And thank you for the compliment." I squeezed him closely and Mackie smiled.

We lay in one another's arms. To my surprise, it didn't feel wrong or bad. I wasn't betraying Sam, I was merely cuddling platonically with a dear, sick friend. Mackie spoke.

"I used to dream about this," he told me softly. "Cuddling with you like this; I never thought it would happen for real."

"Well, it has happened. It is happening. Right now," I said and kissed his forehead. "You're a wonderful man, Mackie. You know, had things been different, it would have been you and me."

Mackie nodded. "I know. I think we would have been a great couple. I only hope Sam appreciates you."

I cuddled Mackie to me and watched as he drifted into a peaceful doze. I held him close, cuddling him. He stirred a little, then murmured something; I thought it was my name, but I couldn't be sure. I stroked his hair gently. There was a small smile on his face when Mackie, very gently, stopped breathing.

I was unsure how I got through the rest of that day. I wept and sobbed over his body for some time, and held him closely. The shock was indescribable. I felt sick. When I recovered myself sufficiently, I pulled the sheet and blanket over his head, then went to hail a passing boy to take a message to Sam to come at once. As the child sped off, I sat on the edge of the bed. I felt suddenly terrible, like I had ruined Mackie's life. I could have, and would have, made him happy, but not at the expense of Sam and our sons. I knew I could never tell Sam about the final moments, only say what was true, that he had died in my arms and had been peaceful. Sam, I knew, would never begrudge me or Mackie that.

CHAPTER TEN

August 1879

I jogged our first granddaughter up and down as I sang an old music hall song to her. It was called 'Champagne Charlie', a lively little tune, and she gurgled with pleasure. Sam didn't think it the most appropriate of lyrics for a two-year-old but she didn't understand them and it was the tune she enjoyed.

As it was summer, I would often take her to the beach. She loved the water and would happily toddle straight to it, at alarming speed, whenever she was set down. I devised a small pair of reins, which I looped around her middle to hold on to. At first, Sam had been incredulous about these, and Charlotte even more so. She had been shocked and had voiced her objection. I explained that Dawn was forever speeding off, and could not only race straight into the sea, but wander away in the town as well. Charlotte did not at all like her daughter wearing a leash 'like a dog', she told me. She also found fault with the way I dressed Dawn. I had never liked the fripperies, bonnets and bows which I considered dangerous, since such articles might be chewed and swallowed; ribbons get tight around necks. I had put Dawn into the all-in-one suits; the same kind that the boys had worn, much to my daughter-in-law's horror. But I continued to put her in one, no matter how fussily she was dressed when Charlotte brought her round, and she could get as grubby as she liked, and move more freely.

Kit proved his love for me when, one morning, Charlotte had come along with Kit to pick up Dawn. I had just changed her back into the dress she had arrived in and was busy filling a tub to wash the all-in-one suits. The pair had just taken Dawn outside when Charlotte spoke.

"Kit! You must speak to your mother. I can't bear for Dawn to be seen in those things. She looks like a boy! I don't like it!"

"I shall not!" he stated. "They're a good idea. Dawn would mess up her dresses otherwise and you wouldn't like that!"

"She ought to be being taught how to be ladylike, sitting playing quietly or being read to!"

Kit shook his head. "She's only two. There's plenty of time for her to learn to be more ladylike," he objected.

"And whilst we're about it, she needs to sing something different to her! I've heard her with those songs, and that one about a man getting drunk. Really, Kit!"

Kit frowned; "she doesn't know what the words mean!"

"No, but she will soon and what if she starts singing it? What'll people think?"

Kit merely gestured with his hand, miming opening and closing of a mouth.

"The trouble with your mother, Kit, is that she wants to take over Dawn completely."

Kit had then whirled her round. "Don't you *dare* to speak of my mamma like that!" He had raised his voice, and at the washtub, I cringed a little. So did Sam. "She has been the best mother I could ever hope to have and if she feels that dressing Dawn in an all-in-one is a good idea, then I agree. You will apologise!"

Little Sam gave a low whistle. "That told her!" he said, grinning.

Oscar had begun walking out with a girl. He and Ollie had just passed their 22nd birthdays. She lived with her family in Tooke the Baker's Row and her father was a butcher. Sam had joked that if they married, Oscar would at least never go hungry, what with a butcher and a baker in the same row.

She was an extremely plain girl, with coarse brown hair and spectacles, but I liked her much better than I did Charlotte. She had a very dry sense of humour and was named Jemima. She had a great love of animals and all manner of flowers.

Kit was now a well-established architect, working with a senior architect who went by the name of Mr Bottle, and this had caused hilarity back at home. When Kit had mentioned him, casually, I had gone into hysterical laughter at such a name.

"Really! Mamma!" Kit had said, embarrassed. "He's holding a wine and cheese party this weekend. I hoped you would both come, but for goodness' sake, if you're going to laugh at his name, do you get it out of your system now! I can't have you laughing like that at the party. He's my senior, don't forget!"

Kit wasn't ashamed of us, but he knew my habit for putting my foot in it. Later that week, he proudly introduced us along with Oscar and Ollie.

Mr Bottle and his wife were charming. It was most unfortunate, however, that Mrs Bottle resembled just that. She was wide-hipped but slender from the waist up and wore, to Kit's horror, a green high-necked dress. He glanced at me and frowned. I beamed hugely at the pair. Obvious to Kit, I was straining not to laugh. Sam too struggled to hold back laughter. It might have been easier had not Kit introduced them as 'The Bottles.' I felt my face aching from schooling my expression.

Once we had been introduced and greeted, I had hoped we could go off and mingle with the guests, but the pair seemed eager to talk, with us being Kit's parents, so there was little chance to avoid contact. Sam chatted about our offspring, when they were young, in order to allow me to laugh. Sam decided to sacrifice Kit's dignity and told them about the time he had tried to 'sell the twins.'

We only attended for our second son's benefit, and I tired of the others quickly; they seemed to have no interesting conversation at all, only being concerned with emulating their betters, and the women talked of nothing but fashion.

Despite this, we managed to acquit ourselves well, causing no embarrassment to our second son, and made our way home along the sea front, where we could see lights from fishermen. Strolling back to the main town, we held hands walking under the yellow glow of the gas lamp. There was singing and piano music as we walked past the various inns; a drunk staggered out of one, tripping on the cobbles and landed on his large rump. At the top of the row, we stopped, looking back down it and a warm, yet sad feeling surged through me.

"Alice?"

"It's alright, Sam. Just enjoying the night." I put both arms round him and kissed him. "Let's get to bed."

5ᵗʰ January 1881

The entire family stood, silently, around Mr Dwyer's graveside. Every single one of us, silent. The cold was biting through the bare tree branches, but nobody cared, so great was our grief. Our much-loved patriarch had passed, peacefully, in his sleep at the age of 94. I held Sam's arm tightly. He was struggling to keep his composure. I could tell, but I attempted to reassure him that his father had been warm, happy and peaceful at the end. Maria stood with her husband and their children. We were all devastated. Simon's passing would leave a massive hole that nobody could ever hope to possibly fill.

"I know he was old," Sam told me sadly, "but, well, he just seemed he would go on and on forever." I nodded.

"I know, darling, but people don't. I am sorry, Sam, and I'm just as sad as you are."

I was as distressed and miserable as anybody who was blood kin. He had become as much of a father to me as had my own been. But at least he had died peacefully. We would all wear black for six months, then it was acceptable to slight the mourning. I knew he would have hated the thought of us all in black, and the accepted colours which were grey or white. Sam chose mostly grey colours since they suited him better and I went for the mauve, but Maria continued in her black dress.

That January was hellishly cold, but we took great pleasure in our grandchildren at least. Kit had now presented us with another grandchild, a boy, named Samuel. Oscar and Jemima had given us twin granddaughters named Mary and Helena. I had been delighted at the choice of names. The Dwyer family was growing.

At the end of July, good news came from Manoa. Iffey had married well; even Helen would have approved, he had written, and she had been safely delivered of a girl and was now the mother to eight children, five boys and three girls. And what was more, Iffey was extremely happy with her lot.

Manoa himself could no longer walk but was enjoying his days in the Caribbean sunshine. He was surrounded by his grandchildren, his daughter and son-in-law and wanted for nothing more. He still thought of Helen, but Helen had evidently never truly stopped loving William.

Unexpected news came too, of Susan. By sheer chance, Albert had been speaking to a man on the jetty, who had returned to Yarmouth ten years previously, having served five years in Botany Bay, and had gone out on the same ship as Susan. A good many of the convicts had died due to a cholera outbreak and Susan had been among them. When Sam and I heard this, we looked at one another with awe. Cholera was a terribly painful way to die.

"Apparently, she had some last words, but they didn't make much sense," Albert told us over dinner that evening. "She said sorry for the stabbing; he guessed that had been the reason for her transportation."

I felt a jolt. Did she mean that of my parents? Surely not. Had it been her all along? In my mind's eye, I saw again the assailant of that terrible night – the black, long, and hooded cloak. The figure had run off, but, I suddenly realised, it had been wearing a skirt!

August 1881

The twins were 24 now, and Ollie, also now married, taught at the Charity School. Oscar worked in the parks and gardens, alongside Kit, who was to design the bridges, bandstands and other pieces. This was something that gave them, and us, a good deal of pleasure, not to mention pride. The garden for the blind was finished too, and everybody could sit to enjoy the flowers.

At age 56, I had no need for wild carrot seeds and Sam, at 64, was just as passionate as he had been at 30. Sam had now stopped working, and Little Sam oversaw the business. Sam had retired, and it allowed our eldest be as independent as possible.

Our neighbour, Mrs Floyd, had since died, Robin having preceded her by some years. The house had then remained empty for some time, and I wondered whether in fact, Ollie and Martha could move in. Sam and I had the money to purchase it, and the Floyds, having had no children, and Mrs Floyd's niece in disgrace, had nobody to leave it to. I hated to think of what might happen. Either it would begin to fall to bits with nobody caring for the outside, or suddenly, we'd find neighbours move in who would be noisy or disruptive. Having talked to Sam about it, he was of the same opinion. Sam at once hastened to Market Row to a solicitor we had had dealings with before when we had sold Manoa's old house. He went to discuss the property, and determine if it had been in the Floyd's possession, or had it had a landlord? Was it possible to buy the house?

Sam was delighted to discover that the house had in fact been their own, and after having words with Ollie and Martha, who appeared thrilled at the prospect of living next door, through the solicitor, Sam and Ollie started the negotiations that went into purchasing the house. On their return, I was surprised to find they had the keys to the house, much sooner than anybody had expected. I smiled brightly, keen to go inside the new house, a smile that vanished when we opened the door and went in.

"It STINKS in here!" I wailed loudly, covering nose and mouth at once, and horrified at the prospect we had bought a filthy disgusting house for our dear son and daughter-in-law. Why had it not occurred to me before? Was I going daft in my old age? We hadn't been in the house since Robin had died. It had been bad enough then.

"Don't worry," Sam said, an arm about my shoulders. "It was bound to be dirty; we'll find someone to clean it for us. I don't want you on your hands and knees scrubbing!"

"Me neither," Ollie told me firmly.

I groaned. I should have known better, but I had been so excited at the idea our son would be right next door that I had forgotten the occupants of the house had never bothered to clean either themselves or their house. I marched about the ground floor, and flung open every single window I could see, retching at the smell in their main living area. I looked in despair at the range, filthy from years of thick, smelly, congealed grease, ash and soot, the fireplaces in the room similar. What disgusted me more than anything was the fact that cooking pots still sat on the range bearing traces of the final meal. Sam peered inside, regretting it at once, and pulled a face, hurriedly covering nose and mouth with a handkerchief. The pot appeared welded to the surface of the range.

"I don't think she ever took them off the stove, Mamma!" Ollie told me. "Just scooped out whatever was inside and ate, then stuck the next lot in after!"

Some of the furniture had been cleared out, and what was left was fit only for a bonfire – a kitchen table, that I at once told the men to put outside and burn, and some rickety wooden chairs that went the same way. Cobwebs hung in every corner, black with filth and very ancient-looking.

Sam looked to where Martha and I were hastening upstairs. "I don't think your mother expected it to be this bad," Sam told Ollie. "She wanted you to have a home of your own. To be honest, I didn't think things through either. This unholy mess!"

But Ollie was untroubled. "It'll be fine, Papa. Like you said, a new pin! The house is sound. All it needs is a little love and care."

Martha and I went to look around the upstairs bedrooms. I dissolved into tears. It would take forever to get this house clean.

"What must you think of me?" I sobbed. "It's terrible! Why didn't I think? I've seen cleaner pigsties!"

"Ah, come on, Mamma, it'll be fine! We couldn't be more grateful. I know you wanted us to share your home, but think, you won't want grandchildren under your feet all the time, will you? This is the finest gift you could both give to us, truly, and we will have the best of neighbours too!" She kissed my cheek.

The cleaning work next door began. Their yard filled with old furniture, which was then carted away, time and again. I had refused to venture inside a second time until it was clean. But the cleaning women hired were quite brilliant. They started from top to bottom of the house. Every day, I saw them come in and the work would begin, sounds of scrubbing, singing as they worked. Windowpanes became clean and sparkling. Bit by bit, the house was being transformed. Fresh whitewash was painted on the walls, the front door was painted a deep, dark blue, and the doorstep scrubbed.

At the end of the month, we were invited for dinner.

On entering the house, we all stood and stared. What a transformation! I could hardly believe it. Walls had been scrubbed and freshly painted. The floorboards polished, with colourful rugs here and there. The furniture, simple and plain, but clean. The oven looked brand new – I wondered how long it had taken whoever had cleaned it to bring it up to a black shine – the fireplace neat as my own, fire irons polished and gleaming. I was thrilled and hugged them both.

10th August 1885

I felt the weight of the years on me, now that I was 60. But it was more vanity. I had kept remarkably fit, as had Sam who was 68. He had gone grey now, despite the henna washing. But at least he had his hair and teeth. My hair had turned a silvery greyish colour, but much of the blonde remained and so did the curls. I had kept facial lines at bay by applying cream over the years. It was only I was stiff in the joints now if I sat for too long or on waking.

It was our 35th wedding anniversary and the children had arranged a beautiful weekend at the Grand Hotel, one of the very best in Yarmouth, paid for by them, breakfast and dinner included. It was a wonderful present, but two days before, I had come down with a streaming cold, as had Sam himself.

"Mamma, are you sure you want to go?"

Little Sam looked at me as I sat at the kitchen table. I smiled at him and nodded. "Of course, sweetheart. Why wouldn't I? Your father wants to as well, isn't that so, Sam?"

My husband nodded from his seat by the fire. "Of course. Goodness me, son!! This is our 35th wedding anniversary. Think we'd miss this?"

The Grand Hotel. It was a beautiful building on the sea front and had a wonderful view of the town from the top rooms, which was where he had booked for us to stay. However, for all we felt weighted down by our colds, we couldn't possibly miss this.

Little Sam was concerned that we were not well enough. We both seemed to have dwindled a little since his grandfather had died. What was more, he had had a bad feeling growing within him for a few days now. He was unsure what it was, or if it even meant anything.

"Why not stay here, where I can look after you?" he asked, trying to keep us for as long as he could, in the hope that we would get tired and decide to not go after all.

"Ah, Sam! You are thoughtful and we love you for it, but truly, it'll be nice to have a bit of a break in a hotel," Sam told him.

"Alright," Little Sam acquiesced, but far from convinced and wishing he had never thought of the idea in the first place. "You'll be waited on hand and foot in any case."

I grinned at him. "And I trust the evening meals are sorted out as well?" Sam looked at me with a grin. I chuckled, recalling our fish and chip evening the previous time we had gone to an hotel. But of course, money was not any issue anymore. "We can still bring in fish and chips if you prefer," I said, getting up. "Come on, my love, the cab will be waiting."

Sam and I left, having hugged and kissed Little Sam, and walked down our row. Little Sam watched as we walked, hand in hand. We met Ollie coming up the row as he made his way home and greeted him with a hug. As he made his way up to our home, Little Sam came out to see him.

"You alright, bor'?" Ollie asked Little Sam. He looked worriedly at his eldest brother. Little Sam frowned.

"I don't know," he answered quietly. "I just had a bad feeling. Just uneasy, you know, like you get the first day at school."

Ollie regarded his elder with some concern. "Ah, come on, our Sam, there's nothing wrong. They've had colds before."

"I know, but they're old now," Little Sam said, concerned. Ollie screamed with laughter.

"Don't let them hear you say that, bor'! Mamma would chase you round the house with a broom!" He grinned and put his arm round his brother's shoulders. "Come on. How about a rare trip to the ale house, eh, bor'? Whilst the cats are away and all that!"

We took the carriage along the sea front and looked out at the impossibly blue sky; the waves lapped gently onto the beach which was busy with people. We still felt bad with the colds we had, but as Sam assured me, with a hot bath, soothing lemon and a soft bed, we would be able to rest and the enjoy the remainder of the stay.

Our hotel room was fabulous... exquisite in fact, and we made full use of the bath that evening. We recalled our wedding day, for all we had felt married, merely making simple vows the day we had left for Devon, in front of Mrs Elgin, but it had been a relief to have been truly married after Susan's transportation. I kissed Sam gently. He smiled and looked into my face. "I am so glad I met you," he whispered softly. I touched his lips.

"So am I," I told him.

Neither of us felt much like eating and so, at around eight o'clock that night, we retired to our room. "Sam, let's stay up a while," I told him. "I want to watch the moon on the water." Sam thought then nodded.

We sat at the window seat, wrapped in each other's arms. The sun was setting around the time we returned to our room.

"Thirty-five years married," Sam mused. "It's been incredible. I couldn't have asked for more." I smiled.

"Me neither." I kissed his cheek. "It's gone so quickly though." Sam nodded and rested his chin on my head. The dusk fell and lanterns twinkled out on the water and along the promenade. The lanterns on the cabs glowed eerily as horses pulled them along the front. We heard voices of the holidaymakers down below in the road. The smell of fish and chips wafted along the sea front.

The moon was full. It shone on the water, beautifully, a bright silvery light, with a calm sea. "Isn't it lovely?" Sam murmured into my neck. I murmured agreement. Sam kissed my neck. We watched as some clouds gently blew across the moon. Sam hugged me tighter. "Do you feel well enough to make love?" he asked me and I smiled.

"You bet I do!" I told him. "One lousy cold isn't going to stop me!"

It was sweet, gentle and perfect. Afterwards, Sam lay beside me and smiled. "I love you, Alice," he whispered softly. I stroked his cheek. "I love you too, Sam," I replied, looking into the beautiful blue eyes. Sam held me close, and I nestled into his shoulder. We slept.

17th August 1885

I regret with all my heart that it is I, Kit Dwyer, who must finish this. Our parents, Samuel and Alice, were found in their bed, the day after they had gone to the Grand Hotel. Both had died in their sleep. At first, we could hardly believe it; all they had had were colds, nothing more, but it turned out that they had both died of gas poisoning. This, they would have normally been able to smell, but both having colds, neither of them had.

There had been a small leak in one of the gas lamp pipes in their room. Nothing much, but it had built up over the night, and in the morning, the maid, having not had any summons from my parents, left it until later to go in, and she could smell it at once. She had been horrified to find them, but I was assured, they lay as if asleep, in one another's arms and I find comfort in this, since neither knew anything about it. Nor did one survive without the other, and whilst this is a terrible shock to the family, we know, neither could have lived without the other and that they died together, we must at least be grateful for.

They shall be buried in the churchyard along with our grandparents.

We, as a family, will continue on, but it won't be the same.

Kit Dwyer